In America

IN
AMERICA

[A NOVEL]

Susan Sontag

FARRAR STRAUS GIROUX

NEW YORK

Farrar, Straus and Giroux
19 Union Square West, New York 10003

Distributed in Canada by Douglas & McIntyre Ltd.
Printed in the United States of America
First edition, 2000
Second printing, 2000
Library of Congress Cataloging-in-Publication Data
Sontag, Susan, 1933–
   In America : a novel / Susan Sontag.—1st ed.
      p.   cm.
   ISBN 0-374-17540-3 (alk. paper)
   1. Actresses—Fiction.   2. Polish Americans—California—Fiction.
   3. Utopias—California—Fiction.   4. Frontier and pioneer life—California—Fiction.
   5. California—History—1850–1950—Fiction.   I. Title.
PS3569.06547 I5 2000
813'.54—dc21   99-054641

Title page photograph: detail from Cape Horn near Celilo, 1867,
by Carleton Watkins.
Courtesy Fraenkel Gallery, San Francisco

A signed first edition of this book has been privately printed by
The Franklin Library.

The story of In America is inspired by the emigration to America in 1876 of
Helena Modrzejewska, Poland's most celebrated actress, accompanied by her
husband Count Karol Chłapowski, her fifteen-year-old son Rudolf, the young
journalist and future author of Quo Vadis Henryk Sienkiewicz, and a few
friends; their brief sojourn in Anaheim, California; and Modrzejewska's
subsequent triumphant career on the American stage under the name of
Helena Modjeska.

Inspired by . . . no less and no more. Most of the characters
in the novel are invented, and those who are not depart in
radical ways from their real-life models.

I am, however, indebted to books and articles by and on Modjeska and
Sienkiewicz for material and anecdotes used (and altered), as well as—for help
in getting it right—to Paolo Dilonardo, Karla Eoff, Kasia Górska, Peter
Perrone, Robert Walsh, and especially to Benedict Yeoman. Thanks also to
Minda Rae Amiran, Jarosław Anders, Steven Barclay, Anne Hollander, James
Leverett, John Maxtone-Graham, Larry McMurtry, and Miranda Spieler.
I am very grateful for a month at the Rockefeller Center in Bellagio in 1997.

                                      S.S.

To my friends in Sarajevo

———————————

"America will be!"

—Langston Hughes

In America

Zero

IRRESOLUTE, no, shivering, I'd crashed a party in the private dining room of a hotel. It felt wintry indoors, too, but none of the women in gowns and men in frock coats churning about the long dark-hued room seemed to mind the chill, so I had the tile stove in a corner all to myself. I hugged the fat, ceiling-high contraption—I would have preferred a hearthful of roaring fire, but I was here, where rooms are heated by stoves—then set to kneading some warmth back into my cheeks and palms. When I'd got warmer, or calmer, I ventured across my end of the room. From a window, through the thick scrim of soundlessly dropping snowflakes backlit by a ring of moonlight, I looked down on the row of sledges and horsecabs, on the coachmen swathed in coarse blankets dozing in their seats, on the rigid snow-dappled animals with bowed heads. I heard the bells of a nearby church strike ten. Some guests had bunched near the huge oak sideboard by the window. Half turning, I tuned in to their conversation, which was mostly in a language I don't know (I was in a country I'd visited only once, thirteen years ago), but somehow, I didn't question how, their words reached me as sense. It was something vehement about a woman and a man, a scrap of information I promptly upgraded by assuming that the two were, why not, married. Then with equal vehemence the talk concerned a

3

woman and two men, so, never doubting that the woman was the same, I supposed that if the first man was her husband, the second must be her lover, chiding myself for imagining so conventionally. But whether a woman and a man or the woman and two men, I still hadn't understood why they were being discussed. If the story were familiar to everyone, there would of course be no need to recount it. But maybe the guests were deliberately speaking so as not to be understood too well, because, say, the woman and the man, or both men, if there were two, were also here at the party. This made me think of looking one by one at the women in the room, all buoyantly coiffed and, as far as I am any judge of the clothes of that time, stylishly dressed, to see if one stood out from the others. As soon as I looked, looked with this thought in mind, I saw her, and wondered why I hadn't noticed her before. No longer in her first youth, as people then said of an attractive woman past thirty, of medium height, straight-spined, with a pile of ash-blond hair into which she nervously tucked a few escaping strands, she was not exceptionally beautiful. But she became more compelling the longer I watched her. She could be, she must be, the woman they were discussing. When she moved about the room, she was always surrounded; when she spoke, she was always listened to. It seemed to me I'd caught her name, it was either Helena or Maryna—and supposing it would help me to decipher the story if I could identify the couple or the trio, what better start than to give them names, I decided to think of her as Maryna. Then I looked for the two men. First, I trawled for one who could be thought of as a husband. If he were a doting husband, as I imagined this Helena, I mean Maryna, would have, then I'd find him close to her, never distracted for long by anyone else. And, sure enough, keeping Maryna in my sightline, it seemed obvious now that she was the one giving the party or that it was being given in her honor, I saw her being trailed by an angular bearded man with fine blond hair, combed to the back, that left uncovered his high, powerfully arched and noble forehead, who was nodding affably at whatever she said. That must be the

4

husband, I thought. Now I had to find the other man, who, if he was the lover—or, just as interestingly, turned out not to be the lover—would probably be younger than the amiable-looking aristocrat. If the husband were in his mid-thirties, a year or two his wife's junior though of course he looked much older, this man would be, I guessed, in his mid-twenties, handsome enough, and with the insecurity of youth or, more likely, of inferior social position, a bit overdressed. He could be, let me see, a rising journalist or a lawyer. Of the several men at the party answering to such a description, the one I fancied most was a burly fellow with glasses who, at the moment I spied him, was being familiar with a maid laying out the hotel's hoard of best silver and crystal on the spacious table at the other end of the room. I saw him whispering in her ear, touching her shoulder, toying with her braid. It would be amusing, I thought, if this were the candidate lover of my ash-blond beauty: not an inhibited bachelor but a dedicated rake. It's he, it must be he, I decided with lighthearted certitude, while also deciding to keep another youth in reserve for the part, a slender fellow in a yellow waistcoat, a bit Wertherish, should I become convinced that a more chaste or at least more circumspect swain would better fit with the identities of the other two. Then I wheeled my attention to another band of guests, though after some minutes more of alert eavesdropping I could make nothing further of the story that they too were debating. You might think that by now I'd be hearing the names of the two men. Or at least the husband's. But no one who addressed the man standing not far from me now in the group tightly surrounding the woman, I was sure he was her husband, ever used his Christian name, and so, fortified by the unexpected gift of her name—yes, I know it could have been Helena, but I'd decided that it would be, or must be, Maryna—I resolved to discover his name with or without auditory clues. What could he, I mean the husband, be called? Adam. Jan. Zygmunt. I tried to think of the name that would best suit him. For each person has such a name, usually the name that he or she has been given. Finally, I heard someone call him . . . Karol. I can't explain why this name didn't please me; perhaps, peeved by not being able to fathom the story, I was simply venting my frustration on this man with the long, pale, evenly shaped face whose parents had chosen for him so euphonious a name. So, although I had no doubt about what I'd heard, I couldn't claim to be unsure, as I'd been with his wife's name (Maryna or Helena), I ruled that he could not be a Karol, that I had misheard his name, and gave myself permission to rechristen him Bogdan. I know this isn't as attractive a name as Karol in the language in which I am writing, but I intend to get used to it, and hope it will wear well. Next, I turned in my mind to the other man, as I thought of him, who had dropped onto a leather sofa to write something in a notebook (it seemed too long to be an assignation note to the maid). Certain that I had not yet heard his name, for his name I'd been neither cued nor miscued, I would have to be arbitrary, I decided to plunge ahead and make of him a Richard, their Richard: Ryszard. His understudy in the yellow waistcoat, I was moving quickly now, I would call Tadeusz; though I was starting to think I'd have no use for him, at least in this role, it seemed easier to give him a name now, while I was in the naming vein. Then I went back to listening, trying to ratchet up my sense of the story that, ever more audibly, was troubling most of the people invited to the dinner. It wasn't, at least this much I divined, that the woman was about to leave her husband for the other man. Of that I was sure, even if the scribbler on the sofa was in fact the lover of the woman with the ash-blond hair. I knew there had to be a few romances and adulteries at this party, as in any room filled with lively and fetchingly decked-out people who are friends, colleagues, kin. But this, though the very thing one expects when primed for a story about a woman and a man, or a woman and two men, wasn't what was agitating these guests tonight. I heard, *But her duty lies here. It's irresponsible and without any* . . . and, *But he's asked him to go ahead. It's right that he* . . . and, *But every noble idea seems like folly. After all, she* . . . and, firmly, *May God take them under His protection*, this last uttered by an elderly woman wearing a mauve velvet hat, who then crossed herself. Hardly the way people discuss a love affair. But, like some love affairs, it bore the stamp of recklessness; and it seemed to bring out censors and well-wishers in equal measure. And while at first the story seemed to concern only the woman and the man (Maryna, Bogdan), or the woman and the two men (Maryna, Bogdan, Ryszard), sometimes it seemed to include more than these two, or three, for I heard some of the guests standing about the room, holding their goblets of mulled wine in one hand and gesturing with the other, say *we* (and not only *they*), and I began hearing other names, Barbara and Aleksander and Julian and Wanda, who seemed not to be among the judging bystanders but part of the story, co-conspirators even. Perhaps I was moving too fast now. But, conspiracy or no, the thought of conspiracy came naturally to mind, since these people for all their swank and comforts had not done better than to get themselves born in a country subjected for decades to the variously vindictive decrees of a triple foreign occupation, so that many an ordinary action, by which I mean what people in my country would consider an ordinary exercise of freedom, would have had there the character of a conspiracy. And even if what they'd done or were planning to do turned out to be legal, I had still managed to understand that others, more than a few, had roles in this story of the woman and the man or the woman and two men (you know their names), including some of those nearby continuing to dispute whether it was "right" or whether it was "wrong." I don't know why I've put these words in quotes, it's not just because they are the words I heard spoken; it must be because in the time in which I live these words are used much less confidently, even with apology if you are not a complacent bigot or a lethal avenger, while much of the fascination of these people, of their time, is that they knew, or thought they knew, what "right" and "wrong" were. Indeed, they would have felt quite naked without their "right" and "wrong," their "good" and "bad," which continue to lead a plaintive, withered afterlife

7

in my own time, as well as their, now thoroughly discredited, "civilized" and "barbaric," "noble" and "vulgar," their, now incomprehensible, "selfless" and "selfish"—forgive the quotation marks (I shall soon stop using them), I mean here only to give these words their proper, poignant emphasis. And it occurred to me that this might explain, partly, my presence in this room. For I was moved by the way they possessed these words and regarded themselves bound by them to actions. I heard only ardor, sincerity, in their softly voiced *should we, they shouldn't, how can he, how can she, how can they, if I were they, she still doesn't have the right, but honor demands* . . . I was enjoying the repetition. Dare I say I felt at one with them? Almost. Those dreaded words, dreaded by others (not by me), seemed like caresses. Pleasantly numbed, I felt myself borne along by their music . . . until I heard a bald man with a little pointed beard observe, with more sharpness than I'd heard so far, *Of course they can, if she wants. He's rich.* That was a dose of reality. Whatever they were debating, it seemed to require money, a lot. Further, it seemed more than possible that nobody here was seriously rich, even if one of them had a title, the man I'd decided was the husband, and everybody sported signs of a conventional prosperity. More evidence of their status: that bits of their conversations regularly fell into the one foreign language I do speak well. For I knew that at this time, in their part of the world, the gentry as well as those with a liberal profession often chatted in the language of authoritative, far away France. And just as I was acknowledging that it was a relief to hear French now and then, I heard the woman with the ash-blond hair, my Maryna, exclaiming, *Oh, let's not speak French anymore!* A pity, because she had been speaking the most vibrant French of all. She had a deep-toned voice, which rested deliciously on the final vowels. And she moved as she spoke, in a different rhythm from the others: with a pause at the end of each fluent gesture, each agile turn of her no longer slim body, when she passed, as if to receive their homage, from one cluster of guests to another. But sometimes she appeared irri-

8

tated. And sometimes, I saw it, I don't know if anyone else did, she seemed just tired. I wondered if she had been ill recently. She didn't smile often, except at the little boy, I haven't mentioned that there was a child in the room, with a ripe gaze and floury hair, whom I had to assume was Maryna's son. He looked so much like her, there was nothing in him of the man I'd chosen for her husband, the one I've called Bogdan, which made me wonder whether I had picked the right man. But it often happens that someone resembles one parent while a child, then as an adult resembles the other parent just as exclusively, instead of displaying a unique, ingenious blend of the features of both. The little boy was trying to get Maryna's attention. Where was his nanny? Wasn't it late for a child his age, he was around seven, still to be up? These questions reminded me how veiled was my picture of their lives outside this large, chilly room. Observing them at a party, on something like good behavior, in a state of appealing alertness, I couldn't know, for example, whether the evening would end for husbands and wives in one ample bed, two beds pushed together, or two beds separated by a carpeted canyon or a closed door. My guess, if I had to guess, was that Maryna did not share a bedroom with Bogdan, following the custom in his family, not hers. And I was still unable to name the deed or project whose rightness or wrongness the guests were debating, or so I thought—even as I was receiving a flurry of new clues, now *they* were going too fast, which I'll put in quotation marks too, but only to remember them: words like "abandon her public" and "national symbol" and "crisis of nerves" and "something irrevocable" and "noble savage" and "Nipu." Yes, Nipu. As it happens I'd once read (in a French translation) the book entitled *The Adventures of Mr. Nicholas Wisdom*, which describes Wisdom's sojourn in an ideal, consummately isolated community, in fact it is an island, called Nipu. But I wouldn't have expected anyone here to evoke this classic of their national literature, written exactly a century before the time when the guests were gathered in the private dining room of the hotel and I was thinking about them.

Its account of life in a perfect society, artlessly influenced by both Voltaire and Rousseau, reflected all the quaint illusions of a bygone age. Surely these people would feel remote from such enlightened views, enlightened with a capital E. The history of their implacably dismembered country would, I thought, have kept them immune to any faith in human perfectibility or an ideal society. (And cured, forever, of that other mighty illusion with a capital E: as their greatest poet once declared, bitter experience had taught his country that "the European word had no political value. This nation, attacked by a formidable enemy, had on its side all the books, all the newspapers, all the eloquent tongues of Europe; and from this entire army of words came not a single action.") Yet here they were in this sumptuous room with beamed ceiling and Persian carpets in the heart of this magnificent old city, evoking Nipu, that stern blueprint for a stripped-down life of perfect, rustic comity. I began to wonder if I'd stumbled on a coven of tardy romantics (the romantic age being long over), and I feared for them, for the illusions they might still cherish. But probably they were simply patriots of an unusually grandiloquent stripe. Perhaps I should mention that I had heard, several times, *homeland,* but not even once *the Christ among nations*—as patriots of their time were wont to call their martyred nation. I knew that the memory of injustice colored every sentiment among these people, whose country had disappeared from the map of Europe. Appalled by the lethal upsurge of nationalist and tribal feelings in my own time, in particular (you can be in only one place at a time) by the fate of one small European nation, braided together tribally, and, for that, destroyed with impunity, with the acquiescence or connivance of the great European powers (I'd spent a good part of three years in besieged Sarajevo), I wondered if they could be as exhausted as I was by the national question and by the betrayal, the deceit of Europe. But what could it mean to call someone—it had to be the woman with the ash-blond hair, the woman I'd decided to call Maryna— *a national symbol?* If I assumed she was so distinctively treasured not because she was somebody's daughter or widow but for accomplishments of her own, what could these be? I couldn't rewrite history: I had to acknowledge that a woman of her time and country who was known to and admired by a large public would most likely have been on the stage. For then—only eight years after the birth of the supreme heroine of my earliest childhood, Maria Skłodowska, the future Madame Curie—there was hardly any other enviable career open to a woman (she was not going to be a governess, or a teacher, or a prostitute). She was too old to be a dancer. True, she could have been a singer. But it would have been more illustrious, more patriotic, then, if she had been, I was certain she was, an actress. And that would explain how her good looks imposed themselves on others as beauty; the skillful gestures, the commanding gaze; and the way sometimes she brooded and balked, without penalty. I mean, she *looked* like an actress. And I told myself I needed to make a greater space for the obvious: that, mostly, people do look like what they are. I'd been watching another man, I decided to call him Henryk, a thin man slouched in an armchair who had been drinking too much. With his goatee and careless posture and melancholy stare, he was like the doctor in a Chekhov play, which is what he could be, since there was a good chance of finding a doctor in any cultivated entourage of this time. And if my Maryna was indeed an actress, I could count on there being other theatre people here: say, the leading man in her current vehicle—I picked the tall beardless man with a ringing voice who had started, I didn't understand why, to hector Tadeusz—although the presence of other actresses, at least of Maryna's generation, seemed less certain (they would be rivals). Most likely, I'd find the general director of the city's main theatre, whose season she animated each year with her guest appearances. And she would not have failed to number among her friends a drama critic, one who could be relied upon always to give her the worshipful reviews she had earned (he was a gently rejected suitor from way back). Further, as befits a worldly gathering, someone should be a banker and there should be a judge . . . Maybe I was moving too fast. I turned to the stove and, taking a deep breath, put my hands on the hot dark-green tiles, though really I was not chilled at all now, then went back to the window and gazed into the night. The falling snow was streaked with hail; it rattled the panes. As I turned back to look at the guests, a stout man with a lorgnette was saying, *Listen*. Hardly anyone stopped talking. *Mes enfants,* he bellowed, *that's what hail sounds like. Not like dried peas dropped into a kettledrum!* Maryna smiled. I smiled too, for a different reason (I didn't mind being proven right): so I *was* among theatre people. I decided that this man must be a stage manager, since he was fretting about effects. And I christened him Czesław, in honor of my favorite living poet. On then to the rest of the cast, I said to myself with renewed confidence. Having yet to identify any of the other women, I realized that six could be the wives of the leading actor, the director of the theatre, the critic, the banker, the judge, and the stage manager. The rumpled doctor, since I thought he was a doctor because he looked like Astrov in *Uncle Vanya,* I assumed to be not just unmarried but unmarriable. (And I needed to keep my Ryszard wifeless, too, the better to flirt and pine, though I suspected that he would turn out, when much older, to be not only the marrying but the thrice-married kind.) Then, returning to the other women, I stalled for a moment, wondering if I hadn't misjudged Maryna. If too successful to keep an ex-mentor by her side, while not yet old enough to feel unthreatened by the young, she still might have included one younger actress in her circle of friends; and I found her quickly, a pale delicate woman with a large locket on her bosom, who kept brushing back her auburn hair with a gesture very much like Maryna's. Oh, and one of the women could be a relative and, indeed, somebody I thought looked enough like Bogdan to be his sister was just at that moment talking to the doctor, leaning over his chair; I think she had noticed he was a bit drunk. I also wondered whether I would find a Jew, who would be a young painter named Jakub, recently returned from two years of cosmopolitan art society in

Rome. But as far as I could tell there was just one painter here, and not a Jew, his name was Michał: a red-haired, stiff-gaited man around thirty, who had lost a leg at eighteen in the Uprising. Finally (for the time being), it seemed to me that at a party of this size and composition there should be at least two foreigners, but as carefully as I scrutinized the guests I could find only the one I'd already noticed: a plump man with a full beard and a diamond in his cravat, with whom some people standing near another tall window had been speaking German. He might be an impresario who was on the verge of engaging Maryna's young protégée for some small roles next spring at his theatre in Vienna. I surmised this, that he was from Vienna, because I recognized his accent, my memory has a good ear, even though I've never learned to speak or understand German properly. Of course I didn't marvel at what superior linguists they all were; to this day the educated of this country, restored to the map of Europe a mere eighty years ago, are notably polyglot. But I, with my command only of Romance languages (I dabble in German, know the names of twenty kinds of fish in Japanese, have soaked up a splash of Bosnian, and understand barely a word of the language of the country in which this room is to be found), I, as I've said, somehow did manage to understand most of what they were saying. Still, I had yet to understand what they were really saying. For supposing I was right, I mean about who was an actress and who a stage manager and the rest, this wasn't helping me much to untie the knot of their argument about whether what the woman, Maryna, and the man, Bogdan, or the two men, Bogdan and Ryszard, were doing or were planning to do, was right or wrong. (As you see, I've dispensed with my little crutches, the quotation marks.) But even those who said it was wrong seemed to temper their judgment when it came to Maryna. It was obvious how much everyone admired her, not only her husband and the man (Ryszard, possibly Tadeusz) who may or may not be her lover. I had no doubt that all the men and several of the women must be at least a little in love with Maryna. But it was more, or less, than love. They were enthralled by her. I wondered if I could be enthralled by her, were I one of them, not merely someone watching, trying to figure them out. I thought I had time, for their feelings, their story; and my own. They seemed—and I pledged myself to be like them, on their behalf—indefatigable. Yet this didn't strip me of my impatience. I was waiting for quick relief: to hear something, a sentence, that would bring me the nub and drift of their concern. It occurred to me that perhaps I had been listening too avidly. Perhaps, I thought, it wasn't that I had to listen harder but should mull over what I'd already heard. (The phrase *crisis of nerves* had started to buzz in my head.) Perhaps, I thought, I should simply take off. (And what about *abandon her public?*) Perhaps only if I went downstairs and out into the blizzard and walked for a while (or simply parked myself in a snowdrift near the coachmen perched on their boxes, near the patient horses) would I manage to understand what was engrossing them. I had to admit, too, that I longed for a gust of fresh air. When I'd entered the room, none of the guests seemed to mind the chill, but now they didn't seem to mind that it was too warm. The bells of the nearby church struck eleven times, and I heard the faraway echo, raggedly synchronized, from other churches in the city. A fat, red-faced woman in a near-rhyming, tomato-red apron appeared with an armful of wood and, brushing past me, opened the little door of the stove and fed the fire. I wondered if the flue was drawing as well as it should, knowing that I could expect nothing better of the gas jets, unevenly fed and therefore leaking and sputtering as they always did then, before the advent of natural gas; but, however inevitable that I, a child of neon and halogen, would appreciate the look of gas lighting, unlike everyone else in the room I was not used to its acrid smell. And of course many of the men were smoking. Ryszard, who had been drawing caricatures of the guests to entertain the drowsy child I thought must be Maryna's son, was puffing away on a large, ornately carved meerschaum pipe—exactly the fetish one might expect an insecure, ambitious young man to possess. Several of the older men had lit Virginia cigars. And Maryna, now installed in a vast wing chair, held a long Turkish cigarette in her languid hand—just the sort of mildly disreputable thing a celebrated actress would be given license to do. She could even wear trousers like George Sand if she liked, and I could perfectly imagine her as Rosalind; she would make a splendid Rosalind, though a bit old for the role, but that's never stopped any famous actress: fifty-year-olds have appeared, and triumphed, as Juliet. I could also see Maryna playing Nora or Hedda Gabler, this being the period of the ascendancy of Ibsen . . . but maybe she wouldn't want to play Hedda any more than she would want to play Lady Macbeth, which would mean she wasn't a truly great actor, who's never afraid of playing monsters. I hoped she hadn't been made less of an artist by high-mindedness. Or by self-regard. She was talking to the impresario from Vienna, he was smiling cautiously, and others had drawn close to listen. My Tadeusz, having finally broken free of the speechifying leading actor—I heard, their last words, *Sheer folly* (from the actor) and *Nothing is irrevocable* (from Tadeusz)—now stood beside Maryna's chair, his thumbs in the armholes of his yellow waistcoat: a most un-Wertherish gesture, but who could reproach him for falling out of type, for being happy, for becoming confident, simply because he was standing near her. Ryszard, a little apart, had taken out his notebook again. She looked up and said, *What are you writing?* Hastily pocketing the notebook, he murmured, *A description of you. I shall put it in a novel*—he shook his head—*if I ever find time, with all we have now to do, to write a novel.* The man I'd decided was a drama critic clapped him on the back. *One more reason, young man, not to embark on this foolishness,* he said jovially. But Maryna had already lowered her gaze. She was addressing the impresario with a controlling calm. *Oh, that's not good enough at all,* she said. More and more I saw the imperious woman, who did not have to persuade, whose word was law. I remember the first time I ever saw a diva up close: it was more than thirty years ago, I was new in New York and seriously poor and a rich suitor took me to lunch at Lutèce, where, shortly after the first delicacies had materialized on my plate, my attention was galvanized by the (come to think of it) familiar-looking woman with high cheekbones, raven-black hair, and full, red-painted mouth eating at the next table with an elderly man to whom she said loudly: "Mr. Bing. [Pause.] Either we do things the Callas way or we do not do them at all." And the Mr. Bing in question fell silent for some minutes—as did I. Now I knew that Maryna, my Maryna, must have had her Callas-like moments, if she was what I thought she was, though not tonight, I supposed, when she was among friends, when she would have preferred to cajole. But I could see her blue-grey eyes widen with irritation. How she must have longed, I was getting to know her, I think, how she must have longed to rise from the chair, upsetting everyone, and walk out of the room. To escape; to make an exit; not merely to get some fresh air, as I wanted to do. For I wouldn't have minded ducking out for a quarter of an hour, even to be hailed on—though I usually do mind the cold (I grew up in southern Arizona and southern California). But I didn't dare leave, for fear of missing something said the moment I'd quit the room that would have made everything clear to me. And, I saw, this was hardly the moment to descend into the snowy street. On the far side of the long table the headwaiter was making a discreet signal to Bogdan, as his four underlings bent over almost in unison to light the four triple-branched silver candelabra. Maryna rose, smoothing down the front of her sage-green robe with one hand while extinguishing her cigarette with the other. *Dear friends,* she began. *You have waited so long. You have been so patient.* She glanced slyly at Bogdan. *Yes,* he said. Adding something slothful as well as tender to the play of husbandly expressions crossing his face, he took her arm. How glad I was that I hadn't copped out when I'd wanted to but had remained at my station. My hope was that, once the guests were at dinner, the bits of overheard conversation would unite, and I would finally grasp what was absorbing them. For I thought it even possible that everyone turning, rising, tarrying, sidling toward the long table at one end of the room on the hotel's first floor (in my country it's the second floor) was privy to this deed or plan whose rightness or wrongness was still being disputed, keeping in mind that however many I might eventually discover were in on it, in anything undertaken by as few as two, one person is more responsible than another (though no one is entirely without responsibility, wherever there is consent there is responsibility), and with, say, twenty—actually I'd counted, there were twenty-seven people in the room—not only would one person be more responsible than the others, but someone would have been at the helm, however much that person, if a woman, would probably, in that time, have disavowed the name of leader. To be explained, nevertheless: why anybody follows anyone else. Or, just as puzzling, why anyone ever refuses to follow. (What writing feels like is following and leading, both, and at the same time.) I watched how everyone obeyed the long-awaited command to sit and be served. I didn't mind just watching, listening, I don't ever mind, especially at parties; though I did imagine that, could the guests at this party have become aware of my presence, of the intrusion of so exotic a stranger, a place would have been made for me at the table. (That I might be pushed out on the snowy street never crossed my mind.) Uninvited, unseen, I could look at them as long as I wanted, stare at them even: a piece of bad manners I usually can't practice because it's likely to incur a stare in return. As a child, I mean like many solitary children, I often wished I were invisible, the better to watch—I mean, to not be watched. But I also played, sometimes, at not seeing at all. Around thirteen, after the family pulled up tiny stakes and moved from Tucson to Los Angeles, this walking around with my eyes shut when I was alone or unobserved in the new house became, I recall, a favorite game. (My most memorable venture in blindness was when, on a middle-of-the-night trip to the bathroom, there was an earthquake.) I like the feeling of being reduced to my own resources. Of having to do nothing but cope. *About time*, the judge murmured irritably to his wife. She smiled and put two fingers to her lips. *Will there be ice cream?* said the little boy. The guests were approaching the table, Ryszard edging ahead, impatient to see how close to Maryna he had been seated, with Tadeusz right behind him, but it was Ryszard, hurrying his step, who reached the table first. I saw him scan for his place card and his grin told me that he was not dissatisfied. Once the guests had occupied all the chairs, while they were still unfolding their starched upright napkins, the squad of waiters began distributing the bounties of the first course. I had moved forward, too, and was sitting cross-legged in the embrasure of a tall window at that end of the room, and while I was trying to take in some first words at the table had to silence some words in my head: "sorrel soup," "carp à la juive," "sole au gratin," "boar's meat in cherry sauce" . . . the quotes are just to mark what I lack the patience right now to describe; I would have plenty of time to describe, I thought, after I'd understood the story. Though I knew they had been kept waiting (as, in another way, had I), I was a little surprised that everyone tucked in without ado. Did I expect them to say grace? I suppose I did. And, actually, one person, Bogdan's homely sister, did mutter at length to herself before lifting her fork; I'm sure she was reciting a prayer. Though I hoped that they wouldn't have tired of arguing, for the moment everyone seemed diverted by the sumptuous meal. What I was watching was the gamut of eating behavior, from dainty to wolfish, dotted with colorful comments about the food, and, even, the snowstorm. Good Lord, not the weather! Come back, noble idealists whom I've conjured up from the past. To be sure, not everyone was just eating. The doctor, I saw, much preferred the champagne and the Hungarian wine to the second courses. ("Turkey stuffed with walnuts," "baked black grouse and partridges" . . .) And the young actress, who never took her eyes off Maryna's pearly, unlined face, was chewing in slow motion; hardly anything was missing from her plate. Like her, like most of the guests, I found it hard not to keep Maryna at the center of my attention. I wondered what her real age was; after all, she was an actress. If this were happening now,

I would have said she was in her mid-forties (the ample bosom and heavy jaw, the judicious movements, the bulky gown). But, knowing that even the well-off aged faster then, and that everyone not poor was, by our standards, overweight, I gave her no more than thirty-five. I haven't said that I've been fiddling all along with the apparent age of everyone in the room: Ryszard, since he looked deep in his thirties, had to be twenty-five, and so forth. Traveling back to the past, I expected there to be some frustrations (the towering, fire-concealing stove instead of a waist-level, blazing fireplace) and a few adjustments (to estimate the age of anyone past his or her mid-twenties, deduct ten years), as well as the evident compensations and illuminations. The talk had evolved from pleasantries about the food to a rush of praise for Maryna's performance this evening. She accepted the compliments with a modesty that seemed as adamant as it was charming. *How splendid it was,* said Ryszard, his face aglow with admiration. *You really did surpass yourself, if such a thing is possible,* said the young painter. *She always does,* the leading actor said graciously, reprovingly. Dissociating herself from all this wet appetite, Maryna sat very still, she appeared scarcely to be breathing, a cambric handkerchief to her left cheek. *È sempre brava,* the doctor confided to the mystified waiter who was refilling his glass. Following a lull in the voices and a return to more dedicated eating, of course I was hoping for something else, the critic rose unsteadily, vodka in hand. *To you, Madame.* Every glass except Maryna's was lifted. *To this evening's triumph.* The doctor eased his glass toward his mouth. *Hold on, not so fast, Henryk,* the critic exclaimed with mock severity. *Don't you see I haven't finished?* Groaning, the doctor returned his arm to toast position. The critic cleared his throat, then intoned: *And to that sublime and patriotic art which you honor with your beauty and genius. To the theatre.* Maryna nodded to him and the others, pursing her lips, then whispered something to the impresario, who was seated at her right. *That wasn't fair, that's not one toast but three,* said the doctor gaily. *Three toasts, three infusions of this excellent vodka!*

He hailed one of the waiters. *Not, dear Maryna, that I don't sub-scribe with all my heart to the sentiments just uttered,* he said as his glass was again refilled. Then, raising it once more: *To your per-formance tomorrow.* And he emptied the glass. Next Bogdan, at the other end of the table, rose to his feet. *Not wishing to vex our thirsty friend,* he said, *I shall limit myself to one toast. And it is*—glass in the air—*to friendship. Hear, hear,* Ryszard called out. *Yes,* said Bogdan, *and to our sodality.* Sodality, I thought. What does that mean? *Look, he's doing it too,* the doctor had shouted, vodka already to his lips and drinking so avidly that he had spilled some on his linen shirt. *He can't help himself,* cried the judge, laughing. *Who, me?* said the doctor, wiping his mouth. Everyone laughed except Maryna and Bogdan. *I mean,* Bogdan continued solemnly, *to what we can accomplish together.* Applause. *Hear, hear,* said Tadeusz. *I am ready.* An abashed silence, in which everyone turned to Maryna. She reached for her glass and pressed it against her brow. Then, without rising, she lifted it above her head. *I really have only one toast to offer, not three pretending to be one.* She directed a fond smile at Bogdan. *I drink to one . . . divided into three. That will someday be one.* Dramatic pause. *To our homeland.* Everyone broke into applause. *Brava,* said the painter. Crowd-pleasing toasts, all—whose main effect, it seemed, was to drench everyone in melancholy. The little boy (Piotr? Roman?) left his chair to tiptoe over to Maryna and whisper something I couldn't hear. She shook her head, looking (I'm sorry to report) a bit cross, and he returned to his seat next to Bogdan's sister, was received in her lap, and fell asleep against her neck. Of the ensu-ing murk of conversation, I didn't register much. I wish I could say that I was just feeling thinky, and so had closed my eyes to mount the next rung in the dark. *You have given me so much to ponder,* said a glum voice. *Of course I want to broaden my hori-zons,* said a lilting voice. *No misgivings, none at all?* said a pep-pery, self-assured voice. *How I admire you,* said a sad voice. *Irrevocable,* I heard again. And opened my eyes. This might have been the doctor, who'd plunged his head into his hands. Had I missed something? Silly thoughts had started to buffet my mind. Hearing someone trail off (it was all I retained) . . . *along with my milk brother, Marek, their son,* and identifying the speaker as the man with the plump unshaven cheeks sitting next to the banker's wife, I thought: what a greedy baby you must have been at that countrywoman's breast! The eating seemed to me interminable, and I had not tried to follow the plot of the meal, assuming that it was, *à la française,* a three-act dinner, and that, whenever I wanted, I could peek at one of the small handwritten menus provided with every setting, like theatre programs, to see how much there was still to go. As if he had read my mind, even though I was here to read his, Bogdan murmured, *We don't have to eat like this. I, for one, would be happy to eat simply.* I hoped they were nearing the dessert now. Bogdan had set down his knife and fork. *Quo vadis?* said the judge. *Where goest thou?* Ryszard smiled and took out his notebook. *Where, yes. And how,* said the banker. *Everything must be thought through carefully. No reason for haste.* There was a moment's quiet, as if everyone were indeed reflecting. Then I heard, in a singsongy voice, something like:

> *From the mountains, carrying their heavy, awesome crosses,*
> *They could see in the distance the promised land.*
> *They could see the blue light in the valley,*
> *Toward which their tribe was heading—*

from the elderly woman in the mauve hat. *We need a piano,* interrupted the stage manager. *I can no longer hear this poem except in Chopin's setting.* The elderly woman, I had never decided whether she was somebody's wife or a maiden aunt, perhaps Bogdan's, looked offended. *Please go on,* said the young actress, Krystyna, I forgot to mention that I'd figured out her name. *I had every intention of doing just that,* said the elderly woman tartly. *How does it go?* Exclaimed the painter, *How does it go? You know very well.* And he continued in his ringing baritone:

And yet they themselves will never arrive!
They will never sit down to the feast of life,
And perhaps be forgotten, forgotten, forgotten.

He was a fine elocutionist. *Exactly,* said the elderly woman. Then something happened that was mildly confounding. Maryna lifted her arms and declaimed in her warm alto tone:

Like as the waves make towards the pebbled shore,
So do our minutes hasten to their end;
Each changing place with that which goes before,
In sequent toil all forwards do contend.

And for a few moments I didn't realize that she was reciting in English. I can't say what I thought at first I was hearing, since I wouldn't have been startled to hear any language spoken at this gathering (any except Russian, the language of the most hated of the nation's three oppressors). Another foreign language I don't know but somehow, tonight, was able to understand? Meanwhile, the young actress had burst out with:

Therefore devise with me how we may fly,
Whither to go, and what to bear with us.
And do not seek to take your change upon you,
To bear your griefs yourself and leave me out;
For, by this heaven, now at our sorrows pale,
Say what thou canst, I'll go along with thee.

Her shiny voice trembled, stopped. If you were familiar with *As You Like It,* you would have recognized the lines—of course, she would be Celia to Maryna's Rosalind—though they were barely intelligible, her accent being even thicker than Maryna's. She, Maryna, was not looking pleased. *I butchered Shakespeare's glorious English,* I heard her say to the drama critic, who was sitting on her left. *Not at all,* he exclaimed, *you said it beautifully. I did not,* Maryna answered sharply. And, in truth, she had not. I hoped they would do better when they spoke more English, as I suspected they were going to do, if I'd understood anything about what was being discussed. Undoubtedly, they will continue to speak English with an accent, as do many people in my country, as did my great-grandparents (maternal) and my grandparents (paternal), though naturally their children did not. For it should be mentioned, why not here, that all four of my grandparents were born in this country (hence, born in a country that had ceased to exist some eighty years earlier), indeed, born around the very year to which I'd traveled in my mind in order to co-inhabit this room with its old-timey conversations, though the folks who engendered the couple that engendered me were quite unlike these people, being poor unworldly villagers with occupations like peddler, innkeeper, woodcutter, Talmud student. Having assumed that nobody here was a Jew, I hoped, this was a new thought, that I wouldn't hear an anti-Semitic outburst from someone; I hadn't, and somehow intuited that they were, if anything, philo-Semites. That this was the country my forebears chose to leave by crowded steerage hardly links me to these people, though conceivably it might make the name of this country resonate for me, might draw me to a room here rather than elsewhere; having tried conjuring up a hotel dining room from the same era in Sarajevo, and failed, I had to accept where I had alighted. But the past is the biggest country of all, and there's a reason one gives in to the desire to set stories in the past: almost everything good seems located in the past, perhaps that's an illusion, but I feel nostalgic for every era before I was born; and one is freer of modern inhibitions, perhaps because one bears no responsibility for the past, sometimes I feel simply ashamed of the time in which I live. And this past will also be the present, because it was I in the private dining room of the hotel, scattering seeds of prediction. I did not belong there, I was an alien presence, I would have to lean very close to hear, and I would not understand everything, but even what I misunderstood would be a

23

kind of truth, if only about the time in which I live, rather than the one in which their story took place. *We must always ask more of ourselves*, I heard Maryna say sternly. *Always. Or am I speaking only for myself?* Ah, that was an endearing note. I have a weakness for the earnest, the strenuous. If I thought of Maryna as a character in a novel, I would have liked her to have something of Dorothea Brooke (I remember when I first read *Middlemarch*: I had just turned eighteen, and a third of the way through the book burst into tears because I realized not only that *I* was Dorothea but that, a few months earlier, I had married Mr. Casaubon), yet there was nothing submissive or self-effacing, I could see that, in this woman with the ash-blond hair and the candid, intense blue-grey eyes. She would want to do good for others, but she would never be seduced into forgetting herself. For someone whose ambition was to go on the stage, being female was not an obstacle: she had lived the competitive life, and she had won. But I thought I could put up with a good deal of vanity and self-love as long as she kept the desire for self-improvement, which I guessed she would as I studied the contrast between the impatient, overwatchful expressions crossing her face and that peculiar way she had of holding herself very, very still. Odd to think that somebody could have described me, snugly ensconced in the deep recess of the window, as I'm describing her. In fact, I'm rather impulsive (I married Mr. Casaubon after knowing him for ten days) and have something of a taste for risk-taking, but I'm also prone to the long, drawn-out huddle in a corner that caring about duties brings on (it took me nine years to decide that I had the right, the moral right, to divorce Mr. Casaubon), so it was easy for me to feel indulgent toward these people mired in their dinner, in their debate about what some of them were going to do. And easy for me to become exasperated with them. No one fidgeted. I hadn't spied any hanky-panky under the table. No one had faded, except of course the little boy curled up on another woman's lap, rubbing his eyes, instead of home tucked in his bed. He must be an only child, his mother must have wanted him near tonight, even if I hadn't seen her pay any attention to him for these last two hours at the table. They did seem to me, for all their flashes of agitation about the subject engaging them, a bit too sedate. To what could I attribute their immobility? The overcooked food continuing to be urged on the table? The perennial ineffectuality of the thinking classes? The ponderousness of the late nineteenth century? My own reluctance to imagine anything livelier? True, there was still time for something really vivid to happen. Someone might have a heart attack or whack a dinner partner over the head or sob and groan or toss a glass of wine in an offending face. But this seemed as unlikely as my charging out of my window seat to dance on the table or spit in the soup or fondle a knee or bite someone's ankle. Humid thoughts: I needed some air. On Bogdan's signal, one of the waiters opened the window at the other end of the room, where I'd been lurking when I arrived. I heard an eruption of street shouts and neighing horses. It was just after one o'clock by the church bells (and, yes, by my watch; I've admitted to turning restless). I hadn't been at the theatre at seven o'clock for tonight's performance, of course I wished I had seen it, as they had. Some of them must have been restless, too. But no one would stand until Maryna did. I'd almost given up hoping that their argument about the rightness or wrongness of whatever they were discussing would reach a climax this evening, no matter how long they stayed at the table and I remained nearby, gazing at them, listening to them, thinking about them. For it's the nature of such debates, the debate about rightness and about wrongness, that you can always have misgivings and a new thought the next day, that looking back on the evening's conversation you may exclaim, what a fool I was to say that, or agree to that. Was I under the influence of so-and-so, or just being dopey or thoughtless, my moral thermostat turned down? So the next morning, you are of the opposite mind (perhaps you think the opposite precisely because of what you argued for the night before, that opinion having needed an airing in order to make way for this, the better one), you have something like a moral hangover, but you feel calm because you know now you're on the right track, while uneasily suspecting you could still think something different tomorrow; and meanwhile, the time for the decision you are weighing, the course of action you may or may not follow, is approaching. It may be right now. Then Maryna did rise, and took a cigarette from her gold-beaded reticule and glided to the center of the room. The others stood up, and I assumed they would all leave now. But only Ryszard exuberantly kissed Maryna's hand, then made the rounds, touching his lips to the wrist of each of the other women in the room, I supposed that he was looking forward to capping the evening with a stop at his favorite bordello. Then the director of the theatre and his wife took their leave, followed by the banker and the judge and their wives, then the leading actor and the stage manager and a few others. Nobody else seemed about to go. The doctor opened the bottle of Tokay on the sideboard. The little boy, Piotr (so I belatedly named him), who had been awakened and made ready for departure, was set to wait on the wing chair. Maryna leaned with a fetching show of languor against the back of the chair, surrounded by Bogdan, Tadeusz, the young actress, the impresario, Bogdan's sister, the doctor, and the one-legged painter. Here was one last chance for the conversation to ripen and their decision to be cinched like a purse. *Well, of course,* said Maryna, laughing emphatically, *I don't always agree with myself.* An encouraging thought. They went on talking quietly. I would go on listening. As a child, while I did concede that I was good at learning, I was sure I wasn't "really intelligent" (please ignore the quotes) as I understood what that meant from books, from biographies, there being no one in my vicinity who seemed "really intelligent" (same request) either. Still, I did think that I could do whatever I set my mind to (I was going to be a chemist, like Madame Curie), that steadfastness and caring more than the others about what was important would take me wherever I wanted to go. And so, now, I thought if I listened and watched and ruminated, taking as much time as I needed, I could understand the people in this room, that theirs would be a story that would speak to me, though how I knew this I can't explain. There are so many stories to tell, it's hard to say why it's one rather than another, it must be because with this story you feel you can tell many stories, that there will be a necessity in it; I see I am explaining badly. I can't explain. It has to be something like falling in love. Whatever explains why you chose this story—it may, indeed, draw sap from some childhood grief or longing—hasn't explained much. A story, I mean a long story, a novel, is like an around-the-world-in-eighty-days: you can barely recall the beginning when it comes to an end. But even a long journey must begin somewhere, say, in a room. Each of us carries a room within ourselves, waiting to be furnished and peopled, and if you listen closely, you may need to silence everything in your own room, you can hear the sounds of that other room inside your head. You can hear the fire crackling or the clock ticking or (if the window is open) the cry of a coachman or the *vroom-vroom* of a motorcycle in the alley. Or you may not hear any of this, if the room is full of voices. Raucous or soft-mannered people may be sitting down to dinner, saying something you don't quite understand, let's hope not because the television is on, and full blast, but you'll catch the gist. First it will be only phrases, or a name, or an urgent whisper, or a cry. If there are cries, no, screams, and you see something like a bed, you can hope that this isn't a room where someone is being tortured, but, rather, where someone is giving birth, although these sounds are also unbearable. You can hope that you have found yourself among largehearted people, passion is a beautiful thing, and so is understanding, the coming to understand something, which is a passion, which is a journey, too. The servants were bringing Maryna and the others their wraps. They were ready to leave now. With a shiver of anticipation, I decided to follow them out into the world.

One

PERHAPS IT WAS the slap she received from Gabriela Ebert a few minutes past five o'clock in the afternoon (I'd not witnessed that) which made something, no, everything (I couldn't have known this either) a little clearer. Arriving at the theatre, inflexibly punctual, two hours before curtain, Maryna had gone directly to her star's lair, been stripped to her chemise and corset and helped into a fur-lined robe and slippers by her dresser, Zofia, whom she dispatched to iron her costume in an adjoining room, had pushed the candles nearer both sides of the mirror, had leaned forward over the jumbled palette of already uncapped jars and vials of makeup for a closer scrutiny of that all too familiar mask, her real face, the actress's under-face, when behind her the door seemed to break open and in front of her, sharing the mirror, hurtling toward her, she saw her august rival's reddened, baleful face shouting the absurd insult, threw herself back in her chair, turned, glimpsed the arm descending just before an involuntary grimace of her own brought down her eyelids at the same instant it bared her upper teeth and shortened her nose, and felt the shove and sting of a large beringed hand against her face.

It all happened so rapidly and noisily—her eyes stayed closed, the door banged shut—and the shadow-flecked room with its hissing gas jets had gone so silent now, it might have been a bad dream: she'd been having bad dreams. Maryna clapped her palm to her offended face.

"Zofia? Zofia!"

Sound of the door being opened softly. And some anxious babble from Bogdan. "What the devil did she want? If I hadn't been down the corridor with Jan, I would have stopped her, how dare she burst in on you like that!"

"It's nothing," Maryna said, opening her eyes, dropping her hand. "Nothing." Meaning: the buzz of pain in her cheek. And the migraine now looming on the other side of her head, which she intended to keep at bay by a much-practiced exercise of will until the end of the evening. She bent forward to tie her hair in a towel, then stood and moved to the washstand, where she vigorously soaped and scrubbed her face and neck, and patted the skin dry with a soft cloth.

"I knew all along she wouldn't—"

"It's all right," said Maryna. Not to him. To Zofia, hesitating at the half-open door, holding the costume aloft in her outstretched arms.

Waving her in, Bogdan shut the door a bit harder than he intended. Maryna stepped out of her robe and into the burgundy gown with gold braiding ("No, no, leave the back unbuttoned!"), rotated slowly once, twice, before the cheval glass, nodded to herself, sent Zofia away to repair the loose buckle on her shoe and heat the curling iron, then sat at the dressing table again.

"What did Gabriela want?"

"Nothing."

"Maryna!"

She took a tuft of down and spread a thick layer of Pearl Powder on her face and throat.

"She came by to wish me the best for tonight."

"Really?"

"Quite generous of her, wouldn't you agree, since she'd thought the role was to be hers."

"Very generous," he said. And, he thought, very unlike Gabriela.

He watched as three times she redid the powder, applied the rouge with a hare's foot well up on her cheekbones and under her eyes and on her chin, and blackened her eyelids, and three times took it all off with a sponge.

"Maryna?"

"Sometimes I think there's no point to any of this," she said tonelessly, starting again on her eyelids with the charcoal stick.

"This?"

She dipped a fine camel's-hair brush into the dish of burnt umber and traced a line under her lower eyelashes.

It seemed to Bogdan she was using too much kohl, which made her beautiful eyes look sorrowful, or merely old. "Maryna, look at me!"

"Dear Bogdan, I'm not going to look at you." She was dabbing more kohl on her brows. "And you're not going to listen to me. You should be inured by now to my attacks of nerves. Actor's nerves. A little worse than usual, but this *is* a first night. Don't pay any attention to me."

As if that were possible! He bent over and touched his lips to the nape of her neck. "Maryna . . ."

"What?"

"You remember that I've taken the room at the Saski for a few of us afterward to celebrate—"

"Call Zofia for me, will you?" She had started to mix the henna.

"Forgive me for bringing up a dinner while you're preparing for a performance. But it should be called off if you're feeling too . . ."

"Don't," she murmured. She was blending a little Dutch pink and powdered antimony with the Prepared Whiting to powder her hands and arms. "Bogdan?"

He didn't answer.

"I'm looking forward to the party," she said and reached behind for a gloved hand to lay on her shoulder.

"You're upset about something."

"I'm upset about everything," she said dryly. "And you'll be so kind as to let me wallow in it. The old stager has need of a little stimulation to go on doing her best!"

MARYNA DID NOT RELISH lying to Bogdan, the only person among all those who loved her, or claimed to love her, whom she did in fact trust. But she had no place for his indignation or his eagerness to console. She thought it might do her good to keep this astonishing incident to herself.

Sometimes one needs a real slap in the face to make what one is feeling real.

When life cuffs you about, you say, That's life.

You feel strong. You want to feel strong. The important thing is to go forward.

As she had, single-mindedly, or almost: there had been much to ignore. But if you are of a stoical temperament, and have a talent for self-respect, and have worked hard with another talent God gave you, and have been rewarded exactly as you had dared to hope for your diligence and persistence, indeed, your success arrived more promptly than you expected (or perhaps, you secretly think, merited), you might then consider it petty to remember the slights and nurture the grievances. To be offended was to be weak—like worrying about whether one was happy or not.

Now you have an unexpected pain, around which the muffled feelings can crystallize.

You have to float your ideals a little off the ground, to keep them from being profaned. And cut loose the misfortunes and insults, too, lest they take root and strangle your soul.

Take the slap for what it was, a jealous rival's frantic comment on her impregnable success—that would have been something to share with Bogdan, and soon put out of mind. Take it as an emblem, a summons to respond to the whispery needs she'd been harboring for months—this would be worth keeping to herself, even cherishing. Yes, she would cherish poor Gabriela's slap. If that slap were a baby's smile, she would smile at the recollection of it, if it were a picture, she would have it framed and kept on her dressing table, if it were hair, she would order a wig made from it . . . Oh I see, she thought, I'm going mad. Could it be as simple as that? She'd laughed to herself then, but saw with distaste that the hand applying henna to her lips was trembling. Misery is wrong, she said to herself, mine no less than Gabriela's, and she only wants what I have. Misery is always wrong.

Crisis in the life of an actress. Acting was emulating other actors and then, to one's surprise (actually, not at all to one's surprise), finding oneself better than any of them were—including the pathetic bestower of that slap. Wasn't that enough? No. Not anymore.

She had loved being an actress because the theatre seemed to her nothing less than the truth. A higher truth. Acting in a play, one of the great plays, you became better than you really were. You said only words that were sculpted, necessary, exalting. You always looked as beautiful as you could be, artifice assisting, at your age. Each of your movements had a large, generous meaning. You could feel yourself being improved by what was given to you, on the stage, to express. Now it would happen that, mid-course in a noble tirade by her beloved Shakespeare or Schiller or Słowacki, pivoting in her unwieldy costume, gesturing, declaiming, sensing the audience bend to her art, she felt no more than herself. The old self-transfiguring thrill was gone. Even stage fright—that jolt necessary to the true professional— had deserted her. Gabriela's slap woke her up. An hour later Maryna put on her wig and papier-mâché crown, gave one last look in the mirror, and went out to give a performance that even she could have admitted was, by her real standards for herself, not too bad.

BOGDAN WAS so captivated by Maryna's majesty as she went to be executed that at the start of the ovation he was still rooted in the plush-covered chair at the front of his box, hands clenching the rail. Galvanized now, he slipped between his sister, the impresario from Vienna, Ryszard, and the other guests, and by the second curtain call had made his way backstage.

"Mag-ni-fi-cent," he mouthed as she came off from the third curtain call to wait beside him in the wings for the volume of sound to warrant another return to the flower-strewn stage.

"If you think so, I'm glad."

"Listen to them!"

"Them! What do they know if they've never seen anything better than me?"

After she'd conceded four more curtain calls, Bogdan escorted her to the dressing-room door. She supposed she was starting to allow herself to feel pleased with her performance. But once inside, she let out a wordless wail and burst into tears.

"Oh, Madame!" Zofia seemed about to weep, too.

Stricken by the anguish on the girl's face and intending to comfort her, Maryna flung herself into Zofia's arms.

"There, there," she murmured as Zofia held her tightly, then let go with one arm and delicately patted Maryna's crimped, stiffened mass of hair.

Maryna released herself reluctantly from the girl's unwavering grip and met her stare fondly. "You have a good heart, Zofia."

"I can't stand to see you sad, Madame."

"I'm not sad, I'm . . . Don't be sad for me."

"Madame, I was in the wings almost the whole last act, and when you went to die, I never saw you die as good as that, you were so wonderful I just couldn't stop crying."

"Then that's enough crying for both of us, isn't it?" Maryna started to laugh. "To work, you silly girl, to work. Why are we both dawdling?"

Relieved of her regal costume and reclothed in the fur-lined robe, Maryna sponged off Mary Stuart's face and swiftly laid on the discreet mask suitable to the wife of Bogdan Dembowski. Zofia, sniffling a little ("Zofia, enough!"), stood behind her chair embracing the sage-green gown Maryna had chosen that after-noon to wear to the dinner Bogdan was giving at the Hotel Saski. She put the gown on slowly in front of the cheval glass, returned to the dressing table and undid the curls and brushed and re-brushed her hair, then piled it loosely on her head, looked closer into the mirror, added a little melted wax to her eyelashes, stood again, inspected herself once more, listening to the ascending din in the corridor, took several loud, rhythmical breaths, and opened the door to an enveloping wave of shouts and applause.

Among the admirers well connected enough to be admitted backstage were some acquaintances but, except for Ryszard, clasping a bouquet of silk flowers to his broad chest, she saw no close friends: those invited to the party had been asked to go on ahead to the hotel. And more than a hundred people were wait-ing outside the stage door, despite the foul weather. Bogdan offered the shelter of his sword-umbrella with the ivory handle so she could linger for fifteen minutes under the falling snow, and she would have lingered another fifteen had he not waved away the more timid fans, their programs still unsigned, and shepherded Maryna through the crowd toward the waiting sleigh. Ryszard, finally pressing his bouquet into her hands, said the Saski was only seven streets away and that he preferred to walk.

How strange, in her native city to be receiving friends in a hotel, but for the last five years—her talents having led her inexorably to the summit, an engagement for life at the Im-perial Theatre in Warsaw—she no longer had an apartment in Kraków.

"Strange," she said. To Bogdan, to no one, to herself. Bogdan frowned.

A thunderbolt, like the crack of gunfire, as they arrived at the hotel. A scream, no, only a shout: an angry coachman.

They walked up the carpeted marble staircase.

"You're all right?"

"Of course I'm all right. It's only another entrance."

"And I have the privilege of opening the door for you."

Now it was Maryna's turn to frown.

And how could there not be applause and beaming faces, customary welcome at a first-night party—but she really had given a splendid performance—as Bogdan opened the door (in answer to her "Bogdan, are *you* all right?" he had sighed and taken her hand) and she made her entrance. Piotr ran to her arms. She embraced Bogdan's sister and gave her Ryszard's silk flowers; she let herself be embraced by Krystyna, whose eyes had filled with tears. After the guests, gathering closely around her, had each paid tribute to her performance, she looked from face to face, and then sang out gleefully:

May you a better feast never behold,
You knot of mouth friends!

Upon which words everyone laughed, which means, I suppose (I had not arrived yet), that she said Timon's lines in Polish, not English, but also means that nobody except Maryna had read *Timon of Athens*, for the feast in the play is not a happy one, above all for its giver. Then the guests spread about the large room and began talking among themselves about her performance and, after that, about the larger question afoot (which is more or less when I arrived, chilled and eager to enter the story), while Maryna had forced herself toward humbler, less sardonic thoughts. No jealous rivals here. These were her friends, those who wished her well. Where was her gratitude? She hated her discontents. If I can have a new life, she was thinking, I shall never complain again.

"MARYNA?"

No answer.

"Maryna, what's wrong?"

"What could be wrong . . . doctor?"

He shook his head. "Oh, I see."

"Henryk."

"That's better."

"I'm disturbing you."

"Yes"—he smiled—"you disturb me, Maryna. But only in my dreams, never in my consulting room." Then, before she could rebuke him for flirting with her: "The splendors of your performance last night," he explained.

He saw her still hesitating. "Come in"—he held out his hand—"Sit"—he waved at a tapestry-covered settee—"Talk to me." Two steps into the room, she leaned against a bookcase. "You're not going to sit?"

"*You* sit. And I'll continue my walk . . . here."

"You came here on foot in this weather? Was that wise?"

"Henryk, please!"

He sat on the corner of his desk.

She began to pace. "I thought I was coming here to besiege you with questions about Stefan, if he really—"

"But I've told you," Henryk interrupted, "that the lungs already show a remarkable improvement. Against such a mighty enemy, the struggle waged by doctor and patient is bound to be long. But I think we're winning, your brother and I."

"You talk rubbish, Henryk. Has anyone ever told you that?"

"Maryna, what's the matter?"

"Everyone talks rubbish—"

"Maryna . . ."

"Including me."

"So"—he sighed—"it isn't Stefan you wanted to consult me about."

She shook her head.

"Then let me guess," he said, venturing a smile.

"You're making fun of me, my old friend," Maryna said somberly. "Women's nerves, you're thinking. Or worse."

"I?"—he slapped the desk—"I, your old friend, as you acknowledge, and I thank you for that, I *not* take my Maryna seriously?" He looked at her sharply. "What is it? Your headaches?"

"No, it's not about"—she sat down abruptly—"me. I mean, my headaches."

"I'm going to take your pulse," he said, standing over her. "You're flushed. I wouldn't be surprised if you had a touch of fever." After a moment of silence, while he held her wrist then gave it back to her, he looked again at her face. "No fever. You are in excellent health."

"I told you there was nothing wrong."

"Ah, that means you want to complain to me. Well, you shall find me the most patient of listeners. Complain, dear Maryna," he cried gaily. He didn't see the tears in her eyes. "Complain!"

"Perhaps it is my brother, after all."

"But I told you—"

"Excuse me"—she'd stood—"I'm making a fool of myself."

"Never! Please don't go." He rose to bar her way to the door. "You do have a fever."

"You said I didn't."

"The mind can get overheated, just like the body."

"What do you think of the will, Henryk? The power of the will."

"What sort of question is that?"

"I mean, do you think one can do whatever one wants?"

"*You* can do whatever you want, my dear. We are all your

37

servants and abettors." He took her hand and inclined his head to kiss it.

"Oh"—she pulled away her hand—"you disgusting man, don't flatter me!"

He stared for a moment with a gentle, surprised expression. "Maryna, dear," he said soothingly. "Hasn't your experience taught you anything about how others respond to you?"

"Experience is a passive teacher, Henryk."

"But it—"

"In paradise"—she bore down on him, her grey eyes glittering—"there will be no experiences. Only bliss. There we will be able to speak the truth to each other. Or not need to speak at all."

"Since when have you believed in paradise? I envy you."

"Always. Since I was a child. And the older I get, the more I believe in it, because paradise is something necessary."

"You don't find it . . . difficult to believe in paradise?"

"Oh," she groaned, "the problem is not paradise. The problem is myself, my wretched self."

"Spoken like the artist you are. Someone with your temperament will always—"

"I knew you would say that!" She stamped her foot. "I order you, I implore you, don't speak of my temperament!"

(Yes she had been ill. Her nerves. Yes she was still ill, all her friends except her doctor said among themselves.)

"So you believe in paradise," he murmured placatingly.

"Yes, and at the gates of paradise, I would say, Is *this* your paradise? These ethereal figures robed in white, drifting among the white clouds? Where can I sit? Where is the water?"

"Maryna . . ." Taking her by the hand, he led her back to the settee. "I'm going to pour you a dram of cognac. It will be good for both of us."

"You drink too much, Henryk."

"Here." He handed her one of the glasses and pulled a chair opposite her. "Isn't that better?"

She sipped the cognac, then leaned back and gazed at him mutely.

"What is it?"

"I think I will die very soon, if I don't do something reckless . . . grand. I thought I was dying last year, you know."

"But you didn't."

"Must one die to prove one's sincerity!"

FROM A LETTER to nobody, that is, to herself:

It's not because my brother, my beloved brother, is dying and I will have no one to revere . . . it's not because my mother, our beloved mother, grates on my nerves, oh, how I wish I could stop her mouth . . . it's not because I too am not a good mother (how could I be? I am an actress) . . . it's not because my husband, who is not the father of my son, is so kind and will do whatever I want . . . it's not because everyone applauds me, because they cannot imagine that I could be more vivid or different than I already am . . . it's not because I am thirty-five now and because I live in an old country, and I don't want to be old (I do not intend to become my mother) . . . it's not because some of the critics condescend, now I am being compared with younger actresses, while the ovations after each performance are no less thunderous (so what then is the meaning of applause?) . . . it's not because I have been ill (my nerves) and had to stop performing for three months, only three months (I don't feel well when I am not working) . . . it's not because I believe in paradise . . . oh, and it's not because the police are still spying and making reports on me, though all those reckless statements and hopes are long past (my God, it's thirteen years since the Uprising) . . . it's not for any of these reasons that I've decided to do something that nobody wants me to do, that everyone regards as folly, and that I want some of them to do with me, though they don't want to; even Bogdan, who always wants

39

what I want (as he promised, when we married), doesn't really want to. But he must.

"PERHAPS IT IS a curse to come from anywhere. The world, you see," she said, "is very large. I mean," she said, "the world comes in many parts. The world, like our poor Poland, can always be divided. And subdivided. You find yourself occupying a smaller and smaller space. Though you're at home in that space—"

"On that stage," said the friend helpfully.

"If you will," she said coolly. "That stage." Then she frowned. "Surely you're not reminding me that all the world's a stage?"

"BUT HOW CAN you leave your place, which is here?"

"My place, my place," she cried. "I have none!"

"And you can't abandon your—"

"Friends?" she hooted.

"Actually, Irena and I were thinking of your public."

"Who says I am abandoning my public? Will they forget me if I choose to absent myself? No. Will they welcome me back should I choose to return? Yes. As for my friends . . ."

"Yes?"

"You can be sure I have no intention of abandoning my friends."

"MY FRIENDS," she repeated, "are much more danger-ous than my enemies. I'm thinking of their approval. Their ex-pectations. They want me to be as I am, and I cannot disabuse them entirely. They might cease to love me.

"I've explained it to them. But I could have announced it to them, like a whim. Recently, I thought I was ready to do it. At dinner in a hotel, the party after a first-night performance. I was going to raise my glass. I am leaving. Soon. Forever. Someone would have exclaimed, Oh Madame, how can you? And I'd have replied, I can, I can. But I didn't have the courage. Instead, I offered a toast to our poor dismembered country."

LOVE OF COUNTRY, of friends, of family, of the stage . . . oh, and love of God: love, the word, came easily to Maryna's lips—however little she expected from romantic love, the stuff of plays.

She had been a stern, dutiful child. She thought God was always watching her and recording in a large brown ledger (as she imagined it) her every thought and action. She kept her back straight and always met people's gaze. She was sure God approved of that. She understood, early on, that it was futile to complain, and best not to confide in anyone. God knew how weak she was, but forgave her because she tried so hard. In return, she determined not to ask God for anything she might not deserve, either by her own talents or by the strength of her wishing. She did not want to strain His generosity.

Granted, she could not tell the truth. But there was so much energy in her for saying *something*, and making others listen. A woman could not say much. A diva could say too much. As a diva, with a diva's permissions, she could have tantrums, she could ask for the impossible, she could lie.

It would have been appropriate if she had arisen from nowhere to become a star. It was equally appropriate that she should be the scion of a charming, vastly talented clan. The family story that she constructed, her happy though penurious childhood, artfully blended elements of the two.

She was the youngest of her mother's ten children—there had been six by a first marriage, then four more after marriage to a secondary-school Latin teacher—and, as Maryna used to say, with two of her half brothers already on the stage by the time she was four and learning to read, how could she not have wanted to follow them? In fact, Maryna had not at first dreamed of the actor's life. She wanted to be a soldier; and when it occurred to her that, being a girl, she would never be allowed to bear arms, she wanted to be a poet whose patriotic odes men would recite as they marched to demand their country's freedom. But her father, though he did not discourage her appetite for reading, seemed to think it more becoming for a girl to be musical than bookish. He, after preparing the next day's lessons, retreated from the evening's family noise by playing the flute.

From all this, what she distilled for her friends was that her father had taught her to play the flute.

Banished from telling: the frightening disharmony of her parents, her mother's tirades, her father asleep over his Caesar or Virgil, the taunts of the neighbors' children when she was six that the Latin teacher was not her father but someone who had rented a room in the flat (they'd always needed to take in boarders): someone like the older man, half-German, half-Polish, who moved into the flat with the title of boarder when she was eleven, two years after her father died, and who did not begin to visit her bed (extracting a promise from her not to tell her mother) until she was fourteen—she should count herself fortunate to have remained unmolested until such a late age, was her mother's comment.

"I COME FROM a family of many brothers and sisters, all as children in love with the theatre, though just four of us—Stefan, Adam, Józefina, myself—went on the stage. Of course only one among us had real genius, and it was not I. No"—she raised her hand—"don't contradict me."

Maryna liked declaring that Stefan's was the more natural talent, that she had achieved everything by hard work and application: she'd never ceased to feel guilty about the speed with which her career had eclipsed his.

"And we were poor. Even poorer after our father died, when

I was nine. After he died my mother worked in a pastry shop on the same street as the flat in which we all had been born, which was lost in the Great Kraków Fire." She paused. "When I was young I thought I could not live without comfort and luxury." A spindly waiter was pouring the champagne. "Then I thought I couldn't live without my friends."

"And now?"

"Now I think I can do without everything."

"Which is the same as wanting everything," replied her clever friend.

SHE WAS SEVEN when she first entered a theatre. The play was *Don Carlos*. It seemed to be about love, and then it was about being heartbroken, but then it was about something much better, when at the end the unhappy Carlos went off to fight for the liberty of enslaved Holland. (That he will never go to Holland—that in the final moment of the play the King, Carlos's father, orders his son's arrest and execution—was too horrifying to take in.) She was completely swept up by Schiller's message of liberty, so much so that, eventually, it dislodged from her mind the reason that, young as she was, she had been taken to the theatre. It was to see her half brother Stefan, performing in Kraków for the first time, in one of the principal roles. For, as the play went on, she had realized with a mounting sense of humiliation that she did not recognize him. She'd looked at all the men who came and went on the stage, and hadn't seen her handsome brother among them. One was too fat, another too old (Stefan was nineteen), another too tall. The only one who wasn't too fat or too old or too tall, a man with a silver wig and red paint on his face, playing the part of the faithful Posa, didn't look at all like him. But she couldn't ask her parents who Stefan was. She would be judged hopelessly stupid and never be taken to the theatre again.

After the performance, when she accompanied her mother backstage and Stefan emerged, beaming, his bony face with its

43

strong jaw and high forehead cleansed of makeup, she could hardly ask him which part he had played (*could* he have been Posa?) and just told him that he was wonderful, wonderful.

Then it occurred to her—it seemed a very ingenious, grown-up calculation—that there was one way to ensure that she would be allowed again into a theatre. That was to become an actor herself. Who could bar an actor from the theatre? Indeed, so welcome were actors that apparently they didn't have to use the regular entrance (though she supposed they were still required to buy tickets) but went in by a back door.

"That night"—she was telling the story, laughing at herself, to a friend—"I swore a vow standing with my mouth pressed to the icy pane of the little window of the room I shared with five of my sisters and brothers . . . no, not in the flat where I was born but the new one (it was a year after the Fire) . . . that I would live only for the theatre. Of course I didn't know if I could be an actress. And for a long time Stefan, and even Adam, did all they could to discourage me with fearful pictures of the actor's life: the hard work and the tedium, the bad wages, the dishonest theatre managers, the ungrateful ignorant audiences, the malicious reviewers. Not to mention the unheated filthy hotel rooms and their creaking floorboards, the greasy food and the cold tea, the interminable journeys over unreliable roads in badly sprung carriages, but"— she broke off, to explain—"that was what I liked."

"The discomforts?"

"Yes, the traveling! Being a vagrant. You go somewhere, you please people, and then you never have to see them again."

"But it must be more comfortable now, since you can travel by train."

"You're not listening to me. You don't see," she cried. "It felt right not having a home!"

"I CAN STILL SEE that fire"—she was telling this to Ryszard—"and smell it. I'll always be terrified of fire. I was ten.

44

From across the square, sheltering at first with so many others in the door of the Dominican church, we watched our windows melt, the windows from which my brothers used to take aim with their wooden guns at Austrian soldiers—how that had frightened our mother. She said we were lucky to escape with our lives, which was all we escaped with, for everything burned, even the church, and the flat we moved to after the fire was even smaller. Still, small as it was, my mother took in another boarder—we'd always had boarders in the flat on Grodzka Street—and that was Mr. Załężowski, Heinrich Załężowski, who was very kind and gave me German lessons. Of course, Latin had come easily to me; our father had drilled us in Latin; but I didn't know that I had a talent for learning languages. Though he was a foreigner, from Königsberg, his real name was Siebelmeyer, Mr. Załężowski had become one of us and taken a Polish surname. Mr. Załężowski was a patriot. At seventeen, he'd fought in the Uprising of 1830. My brothers worshipped him. And my mother seemed very fond of him as well, and for a while my brothers and I thought my bearded, gruff German tutor would soon become the stepfather of us all. But it turned out that he had become quite fond of me, young as I was, and though the gulf of twenty-seven years lay between us, I didn't find it in my heart to refuse the affections of so fine a man, who could teach me so much. It was he who believed in my future in the theatre when Stefan was still discouraging me, and after I'd had a catastrophic audition with a celebrated actress in Warsaw (no, I won't tell you who it was) who told me I had no talent at all, none. None! And he offered to launch me on the stage. For some years earlier, while hiding from the police, Mr. Załężowski had managed a traveling theatre company, and he proposed that we go to Bochnia for a time and revive that troupe with some actors he knew there who were seeking work. Thereby he would have an instrument to undertake the direction of my career.

"And so, when I was sixteen, with my mother's tearful blessing, for I wouldn't have done it without that, Mr. Załężowski and

I were married and left Kraków for that town where he still had his connections, and there I made my debut at seventeen, in *A Window on the First Floor* by Korzeniowski, in the part of the wife who, as you'll remember, on the point of being unfaithful to her husband is saved by the cry of her sick baby. Audiences were not sophisticated then. They loved healthy sentiments and a moral. But Mr. Załężowski wanted me to do great plays, German plays and Shakespeare, and within a few months I had learned the roles of Gretchen and Juliet and Desdemona and—

"Why am I telling you all this?" she said fretfully. "I'm making it sound easy!"

"OF COURSE it wasn't easy," said the friend soothingly.

"But it was!" she exclaimed. "For I, who was all ambition, was myself as unsophisticated as the audiences of those days. I remember the effect on me of a little book called *The Hygiene of the Soul*, in which the author, someone named Feuchtersleben, tries to prove that everything we wish can be obtained if we wish it strongly enough. Obedient to the spirit of this utopian, I rose from my bed—it was late at night—and, stamping the floor, I shouted, 'Well then, I must and I will!' This woke up the nurse, and my baby began to cry, so I crept back to bed, dreaming of future laurels."

"You were very young then."

"I was already twenty. No, not so young. And my daughter, my baby—you know what happened. Diphtheria. While I was away on tour."

"Yes."

"I couldn't go to her. Mr. Załężowski, my husband, pointed out that the plays could not be performed without me and we would never be engaged again at the theatre should we fail to fulfill our contract."

"It must have been dreadful for you."

"It still is. I mourn her every day of my life. I love Piotr, but I hadn't pictured myself with a son. I always imagined a daughter."

"But the laurels—you were right about the laurels."

"Yes, I admit that from the beginning I never played anything but principal roles. But it doesn't help. It's astonishing how one becomes accustomed to applause."

AS STEFAN and others had discouraged her, Maryna felt it her duty to discourage young aspirants to the stage who sought her support. "You can't imagine the slights you'll have to endure," she had warned Krystyna. "Even if you become successful"—she shook her head—"and then, one day, *because* you are successful."

But even though Maryna did not mean to encourage, she did, simply because she liked to instruct, and to tell stories about her life.

"Mr. Załężowski, Heinrich Załężowski, used to say, 'It won't help you to grind away day and night at your roles. It will ruin your health and give you too many ideas. Believe me, actors don't need to think!' " She laughed. "Of course I thought this was preposterous. I *like* ideas."

"Yes," interjected one of her protégés, "ideas are—"

"But I knew there was no point in arguing with him. So I replied humbly, I was still very young and he was much older, and my husband: 'Then what should I do?' 'Diligence, day-to-day diligence!' he shouted (why do theatre people shout so much?). As if I'd not been diligent!"

She pressed her fingers to her temples. Another headache in the wings.

"And diligence isn't enough. I can study a part for a long time and still not be ready to play the role. I learn the lines, say them walking up and down, imagining how I'll turn my head and move my hands, feeling *everything* my character feels. But that isn't enough. I have to *see* it. *See* myself as her. And

47

sometimes, who knows why, I can't. The picture isn't sharp or it won't stay in my mind. Because it's the future—which nobody can know."

This was the moment when the young actor listening to Maryna became a little apprehensive.

"Yes, that's what preparing a role is, it's like looking into the future. Or expecting to know how a journey will turn out."

MUSING, she said: "I am not brave, you see. I know myself very well. And I am not quick, either. I should describe myself as . . . slow."

"But—"

"Not quick. Not clever. Just a little above mediocre. Really. But I've always understood"—she smiled implacably—"that I can triumph by sheer stubbornness, by applying myself harder than anyone else."

"PERHAPS you should rest."

"No," she said. "I don't want to rest. I want to work."

"Who works harder than you?"

"I want peace."

"Peace?"

"I want to breathe pure air. I want to wash my clothes in a sparkling stream."

"You? You wash your own clothes? When? When would you have the time? And where?"

"Oh, it's not the clothes!" she cried. "Does no one understand me?"

"PARIS," someone suggested. "Despite the presence there of so many of our melancholy, noble-spirited compatriots,

Paris is full of gaiety and opportunity. And you would never be an exile *comme les autres*. You would like—"

"No, not Paris."

"IT'S TRUE I'm not satisfied. Most of all," she added, "with myself."

"You mustn't—"

"It's good to be happy, but it's vulgar to *want* to be happy. And if you *are* happy, it's vulgar to know it. It makes you complacent. What's important is self-respect, which will be yours only as long as you stay true to your ideals. It's so easy to compromise, once you've known a modicum of success."

"OF COURSE I am not fanatical," she said, "but perhaps I am too fastidious. For instance, I can't help thinking a person who sneezes in an absurd way is also lacking in self-respect. Why else consent to something so unattractive? It ought to be a matter of concentration and resolve to sneeze gracefully, candidly. Like a handshake. I remember a conversation with someone I've known for years, a subtle man, a doctor, whose friendship I cherish, when, in the middle of a sentence, we were talking about Fourier's theory of the twelve radical passions, he seemed suddenly overwhelmed with emotion. He made a sharp shrieking sound and then said 'Kissh'—said it twice and closed his eyes. What did he say, I wondered, staring at his mottled face. I understood when I saw him groping for his handkerchief. But it was difficult to continue with Ideal Harmony and the Calculus of Attraction after that!"

"I THINK," she started off grandly.

And then she stopped.

What nonsense it all is!

"Go on," said Bogdan.

Yes, nonsense to feel what she was feeling. Or perhaps not. How awful to impose this unhappiness, if that's what it was, on Bogdan, who took whatever she said so literally. Why did she always feel like saying something that would crease his brow and tighten his jaw? "I'm thinking how good you are to me," she said, pressing her face against his throat, seeking the comfort and forgiveness of his body.

SHE FROWNED. "Yes, I hate to complain, but . . ."

"But?" It was Ryszard speaking.

"I do love to show off." She clapped her hand to her forehead, moaned "Oh, oh, oh!" then smiled slyly.

The young man looked stricken. (Yes she'd been ill. All her friends said it.)

"Am I showing off?" she said, her eyes glittering. "You tell me, faithful cavalier."

Ryszard didn't answer.

"And if I am," she continued relentlessly, "why?"

He shook his head.

"Don't be alarmed. Aren't you going to say, Because you're an actress."

"Yes, a great actress," he answered.

"Thank you."

"I've said something stupid. Forgive me."

"No," she said. "Maybe it's not showing off. Even if I can't control it."

" I DO TRY to master my feelings, believe me!"

"Master your feelings?" cried the critic, a very friendly critic. "Whatever for, dear lady? It's the profusion of your feelings that delights the public."

"I've always needed to identify myself with each of the tragic heroines I play. I suffer with them, I weep real tears, which often I can't stop after the curtain goes down, and have to lie motionless in my dressing room until my strength returns. Throughout my whole career I've never succeeded in giving a performance without feeling my character's agonies." She grimaced. "I consider this a weakness."

"No!"

"What would my public say if I decided to play comic roles? Comedy"—she laughed—"isn't thought to be my strong point."

"What comic roles?" said the critic cautiously.

START TOO HIGH, and you have nowhere to go.

"I remember"—she was confiding this to Ryszard—"I remember once when I lost control, and the result was a disaster though I was not made to pay for it. The play was *Adrienne Lecouvreur*, a favorite of mine. An actress is a plum role, and Lecouvreur was the greatest of her era. Well, the call-boy had come, I had left my dressing room, I was standing in the wings, it was time for me to go on and, although it was hardly my first time in the role, I realized I had stage fright. That often used to happen to me. If it was just enough to make my heart pound and my palms sweat, it didn't bother me. On the contrary, I considered it a sign of professionalism. If I didn't have some flutter and fever before I went on, I was probably going to give a bad performance. However, it was a little worse than usual that night—not the kind of fear that paralyzes (I've had that, too!) but the kind that makes you lose your head. I entered the stage, and the whole house started clapping, and went on applauding for several minutes. In acknowledgment I sank into a deep stage curtsy, my crossed hands just touching my right knee and my head bent, and as the homage subsided and I raised my head I said to myself, You'll see, you'll see what I can do. Rachel had created this role, her voice was stronger, deeper than mine, and people still remember when she brought the play to Warsaw many years ago, but everyone thinks my Adrienne is superb, and that night I thought I was about to give the best performance of my life. And in this clenched state of mind, I started my scene—and took my first lines too high. I was lost. It was impossible to lower the pitch once I had begun. Adrienne is backstage at the Comédie-Française studying a new part, but she can't concentrate, her pulse is racing, for she's expecting to meet again the man with whom she's just fallen in love. And when she tells her confidant, the prompter, who is in love with her, though he dares not avow it, of her new, secret passion, I shouted, shouted like the most untalented of actresses. Having started on that note, imagine what I became when the prince, this man whose true identity is unknown to Adrienne, enters the greenroom. As any experienced actor will tell you, I had no choice, I had to keep it up. I could only rise higher as the sentiment I had to express became stronger and more pathetic. I sighed, I writhed, and all was genuine. By the fifth act, after Adrienne has kissed a bouquet of poisoned flowers sent by her rival for the prince's affections, my physical suffering was atrocious, and the arms that stretched out to my leading man as I lay dying were contorted with real desire. When the curtain fell, he carried me senseless to my dressing room."

"I LOVE YOUR STORIES," said Ryszard. Meaning, of course: I love you. "And because I love your stories," he continued (but this didn't make any sense at all), "I shall make the greatest sacrifice a writer can make."

"And what might that be?"

"Even if I write a hundred novels—"

"A hundred novels!" she exclaimed. "Vast program. And to think"—she smiled—"you've only written two."

"Wait," he said, "this is a solemn moment. I am taking a vow."

"Actor!"

"My vow, Maryna." He raised his hand. "Even if I write a hundred novels, there will never be one whose main character is a great actress."

THEY WERE in her dressing room. Ryszard was on a low stool, sketching her. She was pacing back and forth, offering him her astonishing silhouette.

"Something about makeup," she mused. "I have a foolish picture in my mind that I don't put all of this"—she pointed at the tray of jars and vials—"on my face, this old face"—she laughed—"that I don't transform myself to look different from the way I really do"—she sighed—"that I can stay myself and still be all the roles I love"—she shook her head—"which is impossible."

"Why impossible?" said Ryszard. "Why can't you?"

"Spoken like the writer you are." She smiled. How he ached to seize her hand. "No writer can understand that acting isn't about sincerity. It isn't even about feeling, that's an illusion. It's about seeming. It's about deciding. It ought to be about *not* feeling."

"That can't be true. You've told me that you feel, to the point of physical discomfort, all the emotions of the characters you play."

"Oh, what does it matter what I say about myself!"

"But you—"

"Ryszard, I'm talking about how to become a better actor. I don't know that I'm so good, I'm only better than the others. And why are most actors so bad? They think that being overwrought is the way to show a strong feeling. They don't know how to act. They don't know how to hide. I try to tell this to our young actors. I remember what Mr. Załężowski said more than once when he was admonishing me. 'Don't mistake this impetuosity of yours for genius,' he'd say. 'There's much to be shorn away before you turn out to be . . . somebody.' He was right. More right than he could ever have known, for Mr. Załężowski was a very"—she was choosing her words carefully—"old-fashioned man."

"IMAGINE," she said to Krystyna, "that you're a young girl living with a man much older than you, a foreigner. He has promised marriage but there is a legal impediment, a wife some-where, though of course you say he's your husband. And there is a baby now. Sometimes he is harsh, but you love him and make excuses for whatever he does that pains you. For the moment your home is an ill-furnished room in a drab mining town, far from the beautiful city where you were born and the love-filled home of your childhood. Imagine the room. A dirty window. A stove. An armoire. A large bed. A cradle in the corner with your little girl, blessedly asleep. The plain wooden table and two chairs. You're at supper. And he, after wolfing down the frugal meal you've prepared and wiping his mouth on his sleeve, has an-nounced that he is leaving you. He rises from the table. You fol-low him to the door, pleading. He slams the door. In fact, he will be back. Oh yes, you'll not be rid of the brute so easily, but you can't know that. For you, he is gone forever. Now, what would you do? Show me. You're in an agony of despair. Show me. No. Go over there, by the door."

Standing by the door, Krystyna hesitated a moment, then began to sob. She staggered, shoulders heaving, to the middle of the room; then collapsed in the chair and threw her upper body on the table, arms extended straight out in front of her, and dropped the right side of her head on her arms; then sank to her knees, lifting her arms at a forty-five-degree angle, and clasped her hands together; then—

"No! No! No!!"

Krystyna flushed and rose to her feet.

"But, Madame, I've seen you do that. Remember, when you played—"

"No!"

"Tell me what to do."

"You walk back into the room slowly . . . but not too slowly . . . you collect the dishes . . . you sit down in the chair, slumping a little. You stare at the table."

"That's all?"

"Yes."

"I don't pray?"

"I said, That's all."

GOD, OH GOD, she said to herself, it's not as if Maryna were really religious except when tormented (but when was she not tormented now?), oh almighty God be merciful! Take this dissatisfaction from me, or give me the means to accomplish my desire. For a while the anguish ceased, but now all Bogdan sees are the obstacles, he has decided it is folly, and asks why he should leave everything, and for me to promise that we will return. I must speak to Bogdan tonight. I'll sit him down on his bed and take his dear hands in mine and gaze into his eyes, but, no, I don't want to bribe him with a show of emotion, when I persuaded him, it was without any actorish wiles—oh God, how discouraged I am now. And yet, Bogdan must admit this: I have done all that I, with my abilities, could do. I've given what I have to give to our country, mindful of its patriotic importance. To think that in Warsaw the only official platform from which Poles are permitted to speak in Polish is a stage! I have been humble, I have been prudent. And I have been grateful, where I should have been grateful. To Heinrich too, for all his betrayals, for all his brutal returns to my life and my bed whenever it pleased him—to Heinrich above all others. He could not reproach me for ingratitude. And my dear friend, the wife of the Russian administrator of theatres, knew how grateful I was for her protection. Everything that became possible here in Warsaw was due to her intervention. When I decided it was time to show my Ophelia to the Warsaw public and the censor-in-chief denied the theatre a license to put on *Hamlet*—because it showed the murder of a king!—she invited the man to her house and persuaded him that the murder was a family affair only, and therefore perfectly harmless, and the license was granted. That was only one example of her goodness to me. But ever since Madame Demichova died there has been no one to protect me. If she were alive they would not have dared to put on that play, that . . . comedy, about an aging actress with a husband from a rich landowning family, whose Tuesday receptions are represented in such an unfriendly manner. Of course, I see it now, a popular actress whom marriage has brought into the ranks of society was bound to arouse mockery. The impudence! Frivolous salon chitchat, our elevated, patriotic conversations? Doesn't it count that they are elevated and patriotic enough to have stirred the vigilance of the Russian authorities, who post two policemen at our door every Tuesday, observing and writing down the names of each of our guests and asking those who come from abroad their addresses and their business with us? But what our oppressors do never surprises me. It's the critics here! It's the jealous actors and mediocre playwrights! If I knew how to hate, perhaps hatred would bring me relief. I ought to have a steel brow and a heart of stone—but what true artist possesses such armor? Only one who feels can produce feeling, only one who loves can inspire love. And would I suffer less if I appeared cold and haughty? No, no, I should just be acting! Yes, a public life is not suited to a woman. Home is the proper place for her. There she reigns—inaccessible, inviolable! But a woman who has dared to raise her head above the others, who has extended her eager hand for laurels, who has not hesitated to expose to the crowds all that her soul contains of enthusiasm and despair—that woman has given everyone the right to rummage in the most secret recesses of her life. To the curious there is nothing more amusing than some overheard snatches of an actress's candid talk, or the rumor of an irregular liaison or a misunderstanding in her home. Oh God, God, is my life to be an eternal expiation for sins, mine and not mine? Yet none of this would matter if it touched me only. But when cruelty and malice claw at those who are dear to me, then I start to hate that pillory called the Stage. Bogdan, selfless generous Bogdan, cannot protect me. That the actress in this play has an uxorious husband born and reared in Poznań he cites only as evidence that the actress is I, as if he were indifferent to how he himself is being insulted. But to a man like Bogdan it's either this silence or what happened two years ago, when behind my back he challenged a critic here in Warsaw to a duel; luckily for Bogdan, critics are cowards. My heart is breaking. Now Bogdan's brother will really hate me. I hear that everyone is talking about it since the play opened last week, but of course no one speaks of it with us. On Saturday we dined with the *Gazeta Polska* critic, but Bogdan said nothing and he didn't say anything either. The next time I saw the man, he always comes to our Tuesdays, my impulse was to lead him to a corner and ask if he was angry with me—I think many people are angry with me because I do so many foreign plays—but the conversation, which was about true liberty and the sufferings of our nation, was so enthralling that I felt ashamed to be preoccupied by my own torments. Instead, I wrote two letters, calm, indignant, dignified, one to his newspaper, the other to the theatre's manager, an admirer of mine, or so he said, but I didn't mail them. I should have known that if you have success, one day, long before you are tired, the public will turn against you—I'm not thinking only of that play. The public is fickle. My public wants to love a newer, younger face. Yes, the public must be dissatisfied with me, and I can't perform any better, not in Warsaw. We must escape from here. Bogdan must not pay for the enmity that surrounds me, though to be sure there are many people who defend me. Friends will blame the play for driving me away, even those who know that for some time I've been thinking of going abroad. But they will also blame me for being offended, offended to the point of finally doing it. Bogdan, who regrets that he ever agreed to our leaving, never lets me out of his sight, and I can see that he hopes to guide my confused spirit—as my husband, no doubt he regards it as his duty. I ought to be grateful to him. I am grateful. Oh God, oh God, I've been looking forward so fervently to this change—it's been so hard to organize everything—and now it's all ruined! I don't look forward to leaving anymore, people will think I'm running away, and I've always looked forward to something. In my childhood I had Christmas, though we were so poor and there were never any presents, and I looked forward to growing up, oh how I looked forward to it, I won't pretend to have been happy in that dark tiny room with the other little ones, but I didn't feel little, I was dreaming of when I would be free and strong and far away and people would— No, I won't slander my childhood. I *was* happy, I knew there was light inside me, I thought with such confidence of the future. Oh God, do not forsake your weak child. I am muddleheaded and tired of acting!

Two

GOD IS an actor, too.

Appearing for countless seasons in a variety of old-fashioned costumes, animating many tragedies and a few comedies; multiform—though usually in male roles—and always statuesque, commanding, lately (this is the second half of the nineteenth century) He has been getting some bad reviews, though not enough bad reviews, yet, to close the show. His dear familiar name continues to froth on everyone's lips. His participation still bestows unquestioned importance on any drama.

Wind rising. Constellations pulsing. Earth turning. People breeding. (Soon there will be more of them walking on the ground than lying under it!) History thickening. Dark people groaning. Pale people (God's favorites) dreaming of conquest, escape. Deltas and estuaries of people. He tilts them westward, where there is more space waiting to be filled. It is eleven in the morning, European time. Wearing neither the kingly robes nor the peasant garb He often affects, today He is God the Office Manager, His costume a three-piece worsted suit, starched white shirt, cuff protectors, bow tie, and—God, too, wants to be modern—He is chewing tobacco. The dominant hues of the set are yellow and brown: the blond wood of His swivel chair and immense desk; the smooth brass fixtures of the desk, whose drawers are crammed with papers; the worn, slightly dented brass of the gooseneck lamp, of the nearby spittoon. Elbows on the desktop, which is stacked with ledgers, He has been consulting population reports, economic bulletins, land surveys. Now He has made an entry in one of the ledgers.

Histories fusing. Obstacles faltering. Families sundering. News arriving. God the Travel Agent has dispatched messengers everywhere to proclaim that a New World beckons, where the poor can become rich and everyone stands equal before the law, where streets are paved with gold (this to illiterate peasants) and land is being given away (ditto) or sold on the cheap (this to those who can read). Villages are starting to empty out, the bravest or most desperate going first. Hordes of landless are surging toward the water (Bremerhaven, Hamburg, Antwerp, Le Havre, Southampton, Liverpool), surrendering themselves to be packed into the bottom of stinking ships. From the encrusted cities, which lie under the canopy of night with their lights on, the swell of departures is less noticeable—but steady. God is looking over shipping schedules. No more Middle Passage horrors, He thanks Himself: only those who *want* to go. Also—thanks, too—it is becoming much safer to cross the Atlantic, even if five of His faithful Franciscan nuns did perish last year when the *Deutschland*, soon after leaving Bremerhaven for North America, foundered off the treacherous Kentish coast. And quicker: by the new steamships it takes only eight days. Of course, God looks forward to the day when people can be moved across oceans in much less time. And eventually, and even more quickly, through the sky. God likes speed as much as the next pale person. Everything is speeding up now, getting faster. This is perhaps a good thing, since there are so many more people.

God professes to be impatient. Which does not mean He is really impatient. He is . . . acting. (That's one kind of great actor, one who feels or tries to feel nothing; to stay remote, impassive. In contrast to Maryna, who feels everything, and is so nervous.) But the people whom God the Prime Mover is shooing off to new

destinies really are impatient, impatient to leave for places understood as free of inherited encumbrances, places that don't have to
be preserved but instead offer themselves endlessly to be remade,
to shuck off the expectations of the past, to start anew with a
lighter burden. The faster they go, the lighter will be their
burden.

And God is abetting all this. This longing for newness,
emptiness, pastlessness. This dream of turning life into pure future. Perhaps He has no choice—though, in so doing, God the
Star is signing His own death warrant as an actor, as the star of
stars. No longer will He be guaranteed the major role in any
drama of consequence attended by the most coveted, educated
audiences. At best, minor roles from now on—except in
picturesque backwaters, where people have never seen a play
without Him. All this moving the audience about will amount to
the end of His career.

Does God know this? Probably He does. But that won't stop
Him: He's a trouper.

God spits.

IN MAY 1876, when Maryna Załężowska was still thirty-
five and at the pinnacle of her glory, she canceled the remaining
engagements of her season at the Imperial Theatre in Warsaw—
and her guest engagements at the Polski Theatre in Kraków,
the Wielki Theatre in Poznań, the Count Skarbek Theatre in
Lwów—and fled seventy miles south of Kraków, her birthplace,
where the party in the private dining room of the Hotel Saski
took place in December 1875, to the mountain village of Zakopane, where she usually spent a month in the late summer.
With her went her husband, Bogdan Dembowski, her seven-year-
old son, Piotr, her widowed sister, Józefina, the painter Jakub
Goldberg, the *jeune premier* Tadeusz Bulanda, and the schoolmas-
ter Julian Solski and his wife, Wanda. So displeasing was this
news to her public that one Warsaw newspaper exacted revenge

by announcing that she was taking an early retirement, which the Imperial Theatre (she was under life contract) promptly denied. Two unkind critics suggested that the moment had come to acknowledge that Poland's most celebrated actress was a little past her prime. Admirers, particularly her ardent following among university students, worried that she'd fallen seriously ill. The year before, Maryna had had a bout of typhoid fever and, although bedridden for just two weeks, did not play again for several months. It was rumored that the fever was so high she had lost all her hair. She *had* lost all her hair. And it had all grown back.

Then what was it this time, friends not in the know wondered. Frail lungs were endemic in Maryna's large family. Tuberculosis had taken her father at forty, and later claimed two sisters; and last year her favorite brother, once a well-known actor, whose claim to fame now rested on his being *her* brother, had fallen ill. Stefan's doctor in Kraków, her friend Henryk Tyszyński, had hoped to send him with them to inhale the pure mountain air, but he was too frail to support the arduous trip, two days of lurching along narrow rutted roads in a peasant's wagon. And could Maryna herself be——? Was it now her turn to come down with——? "But no," she said, frowning. "My lungs are sound. I'm as healthy as a bear."

Which was true . . . and Maryna, long inclined to recast her discontents into an ideal of health, had dedicated herself to becoming healthier still. Warsaw, any populous city, was unhealthy. The life of an actor was unhealthy; exhausting; rife with demeaning anxieties. More and more, instead of assuming that whatever time she could free for travel should be spent educating herself in the theatres and museums of a great capital, Vienna or even Paris, or practicing the ways of the world in a resort like Baden-Baden or Carlsbad, Maryna, her intimates in tow, was choosing the purifying simplicities of rustic life as lived by the privileged. The allure of Zakopane, among many other candidate villages, was its particularly ravishing setting among the majestic peaks of the Tatras, Poland's southern boundary and only altitudes, and the dense customs and savory dialect of its swarthy native people, who seemed as exotic to these city folk as American Indians. They'd watched tall lithe highlander men dancing at a midsummer festivity with a tamed brown bear in chains. They'd made friends with the village bard—yes, Zakopane still had a bard, charged with the melodious misremembering of the lethal feuds and unhappy love stories of the past. In the five years that Maryna and Bogdan had been part-summering there, they'd reveled in their increasing attachment to the village and its dignified, uncouth inhabitants, and had spoken of one day retreating there for good with a band of friends to devote themselves to the arts and to healthy living. On the clean slate of this isolated, politely savage Zakopane they would inscribe their own vision of an ideal community.

Part of its appeal was the difficulty of getting there. Winter made the roads impassable for months on end, and even when, in May, the trip became feasible, a vehicle from the village was the only transport. This was not the familiar, homely farmer's wagon of the more nearby countryside but a long wooden affair topped with canvas stretched over a bowed hazel frame, like a Gypsy wagon—no, more like those in engravings and oleographs of the American West. A few such wagons were to be intercepted in Kraków, at the main food market, where there were always some highlanders on a weekly run from Zakopane to the city; once voided of their load of mutton carcasses and sheepskin jackets and intricately incised logs of smoked sheep's cheese, they would be returning to the village empty.

Merely to set out was already an adventure. Leaving the dawn light to pile into the wagon's dark pungent interior, with the driver gallantly pressing his own sheepskin jacket on Madame Maryna for a pillow, they huddled among their soft bags, chattering and grimacing with delight as the highlander screwed his broad-brimmed hat down on his head and urged his two Percherons forward, out of the city and down the plain south of Kraków. Peace to their bones! A quaint wayside cross or shrine or, better, one of the small Marian chapels at a crossroad, would provide an excuse to clamber out and stretch their legs while the driver genuflected and muttered some prayers. Then the wagon started up the Beskid hills and, as the hills closed in, the horses' pace dropped to a walk. With time out for a hasty picnic of food they had brought from Kraków, they would reach the hamlet at the top by late afternoon and, as negotiated by their driver, be fed by their peasant hosts and be deeply asleep, the women in huts and the men in barns, before dark. It would be dark, three in the morning, when they were pulling themselves up into the creaking wagon for the second half of the journey, which—after the long, bone-jarring stretch downhill, mostly at a trot—had a much-awaited halt a little before midday at the only town on the route, Nowy Targ, where they could wash and eat a hearty meal and drink the Jewish tavernkeeper's execrable wine. Sated, and soon to be hungry again, they regained the wagon, which continued along meadows lush with grass and herbs and bordered by a lively stream. Beyond, ahead, rising into a bluer and bluer sky, was the limestone and granite Tatras wall, crowned by the double peak of Mount Giewont. They were munching on some dried cheese and smoked ham purchased in Nowy Targ when the valley narrowed and the wagon began its last uneven ascent. Those who chose to walk behind the wagon for a spell, Maryna was always one of them, were invariably rewarded by a glimpse, through the stands of pine trees and black firs, of a bear or a wolf or a stag, or an agreeably equalizing roadside exchange of greetings ("Blessed be the name of Jesus!" "Through all ages, amen!") with a shepherd wearing a long white cloak and the distinctive male headgear, a black felt hat with an eagle feather stuck in it, which he doffed at the welcome sight of the quality folk from the big city. It would be another three hours before they reached the upper valley, some nine hundred meters high, where the village nested, and the weary horses, longing for home and a horse's oblivion, picked up speed. With luck it would be just sunset when they came clattering into the village to take up their borrowed peasant life.

For some weeks, as long as a month, they occupied a low square hut with four rooms, two of which could be used as sleeping chambers: the women and Piotr slept in one room, the men in the other. Like every dwelling in Zakopane, this hut was an ingenious sculpture of spruce logs (the region abounded in spruce forests) with the joints dovetailed at the end, while its few heavy chairs, tables, and slatted beds were carpentered from the more expensive, pinkish larch. Within minutes of their arrival they had flung open the dull-paned windows to air out the garlic reek, distributed in cupboards and on wall pegs their minimum of possessions—bringing so little was also part of the adventure—and were ready to start enjoying their unencumbered freedom. In principle, country life for city people is a delicious blank, time sponged clean of work and the usual habits and obligations. Were they not on holiday? Of course. Did this give them more time to themselves? No. The engrossing, compulsory routines of city people in the country managed to fill the whole day. Eating. Exercise. Talking. Reading. Playing games. And of course housekeeping, for another part of the adventure was dispensing with servants. The men swept and chopped wood and collected the water for bathing and laundry. Washing, beating the wash, and hanging it out to dry was the women's task. "Our phalanstery," Maryna would say, evoking the name of the principal building in an ideal community as envisaged by the great Fourier. Only the cooking was left to the hut's owner, Mrs. Bachleda, an elderly widow who moved in with her sister's family during the lucrative stay. The day was organized around her ample meals. Over breakfast, sour milk and black bread, they would apportion tasks and plan excursions. In the late morning, the whole party would set out for a collective walk in the valley, taking a picnic of black bread and ewe's cheese and raw garlic and cranberries. Evenings, after a supper of sauerkraut soup, mutton, and boiled potatoes, were for reading aloud. Shakespeare. What could be healthier than that?

As people of active conscience, Maryna and Bogdan could not have accepted being mere summer folk, and had made a tacit contract of benevolence with the village that went far beyond the infusion of cash their annual presence brought into its near-subsistence economy. Maryna and her friends were hardly unaware that, salutary as Zakopane was for them, the health of the two thousand villagers left much to be desired. Luckily, one of the friends who had followed Maryna to Zakopane was the faithful Henryk. Soon he was spending more time there than she, confiding his practice in Kraków to a colleague for a full three months, and treating the villagers without charge. At first they were suspicious, seeing no impediment in a mouthful of rotten teeth or throat goiters or rickets and nothing unnatural in the death of infants or the sickening of anyone over thirty-five. His little speech about the principles of sanitation was city gibberish to their ears—until they saw how many lives were saved by his ministrations (and food he brought from Kraków) the second summer he was there, in 1873, when cholera struck. And he alone among Maryna and her friends understood most of what the Tatras highlanders were actually saying, even when they spoke rapidly, their dialect containing scores of words for common things which are nothing like their equivalents in standard Polish. His tutor, a grateful patient, was the village priest.

The villagers' part of the contract (to that they'd not consciously assented) was: not to change. Their cosmopolitan visitors thought they could help in this. Bogdan had the idea of starting a folkloric society, and Ryszard of learning the dialect in order to transcribe the fairy tales and hunting stories of the village bard. Henryk was planning a scientific museum that would display for the villagers' edification the glories of the Alpine stronghold looming above them, such as the impressive variety of mosses he had garnered on his rocky climbs. Maryna was for starting a lace-making school for the village girls, which would aid the faltering economy and help preserve an endangered local craft. The previous summer she had taken lessons from a one-eyed crone reputed to be Zakopane's champion lacemaker and, to the titters of the village women, tried her hand at wood carving.

Difficulty of access had until now protected the village, its archaic customs and uniformity of behavior and rich traditions of oral recitation. Faces were cast from only a few molds, as there were just a few family names. The village still had one muddy street, one wooden church, one cemetery. A real community! But Maryna and her friends were not the only outsiders. There were not yet any chalets (imitating, floridly, the wooden plainness of the highlander huts) or tuberculosis sanatoria (it would be a decade more before Zakopane achieved the official status of a health resort), and a railroad link to Kraków (guaranteeing year-round access to the village) would not be built for another thir-teen years. Yet it was on the verge of becoming fashionable in the summer months, because Poland's most famous actress and her husband took their holidays there. When they first came, there was one way to stay in Zakopane: to sleep and be fed in a high-lander's hut. Two summers later, when Ryszard was first invited to accompany them, the village had one ill-kept public lodging and two cottages nearby serving expensive monotonous food and undrinkable wine. And there were tourists, a handful, to stay at the hotel and frequent the restaurants.

How different the occupations of these tourists from the healthy regimen Maryna was following. Each day, whatever the weather, began with dawn bathing in the brook behind the hut, followed by a solitary walk before breakfast. She roamed the damp meadows, plucked unfamiliar mushrooms from rotting tree trunks and dared herself to eat them on the spot, recited Shake-speare to goats. She depleted a rich repertoire of manias, enthusi-astically taken up and then dropped. Some were dietary: for days on end she consumed only sheep's milk, then nothing but sauer-kraut soup. There were also breathing exercises, from a book by Professor Liebermeister, and mental exercises, too: for one hour a day she stretched out motionless on the grass and concentrated on recalling a happy memory. Any happy memory! It was the beginning of the era of "positive thoughts," which specialists in self-manipulation were preaching to men, to make them more robust salesmen of themselves, and doctors were prescribing to women, especially those suffering from "nerves" or "neurasthenia"—when they were not prescribing to women simply not to think at all. Thinking (like city life) was supposed to be bad for one's health, especially a woman's health.

But Henryk was not like this, not like other doctors. He might say, Trust the good air of Zakopane to work its curative powers. Henryk was a great believer in air. But he did not say, Rest, have a mental blackout, confine yourself to womanly occupations like lacemaking. There was nobody Maryna liked talking to as much as Henryk. If only he weren't so obviously enamored. It was one thing for young men like Ryszard and Tadeusz to fall in love with her; she knew the power of a reigning actress to inspire such reckless, perfectly sincere but shallow infatuations. But that this intelligent, melancholy older man was pining with unavowed love was painful to her. She wished he would sneeze.

"Sneeze, Henryk!"

"I beg your pardon."

"I like to hear you sneeze. It makes me find you ridiculous."

"I *am* ridiculous."

Maryna sneezed. "See how handsomely I do it?"

It was last September and they were sitting in a sun-filled room in the hut Henryk had rented for the summer. With one larch table, two chairs, and a bench, the walls bare except for a row of crudely colored pictures on glass of shepherds and bandits painted by local shepherds and bandits, it was scarcely a parlor, much less a consulting room. Only the cupboard's worth of scalpels, forceps, catheters, tenon saws, specula, microscope, stethoscope, stoppered vials, and dog-eared medical books—a modest selection from his well-stocked office in Kraków—confirmed his profession.

"Are you telling me you have a cold? It would hardly surprise me since you insist on walking barefoot in the grass and bathing in an icy stream at dawn."

"I don't"—she started coughing—"have a cold."

"Of course not." He came toward the bench where she was sitting and extended his open hand.

"Ah, the good air of Zakopane," Maryna said, surrendering her delicate wrist.

He shut his eyes as he stood over her. A minute passed. With her free hand Maryna reached for the plate of raspberries at the end of the bench and slowly ate three. Another minute had passed.

"Henryk!"

Opening his eyes, he grinned mischievously. "I like taking your pulse."

"I've noticed."

"So I can reassure you"—he placed her hand back in her lap—"how healthy you are."

"Stop it, Henryk. Have a raspberry."

"And your headaches?"

"I always have a headache."

"Even in Zakopane?"

"All I have to do is relax. As you know, I rarely have a full-blown headache when I'm working too hard."

He had returned to the table. "And yet your instincts are right to tell you to seek refuge here whenever you can from the hurly-burly of Warsaw and all the touring."

"What refuge!" she exclaimed. "Admit it, friend, it's hardly the undiscovered village it was when we arrived here four years ago."

"When *you* arrived, dear Maryna. Please recall that you were the first well-known person to come here every summer. I merely followed."

"Not you," she said. "I mean all the others."

Henryk tilted his head, forefinger to bearded chin, and

gazed out the window at his inspiriting view of the Giewont and the distant summit of the Kasprowy.

"What do you expect, since each time you and Bogdan come a few more people discover the beauties of the place. You are the village's biggest populator."

"Well, at least they are my friends. But now there are people I don't know in that so-called hotel old Czarniak has opened. Zakopane with a hotel!"

"Where you go everyone follows," he said, smiling.

"And the foreigners. Don't tell me they are here because of me. English, God be praised." She paused, she dramatized. "If one must have tourists, let them be English. At least we don't have any Germans."

"Just wait," he said. "They'll come."

THIS YEAR'S stay was different. For one thing, they had arrived much earlier, and they were not on holiday. Bogdan had proposed they assemble everyone involved in the plan—their plan: it had not been hard to bring Bogdan around again. Maryna thought they should invite just a few friends, those who were wavering. Ryszard and the others on whom she already knew they could count need not come.

After journeying to Kraków, and recovering Piotr—two years earlier Maryna had sent the child away from Warsaw, where the language of instruction in schools was Russian, to live with her mother in Kraków, where the more lenient Austrian rule permitted Polish-language schooling—Maryna and Bogdan spent a week of afternoons in Stefan's flat, often joined by the guardedly reassuring Henryk. Stefan was now confined to bed much of the time. The morning after their arrival Bogdan himself went to the food market square to arrange everything with one of the highlanders sure to be loitering there after selling off his load of mutton and cheese. Familiar faces crowded around him, offering their services, their wagons. Bogdan picked a tall fellow with lank black hair who spoke a shade more intelligibly than the others and, in his comical farrago of educated Polish and highlander patois, instructed the man to tell the old widow whose hut they'd rented last September to ready it now for the arrival of himself and his wife and stepson with five others. The man, a Jędrek, was to be prepared to bring them to the village one week from today. He declared that it would be an unforgettable honor to carry the Count and the Countess and their party in his wagon.

They had known only the summer, when the mountains above the tree line look clear of snow and the meadows have gone bare of flowers. The high mountains now were still covered with snow—winters are long and harsh in the Tatras—but as the wagon passed along green meadows carpeted with purple crocuses, purple with a dash of dark blue, Jędrek's passengers could hardly refuse to call it spring. Maryna reached the village excited, then edgy—feelings she identified as the elation that follows the making of a great decision and the restlessness that succeeds the familiar discomforts of the journey. It could not be a headache, she was sure, although this giddiness and pointless energy were not unlike what she would feel, sometimes, three or four hours before the onset of one. No, it could not be a headache. But as she stood with Bogdan admiring the sunset, she had to acknowledge that there was something wrong with the way she was seeing, it had become full of dazzles and zigzags and flicker and sprays of light, the sun seemed to be boiling, and she could no longer deny the throbbing in her right temple and the pressure in the nape of her neck. She who had never canceled a performance because of a headache collapsed for twenty-four hours, lying in the dim sleeping chamber with a towel wrapped tightly around her head in a leaden stuporous daze. Piotr tiptoed in and out, and asked when she was going to get up and clearly needed to be comforted, and she made the effort to keep the child with her for a while. It was all right if she patted his hair and kissed his hand with her eyes squeezed shut. Whenever she opened them, Piotr seemed very small and far away, as did Bogdan, crouching by the bed, asking again what he might bring her—they seemed to have lattices on their faces. There were faces enough peering out of the dark knots in the beams that supported the ceiling, which seemed to be just above her, pressing down on her, shimmering, scintillating. All she wanted was to be left alone. To vomit. To sleep.

The headache she had later in their stay was mild compared to this, one of the worst Maryna could remember. But after she recovered she was very fretful. There were long insomniac nights watching the shadows on the wall (she kept one oil lamp lit) and listening to Piotr's adenoidal breathing, Józefina's snoring, Wanda's coughing, a sheepdog barking. Once a night Piotr would crawl into her bed to tell her that he needed to use the outhouse and she had to come with him because a horrible witch lived in the yard who looked like old Mrs. Bachleda. And when they returned to the sleeping chamber, he would want to get back into her bed because, he explained, the witch would try to kill him in his dreams. Useless for Maryna to tell Piotr he was far too big to have such childish fears. But soon, hearing the noisy mouth-breathing that signified sleep, she could carry him to his mattress and go outside again to gaze up at the blackness spattered with stars. Then, finally, a few hours before dawn, it was her turn to sleep. And to have odd dreams, too: that her mother was a bird, that Bogdan had a knife and hurt himself with it, that something terrible was hanging from a tree.

She was often tired. And some days she would feel "dangerously well," as she put it, for any exceptional energy or high spirits might be a sign that she was to have one of her disabling headaches the following day. The antic thoughts, the uncontrollable urge to laugh or sing or whistle or dance—she would pay for these. Convinced the headaches were due to a slackening of effort, she took more strenuous walks than ever; it seemed that she had gathered her friends around her mostly in order to leave them.

She walked partly to exhaust herself—and had no need of company. Bogdan helped her dress, tenderly booted her, and watched her until she disappeared, heading southwest. From the village to the higher meadow leading to Mount Giewont was about seven kilometers. From there she crossed into the forest and followed the trail that brought her, breathless, to a still higher plateau with grass, dwarf shrubs, and Alpine flowers; in giddy homage to the murder of Adrienne Lecouvreur by the gift of poisoned flowers, she picked a bunch of edelweiss, kissed the odorless blossoms, and lifted her face to the sun. She would have liked to climb to the crest of the Giewont, which she'd done in previous summers with Bogdan and friends and a guide from the village. But, afraid of the dark fancies crowding her mind, she didn't dare attempt it alone. Even to venture into the foothills through patches of melting snow, and partly up the slopes, she wanted Bogdan, Bogdan only, to accompany her.

Bogdan's stride was faster than Maryna's, and she didn't mind walking behind him. That way she could feel both accompanied and alone. But sometimes she had to bring him to her side, when she saw something he might be missing. A crow in a tree. The silhouette of a hut. A cross on a hill. A grouping of chamois or an ibex on a nearby crag. The eagle swooping down on some luckless marmot.

"Wait," she would cry, "did you see that?" Or: "I want to show you something."

"What?"

"Up there."

He would look in the direction she pointed.

"From here. Come back here."

He would come halfway and look again.

"No, right here."

She would take his arm and bring him back to where she had stopped to admire, so he could place his booted feet just . . . there. Then, standing at his side, she could watch him seeing what she had seen and, thoughtfully, not moving for a minute to show he really had seen it.

What a tyrant I am, Maryna did sometimes think. But he doesn't seem to mind. He's so kind, so patient, so husbandly. That was the true liberty, the true satisfaction of marriage, wasn't it? That you could ask someone, legitimately demand of someone, to see what you saw. Exactly what you saw.

FROM A LETTER that Maryna entrusted to one of the highlanders leaving for the market in Kraków, to post as soon as he arrived:

Ryszard, what have you been doing, thinking, planning? Given your habitual fine opinion of yourself, perhaps I shouldn't confide that you have been missed here by all of us. Do not feel too self-important, however. For this may be because our usual occupations have been taken from us. First it was snowing for two days—yes, snow in May! And now we've had three days of cold rain, so Bogdan and I and the friends have had no choice but to decree ourselves housebound. And now I remember what it was like to be a child in a large family who has been denied permission to go out. For, thus cooped up, we have tired of all subjects of conversation, even that most on our minds, and despite the extreme interest of what Bogdan has told us about a colony in one of the New England states called Brook Farm. Well then, you'll say, amuse yourselves. But we have! I have devised charades for those who wanted to exercise their acting skills (it wouldn't have been fair for me to participate)—Bogdan has beaten Jakub and Julian at chess—we have composed songs both jolly and sad (Tadeusz is learning to play the *gęśle*, that fiddle-like instrument we've heard at the shepherds' encampments)—we have recited Mickiewicz to each other and got through all of *As You Like It* and *Twelfth Night*. And, yes, it's still raining.

Guess what we did today. We were reduced to entertaining

ourselves by killing flies. Truly! This morning among Piotr's toys I found two tiny bows, Julian made arrows of matches with a needle at the end, and we took turns aiming at the drowsy flies ornamenting the wooden walls of the room where we sit, applauding as one by one our victims fell at our feet. What do you say to such an occupation for Juliet or Mary Stuart?

Nevertheless, don't suppose it's because I am bored that I am inviting you to join us. We're certain to remain at least another two weeks, in which time the weather is bound to improve and much could be discussed, and it occurs to me that since Julian now seems quite committed and eager, you should be here too, so that we may settle some details of the new plan in which you have a leading role. And you can reassure Wanda, who is distressed over their impending separation, that you will keep an eye on her husband and make sure he does not court any unnecessary danger, although, knowing you both, I think it should be the other way around! So, consider yourself invited—if (yes, there is an if) you give me your word on one delicate matter. What does dear Maryna want of me that I would not willingly grant her, you will be thinking. I know your warm heart. But I also know something else about you. Will you forgive my frankness? You must promise to behave like a gentleman with the local girls. Yes, Ryszard, I am aware of your bad habits. But not in Zakopane, I beg you! You are my guest. I may yet come back here, I have made a commitment to these people. Do we understand each other, my friend? Yes? Then come, dear Ryszard.

MORTIFIED WHEN he received Maryna's letter, and determined to do anything and everything she asked of him, Ryszard left Warsaw the next day. Arriving in Kraków, he called on Henryk to ask his help in arranging the trip to the village. Henryk not only accompanied him to the market to assist him in finding a reliable driver but decided impulsively that he would go, too. Surely Stefan's condition could not significantly worsen if he were gone for only ten days. If Ryszard were invited, and by Maryna herself, how could he stay away?

Ryszard took his room in the hut of the village bard, partly to continue the task begun last summer of making a compilation of the old man's tales, partly to escape Maryna's vigilant eye if, despite his best intentions, he should succumb to the unwashed charms of one of the village girls.

"Ah, communal life," Henryk said to Bogdan when told there was a mattress waiting for him in the men's sleeping room. "Please don't be offended if I stay at Czarniak's place."

"The hotel?" said Bogdan. "You can't be serious. I trust you carry a disinfectant in your physician's satchel for the mattress you'll be given there."

Except when he was called to some medical emergency (a breech birth, a smashed leg, a ruptured appendix), Henryk was almost always at the hut, available to Maryna, entertaining Piotr. The boy seemed bright to him, and so he decided to teach him about the new doctrines of evolution.

"If I were you," he said to Piotr, "I'd think twice before you tell the priests at school that a friend of your illustrious mother has even mentioned the name of that great Englishman, Mr. Darwin."

"But I can't tell them," said the boy. "Mama says I'm not going back to that school anymore."

"And do you know why you're not going back?"

"I think so," said Piotr.

"Why?"

"Because we're going on a ship."

"And what will you do on the ship?"

"See whales!"

"Which are what kind of creature?"

"A mammal!"

"Excellent."

"Henryk!" It was Ryszard, who had just sauntered over. "Don't fill the lad's head with useless facts. Tell him stories. Stimulate his imagination. Make him bold."

"Oh, I'd like a story," cried Piotr. "Tell one about a witch and how she gets killed. Fried. In a stove. And then she—"

"You should be telling the stories," said Ryszard.

"I have stories, too," said Henryk. "But they don't make me bold."

SHE WAS GROWING silent, she who had always been so talkative. How those who had gathered here wanted to please her!

Maryna watched Tadeusz and Ryszard watching her with adoring eyes. She wished she were in love, for being helplessly in love awakens one's better self. But when marriage puts an end to that, it is a deliverance. Love makes men strong, self-confident. It makes women weak.

Friendship, though . . . that was another matter. Friends make you strong. How was she to do without Henryk? They were in the forest sitting on the stump of a fir tree near a berry patch. Piotr was playing with his full-size bow and arrows nearby.

"I've never liked forests," said Henryk. "But I'm starting to. All I have to do is imagine that each tree is a fellow creature. Stuck in this gloomy forest. Rooted here. Waving its leaves about. Help! Help! cries the tree, I'm—"

"Don't be pathetic, dear Henryk."

"Why not? I'm enjoying myself."

"Be pathetic, dear Henryk."

"Good. Where was I? Oh, my trees. No Birnam Wood to Dunsinane for them. And then they're cut down, which is not the escape they had in mind. Try some of this."

Maryna took the proffered flask of vodka.

"Imagine," she said after a while, "what it is to have got in your head that there is something your Fate has willed, that you must obey your star. Whatever others think."

"Maryna, you speak about yourself as if you were completely alone. But what strikes me is how set you are on bringing others along with you."

"One can't do plays without other people."

"Actually, I was thinking of Zakopane. You are vexed that you can't keep the Zakopane you discovered, but you have to know it can't remain what it was. I think it shouldn't. The lives of people here are hard. But they're not a tribe of nomadic Indians in North America. They're a hemmed-in settlement of shepherds in Europe whose miserable livelihood is shrinking. The land has always been too poor for serious farming, and you know, don't you, the iron mine is bound to close within the next few years. How will they live then if they don't peddle their humble finery and wooden geegaws, their mountains, the views, the good air?"

"Do you really imagine I don't care about——"

"And, as I've often pointed out," he continued heatedly, "you, abetted by the dear indispensable Bogdan, set all that in motion. Though it was bound to happen anyway. How could more and more people not hear about Zakopane? You wanted others around you. Your community."

"You think me naïve."

He shook his head.

"You think I'm being pretentious."

"Oh"—he laughed—"there's nothing wrong with being pretentious, Maryna. I confess to the adorable failing myself. It's a Polish specialty, like idealism. But I do think you shouldn't confound a spartan house party with a phalanstery."

"I know you don't like Fourier."

"It's not for me to like or dislike your utopian sage. I can't help it if I know something about human nature. It's hard for a doctor to avoid that."

"And you think I could be the actress I am without knowing something about human nature?"

"Don't be angry with me." He sighed. "Maybe I'm jealous, because . . . I can't be a member of your party. I have to stay here."

"But if you wanted, you could, when we—"

"No, I'm too old."

"What nonsense! How old are you? Fifty? Not even fifty!"

"Maryna . . ."

"Do you think I don't feel old? But that doesn't stop me from—"

"I can't." He raised his hand. "Maryna, I can't."

THE WEATHER turned warmer, and the whole party, except for Henryk and Ryszard, had spent the afternoon in the forest and were now assembled outside the hut in the failing light. Pleasantly tired, more than a little talked out, they were looking forward to their dinner of soup and two kinds of mushrooms, the delicately shriveled brown ones they had found in a grove of firs today and the savory dark-orange pickled *rydz* they had harvested on forest excursions last September. Bogdan had laid down a track on the grass for Piotr to play with his wooden trains. Maryna was writing a letter at a little table by the oil lamp Tadeusz had lit for her: a crescent moon and a pair of planets had appeared in the pale sky. Wanda was changing the buttons on an embroidered flax shirt she had purchased for Julian. Józefina and Julian were having a whispered dispute over a card game. Jakub was sketching the cardplayers. The screech of an owl heralded the baaing of some wayward sheep, while from indoors came the sound of sizzling butter in Mrs. Bachleda's crude skillet—delicious noise!

Henryk had strolled over, poured himself some arrack, sat down in the extra chair at the cardplayers' table, and was trying to concentrate on a book. Ryszard, who'd elected to spend his forest day with his landlord (killing animals in the company of another man was the most enjoyable way of staying clear of the temptations alluded to by Maryna), arrived last. He had pulled up a chair to Maryna's table, taken out his notebook, and was writing up a hunting tale the old man had told him after they'd shot their second fox.

Bogdan was pacing. "I've done nothing strenuous but I am tired," he said.

Henryk snapped the book shut. "You're not feeling ill?"

"I don't think so."

"You didn't sample any strange mushrooms today?"

"I did," said Tadeusz.

"And how are you feeling, young man?"

"Couldn't be better!"

"Because you're not supposed to eat whatever looks enticing to you in a forest."

"Everyone knows that," Bogdan muttered. "But should someone have been imprudent, we have a doctor among us for the week."

"If I were you," said Henryk, "I'd place no more confidence in doctors than in mushrooms." He was toying with his empty glass. "Would you like to hear a cautionary tale about both?" He laughed. "It's a dreadful story."

Ryszard looked up from his notebook.

"You probably never heard of Schobert. Nobody plays his compositions now, which were written for the harpsichord." He paused. "He lived in Paris. He was famous throughout Europe."

"Don't you mean Schubert?" said Wanda.

"Don't answer her," said Julian.

"I'm afraid it's Schobert," said Henryk.

He stood, slowly lit a pipe, and buttoned his jacket, as if he were off for a stroll.

"So at last," said Ryszard, "you're going to tell us a story."

"Well, this is quite an unpleasant one." Henryk sat down again. "I wonder why I thought of telling it."

"Henryk, don't tease us," Maryna said.

Henryk knocked his pipe against the sole of his boot. "Could it be," he said, "that I'm a little thirsty?" Józefina fetched him the bottle of arrack.

He took a swig. "Courage," said Maryna.

Henryk looked about at his expectant auditors and smiled.

"Well, it seems that this man, this valuable man, this admirable artist, was extremely partial to mushrooms, and so had arranged a day's outing in the country, I think it was the forest of Saint-Germain-en-Laye, no matter, with his wife, the older of his two small children, and four friends, among whom was a doctor. They arrived in two carriages at the edge of the forest, descended, and began to walk. Schobert started scouting for mushrooms, and during the course of the day picked what he thought was a choice basketful. Late in the afternoon, the company went to Marly, to an inn where Schobert was known, and asked for a dinner to be prepared to which they would contribute the mushrooms. The cook at the inn glanced at the mushrooms, assured his guests that they were the wrong sort, and refused even to touch them. Schobert told the cook to do what he had been asked. But could they actually be the wrong sort, asked one of the friends. Nonsense, said the friend who was a doctor. Nettled at the cook's obstinacy, though of course it was they who were being obstinate, they left and went to an inn in the Bois de Boulogne, where the head-waiter also refused to prepare the mushrooms for them. More obstinate than ever, for the doctor still insisted that the mushrooms were good, they left that inn, too."

"Heading for disaster," murmured Ryszard.

"Night having fallen and everyone admitting to being very hungry, they returned to Paris, to Schobert's house. There he gave the mushrooms to his maidservant to cook for supper—"

"Oh," said Wanda.

"—and all seven of them, including the doctor who claimed to know all about mushrooms, as well as the maid, who must have nibbled while cooking, and the dog, who must have begged a taste

8 1

from the maid, were poisoned. Since they succumbed together, they were without any assistance until the following midday, a Wednesday, when a pupil of Schobert, arriving for his lesson, found them all thrashing about in agony on the parquet floor. Nothing could be done for them. The child, who was five years old, died first. Schobert survived until Friday. His wife did not die until the following Monday. Two lived as long as ten days more. Of Schobert's little family only the three-year-old, who hadn't been taken along on the outing and was asleep when everyone returned, was left."

Piotr giggled loudly.

"Go inside and wash your hands, Piotr," said Bogdan.

The child went on pushing his trains about. "Crash!" he said. "It's a train wreck."

"Piotr!"

"What a grisly story," said Jakub, who had been standing in the pegged doorway of the hut. "They had only to listen to the cook at the first inn, or the headwaiter at the second."

"Servants?" Ryszard exclaimed. "Who then did not feel superior to servants? It's a perfect story of the *ancien régime*."

"Imagine placing such faith in a doctor," said Henryk.

"Imagine a doctor being so confident he was an expert on mushrooms," said Ryszard.

"But Schobert was the one who was so fond of mushrooms," said Bogdan. "It's Schobert's fault. He was the head of the family, he was in charge of the excursion."

"But a doctor," Wanda said. "A man of science."

"While I suppose I should protect my wife's illusions about men of science," said Julian, "the truth is, both are equally to blame."

"No, the responsibility has to be Schobert's," Józefina said. "Nobody wanted to contradict him. Think of the force of his personality. A great musician, a man admired by everyone . . ."

"What do you think?" Tadeusz said, the first to feel uneasy

that Maryna was not taking part in the conversation. She shook her head. "If someone said that the mushrooms we had picked were poisonous but *you* wanted to eat them—"

"Surely you would not follow me."

"Perhaps I would."

"Bravo!" said Henryk.

Everyone looked expectantly at Maryna.

"But I am not so stubborn," she cried. "I would never insist on eating mushrooms that someone said were poisonous." She paused. "What do you take me for?" (What did they take her for? Their queen.) "Oh, my dear friends . . ."

MARYNA HAD no desire to linger beyond early June, when the first summer tourists would be arriving. The men spent their last hours in the village purchasing sheepskin blankets and six of the sturdily crafted hatchets that double as weapons for the highlanders. Back in Kraków she visited Stefan, now alarmingly paler and thinner, before continuing on with Bogdan and Piotr, accompanied by Ryszard and Tadeusz, to Warsaw. There Tadeusz learned that he was finally to be offered a contract at the Imperial Theatre, which Maryna, seeing how much he dreaded disappointing her, warmly counseled him to accept, and abandon all thought of joining them. She did Tadeusz the honor of accompanying him when he signed the contract, and stayed on for a quiet talk about her own plans with the Imperial's blustering, kindly managing director, who would not hear of anything but a year's leave of absence, no more. Bogdan was busy raising the money needed for their great venture, and this furnished the detective assigned to follow him everywhere with a new list of names for other detectives to follow: those who came to look at their apartment and its furnishings, which Bogdan had put up for sale.

Within two weeks, however, they were hurrying back to

Kraków for Stefan, who, long separated from his wife, was now unable to care for himself at all and had gone home to their mother's flat. The evening of their arrival Stefan closed his eyes and, with a loud sigh, tumbled into a coma. Kneeling by the bed, Maryna touched her lips to his brow and wept soundlessly. The clammy face on the pillow was eerily juvenile, bony, as when she had first seen him on a stage, without recognizing the beloved friend of both Don Carlos and his wicked father; the face of the gloriously handsome young man she had worshipped as a small child. Unbelievable to think that it was now his time to die!

Mother was quite overcome with grief, she wrote to Ryszard, but Adam was there, and Józefina, and Andrzej, and little Jarek. Henryk, who never left us, did what he could, but there was no detaining my precious willful brother. I held him all night in my arms, his body felt dry and light as kindling while the blood came pouring from his mouth, and then he was gone.

Stefan's death was also Maryna's farewell to her family.

BOGDAN, TOO, had to make a farewell visit: his family were rich landowners, living on large holdings in western Poland under Prussian rule. Maryna had been at the principal Dembowski estate once, in 1870, after she accepted Bogdan's proposal of marriage—but not to stay, for Ignacy, Bogdan's older brother and the head of the family, refused even to meet her, while telling Bogdan that he, of course, would always be welcomed with open arms. They took rooms at a nearby inn.

Before they left two days later, Bogdan brought Maryna into the sprawling white-pillared manor to meet his grandmother, who had sent word to him that she, naturally, did not oppose his marriage. Squeezing his wife's hand, Bogdan had pulled her through room after room over the brightly polished wooden floors (she remembered their shine) as if they were naughty children, fleeing a justly wrathful adult, or children in disgrace, fleeing an ogreish tyrannical adult—so much did he dread coming upon his brother in one of those large, sparsely furnished rooms. Bogdan in a hurry, panting, seemed to have relapsed into a disquieting vulnerability in this house where he'd been a child. Maryna didn't want to feel like a child. It was partly so as not to feel like a child, ever, that she had become an actress.

They gained his grandmother's upstairs sitting room. Bogdan bent his knee as he kissed her hand, then sank to both knees to let her hug his head while behind him Maryna offered a curtsy that was, pointedly, not a stage curtsy, and in her turn kissed the old woman's hand. Then he left them alone.

Maryna had never met anyone like Bogdan's grandmother. Born in 1791, the year before the Second Partition, when the last king of Poland, Stanisław August Poniatowski, was still on the throne, she was a survivor of a distant, more free-spirited era. She thought her grandchildren, with the possible exception of Bogdan, were fools. Above all, Ignacy, the eldest—as she explained to Maryna at a rapid clip and with a twinkle in her rheumy eye.

"He's a prig, *ma chère*, that's all there is to it. A frightful prig. And don't expect him to soften and come around. The well-being of his younger brother counts as nothing to him compared to some vain idea of the family's dignity. Is this what our bold, virile Polish gentry has come to? Disgusting! I can hardly believe I'm related to this sanctimonious, Mother-of-God-worshipping fool. But there you have it, *mon enfant.* Modern times. *Que voulez-vous?* And he calls himself a son of the Church. As far as I understand, Jesus did look favorably on brotherly love. Now you see the true face of our ridiculous religion. Should not a Christian rejoice that such a charming accomplished woman as you has arrived to make his brother happy? *Mais non.* You do make him happy, I hope. You know what I mean by happy?"

Maryna was more surprised by the old lady's scorn for religion—she had never heard anyone rail against the Church—than by the impertinent question she'd sprung at the end of her tirade. Bogdan had mentioned that his grandmother was reputed to have taken many lovers during her long, contentious marriage to the man with the sword, General Dembowski. Considering that she had a right not to reply, Maryna mustered a becoming, modest blush: she could blush as easily as weep on inner command. But the old lady was not to be put off.

"Well?" she said.

Maryna gave in. "Of course I try."

"Ah. You try."

Maryna didn't, wouldn't, answer this time.

"Trying is a very small part of it, *ma chère*. The attraction exists or it doesn't. I would have thought you, an actress, would know all about these matters. Don't tell me that actresses don't in any way deserve their interesting reputation? Just a little? Come now"—she bared her toothless gums—"you disillusion me."

"I don't want to disillusion you," Maryna answered warmly.

"Good! Because there's something that troubles me about Bogdan. *C'est un sérieux. Trop sérieux peut-être.* Of course, he's too intelligent to think himself bound to grovel before ignorant priests mumbling in barbaric Latin. Unlike Ignacy, Bogdan has a mind. He has the makings of a free spirit. Which is why he chose you. But still, I've worried about him. He's never had dalliances like his brother or all the other young men in his circle. And chastity, *ma fille*, is one of the great vices. To be twenty-eight and still know nothing of women! You have a great responsibility. It's the one defect for which I reproach him, but you have arrived to correct that, unless of course, which would explain the mystery, for there are men like that, as you must know, being of the theatre, he—"

"He really loves me," Maryna interrupted, feeling a stab of anxiety. "And I love him."

"I see that I displease you with my candor."

"Perhaps. But you honor me with your trust. Surely you wouldn't say these things to me if you did not believe I love Bogdan and intend to do everything in my power to be a good wife to him."

"Prettily said, *mon enfant.* A charming evasion. Well, I will not press you on this matter. Just promise me you won't leave him when he ceases to make you happy—for he will, you have a restless spirit, and he is not a man who knows how to possess a woman entirely—or when you fall in love with someone else."

"I promise," said Maryna gravely. She sank to her knees and bowed her head.

The old lady burst out laughing. "Get up, get up! You are not on a stage. Of course your promise is worth nothing." A bony hand reached out and seized her arm. "But nonetheless I shall hold you to it."

"*Grand-mère?*" It was Bogdan at the door.

"*Oui, mon garçon, entre.* I have done with your bride, and you may take her away with the knowledge that I am quite pleased with her. She may be too good for you. You may both visit me once a year, and, *rappelle-toi,* only when your brother is traveling. You will have a letter from me when you may come."

MARYNA WAS FURIOUS not to be regarded as a worthy wife to Bogdan by his family for . . . what? Being a widow? They couldn't know that Heinrich had been unable to marry her or that he wasn't dead; having decided to return to Prussia, his health failing, he had given his promise, she believed a sincere promise, never to enter her life again. Having a child? Could they be so base as to suspect that the late Mr. Załężowski, her husband, was not Piotr's father? But he was! No, she was certain the reason was Ignacy's disapproval of his younger brother's lifelong passion for the theatre. Gratifying as it was that the Dowager Countess Dembowska did not share the family scorn of actresses, Maryna knew that until she was accepted by the older brother she would never be accepted by the others. Maryna supposed the distinguished old lady had some influence on Ignacy—but either she didn't or she disdained to use it, and Maryna had never seen her again. Whenever Bogdan was summoned for his yearly visit, Maryna was mid-season in Warsaw or on tour.

They had never accepted her. Eventually she had won the love of Bogdan's maiden sister Izabela, but Ignacy's opposition only hardened with time, and Bogdan ceased to have any relation with his brother, pride dictating even that he decline, out of his income from the various family properties, the portion due him from the estate managed by Ignacy. But Bogdan had no choice except to ask for a proper assignment of this money now. He wrote Ignacy explaining the reason for his impending arrival. An investment, he said. An excellent investment. He wrote to his grandmother asking her permission for an unscheduled visit. Maryna said that she wished to say good-bye to his grandmother, too.

As soon as they arrived and had installed themselves in their rooms at the inn, Bogdan and Maryna hired a carriage and drove to the manor. The chief steward told Bogdan that the Count would receive him in an hour in the estate office, and that the Dowager Countess was in the library.

They found her heaped with shawls in a high deep chair, reading. "You," she said to Bogdan. She wore a white lace headdress and there were patches of rouge on her seamed, knobby face. "I don't know whether you are late or early. Late, I suppose."

Bogdan stammered, "I didn't think—"

"But not too late."

Beside her was a low table with a tall glass of something thick and white that Maryna could not identify until she and Bogdan were brought glasses of their own: it was hot beer with cream and morsels of finely chopped white cheese floating in it. *"À votre santé, mes chers,"* murmured the old woman, and raised the glass to her sunken mouth. Then, looking at Maryna, she frowned.

"You're in mourning."

"My brother." Recalling the Dowager Countess's style of impertinent declaration, Maryna added, "My favorite brother."

"And he was how old? He must have been very young."

"No, he was forty-eight."

"Young!"

"We knew Stefan was very ill and unlikely to recover, although of course one is never really prepared for—"

"One is never really prepared for anything. *Ah oui.* But the death of someone is always a liberation for someone else. Contrary to what is usually said, *la vie est longue. Figurez-vous,* I am not speaking of myself. It is very long even for those who don't attain any spectacular longevity. *Alors, mes enfants*"—she was looking only at Bogdan—"here is what I have to say to you: I like your folly, *çela vous convient.* But may I ask why?"

"Many reasons," said Bogdan.

"Yes, many," said Maryna.

"Too many, I suspect. Well, you'll find the real one *sur la route.*" Suddenly her head dropped forward, as if she had fallen asleep, or . . .

"Bogdan?" whispered Maryna.

"Yes!"—she had opened her eyes—"a long life is altogether wasted on most people, who quickly run out of enthusiasm or dreams and still have all those years ahead of them. Now, a fresh start, that would be something. Something rare. Unless, as people usually do, you manage to turn your new life into the old one."

"I think," said Bogdan, "there's little chance of that."

"You aren't getting any more intelligent," said his grandmother. "What kind of books are you reading now?"

"Practical books," said Bogdan. "Books on livestock farming, on viticulture, on carpentry, on soil management, on—"

"Pity."

"He reads poetry with me," said Maryna. "We read Shakespeare together."

"Don't defend him. He's an idiot. You're not so clever yourself, at least you weren't when I met you six years ago, and now you're more intelligent than he is."

Bogdan leaned over and kissed his grandmother tenderly on the cheek. A tiny hand gnarled by arthritis reached up and patted the crown of his head.

"He's the only one I love," she said to Maryna.

"I know. And you're the only one it distresses him to leave."

"Nonsense!"

"*Bonne-maman!*" cried Bogdan.

"*Pas de sentiment, je te le défends. Alors, mes chers imbéciles,* it's time for you to go. We won't meet again."

"But I'll be back!"

"And I'll be gone." Unclenching her right hand, she stared at the palm, then lifted it slowly. "An atheist's blessings on you, my children." Maryna bowed her head. "*Bis! Bis!*" said the old lady merrily. "And some advice, yes? Don't ever do anything out of despair. And, *écoutez-moi bien*, don't invent too many reasons for what you've decided to do!"

EVERYONE WONDERS why we are going, Maryna said to herself. Let them wonder. Let them invent. Don't they always tell lies about me? I can lie, too. I don't owe anyone an explanation.

But the others need reasons, or so they tell themselves:

"Because she's my wife, and I must take care of her. Because I can show my brother that I'm a practical man, a virile son of the land, not just a lover of theatre and the editor of a patriotic newspaper that was quickly shut down by the authorities. Because I can't bear always being followed by the police."

"Because I am curious, that's my profession, it's what a journalist should be, because I want to travel, because I am in love with her, because I am young, because I love this country, because I need to escape this country, because I love to hunt, because Nina says she is pregnant and expects me to marry her, because I've read so many books about it, Fenimore Cooper and Mayne Reid and the rest, because I intend to write a great many books, because . . ."

"Because she's my mother and she promised me she would take me to the Centennial Exposition, whatever that is."

"Because I, a simple girl, am to be her maid. Because, out of all the other candidates at the orphanage, all prettier and more skilled at cooking and sewing, she chose me."

"Because that's where the future is being born."

"Because my husband wants to go."

"Because maybe I can't be just Polish, even there, but I won't be only a Jew."

"Because I want to live in a free country."

"Because life there will be better for the children."

"Because it's an adventure."

"Because people should live in harmony, as Fourier says, though—it must be very uplifting from all that I've heard—I confess that each time I try to read his article on work as the key to human happiness my eyes start to—"

"Then forget about Fourier! Shakespeare," Maryna said. "Think of Shakespeare."

"But there's everything in Shakespeare."

"Exactly. As in America. America is meant to mean everything."

And in an old-style actor's declamatory voice, a voice that intends to be heard to the last row of the highest balcony:

"Make haste, make haste. Hordes of people are surging past you. History is roaring by, turning itself into geography: open land as far as the mind can see. Drivers of covered wagons are flogging their horses onward, as if they could catch up with the trains that now link the two coasts—there is a tempest of spitting!"

And so they went to America.

Three

RYSZARD AND JULIAN went first, to scout out a place on the western rim of the continent that would answer to the prospective emigrants' dreams. In late June they traveled to Liverpool, home port of the famous ships flying the red swallow-tail burgee with the five-pointed white star, one of which left for New York every Thursday. The White Star Line's six steamers dedicated to the North Atlantic crossing were advertised as the most opulent, the fastest, the safest; and the one on which they booked passage, the S.S. *Germanic*, was also the newest, having been built to replace the *Atlantic*, which, in 1873, after being chased by lethal gales all across the ocean, emerged into a patch of clear weather and smashed head-on into the granite coast of Nova Scotia, taking down with it five hundred and forty-six lives: the century's worst transatlantic disaster, twelve times the number lost six months before on the North German Lloyd's *Deutschland*, sailing from Bremerhaven.

"You know," Ryszard said, "assuming I would survive it, I'd rather like to be in a shipwreck."

"I'll take my adventures on land," said Julian.

It had been Julian's idea to leave from Liverpool rather than Bremerhaven, the usual port for Polish departures to America. He had once spent a year in England and commanded the basic phrases of polite conversation in that important, difficult language so oddly deficient in cases and genders. Ryszard, who had been working hard in the last months to master English, had traveled abroad very little: he knew Vienna, Berlin, and St. Petersburg, the capitals of the masters of Poland. Ryszard, who wanted to experience everything, had never been to England.

He was glad to be partnered for this voyage into the unknown; he would not have wanted sole responsibility for their mission. But he was irked by the way the relentlessly amiable Julian, older by ten years and the more proficient traveler, simply took charge of their arrangements and experiences: introducing Ryszard to the bounties of an English breakfast, lecturing Ryszard on the miserable condition of the English working class, explaining the transformations wrought by the ever more extensive use of steam power in transport and industry, laying out their money at a broker's office on Waterloo Road for first-class tickets. Ryszard had pointed out that they could be traveling more economically—the *Germanic*, unlike other White Star express liners to New York, had no second class—but Julian, as always, had his own ideas. "We'll be frugal in America," he said, with a wave of his hand. As if he, Ryszard—but Julian, never—were the provincial Pole. Or one of Julian's pupils. Or, God forbid, the docile Wanda; he'd heard Julian patronize his wife in the same teacherly tones. That had to change, would change, Ryszard vowed, as they reached dockside to board the glorious vessel with its four tall masts and two stumpy salmon-pink funnels with raked black tops, its shouting sailors and mute, intimidated emigrants being directed with their bundles of bedding and wicker crates and cardboard suitcases down steep iron stairs toward the ship's cellar: this is when he would change into a man of the world, someone who always knows how to behave. You are whatever you think you are, Ryszard said to himself. Whatever you *dare* think you are. And to be free to think yourself something you're not (not yet), something better than what you are—isn't that the true freedom promised by the country to which he was journeying?

Son of a clerk and grandson of peasants, Ryszard was keenly aware how much deportment and savoir faire figure in the impression one makes on others, and was not about to relax his standards for himself because he had read (all travelers were in agreement about this) that fine manners counted for little in the New World. He'd watched Julian slip some coins to the porters who hauled their trunks and portmanteaus up the gangway, and to the brawny fellow who brought them midship to their cabin. Tipping, always a vexing question for the inexperienced traveler. And how the devil was Julian so versed in shipboard protocol as to know that after going on board they were immediately supposed to settle where they would be sitting for their meals throughout the eight days of the voyage? He trailed after Julian as the older man headed unerringly for the Saloon ("the dining hall," he said to Ryszard), an immense domed room extending the entire width of the ship, with walls paneled in bird's-eye maple and pilasters of oak inlaid with rosewood, two marble fireplaces, a platform at the far end with a grand piano, and four long tables framed by rows of upholstered armchairs bolted to the floor. At the entrance a dozen passengers clustered around a podium presided over by a bearded man in an impressive black uniform with two gold stripes separated by a white band on the sleeves. "The captain?" whispered Ryszard imprudently. "Chief steward," said Julian.

As soon as Julian had negotiated their places—they were to be at the second table—and gone off to their cabin to unpack, Ryszard arranged for a seat at table number three. Then he joined Julian, who reminded him once again that outside Poland a man does not automatically, upon being introduced to a woman, kiss her hand ("I'm afraid that's considered rather old-fashioned, especially where we are going"), and immediately after, as if wishing to cancel this hint that he was already nostalgic for the Old World by demonstrating his utter harmony with the new, drew Ryszard's attention to a cleverly designed folding washstand and pointed out the other amenities, such as the gas lamp and the electric bell to call a steward, to be found only on the White Star ships. "Modern improvements often start as luxuries," Julian explained. "Let's hope that before long such devices will be available to better the lot of everyone."

"Yes," said Ryszard, who wondered how he was going to make Julian accept what he'd just done.

"We should open this trunk."

"Yes."

"What's wrong?"

"You're a teacher, a man of science, you appreciate inventions, but I'm a writer."

"And?"

"I'm fond of games."

"Are you?"

Ryszard went on silently assisting in the unpacking.

"What kind of games?"

"What I had in mind," said Ryszard, feeling his face flush, "if you could consider going along with it, was that, it's just a little game, that we'd pretend we're not traveling together."

"Pretend *what*?"

"Well, we could know each other from Warsaw. No, it's better to have become acquainted just before boarding the ship." He carefully lifted Julian's shirts out of the trunk. "I'll be Mr. Kierul to you and you'll be Professor Solski to me, and we'll tip our hats to each other when we meet on the deck."

"While we're sharing the same cabin?"

"Who is to know that? Except for a few hours of sleep, I for one intend always to be on deck or exploring the ship."

"And eating side by side?"

"Actually, we're no longer at the same table. I need to practice my English. If you're there, I'm sure to be lazy and just talk Polish to you."

"Be serious, Ryszard."

"I am serious. I'll be gathering material for my articles about my impressions of America—"

"We're not in America yet!"

"This ship is full of Americans! I have to talk to them."

"You're not fooling me," said Julian. "I know the real reason."

"What?"

"To have a clear field with the available girls. Or do you think this old married man is going to preach to you about lechery? Go ahead!"

Ryszard grinned. (As if another man could cramp his zeal for seduction!) The real reason was that he wanted to be alone with his own thoughts, without the obligation of dialogue. But he was content to let Julian settle on this explanation. As it turned out, he need not have schemed how to lighten Julian's overbearing presence on the voyage. Julian was at the first night's dinner, gleefully holding forth (Ryszard observed from the table to which he had reassigned himself) on God knows what tedious topics to a middle-aged Englishwoman; he ate a copious breakfast the next morning; but he failed to appear for lunch. Ryszard went to see what was wrong and found him in his nightshirt retching helplessly into the vomit-filled washstand, and helped him back onto his bed. From then on, though the sea stayed calm for most of the crossing, Julian was almost continuously seasick, and rarely emerged from their cabin.

Ryszard was never seasick, not even during the one spell of bad weather, and that seemed to him an omen of future unlimited powers. This journey will make a writer of me, he said to himself, the writer I have dreamed of becoming. If ambition is the surest goad to writing better, writing more, then ambition must be cultivated: by keeping in sight, always, the romance of one's own life. To travel to America had not figured in his dreams of a romantic life before Maryna broached the idea last year, and Ryszard had decided it would be there—on some prairie or desert, perhaps rescuing her from an Indian raid, or finding a spring and bringing her water in his hands, or with those same bare hands trapping a rattlesnake to roast over a campfire when they were stranded, parched, famished—that he would finally win her away from the genteel Bogdan. Now, on the ship, dreams about his enhanced prospects as a suitor were joined by the conviction of his enhanced energies as a writer. The articles he would send back to Warsaw as the newly appointed American correspondent for the *Gazeta Polska* could make an important book. Mentally consigning to oblivion those two mawkish novels he'd had the temerity to publish while still at university, he exulted: My first book!

He had never felt so much a writer, so delightfully alone. Julian was mortified by being seasick: he certainly didn't want his cabin mate to stay at his side and tend to him. Ryszard was usually sharply awake by five o'clock, but lingered in his bed a little longer—he found the rocking of the ship excited him. (The first morning he masturbated to the mental image of a fat brown walrus slowly turning from side to side. Strange, he said to himself; I must think of Nina tomorrow.) Then he rose, washed, and shaved; Julian groaned softly, opened his unseeing eyes, and turned his head to the wall. There was no one in the corridor—how indolent these rich people are!—and for the hour or so until breakfast he had the luxurious Smoke-Room, with its couches and chairs sheathed in scarlet leather, all to himself to con his maps and atlases and English dictionaries and grammars. Then, over the tasteless porridge and the bizarre kippers, he could listen and respond to English untainted by a single Polish word. He was at the far end of his table and by chance the passengers nearby were all native English speakers—plain-faced, smartly dressed Americans, male and female, and a Canadian bishop, who'd been in Rome to receive the Pope's blessing, and his young secretary. Breakfast done, whatever the weather he went outside for a tour of the upper part of the ship—his walking stick from Zakopane with the carved bone knob, a bear's head, might seem an affectation on the pitching deck—then settled into a reclining chair and opened his notebook. The time until noon was devoted to jotting down descriptions of whatever he saw: sailors swabbing the deck and polishing brass fixtures, passengers dozing and chatting and playing quoits, the shapes of clouds and the patterns of gulls following the ship, the exact color and striations of the magnificently monotonous sea.

Before lunch he went to sit with Julian, to encourage him to eat the broth and rice that had been brought to their cabin, and returned after lunch for a longer visit to report on his shipboard encounters and observations and listen to Julian's lectures about America: though nausea prevented him from even opening the copy of *Democracy in America* he'd brought to read on the voyage, Julian was full of ideas about what Tocqueville must have said in his celebrated book. Then Ryszard hurried to the somber room with its uniform editions of Sir Walter Scott, Macaulay, Maria Edgeworth, Thackeray, Addison, Charles Lamb, and such, locked up behind high glass-fronted bookcases, names of famous authors carved in scrolls on the oak wainscoting, and quotations with a maritime theme inscribed on stained-glass windows: there, in the Library, he wrote his letters—to his mother and aunts, to friends, to various abandoned women to each of whom he had promised to return, and of course to Maryna and Bogdan (how he wished he could write to Maryna only). Some two hours later he released himself and went back to the Smoke-Room, ordered a whiskey (a new drink!), lit his pipe, and in that boisterous all-male preserve offered himself the pleasure of a chaste daydream about Maryna. Then he reclaimed his deck chair to continue reading Julian's copy of Tocqueville or honing his skills of description in his notebook; or he prowled the deck where, ever bent on honing his skills of seduction, and as if to test Tocqueville's statement that the United States was morally stricter than Europe and American women more chaste than English ones, he flirted gamely with a pretty, self-assured young American from Philadelphia, whom he was trying to persuade to call him by his first name.

"I certainly don't know you well enough to call you by your Christian name," she said. "Why, we've only known each other for three days, and one of them I didn't even come on deck because I was, I was . . . indisposed."

"It is like your Richard," he persisted, fondling her in his mind, "although we spell it differently."

"What if my mama overheard me calling a gentleman I barely knew by his Christian name?"

"Pronounced the same," he said. "*Rishard.* Is that so difficult?" How long, he wondered, would it take to bed her on land?

"But you *don't* say it the way we do!"

"I will"—he laughed—"as soon as I am in New York."

"Are you sure?" she replied pertly. "I'm not so sure, Mr. . . . oh, I can't pronounce it! They have very funny names in your country."

"Then teach me how to pronounce it like an American."

"Your family name?"

"No, you impossible creature. *Rishard!*"

And impossible—if Ryszard had any thoughts of further intimacy—she was.

A WRITER is never, need never be, bored—fortunate aptitude! The ship, Ryszard learned from notices posted about the promenade deck and at the entrance to the Saloon, proposed a great deal of daily entertainment: lectures, religious services, games, musicales. But nothing was so entertaining as drawing out his fellow passengers in conversation—like most writers, he was a sly, ingratiatingly receptive listener—and there wasn't much point in trying to talk about himself.

He was confident that he would soon be able to understand them. But there was no chance they could understand him. As he had discovered while he and Julian were practicing their English with strangers in pubs and restaurants during the few days in Liverpool—and confirmed in his first mealtime conversations on the ship—foreigners hadn't the faintest idea about Poland, its history, its sufferings. He had supposed that Poland's near-century-long ordeal had made it known to everyone in the civilized world. In fact, he could have been from the moon.

Over every meal he was assured by Americans that theirs was the greatest country on earth, the proof being that everyone knew about America and everyone wanted to come there. Ryszard also came from a country which considered itself chosen for a unique destiny. But election for martyrdom produces a different turning inward of a people than the self-absorption of these Americans, which stemmed from their conviction of being uniquely fortunate.

"In America, this is the whole point, if you follow me, everyone is free," said one of his tablemates, a gruff fellow with a freckled pate who had ignored him until, on the third evening out, he abruptly thrust his card at Ryszard while intoning, "Augustus S. Hatfield. Businessman from Ohio."

"Cleveland," said Ryszard, pocketing the card. "Shipbuilding."

"That's right. Since I wasn't sure you'd heard of Cleveland, I said Ohio, because everyone has heard of Ohio."

"In my country," said Ryszard, "we are not free."

"Really? And what country is that?"

"Poland."

"Oh, it's very backward there, I've heard. But so is everywhere I've traveled, except perhaps England."

"The tragedy of Poland is not backwardness, Mr. Hatfield. We are a conquered people. Like the Irish."

"Yes, Ireland's very poor, too. Didn't you see all those filthy wretches getting on when the ship called at Cork? I know White Star has to take them, as many as they can fit down there. And good business it is, for they can't be making a whole lot from us, what with all this fancy food and so many to wait on us hand and foot. But, Lord, when I think of them all, if the ladies present will excuse my alluding to it, packed together in bare bunks on top of each other with no sense of decency at all, but you know those people, it's what they like to do, that and drinking and stealing and——"

"Mr. Hatfield, I mentioned the Irish because they don't have their own state, either."

"Yes, the British have a hard time keeping them under control. I bet sometimes they don't think it's worth it, and wish they could just give up and go home."

"Everyone wants to be free," said Ryszard calmly, after reminding himself that a man of the world considers expressing indignation to be vulgar. "But no people thinks so much of freedom as one that has long suffered under foreign domination."

"Well, they should come to America. I mean, if they're prepared to work—we don't need any more dirty lazy people. As I said, in America everyone is free."

"We Poles have been dreaming of being free for eighty years. For us the Austrians and the Germans and especially the Russians—"

"Free to make money," said the man firmly, ending the conversation.

How they relished the signs of their own privilege, these Americans, never tiring of pointing out to each other the luxurious furnishings of the ship—their part of the ship. How oblivious of the life beneath their feet in that warren of unventilated spaces between the upper deck and the cargo hold where seven-eighths of the *Germanic*'s passengers were berthed—some fifteen hundred of them, after the ship had picked up its remaining complement of several hundred Irish emigrants before setting out across the Atlantic.

Ryszard was hardly unaware that human populations divided into the comfortable, some very comfortable, and those who were not. But in Poland the harshness of class relations was diluted by the sentimental solidarity of the national identity, of the national sorrow. A vertical, floating world offers nothing to soften the starkness of privilege: you were here, on top, spaciously distributed, overfed, in the light, and they were there, on the bottom, crowded together, dispensed rations, in malodorous darkness.

What were the overflow crowd of first-class passengers thinking as they listened yesterday morning in the Saloon to the Reverend A. A. Willit's lecture, "Sunshine, or the Secret of Happiness"? Nothing, except that sunshine—and happiness—were wonderful things. And why should he be surprised at that? A man of the world is never surprised by anything.

AND A WRITER—comfortable assumption!—is never an intruder, or so writers believe. Ryszard had made a brief descent into the steerage maze after lunch on the second day of the voyage. ("You should also go to where the stokers are," Julian said, when he announced his intention. "Remember what I told you about the factories in Manchester.") Having neglected to procure a plan of the ship, he wasn't sure where he was heading as he veered and tacked across the tilting floor. He skirted an ill-lit space reeking of food and flatulence; overriding the general din he distinguished wailing infants, the rattling of tin dishes, coughing, shouts and imprecations in a Babel of languages, a jaunty air on a concertina. The rolling of the ship seemed more pronounced below, and at the first sounds of someone vomiting he felt like vomiting, too.

In the old days, a steerage ticket purchased a bed-sized shelf in a dank airless space shared by dozens of passengers of both sexes, but after this was discovered to be an offense to decency, newer ships such as the *Germanic* segregated male and female single passengers from one another and from people traveling as families. Ryszard entered one of the dormitories where close to a hundred men were berthed. "Oh, look at the toff," he heard from somewhere in the rank dimness. And laughter. And: "He's come to see the animals in the zoo." From the fourth tier of the bunks just in front of him, a large very white face peered upside down into his. "You got a friend in here?" said the face. "Leave him alone," shouted a fat woman in a kerchief at the doorway. When he left, she asked him for a shilling.

The following afternoon he decided to try again at another entrance. He'd hesitated at the top of the stairs, eyeing the disconcerting notice posted nearby—"Saloon passengers are requested not to throw money or eatables to the steerage passengers, thereby creating disturbance and annoyance"—and then met the bold stare of a deckhand repainting a lifeboat davit nearby.

"I am not going to throw anything at them," he said jocularly.

"Did you want to go to steerage, sir?" said the man and put down his brush.

"Actually, yes," said Ryszard.

"And for me to take you?"

"Why? Am I not allowed to go alone?"

"Well, it's up to you, sir. If I come with you, I could show you where to go."

Ryszard was mystified by the interest in escorting him— even more mystified when, as they were descending the stairs, he heard, "You're one of the first gentlemen this trip to come down." He had assumed that the visit of someone from first class would be more than a rarity. The sailor pushed open the big iron door. At first, as the day before, he couldn't see much. "Follow me," said the sailor. They were in the area where families were quartered, smaller rooms with berths for twenty or thirty people, each room, like each of the several families camping there, with its own distinctive degree of distress, hilarity, resignation. In one, a fiddler was playing for three dancing couples and an old man was clapping his hands to the tune; in another, dark as a dungeon, women in shawls were feeding children on the floor while from the bunks came the sound of loud male snoring; in another, four men huddled around an oil lamp were arguing over a poker game, and an old woman was rocking and crooning to a crying baby. He was led down a narrow passageway that gave onto a wider passage curtained off near the end by two brown blankets.

"Mick," shouted his guide. From a cubicle beside the makeshift curtain emerged an elfish man with russet, no, fox-colored hair—Ryszard's hand was already in his pocket, twitching at the spine of his notebook. "Here's the fellow you want. And now I'll be leaving you in his good hands."

"Very kind of you," said Ryszard.

"At your service, guv'nor," said the seaman and held out his hand. Ryszard put a shilling in it; the hand stayed open—he added another shilling. "Much obliged. And, Mick, don't forget—"

"Clear out, you dog!" snarled the irate elf. "And the name isn't Mick!"

"English bastard," he growled at the sailor's back. He was holding a bottle in his hand. "Have a drop," he said to Ryszard.

"I am a Polish journalist," Ryszard began, "and I want to speak to some passengers in steerage class for an article I am writing about our ship."

"Writing an article, are you?" The elf could grin, too. "And how many would you be wanting to meet?"

"Well," said Ryszard, "if I could interview five or six of your friends—"

"Five or six!" exclaimed this non-Mick. "You're going to interview them. Interview them all at once, you are?" He stamped his foot and chuckled. Sinister elf, thought Ryszard. "Here, sit here on this." As he was pushed onto an upturned basket next to the curtain, Ryszard felt a stir of alarm: was he about to be set upon and robbed? Not in an Apache ambush, by a statuesque brave looming over him with his tomahawk, but in a Fenian one, by a little man with fox-colored hair waving a whiskey bottle at his head? But no . . .

"Do you think my nieces would do? Six is all I have, my lovely nieces that I'm bringing to America." Oh. Ryszard was less relieved than he was annoyed at his own naïveté. "Drink up, man. I'll not be charging you much for the booze. You're a hale young fellow, I can see that. Ready for it, are you?"—Ryszard had stood—"Well, here you go."

"Some other time," said Ryszard.

Then the man launched into a stream of whining words to the effect that (Ryszard did not understand everything) quite a few gentlemen from the first class had already availed themselves of his girls' services, and the foreign gentleman need have no worry, his girls were very clean and healthy, he could vouch for that. He lifted the hanging blankets. Inside, sprawled on a couch whose brocaded pillows and throw might have come from someone's trousseau, was a tangle of red-eyed girls, none of them appearing older than eighteen. One was crying. "Very clean and healthy," he repeated. They looked thin and miserable, not at all like the plump cheerful girls in the brothels of Kraków and Warsaw. "So what do you think of my lovely girls?"

One was pretty.

"Good afternoon," said Ryszard.

"Her name's Nora. Isn't it, my girl?"

The girl nodded meekly. Ryszard took a tentative step forward. There was some low bedding in the other corner. What if he caught syphilis and—and would have to renounce Maryna forever? But he was already inside.

"My name is Ryszard."

"So just one will do, eh?"

"You have a funny name," she said. "Are you going to America, too?"

"On your feet, my beauties!" shouted the man. He shooed the others out and dropped the curtain.

As Ryszard lowered himself on the bedding beside the girl, the ship listed sharply. "Oh," she cried, "I do get afraid sometimes"—she was chewing the ends of her fingers like a child—"I never been on a boat before, and drowning must be something awful." A wave of pity that grew and grew swept over him as the swell of the ocean subsided. She was, he saw now, even younger than he had supposed.

"How old are you, Nora?"

"Fifteen, sir." She was fumbling with the buttons of his pants. "Almost fifteen."

"Ah, you don't have to do that." He took away her hand with its bitten nails and held it in his. "Have there been many other visitors from—from upstairs?"

"You's the first today," she mumbled.

"Making your way all right, boyo?" shouted the voice from the other side of the curtain.

"What is he saying?" said Ryszard.

"Let me be nice to you," said the girl. She had pulled her hand free from his loose grasp, and flung herself on his chest. He held her tightly, his palm against the small of her back, and stroked her matted hair.

"He does not beat you, does he?" he whispered into her ear.

"Only if the mister complains," she replied.

He let himself be pushed over on his back and felt her chapped lips brush against his cheek. She had hiked up her cotton shift and was rubbing her bony loins against his body. He was becoming aroused, despite himself. "I would rather not," he said, slipping his hand beneath her and lifting her torso a few inches above his. "I will give you the money and you can say—"

"Oh, please, sir, please," she squealed. "You can't give the money to *me*!"

"Then I—"

"And he'll find out you didn't like me, and he'll—"

"How can he find out?"

"He will, he will!" He felt her tears on his neck, the grinding of her pubis. "He knows everything! He'll see from my face 'cause I'll be ashamed and worried, and then he'll look, you know, between my legs."

Sighing, Ryszard shifted the frail body to the side of his torso, unbuttoned his pants, and took out his semi-erect penis, and moved her back on top of him. "Do not move," he said, as he gently inserted it between her scrawny thighs, just above her knees. "What are you doing?" she moaned. "That's not the right place. You're supposed to put it where it hurts me." Ryszard felt tears prickling his eyes. "We are playing a game," he whispered hoarsely. "We pretend we are not on this big horrible ship, we are on a little boat, and the boat is rocking and swaying, but not so much, and the boat has this little oar that you must hold tight with your legs because otherwise it will fall into the water and then we can never row home, but you can shut your eyes and pretend to sleep . . ."

Obediently, the girl closed her eyes. Ryszard closed his eyes too, still stinging with pity and shame, while his efficient body did the rest. It was the saddest story he had ever invented. It was the saddest game he had ever played.

"JULIAN . . ." Ryszard began. He was in their cabin, watching the older man sipping some broth. "Do you ever go much to brothels in Warsaw, I mean did you go before you married Wanda?"

"Even then not as much as you, I'll wager," said Julian, managing a smile. "Now? Hardly ever. Marriage has tamed me."

"It can be dispiriting," said Ryszard, torn between the hackneyed desire he was feeling at this moment to confide in Julian and a wiser determination to keep this experience to himself. "Dispiriting," he repeated, waiting for Julian to draw him out.

"Not as dispiriting as marriage," Julian said. "What's the sadness of a loveless hour, compared with a lifetime of loveless cohabitation?"

Ryszard realized that what he had unwittingly provoked in Julian was a desire to confide in *him*. For a moment the weakness of the young man who had never had a father (he'd died before Ryszard was born) stood off the second nature of the writer whose favorite pastime was inciting other people to talk about themselves. Then the writer won.

"I'm so sorry to hear there is discord between you and Wanda."

"Discord!" Julian howled. "Do you know what I dream of alone in this cabin, vomiting up my guts all these days? Let me tell you. That we reach America, that we locate a site for the phalanstery, and then, just before the rest arrive with Maryna, I disappear. Nobody knows where I've gone. But I won't have the courage, you'll see. There will be no New World for me."

"You don't love her at all?"

"Do I seem to you to be a man who could love such an imbecile?"

"But before you married her you must at least have had an inkling of—"

"What did I know about women? She was young, I wanted a companion, I thought I could mold her and she would look up to me. Instead, she's simply afraid of me. And I can't keep from showing my exasperation. My disappointment." He groaned. "You can't imagine how I envy you. Blessedly unmarried, you can toddle off to whores whenever you like with a clear conscience, while courting an ideal woman whom you will never win—"

"Julian!"

"I'm not supposed to mention your designs on Maryna, am I? Everyone knows."

"Even Bogdan."

"How could he not? He'd have to be as stupid as my Wanda."

"And everybody finds me quite ridiculous."

"Let's say . . . youthful."

"I *will* win her! You'll see. There's sadness in that marriage, too. I could make her much happier."

"How?"

Ryszard could hardly say to Julian that his intuition told him a man like Bogdan does not know how to make a woman happy sexually. "I'd write plays for her," he said.

"Ah, youth," exclaimed Julian.

It suddenly occurred to Ryszard that Julian wasn't really sick, that he had only fallen into a fit of despondency, that he'd been hiding.

"Dress and come on deck with me," said Ryszard. "You'll feel better, I promise."

"And flirt with the girls? You'll share some of your conquests?"

"Oh, my conquests." Ryszard laughed. "Which one do you want? The Englishwoman with the lorgnette and the copy of *A History of White Slavery* in her reticule? The Spanish dancer with the finger cymbals? The French widow you'll hear crooning 'You come wiz me, my love' to the little white dog she walks about the deck? The Roman countess bedecked with paste jewels, who hopes to restore the fortunes of her ancient family by capturing a rich American husband? The lady from Warsaw, yes, Warsaw, we are not the only Poles in Saloon class, who announces to all and sundry that she is going to America to escape the yoke of the Muscovite, or her sister, who is already so homesick (I'm afraid she reminds me of Wanda) that she will certainly want to show you the little silk bag of Polish soil she keeps between her breasts? The unhappily married German who confides that she could never be attracted to a man who did not share her adoration of Wagner? The American (Julian, you'll not believe these American girls!) who recommends, for your health, a trip on her papa's railroad? The sickly Irish girl who is traveling with her uncle in steerage—" He had started to laugh at his own rollicking inventiveness, of course one isn't supposed to laugh when one is trying to be amusing, so why couldn't he stop laughing, laughing so hard his eyes filled with tears, but he staggered on, finishing breathlessly with: "You're welcome to all of them."

"Bravo," said Julian.

"So will you get dressed now?"

Julian shook his head. "Let me live vicariously. I shall look forward to reading a story about each of these ladies in your next book. Don't disappoint me. And now, if you'll excuse me, I'm afraid I am about to be sick."

HOW IRRITATING that Julian would not accept his offer of rescue from naïve self-pity and unhealthy inactivity. How odd for him to have extended it, after being so bent on disburdening himself of Julian's company during the voyage; but a change of inner weather can no more be ignored than the coming of an ocean squall.

Leaving the cabin, after dutifully cleaning up after Julian, he regained the sun and wind and his own perch of scornful acuity. Like most writers who are intelligent, Ryszard had long since accustomed himself to being actually two people. One was a warmhearted, anxious man, rather boyish for his twenty-five years, while the other one . . . in the other one, detached, reckless, manipulative, flourished the temperament of someone much older. The first self was forever being surprised by the evidence of his own intelligence; it never ceased to astonish him, thrill him, when words, eloquence, ideas, observations just *came,* like birds flying out of his mouth. The second was condemned to finding nobody clever enough—and everything he saw a challenge to his skills as an observer and describer, because so blindly, thickly steeped in itself ("the world" is not a writer).

The first self was the insecure youthful Pole who aspired to be a man of the world. The second had always, in the recesses of his furtive heart, considered himself to be someone unlike anyone else. One of those extremely intelligent people who become writers because they cannot imagine a better use of their watchfulness, their sense of being different from others, Ryszard knew that his intelligence could also be a handicap: how good a novelist could he ever become if he found everybody he met either preposterous or pathetic? One must believe in people to be a great writer, which means one must continually adjust one's expectations of them. Ryszard could never be so contemptuous of a woman for being less intelligent than he, since stupidity was a quality Ryszard found to be in ample supply among everyone he knew, including Maryna (whose intelligence he found . . . endearing). And, despite what he had said to Julian, Ryszard would have been affronted if everyone back in Poland did *not* think him in love with her; and to these easily mocked yearnings of a younger man for a famous actress, the man who was always seeing through people, the writer, gave his fervent assent. He thought it becoming, even improving, to be humbled by love.

Love, a voluptuous sacrifice of judgment. Love, the shapeshifter—changing as much in the absence as in the presence of the beloved. The variety of his feelings for Maryna enchanted him. One day it was lust, pure lust. He could conjure up only the smooth white nape of her neck, the curve of her breasts, the pink heaviness of her tongue. The next day it was fascination. She is the most interesting subject I've ever come across. Another day: it's only (only!) her beauty. If she didn't look exactly like that, that face, those gestures, if she didn't have that voice, if she weren't so tall, if she didn't wear those soft, silkily expressive clothes, she could never have burned a hole in my heart. And sometimes, often: no, it's admiration. She has a great talent, and a great soul; she is sincere, which I am not.

Maryna, he knew, would approve of his sympathy for the steerage passengers, and when, two days later, he went down once more to steerage—whether because Maryna would want him to or simply because he had to re-experience, but more coldly, that dismay, at that moment Ryszard was delightfully unable to say— he also came away with more than enough material for his article about the trip from conversations he succeeded in conducting with some dozen stuporous or bewildered emigrants. (The old man who recited from the Book of Revelation, explaining how it had been ordained by God that before the end of days everyone in the world would come to "Hamerica"—Ryszard would save him for a short story.) It took two days before the smell of putre-fying food and shit-clogged toilets was out of his nostrils.

It was still in his nostrils when the captain of the *Germanic* took Ryszard aside to remonstrate with him about his forays, say-ing that while he could not of course forbid "communication" between Saloon and steerage passengers, he had instructions from the company to discourage it strongly. "For reasons of health," he said. He was a large man, a whale of a man, on whom this mincing language seemed ill-suited, Ryszard was thinking—for he assumed that the captain was referring to the wretched sexual commerce offered below. But no, it turned out to be a more immediate inconvenience: should the Health Officers in New York who would be examining the steerage passengers for signs of contagious or infectious disease find out there had been any visits from Saloon passengers during the voyage, those passengers might also be made subject to quarantine.

"I thank you for your concern," said Ryszard.

They were in the Smoke-Room, to which all the men were expected to adjourn once dinner was over (wives and daughters had the Ladies' Boudoir for their own off-duty chatter), and where Ryszard had excused himself from the obligation of making polite conversation and sat a little apart with his pipe, watching, listen-ing. The men, flushed with drink, mostly talked of stocks and per-centages (he understood little of what they were saying) or related stories of their sexual exploits (he wondered which of them had been with Nora) while Ryszard—Ryszard was cultivating elemen-tary forbearance and good-humored indifference. What a great distance I have come on this ship, he thought. He felt not only many miles but many years from the callow young man who had come aboard at Liverpool. How fast the intelligence travels. Intel-ligence travels faster than anything in the world.

TOWARD THE END of the voyage the weather turned rough (one day of real gales) and, as if needing only this challenge, Julian ruled himself recovered from seasickness and able to resume the routines of shipboard life. "I feel quite refreshed," he announced to Ryszard. "As if I'd taken a cure."

They were standing together at the railing above a now calmer sea and Julian was alerting Ryszard to some differences between British and American English ("A booking office is a ticket office, luggage is baggage, a station is also a depot . . .") when the girl from Philadelphia came onto the deck.

"Oh, there you are! I've been looking for you everywhere."

"Aha," said Julian.

She was upon them now.

"Good morning, Miss," Julian said. "It's a beautiful day, is it not? What a pity, is it not, that this delightful voyage is about to end."

"Want her?" said Ryszard in Polish. "She's yours."

"What are you saying?" said the girl. "My mama says it's not polite to say something other people don't understand."

"I am telling Professor Solski that you have found me so charming that you are very eager to meet as many Polish gentlemen as you can."

"Mr. Krool, how can you say such a thing! Why, that's a lie!"

"Excuse me," said Julian, "excuse me, Miss," and fled.

"How naughty you are," cried the girl. "Now your friend has left. If you did want me to meet him, that wasn't the way to go about it. Why, I believe he was even more embarrassed than I was." She paused, and then wagged a finger at Ryszard. "Oh, you are very, very naughty. Were you *trying* to embarrass your friend?"

"Yes. To be alone with you."

"Well, we can only be alone for a minute. I have to go right back to the cabin to help Mama decide what to wear for the farewell banquet tonight. But I brought you this." She was holding out a small red plush album with gilt edges.

"A present?" said Ryszard. "You have a present for me, you adorable girl?"

"Oh no, it's mine!" she exclaimed. "It's my most precious possession, except for—" She stopped, abashed. The list of her precious possessions was rather long.

"Still, you want to show me your most precious possession. And that proves you do like me. What is it?"

"My autograph book!" she called out triumphantly. "And my showing it to you doesn't prove anything at all. I show it to everyone I know and everyone I meet, even if I like them only a little."

"Oh," said Ryszard in mock dismay.

"You have to look inside. It has verses people have written to me. Every young lady owns one."

Ryszard leafed through the pages of robin's-egg blue, salmon, grey, pink, buff, and turquoise. " 'Be good, dear child, and let who will be clever.' Who wrote that?"

"My father."

"Do you agree?"

"Mr. Karool, you do ask the silliest questions!"

"Richard. And this?"

"Which?"

How he enjoyed reciting, in his ridiculous Polish accent, "In the tempest of life / When you need an umbrella / May it be upheld / By a handsome young feller." If Maryna could see him now! "Who is the author?"

"My best friend, Abigail. We were at Miss Ogilvy's Academy together, she was just a year ahead of me, but now she's married."

"Which means you envy her?"

"Maybe I do and maybe I don't. That's a very intimate question!"

"Not so intimate as I can be."

"Mr. Kreel, you just have to stop that. And write something in my book, didn't you say you were a writer? If you write something in it, then I'll never forget you."

"I must write something for you to remember me? You would not remember me always if I follow you to Philadelphia?"

"You're coming to Philadelphia?"

"To see the Centennial Exposition, of course. You said that I must see it."

"But I—"

"And you shall be my guide." He pulled her toward him: why not, they were landing in New York tomorrow. "I press you to my heart. Don't say that we must part. Or I shall find a—" And she, too, fled. Farewell, Philadelphia Miss.

NARROWING WATER, islands, tugboat, then *the* island, Manhattan, sultry wind, and the gulls, cormorants, falcons wheeling and circling overhead as the *Germanic* started upriver, eventually shuddering and bumping into White Star's pier at Twenty-third Street. On their right, the relentless *contra naturam* of a modern city, a city devoted to the recasting of all relations into those of buyer and seller. A successful city, a city to which people wanted to emigrate. At any cost, whatever the indignities.

The steerage passengers were still being herded off the *Germanic* onto the barge that would transport them back down the river to Castle Clinton, the former fort at the bottom of Manhattan where they would be interrogated and examined, when the customs officials who had come aboard to interview the first-class passengers and check their baggage had finished with them and welcomed them to America. Ryszard and Julian descended into the steaming street and hired a hackney carriage to take them to their hotel.

Its size astonished even Julian. By telegraph from Liverpool he had booked a double room at the Central Hotel—for the name. "It looks like a bank," said Ryszard.

Is this normal weather, he inquired of the clerk after they had registered (in a free country, as Julian pointed out, one need not show any identity document) and after asking him where to purchase stamps to mail his stack of letters ("Just give him the letters," whispered Julian. "He does it and puts the postage on our bill").

"You mean the hot wave?" said the clerk. "Oh, it's not so hot as it can be. Not in July. No, sir. This is nothing. You should come back next month!"

Following the two black porters who sprang forward to take charge of their trunk and bags, they crossed the huge lobby, with its several aroma zones of polished brass and oiled wood and chewing tobacco, looked into the cavernous dining room where four times a day the guests descended for their meals (Ryszard noting that the heat apparently authorized men to dine without their jackets, Julian explaining that, as on the ship, in American hotels there is no separate charge for meals, their cost being included in the price of the room), reached their immense room with its handsome but, their skin told them, useless ceiling fan, and decided to go out immediately for a walk. And it was when they stepped back on the street that Ryszard, who had been busy observing, judging, concluding from the moment they had landed two hours ago, had his epiphany. Perhaps it was seeing the sign as they emerged from the hotel. Broadway. They were on Broadway! His agile mind slowed and all he could think was: I'm here, I'm actually here.

On the ship, that cruel microcosm, Ryszard was nowhere; therefore he could feel he was everywhere, the king of consciousness. You pace your world, as it moves across a surface of unmarked sameness, from one end to the other. It's small, the world. You could put it in your pocket. That is the beauty of traveling on a ship.

But now he was somewhere. He had not felt dumbfounded when the destination had been St. Petersburg or Vienna (though his head had long been stocked with pictures of those, to him, mythical cities), had not felt stunned the first time by the sheer this-ness of where he was, and that it looked as pictured. It was

New York that produced this spell, or maybe it was America, Hamerica, made too mythical by a suffusion of dreams, of expectations, of fears that no reality could support—for everyone in Europe has views about this country, is fascinated by America, imagines it to be idyllic or barbaric and, however conceived, always a kind of solution. And all the while, deep down you are not entirely convinced it really exists. But it does!

To be so struck that something really exists means that it seems quite unreal. The real is what you don't marvel over, feel abashed by: it's just the dry land surrounding your little puddle of consciousness. Make it real, make it real!

That evening they returned on foot almost to the bottom of the island. As night fell the streets were still aswarm, shoppers and office workers giving way to the entertainment crowd, which included a multitude of streetwalkers. Lingering in Union Square, watching the well-dressed go into the theatres; peering into a bar on Bleecker Street at half-naked women on the laps of shirtsleeved men canted back in their chairs ("This is what, oddly enough, Americans call a saloon. Also a dive," said Julian); passing streets where suffocating tenement dwellers had dragged pallets and planks out on fire escapes and sidewalks to sleep . . . Ryszard remaining silent; Julian commenting that a slum in New York had a different meaning from a slum in Liverpool because here people had hope ("Ships aren't leaving New York weekly packed with poor people emigrating to Liverpool," he said). But Ryszard didn't mind, hardly heard Julian's platitudes. He was listening to the voice in his own strangely empty head. I'm here. Where did I think I was going? I'm here.

It exists . . . but then, do you?

OF COURSE you have your things you do. Your ways of behaving. If you are a man, anywhere you go, you can always hunt for sex. If, man or woman, you are someone given to more exotic entertainment, such as art, you can spend time checking out the local facilities, if only to deplore their insufficiency. If you are a journalist, or a writer of fiction playing at being a journalist, you will want to get your fill of the local misery. The unrelenting servility of the Negro waiters in the hotel restaurant, exclaiming "Yes sir! Yes sir!!" to every request, confirmed his impression that the politest people to be encountered in New York were those from Africa, who had been brought here in chains, while the people felt to be a menace were Europeans who had most recently chosen to come here. Wherever he was warned not to venture he went: the valley of hovels and shanties that started a few streets west of the Central Park, dark and fearful backstreets such as Bayard and Sullivan and West Houston, even the infamous Rag Pickers Row and Bottle Alley, where the most impoverished, most miserable, and therefore most dangerous lived. The risk of having his wallet lifted was the least of the dangers he was told he would be incurring. You would think he had landed on an island of cannibals.

Ryszard had the writer's perpetually available blankness of mind. Julian had the comfort of his interests—science, inventions, progress. What he saw when he traveled illustrated or added to what he already knew. It was Julian, alone, who went off to the Centennial Exposition two days after they arrived. The latest prodigies of American inventiveness were on display—the telephone! the typewriter! the mimeograph machine!—and he returned after a day in Philadelphia enchanted with what he had seen. Ryszard, although his paper wanted a firsthand account of this national jubilee and world's fair, had begged off: he could not bear another round of Julian explaining the modern and the sensible to him. It was New York, its rawness, its irreverence, that attracted Ryszard. Indeed, he suspected he might have felt even more at home in the city of thirty years ago that Dickens had excoriated, when pigs were still to be seen on the cobblestone streets. Of the three articles he sent back to the *Gazeta Polska* before they moved on—"The Life of a Great Transatlantic Steamship," "New York: A First View," and "American Manners"—the second and third were full of lively description and judicious admiration for the city's energies.

Ryszard's one advantage as a traveler over Julian: his taste for sexual entertainment. Having, by chance at sea, for the first time in his life glimpsed something of the abjection of prostitution, Ryszard determined to efface this disturbing knowledge by a jolly visit to a whorehouse on land. The evening ended memorably on an exchange with a fellow client in the lounge of the house in Washington Square where, returning downstairs from his hour with a luscious Marianne, he stopped to drink a glass of champagne and bask in pleasure's boost to the gradual refilling of his mind.

"Can't place the accent," said the man amiably.

"I am a journalist from Poland," Ryszard said by way of introducing himself.

"I'm a journalist too!" Not the profession Ryszard would have guessed for this pleasant-looking older man with the creased face and the build of a sportsman. "Have you come over to write about America?" Ryszard nodded. "Then you should read my books. I can't resist recommending them."

"I want to read as many books about America as I can."

"Great! That's the spirit! The subjects may seem a little narrow to you. I mean, I'm no Tockveel—"

"Who?" said Ryszard.

"Tockveel, you know, that Frenchman who came here, must be almost fifty years ago."

"Right," said Ryszard.

"But, you'll see, in my books you'll be learning about things most foreigners don't know anything about. There's the one last year, *The Communistic Societies of the United States,* and the one three years ago, *California: For Health, Pleasure, and Residence,* and—"

"But this is, this is"—Ryszard, happily excavating the word from his passive vocabulary—"uncanny, Mr. . . . ."

"Charles Nordhoff." He held out his hand and Ryszard seized it warmly.

"Richard Kierul." My God, Ryszard thought to himself. I'm changing my name. In America I really am going to be Rich-ard. "Uncanny," he repeated. "Because California is where I am going and expect to stay for a while. And I am very interested in communities which live according to a higher standard, one of mutual cooperation." He paused. "That is, I presume, what you mean by communistic."

"Yes, and there have been plenty of them, in Texas and Pennsylvania and California, all over, though they don't work in the end, of course. But that's what this country's about. We try everything. We're a country of idealists. Or isn't that your impression?"

"I confess," said Ryszard, "I have not seen much of that so far."

"No? Well, you haven't seen the real America. Get out of New York. Nobody cares about anything here except money. Go out west. Go to California. It's paradise. Everyone wants to go there."

DOESN'T IT SEEM very American, he said to Julian, to whom he reported this exchange (though not its setting) on his return to the hotel, that America has its America, its better destination where everyone dreams of going?

Ryszard realized he had fully outlived his shock and astonishment only when he and Julian set their date of departure. He was no longer marveling; it was all quite real. Indeed, by that operation which an acute mind has always at the ready to master wonderment, he had decided that what stunned him with its uniqueness was not unique: this Noah's Ark of escapees from every flood, every disaster on earth, already the third largest city in the known world, was not going to be the only one of its kind. Wherever there is promise there will be this ugliness, this vitality, this discontent, as well as this self-congratulation. On Sunday, the third day of their stay, Ryszard went to a church in Brooklyn to hear its eminent minister, the author of a recent best-selling volume entitled *The Abominations of Modern Society*, preach a sermon on the inhumanity and godlessness of New York. Such denunciations struck Ryszard as of a piece with the boasting about the extremes of weather. We have the greatest country. And we have the most sinful metropolis. Surely not. Immobilizing traffic, swirls of paper detritus, construction sites, homely buildings layered with shop signs and advertising, faces of every color and shape, this continual arriving, and building, and leaving—soon the world will be full of cities like this.

They left on the cross-country train a week after their arrival. Completing his article on the transatlantic trip, Ryszard had spent some hours at Castle Clinton observing the morning deposit of steerage passengers awaiting their fate in the huge hall and, amid the signs informing the immigrants in stern lettering who was welcome and who was likely to be excluded, spied this more inviting message:

HO! FOR CALIFORNIA!
THE LABORER'S PARADISE.
SALUBRIOUS CLIMATE. FERTILE SOIL.
NO SEVERE WINTERS. NO LOST TIME.
NO BLIGHTS NOR INSECT PESTS.

So read the poster with a drawing of a giant cornucopia disgorging a fall of colorful fruit, fish, vegetables, ploughs, houses, people. He saw it again in the equally crowded hall of the railway station, and pointed it out to Julian, as they looked for the platform from which the train departed. They would be seven days and seven nights on the train, which made many stops, none, except at Chicago, for more than an hour or two. Ryszard was enchanted at the prospect, Julian much less so since having learned that it was now possible to go even faster. Inaugurated on the first of June, the express train, which made few stops and went at an unimaginable fifty to sixty miles an hour, took only three days and nights to reach San Francisco. That was the train, Julian decided, that they should take. But Ryszard had balked. "There's so much to see," he said. "I have to *see*." Ryszard had refused to agree to changing their tickets.

"No lost time," muttered Julian, with a nod to the poster.

"The Laborer's Paradise," exclaimed Ryszard. "Cheer up, comrade."

"Well, at least . . . all right. No blights nor insect pests," Julian sang out, grinning. "Ho! For California," they chanted, happily, together.

Four

Hoboken, New Jersey
United States of America
9 August 1876

Dear friend,

Yes, a letter. And you were thinking, The continent ate her. A letter I've been composing for days in my head, though I have taken in too much to recall everything. And what is the first thing that comes to mind? Those last moments in Warsaw. Your scowling face at the railway station. I don't see the crowd, I don't hear the students serenading me with patriotic songs. I see the sadness of my friend. Dear friend! We are not lost to each other, I promise. You are, you always will be, so dear to me. But have I missed you? I shall be honest, with whom can I be honest if not with you? No, not yet. I was relieved to see you slouch, turn, and quit the platform before the train departed. One more burden lifted: your sadness. You wanted to enroll me in your gloom, your conviction that life cannot be restarted, that we are all prisoners of whatever we have become. But I do not accept that, Henryk. I can change, I know it. Already I am no longer "the same person." Illusion of an actor, you will say: of one used to changing characters, putting on the garments of another. Well, I shall show you that it can be done *without* being on a stage!

Did you then go off and get drunk? Of course you did. Did you say to yourself, my Maryna has abandoned me forever? Of course you did. But not forever—though who knows when we shall see each other again. Your distress over my departure makes me seem more necessary to you than ever, in your memory you will exaggerate my charms, and forget how much unhappiness my presence in your life, and your rueful affection for me, have brought you. You follow in your mind: she is on the train, she is on the ship, now she has reached America, she has begun that new life in scenery I cannot imagine. She has forgotten me. After a while, you will be angry. Perhaps you are angry now. You will feel older, and then think, *she* is aging, too. Soon she will not be beautiful at all. This thought will give you some pleasure.

If it consoles you, then imagine me as the train pulled away from the station, closing the compartment door, taking off my gloves and hat, pouring some water from the pitcher and burying my face in a damp cloth, which ruins my makeup, exposing the puffy circles under my eyes and the lines from my nose to my mouth, then collapsing in my seat, trembling, not knowing whether to laugh or to cry. All those farewells! Were you aware how nearly I was undone by them? The tearful young actors gathered on the bare stage of the Imperial Theatre on the after-noon I went to say good-bye, the siege of reproachful devotees at the stage door when I left the theatre at twilight, on the sidewalk beneath our apartment through the last days, and then, since I couldn't stop the time of our departure being published in the papers, the procession of university students who accompanied the carriage, shouting, singing, to the station, and the wreath of white and red ribbons signed "To Maryna Załężowska—from Polish Youth" which they presented to me as I boarded the train. "They want to make me feel guilty," I said to Bogdan. "No," he replied, you know how gentle he can be, "they want to make you feel loved." But, I thought, isn't that the same thing?

I don't see why I should be made to feel guilty for leaving!

By the time we reached Bremen, and this but the start of

our journey, I felt I had already aged a year. We had two days before the *Donau* sailed, two days of nothing to do, and I wanted only to rest. But don't imagine I was ill. And no headaches, none at all. I was feeling weak because something was flowing out of me. Or I was girding myself for a final struggle. "You have passed a sentence on yourself," you said to me in Zakopane. "Now you feel obliged to carry it out." No, Henryk. Driven, I'll grant you; obliged, never. But I did wonder if, at the end, I would falter. Perhaps I still thought someone would stop me. Perhaps I've always thought someone would stop me. So many tried. So many, yourself included, reminding me who I am, this Madame Maryna who is so important, so necessary to them. Or to the theatre. Or to Poland. When all she wants is to become no one!

In Bremen, I had to endure one last farewell. One last attempt to stop me. He was waiting at the Hotel Cordelia, he of whom I can speak only to you. And with flowers! Not one of those admirers who loiter in lobbies, usually young men with student caps, stammering, pushing flowers at me, but a surly-looking old man with an odd felt hat. That's all I took in with my glance, as Bogdan, who doesn't know what he looks like, intercepted the flowers. Until he spoke—"Welcome to Bremen" is all he said—I didn't recognize him. How is that possible, Henryk, how? He has not changed *that* much.

I looked back but he had vanished. Piotr was behind me, with Wanda. I was shuddering, I must have been pale, I know my voice had gone hoarse when I joined Bogdan at the desk. There we found letters for Wanda from Julian, for us from both Julian and Ryszard, the last mailed from New York, for Bogdan from his sister, who was to arrive that afternoon (she insisted on coming to see us off), for me a letter from the Bremen Shakespeare Society requesting the honor of my presence at a reading of *Julius Caesar* by some promising young actors—and a note from the man in the felt hat. He had read in a German paper that I was going to America. He had come, all the way from Berlin, to see Piotr, he said. Surely I would not dispute his right to bid his son farewell.

You can imagine the dread I felt at the prospect of this encounter, but—you know this about me, too—I was more afraid of being a coward. I left a note with the concierge, as he asked, setting our assignation for the following afternoon on the promenade nearby, along the Weser. I told Bogdan, who had all he could do to console poor Izabela, that I was going for a stroll with the boy. I told Piotr that he was going to meet an old friend of his grandmother. (Don't accuse me of opening ancient wounds, Henryk!) Of course he was late, and then without a word lunged at the child, hugging him to his old coat, whereupon naturally Piotr started to bawl. I told the maid to take him back to the hotel. Heinrich didn't object. No good-bye, no fond paternal glance—he's still a brute, Henryk, this stiff, sad old man. Then we walked on, but it proved impossible to converse side by side. "What?" he kept saying. "What??" "Have you gone a bit deaf?" I said. "What??" We went to the café in the Altmannshöhe and sat by the water. Straight off I told him that I would not permit him to reproach me. "Reproach you!" he shouted. "Why should I do that?" I said I would not permit him to shout at me either. "But I don't hear my voice," he whined. "You can see that I don't hear well." And then he described these last years in Berlin, and the woman he lives with, who has stomach cancer. "Soon I will be completely alone. *Bald ganz allein, der alte Zalezowski.*" He too accusing me of abandoning him? I asked him if he needed money. This provoked an extravagant show of indignation, which means that at the end he did take money from me. And yes, he did try to dent my resolve. First he evoked the dangers of an ocean voyage, as if I were unaware of these, and even reminded me of the attack last year on the *Mosel*, sister ship to our *Donau*. Do you recall reading about that? The bomb exploded prematurely, just before it left Bremerhaven, killing eighty-nine and wounding fifty passengers and crew. Then he offered his solemn prediction that I won't like America. There's no respect for culture, theatre as we know it means nothing to them, plebeian entertainments are all they want, and so on and so forth, whereupon I assured him that I was hardly going to America to find what I was leaving behind in Europe—*au contraire*! Last, he declared I had no right to deprive him of the possibility of seeing his son— as if he has ever shown the slightest interest in the boy! Feeble tirades these were, with nothing of the old force. He had a hacking cough and kept running his fingers through his thin sandy hair. I don't think he really believed he could stop me. He just wanted to exhibit himself. He wanted my pity. He was pitiable. I did not pity him. I was free of him, at last.

And yet . . . I knew then that I really had loved him. Perhaps I have never loved anyone as much. I loved him with that part of me that wanted to be someone, someone who would do great things in this world.

Even this pitiable spectre could not mar the elation I felt boarding the ship.

There *were* dangers on the voyage, but not of the kind Heinrich had invoked. The sea was calm, our accommodations comfortable, though the ship seemed small, I suppose *is* small; it was built nearly ten years ago. But then there is German servility, which is meant to make you overlook the German taste for giving orders. The captain so fawned and fussed over us—he had learned I was a famous actress and Bogdan a count—you might have thought the faltering reputation of the Norddeutsche Lloyd fleet rested on our approval. At first I was irritated by the monotony of life on an ocean liner, which is so regimented and pampering. *L'indolence n'est pas mon fort.* But a long trip over water has its special magic, to which I eventually succumbed. It made me quite unsociable, even with the members of our party, and especially at dinner, with its obligatory light conversation to the music of a string trio playing Bizet and Wagner. I preferred to commune with the sea, which reminds one of the enormous emptiness of the universe.

Again and again I was drawn to the upper deck to stand at

the railing and look down at the heaving water. Near the ship it was dirty green, farther out the color of tarnished pewter. Sometimes I saw other ships, but they were far, far away. Even when I watched them for a long time they seemed not to be moving—they looked bolted to the horizon—while our little, creaky *Donau* was a speeding projectile of steam and iron, ploughing the ocean. Our venture began to rhyme in my head with the inexorable thrust of the ship through the water, with my dizzying awareness that it was I who had set us all in motion: no way to stop it now! I can tell this only to you, Henryk. I was haunted by the idea that I might throw myself in the ocean. I might have done it, who knows. But I was brought to my senses by someone else's folly.

It was the fourth evening out, around eight o'clock. We had been released from dinner half an hour earlier and I'd accompanied Piotr to the cabin he shares with Wanda to see the child readied for sleep and tucked in, and had just returned to our stateroom where Bogdan was sitting with an unlit cigar, waiting for me. I remember that I leaned over to look with him through the porthole at the newly risen moon, as we recalled to each other, laughing, something fatuous the captain had said at table about the moon and melancholy—I had already hung up my cape, had put away my rings and necklace and earrings, had laid out my peignoir—when the ship seemed to stagger like an old trotter suddenly gone in the hamstrings. Then all went still, ominously still, beneath our feet. We could hear shouts in the corridor; Bogdan said he would go on deck to see what was amiss and I quickly followed. The ship had stopped. The crew was scurrying about, some slackening sails, others lowering a lifeboat over the side. Bogdan found me to tell me the news. The second officer had spied someone in the water. A cabin boy had found a pair of large lace-up ankle boots by the starboard railing. One of the first passengers who had hurried on deck, an Englishman at our table, remembered the shoes: a gentleman does not wear ankle boots to dinner—except perhaps an American. No doubt then about who was missing. People crowded around us, asking if we'd had any recent conversation with him which could shed light on this tragic accident. Hardly! His seat was at an adjoining table; since the introductions of the first night out we had never spoken. He was traveling alone: a tall young man with pale blue eyes, a squint, steel-rimmed glasses, a solemn face. I'd seen, as he sat down the first night, that his tailcoat was a size too small for him. I certainly hadn't noticed the poor lad's inappropriate shoes. We all stood at the railing in silence and watched the little boat moving round and round the ship in ever widening circles. There was still light in the sky, but the sea was black. From the bridge the captain was shouting instructions through a megaphone at the sailors in the boat. The sailors were waving their torches and shouting at the water. Then we began to shout, too, for the sky was darkening, soon the color of the sea would swallow that of the sky, already we had to strain to tell sea from sky. But the American never reappeared on the water's surface. Another half hour, and the captain ordered the boat to return, the engine was started up again, and the ship went on.

Of course, it is possible it was an accident: that he'd longed for the peace of the deck after the tedious dinner, that at the railing, being American and young, hardly more than a boy, he had insouciantly removed his shoes to stretch his toes and feel the clammy planks under his stocking feet (Piotr might have done that; *I* might have done that when no one was watching!) and then glimpsing something large, silvery, a whale he thought with excitement, leaned over, and when the sea heaved and the ship rocked—

But it wasn't like that, was it? Still, maybe he didn't *plan* to do it. Perhaps he just went outside for a turn under the night sky, quite tranquil, with nothing much on his mind except the usual, bearable forebodings and regrets. And then, like me, he was mesmerized by the lure of the sea. Suddenly it seemed so easy to fall. But what could have made him want to give up the security of feet planted on the deck and chest pressed against the guardrail and cheeks and brow receiving the moist caressing breeze for a flailing, heart-stopping plunge toward the blow of icy water; to surrender the air of a deep openmouthed inhaling for a wall of water pushing into his face, flooding his throat, swaddling his hips and legs, dragging him away from the ship? What failure of imagination made him cast himself overboard? Or what callow despair? But we are always being borne inexorably toward something. Who, what, was waiting for him when the ship docked in New York? A family business he didn't want to enter? A fiancée he no longer wished to marry? A mother to whose doting attentions he would again be enslaved? How I wish I could have explained to him that he didn't have to be what he thought himself sentenced to be. For isn't that why one thinks of ending one's life?

Quite a few of us remained on deck for a while, still hoping to spy something in the water—as if returning below meant acquiescing in his death. At breakfast next morning people talked of little else. It was agreed that he dressed badly, it was observed that he had been acting oddly, it was concluded that he must have been out of his mind. Bogdan seemed much affected. Piotr, who had been listening somberly, asked me in a whisper, "Why did he take off his shoes?" When I didn't answer—suicide is not something one wants a child to be able to picture clearly—he declared that the American took off his shoes because he was going for a swim. And if he wanted to swim in the ocean he must have been a very good swimmer, so it was possible, wasn't it, that he was still swimming. Then another ship could pick him up. I told him it was possible. That afternoon the captain held a memorial service in the Saloon. I was asked to recite something and, thinking it should be a German poem since we were on a German ship, plunged somewhat distractedly into

Vorüber die stöhnende Klage
Elysiums Freudengelage
Ersäufen jedwedes Ach—

Elysiums Leben
Ewige Wonne, ewiges Schweben,
Durch lachende Fluren ein flötender Bach

and so on, you remember, Schiller's "Elysium." But at *Hier mangelt der Name dem trauernden Leide,* Here grieving sorrow has no name, I could no longer hold back my tears. On my request the country girl I've taken with us to help with household chores sang a hymn to the Madonna; she, Aniela, sings beautifully. How it saddens me to remember him, this young man I never knew—

I shall stop now.

10 August

I can continue. Have I alarmed you, dear friend? Don't worry for me. I am quite solid. You know I have these wild fantasies. It is my nature to imagine, vividly imagine, what others feel.

What else shall I tell you about our voyage on the *Donau?* That I ate heartily, that I took deep breaths of sea air, that I waited for the voyage to end. Unlike more than one member of our party, I harbor no romance about travel. To combat idle or morbid thoughts, I worked through another manual of English grammar and I read. Losing oneself in a book is a great consolation. Bogdan had his books on farming, but he was enjoying the journey too much to feel like immersing himself in preparations for the tasks awaiting us when it came to an end. Indeed, he said to me one evening that he almost wished we would never arrive, that the ship would sail on forever. Piotr, who seemed equally enchanted, scarcely opened his precious illustrated volume of Fenimore Cooper, familiar tales of noble Indians retreating before the onslaught of civilization having yielded to the exotic reality of the steamship advancing across the ocean under the stars. He put questions to everyone about the workings of the ship's engine and the names of the constellations. The chief engineer, whose pet he became, took the boy down into the stokehold. Bogdan, adorably paternal, spent hours with Piotr poring over an atlas of astronomy borrowed from the captain's private library. And I had the volume you gave me as a farewell present, *The Expression of the Emotions in Man and Animals*, and was pleased to find my English up to the challenge of reading it. Of course, as you had to know, Mr. Darwin's account of how similarly to us animals express fear, hate, joy, shame, pride, and the rest was bound to interest me. And I see why *he* would be drawn to this subject, for if we are so like animals, that is further evidence for his notion that we descend from them. Well, maybe we do! Had I read the book on land, I would have been made queasy by this thought, but reading it at sea, where human beings seem insignificant, seem nothing, made me receptive to Mr. Darwin's blasphemies. Henryk, I did not resist your book!

Yes, I accept that animals do resemble human beings, resemble us to a fault. They are like old-fashioned actors, with all too predictable ways of expressing what they feel. Mr. Darwin's book is, in fact, a manual of overacting. Woe to the actors who consulted this book; they would find all their bad habits confirmed. A good actor will be chary of the obvious facial sign, the large gesture—natural as these may be. What is most moving to an audience is a certain holding back, a kind of dignity in distress. This has nothing in common, I hasten to add, with the notorious reluctance of the English to show their feelings at all. For even Mr. Darwin, bent on proving that the language of emotions is universal, must admit that his compatriots shrug their shoulders far less frequently and energetically than the French or the Italians and that the men rarely cry, whereas in Poland, indeed in most parts of the Continent, men shed tears quite readily and freely.

And, I think, there *is* one irreducible difference between human beings and animals. Mr. Darwin's idea that each emotion has a natural way of being expressed assumes that each emotion is distinct. That may be true for my cousin the monkey and *mon semblable* the dog. But aren't we humans apt to feel—moments of emergency excepted—at least two emotions at once? You, dear friend, are you not feeling contradictory emotions about my departure? Are you biting your lip, raising your eyebrows, contracting the grief muscles around your eyes? No, probably there's nothing to be observed on your face. Am I saying then that you are a good actor, Henryk? Perhaps I am. Nothing to be observed in your body, other than a slower gait—except when you drink. And, forgive me for hectoring you, but are you drinking as much as you usually do? More?

Ah, but you will say, what I feel about dear Maryna and her abandonment of me is not an emotion. It is a passion! Exactly. Exactly, dear friend. And Mr. Darwin is describing not passions but only reactions. By emotions all this Englishman seems to mean is what we feel when we are caught unawares, surprised. Someone I don't at first recognize but do have reason to fear is lurking in a crowded place where I expect to meet no one, like, yes, a hotel lobby in a foreign city. Or someone I know to be furious with me—I never told you about this incident—bursts into some place where I feel utterly safe when I am alone, like my dressing room. I am startled and, of course, frightened. My lips part, my pupils dilate, my eyebrows rise, my heart beats violently, my face pales, the hairs on my skin stand erect and the superficial muscles shiver, my mouth goes dry and my voice turns husky or indistinct—all this reacting quite out of my control. When the stimulus is withdrawn, I return to calm. But what about those long-held painful feelings that seem to have been mastered, and then, without any warning, flood the soul? Where is unrequited amorous longing? What about jealousy? What about regret?—oh, yes, regret! And anxiety, anxiety about everything and nothing? Mr. Darwin's repertoire seems very British!

Speaking of the British mentality, I must tell you about the other book in English I brought to read on the ship—a novel, not at all recent, called *Villette*. It is the portrait of a young woman of high principle and small expectations. You know how I always sympathize with such a character. I like heroic women and I wait for a dramatist who will depict the heroism of women in modern life, women who are not beautiful, who are not wellborn, but who struggle to be independent. I was even imagining how one might adapt the novel for the stage; it would be a challenging role—a relief from actresses and queens!—which I might like to have played. That was not why I was given the book, a parting gift from a colleague at the Imperial who had spent her childhood in England. She thought I would be interested in a scene where the heroine sees Rachel performing in London. I was making my way tenaciously through the book (Miss Brontë has a bigger vocabulary than Mr. Darwin!), quite entranced by the character of Lucy Snowe, a plain, self-aware girl full of hidden passion, until I finally reached the chapter where she is taken to the theatre. Imagine my dismay when I discovered that the heroine, with whom I had been feeling such sympathy, does not like Rachel at all. Although she is beguiled, enthralled, by Rachel's power—who was not?—she is also repelled by the passionate woman she sees on the stage. She actually disapproves of her! She judges the expressiveness of the stage empress to be excessive, unwomanly, rebellious—satanic!

Don't you find it odd that watching a great actress could have aroused such animosity, such fear? In Poland, as in France, an actress might be taxed with being too free with her sexual favors, but not with being too fervent. Perhaps the theatre means something in Poland that it cannot mean elsewhere, even in the land of the divine Shakespeare. Why could Lucy Snowe not simply have enjoyed herself? Why did she not wish to be transported? Why did she feel threatened by the passion of Rachel? And yet the novel Miss Brontë has written is very passionate. Perhaps the author was quarreling with herself. She feared that her own passions would overturn her life. She did not wish to change, or be changed.

But you see, I am imagining my own task—and the resistance to it, from outside and from within—everywhere I turn. It is harder for a woman to want a life different from the one decreed for her. You men have it much easier. You are commended for recklessness, for boldness, for striking out, for being adventurous. A woman has so many inner voices telling her to behave prudently, amiably, timorously. And there is much to be afraid of, I know that. Don't assume, dear friend, that I have lost all sense of reality. Each time I am brave, I am acting. But that is all that's needed to be brave, don't you agree? The appearance of bravery. The performance of it. Since I know I am not brave, not brave at all, this spurs me on to act as if I were.

No one in our country would charge an actress who flaunts her feelings on the stage with being a demon, yes, a demon, and with glorifying the figure of a rebel—this is a moralism with which I am unfamiliar. In Poland we cherish the idea of rebellion, of the insurgent spirit, do we not? I cherish the rebelliousness in myself, being all too aware of how much I am drawn to yielding, to following slavishly the expectations of others. How I fight that large part of me that is a conquered spirit, eager to obey—larger, surely, because I am a woman, reared to be servile. This is part of what drew me to the stage. My roles schooled me in confidence and in defiance. Acting was a program for overcoming the slave in myself.

Imagine then what it means for me to give up the stage, where I have permission to act imperiously. Don't think it is not a sacrifice. I have been married to the stage for nearly twenty years. Perhaps one day in California—even now, already in America, it thrills me to write CALIFORNIA—by the brook behind our little hut, for the amusement of our colony and some Indian maidens, I shall perform a scene from one of my favorite plays. Yes, I confess, I have taken some of my costumes—Juliet, Rosalind, Portia, Adrienne—with me. No doubt it will feel quite ridiculous to put one of them on after a day of vigorous toil in our fields under the blue skies or in the hills on horseback with a gun over my shoulder. How artificial will all this appear to me then! Still, if ever I am tempted to return to the theatre, may I remember what I have learned about the Anglo-Saxon suspicion of great actresses. Thank goodness I have not come to America to go on the stage!

12 August

But she has not told me anything about America, you must be thinking. Well, I can tell you something about New York, which everyone insists to us is now so overrun by immigrants as to be but an extension of Europe—not America at all! As you saw at the beginning of this already too long letter, we are not staying on the island of Manhattan. Since Bogdan thought accommodations there for all of us in a decent hotel a waste of our capital, we sought the advice of the captain, who recommended an inn, comfortable and not expensive, close by where the Norddeutsche Lloyd line has its piers on the other side of the Hudson River. Here, in this waterfront town whose charming Indian name means tobacco pipe, and in full sight of Manhattan, we are actually in another of the thirty-eight states!

Each morning the more intrepid among us board the ferry and spend the day exploring the city—I say the more intrepid, for those who cross the river are now a smaller group. Manhattan has proved intimidating to most of our gentle companions; and they think only of moving on, and of our waiting pastorale. Wanda is altogether lost without Julian. Aleksander, though indefatigable, is handicapped by his lack of English. Danuta and Cyprian must attend to the needs of their two little girls. Only Jakub, who goes about everywhere with his sketchbook, has made himself almost at home here. I fear he will be quite sorry to leave so soon, but I have promised him that California will prove just as rich a subject for the artist. I shall be a little sorry, too. An actor is generally an eager spectator, and no spectacle could be more enthralling than what we see enacted, in every known language, on this rude stage. Every race and nation and tribe in the world is represented, at least among the poorer classes—and most people appear to be very poor once one ventures beyond the grand streets. I'm not surprised to find the city so ugly. But I had not expected to see so many paupers and vagrants. We are told that the poor are more numerous than a few years ago, not only because there are more and more immigrants, most of whom arrive with nothing, but because—Bogdan had received some dire warnings from his brother about this—the economy has yet to recover from the great crisis ("panic" it's called here) of three years ago. Employments, especially menial ones, are scarce and wages continue to fall. But obviously this doesn't deter anyone from coming here, expecting better days!

Last night Bogdan and I claimed an evening for ourselves, and dined at Delmonico's, a restaurant reputed to be the best in the city. I can report that the nabobs here are as richly fed and sedate in their movements as those in Vienna and Paris. Outside, all is restlessness and noise. Wagons, carriages, omnibuses, horsecars, streetcars, jostling pedestrians make each corner crossing an adventure; every building is covered with signs and there are men hired to be walking kiosks, festooned front and back, even on their heads, with advertisements, while others shove leaflets into the hands of every passerby or toss them by the fistful into the streetcars; bootblacks plead for clients from their little stands, peddlers shout from their carts, and bands of musicians, mostly German, blare their horns and tubas at you. I was surprised to see so many Germans, more numerous even than the Irish and Italians, with each nation having its own quarter. Henryk, there is so much misery and poverty here. And crime: we are constantly being warned not to venture where the poor live, for the danger of being attacked and robbed by bands of roughs is very great. Jakub is the most daring among us in exploring these teeming parts of the city; he has already filled five albums with sketches. Yesterday he spent the afternoon in the neighborhood of Jews, poor Jews of course, who look much as they do in Kraków, the dark-bearded men in skullcaps still wearing their long black coats in this atrocious heat.

Which brings me to my only complaint. I have never known

such heat. All of us are suffering. Piotr has a rash. Danuta's younger girl cries all the time. Feeling hot means that I feel over-dressed—I suppose I *am* overdressed—though less than the women here, who still wear hoops and, as Danuta, Wanda, Barbara, and I have noticed, stare enviously (so I imagine) at our slim skirts. Of course, we walk a great deal after we disembark from the ferry. Yesterday, while we were strolling on Broadway, the principal street here, a large woman girded by an enormous hoop under her heavy black skirt crumpled to the sidewalk before our eyes. I thought she was seriously ill but, no, a fellow stroller said this happens often in August, and a cabman unfastened his horse's pail of water and unceremoniously sprinkled some on her face, whereupon she was helped to her feet and without any em-barrassment went on her way. I know it is imprudent to remain so much in the sun, but we have no hotel to retreat to. If Piotr had his way, we would be taking refuge once an hour in an ice-cream parlor. Ice cream here, made by Italians, is delicious. He's also fond of an Indian delicacy sold on the street, dry airy lumps made by exploding kernels of white corn, and the small brown pea-nuts sheathed in a pale soft pod, but these I find quite indi-gestible. People here drink even more water than wine with their meals, and in winter as well as summer the water is drunk very cold: the glass is filled with small cube-shaped pieces of ice—I'm sure you will think this quite unhealthy. Today, in vain search of coolness some of us visited the vast park just completed north of the city; it is called the Central Park, though there is nothing cen-tral about it. Nor much that is parklike either, if truth be told—do not imagine anything like a newer park in Kraków, much less our stately, leafy Planty—for most of the trees are too young yet to give any shade.

The Polish community is small, many more of our compa-triots having settled in the west, in Chicago. Bogdan has visited some of the leaders, who told him of their desire to organize a re-ception in my honor. I feel that I must decline, much as I regret disappointing them. They want to welcome the person I have ceased to be. But the actress who was cannot stifle her curiosity about the theatre, and August, besides being the hottest month, is also the beginning of the season. Indeed, as Heinrich rudely warned me, theatre here does seem to mean something other than what it means *chez nous* and in Vienna and Paris. The public expects to be entertained, not elevated, and is most entertained by the grandiose and the bizarre. We had thought of seeing Offenbach's *La Grande-Duchesse*, playing on one of the largest stages here, until we learned that it was being performed by the Mexican Juvenile Opera Company and that the prima donna, Señorita Niña Carmen y Morón, was eight years old. Can you imagine hearing the Duchess's *"Dites-lui qu'on l'a remarqué"*—is there a more ravishing love song?—in the shrill squeaking voice of a small girl! Something for Piotr perhaps, though I suppose he would have enjoyed even more the program at another theatre, which included George France and his dogs, Don Caesar and Bruno, the Hansell Troupe of Alpine Warblers, Jenny Turnour the Trapeze Queen, and a Herr Cline, who dances a *pas de deux* on the high wire with his grandmother. No Shakespeare in any of the theatres, alas, even though I have been assured that no dramatic author is performed as often in America as Shakespeare. Apart from farces and melodramas that seem not worth risking, even out of curiosity, there is only a light comedy, English of course, called *Our American Cousin*, which has enjoyed an unstoppable popularity throughout the country for the last eleven years because it was while watching this play from a box with his wife and members of his government that President Lincoln was murdered—by a deranged actor, as you'll recall. Proper plays are almost all English or French but, while Wagner is adored by the New York public, there is no interest in the great German dramatists. Should you want to see some Schiller, you must go to one of the German-language theatres, where you will see him performed by a second-rate touring company from Munich or Berlin. And, since it's unthinkable to present a play by Krasiński or Słowacki or Fredro in English and there are not enough Poles in

New York to support a Polish-language theatre, our own sublime dramatists remain quite unknown here.

I would dearly have liked to see one of the eminent American actors whose reputations have reached Europe, but none are on view now. We did go to the magnificent theatre owned by one of these actors, Edwin Booth (it was his younger brother who assassinated Mr. Lincoln), which has opened with a tragic drama by Lord Byron, *Sardanapalus*. It seems petty to note that the acting left little to the imagination—your Mr. Darwin would have approved!—given that the play has been turned into a vast and ingenious spectacle. Loud music, towering décor, a hundred performers milling about an immense stage—that's what the public here most appreciates. Besides a dozen actors in the principal roles, the "Italian ballet" in Act Two had—I am looking now at the program—"four first-class dancers, eight coryphées, six ballet ladies, ninety-nine supers, twenty-four negro boys, twelve chorus women, eight chorus men, and forty-eight extra ladies"! Imagine all these cavorting about while the stage machinery produces the most astonishing effects: an entire scene may rise from the floor or drop out of sight. The last act ended with a stupendous conflagration, which the audience appreciated mightily, as did we.

Here biggest is best—a prejudice perhaps no more unsound than thinking oldest is best. Booth's Theatre, which seats almost two thousand people with standing room for hundreds more, is far from the largest. Larger still is Steinway Hall, where, we were solemnly informed, Anton Rubinstein made his American debut. Seeking to impress Bogdan, I refrained from mentioning, ever so casually, that the great pianist was a frequent guest at our Tuesday evenings in Warsaw. It occurs to me that, for all their boasts about having the biggest and the most of everything, Americans, when it comes to art, are surprisingly devoid of patriotic self-confidence. It is false to say that the public craves only plebeian entertainments. But it is assumed that performances of quality come from abroad. Foreign actors make quite a splash here and, if

French or Italian, are expected to perform in their own language, which no one understands. Rachel triumphed with *Adrienne Lecouvreur* at the biggest theatre in the city, the Metropolitan, some twenty years ago; and ten years ago Ristori made a very successful, lucrative tour throughout the country. Thinking about this now, I confess to feeling a twinge of envy. But, no, don't conclude that I dream of resuming my career here. In what language? No one would want to hear our native tongue, and the other in which I have been trained to act, German, is also considered fit only for the immigrant public.

I shall not grumble about a play called *The Mighty Dollar* that we saw at Wallack's Theatre, ending our sampling of what is on at the theatres. At Gilmore's Garden we heard Madame Pappenheim, Emilie Pappenheim, a soprano, in concert; Bogdan and I found her less interesting than her audience, which was most enthusiastic, applauding at every trill. At a French art gallery, Michel Knoedler's, we saw a room of dull paintings, and at the New-York Historical Society (there is no museum here worth speaking of) we came upon marble bas-relief sculptures taken from the palace of Sardanapalus—a nice surprise after having seen their fanciful rendering in papier-mâché during our Byronic evening. We take Piotr with us everywhere, and viewing the city through his eyes keeps me from being too fastidious: the child is enchanted by everything. This can't be said of the other child in my custody—I mean Aniela, our new servant—to whom everything is merely incomprehensible. She was told she was going to America, but Warsaw must have been an America to her (she had never been out of her natal village), after which she found herself on a train (she had never seen a train), in a hotel in a foreign city, in a hotel on water, as she called our steamship, and now here. When we walk I hear the constant refrain, "Oh, Madame! Oh, Madame!" Imagine me with my little boy on one side and this pudgy horse-faced girl on the other, both of them clasping my hands in apprehension and astonishment. You had a glimpse of her at the station and, knowing my appreciation of beauty in all forms, may wonder that I engaged her. I also surprised every-one at the orphanage in Szymanów by choosing her among the six girls reared there who had been selected for me to interview. One of the nuns took me aside to warn me I was making a mistake, that Aniela's proficiency in sewing and cooking was far inferior to that of the others. Why then did I take her? Well—you'll smile—it was because of her voice. When I asked her if she knew how to sing, she stared at me, mouth agape, then without first closing her mouth (but closing her eyes tightly) sang two Latin hymns and "God Save Poland," one after another. I know it sounds comical, but her singing moved me to tears. I could tell she had a sweet disposition, the girl is only sixteen, and Danuta and Wanda will teach her to cook and sew. To tell the truth, I need a few lessons myself! Any female can learn to keep house, but who would think of teaching this child how to sing?

I can see, though, that I shall have to teach her everything else. First of all, not to be afraid of the world. Second, not to be afraid of me. I had asked her before we left Warsaw if she had everything she needed for her new life, which I tried, with little success, to describe to her. As if this were a test she must not fail, she cried, "Oh yes, Madame. Everything!" I discovered after we started the journey that she had only one dress, a scarf, a torn smock, and a quilted fustian jacket to her name. The proprietor of the inn in Hoboken has advised us to buy clothing here before setting out for California, since everything in the big stores is marked down because of the "panic" I mentioned earlier. So you may imagine your Desdemona yesterday going from store to store, engaged in earnest conversation with clerks over a coat, a skirt, a shirtwaist, and some very practical undergarments. The store of stores here, A. T. Stewart, a cast-iron palace occupying a whole city block, is said to be the largest in the world; but I prefer a smaller emporium, Macy's, which has just opened a boy's clothing department whose sensible array of goods bitterly disappointed Piotr. He was expecting that I could purchase for him there an Apache feather headdress and loincloth, and for the rest of the day remained quite inconsolable!

Piotr has forgiven me for disappointing him: yesterday we visited the Centennial Exposition.

The trip was itself a spectacle, inside the train as well as looking out the windows, since it appears that the cars on American trains, even in so-called first class, are not divided into compartments. For some two and a half hours we had an intimate view of a fixed number of perspiring strangers, and they of us, perspiring just as profusely while trying to keep some shred of useless Old World dignity. Most passengers were *en famille* and carrying hampers of food and drink, the genial offering of which, whether accepted or not, gave them the right to be friendly— which, in America, means asking questions. What country we came from, if we were going to the Centennial, and what we wanted to see. "It's too big to see everything," we were told again and again. There were only seven of us, for Barbara and Aleksander, once they learned that Philadelphia lay to the south and was likely to be even hotter, remained in Hoboken; nothing could persuade them to share this keenly anticipated excursion with us. Danuta and Cyprian were able to come because they could leave their little girls with Aniela, but Danuta has sought reassurance that they will not suffer so much when we reach California. Suffer! Even as I remind them that California is famed for its ideal, temperate climate, I worry that they haven't understood how arduous in other ways our life there, at least for the first months, may be.

Philadelphia, what we saw of it between the station and the Exposition grounds outside the city, is older, handsomer, and cleaner than Manhattan. I missed the hubbub of Manhattan! But enough people for the most avid connoisseur of crowds were awaiting us at the Exposition, which has already received several million visitors since it opened in May.

There was no way we could see everything of interest in one day. Imagine, Henryk, the largest edifice in the world, the Exposition's Main Building, a colossal structure of wood, iron, and glass five times longer and ten times wider than the *Donau*! Imagine—but you have undoubtedly read about it in our papers or the German papers. Indeed, you should have been able to read an account by Ryszard; I know he promised the *Gazeta Polska* at least one article about the Centennial. But, as we learned from the letter waiting for us at the hotel in Bremen, our carefree young journalist never went to Philadelphia. He wrote that he was too impatient to leave, and would make some articles out of the transcontinental journey instead, such as Chicago rising from the ashes after their Great Fire of five years ago. And once he reached the Western Territories, he would finally see live Indians, if only in mournful procession, fleeing the invincible government troops who protect the pioneers. This made me smile. For Chicago, where Ryszard would have spent only a few hours, must be already completely rebuilt; Henryk, in America five years is a very long time! And the most recent battle with the Indians, early this summer, resulted in ignominious defeat for the cavalry and the death of their leader, General Custer. Since Ryszard has such a great imagination—perhaps even more necessary for a journalist than for an actor—I won't be surprised if you tell me he did send back an article on the Centennial Exposition!

Since you must already know something about the marvels to be seen there, I shall mention only what is amusing and oddly scaled. (You see, I am already becoming an American!) Imagine a cathedral six meters high made of spun cane sugar surrounded by candy historical figures, a solid-chocolate vase weighing a hundred kilos, and a half-size replica of the tomb of George Washington, who at regular intervals—this particularly enchanted Piotr—rises from the dead and is saluted by the toy soldiers standing guard. My favorite was the Georama: huge, uncannily detailed dioramas of Paris and of Jerusalem—that and a Japanese house, which unfortunately had no furniture.

We'd no time for visits to the Bible Pavilion, the New England Log House, the Turkish Coffee Building, the Burial Casket Building (no, Henryk, I am not making this up!), among the smaller edifices, but we did walk quickly through the Photograph Gallery and the Women's Pavilion, where we missed the daily breaking of a chair by a lady weighing two hundred and ninety kilograms, but did gaze in wonderment at the huge statue of a sleeping Iolanthe carved in butter by a woman from Arkansas. Butter? In this heat? Yes, and it is fresh butter, for she sculpts it anew every day! Then at least two hours had to be set aside for the Indian exhibits in the Government Building. Besides examples of their pottery, weapons, and tools, there were wigwams and wax figures of celebrated Indian braves, life-size and in full regalia, bringing Piotr his long-awaited sight of peace pipes and tomahawks. Poor child, he kept asking me for assurance that these were real, meaning that they were not costumes and props for actors. I was struck by the modeling of the faces. The small cruel black eyes, coarse unkempt locks, and large animal mouths were clearly designed to inspire hatred for the Indian as a hideous demon. Here you would not find a trace of that reverence for the Indian race we imbibed in the adventure books of our childhood.

You have heard about the astounding new inventions: a porcupine-like machine for stamping inked letters on blank paper, another that can make many copies of a single page produced by the writing machine, and a small box that sends the human voice over an electric wire. About this instrument for hearing at great distances, the telephone, we were told that its inventor hopes to improve the audibility of what is transmitted: while the occasional sentence comes through with startling distinctness, for the most part only vowels are faithfully reproduced and consonants are unrecognizable. But surely it will be perfected. And what a boon to humanity that will be, when, by means of this device, anyone can have an Italian opera, a play of Shakespeare, a debate in the Congress, a sermon by their favorite preacher laid on like gas in one's own house. The possibilities for public instruction are unlimited. Think of those who cannot afford theatre tickets being able to hear the performance over their telephone. Still, I worry about the consequences of this invention, human laziness being what it is, for nothing can replace the experience of entering a temple of dramatic art, taking one's seat among the other spectators, and *seeing* a great actor perform. Once there is a telephone in every home, will anyone still go to the theatre?

Of the many monuments on the Exposition grounds you would have been especially amused by the Centennial Fountain, which was erected by the Catholic Total Abstinence Union of America. (Consider the prospects of such a league in Poland!) In the middle of a vast basin an immense statue of Moses rises from its rough granite pedestal, and circling the basin are tall marble statues of prominent American Catholics, whose names and deeds are of course unknown to me, with a drinking fountain at the base of each statue. Slake your thirst at this pure source and you will never crave alcohol again? How could I not help thinking of you, dear friend? An attendant told us that, unfortunately, it had proved impossible to complete the fountain before the Exposition opened. It would never have occurred to me that something was lacking. Even more fountains to encourage sobriety?

So ready was I to embrace the American love of eccentric achievement that I failed to identify another monument as obviously unfinished—rather, part of something unfinished. The French government has sent over to the Exposition a gigantic forearm whose invincible hand clasps a torch; it is hollow, and stairs inside lead to a balcony below the torch. I was prepared to envisage this sculpture, made of copper and iron, planted on a pedestal in the center of the city of Philadelphia, and was almost disappointed to learn that there will be a whole figure attached to the heroic arm, Liberty herself, a modern Colossus being fabricated in Paris which one day will be placed (like the one in ancient Rhodes) in the harbor of New York to welcome arriving immigrants. How, I ask myself, does one ever know what is finished in this country, and what is merely under way?

17 August

It is late afternoon and I am continuing this letter in the shade of an elm tree behind our inn in Hoboken, after an exhilarating day in the city. We went directly from the ferry to the main post office and found, as we had hoped, more letters from Julian and Ryszard. After two weeks in the southern part of the state, they have found a parcel of land, complete with house and barns, near a small vineyard colony. Ryszard proposes to stay on for a month in the neighborhood of our new home; he wishes to isolate himself to write some stories and also to enjoy the outdoor life in the company of Indians and Mexicans; he will go north again just before our arrival. Julian prefers to wait for us in San Francisco, where there is a lively Polish community. Bogdan and I spent the rest of the morning making our travel arrangements. Tomorrow he will take Piotr back to Philadelphia; the child has been clamoring for another visit to the Exposition. The day after, we leave on the *Colón*, bound for Panama. There we will cross the isthmus by train and board another ship, which will take us to San Francisco, where I don't expect to tarry (unless, as seems possible, Edwin Booth is performing there) but, with all our group reunited, immediately take the train south.

Since these ships are not modern iron steamships but paddle steamers, the trip will take more than a month. Why not take the transcontinental train and arrive in one week, you will ask. Well, I am deferring to the wishes of my dear husband and son. Piotr begged me not to deprive him of the chance to live on a wooden boat, Bogdan has fallen in love with sea travel, as I told you, and I—I rather liked the idea of savoring the contours of the continent. Don't let what I have told you of my romance with water make you apprehensive, dear friend. Your Rusałka—did I ever tell you Rusałka was my favorite story as a very young child?—is looking forward to having a very long life on land.

Aspinwall, Panama
9 September

In haste. The start of our trip was a fiasco. The *Colón* was very small—we would have been more comfortable sleeping in tents on the deck than in its fetid tiny cabins below—and maintained with shameless negligence. After two days at sea, the main steampipe exploded: it took us twice as long to crawl back to the Hoboken docks! You can imagine the dismay of our party, and the reproaches of Danuta and Cyprian, who long to arrive as quickly as possible. It seems that some of the others also wanted to take the train, but no one had the courage to oppose me. I should feel a little guilty. Perhaps I do. No, I think not. You know how I hate to change my mind, to give up something once I have decided to do it. We were pledged to going by sea.

Each day I commit to memory at least twenty new English words. Seaworthy—isn't that a lovely word?

After a brief wait in Hoboken we departed again on another paddle steamer, larger and better fitted, the *Crescent City*. The trip passed without incident. At sunset the passengers would gather on the deck for the unison singing of folk songs such as "Darling, I Am Growing Old" and "In the Sweet Bye and Bye"; it was soothing to the nerves to join them. Until the last days, when the ship veered eastward to pass between Cuba and Haiti, we were never out of sight of one of the American states.

This morning we disembarked at the port on the Caribbean side of the isthmus, which is on a little sand-covered island about a kilometer long and connected to the mainland by the railway embankment. I expected a town. It is a village with only one street, or rather one long row of houses mostly occupied by stores whose thuggish-looking proprietors all wear flat straw hats and white pajama suits—and is unspeakably ugly. As for the heat, forget my earlier complaints; this is beyond anything we endured before. *N'en parlons plus!*—one must simply surrender oneself to it. For a while it was raining and we were obliged to take shelter in a sinister grogshop, where we learned from an inebriated old Negress that the rainy season here, which begins in April, lasts nine months! The rain has stopped for now, and we have come outside to dispose ourselves on wet chairs in what passes for a café. Everything is wet. The air is wet. The beetles—there are beetles everywhere—are wet. It is so humid that I could wring out my blouse and deepen the puddles at my feet. Plump dusky women, beautiful in purple and red garments, promenade up and down before our shy gaze. And vultures too, strolling and flopping about with impunity: because they eat the dead rats and the refuse everyone throws into the street, it is forbidden to shoot them. I don't know where the other passengers have put themselves. Bogdan and Cyprian have gone to fetch water and tropical fruits for our two-hour train ride through swamp and jungle to the other side of the isthmus.

So, imagine me sipping a glass of tea laced with rum at my rusty table, looking with impatience and amusement at my charges. Wanda sitting across from me, sighing loudly. Barbara and Aleksander, their heads down on their table, too weary even to complain. Danuta off somewhere with the little girls, who have diarrhea. Jakub and Piotr at another table, both drawing. Jakub says this is a painter's paradise—now he will wish to linger in Panama! Piotr's drawing is a map: he has just announced that when he grows up he will dig a shipping canal across the isthmus. He seems already grown up to me, Henryk. You would be astonished to see how changed he is by this trip, less babyish, indeed quite the little man. Now it is he who takes Aniela by the hand and tries to comfort her. The poor girl is terrified. Our friends are more stoical, but I know they are shocked by how exotic everything is. Barbara has just inquired in a tremulous voice if there are many Africans in California! I shall transcribe for you what is being said right now.

Piotr (jumping up): "No, Indians!"

Barbara: "But aren't they black?"

Piotr: "No, red!"

Barbara: "Red?"

Aleksander: "Don't be silly, Barbara."

Wanda: "I'm covered with mosquito bites!"

Jakub: "And don't forget the yellow people."

Barbara: "Yellow people!!"

Jakub: "Yes, Chinese. And the men have a long black braid down their backs."

Aniela (wailing): "Oh, Madame, are we going to China? You didn't tell me we were going to China!"

Now I shall have everything to do to calm her.

Later

Bought a parasol and a pair of sandals. Blister. See Bogdan and Cyprian far away, arms laden, coming toward us. Starting to rain again. Danuta's girls are crying. A hideous giant brown cockroach ambling across the table; Wanda shrieking. Owner of the café laughing at Wanda. *Cucaracha!* he shouts, hurling himself at the table, brandishing a towel. My first word of Spanish. Henryk, it's just flown away. Flying cockroaches, Henryk.

Train about to leave.

11 September
aboard the *Constitution*

Henryk, I have written you a letter of truly American proportions.

And now I can't think of anything to say. The coast of Mexico is— No, you don't want guidebook descriptions from me.

But is it I, your Maryna, who is writing to you? I boasted to you of my desire to change, but I was not prepared for the change the trip itself has already wrought on me. I swim in vacancy. The rigors and distractions of traveling are my only theme. I see why neurasthenics are advised to travel. I scarcely think about myself at all anymore. There are only practical questions. My inner life is quite evaporated. Poland, the stage, seem very far away.

The next time I write will be from California. Henryk, can you imagine that?

Your

M.

Five

CALIFORNIA. Santa Ana, the river; *Heim*, home. Anaheim. Germans. Poor German immigrants from San Francisco who came south twenty years ago to colonize, to farm, to prosper. Stolid, frugal German neighbors. Surprised to see we are so many, and not all related to one another, to share one small house on the outskirts of their town. They ask how many guns we have. They ask if we are a religious sect. They ask if our men can help with the digging of a new irrigation ditch. They ask if Piotr will be attending the school, or will we be keeping him at home to help with the farmwork. Of course he'll go to school! The house, of banal sycamore boards instead of adobe bricks, *is* too small—what could Julian and Ryszard have been thinking!—with every floor except the kitchen completely carpeted, apparently an American custom. Yes, we are here to make this new life together, yes. But with all this adjacent emptiness—America is nothing if not spacious—it's absurd that we should be so crowded . . .

They have a rousing view of the Santa Ana range to the east and the San Bernardino Mountains farther north and east. To the back and sides of the house are tamaracks, pepperwood, fig trees, and a live oak. Beyond is a field of tall grass where shocks of hay and maize are drying in the sun, and a vineyard that stretches on and on—everything that looks away from the house is splendid. Closer views are more deflating. The fenced-in front yard with its cypresses, shaggy grass, and scatter of roses looked, Maryna said, like a poorly kept small graveyard.

"A graveyard, Mama? A real graveyard?"

"Oh, Piotr," she said, laughing, "you mustn't listen to everything I say."

But they were listening, all of them, they were waiting for her to cue them, remind them, overwhelm them, steady them with her unwavering intentness. It was her certainty, compounded by her powers of self-absorption, and her impatience with their occasional lapses into faintheartedness, her barely concealed exasperation with their frailties, her never being wholly satisfied with their best efforts, above all her silences, admirable intimidating silences, her standing aside from the common chatter, not responding to a trivial observation or conventional social nicety or an unnecessary question (for that's all it was), probably not even hearing what had been said, that made them want to please her, made them feel they would not want to be anywhere else on earth than here with her, acting out her vision.

But how to create the utopian household on so cramped, so ungenerous a stage? First, by making do and putting up with—skills Maryna had mastered during the early years of touring in Heinrich's troupe throughout small-town Poland (those barebones theatres, those tumble-down lodgings); and the present discomforts would soon be allayed. Yes, Maryna assured everyone the morning after their arrival, there would be a second, adobe house: she and Bogdan would ask around in the village for Mexican laborers to help them build it. In the meantime . . . Danuta and Cyprian and their girls must have the large bedroom, she and Bogdan the second bedroom, Wanda and Julian the smallest of the three bedrooms. Piotr would sleep on the parlor sofa; Aniela on a camp bed in a nook in the kitchen. Barbara and Aleksander gamely accepted assignment to a storage shack not far from the corral; lumber, ladders, barrels of nails, paint buckets, lathes, hammers, and saws into the barn. Maryna wished she could sleep in the barn, just for the first days, alone. The space she coveted, quite separate from animals and farm equipment and hayloft, was cozily furnished with rugs, saddles, mattings, harnesses, and coyote skulls . . . but, no, she could not do this to Bogdan. Our two bachelors, Ryszard and Jakub, in the barn.

Leaving the unpacking and the care of the three children to Aniela, the newcomers had been shown about the land by the family renting it to them and toward the end of the first day felt they had taken possession of it with all their senses. They had welcomed into their nostrils a rich assault of barnyard and plant odors, they had tramped the amply watered earth, fingering its bounty of vines laden with Mission grapes, they had knelt at the edge of a ditch and passed their hands through the water. Just beyond the vineyard was nature in a more armored, truculent mood: a vast solemn plain dotted with cactus and scrub, steeped in silence. They gazed out at the deep-blue sky and, as the sun hovered nearer and nearer the mountain's crest, feeling the need to absorb in quiet their surfeit of new impressions, with no more forethought than precedes sinking into a chair and staring at the ceiling or taking off for a stroll in a leafy park, they drifted apart, and one by one wandered into the desert.

No landscape, not even the swampy jungle of the Isthmus of Panama, had struck any of them as this awesomely strange. And they were not being borne through it, receiving it as a view, but walking in it, on it, for it was all pale surface, the sky so lofty and the ground so level, and they had never felt as erect, as vertical, their skin brushed by the hot Santa Ana wind, their ears lulled by the oddly intrusive sound of their own footfalls. Pausing, they could hear the hiss of skinny desert-colored creatures scurrying along the pebbly surface. Slithery fanged creatures (a snake!), but down there, speeding off. Hardly anything is near anything here: those slouching braided sentinels, the yucca trees, and bouquets of drooping spears, the agaves, and the squat clusters of prickly pears, all so widely spaced, so unresembling—and nothing had to do with anything else. Each alone, each separate. The sense of jeopardy that couldn't altogether be stifled (was that a scorpion?) quickened their pace for a while, as if they thought they might soon be arriving somewhere. In the clear air the mountains looked deceptively near. And how small, when they turned around for a moment to see how far they'd gone, their little green world. They walked on, lost in the brightness of their sensations, walked and walked: the mountains came no closer. Their fears had long since subsided. The purity of the vista, its uncompromising bleakness, seemed first like a menace, then an excitement, then a numbing, then a different arousal. Their real initiation into the seductive nihilism of the desert had begun. The soundless, odorless, monochrome landscape, so drastically untenanted, had the same effect on everyone: an intoxicating impression of aloneness, which gradually gave way to a more active assent to the experience of solitude. All were visited by a yearning something like Maryna's—to be alone, really alone (what if I, what if she, what if he . . . ?)—and allowed themselves to imagine the disappearance, without drama, without guilt, of those nearest to them, somewhere out here, too. And isn't to imagine to desire? The surrender to the desiccating of feeling was swift but it palled almost as rapidly, as something, a deeper fear, made them pull away from it, purged, chastened, and then it was time to turn around and walk back to dampened land and their moist lives.

Only one among them, wandering about in the same empty-headed daze, had excluded herself from the tapering off of this delicious, subversive fantasy, for despite the warnings to everyone by Ryszard and Julian to stay clear of the cactus plants, Wanda had been unable to restrain her curiosity about what it would feel like to touch one, and chose the downy-looking pad of a beaver-tail. "It doesn't have any spines," she wailed. "How could I know it would have these horrible—" she whimpered. "But both hands, Wanda? You had to use *both* hands?" Julian fumed. He had brought her to the porch, to the tweezers and the candle. "No-

body on earth but you would think of touching a cactus with—"
Wincing and sighing, he stood behind her, holding her shoulders,
as Jakub and Danuta picked for an hour at the hundreds of tiny
hairy needles embedded in her fingers and palms. When over
Wanda's moans they heard an unmistakable shriek from somewhere nearby, everyone's first thought was of another cactus disaster. "Madame! Madame!" Maryna hurried to the rescue. But it
was just the three huge purple eggplants Aniela had stumbled
across, lolling like fat bombs dropped behind the house, and had
then tried to pick up, only to discover that each was closely fastened to the stony earth. Ryszard, hacking at the cord-like vine
with his hunting knife, freed them.

While they were jubilantly preparing the first meal of their
new life—the eggplants, roasted over a fire in the yard, supple-
mented by provisions bought in the village—the luminous severe
sky darkened into night, a blackness holding brighter stars than
they had ever seen in Zakopane. Stars set in ebony, Jakub said.
Danuta and Cyprian went indoors, Cyprian to fetch one of the
telescopes Bogdan had brought from Poland and Danuta to put
their little girls to bed; Piotr, feeling neglected as well as pleased
at not being sent to bed, too, stationed himself on the porch and
practiced answering the coyote's howl. Soon everyone was driven
indoors by big-bellied mosquitoes which could bite through
clothing and made sleeping that first night (and for weeks after)
a torment. But even without mosquitoes they could hardly have
slept well when they were so excited by their own intrepidness,
and were being pulled in and out of sleep by such vivid dreams.
Julian of Wanda's bleeding hands. Ryszard of his knife. Aniela of
a mother she had never known, who looked like the Virgin Mary
in the orphanage chapel; she often dreamed of her mother. Piotr
of dead people crawling out of their graves and besieging the
house. Bogdan that Maryna had left him for Ryszard. And
Maryna of Edwin Booth, whom she had finally seen, just a week
ago. For only hours after the *Constitution* docked in San Francisco

Bay, Maryna had learned that the great Booth was performing there, at the California Theatre, and the very next day she saw his Shylock and two days later his Mark Antony. She was not disappointed. She had wept with admiration. In her dream, he bends toward her. He cups his palm on her cheek. He is telling her something sad, about something that cannot be undone, someone who has died. She wants to touch his shoulder; his shoulder is sad, too. Then they are on horseback, riding side by side, but there is something wrong with her horse, it's too small, much too small; her feet scrape the ground. He is swathed in the Oriental draperies he wore as old Shylock, he even has on the reprobate's soft yellow cap and the pointed red shoes, though he is really Mark Antony. They dismount near a giant cholla. Then he flings his cap to the ground and, to her horror, seizes a spiny branch of the cactus with one bare hand and hoists himself up with the agility of a young man. Don't do that! she shouts. He continues climbing. Isn't he being martyred by those horrid needles? Please come down! she cries. She is weeping with fear. He is laughing. Was it still Booth? He looked a little like Stefan. But no, it cannot be her brother, who is back in Poland, no, who is dead. Holding on to the topmost branch of the cholla, he begins the great speech of reproach and incitement, declaiming to the lofty air and then to her when he comes to

> *O, now you weep, and I perceive you feel*
> *the dint of pity. These are gracious drops.*

But there was something novel, no, unfamiliar, no, familiar, in the words streaming from his mouth. She had understood him perfectly in San Francisco, she understood him now, though the speech didn't sound the way it had at the theatre. Could he be saying it in Latin? Antony was a Roman. But Shakespeare was an Englishman. Then is this how English should sound? If so, all her studying and practicing had been in vain. That was what she was fretting about as she awoke and realized, laughing to herself, that she had dreamed Edwin Booth into acting in Polish.

ONE OF THE REASONS Julian and Ryszard had chosen this site was its proximity to a community—German-speaking to boot, so there would be no language barrier—of first-generation farmers, who once knew no more than they of the grape and the cow, the plough and the irrigation ditch.

Only twenty years ago these fertile fields and thriving village were twelve hundred acres of waste, sandy land, a mere corner of a vast ranch whose Mexican proprietor, convinced that this patch couldn't support a goat, was glad to sell off. It took European immigrants, to whom the desert was not only alien but a kind of mistake, correctable by the introduction of water, to think that southern California, with more or less the same climate as Italy, had to be propitious for growing grapes.

The land rented with Bogdan's money had been worked by its owners (now relocated to a ranch in the foothills) right up to their arrival in early October, near the close of the vineyard cycle: most of the grapes had already been picked and sold. It seemed a fortunate moment to begin their tenancy, to ease into their stewardship.

They refused to allow that their inexperience was an insuperable obstacle. All that was needed was industry, stamina—humility. Maryna arose at six-thirty each morning and instantly seized her broom. Ah, Henryk, if you could see your Desdemona, your Marguerite Gautier, your Lady Anne, your Princess Eboli now!

Caught between two inclinations, to hand out tasks to everyone and to impose the principle that all work be voluntary, Maryna had decided simply to set an example. She enjoyed sweeping: the robust strokes and jabs accorded with her thoughts. And shelling beans, which she liked to do in an armchair made of manzanita branches on the porch: the mindlessness of it drew on deep calming reserves of vacuity she had made good use of as an actor. She didn't miss being on stage. She didn't miss anyone. Bogdan was out in the vineyard with Jakub and Aleksander and Cyprian. Ryszard was off somewhere writing. Barbara and Wanda had gone to the village to buy the day's bread and meat. Danuta was with her little girls. Piotr came running to show her a dead lizard he had found; Aniela and he were going to bury it in the yard with a little cross. She heard them laughing together. The girl was a wonderful playmate. She's a child herself. If Kamila had lived, she would be sixteen now, Aniela's age. The babbling toddler she could only imagine here on her lap, in the warmth of her lap, toying with the shelled beans in the bowl . . . a daughter of sixteen. That memory still ached—she missed neither her mother nor her sister, neither her Good H. nor her Bad H. (as she'd dubbed Henryk and Heinrich), not even Stefan. Only her lost daughter.

To be done with mourning! To live in the present! In the sun! She was soaking up light. She thought she could actually feel the desert's glare sealing her skin, drying up tears shed and unshed. It was almost palpable, the receding of the immense anxiety in which she had thrashed about for so many years, and the upsurge of vitality, freed from the need to husband it for performances. The exertions she had abandoned—being on stage or (in that distraction, her life) recovering from or preparing for the time on stage—had seemed so inevitable, so enclosing. She had wrenched herself away, only half convinced of the necessity of what she was doing. Now it was this new life, this new landscape and its horizon, which felt, already, complete. How easy it had been, after all. Henryk, are you listening? To change one's life: it's as easy as taking off a glove.

No one was shirking, everyone was eager to do something useful. Wanda told Julian she thought the house should be repainted. Several acres of grapes remained to be gathered and the vines, once stripped, needed to be fertilized—the lull in the implacable sequence of the agricultural year being only a relative one. Aleksander fabricated a scarecrow dressed like a Russian soldier to place in the vineyard. After a few days Bogdan and Jakub started gathering the remaining growth of grapes. But they had just arrived, they were just settling in, and the glorious weather seemed like an invitation to confound effort with self-improvement. Julian took to explaining to all who would listen the chemistry of winemaking. Danuta was helping Barbara do the drill in her English phrase manual. Aleksander was assembling a collection of rock specimens. Jakub had set up his easel. Ryszard offered riding lessons on the sorrel mare after his morning stint of writing. They lay in the hammocks Cyprian had strung from tree to tree and read novels and travel books; at twilight they raised their faces to the rosy sky, and watched sky and clouds and the mountain-framed vastness darken in tandem, until the bronze harvest moon came arching over the mountain and relit the clouds; one night it emerged bigger and redder, with an inky thumbprint: Julian had alerted everyone that there would be a lunar eclipse. They were waiting for it. Nothing equaled simply being still. And riding, slowly at first, then at a gallop once they learned to trust the freedoms of the high Mexican saddle, into the desert, sometimes to the foothills, occasionally all the way to the ocean twelve miles to the west.

On the eve of their long journey to California, Cyprian had been sent to Washington to spend a day at the Department of Agriculture, where he collected a box of pamphlets about viticulture in the southern part of the state. Clearly, it would make sense to follow in the footsteps of the Anaheim settlers: the village had been founded as a vineyard colony. But Bogdan thought their forty-seven acres, more than twice the stake exploited by each of the original fifty families, should also include ten acres of orange grove and another five of olive trees. If they had only one cash crop, an infestation or a cold snap could wipe them out. With several crops, something would always be flourishing.

While the men debated from house to perimeter and hammock to hammock the order of their projects, the only tasks that couldn't be postponed—feeding the animals, feeding themselves—fell to the women. Nobody could go out to fill the cows' trough with hay and oats or scatter grain to the hens or bring barley, corn, and clover to the horses, much less call on wine-producing neighbors about buying their grapes, until they had put away a good breakfast, a breakfast they'd enjoyed. Some wanted tea, others coffee, others milk or hot chocolate or wine soup; everybody wanted eggs, cooked three or four different ways—when there were some, for the hens were accustomed to laying everywhere and the stray dogs often found the eggs first. All those salivating palates and pink churning guts, theirs no different from the animals', except that theirs had the accents of individual taste, of history, and the burden of fickleness.

Ensuring the communal meals took up much of the women's day. None of them had much experience cooking, least of all Aniela, who proved as inept at common domestic tasks as Maryna had been warned. They grumbled behind Maryna's back—and sprang at the chance to do whatever she asked of them. Wanda, whose bandaged hands rendered her useless for the first week, burst into tears when she was told she was not needed in the kitchen. Danuta undertook to feed the three children separately. Barbara was charged with replenishing the coffee, tea, sugar, bacon, flour, and other staples (invariably underestimating how much they needed) as well as purchasing most of their daily diet until they would be eating only vegetables they grew, drinking their own wine, broiling their own poultry (each had a go at chasing a hen or a turkey with an axe, and returned empty-handed to the kitchen). Their hunter, Ryszard, brought back rabbits and quail from his dawn rides in the foothills. Lingering in the kitchen if Maryna was there, when no one was looking he would slip a paper in the pocket of her apron . . . a poem or a story fragment; one simply read, "May I tell you my dream?" She had taken Ryszard's attentions for granted in Poland, part of a landscape of flattering attentions; here, in the throes of learning to master the flapjack and the omelette, they distracted her. Once she looked up and saw he had returned and was standing in the doorway watching. With a gesture that was almost theatrical, wiping sweat from her brow with her bare forearm, she smiled at him mockingly. "Either come inside and help," she said, "or go back to the barn and write."

It would be a while before the cooking could be left to Aniela, who also hovered about, desperate to please Maryna, having nothing she could do that pleased except sing the old plangent hymns to the Madonna and to Poland. But the kitchen was already crowded and Aniela couldn't help but be in the way. Maryna gently sent her off to play with Piotr and the girls. Then Barbara, quite uninvited, took up the singing relay. She had learned one song, just one, in English, "Suwannee River," and she sang it over and over. What exasperated Maryna wasn't Barbara's ridiculous accent, well, only a little that; it was the song. Here they were in the farthest, westernmost part of America, and Barbara was yowling in her tuneless voice about some river back East, or perhaps in the South (Maryna was a bit vague about where it was), which she, Barbara, had never seen, would never see. True, Maryna didn't have any songs about the mighty Pacific Ocean, much less about the little Santa Ana River, to propose in its stead. That didn't stop her thinking this song an impertinence, a lack of respect for where they were, for the god Geography himself.

WHERE were they?

They were far away, yes . . . but far from where? It would be weak-minded, even unsporting, to aver: from Europe, from Poland. Further, that would be true of anywhere they might be in America. Better to think of themselves as far from some place in America—say, the one real city in the state (the biggest west of the Mississippi) with three hundred thousand inhabitants, flourishing theatres, and a knot of Polish émigrés, mostly families that had fled after the failed insurrections of 1830 and 1863. Yes, they were far from San Francisco. This little Anaheim, with half the number of inhabitants of Zakopane, was nothing. Still, you could hardly call it primitive. Or a village, in their sense: a place where people had collected, immemorially, to live. This was a place people had chosen, wrested from nothingness, were zealously developing—modern.

And all that seemed very American, as the new arrivals understood their new country, even if it felt sometimes as if they weren't really in America. They spoke Polish among themselves and German with their neighbors, indisputably a convenience for those like Aleksander who were having trouble learning English, though it seemed queer to have come all this distance and still be conversing in the all too familiar language of one of their conquerors. But—as Bogdan pointed out—that was America too, an odd country, perhaps the oddest country of all, welcoming every European nationality, and—Ryszard, who'd begun the study of Spanish, broke in—English wasn't the language of California's natives, either.

They had imagined a sleepy agricultural commune. This was a miniature town, its streets laid out self-importantly on a grid, full of business energies. It was the end of the vintage, and the village was crowded with those who had gathered the grapes and trampled them. Some were the Mexicans who performed most of the menial jobs in the village and lived in their own hamlet nearby. Most were Indians, Cahuilla Indians, who rarely came down from the wild mountains of San Bernardino except for the harvest and were camped just beyond the living fence of willows surrounding the village, sleeping in tents or on piles of rawhides under the night sky. The Mexicans and Indians vied with each other in drinking contests, from which the Mexicans broke off on their own, some to wander about and bellow compliments at the German girls still outdoors, accompanied by their frowning fathers and brothers, others to build a bonfire in the middle of Lemon Street and dance the bolero. The Indians watched on one side, the Germans on the other. Then the Germans went to bed, leaving their streets to the carousing vineyard hands.

When Maryna and Bogdan went to the Town Hall to introduce themselves to the mayor, Rudolf Luedke, he assured them that such public rowdiness was altogether exceptional, Anaheim being a respectable community of God-fearing hardworking families, unlike that helltown thirty miles away whose lawless, tequila-swigging denizens amuse themselves with bearbaiting and knife fights (until recently they averaged a murder a day, almost all unpunished) and, in certain houses, entertainments that can't be mentioned in the presence of a lady . . . which reminded Maryna that Ryszard had intimated how much he had enjoyed his side trips to Los Angeles when he and Julian first came to Anaheim. Herr Luedke gave them a tour of the irrigation canals —interrupting the flow of German to use the Spanish name, *zanjas*—which interlaced the village, noting that water was always breaking out of its channels into the streets, whereupon Bogdan remarked that this need for constant maintenance and repair of canals and streets must be a great incentive to regular habits on the part of the citizenry. "Exactly," said the mayor. He showed them the churches and the turnverein and the Water Company, a room of which had been used as the village school, and the proper schoolhouse the community had now, two rooms, where Piotr would be going. He brought them home to meet Frau Luedke, who presented their daughters, laid on coffee and schnapps, and invited them to join the Anaheim Cultural League, which met at the Planters Hotel on Lincoln Avenue on the first Wednesday evening of every month. Maryna did not mention that she used to be an actress.

Several days later the celebrations reached their climax with the arrival of the Stappenbeck Circus from Los Angeles. In the afternoon a procession of caged and uncaged creatures invaded

164

Orange Street: an elephant bearing a rickety tower on its back, two bears, a mangy mountain lion, monkeys, and parrots. Piotr was disappointed when Ryszard told him that a mountain lion wasn't a lion at all, but a puma; "I thought there would be real lions in California," he said, pouting. And Friedrich Stappenbeck's menagerie of sad animals could not impress those who lived among free animals, whom they considered their kindred spirits. But the Indians—and everyone else—went wild over the performing humans under the tent: the fire-eaters, the jugglers with knives, the contortionist, the magician, the Uncle Sam clown, the tiny woman who hurtled through the air on her trapeze, and the strong-man, a wide sullen-looking youth with a thatch of black hair and legs like logs, in whom there was particular interest, for he was born and raised in the region. The Indians didn't recognize him as one of their own, this offspring of a Cahuilla squaw who had left the mountains and worked for a ranching family in the foothills as a laundress (she had died when he was small) and a *vaquero* who had broken horses for a time on the ranch. But the villagers remembered him well, as a loner and a malcontent, though nobody could accuse him of any misdeed. His real name, U-wa-ka, had died with his mother; in the village and the foothills he was known as Big Neck. Two years ago he had simply disappeared; there had been no news of him since. And here he was again, a foot taller, with a buckskin cord around that enormous neck and a new name, a circus name: Zambo, the American Hercules. He could carry six people around the ring, three on each shoulder. He could take on any two contenders—a half dozen volunteered from the audience—and wrestle them to the ground. And he was at the center of the circus finale, with all the animals cavorting to the crack of Stappenbeck's whip, and Matilda, the Aerial Angel, as the trapeze artist was billed, balanced on top of a pole thirty feet tall carried by the exultant Zambo, while a steam calliope that had been wheeled into the ring, Uncle Sam at the keyboard, emitted a sequence of discordant whistles approximating dear old "Yankee Doodle." The Americans cried "Hurrah!"; the Germans, "Hoch!"; the Mexicans, "Viva!"; and the Cahuillas whooped with joy.

"TELL ME a story, Mama."

"Once upon a time——"

"No, not that kind of story. I mean a real story."

"What's a real story?"

"One with bears. And people getting killed. And everyone crying."

"Piotr! Why should everyone cry?"

"Because they're going to die."

"Piotr!"

"But it's true! You told me it was true when I asked you. And Uncle Stefan died and I saw you crying. And I heard Cyprian say the mule looks sick. And if everybody is going to die then you might die someday and——"

"Piotr darling! Not for a very long time, I promise! You mustn't think about that."

"But I do. Once I think about something, I can't stop. It's there in my head and it keeps on talking to me."

"Piotr, listen to me. There's nothing to be afraid of here. And I'm not going away anymore. All that is finished."

"But I *am* afraid."

"Afraid of what?"

"That I'm going to die. That's why I need a tomahawk."

"Oh my little Piotr, what good will that do you?"

"Well, I can kill them back. They all have guns."

And that was true, too. All the men had guns. And the guns were out.

The morning after the circus performance, the village awoke to startling news that only confirmed their opinion of Los Angeles and everything that came from there. Stappenbeck had been murdered and Matilda abducted, and the killer and kidnapper was the strong-man, Zambo. The show had ended, the audience had departed, and the performers were heading for the sleeping wagons to change from their motley into work clothes for the long night of striking the tent and packing up. They heard Stappenbeck's screams for help and ran back to the tent. The circus owner was writhing on his back next to the monkey cage; Zambo, bestriding him, was shouting "Never! Never! Never!"; and Matilda was sobbing in the shadows. The minstrel trio rushed at the youth and flailed at him with their bones. Zambo slammed them aside with one shoulder and they went tumbling, unhurt, onto the sawdust, beside the dying man. Then Zambo swept the aerialist up in his arms and ran into the night.

The contortionist tried to lift Stappenbeck to his feet. His hair was soaked with blood. He was carried to the mayor's house, and lived long enough to curse his murderer and name the motive for the crime. He had caught Zambo rifling the chest where the box-office receipts were kept. Luedke conferred with the sheriff and at dawn a posse was assembled and sent out after the fugitive.

Where would Zambo have gone on foot? He had often talked about quitting the circus and going to live in the Santa Ana Mountains, volunteered the juggler and the fire-eater. But Zambo a thief? No. Stappenbeck had hated Zambo, though the boy's only crime was to have gone all soft over Matilda, who was Stappenbeck's niece (the magician said she was his adopted daughter). Stappenbeck would whip Zambo for no reason at all; and poor Zambo had never lifted a finger against his tormentor, never even flinched or cried out. They don't feel pain the way we do, said the Uncle Sam clown.

For the villagers, who had no cause to doubt the testimony of a dying man, Matilda's departure with Zambo proved the case against the half-breed. Theft, then murder, capped by the abduction of a white woman—a typical Indian crime. The sheriff was confident that Zambo and the woman would be found. Stappenbeck had been the only one in the circus in possession of a gun.

Maryna and Bogdan and Piotr and the others saw them riding by—grim men with Sharps rifles and Winchesters galloping into the desert.

A plot for Ryszard! He started writing it—his version would be a love story—that afternoon. He kept Zambo's age, sixteen, but lowered Matilda's by a decade to thirteen, and renamed them Orso and Jenny. The beloved of *his* strong-man was an angelic child on the eve of womanhood, and in no way related to the circus owner, who received the name of Brandt. By dinnertime Ryszard had everything but the ending, as he told the others.

"But it's not finished," he protested when he was begged to share it.

"Neither is the real story," said Bogdan. "We haven't heard whether the posse has found them or not."

Ryszard went to fetch his manuscript from the barn and read his tale aloud.

Anaheim in all its robust quaintness: cowboys on snorting mustangs, farmers from outlying settlements tethering their buggies to the hitching posts; local blond beauties, black-tressed señoritas from Los Nietos, farmers' wives crowding the milliner's shop to buy bolts of calico and gingham and examine patterns from the fashion books; gossip, flirting, boasting, haggling; the buzz of anticipation over the circus arrival. The procession of Brandt's menagerie along Orange Street. Introduction of the hulking strong-man and petite aerialist. Orso's feral resentments tamed by unavowable love, Jenny's childish innocence troubled by burgeoning love. Brandt's explosions of jealous rage. Orso's fortitude during these terrible beatings. Putting up with any mistreatment, fearing only dismissal and separation from his darling Jen. The performance under the tent. Orso's feats of strength. Jenny's grace and daring. Admiration of the crowd. After the performance: the two youngsters lingering on a bench in a corner of the darkened tent. Jenny's maidenly expressions of pity at the brutalities visited on her circus comrade. Orso evoking his daydream of leaving the circus and taking Jenny to a free beautiful life in the Santa Ana Mountains. Jenny leaning the back of her little head against Orso's barrel-like torso; Orso gripping the edge of the bench with his meaty hands. Sighing. More sighing. The first avowals of their true feelings for each other. Orso timidly reaching up to touch Jenny's hair. Brandt in the shadows spying on them, then rushing forward. Orso offering no resistance and allowing himself to be slashed with the whip. Brandt turning to Jenny and for the first time raising his whip to her. Orso hurling him to the ground. Brandt's head hitting the corner of the monkey cage. Orso gathering Jenny in his arms. Fleeing together in the night, across the desert and into the foothills, the posse following. A few hours of chaste sleep. Jenny's terrors. Orso's tender protectiveness. Continuing their flight into the blue mountains. Cold, wild animals, hunger, exhaustion . . .

Ryszard looked up from his sheaf of papers. "And that's as far as I've got."

"Very engaging," said Bogdan. "Vivid. Rather touching."

Ryszard didn't dare ask Maryna what she thought. To write a love story and read it aloud in her presence before Bogdan and the others seemed bold enough. And he didn't want to hear anyone else's opinion. He was evading Julian's mocking stare.

"One small detail," said Julian. "The mountains here. I suppose you *could* say they're blue."

"And I do, you . . . scientist!" roared Ryszard. "Just by writing the word 'blue' I make them blue, that's what a writer does, and you, my reader slave, have to see them as blue."

"But they're not—"

"Whereas a painter," Ryszard continued triumphantly, "if he thinks the mountains are blue, must put it before your eyes, must *make* a color out of his pigments which maybe, though it doesn't matter what we say, we'd call blue—"

"Or violet or lavender or purple," said Jakub gaily.

"And how will you end it?" Cyprian asked.

"Heartrendingly, I suppose," said Ryszard. "Either *lento*, with more on their hardships and sufferings until, eventually, they take shelter in a mountain lion's cave and lie down to perish of hunger and exposure in each other's arms. Or, *allegro, allegro feroce*, with the posse running them down in one of the canyons, on the edge of a ravine. You should see it now"—he silently added "Maryna"—"the chaparral up there is still green: what gives them away would be the sequins on Jenny's frayed pink tunic and tights glinting in the sun. As the posse closes in on them, the Aerial Angel takes Orso by the hand and they leap together into the ravine to their deaths."

"Oh," sighed Barbara.

"I hate unhappy endings," said Wanda.

"Ah, the voice of the uncultivated reader," said Julian.

"Actually," said Ryszard, as embarrassed as everyone else by Julian's inveterate scorn for his wife, "I have doubts about the double suicide, too." From chivalry to a dollop of inspiration: "Yes, maybe they shouldn't be captured."

"Yes, yes," said Wanda.

"Can you believe this woman?" Julian said.

"They could elude the posse and remain in the mountains. The bruise-blue mountains, Julian. Beauty and the beast settling down in a remote canyon where no one ventures except the most intrepid trapper."

"But how do they eat, stay warm, defend themselves against wild animals?" Aleksander asked.

"He's an Indian," said Cyprian. "He knows such things."

"Half-Indian," muttered Jakub.

"But Jenny isn't," Danuta said.

"Don't shy away from an unhappy ending," said Bogdan, "if that seems more truthful."

"Readers, readers!" Ryszard exclaimed. "I just want to tell a good story. What's more truthful? What makes you feel less sad? Don't load this dreamer's shoulders with too many responsibilities! You'd think the ending I decide could influence what actually happens to the poor wretches!"

But he was starting to feel just that; so, honoring the superstitious feeling, Ryszard consulted one of the Mexican women who tell *suertes*, or fortunes, about their fate. Her prediction—that they would be hunted down and killed—decided it for him; the end almost wrote itself.

Orso spotted going up a steep hill carrying Jenny in his arms; the guns blazing and thundering; the sound crashing back from the canyon walls, a bullet tearing into Jenny's head, Orso appearing to fall; the posse finding him on the ground, howling with grief, cradling the dead Jenny in his arms, the lariat that went flying toward Orso and sizzled around his neck; then they—

No! No. Lose the posse. Save the children. Invent an old squatter living in reckless solitude—years since he'd last seen anyone in his forbidding stretch of mountain—who would welcome them to his campfire and prove as lavishly benign as the circus owner had been cruel. They were terrified, he would hearten them. They were famished, he would feed them. Raking in the ashes he set on the grill a fine haunch of venison, and as he watched them eat—perhaps he had once been a father—his eyes filled with tears. "Since then these three have lived together," went the last line of the story. This is America, Ryszard thought, where the maudlin happy end is as appreciated as a bout of self-righteous, gleeful slaughter. When, two days later, the posse did catch up with the fugitives and opened fire, hitting Matilda in the spine (she would be paralyzed for life), and then strung up Zambo, Ryszard had no regrets about the dénouement he had chosen. What is the point of turning real events into stories if you can't change everything, especially the end?

AND WHAT IS the point of telling stories, if not to stir up the longing everyone harbors for an alternative life?

Further, Ryszard was not in the mood to relate the story of an impossible love that turns out to be . . . impossible. Writing is conjuring: Ryszard wanted to show impossible love to be possible. His own love for Maryna had become an endless, unfinished story he was constantly revising, embroidering, sharpening, finding more fluent ways to describe to himself. Here he was, living side by side with her but not daring to approach her less puppyishly for fear of a definitive rejection. He suspected that she counted on his attentions, his burdensome attentions, that she would be sorry to see her ardent, infinitely patient suitor become, simply, resigned. But the role was harder to play without the décor in which it had been devised. There were no dressing rooms (he had loved looking at her while she looked at herself in the mirror), no smoky gaslit corridors, no darkened carriages. The bordellos of Los Angeles had mirrors, there were mirrors in San Francisco and not only in the theatres, but what use could an outward-looking village like Anaheim have for the beguiling play between surfaces and what lies behind them? Their new life had no mirrors. Only views.

He might have felt less deflated had he only to endure a husband's presence, but to be conjoined with four couples—all of whom, even the miserable Julian and Wanda, seemed so irrevocably mated—made him feel further from Maryna than he had ever been. (To affirm the bachelor difference, he persuaded Jakub to accompany him to Los Angeles for a weekend of whoring.) They were rarely alone together, except during riding lessons. He recounted solitary adventures he'd had when he and Julian came in August, camping and exploring beyond the settled areas. Was there to be no straying from the marital paddock? No piping in of new erotic energy? "Ride with me," Ryszard said. "Let me show you the mountains." "Soon, soon," she murmured. He had dreamed of protecting her. But there was nothing to protect her from. Unless Bogdan were somehow to disappear. In stories, nothing is impossible. Bogdan could fall from a horse and break his neck, and then she would realize . . .

Maryna, dismounting, unceremoniously tugged at his collar. This journey to a liberating vacancy for which Ryszard offered himself as chaperon, call it the shadowless desert, call it the uninhabited mountains—she was already there.

"Oh, Maryna," he groaned. "Is there no hope for us?"

"Us?"

He bowed his head. "Me."

"I think," she said, "there is hope for you."

"And you, Maryna? So bent on becoming posthumous! Have you really changed that much? Is it possible, Maryna?"

"More than possible."

"And this"—he flung out his arm to the land that surrounded them—"is the only passion that engages you now?"

She didn't answer.

"But couldn't you be deceiving yourself about what you really want? Don't you ever feel stranded? The scenery is beautiful, our Arden, but it doesn't change. Don't you ever feel impatient with everyone—Julian, poor Wanda, Danuta, Aleksander, Cyprian, Barbara, even Jakub . . . no, I won't exclude myself. How can you stand us?"

"Us?"

"And the animal and human roughness, and heavy mud-caked boots and rank clothes, and the reddened rough skin on your own hands, and Aniela's boils, which you lanced with the heated blade of a razor (I was watching you, where did you learn to do that?)—this isn't you. The muck and the ooze and the dryness—you're made for velvet. And all the race hatreds stirring in these new Californians, just below their reconciling greeds. It's hardhearted and empty here. It will make us hardhearted and empty, Maryna. Wait, don't say 'Us?' again, it will make you, even you, hardhearted and empty."

"I'm sorry you find me cruel, Ryszard. But I don't mind being empty."

"You never feel sorry for yourself?"

"I felt sorry for myself in Poland. Now I don't even understand why. But here? No, never. Surely you see that I'm thriving on being stripped of almost all that made me distinctive to others and to myself. It makes me, now you'll really think me cruel, it makes me laugh."

Absences: plush, relics, dimness, corridors, one's own history. How could she explain to Ryszard? Here every story emerged freestanding, without roots in long genealogies of concern and obligation. The sudden drop in the volume of meanings in the new life worked on her like a thinning out of oxygen. She was feeling giddy. And yet it was all so familiar. Groups subdued by difficult routines and impetuous leadership were Maryna's natural element: the communal impulse is strong among theatre people. And this newly rooted life hardly differed from the life of traveling players. If some of the simplest tasks of farm life still eluded them, no wonder, they had prepared hastily, conning their parts as farmers at the last minute, just off stage. For a time they would be "winging it," as actors say, until they had mastered their roles.

In the evening, gallantly ignoring their pulled muscles, aching backs, scraped shins, painful sunburns, they gathered in the living room to pore over their pamphlets from Washington and the books on farming brought from Poland and discuss fertilizers and fencing, the planting of an orange grove, the repair of the henhouse, and the hiring of a few Indian or Chinese laborers to help them. Pacing about, Bogdan outlined his plans for the new dwellings. He spoke in clipped rapid phrases, his hand clenched around a near-empty glass of tea and its clinking spoon. A hand Maryna hardly recognized, with its blackened thumbnail and the fat vein crawling from tanned knuckle to wrist; a Bogdan she had not known before, no longer entirely absorbed by her, doing all this for her. Sinking into the collective—for her.

Everyone was supposed to participate in these discussions. In fact, the women—except for Maryna—hardly spoke, as if they assumed they had nothing to say, or were going to be criticized, or that making decisions was a man's job. Farm life organized the women for new docilities, dictated to everyone new menus of incompetence. And knowing how their neighbors saw them, as coddled impractical gentlefolk, made them shy about asking for help. Herr Kohler had sent over one of his young Mexican farmhands to show them how to care for the vineyard, whose cycle was starting over. The men watched somberly as he demonstrated the way to cut back the large shoots, to apply fertilizer, to pack soil against the base of the vines. And it was kind of Kohler, who was selling them milk, cream, and butter, to tell Pancho to give milking lessons as well; but none of the women had strong enough hands or the right technique: they felt they were torturing the cows. After a few days they started buying milk from another nearby farm.

It was not in Maryna's nature to be charitable to herself, ever, or forbearing with others. But how petty it seemed under this unrelenting sun to be fretting that Barbara and Danuta made reluctant milkmaids.

Fatigue and the drone of communal preoccupations seemed only to fatten her immense sensation of physical well-being. More absences: words, self-dramatization, amorous energies. Healing absences. Carnal presences. The piercing reek of fresh dung and their own sweat. Panting over the kitchen range, at the milking stool, behind the wheelbarrow, and the harmonies of collective fatigue exhaled at the end of a day, in silence, at the dining-room table. All sonorities reduced to this: the sound of breathing, only breathing, theirs, her own. She never felt so attached to the others as then, feeling herself enclosed in a cube of noisy breathing; never felt so optimistic about the life they were laboring to build. Easy to say: it will not last. Every marriage, every community is a failed utopia. Utopia is not a kind of place but a kind of time, those all too brief moments when one would not wish to be anywhere else. Is there an instinct, a very ancient instinct, for breathing in unison? The ultimate utopia, that. At the root of the desire for sexual union is the desire to breathe more deeply, deeper still, faster . . . but always together.

IN NOVEMBER, Maryna and Bogdan received a letter from a compatriot who had been living in San Francisco for almost twenty years, Bruno Halek, a shrewd impertinent old man of indeterminate occupation and, plainly, some means. He had befriended Ryszard and Julian when they were first in San Francisco in July, and had shown the larger group about when they arrived in late September.

Halek asked if he might pay a visit to his friends in their wine-producing Rhineland village in the desert. He had not stretched his mighty legs for a time, he said. He would not have dreamt of making such a long trip if the only transport for his admittedly large self were still that pokey side-wheeler—three days of dried beef and parboiled beans!—as far as the harbor near Los Angeles, and *choo-choo-choo* only for the last thirty miles. And picture this, he said. When the Germans went south in 1859 (he had met some of them then, hardworking dullards all; it would be amusing to see them now), their ship had gone right past Los Angeles, anchoring three miles off the coast where Anaheim was going to be, and the colonists had been taken by rowboat near the shore, where a party of Indians hired by those two clever Germans with the wine company in Los Angeles in which the San Francisco people had bought shares were waiting for them waist-deep in the water, poor devils, and then each German man, woman, and child had been lowered onto the shoulders of an Indian and carried to land. But those epic days were past (though he'd like to see even the brawniest brave with the strength to carry him!), and since there was now a train to Los Angeles he was eager to make the trip, not that he meant to impose on them, he was not one for sleeping in a tent or a log cabin, he expected to stay in a hotel, but come he would, dear Madame Maryna permitting. If only, he added jovially, to sample the wine.

And could he bring them anything from San Francisco?

Out of the question for their guest to stay at the Planters. Maryna and Bogdan had the sofa removed from the parlor and replaced by a bed; during his visit Piotr would sleep in the kitchen with Aniela. Despising that part of herself that wished to impress Halek (more exactly, not to disillusion him), while convinced that it would bolster everyone's self-esteem to participate in the effort of making their new home as attractive as it could be, Maryna took his arrival as an occasion to goad the others into some long-postponed tasks. The henhouse must be repaired (their large guest would undoubtedly ask for four eggs at breakfast); the house repainted, furniture polished, more books unpacked—farm work was put aside and everyone drafted to make the house fit to be visited. And their larder was to be properly stocked, and bottles of the good aguardiente and tequila available in the Mexican settlement laid in (Halek would certainly turn up his nose at Anaheim's profusion of German beers). Then, a week later, leaving Danuta and Barbara to arrange the cut oleander in pretty Cahuilla baskets, Maryna went off with Bogdan in the buggy to the depot. Their visitor descended from the train, even larger than they remembered and further bulked out with a clutch of packages tied with brown twine containing newspapers from Poland, books, kerchiefs and scent cases for the women, a lace mantilla for Maryna, lead soldiers for Piotr, dolls and lollipops for the little girls.

"I'm ravenous," he said as he entered the house.

Aleksander laughed. "We're always hungry, too."

"That's because you're working too hard," cried Halek. "I'm hungry"—he slapped his immense belly—"because I'm hungry." And then he made a sound, something like a bark, something like a groan. "I remember that," said Piotr happily. The sighting of sea lions roaring on rocks from the terrace of a cliffside casino outside San Francisco was an obligatory pleasure for every visitor to the city. "I can do a coyote, Mr. Halek. Listen."

Their chance to show their visitor around. First things first: they took him for a tour of Anaheim's irrigation system. "I see," he chortled, "a Rhineland village with Dutch canals. We're in Holland here."

They showed him their two cows, their three quick-tempered saddle horses, and the sickly mule. He asked them how they got on with their neighbors.

"We don't see much of them," said Cyprian.

"I should hope not," said Halek. "What would you have in common with these moneygrubbing farmers and shopkeepers? Contrary to the legend spread by that journalist Nordhoff, another German, who came here a few years ago and wrote a lot of nonsense about Anaheim, there was never, as you know, anything 'communistic' about this village."

Of course, he was right—to the disappointment of the Polish settlers, their heads full of Fourier and Brook Farm. The Germans in San Francisco had been recruited by a land surveyor working for two of their compatriots who owned vineyards and a wine company in Los Angeles and were looking to expand their business. With the money put up by the fifty investors, a parcel of land was bought and made fit for settlement: Chinese and Mexican workers were engaged to dig the irrigation ditches, Mexican workers to plant the vines, Indian workers to build the adobe houses where the fifty families would live. When they arrived two years later the houses and vineyards were waiting for them. At first the society owned everything, but after a few years, when the place was showing a profit, the cooperative was dissolved, and each of the original settlers recouped his investment and became the owner of his own stake. Anaheim was never, not even at the beginning, an experiment in communal living.

"Now you, Madame Maryna, you and the esteemed Count Dembowski and your friends, with our irrepressible Polish idealism, have decided to make the legend a reality. And for that I take off my hat to you. But I implore you, do not forget the stage, still in mourning for the departure of its queen. I suppose you would not consider, after a year or so of this adventure, again—"

"Not you, too! I didn't expect to endure the same reproaches in America, even from a countryman. No, this is not an adventure, my friend. It's a new life, the life I want. I don't miss the stage."

"You don't miss the comforts to which you were accustomed, Madame Maryna?"

In reply she tossed him, in English:

Ay, now am I in Arden: the more fool I; when I was at home I was in a better place; but travellers must be content.

"I beg your pardon?"

"Shakespeare, Mr. Halek. *As You Like It.*"

"And so I do, which is why—"

"But I am teasing you, Mr. Halek! I repeat: I don't miss the stage."

"You are very brave," he said.

He was delighted, delighted to see his friends so lean and healthy. Undoubtedly it was all the exercise they were getting, which his girth ruled out for himself, alas, although, he admitted, even when he was young and slender, yes, he had been slender once, he said, staring at Wanda (much of this was directed at Wanda, who looked stunned that Halek was flirting with her), even slender he loved nothing more than loafing. Eating, talking, and playing chess (he would sing as he pondered his next move) were favorite pastimes. "It's your little rustic Athens that seduces me," he said. "Not your little Sparta." They enjoyed regaling him with stories of their ineptitude—actually, Halek made them feel like seasoned country folk. "I like the views," he said from the hammock that had been specially reinforced the day after his arrival. "And the animals too, as long as they keep their distance." He was as disconcerted by the charming young badger that Ryszard had captured and made into a household pet as by a truly terrifying giant scorpion scooting across the yard. "I confess to being as afraid of animals as a Jew is of water," he said. And, turning to Jakub: "I haven't offended you, I hope."

For their turkeyless first Thanksgiving—Piotr wept and the shrieking bird was spared—Maryna laid out the damask linen she had brought from Poland and allowed herself to be exempted from kitchen chores. All the other women shared in the cooking, and Halek astonished them by volunteering to prepare the dessert. "How do you think an old bachelor like me would ever get what he wanted if he couldn't do something for himself?" It was called, he told them (a sliver of English), a shoofly pie—"Shoo fly, shoo fly, shoo fly," Piotr began to chant—because one will have to shoo away the flies attracted to its molasses and brown-sugar filling.

"Shoo fly, shoo fly—"

"Stop it, Piotr," said Maryna.

"Sweet on the inside," crooned Halek. "Stuffed with sweetness. Can't keep the flies away."

"It's very tasty," said Wanda. "I'd be grateful if you wrote out the recipe for me."

"Do, Mr. Halek," said Julian. "This will keep her mind occupied for at least a week."

After dessert, when nothing remained but the crumbs on the cloth and the sticky plates and the empty coffee cups, Bogdan recalled that they had neglected the ritual with which this most American of dinners should begin. "I give thanks that we are all here together," he said. "Who will go next?"

"Piotr darling," said Maryna, "tell us what you're thankful for."

"That I'm taller," he said joyously. "Aren't I taller now, Mama?"

"Yes, darling, yes. Come here and sit in Mama's lap."

"I give thanks to America," said Ryszard, "a country insane enough to declare the pursuit of happiness to be an inalienable right."

"I give thanks that the girls are healthy," said Danuta.

"Amen to that," said Cyprian.

"Barbara and I give thanks to Maryna and Bogdan for their vision and their generosity," said Aleksander.

"Friends," murmured Maryna, holding Piotr tightly and burying her face in his hair. "Dear friends."

"Mama, I want to sit in my own chair."

"I give thanks for America's dream of equality for all its citizens, however far that dream must go to be realized," said Jakub.

"I give thanks to Mr. Halek for the dessert," said Wanda.

"Trust my wife to lower the tone," said Julian. "I suppose that I should give thanks that in America it is legal to divorce."

"Don't, Julian. I beg you!" cried Jakub.

"Aniela," shouted Maryna.

"And I thank Mrs. Solski for her gracious compliment," said Halek, grinning. The girl emerged from the kitchen.

"Aniela," said Maryna in a furious tone, "we are giving thanks for our blessings."

"Blessings, Madame? Blessings? Have I done anything wrong?"

Julian buried his head in his hands, then looked up, grimacing. "I apologize, Maryna. I don't mean what I say. I'm sorry."

"It's not just Maryna to whom you owe an apology," said Bogdan.

"Husbands"—Halek roared—"husbands!"

"Are the blessings over, Madame? May I go back to the kitchen?"

"And I shall come with you, child," said Halek, "and you can say your blessing to me."

Of course, he had been brazenly paying court to Aniela as well as to the wretched Wanda (which enraged Julian), but he had his comeuppance the following day. When he took his erect penis out and lunged at Aniela in the kitchen, she bolted and he lumbered after her, trousers agape, as far as the field beyond the barn, where he slid into an irrigation ditch. Aniela halted a little downstream and stared in amazement at the penis bobbing in the water. The wide ditch was only a foot and a half deep but the near-supine Halek, for all his grunting and sloshing about, was incapable of righting himself. "Your hand, child!" He was wetter than a sea lion. "Your lovely hand!" Sure that this was all her fault and that she would be punished—for having been attractive to the fat man or for having fled his attentions, which caused him to fall in the water, she wasn't sure which: all she knew is that she felt guilty, which meant that she must have done something wrong—Aniela turned and ran back to the kitchen.

The barking of the house dog, a stray they'd adopted which Bogdan, to the puzzlement of their German neighbors, had named Metternich, brought Ryszard and Jakub to Halek's rescue.

"I'm an old scamp," he sputtered after they hauled him out of the water. "Madame Maryna, what must you think of me now? Can you forgive me?"

She did. It was easy for Maryna to pardon Halek his scabrous antics: he was ludicrously obese, he was returning to San Francisco in a few days. He became more difficult to pardon when they discovered, an hour after seeing him off at the depot, that their merry friend was a kleptomaniac. Bogdan was missing the brass knuckles he'd brought from Poland, Julian his compass, Wanda her book of recipes, Danuta and Cyprian their older child's christening cup, Jakub a volume of Heine's poems, Barbara and Aleksander a bottle of black currant vodka, Ryszard a leather belt hung with bears' claws and snake rattles he'd bought on one of his trips into the San Bernardinos from a Cahuilla trapper. Halek even went off with Piotr's favorite jigsaw puzzle, The Smashed Up Locomotive. Only Aniela was spared, unless one counts the jar of sugar he filched from the kitchen. And Maryna lost a matching necklace and pair of pendant earrings of oxidized silver: Polish women of fashion had worn such mourning jewelry, as it was called, after the failure of the 1863 Uprising. A present from Bogdan's grandmother, they were among her most treasured possessions.

Bogdan's indignation at the theft of the necklace and earrings dimmed her own sadness. "Don't mourn jewelry, dear heart. Old Halek may cherish them even more than I did. He has been living in America so long."

"You are too generous," Bogdan said icily. "It's unnatural."

"It's he who was too generous, more than his own nature could tolerate."

"You compare those trinkets he brought with—"

"Oh, Bogdan, let's not mind. One should always be ready to part with anything."

Possessing things was a technique of consolation. The silver-backed brushes, the damask tablecloth and napkins, the four large trunks containing a thousand books (where would they ever put them?), the sheet music of Moniuszko and Chopin songs no one had played on the upright piano in the parlor (it was hopelessly out of tune), the costumes she would never wear again—anything brought that was not of purely practical value signified a desire to keep faith with the old life, and the need to be consoled for having abandoned it. But why should she need to be consoled?

She didn't miss their dark Polish woes, or even the dark weather, although the fabled southern California climate, which seemed to them to consist in an absence of weather, had not ceased to surprise. There seemed to be only two seasons here: a hot dry summer, followed by a long temperate spring called winter. They kept expecting something more, a violence of nature, an obstacle. By now, back in Poland, fields and mountains, churches and theatres lay under the wide wet grey sky of real winter—the road to Zakopane would once again be impassable—while Sunnyland's azure days and starry nights augured easier and easier transit from one place to another, one life to another.

Health is a promise of more future, while possessions reinforce ties to the past. Each day, Maryna was feeling stronger, more fit, which is what the boosterish books about southern California guaranteed to everyone who would make the trip, settle here, fill up empty land. To begin with, there had been gold; now there was health. California bestowed health, California encouraged working at being healthier. But you'll be at your most fortified, your fittest, when the furor of need subsides; when needs give way to a soothing, vigorous indifference; when you are simply grateful to be alive, alive again. As you are when just awake, those first unhinged moments—dawning to light, grazing in a thicket of pristine feelings, your body still sodden with sleep while your mind, even as it disentangles itself from a dream (whose plot diverged so alarmingly or comically from the life you recall that you live), your mind floats free.

It's not that you don't know where you are, or what you've settled for. There's Bogdan's tousled head on the next pillow, thought Maryna. There's that sound: the dear man grinds his teeth when he sleeps. It could be Heinrich with his open mouth and reedy snore, or Ryszard, who would be rubbing his eyes and reaching for his glasses on the night table, or any one of a dozen other men, though it is not. And for this moment, this moment only, it would not even matter. For as you look about, your feelings toward both bedmate and bedroom furnishings are equally accepting, equally anesthetized. The iron bedstead with the four copper-ball finials; the plain wardrobe with the sagging door; the mottoes on the walls, E PLURIBUS UNUM worked in beads and HOME SWEET HOME embroidered in wool and trimmed with flowers made of human hair—these seem just right, impersonal and unchosen like the décor of a hotel room where someone has retreated to write a book or pursue a clandestine love affair: a perfect setting for transformation.

But how ungovernable the impulse to add some personal touches, to improve things, to expand the zone of possession. From the beginning it had been clear that they must create more space for themselves and the others. By building one small adobe dwelling for Danuta, Cyprian, and the children, then another for Wanda and Julian where they could conduct their miseries out of earshot, and putting in a new floor and walls in the shack Aleksander and Barbara occupied, they would have a real phalanstery. Of course it would be foolish to sink more money into a property that was rented, whose option to buy did not come into effect before six months of tenancy. Perhaps the owner would be willing to sell it to them now.

Like the bride who, standing in church beside the groom, realizes that while she does love this man and want to marry him, it's not going to last, it's going to prove a mistake, envisages this before her finger receives the ring, before her mouth shapes the "I do," but finds it easier to banish foreknowledge and continue becoming wed, Maryna thought: It is frivolous to interfere with what has been so ardently conceived, so wholeheartedly undertaken. She had to go through with it, because everything had led to this. How could she be standing anywhere but here? And skepticism can coexist with confidence. With all this character-building hope and exertion, how could they not succeed? Hope and exertion, like desire, were values in themselves. Their community would still be a success even if it failed.

Ryszard brought along his lucky sea-green marble inkstand to be used at the ceremony. After Bogdan signed the deed of purchase and handed over the envelope with the four thousand dollars to the farm's owner in the presence of Herr Luedke and the town clerk and Piotr's schoolteacher (a comely Gretchen from San Francisco who had obviously caught Ryszard's fancy), they returned to the house to celebrate. Maryna gazed at Bogdan with sovereign tenderness.

"Wanda, you can't wait until we're all sitting down?" whispered Julian.

"Beef and onion stew!" said Aleksander, helping himself to a large portion from the bowl Aniela was passing around the table.

"It's not beef and onion stew, it's *guïsado*," said Piotr. "I've had it after school at Joaquin's house."

"Let's celebrate today by speaking English," said Maryna.

Who doth ambition shun
And loves to live i' th' sun,
Seeking the food he eats
And pleased with what he gets,

she sang. And, as if on cue, Ryszard chimed in with the chorus's

Come hither, come hither, come hither
Here shall he see
No enemy
But winter and rough weather.

"Bravo," said Maryna. Bogdan frowned. Outside, the sun was shining fiercely.

Six

PRUNES, PAPA, potato, prism.

"I beg your pardon," said Jakub.

"Prunes, papa, potato, prism. You needn't say them all. Prism is the one that counts, that gives the mouth a pleasant expression. But it helps to get a running start with prunes, papa, potato. Are we ready?"

The photographer had planted the camera box near the live oak at the rear of the house.

"Ready," said Maryna from some twenty feet away, her hands resting on Piotr's shoulders. Bogdan, Julian, and Wanda had gathered on her right. To her left were Danuta and Cyprian and their little girls, each clasping a pet bunny.

Knocking back her flat-crowned Spanish hat (it was secured by a chin strap), the photographer ducked under the black cloth and emerged a moment later.

"Can you not find some boxes for those in the second row to stand on?"

"Aniela, something to make you and the others taller," said Maryna in Polish without turning her head.

"I'll help," Ryszard said. "There's just what we need in the barn."

The girls dropped their bunnies and went scampering after

them. Piotr ran ahead to the barn and returned with Ryszard and Aniela atop their wheelbarrow's worth of milk pails. Barbara, Aleksander, Ryszard, Jakub, and Aniela regained their places in the second row.

"You remember what I told you?"

"Piotr, prunes, papa, potato, prism," shouted Piotr. "Piotr, prunes, papa——"

"Excellent, little man. Now if you could just get your mother and father and their friends to say it . . ." Eliza Withington stared judiciously at the group. "Eyes wide open, that's right. Now I would like to see a pleasant expression. You're going to be very glad to have this record of yourselves in the years to come."

And so they will be. And the brash light of the hot March afternoon will become the sepia grace of bygone days. *Then* we were like *that*. Young and innocent-looking. And so picturesque. Maryna barely recognizable in frontier garb, a dark calico dress with a long overskirt, her hair parted in the center and knotted snugly at the back of her head. Bogdan in his natty corduroy sack jacket and wool trousers tucked inside his new Wellingtons. Piotr in plaid shirt and short denim pants, his blond hair blunt-cut at ear level and combed to one side—a little American boy. And look, Ryszard in a sombrero! "The pants were red," Ryszard will say to his wife (his second wife), fingering the picture and staring back at his own old-colored stare. "And the flannel shirt fastened with a hook and eye, that was my favorite shirt. Try to guess what my attire had cost me, all together? One dollar!" Aniela will recall the thrill of putting on the white bibbed apron Maryna had bought for her a week before.

"We think we are wearing a pleasant expression," said Bogdan. "But you are the photographer."

"More pleasant would be better. A little bit of dreaminess, if you catch my meaning. An expression I'd not ordinarily suggest to a farming family but you don't appear to me like the other people I have observed in this community." Leaving her station behind the camera, she approached Danuta—"May I?"—and straightened her bonnet. Then she returned to the camera to examine them once again. "Or if not, perhaps there are too many of you, then more natural. I mean, not too relaxed, but almost a little distracted—as if you were having a good time. Sometimes one can look too dignified, I always say. What country did you say you were from?"

"Poland," said Bogdan.

"Oh my! And you're all from Poland?"

"All," said Jakub.

"Well, isn't it wonderful, all the different people who want to come to America. I mean, I would never think of going to Poland, which is very near Russia, isn't it?"

"Very near," said Cyprian.

"And Russia is vast, isn't it, like America. But I'm sure your country is awfully interesting, too. All those small countries must be wonderful to see and to photograph. Maybe I will get to Europe one day, I've still got time. I'd go about in my wagon just as I do here, and stop whenever I felt the urge, and take all the pictures I wanted. Do you think people would laugh at me? Who's that old bird from California, they'd say. No matter, I'll just stare them down. Oh"—she laughed, pointing at Maryna—"I saw you smile."

THE PORTRAIT of their community had been Maryna's idea, when she saw the advertisement in Anaheim's weekly *Gazette*:

Mrs. Eliza Withington
Photographic Artist
Excelsior Ambrotypes and Daguerreotypes!
Mrs. Withington, having perfected herself in the art,
cannot fail to please.
Will remain in Anaheim for one week in the
Planters Hotel, room no. 9.

Call and see. Prices reasonable.
Likeness guaranteed.
"Secure the shadow 'ere the substance fade."

Maryna dispatched Ryszard to the village to call on Mrs. Withington and ask her if she could come out to take a photograph of
fourteen people, including three children. Ryszard took the occasion to spend an intimate hour with his schoolteacher and then
strolled over to the hotel. In a wagon near the entrance, the one
bearing a sign depicting a camera on its tripod, sat a stout elderly
woman in a Stetson and black alpaca ulster.

"It can only be the illustrious Mrs. Withington," he said,
tipping his new sombrero. "I did not expect to find you outside
taking the sun."

He explained his commission. She explained to him that it
was tedious for her to wait for prospective clients indoors. "I live
by the light and for the light," she said. She agreed to bring her
traveling studio to the farm the next morning.

The Polish settlers were enthralled by this specimen of
independent American womanhood. But they could only watch
while she unloaded box after box holding the fragile glass plates
and the packets and bottles of chemicals, the tripod with its legs
doubled up and tied, and "the pet," as she called her Philadelphia
box camera; set up her dark-tent in which she laid out her salts
and emulsions and arranged the tanks for sensitizing and developing the plates; untied and unfolded the tripod and mounted the
camera. Except for asking for water to fill the tank in which she
cleaned the five-by-eight-inch glass plates, she refused all offers
of assistance from the men. But she brightened when Julian told
her that he had been a chemistry teacher back in Poland before
becoming a farmer in America. "Ah yes," said Mrs. Withington,
"photography is chemistry. Nothing else, is it not?" She invited
him to peer inside the cramped dark-tent while she applied the
photosensitive salts to a sheet of glass and then coated it with the
wet collodion, her reward being some knowledgeable questions

from Julian about the superiority of collodion to the albumen-on-glass process, along with a respectful concern about the explosive properties of collodion's principal ingredient, nitrated cellulose ("Yes, we call it guncotton," she said cheerfully). Jakub was permitted to join them when he divulged that he was a painter as well as a farmer. "Of course, photography is painting, too," she remarked. "Painting with light." Her pair of new Morrison lenses, she told Jakub, would produce a likeness far superior to what could be achieved by any painter.

Though there was a place up north she called home—Ione City, a tiny village in the Sierras—where she had a portrait studio, for several months each year she was out and about in her wagon looking for picture-worthy escarpments and gorges, bizarre rock formations and looming cacti. She subsidized her itinerant life by stopping in villages to offer her services. "Weddings and funerals are best," she observed. Since Anaheim had been a disappointment in both respects, she would be on her way after taking their photograph.

She had traveled up and down the state, she told them, many many times.

"Alone?" Barbara exclaimed.

"Are you not afraid, Mrs. Withington?" said Danuta. "I would be so afraid."

"Never!"

"But surely you would be safer," said Ryszard, "if you took an assistant with you."

"I have my Colt and I know how to use it," she replied, patting her hip.

After the picture-taking they invited her to stay for the noon meal. She said that she never felt so happy as when she climbed back into her wagon and moved on. "I have a restless soul," she said, "and all the patience I am mistress of is used up in mixing my salts and collodion, preparing my plates, and concentrating my mind on my subject before I fix its image. The glory of it is that every day I have something new to look at through my lens." But she accepted their invitation to come indoors for a glass of tea ("You wouldn't have some whiskey, would you? Of course not, you drink vodka, like the Russians"; "Say, rather, the Russians drink vodka like us," said Cyprian) and, once installed with glass and whiskey bottle on the parlor sofa, seemed inclined to linger and chat. "I address myself particularly to the lady who shifted into such a graceful position just as I was about to expose the first plate"—Maryna smiled again—"and smiles so winningly when she wants. Of course, few people would want to have a portrait of themselves smiling. In the paintings by the Old Masters only clowns and fools smile. A photograph should show us in our essence, as we try to be, as we wish to be remembered, which implies tranquillity."

"Dogs smile, Mrs. Withington. Mr. Darwin himself makes something out of that."

"True enough. But what does the dog mean by it? Is the critter happy? Or only trying to entertain its master? It may be pretending."

"What do people mean when they smile?" Ryszard said. "Maybe we are all pretending."

"I think," said Wanda, "that we—"

"Wanda, just listen," said Julian. "Please."

"And then to lock the muscles of the face, to hold a smile, since the camera can hardly take a picture like *that*!"—she snapped her fingers—"is bound to produce an expression that looks counterfeit, or worse. When the negative is developed, the photographer may find that instead of smiling the subject looks about to cry."

"Or both," Maryna said.

"You have posed for the photographer many times, have you not?"

Maryna nodded.

"I thought so. The moment before I uncapped my lens, you

arched your eyebrows ever so slightly, which elongated the oval of your cheeks. I like it when people know what they're doing. Were you ever on the stage?"

"I was, Mrs. Withington."

"But I'll warrant you didn't do comic turns, Mrs. Zawa— Mrs. Zawen— Sorry, your Polish names are too hard for me to pronounce. I'm sure you were very grand and serious and when you smiled, people felt it was a gift, a special gift for them. I feel that, when you smile at me."

"You are very perceptive, Mrs. Withington. Do you go much to the theatre?"

"Oh my, there's no theatre in Ione City! Even when it was a mining camp—it wasn't Ione City yet, the miners called it Bedbug and Freeze-Out—it was never rich enough. But I came only twenty-five years ago, from New York, where I went to all the plays and had my favorite actors and scrapbooks full of clippings about them. I was sure I'd miss all that when my husband heeded the siren call of gold and I followed him to California. But when I was left on my own after he died in an accident, fell from a cliff, poor man, and I set myself to master the heliographic art, the demand then was mostly for pictures of men showing off handfuls of nuggets or staking their claims, and everyone thought it very original for a woman to hang out a photographer's shingle, still more peculiar to become a roving photographer, with all these heavy boxes to lug about, but I knew I was strong—what I really wanted to be was a surveyor, but they don't let women do that yet—well, then I didn't miss going to plays at all. I appreciate when people are just themselves, because they don't know any other way to be. Let me tell you about someone I photographed recently on my travels whose uncommon destiny has made her almost as natural as a landscape." She looked about the room. "How long did you say you've all been in California?"

"It's already six months," said Bogdan.

"And in that time has anyone mentioned to you a remarkable woman, Eulalia Pérez de Guillén? Everyone knows about her. No? She once owned the land that's now Pasadena, but that's not why she's famous. It's because this December past she celebrated her hundred and forty-first birthday. Yes. She's back out in the San Gabriel Valley living with one of her great-grandchildren, her children and grandchildren being long dead, but what can someone expect who saw the light in 1735? That's where she was born and she's returned to assisting at the Mission church as she did a hundred and twenty-five years ago when she was a girl. Last month I made a beautiful ambrotype of her in the Mission garden. Can you picture her? Tiny and bent, the head toothless and furrowed and nearly bald—you would have thought at her age she'd be like a bush in that old garden. But she was fidgety as a calf, she didn't even know how to become solemn as people do when they pose for the camera, and I could not resist photographing her good-natured smile."

"*Quelle horreur,*" said Bogdan.

"She just doesn't know how to die," said Ryszard.

"An inspiration to us all," said Mrs. Withington. She finished the glass. "Well, I must be off. I hope to be in Palm Springs in a few days, and from there go out into the desert to photograph some boulders, and after I'm expected in Los Angeles. There a colleague of mine has a studio where I will make my prints and mount them. I should be passing through Anaheim again in three weeks, and if you don't like the picture, you need not pay me. But I know you will like it. You all have such interesting faces."

"DID YOU EVER SEE such a creature?" said Ryszard. "Only in America could you find a woman like that, who thinks women are no different from men, who spends her life giving orders to other people. She *is* a man! That ginger hair and the man's hat and the Colt in its holster and the morning whiskey and all those boisterous opinions. Wonderful, wonderful!"

"I liked her," said Maryna. "She's courageous."

"I liked the story about the woman who was born in 1735," said Barbara.

"I'd like to see the birth certificate," said Julian. "I don't believe a word of it. Nobody lives that long."

"Mama, do you think—"

Maryna reached out for Piotr and pulled him to her lap.

"Of course, she may well be a good photographer," Ryszard conceded.

"She's certainly a good subject," said Jakub. "I'd love to do her portrait, but she seems the last person who could stay in one position long enough for a painter."

"Oh no, oh my," said Cyprian, mimicking the old woman's nasal drawl, "I don't like to pose. I'm a very restless person."

Maryna laughed.

"It will be sweet," said Danuta, "to have a likeness of the girls when they were still little."

Picture-taking transported everyone into the future, when their more youthful selves would be only a memory. The photograph was evidence—Maryna would send one of the prints she'd ordered back to her mother, another to Henryk, another to Bogdan's sister—evidence that they were really here, pursuing their valiant new life; to themselves, one day, it would be a relic of that life at its hard, rude beginning or, should their venture not succeed (after six months on the new Brook Farm, the colony counted $15,000 spent and almost nothing returned), of what they had attempted.

"I wonder if I'm going to be shocked when I see myself in the photograph," said Maryna to Bogdan when they were alone. "I never think anymore about how I look, now that I'm not obliged to care about looking my best."

Bogdan reassured her that she looked no different (not true), that she was as beautiful as ever, as beautiful to him (also not true). But Maryna was not to be soothed. Posing, posing now, left a queer aftertaste. "It felt natural to be photographed as an actress, in the costume of one of my roles. I knew what I was supposed to do for the camera, and how I wanted to look. Today I was posing in a void. Pretending to offer something. Playing at being photographed."

IMPOSSIBLE TO FEEL SINCERE while having one's photograph taken. And impossible to feel like the same person after changing one's name.

Maryna's little son was the first to rename himself. One day in February he announced that he was Peter, as he was called in school. Maryna, startled by the firmness of his childish treble, had replied that this was quite impossible since he'd been christened Piotr and, besides, what patriotic Polish child would wish to have a German name?

"It's not German, Mama. It's American!"

"They can call you whatever they want, but your name is Piotr."

"Mama, you're wrong! Peter's an American name!"

"Piotr, this discussion has ended."

"I'm not going to answer or obey when you call me Piotr," he wailed, and ran into the kitchen to fling himself into Aniela's arms.

And he meant it, having received the command to change his name from the people who lived in a drainpipe he passed every day going to and from school; they were very tiny, no bigger than his hand, a whole family of them, with many children, and he used to stop and chat with them and they would tell him stories, and what he ought to do. One day Miguel came riding by—Miguel was the strongest boy in the class, Miguel came to school on his own pony—and, seeing him squatting at the side of the drainpipe and talking into it, dismounted and stooped beside him; and his Polish schoolmate had told Miguel about the tiny family in there, and also that his name was really Peter. And that was a bond, Miguel and he were really friends now. So he would have to go through with it, much as he was afraid of angering his mother, especially since she wasn't as pretty anymore.

He won the essential part of his struggle immediately: Maryna stopped using his name to address him. She could say "darling" or "little one"—he would answer docilely to endearments—but the inhibition galled her, and she suspected that behind her back Aniela had already yielded to Piotr's strike on behalf of his new name. This went on for two months. Then one morning, as he was leaving for school, Maryna said, "Come back for a minute."

"I can't, I'll be late!"

"Do as you're told."

She motioned for him to sit at the dining table.

"What is it, Mama?" She sat across from him and began stacking the greasy breakfast dishes. "Mama, they'll punish me if I'm late!"

She put her hands in her lap. She cleared her throat. "All right. I give up."

No need to explain. After a minute of silence he pulled his slate out of his schoolbag and laid it on the table.

"You don't want to go to school now?" she said softly.

He extracted a piece of chalk and laid it on the top of the slate.

"And I'll tell your stepfather and the others—what we've decided."

He pushed the slate across the table at her. She wrote his new name on it in large letters and handed it back to him. He nodded solemnly, returned the slate to his bag, and went off to school.

Shortly after Piotr became Peter, he also inherited a bedroom of his own. With the two new dwellings put up by Indian laborers, there were now separate quarters for Cyprian and Danuta and their children, and for Barbara and Aleksander. Each couple had its own hearth, and Julian had built an outdoor oven with the leftover adobe bricks, but everyone continued to take meals together in the dining room of Maryna and Bogdan's house or at a long table in the yard. Communitarians of the mildest stripe, the friends had quickly dismissed Fourier's call for the abolition of marriage—the unseasoned dream of a lifelong bachelor, observed the contentedly married Aleksander—but agreed that the preserving of family feeling did not require the perpetuation of the lugubrious family meal. And they needed to unite after the day's dispersions of interest and labor: accustomed to talking late into the night, as educated Poles had been doing for generations, they balked at keeping farmers' hours, even if it meant having less energy for the next day's work.

They were still far from attaining their ideal combination of mental and physical exertion. But at least the main house had a library now (the last of the books had been unpacked and arranged on newly built shelves) and a proper piano, with a lid and brass legs, which Maryna had ordered from San Francisco (it cost a fortune, seven hundred dollars). No vehicle of nostalgia is more potent than music: they'd not been aware how much they missed Poland until they started making music together after supper. They had longed for music, they had longed for the music of Polish composers, a song by Kurpiński, a waltz by Ogiński, above all for Chopin's nakedly expressive art. But these resounded differently in their outpost at the far edge of the American vacancy, the American sublime. Chopin's polonaises and the mazurkas, celebrated throughout the world as a musical symbol of the Polish struggle for independence from foreign rule, now seemed an involuntary disclosure of the pathos of patriotism. His nocturnes, with their enlivening flow of moods without boundaries, seemed weighed down by the sadness of exile and homesickness.

They could sigh and sigh, had they been willing to surrender to a rueful feeling. Easier, more intimate, to project it onto those they had left behind.

Did you sigh, Henryk, when you received the photograph? I

see it hanging in your consulting room above your desk in a fine walnut frame. Scrutinizing our faces and quaint clothes with your loupe, as you must have done, did you, even for a moment, imagine yourself in the picture? Don't you regret not having come with us? By now the sun would have baked all that gloom out of you. You can still be one of us, dear friend. Come! And, later in the same letter: No, I never have headaches in California. How transforming it is simply to feel well, entirely well. But everyone feels different. I haven't told you that some of us even have new names! Piotr answers only to Peter, Bogdan is addressed by the locals as Bob-Dan, Ryszard has abandoned himself to Richard, and Jakub is toying with Jake. We are all flourishing, and none more than my wonderful little boy. New Piotr, Piotr as Peter, Peter *tout court*—he's another child. Taller, hardier, less fearful. He has made friends. He can ride bareback, as the Mexicans and Indians do. He takes piano lessons from a young lady in the village. Henryk, you would not recognize him! Maybe we should all change our names!

How could she complain, even to Henryk? Tell him that they were not all changed for the better? Cyprian and Aleksander seemed somewhat dulled by chores and cares, and Julian, though as propulsive as ever, was still persecuting poor Wanda. Tell him that she missed female friendship? Wanda could only be an object of sympathy, and Maryna had realized that she hardly liked Danuta and Barbara, who were blessed with amiable husbands, much better; they too were so, so, how would she have said it politely, tractable. Tell him that she was in revolt against the very state of coupledom, her own special marriage excepted? Only importunate, clever Ryszard and gentle Jakub, their bachelors—and dear Bogdan, of course, tense and overprotective as he was—didn't get on her nerves. Tell him that she feared she was becoming stupid, for want of enough mental stimulation, and that it was becoming harder to summon up the forbearance even more essential to life in a community than to a marriage? No, she would tell him none of these things.

But, yes, she told Henryk, she missed him.

Loyalty to an imperiled group enterprise was a virtue rooted in her professional life. You accept the leading role in a new play, you go into rehearsal, and then realize that, for all your efforts and those of the others, it's not working, the play is less good than you thought; but it's not bad, either, and who understands better than you its virtues, you love it as you love a thankless child; and perhaps it will work after all: everyone is trying so hard to salvage it, cuts and changes have been made in the text and livelier staging devised and the scene-painter has a new idea for the last act, it would be wrong to give up hope; and so with your fellow actors you close ranks, you defend it, no, you praise it to everyone outside your community of effort. You say that all is well. There is often no insincerity in this. You believe in what you're doing. You must believe in it.

Whether the others complained in their letters, she could not know. She only knew how much it depended on her to keep them harmonious, roused, forward-minded: she accepted that responsibility. For she had powers she could not relinquish. Hers was still a transforming presence, lit by the afterglow of all the heroic and expressive roles she had played. The woman churning butter and baking bread and guiding Aniela through the preparation of a dinner had once gone bravely, regally, to the beheading ordered by her cousin Queen Elizabeth of England, piously awaited the strangling hands of the demented Othello, hastened to put an asp to her bosom upon learning of the death of Mark Antony, expired in a lonely bedroom, a reformed courtesan, bereft even of her dear camellias. Done all these final things: majestically, poignantly, irresistibly. She might not look exactly as she did in Poland. But coarsening toil had not changed the way she walked, or turned her head to listen, or kept silent, or, most alluringly, spoke. In the vibrant cello voice urging them to remonstrate more forcefully with the neighbors whose cattle had devoured their winter barley crop they heard the cadences of the voice that had proclaimed the excellence of mercy to Shylock, denied the coming of dawn to the fugitive Romeo, raved with Lady Macbeth's guilty dream and Phaedra's lustful longing for her stepson. It would be a long time before these nested auras of nobility faded.

A queen who has abdicated will always be a queen to those who knew her on the throne. But Maryna had vowed not to explain here in California who she had been; who she was now, an immigrant, needed no explanation. Their arrival (their clothes, their nationality, their ineptitude) had caused something of a stir. But after six months, a long time in California, whose plenitudes accommodated an even faster rate of change than the rest of America, their presence was almost taken for granted. The sharpest impression of singularity Maryna could make on the villagers was to turn up with her husband and friends for Sunday Mass at St. Boniface's, overdignified as ever, in a new hat.

They were no longer the newest interlopers; they were almost old-time residents. There were even Chinese now, who did laundry and labored in the fields, as well as more families with American, that is, British yeoman, names. In February, a community of twenty-seven adults and nineteen children calling itself the Societas Edenica moved onto a hundred-acre ranch north of Anaheim. The gossip in the village was of odd sleeping arrangements, strange group calisthenics, a repulsively spare diet. And it seemed that all these novel coercions were designed to generate both holiness and health. The buildings they put up were round, supposedly to promote a better circulation of air. As the circle was perfection in a shape, so health was perfection, the only attainable perfection, in a body and a soul. Alcohol and tobacco were banned, along with meat, any food touched by fire, whatever else would not have been eaten in Eden's garden. Our fallen state, preached their leader, a Doctor Lorenz, is nothing but our departure from the healthy life of our original progenitors. Adam and Eve, you know what that means, said the villagers, who, whenever they found pretexts to trespass on the colony's property, were frustrated never to come upon anyone Eden-naked.

This was a venture in ideal living not at all to Maryna and Bogdan's liking. But the militant regard for health being enforced at Edenica had some attraction for at least two members of their own undoctrinaire community. Danuta and Cyprian had gone off meat before the arrival of the Edenists, and more recently had requested that their food be cooked separately, salt-free, and that bowls of grated apple, chopped almonds, and pounded raisins be set out at every meal for them to fill up on while the others persisted in compromising their digestions with fatty stews and greasy roasts.

Food being a medium of fellowship, it was felt that Danuta and Cyprian had broken some tacit compact with the community by these stark renunciations.

"I expect you'll soon be eating mashed acorns like the Indians," said Alexander.

"*J'apprécie votre sarcasme*," said Cyprian sourly.

"Peace, friends," said Jakub. "As they say in Rome, *vivi e lascia vivere*."

But Danuta and Cyprian refused to consider themselves mocked, and earnestly continued to press their new strictures about diet on the others. Danuta showed Aniela how to make a dessert that Maryna was sure came from the kitchen repertory over at Edenica, a kind of custard of flour and water flavored with strawberry juice.

"Delicious, isn't it?" said Danuta.

"I wouldn't say it's as good as shoofly pie," said Wanda.

"Really?" said Julian. "Not as good as shoofly pie, Wanda. Are you sure?"

"Quite inedible," said Aleksander. "But as you see, *mon cher* Cyprian, I'm eating it."

They had pooled energies, resources, hopes, a relaxed idea of comity and self-fulfillment. They were sure, Bogdan was sure, it did not seem farfetched to suppose, that the farm would soon realize a profit. They had not given up when it was truly hard, in the first months, and by now tasks that had seemed so daunting, from milking the cows to tending the vineyard, had become routine. The dormant vines had begun showing signs of life, and the soil had been turned to get air to the roots. Arriving as late as they had last autumn, they had found only one buyer for their vineyard's yield—they had sold the grapes for two hundred dollars—but there was reason to think they would do much better this year. Lacking the goad of their own incompetence, they had settled into a wry appreciation of the slowness of the agricultural cycle.

How different for their artists: Jakub, who had completed a cycle of paintings on Indian subjects in the last months, and Ryszard, whose writing had produced some extra income for the colony—he contributed two-thirds of the money earned by his newspaper articles on America, now coming out in Poland as a book—had finished enough stories to make another book, was nearly done with a novel set in a mining camp in the Sierras, and had begun in his head a long novel set in ancient Rome in the time of Christian persecutions under Nero. When not writing he was off hunting—the meat-eating majority still depended on his forays—and had recently acquired a steed of his own, a Mexican horse, for which he'd paid eight dollars; overpaid in fact, since these could be had in Los Angeles for five, while an American horse, good for work or carriages, cost anywhere from eighty to three hundred dollars.

It was a three-year-old, dappled grey, rather tall and strong, and ill-natured like most mustangs. Disregarding the advice of neighbors, Ryszard had not trimmed its long mane and over-grown fetlocks: what he wanted was a wild horse that would be tame for him. At first Ryszard could control the animal only when virtually strangling it with his lasso, but a month of patient struggle, during which the horse learned to tolerate being caressed first while being fed, then while being cleaned and brushed, had turned it into the most responsive, spirited animal companion its owner could desire. Ryszard enticed Maryna into the stable to watch him saddling his Diego, as he'd named the horse, and fitting the bridle to its shaggy muzzle.

"And how many pages this morning?"

"Twenty-three. The last twenty-three pages of *The Little Cabin*. I've finished the novel."

"Bravo."

"Finished. Done. And it's good, Maryna, it really is. And what do you think has been spurring me on to work so well?"

"Ah, you want me to guess what I know," said Maryna. "Ambition?"

"I've always been ambitious. Ambition is only one of the four affective passions according to—dare one still invoke his name?—Monsieur Fourier. No, Maryna, it's not ambition."

"Friendship?" She was smiling. "Yours for me?"

"Maryna, really!"

"Family feeling?" she said, patting the mustang's bristling mane.

"It's the passion you haven't mentioned. Or," he added boldly, "have forgotten."

"I haven't forgotten."

"Because I won't let you forget!"

"And because I'm waiting for you to allow this infatuation to subside. That should be easier here."

"So you think I'm in love only with the actress."

"No. I don't think so little of myself."

"Or of me, I trust. Maryna, don't you know I really love you?"

Sighing, she leaned against the mustang's head.

"What are you thinking?" said Ryszard gently.

"Now? I'm going to disappoint you. I was thinking of my son."

MARYNA, MARYNA, began the letter Ryszard slipped in her pocket. Yesterday's conversation in the stable. What must you think of me? Ryszard the lovelorn, Ryszard the graphomaniac— I badger you with my hopes, I am far too caught up in my writing. Even Jakub will turn from a long stint at his easel to shovel manure off the barn floor, whereas I, I seclude myself to write, I gallop off with my gun (which is hardly work for me). You have proposed that this be a time of common purposes, and I stay separate.

It is obvious that I am not cut out to be a farmer. Were you meant to be a farmer, Maryna? To be a materialist, forever bound to the routines of ploughing and profiting? Were any of us meant to be farmers? I confess it makes me groan to see Bogdan sowing corn or pruning the vines, his mobile face with its sarcastic smile habitually at the ready recast in a stern frown of exertion. And you nearby, your translucent stain of discontent gleaming in the California sun. Are our souls being purified by physical labor, as Russian writers preach? We thought we were choosing freedom and leisure and self-cultivation. Instead, we have committed ourselves to day after day of repetitious agricultural duties. And it will always be like this, Maryna. And even when life here becomes less strenuous, as the farm becomes profitable and we can employ local laborers to do most of the work—is that the life we had envisaged? For it is not rest we want, Maryna. Do you really want to rest?

People like us should not *settle* in this country—least of all in a village, I warrant they are all like our prosaic Anaheim, and not in New York or San Francisco either: any of our middle-sized European cities is handsomer and more civilized than an American city will ever be. No, one must stay on the move to have the best that this country can offer. As a hunter does, here where hunting is far more than a recreation: it is a necessity, not only practical but spiritual, a unique experience of freedom. Beyond the boundaries of what is called civilization here, where land is divided up and constitutes private property, lies territory that can only be frequented by those with the skills of a hunter. It starts just beyond our river. There everything is on a scale you cannot imagine—the deer are twice as big as the deer in Poland, the American grizzly bear is bigger, stronger, more ferocious than every European variety of bear. And the sky, Maryna, the sky is even blacker, more filled with stars than it is in our valley; and one has dreams and visions that are twice as large as life. Oh, I shall not conceal it from you, I have drunk a bitter concoction made of jimson weed which the Indians use for their sacred ceremonies. But no drug is needed to be plunged into a Bacchic mood. At the close of a day spent with my hard-featured hunting companions, when we carve up our prey and then recline around a campfire feasting on pieces of pink steaming meat, I feel in savage unity with all of creation. And afterward, in an enchantment of satiety, I crawl into my tent, a piece of canvas hung on some low branches with room under it for one person (there could be room for two), and being alone (alas), fall straight down, as after a draught of laudanum, into sleep.

I have watched you blissful at an incendiary sunset seen from our valley and at the sight of the heaving great Pacific after a gallop to the coast. I promise you an elation no less keen in the high, dangerous mountains. When you are with me, we shall be characters in some romantic opera, I singing the baritone role of an Alpine brigand and you my mezzo inamorata, a princess traversing the mountain on her way to a loveless state marriage, whom I have rescued from the avalanche in which all the other members of her party perished. And if you like, we could go farther, we could descend on the other side, into empty pale land presided over by cacti thirty, forty feet high. Moon country, Maryna. With sand verbena that covers the desert floor in pink. And when night fell, we would ride full tilt against the stars.

I don't plan to introduce you to any of my companions, unless you so desire. But you will not be disappointed if you do meet them. Their life, edged with danger and free of banal conviviality, has bred a remarkable race of solitaries. They will not remind you of our shepherds from Zakopane who, throughout their long months alone in the high Tatras, remain cocooned in the securities of ancestral place, of family, of religion. The American is someone who is always leaving everything behind. And the void this makes in his soul is a matter of astonishment to him, too.

I am thinking of a squatter named Jack Goodyear—don't you like this American name?—with whom I've stayed several times on my longer trips into the mountains. Though by nature he is little inclined toward headwork, his Robinson Crusoe way of life has fostered a touching habit of introspection. I remember once resting on bare planks inside Jack's small hut; it was late in the evening, a long time had gone by without either of us saying anything, and he had just thrown another bundle of dry laurel on the fire. Then without any prologue he broke the silence to tell me that it sometimes seemed to him as though there were two Jacks: one who chopped down trees, hunted the grizzly bear, tended his apiary, hoisted a new roof on his hut, carried a discarded white beehive inside to use as a chair, cooked his cornmeal and doused it with honey; and the other—"By God," he kept interrupting himself, "by God"—the other who was doing nothing but just gazing at the first. He told me this very simply.

Two Jacks. Two Ryszards. Two Bogdans, I do not doubt. And two Marynas, I am sure. Tell me that you don't feel you are acting in a play. Tell me there isn't one Maryna who is kneading dough for bread, washing clothes in the round wooden tub in the yard, weeding the vegetable plots, and the other, standing beautifully tall as only you do, who gazes at herself with amazement and incredulity. Tell me. I'll not believe you.

Maryna, ride with me . . .

MARCH 22. Visit to the dentist, Herr Schmidt. Not incompetent. Upper left molar extracted. Agitated when I awoke. Did I say anything while under the ether? I was having a tender dream about ———. But surely I would have been speaking Polish, and therefore wouldn't have been understood. But what if I just kept calling out his name?

March 23. Copper-colored skin. Cheekbones. Impure thoughts.

March 24. M. doesn't see how much I have to struggle against my natural inertia. Her penchant for exertion has been a good influence on me. What makes me strong is being strong for her.

March 25. We have been captured for all eternity near the house on a sheet of wet glass by an itinerant photographer, who was female, elderly, and quite droll. M. liked her. A diverting occasion for our community, I thought, but for M. it seemed to bring out a kind of foreboding. Or regret—as if we were taking the first step toward accepting the eventual failure of our colony, by making sure that we would have in our possession an image of what we are now.

March 26. I've always had a horror of making myself conspicuous or seeming different from other people. Beset by qualms, I didn't do anything outrageous. I was merely obstinate, absentminded. Only in a theatre did I feel free to pay attention to everything that went on about me. While watching a play, in the company of actors, I found in myself nearly occult states of awareness. I thought I would never marry. I loved but I never wanted to seduce. Then everything became possible with M. She entranced me. She needed me. The sluggish coals of my emotions burst into flame. Can love be founded on adoration, I asked myself. Yes, replied my heart.

March 27. It is so habitual for me to support M. in anything she has wanted to do. For a long time I thought her wanting to come to America a whim. Worse: I feared it was an act of desperation, not thought out at all. So it was my task to make it *mean* something—or something else. I've heard her parroting my ideas to Henryk, about how the noble doctrines of Fourier could be adapted to our venture, almost sentence by sentence. I suppose it didn't matter that I was listening. That an actress is not the author of the play doesn't make the lines any less hers. Gophers have made havoc of the artichoke patch.

March 28. M. still treats P. like a baby. Actresses make willful mothers, smothering and neglectful. Now he's asked for piano lessons. It would be wiser to encourage his interest in engineering. The boy is already too high-strung. Unless he's a future piano virtuoso, which I have no reason to think likely, a passion for music can only strengthen his morbid, effeminate tendencies. Perhaps M. will be less than enthusiastic about these lessons once she realizes that the piano teacher, the pretty daughter of the town clerk, Herr Reiser, is already an object of Ryszard's lighthearted lust.

March 29. They are alike in many ways, M. and Ryszard. I understand, I suppose I envy, the actress, who has permission to flaunt herself in the guise of another. I feel more censorious toward the writer, who believes he has a mandate to say what he himself thinks to the world. But I can't help admiring his self-confidence and his blithe, almost American pursuit of his own happiness.

March 30. The defect of keeping a diary is that I note mostly what ruffles my temper. Tonight I could pen a whole sermon on the ugliness of a loveless marriage. Wanda has taken to wearing her hair pulled back and in frizzed bangs—*le dernier cri*, apparently, among the ladies of the village—and Julian is merciless.

March 31. I try not to be irritable. M. can't imagine I harbor *any* criticisms of her. She thinks of me as an admiring mirror. Perhaps that's her idea, the actress's idea, of a good marriage. But I know my jumble of feelings is what makes me right for her. Only I register her bad behavior as bad, only I see her vulnerability, her dismay, only I know that she doesn't want, really, to be possessed by anyone.

April 1. A day in the fields has left me feeling optimistic. Most of the grafts we did last month have taken, the vines have flowered, the grapes have appeared, and the leaves to protect them. The sandy land *is* fruitful, and we are working more expertly than ever. Ramon, age 17. My senses are sharper here. I cannot control what I feel. I cannot control its reverberations in my flesh and my heart. But I can control what I do. I will not betray M.

April 2. Jacinto, age 25. Curly hair. Scar on his right forearm. White teeth. Calloused hand inside his partly open shirt. The curve of his breast. Standing there.

April 3. This afternoon I rode with Ryszard out to an Indian settlement in the Santa Ana foothills. Packs of scrawny children came running out of the wigwams and a few grey adobe huts thatched with tule reeds—an impression of mournful poverty. An elder ordered some women to serve us bowls of acorn porridge and their jet-black bread made from acorn flour. The dessert was *tuna*, the red fruit of the prickly pear, and the drink was manzanita cider. On the way back, Ryszard and I argued about whether the insensibility of Indians to pain is proof of their inferiority. I said the more one feels, the higher one is racially, culturally. He accused me of the most benighted prejudice. I'm sure he said to himself, a Dembowski *would* think that. Despite everything, I like Ryszard. He is intelligent. He has a healthy nature. How fortunate for me that he can't offer M. the fidelity she requires, or even notice that she minds his trifling with P.'s schoolteacher and Fraülein Reiser.

April 4. Flashes of hope, like flashes of desire. Beginning again. How much must one give up for the privilege of "beginning again"? For more than fifty years Europeans have been saying, If it doesn't work, we can always go to America. Socially mismatched lovers escaping a family ban on their union, artists unable to win the audience they know their work deserves, revolutionaries crushed by the hopelessness of revolutionary endeavor—to America! America is supposed to repair the European scale of injury or simply make one forget what one wanted, to substitute other desires.

April 5. Staszek, Józek. The shepherd boy who gave me the feather. Mrs. Bachleda's grandson. I never anticipated California would be a new theatre of temptations. Indeed, I thought I was leaving these furtive pinings behind in our unhappy country. Instead, it's as if my weakness had flown ahead of me. While we were exploring New York, descending the Atlantic coast, crossing the isthmus, rising up the California coast, dallying in San Francisco, and then entraining for here, these reincarnated phantoms of endangering desire were already waiting for me. And with them a quiet, firm voice that says, as it never did in Poland, why not? You are abroad, no one knows who you really are. This is America, where nothing is permanent. Nothing supposed to have fixed, unalterable consequences. Everything supposed to move, change, be torn down, mix.

April 6. Transfixed this morning by an idyllic scene of comradeship straight out of Whitman's Calamus poems. Joaquin, age 19. Loose cotton shirt, trousers made of the skin of fallow deer. Seated on a tree stump playing a kind of small harp with one string which they call a *chiote*. Sinewy wrists, broad hands. Beside him on the ground, legs akimbo, carelessly leaning his head against Joaquin's thigh, another boy, no more than 15, was singing. His name, I think, is Doroteo. Level marked brows over large eyelids. His fat busy lips. When I asked him to translate the song, he blushed.

> *In the shade of the magnolia I dreamt of you.*
> *When I awoke and found you gone,*
> *I cried myself to sleep again.*

Then I blushed. I wanted to stroke his leg from the knee to the groin.

April 7. It is eighteen months since M. first proposed coming to America. Spring rains are over, we are told. It will be dry until November. Moments of hard doubt when I think of the money (mostly mine but also Aleksander's, his aunt's legacy) slipping through my fingers. I am the only one who thinks about money, and I am the one least prepared, by nurture and temperament, to think about it. The others must be worrying too, but don't dare express their concern, as if they would be impugning my competence. Still, there is reason to be optimistic. I had not fully understood the scope of the depression in the wine industry, which reached its nadir the year before last. Grapes sold for $8 a ton and were sometimes fed to hogs. But prices are rising, they should soon return to what they were before 1873, around $25 a ton. Come this autumn or the next, we could make several thousand dollars.

April 8. Dream about Francisco. His hand on the iron pommel of his saddle. It is natural to be attracted by beauty. M. was so beautiful.

April 9. In the village this morning to have a horse reshod and buy grain for the livestock, I was struck once again by how plain, how meanly utilitarian, the buildings are. One can easily imagine any or all of them being torn down. Conversation about irrigation with that idiot Kohler.

April 10. Humbling experience to be without a past. Nobody knows, or would care if they did know, who my grandfather was. General who? Perhaps they've heard of Pułaski, but that's because he came to America, or Chopin, but that's because he lived in France. In Poland, I congratulated myself that my sense of my own dignity didn't come from my name or rank. I was too different from my family—I had better ideals, other weaknesses. But I was proud of being Polish. And that pride, like Polishness itself, is not only irrelevant here, it is a handicap, for it makes us old-fashioned.

When we first arrived, most of us were disappointed to have only foreigners, instead of real Americans, for neighbors. The more I know the villagers, however, I see that although they still speak German they really are Americans. What is European, indolent, old-fashioned, has no place here. And it seems easier for someone from Europe to become an American than I would have thought. But it will never be easy for Mexicans. Poor Mexicans will always be lowly foreigners to these newly minted Americans, while the few wealthy Mexicans remind me of our gentry back

home—they are valiant, haughty, extravagant, hospitable, cere-
monious, lazy—and destined to be pushed aside by the Americans with their unrelenting practicality and passion for work.
The old California's doom is sealed.

April 11. Billy's the name, says the carrot-haired boy at the
rodeo. What's yours? White teeth, a scar on his forehead. Bob-
Dan, I say. Nice to meet you, Bob. Whinny and plunge of the
horses. Imprecations of the Mexican cowboys digging their
wooden stirrups into the bleeding sides of their broncos. Bellow-
ing of cattle, thrown, pinioned, branded. No, not Bob, I say, Bob
and then Dan. He calls me Bobby.

April 12. I think I have never felt so healthy, so pleased with
myself, so agreeably simplified, as this morning, with the temperature at 85°F by ten o'clock, pitching forkfuls of hay down from
the loft for the horses. Read Pasteur's *Etudes sur le vin* in the
afternoon.

April 13. I decided to have a candid conversation with Dreyfus, the only Jew in Anaheim as far as I can tell and, not surprisingly, the cleverest fellow in the village. He says the only way to
make a go of our enterprise is to start our own wine company. We
must expand or perish.

April 14. Forbidden desire, straining to be liberated by foreignness. The curse on desire. But there is no puzzle about how I
can be so strongly drawn to these boys and wholly in love with M.
Loving her is the one steadiness I have.

April 15. One answer would be to plant other varieties of
grape. From one grape, brought here by the Spanish fathers who
founded the Missions, so many kinds of wine are made. The
liqueurs, the brandy and angelica and sparkling angelica, and the
port and sherry and other sweet wines, uneven though they be,
are acceptable—the *criolla* grape swells with sugar under all this
sun. But the dry wines, the riesling, the claret, being too low in
acid, are flat and dull. Yet everyone drinks them. And not only in
California. The companies here sell more and more on the East
Coast, and even export to Europe. It is entirely possible that wine

will become American, with an American standard of excellence, just as happiness is destined to become American, with an American standard of what it is to be happy.

April 16. Are we fools for coming here? The possibility is not to be excluded. Am I a fool? Complaisant husband, looking the other way while another man courts his wife? But she will not leave me for him. Ryszard is not the man for her. I am not a fool.

April 17. I was born thirty-five years ago, which makes it my birthday *à l'américaine*. Our custom of celebrating birthdays on the day of the saint after whom one is named is unthinkable here, and not just because this is not a Catholic country, with a religious calendar enshrining the most ancient histories and traditions. What is paramount in America is the personal calendar, the personal journey. *My* birthday, *my* life, *my* happiness.

April 18. Two Indian boys playing leapfrog. One with black hair like a horse's mane and filed teeth. 97°. And it isn't summer yet. I should get a book on pig breeding. And one on beekeeping and how to make mead. Talking to people in the village, I gather that these are the businesses that require the least amount of work and bring the best profit: pigs and bees. Mead is very popular here, but they don't make it properly. Julian and I made some, and it seemed very good. However, it would not hurt to have proper recipes.

April 19. I came too late into her life to entertain the fantasy of molding her. I had no aspirations to change her. I loved her exactly as she was. I was an ideal second husband. The husband of a great actress—that was a role I knew how to play. I wanted her to take me for granted, and now I find that I take her for granted, too. But I have never penetrated the innermost recesses of her heart. Odd how confident I am that M. will never leave me.

April 20. Juan María, Doroteo, Jesús.

April 21. Ryszard has proposed to take us, just M. and me, on a two-day trip into the San Bernardinos. I told M. I can't leave the work I'm doing with Aleksander on the stable, but she should go. To be sure, Ryszard may have counted on my refusing.

April 22. M. off before dawn with Ryszard, old Salvador in attendance. Ryszard was armed with his 14-shot Henry rifle, revolver, and bowie knife. Salvador carrying enough weapons for two bandits. M. took a gun, too. At supper everyone seemed subdued, having no one to perform for. Maybe they're all worrying that she will leave *them.* The most distraught was Aniela. How can Madame sleep outdoors, she kept saying. P. asked if his mother's absence meant he could stay up later and practice at the piano. The house felt empty and I went for a long walk around midnight. Away from our settlement, in the immensity and candor of nature, under the boundlessness of the night sky, I was suddenly gripped by a vision of the enormous falseness of human relations. My love for M. appeared to me as a great lie. Equally a lie are her feelings for me, for her son, and for the members of our colony. Our half-primitive, half-bucolic life is a lie, our longing for Poland is a lie, marriage is a lie, the whole way that society is constituted is nothing but lies. But I don't see what I can do with this knowledge. Break with society and become a revolutionary? I am too skeptical. Leave M. and follow my shameful desires? I cannot imagine a life without her. Returning to the house, sitting down to write this, I think once again: the house is empty.

April 23. They returned this evening. M. exuberant, full of stories of what she had seen. She had a nasty injury, the culprit being not some wild beast but a cup of boiling hot tea; the entire palm of her right hand is one suppurating blister. I don't think she discovered she was in love with Ryszard. But how would I ever know if something transpired between them? I have an actress for a wife.

TRAVELING EASTWARD in the direction of the mountains, their horses crossed the wide sandy bed of Anaheim's seasonal river. After all his entreaties, Ryszard was astonished that Maryna had agreed to the excursion. Now he would surprise her, by showing that he did not assume she had conceded anything further by giving him this. Patience was the cardinal virtue of the hunter: he would not press his suit. Nor would he point out what they were seeing. From the vantage point of silence, that would present itself as an intrusion, as if he thought she could not see for herself the herd of Angora goats, the cock pheasants perched on the cactus, the antelope on the hill, the flock of rose-colored turtledoves hovering above. He felt ashamed of his ready spray of words. Words were easy—they flew out of him and filled everything with light. There was no need to talk.

Toward noon they stopped on a high ridge of the San Bernardinos. Salvador pointed to a large black oak on the edge of the glen and shouted something to Ryszard in Spanish.

Ryszard shook his head. *"No quiero oirlo."*

Salvador crossed himself, dismounted, tied up the horses, and began gathering brushwood for a fire.

"What did he say?" said Maryna.

"That a cattle thief was caught up here last summer."

"Right here?"

"Yes."

"And what happened to him?"

Salvador had kindled the fire, and was setting out his tin-ware—saucepan, kettle, dishes, cups—for a light meal.

"He was lynched."

"From that tree."

"I'm afraid so. Yes."

Maryna groaned and moved toward the fire. Ryszard followed her, took a blanket from his saddlebag, and spread it out on the ground for them to sit.

"I won't ask if you're tired."

"Thank you."

"Do you wish you hadn't come?"

"Ryszard, Ryszard, stop fretting about whether I'm glad to be here. And with you. I am."

"Now I know you love me. You said my name twice."

"Yes, as you do." She laughed. " 'Maryna, Maryna!' "

He thought his heart was going to burst with happiness.

"Are you happy, Maryna?" he said gently.

"Ah, happiness," she said. "I think I have a vast capacity for happiness."

It was not the moment to explain to Ryszard her new arrangement with herself regarding happiness and satisfaction. Happiness depended on not being trapped in your individual existence, a container with your name on it. You have to forget yourself, your container. You have to attach yourself to what takes you outside yourself, what stretches the world. The joys of the eye, for instance—she remembered her mad delight the first time she set foot in a museum: it was with Heinrich, Heinrich had taken her to Vienna, she was nineteen and sorely in need of initiation. She was a girl. One of the strengths that comes with being a woman, and older, was that she had less need to share those bright moments of exit from the self. But she had not forgotten, though Ryszard seemed to think she had, the joys of hand and mouth and skin.

Salvador passed them plates of dried biscuits and beef jerky and pint cups of Japan tea sweetened with honey.

Ryszard, grimacing, set his cup down on the blanket and shook out his burning hand. Maryna, he saw, was still holding hers.

"You don't find it too hot?"

Maryna nodded and smiled. "I'm not sure that I don't love you."

Ryszard felt stabbed to the heart. He reached for his cup, still intolerably hot, and quickly let go of it. "Maryna, put down your tea!"

"Perhaps I do," she continued. "Perhaps I could. But of course I feel guilty when I love someone I'm not supposed to love."

"Maryna, let me see your hand."

"When I was nine, right after my father died"—she set

down the cup and shuddered—"I was put in a convent school for a year."

"Your hand."

She extended her hand, palm up. It was dark red. "Salvador!" Ryszard shouted.

"*Señor?*"

"Idiot! Idiot!" He jumped to his feet and got the jar of honey. "Will you let me put this on it?" He saw there were tears in her eyes. "Oh, Maryna!" He bent over her palm, blowing on it and applying the honey. "Does it hurt less?" When he looked up, her eyes were dry and glittering.

"I had a teacher there, Sister Felicyta, whom I realized I loved more than my mother, more than anyone in the world. So I trained myself not to look at her face, ever. She thought I was very shy, or very pious, with my downcast eyes, and all the while I was burning with desire to press my lips to her beautiful face."

"Let me kiss you, Maryna."

"Don't."

"So I will never hold you in my arms? Never?"

"Never! Who knows what that means? What I do know is that the prospect of being in a . . . of having to hide, of having to choose, is unbearable to me. I need my life to be simple."

"You find marriage simple."

"Oh, that's not simple! Bogdan's not simple. But I suppose Bogdan is complexity enough." They sat in silence for a while.

"Maryna?"

She stood. "I'd like to move on."

After they remounted, seeing that she was using her left hand to hold her reins, while holding the right, wrapped in a kerchief, close to her breast, Ryszard took her reins and walked both horses through a stony ravine and up a steep brambly slope. From behind him she was saying something about a special torment that made life difficult for Bogdan, something about not knowing (but she couldn't explain) who he really was. Then they seemed to be arguing, which was the last thing Ryszard wanted to happen, especially after she had virtually promised that she would be his one day.

"If my grandfather had been a staff officer under Napoleon and my wife were my country's national heroine," Ryszard had turned back to say, unworthily, "I suppose I might brood about who I was."

"You're not being as intelligent as you usually are," she had replied coldly.

But she seemed to forgive him as the terrain leveled off and she took back her reins with her left hand and they galloped together for a time, lifting their faces to the radiant sun and a few white smudges of clouds in the faultlessly blue sky, while Ryszard mused on his joy and Maryna's startling little lesson in how to endure pain.

As night fell they camped on the far side of the mountain, and an anxious Salvador served them salt pork and bread on the tin plates, and once again babbled his apologies and excuses. *"Señora, perdóneme, mil disculpas, perdóneme."* His hands were so calloused, he said, he hadn't realized how hot the cups were. *"Ahora no está caliente, señora, está frío!"* Ryszard translated.

"Not the meat, I hope," said Maryna, laughing.

Maryna was as delighted as a child with the bed Salvador made up for her of finely broken twigs of manzanita and ceanothus, spread with layers of dark moss and glossy ferns. Then, leaving Salvador by the fire with his gun, watching over the sleeping Maryna—he'd assured Ryszard once again that no rattlesnake could glide over the horsehair lasso he had laid in a circle around her—Ryszard removed himself from their camp to walk among the moonlit trees and smoke his pipe. The thought of Maryna asleep, under his protection, in the vastness of nature, beneath the boundless night sky, was the fulfillment of an old fantasy—they were two slender arrows passing through the largeness of the universe—and he was gripped by an exquisite sensation of triumph. He loved. He was loved. He was sure of that now. The wind had risen, and the silent forest seemed to thrum and whisper. Then his moment of rapt attention disclosed, to his dismay, to his fear, a sinister rustling noise. It could be, he reminded himself, the sound of ripe acorns breaking loose from their pedicels and rustling through the leaves as they fell to the ground. It could also be the stealthy approach of *Ursus horribilis*, about to jump from behind the tree and tear open his throat before he could utter a cry. And he had left his gun by the campfire. Lashed by fear, all his senses brought him fresh news. He could even detect, among the forest fragrances, a far-off stench of skunk. And the noises—hooting owls and another fainter rustling sound; and then . . . blessed silence, which he greeted with choking relief and gratitude, as if he had received a reassuring message from nature itself. All was well, all would be well. It was not that he entertained any fantasy of being invulnerable, Ryszard was too rational for that. But nothing could rout his immense feeling of well-being and self-approval. Even if my life ended now, he said to himself, I would still think, My God, what a journey I have made.

APRIL 24. Our community is like a marriage, M. says to me today, and suddenly I'm on my guard. I don't mean *our* marriage, she says, laughing. I mean a marriage that's matured by compromises and disappointments and abiding goodwill—obviously, I'm not thinking of Julian and Wanda either! An old dobbin of a marriage, one that the spouses find dispiriting to think will go on forever but impossible to imagine calling off. It's a flash of the old M., the one I love best: restless, scathing, self-critical, autocratic.

April 25. It seems so American that grapevines here are actually bushes. The local people think it most efficient: no fussing with trellises, etc. But all I can think of is: no mutual support, no clinging, no interpenetration. Every vine on its own. Striving, striving, to outdo its neighbors.

April 26. If I find a good book about drying the grapes for raisins, I could put a few thousand dollars into our coffers. This afternoon Julian and I visited two drying houses in the village, both badly operated. Still, the local grapes are far better for raisins than for wine; moreover, the raisins sell much better. Gardiner told me he sold raisins from twenty acres for $8,000. Jacinto's gleaming brown eyes.

April 27. We could try to diversify further. Olives, and oranges, of course, and lemons, pomegranates, apples, pears, plums—all these pay well. Figs too, which are sold loose, rather than, as in Poland, threaded on a long string. It appears the soil is too dry for bananas, and while watermelons grow nicely they are quite useless—too cheap. People also plant a lot of tobacco here, but mainly for their own use. They don't do much sericulture; although silkworms grow fast and the pods are wonderful, I've been told it is "too much work" for the American.

April 28. In Poland I thought that I was what I had to be. America means: one can strive with fate.

April 29. We were awakened during the night by our bed moving across the floor. A "small" earthquake, according to the villagers, and apparently common in southern California, though it is the first we have felt. Both M. and P. said they enjoyed it, M. claiming to have been warned in her dream. Just as she woke she heard the trumpet call from the tower of St. Mary's! P. now lives in hope of a big earthquake, like the one twenty years ago, before the Anaheim colonists arrived.

April 30. Our mare has been bitten by a rattlesnake, but it seems she will recover. As for me, I have been feeling resentful. M. knows I didn't want this. Now I want it more than she does. Perhaps you're having some doubts about your own sincerity, I say caustically. Of what use is sincerity without wisdom, she answers in her most adorable, ripest tones. I am appeased, but not entirely. She thought she was affirming freedom and purity, not a household and housework. I don't think she really wanted a home.

May 1. That I don't feel free to pursue my desire is surely not just because I am abetting the desire of someone else. Even in matters of the senses, I remain an amateur, a dilettante.

May 2. Last week, near Temescal, an Indian laborer entered the privy while it was being used by the rancher's wife and, she claimed, tried to assault her, though her screams brought rescue before "the worst" could take place. The poor fellow was tied up and castrated by the irate husband on the spot, and put in the barn, where he bled to death that night. We heard about it today. It seems vile to think, We didn't *have* to hear this horrifying story.

May 3. Jakub lectures me on the crimes committed here against the Indians. It seems that Indians were actually made slaves here after the Gold Rush, and this went on until about five years ago. He acts as if he were the only one among us with any moral feelings.

May 4. It can fail. But I must not fail. I must not fail M. We don't produce most of what we need. We don't sell most of what we produce.

May 5. 99°. The relentless success of these Californians gets on my nerves. I am bred to a distinctively Polish appreciation of the nobility of failure. (It seems vulgar to succeed, and so forth.) A plague of grasshoppers has descended on our fields.

May 6. Wanda seems unwell and left supper early. Julian said she has a fever. We are all concerned. Danuta, predictably, proposed a diet change, reminding us that when one of the little girls fell ill she'd fed her only fruit and sprouted grains, and within two days her fever had gone.

May 7. Cyprian took me to meet Doctor Lorenz. Slender, pale, with massive eyebrows overhanging penetrating eyes, a patriarchal beard, and a resonant powerful voice. The very model of the leader of a religious sect. Each member of the community has the title of Worker in God's Garden, but I saw that their daily routines include no farmwork—the ranch is tended entirely by Mexican labor—which may explain why the colonists feel in need of several hours of strenuous exercises following their morning prayers. I had a tour of the men's house and the smaller house where the children are lodged. These buildings, like the one where the women sleep, are perfectly round. Wives and husbands are permitted to spend Saturday night together. The principles of the Edenic Diet were explained to me, and we were invited to partake of a vile repast of wheat groats and barley, ground fine, moistened with fruit juice.

May 8. M. tells me that Ryszard asked Julian why he and Wanda don't have a child. It seems, according to Julian, that she can't have children. M. is thinking of starting a crafts school for Indian girls.

May 9. The people who settled Anaheim came here to live better than they had in San Francisco. Our settling here was mere happenstance, and we live worse than we did in Poland. If our community fails, it won't be because of the impracticality of all utopian schemes but because we have renounced too much of what was gratifying. We wanted to create a life, not a livelihood; making money was not, never could have been, our main incentive. It's rankling to know that if we give up, our neighbors will say we didn't work hard enough—that after we planted our crops we expected to sit on the porch or lie in hammocks while things grew. It's not true. If anything, we work harder than they do. But we are distracted. We lack a common sense that comes naturally to them.

May 10. I rode alone to Anaheim Landing, almost twenty-six miles there and back, and felt much the stronger for it. One patch of shore was strewn with iron pyrites—fool's gold they call it here—and I filled a pouch with it for P.

May 11. Others have failed before us. Brook Farm. The Fourierist colony that Kalikst Wolski founded in La Réunion, Texas. We knew that. Indeed, it was while we were making our own plans for emigration that I read Wolski's rueful account of his venture, published after he and his friends had returned to Poland. But even now I think we were right not to be discouraged by another group's failure to sustain a cooperative community along Fourierist lines here in America. If everyone were so prudent, nothing would ever happen. It would be like losing faith in marriage because of Wanda and Julian. One has the right to say, *My* marriage will be different.

May 12. Perhaps our venture will seem very Polish. I know the reputation we have abroad among those sympathetic to our nation's tragic history. That we lack political wisdom—look at our insurrections, which never had any chance of success. That we are gullible—Napoleon had no trouble convincing us that our nation's legions must shed blood for him; it was enough for him to wave the White Eagle in front of our noses, and off we rode into Russia in 1812, my grandfather in the lead. That our proneness to enthusiasm is childish, incapacitating; certainly not compatible with good management, cleverness, discipline, moderation, and other qualities necessary in the coming giant struggles of all nations for survival in an era of industrialization and militarism. That we can always be counted on for gallantry and acts of personal courage, but that there is a certain conceit in our high-mindedness. The most stinging charge: that we are a nation of dilettantes.

May 13. Poland is full of monuments. We commemorate the past because the past is a fate. We are natural pessimists, believing that what has happened will happen again. Perhaps that is the definition of an optimist: someone who denies the power of the past. The past is not really important here. Here the present does not reaffirm the past but supersedes and cancels it. The weakness of any attachment to the past is perhaps the most striking thing about the Americans. It makes them seem superficial, shallow, but it gives them great strength and self-confidence. They do not feel dwarfed by *anything*.

May 14. About five o'clock this afternoon Wanda attempted to hang herself in the barn. She failed to secure the rope properly to the beam and it must have held for only a moment after she jumped off the ladder, but the fall tightened the noose—she would have choked to death in a few minutes had Jakub not been upstairs in his eyrie, heard the crash, and arrived in time to pull the ladder off her and undo the noose and run for help. We carried her unconscious to our house and I rode to the village to get Higgins, who has made a poultice for the bruises on her neck, set her broken arm, and given her some chloral hydrate. It's two in the morning; he has just left. Of course, she must stay here for several days. M. is still with her. Aleksander and Barbara have taken Julian in for the night. He was making a spectacle of himself outside the house, weeping and shouting that he was going to kill himself too, that was the only thing that would satisfy everyone, only *he* wouldn't botch it. But now, according to Barbara, he only sits with his head in his hands. M. has forbidden him to come near Wanda.

May 15. Wanda is still in great pain, unable to eat or even drink. Higgins, who came by today, says she is doing well, and urges us to keep her in bed for a few days. No one knows what to do. Julian is contrite, but how long will that last? "I know I'm not intelligent" was all she managed to say to me in a hoarse whisper. It is all so pitiable, but sordid and lowering, too. She has been pleading with M. to let Julian visit her.

May 16. We have almost as much reason as Julian to feel remorseful. Living in community means assuming responsibility for others, not just for oneself and one's family. Everyone disapproved of how Julian treated Wanda; as a community, we should have reined him in.

May 17. Wanda has returned to Julian. After she left the house, M. was almost in tears. Now she is irate. I remind her, no one can know what goes on inside someone else's marriage.

May 18. Since Julian and Wanda are no longer coming to meals, M. has told Aniela to bring them their food. When we visited them this evening, Wanda spoke of an attack of nerves, probably brought on by hard work, and Julian agreed that she had been working too hard.

May 19. Julian and Wanda will return to Poland at the beginning of next month. What has happened is so appalling that no one dares to urge them to stay, although, God knows, it is unlikely to go better between them when they are home. Julian will have a new reason to blame Wanda, that they have left their friends, abandoned the great adventure, given up America, that he has been disgraced by her weakness. M. is very sad. Jakub may take their house. Ryszard prefers to remain in the barn. Nothing else has changed, but everything has changed, I can feel it. We are going to fail.

May 20. I don't feel like writing anything this evening.

May 21. Nor today.

May 22. In America, everything is supposed to be possible. And everything *is* possible here, abetted by the American inventiveness and the American talent for desecration. America lived up to its part of the bargain. The fault, the failure, is ours.

May 23. Dinner today was acrimonious. Barbara mentioned hearing from a neighbor that there is a sick child at Edenica who is slowly starving to death on a diet of grated apple, rice, and barley water, and that no doctor has been summoned to visit her. Danuta and Cyprian insist there is a campaign to vilify the colony.

May 24. Taking down a dead tree near the barn with Aleksander. At one end of the crosscut saw, I lost the rhythm and the blade buckled. In America it is hard to think that failure has its nobility.

May 25. Don't wait to be a setting sun. (I have read this maxim somewhere.) Prudent people abandon things before being abandoned by them. Wise people know how to make every end into a triumph.

May 26. It can't simply be that we had no experience: neither did the Germans who came to tend vineyards twenty years ago, who included an engraver, a brewer, a gunsmith, a carpenter, a hotel keeper, a blacksmith, a dry-goods-store owner, a hatter, two musicians, and two watchmakers. Surely we were no less capable of learning what was needed to make our venture a success. But their primary purpose was to succeed as farmers. We were willing to be farmers, in order to have a quiet rural life.

May 27. Argument with Danuta and Cyprian. The little girl at Edenica has been taken by the village authorities, and formal charges of endangering the life of a child brought against Lorenz. He is to appear in the village court next Monday. Danuta and Cyprian assure us that he will be exonerated. M. particularly loving this evening. Sleeping now.

May 28. I rode to the mountains this morning and came back at dusk. About fifty miles. I didn't feel tired at all.

May 29. Meeting to decide what to do. Danuta and Cyprian want to continue. Jakub says he is willing to go on, and, whatever happens, he wants to stay in America. Barbara is very distressed by a letter from her mother—her father is ill and not expected to live long—but she and Aleksander are not considering making a trip back home, since they probably could not reach Warsaw in time. Aleksander has already assured me that the dismay he has expressed about our prospects does not mean that he regrets joining our venture, and I want to believe him. It is agreed we will continue until October and the vintage, and see if we can sell the grapes at a good price. M. says she could raise some money to keep us together until the farm becomes profitable by going back on the stage for a while.

May 30. 97° at noon. I should not like to think I am pushing M. back on the stage, to have an excuse for giving up our life here, which we will call an adventure, an interlude. And then I think: But she does want to go.

May 31. I suppose it's worth noting that the charges against Lorenz have been dropped. Apparently the community pledged a substantial sum to the building fund for the new school. Saw Doroteo admiring a straw hat in the window of a store in the village. He showed me that he had 15 cents—the hat cost "two bits," he said, California(?) slang for 25 cents—and asked me to buy it for him. Feelings of shame.

June 1. We saw Julian and Wanda off at the depot this morning. They board the transcontinental express in San Francisco tomorrow. Their ship leaves New York for Bremerhaven in ten days.

June 2. I am plagued with useless questions. What moves us to take one direction in life and not another? How did it become inevitable that we would travel to California and not another place? Found Doroteo in the kitchen, trying to make himself understood by Aniela. Asking if we need an extra field hand. Wearing the hat.

June 3. A day of idleness and conversations about our future. Barbara received another letter from her mother: her father has died.

June 4. Barbara and Aleksander took me aside after supper. They have decided to return to Poland sometime this summer.

June 5. Danuta and Cyprian have announced their intention to remain in California: they will be moving to Edenica. M. remonstrated with them, to no avail. There's no arguing with fanaticism. Clearly, this folly has been in the making for a long time. And Lorenz's preposterous community has a better chance of surviving than ours had. Maybe we weren't radical or eccentric enough. Ay, Doroteo.

June 6. In retrospect, it is easy to say that we were bound to fail, were naïve, should have known: European intellectuals who thought they could be pioneers, and so forth. We are hardly the first and surely not the last to believe in the possibility of a better life, perhaps on foreign territory, where, one has been told, a fresh start is being made. Those incapable of any idealism will heap scorn upon us. But there is nothing shameful in wagering on our better nature. It would be a poorer world if no one ever felt like us again.

June 7. Jakub left today for New York. In farewell he presented M. and me with three paintings that he thinks the best of the work he has done here. A small portrait of two sad heads, a young woman and a bearded man: Jessica and Shylock. Full-length portrait of M. seated, reading. A scene in Los Nietos: a Mexican woman with a tumult of small children at her knees hanging long strips of jerked beef on a sort of clothesline running between a pair of eucalyptus trees. The paintings are splendid. M. is despondent over Jakub's departure.

June 9. M. is engaged with Aniela in a ferocious bout of housecleaning. She says she feels very calm. I must talk to August and Beate Fischer.

June 12. M. and Ryszard and I rode out this afternoon to Anaheim Landing to eat freshly caught flounder at the tavern there and watch the sun set over the ocean. Purged of wanting something from this beautiful setting, we felt almost as we did when we first arrived, full of euphoric appreciations. On the eve of departure, we behaved like newcomers. Or future tourists. So final and vast and indifferent did the Pacific appear, it felt as if one could not go farther than here, that one could only go back, retracing one's steps. But of course that is an illusion.

June 13. It wasn't a new life M. wanted, it was a new self. Our community has been an instrument for that, and now she is bent on returning to the stage. She will not consider going back to Poland, she says, until she has shown what she can do before the American public, and dares me to cite all the obstacles that lie between her and stardom in America.

June 15. M. getting ready to go to San Francisco. As soon as she is settled, P. and Aniela will join her.

June 16. The Fischers, well aware of all the improvements we've made on the property, including two new dwellings, say they are willing to buy back the farm for $2,000 less than I paid them for it in December. I shall stay to look around for other offers.

June 17. Had any of us really taken in the volatility of the economy here? Or how much work there was to running a farm? Maybe we should have gone to the South Seas.

Seven

IT FELT LIKE an escapade; like leaving home; like telling lies—and she would tell many lies. She was beginning again; she was rejoining her destiny, which conferred on her the rich sensation that she had never gone astray.

Maryna arrived in the city in late June. Her skin had forgotten San Francisco's brisk maritime climate, she had let slip from her mind the noble bay and ocean views, fog permitting, from the top of the steep streets in the heart of the insouciantly planned city, but she recalled every detail of the wide, pillared entrance to the building below Nob Hill on which all her desires were trained.

Bogdan had arranged for Maryna to stay with old Captain Znaniecki and his wife. A respectable woman temporarily severed from her family would hardly want to live on her own. The Znanieckis had been chosen because they were kindly and protective, and because the Captain had married an American, so Maryna would not be speaking Polish all the time. Further, Znaniecki, a senior surveyor and title searcher with the Land Office, apparently knew everybody—from members of the Bohemian Club to the governor of the state—and it would take concerted lobbying to secure an audition with the formidable Angus Barton, the California Theatre's manager in charge of the stage. The morning after her arrival, Maryna had walked over to Bush Street and slipped into the theatre. Like a gladiator whom bravado and fear have lured to the last row of the empty stadium the day before the game, high above the arena's neatly raked, unbloodied sand, Maryna entered one of the boxes for a view of the red velvet curtain and the width of the peacefully darkened stage. But the stage was not dark: a rehearsal was under way. A tall, stooped man dressed in black had bounded from his seat in the tenth row and was rushing down the aisle: she wondered if he could be Barton. "Don't tell me you'll be 'all right' this evening," he shouted at one of the actors. "If there's anything I *hate*, it's that. If you're ever going to be 'all right,' you can be 'all right' *now*." Yes, that must be Barton.

The problem, as she confided in a letter to Henryk, was that she was rarely alone. Word of her arrival had spread (but how could she go anywhere in the world there were Poles and remain incognito?) and everyone in San Francisco's Polish community wanted to be invited to meet her. It was difficult to stoke the banked fires of ambition and the fear of failure while being lapped by the effusive adoration of her uprooted compatriots. And then in the evening only Polish was spoken, though Captain Znaniecki, a refugee from the wave of slaughter and arson incited by Metternich (and, horrifyingly, carried out by Polish peasants) which had decimated the liberal, insurrection-minded gentry and intelligentsia of the Austrian part of Poland thirty years earlier, was as engrossed by the politics of his adopted country as by the catastrophes that punctually befell his homeland. He called himself a Socialist—while telling Maryna he suspected that Socialism had little future here in America, where the admiration of the poor for the rich seemed even more unassailable than the fealty enjoyed by monarchs and priests in Europe—and took it on himself to elucidate for her the difference between the two American parties, but in the end Maryna understood little more than that the Republicans wanted a strong central government and the Democrats a loose, federal union of the states. She supposed these party matters must have been easier to grasp in antebellum times, before the slavery issue was settled, when no right-thinking person could have failed to be a Republican; it was unclear to her what Americans were quarreling about now. One evening Znaniecki invited her to hear "the Great Agnostic," Ralph Ingersoll, who was drawing huge crowds in San Francisco with his atheistic sermons. Maryna was impressed by the responsiveness of the audience.

She had interrupted the accumulations of approval that embolden a performer, with what consequences to her art Maryna had now to determine. I adore recklessness, she wrote to Henryk, and wondered if she was telling the truth.

She left the Znanieckis, secluding herself from her fawning compatriots in furnished rooms half a neighborhood away. By pawning all her jewels, none of them worth much in dollars, she would have enough to live on, very frugally, for two months. She required solitude to reconstruct the instincts, the technique, the dissatisfactions, and the taste for effrontery which had made her the actress she was. The art of walking, the effortlessly upright carriage and certainty of step, needed no refurbishing. The art of thinking only of herself, essential to true creation—that she could only recover alone.

Now there were only herself and this city, herself and her ambition, herself and the English language, this cruel master she would subdue and bend to her will.

"Will," said Miss Collingridge. "Not *weel*."

She had found Miss Collingridge by crossing the sloping wooden floor of her parlor and looking out the bow window, a volume of Shakespeare pressed to her bosom. Gazing dreamily into the street while reciting to herself from *Antony and Cleopatra*, she became aware that a short plump woman with corn-colored hair topped by a large straw hat was staring up at her. Involuntarily, Maryna smiled. The woman clapped her hand to her mouth, then took it away slowly; smiled; hesitated a moment; flung herself into a cartwheel (her cape went swirling); and walked on.

They met again a few days later, when Maryna had let herself out in the afternoon for a stroll in the Chinese quarter—the apartment was a few blocks from Dupont Street—after eight hours of studying and declaiming. She had turned into a lantern-hung alley, drawn by the sinuous racket of music and voices shrilling over the gilded balconies of teahouses; through the open doors of the shops adorned with pennant flags beckoned a bright disorder of carved ivories, red lacquer trays, agate perfume bottles, teakwood tables inlaid with mother-of-pearl, sandalwood boxes, umbrellas of waxed paper, and paintings of mountain peaks. Sauntering beside her among the faster-gaited coolies in blue cotton tunics were several gentlemen in lavender brocade coats and puffed silk trousers, their long queues braided with strands of cherry-red silk, and coming very slowly behind her—Maryna stepped aside to admire them—two women with beautiful sleek heads and jade bracelets falling over their hands, each leaning on an attendant maid; her gaze dropped casually below the hem of their sumptuous robes to the three-inch-long stumps shod in gold-embroidered silk, and before she could remind herself that she'd once read about the custom in prosperous Chinese families of breaking the bones of their small daughters' feet and keeping the toes tied back against the heels until the girls were fully grown, her stomach heaved and her mouth filled with acrid phlegm. The shock had gone straight to her innards.

"Are you ill? Shall I run for a doctor?" Someone was at her side as she held back a faint. It was the young woman whose eyes she had met from her window the other day.

"Oh, it's you again," said Maryna wanly. Struggling to contain another surge of nausea, she smiled to see the galvanizing effect this greeting had on her rescuer, who darted into a shop and emerged with a fan of white feathers, which she waved energetically at Maryna's face.

"I'm not ill," said Maryna. "It's that I just saw two Chinese ladies who— two women with—"

"Oh, the little-foot women. It gave my stomach a turn too, the first one I saw."

"How kind of you to— very kind," said Maryna. "I'm quite recovered now."

By the time the young woman had walked her home, each had learned all she needed to know about the other to feel they were destined to be friends. Why should I have been looking out the window at that exact moment, she wrote Henryk. And why should I have smiled at her? There is something a little romantic about it. And I had not yet heard her silky contralto or her admirable enunciation! Well, there it is, dear friend. The first *coup de foudre* I have experienced after a whole year in America is for a bossy, hoydenish girl who wears silly hats and shapeless serge capes and tells me that she keeps, for a household pet, a full-grown young pig. But you already know how I can be seduced by a mellifluous voice.

Maryna's new friend had commended her mastery of English vocabulary and grammar, and ventured to say that this was a disinterested, professional judgment. Miss Collingridge—Mildred, she said shyly, Mildred Collingridge—was a speech teacher. She gave elocution lessons to the rich wives in the new mansions on Nob Hill.

Maryna had told her that she had given herself two months, no more, to prepare for the audition. She would show this Mr. Barton what she could do.

"Mister," said Miss Collingridge. "Not *meester.*"

Diving into Maryna's employ for the pittance gratefully offered (Maryna could not afford a penny more), she came each morning at eight o'clock to Maryna's lodgings to work with her on the roles she was relearning in English. Seated side by side at a gate-leg table near the parlor window, they went at the lines a word at a time, and, when vowels had been hammered and consonants chiseled and an entire passage polished to the satisfaction of both, Maryna marked her play script for pauses, stresses, breathing marks, aids to pronunciation. Then she would rise and pace and declaim, with Miss Collingridge remaining at the table and reading (in the flattest of tones, as Maryna had instructed her) the other roles. It was never her tutor who ended their long days together: Maryna had found a partner in work as tireless as herself. But sometimes, at Maryna's insistence, they would break for a stroll. Maryna had not realized, while she was letting herself be pacified by rural austerities, how much she had missed the pulse and perfume of city life.

"City," said Miss Collingridge. "Not *ci-ty*."

Captain Znaniecki came often in the early evening to bring covered platters of the good Polish dishes he had taught his wife to cook and to see how Maryna was getting along, and when she told him about Miss Collingridge, he said: "Dear Madame Maryna, you don't need any professor. Pronounce the words just as they are written, as you would pronounce them in Polish—that's more than good enough, and you'll only spoil the shape of your mouth or harden your voice trying to make impossible or harsh sounds. And above all, don't try to pronounce the *t-h* as they do, for you'll never manage it. Plain *t* or *d* are far more pleasant to the ear than their lisping *th*—and besides, I assure you, Americans are charmed by foreign accents. The worse they think your accent, the better they'll like you."

He had said she could never learn to pronounce English correctly. What if he was right? She would become a sort of freak, to be applauded because she was ridiculous rather than wonderful. How then could she ever represent something ideal as an artist? But she would not do what he advised.

Over and over she practiced the infernal *th*—impossible to place her tongue so as to form the sound without first halting the flow of a phrase. Perhaps one needs a pair of American dentures, she joked with Miss Collingridge. She had seen a large sign at the corner of Sutter and Stockton: DR. BLAKE'S INDESTRUCTIBLE TEETH.

"Teeth," said Miss Collingridge. "Not *teece*."

Each word was like a small, oddly shaped parcel in her mouth. Theatre, thespian, therefore, throughout, thorough, Thursday, think, thought, thorny, threadbare, thicket, throb, throng, throw, thrash, thrive . . . That, that, that. This, this, this. There, there, there.

Besides Miss Collingridge the only person Maryna had seen gladly in the first weeks in San Francisco was Ryszard. But in the end she had to send him away.

Ryszard had left Anaheim before she went north. He had been waiting for her when she arrived. On the Fourth of July, they listened to vehement oratory and music and watched the parading and the fireworks and the firemen rushing by in their red wagons to put out the many fires. Another day they hired a four-wheeled stanhope for an afternoon's drive along the ocean shore. She felt drawn to him. They held hands. Their hands were damp. She felt happy, and surely that was part of being in love. She was no longer the head of a clan, temporarily neither a wife nor even a mother—not responsible for others; free to act solely for herself. (Had she ever done that?) But having for a time forgone both husband and child, did she want to assume the obligations of a lover?

All she wanted was to think about the roles she was preparing.

Ryszard suggested they go to the theatre. "Not yet," she said. "I don't want to be influenced by anything I see here and think, Oh, this is what an American actor does, or what an American audience applauds. To find what is deepest in my own talent I have to look for everything within myself."

Ryszard was enchanted to see her molting back into the imperious artist. "It has never occurred to me," he said humbly, admiringly, "to suppose I should do without the inspiration to be found in the books of other writers."

"Oh, dear Ryszard, don't apply what I say to yourself," she said grandly, tenderly. "I must be concentrated. It's the only way I know how to be."

"It is your genius," he said.

"Or my handicap." She smiled. "I'll admit that I miss going to the theatre."

The next evening Ryszard took a box at the China Theatre, on Jackson Street, a bluntly colored two-story building with a tiled roof upturned at the corners. After the first clang of gongs and cymbals from the shirtsleeved orchestra at the rear of the stage, as one, two, three, eventually some twenty brightly encumbered actors surged into view through a flap of cloth on the left and began shouting in falsetto voices at one another, Maryna tugged at Ryszard's jacket like a child. Then something transpired, some lurch of story, for suddenly six of the actors dashed away through the opening, similarly draped, on the right.

"Brilliant, isn't it?" said Ryszard. "No entrances and exits to decide—actors always come on at a trot from the left and go off at the same velocity on the right. No character to construct out of one's inner resources—*that* one is a man of valor because he has painted a white mask on his face and *that* one a cruel man because he has painted his face red. No concealment of the mechanics of spectacle—when a property is needed, someone brings it on the stage and hands it to the actor; when a costume needs adjusting, the actor stands a little apart from the others and the dresser arrives to fix the costume. No—" Why am I chattering like this, Ryszard admonished himself, when she can see everything I'm seeing, and more?

At the tumblers and the pasteboard lions and dragons Maryna clapped her hands gleefully. "I could sit here all night!" she exclaimed, she exaggerated. "I want it to go on forever." Ah, said Ryszard to himself, it's still all right.

The next morning Miss Collingridge was taking her pig, stricken with a stomach ailment, to a veterinarian; she'd told Maryna she might not arrive for their work together until the late afternoon. Seizing on the time freed by this happy misfortune to propose, exceptionally, a daytime excursion, Ryszard came to fetch Maryna for a ferry ride around the Bay with a stop in Golden Gate Park. She was still thinking, she told him, about the glorious artifice of last night's entertainment.

"There is another Chinese theatre here I wish I could show you," said Ryszard. "But it has only a pit with benches and standing places, there are no boxes for ladies, and the night I went it was packed and the stuffiness and heat were unbearable, the audience numbering, besides Chinese men, quite a few louts and, as I can testify, pickpockets. The interest of the experience (no, I lost only two dollars and my handkerchief) is that they do neither opera nor circus. The stage is much smaller than where we were last night, so I was prepared to see a simpler pageant. You know, one of those plays in which the sun emerges, followed by a dragon, the dragon tries to swallow the sun, the sun resists, the dragon flees, and then the sun performs a dance of victory, which is rapturously acclaimed by the audience. Not at all! *Loin de cela!* To my surprise, everything was quite compatible with reality."

"I should like to know what you mean, dear Ryszard, by reality."

"First of all," said Ryszard, "the plot of the drama I saw. Of course I didn't understand a word of what was said, but the story seemed clear. It concerned a writer who was hopelessly in love, well perhaps not altogether hopelessly, with a beautiful lady much wealthier than himself."

"And married, no doubt."

"Happily, not. No, the lady was quite free, except for the impediment of their difference of fortune, to return the writer's love."

"Ryszard"—Maryna laughed—"you are making this up."

"No, I swear I'm not."

"And did she give herself to the impecunious writer?"

"Ah, that's what made the drama I saw that evening so much like life. The actors walked back and forth, arguing with one another, some even jumped up and down, but in the end there was neither a marriage nor a funeral. Apparently, to the logical Chinese mind, it makes no sense for a story that unfolds over several months—even years—of its protagonists' lives to be represented in one evening. No, a play ought to last as many months or years as the story it tells. Whoever wishes to follow, let him come again."

"And how do you—I'm asking the writer—how do you think the play ends, when it does end?"

"I think that, since in China events occur which according to our conceptions are exceedingly improbable, the lady will bestow her love on the penniless writer."

"*Do* you?"

"However," he continued, "the laws of dramatic suspense require that the courtship take a very long time."

"Are you sure? Perhaps you're being pessimistic."

"It's a month since I saw my episode. I presume that the enamored writer has not yet succeeded in winning the hand of the comely 'Flower of Tea'—"

"Ryszard—"

"But he may have already won over several influential relatives who have promised to plead his suit." He smiled gravely. "You see how patient I am."

"Ryszard, I want you to go somewhere else while I prepare for the audition."

"You are sending me away," he groaned.

"I am."

"For how long? Is it like the Chinese play? Weeks? Months?"

"Until I summon you. If I'm successful, I shall welcome you back."

"And then what happens?"

"Ah, you want to know the end," she cried. "You cannot be both a character in the play and its author. No, you must wait in suspense. As I do."

"What suspense? How can *you* fail?"

"I can fail," she said solemnly.

"If Barton turns you down, he's an idiot and doesn't deserve to live. I shall come back and kill him."

She repeated this to Miss Collingridge, expecting to make the young woman laugh.

"Idiot," said Miss Collingridge. "Not *eediot.* And kill, not *keel.*"

"Miss Collingridge predicts," she told Ryszard, "that it is my destiny to be loved by the fair sex." Ignoring Ryszard's grimace, Maryna went on: "And you should be happy about that. For so far, I must tell you, no Yankee has yet looked me over, none has paid me a compliment. But since, if one is to believe the saying here, a woman's will is God's will, I am content."

A few days later Ryszard left the city, choosing to stay away from Maryna in the company of a pair of elderly Polish émigrés, veterans of the 1830 Uprising against Russia, who lived in Sebastopol, a village about forty miles north of San Francisco. It is perfect here for writing, he told her in his first letter, for I have absolutely nothing else to do; the two old soldiers will not let me meddle with the household chores. I am writing many things, he told her in his next letter, among them a play for you, which, as you needn't remind me, I once promised, oh it seems long ago, I would never attempt. On some mornings, rereading it at my table, I think it quite splendid. Will you think so, too? Maryna, my Maryna, comely Flower of My Heart, I count on your covering the poverty of my play with your royal cloak.

She wrote him, asking his advice about what she should propose to Barton for her opening vehicle. She would much rather do Shakespeare (Juliet or Ophelia) but thought it wiser to start with a play whose original language was not English: her accent would grate less. *Camille*, perhaps. Better still, *Adrienne Lecouvreur*; playing an actress, at the worst she would appear to be . . . an actress. The play was popular on American stages and a favorite with visiting European stars, starting with Rachel herself, who had opened her only American tour with it in New York twenty years ago.

Camille, wrote Ryszard. It is a much better play. If you'll permit me, I've always thought *Adrienne Lecouvreur* rather maudlin and shrill. You must know that, Maryna, no matter how much you relish the part. I will confess that the ending leaves me quite dry-eyed, except when you do it. And that's because, etc., etc.

She asked Bogdan's opinion, too. *Adrienne Lecouvreur*, replied Bogdan. Definitely *Adrienne*. His letters from Anaheim were always laconic. They contained reassuring news about Peter, discouraging news about efforts to sell the farm, but little of Bogdan's own state of mind. She was grateful that he never made her feel uneasy about leaving him with the child. She would send for Peter and Aniela soon—as soon as she'd had the audition. She had to devote all her time to preparing. She needed to be entirely single-minded. She wanted to experience herself as completely alone. It occurred to her that she might never be alone again.

"NOW, YOU mention genius," said Angus Barton, although Maryna hadn't mentioned it. "And genius speaks in every tongue, I'm not saying that isn't true. And I'm not saying I don't believe you weren't some kind of star in your own country, all your compatriots here in San Francisco who have been writing me letters and coming by the theatre and imploring me to see you and leaving me articles about you, which of course I can't read, they couldn't be making it all up, could they, but this is America, and you say you want to act in English even though it makes no sense for a foreign actress to come here and not act in her own language, since our public is used to that, and think they do understand as long as they know the story, though I hold to the old-fashioned idea that when it comes to a play the audience ought to understand the words. And I'm not saying that the public in America hasn't opened its arms to foreign actors, but they come from countries that Americans like the sound of, like France and Italy, and I'm afraid your country isn't one of those, and they come here on a tour, with everything nicely prepared, and everyone eager to see them, and then they go home. And I'm not saying that I won't give you an audition, if only to get your friends to stop badgering me, I'm willing to do that, but you must agree I can be honest with you, I shall criticize you frankly, I'm not going to mince my words."

"Yes," said Maryna.

"And I'm not saying I think it's a complete waste of my time for me to give you an hour on Wednesday morning, sorry that I can't spend any more time with you now, I have an appointment in a few minutes, but I don't want you to get your hopes up, you seem like a nice woman, very dignified, with your mind all made up, I like that, I like a woman with spark, a woman who knows how to stand up for herself, but you have to bend in this country too, everyone does. And I'm not saying that you've not heard this before, but theatre has to be good business, people here don't go so much for highfalutin ideas of theatre such as they keep on with in Europe. And I'm not saying that you don't know that, but what I see before me is a lady, and perhaps back in your country a refined woman like yourself would make a great impression, you can impress the public with that here too, but they don't want a steady diet of lady, not even our rich folk in San Francisco, and we have plenty of them now with all the Comstock bullion, like the late Mr. Ralston who built this theatre and the Palace Hotel too, he liked a lot of fancy European things. And I'm not saying that they're just a bunch of snobs living in the mansions on Nob Hill, who all take boxes at the California, because rich people want to think they have culture, that's why the city has so many theatres, and there are quite a few Jews in society here, and I guess they're the most cultivated, but you can't play only to them. So I'm not saying that San Francisco doesn't have some people who know what they're seeing, when Booth does a turn here or one of the big stars on tour from Europe comes through, all of them hoping to play at the California, since everyone knows that after Booth's Theatre in New York it's the best theatre in the whole country, and that makes our public extra hard to please, especially the newspapermen here, who are just waiting to puncture the balloon of some big foreign reputation. But I'm not saying that ordinary people don't go to the theatre too, and if you don't please them it doesn't work at all. They have to cheer and laugh and poke each other in the ribs and cry. I wonder if you could do comedy roles. No, from the look of you, probably not. Well, that settles it. You have to make them cry."

"Yes," said Maryna.

He looked at her sharply. "I don't discourage you, or disarm you, with all this prattle?"

"No."

"Ah, I see. You are proud, you are confident. You are probably intelligent. Well," he snorted, "that's no asset for an actor."

"I have been told that before, Mr. Barton."

"I suppose you have."

"But you could be more condescending. You could have said to me that intelligence is no asset for a woman."

"Yes, I could have said that. I shall hereby make note not to say it to you." He stared at her with curiosity and irritation. "I tell you what, Madame I-can't-pronounce-your-name. Let's get this over with. Are you prepared to do something right now?"

Of course she was not. "Yes."

"And we'll part as friends, right? No hard feelings. And it will be my pleasure to invite you to my box any evening this week."

"I shall not waste your time, Mr. Barton."

Barton slapped the desk. "Charles! Charles!!" A young man peeped through the door. "Go run over to Ames's office and tell him to hold tight, I won't be free for another half hour. And send William to put some lamps on the stage, and a table and chair."

"A chair is enough," said Maryna.

"Forget the table!" shouted Barton.

As Barton led her from his office through a maze of corridors, he said, "And what are you going to do for me?"

"I was thinking of Juliet. Or Marguerite Gautier. Or perhaps Adrienne Lecouvreur. These are all roles I have played many times in my native country and have now learned in English." She paused, as if hesitating. "I think, if you have no objection, I shall show you my Adrienne. That was the role in which I made my debut at the Imperial Theatre in Warsaw, and it has always brought me luck." Barton whistled, and shook his head. "Yes, the climax of Act Four, when Adrienne recites to her rival, in front of a glittering assembly, the insulting tirade from *Phèdre*, and from that straight into Act Five."

"Perhaps not all of Five," said Barton quickly. "And I won't need *Phèdre*."

"In any case," Maryna continued imperturbably, "I shall require the good offices of a young friend, who is waiting in the lobby and has my copy of *Adrienne* with her, to join me on the stage to read."

"We had Ristori in San Francisco with her troupe doing that only two years ago. But she was at the Bush. Of course she did it in Italian. Maybe she did one speech in English—no matter, you couldn't understand a word she said. After she paid for most of her reviews, the public came, and in the end it was quite a success."

"Yes," said Maryna, "I was sure that you were familiar with the play."

They had reached the wings. Before her was the dim stage, and waiting at the center a plain wooden chair. A stage! She would be walking again onto a stage! Maryna paused for a moment, a moment of genuine hesitation, so overcome was she by excitement and joy, which she supposed Barton would interpret as stage fright. No, not even stage fright, but ordinary panic, the panic of the amateur who, having passed herself off as a professional, is about to be caught out in her deception.

"Well," he said, "here you are."

"Yes," she said. Here I am.

"The stage is yours," he said, and left by the steps on the right, pausing midway to pull an envelope out of his pocket and slice it open with a stiletto.

"Put aside your doubts," said Maryna, meaning his damned letter, "and *If you have tears, prepare to shed them now.*"

"Ah, Mark Antony to the plebs." Barton turned back to look at her. "You should hear how Edwin Booth delivers those lines."

"I have."

"Really. And where, may I ask, did you see our great trage-dian? I'm not aware that he has yet made any European tours."

She stamped her foot lightly. "Where I am standing now, Mr. Barton. Last September. His Mark Antony, and his Shylock."

"Here? So you've been to the California Theatre! But of course, you told me you've been in the state for a while." He had reached his seat in the middle of the tenth row. "Now, you *must* be my guest sometime this week."

Maryna beckoned to a timorous Miss Collingridge to re-move her sailor hat, come on the stage, and occupy the chair, from which she would read (without emotion) the lines of Mau-rice, Adrienne Lecouvreur's beloved, and, at the end of the act, the few lines of Michonnet, the prompter at the Comédie-Française, Adrienne's dearest friend as well as hopeless candidate for her love.

"Remember, don't act. Just give me the lines."

"Give," mouthed Miss Collingridge. "Not *geeve.*"

Maryna smiled. "And don't worry for me," she whispered. "I shall be"—she was still smiling but now to herself—"I shall be 'all right.' "

Maryna looked about the empty theatre. How was she to do her best in these dismal circumstances? There were no admiring friends in the seats, no other actors, no painted scenes, no proper-ties (should she have asked for something, a candle, a shoehorn, a fan to serve as the bouquet of poisoned flowers?), no audience to stimulate her. Only the chair to talk to, with Miss Collingridge in it, and one unsympathetic man to judge. And Miss Collingridge looked so abject and small. Perhaps she should imagine it was Ryszard in the chair instead. And would she have her voice, the commanding voice audible without effort (without effort!) at the rear of the second balcony, to say Adrienne's lines in English? In America!

"Just the death scene, the second half of Act Five, Mr. Barton. Do not despair. I shall begin," she said, the voice was not the actress's voice, "after I have opened the small casket containing the poisoned flowers sent by the Princesse de Bouillon, which I believe are from Maurice, and kissed them. Begin with my reply when Maurice, who has just been shown into my apartment, says to me"—a little fuller than flat-voiced—"*Adrienne! But your hand is trembling. You're ill.* Miss Collingridge . . ."

Maryna stared at the chair.

Adrienne! But your hand is trembling. You're ill, said Miss Collingridge evenly, unexpressively.

The gauntlet had been thrown down.

No, no, not anymore. The words arched from Maryna's mouth. In the actress's voice. She placed her hand over her heart. *The pain is not there.* She brought her hand to her head. *It's there.* Said.

It's strange, it's bizarre, she continued. *A thousand different, fantastic things without order or connection are passing through my mind.* It was the opposite of what was going on inside Maryna's head, in which a firm, slicing clarity had descended.

And the delirious words gushed from her throat.

What did you say? Ah, I've already forgotten . . . my imagination seems to be wandering, where is my reason? But I must not lose my mind, no . . . first of all, for Maurice's sake . . . and . . . and for this evening. Delirium, produced by the working of the subtle poison on the brain. *The theatre has just been opened . . . the house is already full.* No physical pain yet. No writhing. *Yes, the curtain will rise soon . . . and I know how impatient and curious the audi-*

ence is. They have been promised this play for a long time . . . yes, such a long time . . . since the first day I saw Maurice . . . There was an objection to staging it again. It is too old, some said, it seems passé. But I said no, no . . . and I have a reason. Ah, little do they guess that reason: Maurice has not yet said to me "I love you" . . . nor have I said so to him . . . I don't dare. Now in this play there are certain lines that . . . I can say before everybody and no one will know that I am addressing them to him. It is a clever thought, is it not?

My love, my best love, return to yourself, said Miss Collingridge for Maurice, still admirably flat. Maryna looked at Miss Collingridge. She was rocking back and forth in the chair and lifting her face, gone all naked with passion, toward Maryna, and Maryna felt the push of Miss Collingridge's emotion passing into her, stirring and soothing some soft uneasy place. *Hush, hush*, she said, as Adrienne, to Miss Collingridge, *I must appear on the stage.*

She was grateful to Miss Collingridge: one cannot do one's best on a stage if one does not feel loved. An actor withers without love. Imagine having to do the scene in this empty theatre only for Barton, to whom she now directed all her watchfulness. *What a splendid audience—how numerous, how brilliant! How my movements are watched by every glance. They are kind, very kind to love me thus.* At first he could not have been paying attention at all, he was reading his letter, then he leaned back, clasped his hands behind his head, and seemed to be gazing at the top of the proscenium arch: she dismissed him contemptuously from her thoughts; but looking again she saw—he was leaning forward, his arms folded across the top of the seat in front of him—that she had finally interested him.

Adrienne! She does not see me, she does not hear me. The brisk, plump, diction-perfect voice of Miss Collingridge, in the role of Maurice.

Yes, Maryna saw, she had Barton now. Now he would see what she could do.

Can no one aid her? Has she not a friend? continued Miss Collingridge as Maurice, still tenaciously under control. And then she had to go on, old Michonnet having just entered—*What has happened? Is Adrienne in danger?*—a doubling of distress that fractured Miss Collingridge's composure, for she rose from her chair as she answered hoarsely, for Maurice, *Adrienne is dying!* and fled to the side of the stage.

What is the silly girl doing, Maryna thought, before realizing that she'd done her a real service by ceding the chair.

Who is near me, Maryna whispered plaintively. *How I suffer! Ah, Maurice, and you too, Michonnet. It is very kind. My head is calm now, but here in my bosom there is something like burning coal consuming me.*

Poisoned, wailed Miss Collingridge as Michonnet from her dark corner.

Maryna glanced at Barton's staring face in the tenth row. He seemed aroused. But had she made him cry? *Ah, the pain increases. You who love me so much, help me!* Then, oh so softly, in tones of accusatory wonderment: *I do not want to die.*

That was the line that never failed to ignite a burst of sobs in the audience, a line that touched every heart but those of the callous or the prejudiced. Listening to its echo in her head, Maryna allowed that she had never delivered the line better. *I do not want to die!* She permitted herself a few tottering steps before she sat, slowly.

An hour ago I should have prayed for death as a blessing, she said quietly, *but now*, without raising her voice, *I want to live*. A little more firmly: *Oh Heavenly powers! Hear me!* Not too loud. Barton can receive every syllable in that hollow heart of his. *Let me live . . . a few days more . . . just a few short days with him, my Maurice . . . I am young and life starts to seem so beautiful.*

Ah, it's unbearable, moaned Miss Collingridge as Maurice.

Life! Maryna cried. Now the decrescendo would be best. *Life!*

Ristori's Adrienne, following Rachel's, would attempt to stand after these words, attempt in vain, and then sink back into the chair. Maryna had always played the moment that way, too—

audiences expected it—but inspiration now led her to a new, a better idea. She wrenched her body around to face squarely upstage, as if Adrienne wished to spare her lover and her old friend the sight of the agony devastating her features, keeping her back to Barton a full, endless thirty seconds. Then, slowly, she turned, turned toward him another Adrienne, another face, that of someone already dead. *No, no, I shall not live; every effort, every prayer is in vain. Do not leave me, Maurice. I can see you now, but I shall not be able to see you much longer. Hold my hand. You will not much longer feel its pressure . . .*

Adrienne! Adrienne! cried Miss Collingridge.

There were to be no more words from Michonnet or from Maurice, she had launched Adrienne's final speech, only a few more lines to the end, and though she could see every furrow in Miss Collingridge's waxy face at the side of the stage, she could no longer make out Barton's face at all. *O triumphs of the theatre! My heart will no longer beat with your ardent emotions! And you, my long study of the art I have loved so much, nothing will remain of you when I am gone.* Tone of noble lament as if, for a moment, Adrienne had quite forgotten herself. *Nothing survives us, nothing but memory.* But she remembers now! Maryna looked blindly about her. *There, there, you will remember me, will you not?* (She saw Miss Collingridge nod through her tears at that passable *There, there.*) And, as in a dream, she finished, *Farewell Maurice, farewell Michonnet, my two, my only friends!*

There was a moment of silence. She could hear Miss Collingridge sniveling. Then Barton began to applaud rhythmically, echoingly, very slowly. Maryna felt slapped by each sound. Then he took out a handkerchief, blew his nose loudly, and shouted into the dark theatre, "Tell Ames I can't meet him at all. Madame, I . . . No, wait, I'm coming on stage."

"Miss Collingridge," Maryna said softly, "will you meet me at my rooms this afternoon at four o'clock? I must hear Mr. Barton's verdict without a witness." It was cruel to send the girl away, but she had to confront her destiny alone. Barton, wheezing, came forward and grasped her hand. "May I invite you to lunch with me?"

"Perhaps. But first you will tell me, what is my fate?"

"Fate?"

"Will you give me a week?"

"A week!" he exclaimed. "I'll give you weeks. As many as you want."

"I'M A BILIOUS MAN, Madame," said Barton, tucking into the ample noon repast offered at the Fountain Bar. "Can you forgive me?"

"There is nothing to forgive."

"No, no, I beg your pardon from the bottom of my heart. I thought you were a novice. Not even that, I thought you were some society lady with dreams of going on the stage. Never did I imagine that I was about to see a great artist." He sighed. "You may be the greatest actress I have ever seen."

"You are kind, Mr. Barton."

"You mean I'm a fool. Well, I shall make it up to you."

He says he will make it up to me, Henryk. All went well, Bogdan. Ryszard, come.

They were sitting in one of the more select bars in the city, at the corner of Sutter and Kearny Streets, a popular place, Barton remarked, for bankers.

"As you see," he added, with a nod at the to-and-fro of men about the room going up to consult a slender ribbon of paper trickling down one of the walls into a basket on the floor, followed by an explanation: these were choice gleanings, fresh at every moment, from the sub-marine cable, which were needed to conduct great mercantile transactions here in San Francisco. "News from the whole world, transported across intervening oceans to arrive on a strip of paper scarcely wider than my cigar band."

"How convenient," said Maryna.

"Even Ralston used to come to the Fountain. It's a pity you can't meet him, he was the richest man in the city, but damned, pardon my French, Madame, if he didn't go for a swim in the Bay and drown by accident the very afternoon he learned that his bank failed. Some problem with his partner." He laughed. "That fellow over there fiddling with the solid-gold watch fob crossing his waistcoat."

"Shall we turn now to *our* business, Mr. Barton?"

"Right," said Barton.

They began with a disagreement. Barton did not think she should open with *Adrienne Lecouvreur. Camille*, he thought, would be much better.

Adrienne first, Maryna said. Toward the end of the first week, *Camille*. And then one, perhaps two, plays of Shakespeare. She thought she should begin with Ophelia or Juliet, whose pathos was second nature to her. For although there was no Shakespearean role she liked better than Rosalind, she preferred to wait to do *As You Like It* until she had further reduced her accent. With Shakespeare's comedies, she said, she had the impression that the audience listens differently. One expects, she explained, a more prominent linguistic grace.

"Am I being clear?" she added.

"Very clear," said Barton.

"But perhaps you disagree."

He smiled. "I can see it will be hard to disagree with you."

"While you are in that mood, Mr. Barton," she said briskly, "I think we should proceed to discuss my contract, my salary, and the dates you can propose. And the other actors, of course—I trust you can supply me with a Maurice de Saxe as princely as the Maurices I played with in Poland. Also you will tell me something, but not too much, about the drama critics here. Though I can hardly complain of the treatment I have received from critics, I have never liked them. They always start out thinking you are going to fail. I remember when I made my debut at the Imperial Theatre in Warsaw, the critics were most skeptical. That I had chosen, yes, *Adrienne Lecouvreur*, was regarded as a great act of presumption. How could I, a mere Polish actress, dare to touch the role written for the immortal Rachel, which had then become the property of Adelaide Ristori? But I triumphed. With that role I was proclaimed queen of the Polish theatre, and from then on I could do no wrong." She smiled. "A triumph is sweeter when one has first to surmount a wall of skepticism."

"Indeed," said Barton.

When they returned to the theatre, Barton took her for a tour of the neatly labeled interiors and exteriors in the scene-dock (Oak Chamber, Gothic Palace, English Drawing-Room, Old Venetian Palace, Forest Glade, Juliet's Balcony, Humble Parlor, Tavern, Lake by Moonlight, Rustic Kitchen, Dungeon, French Ball-Room, Rugged Coast, Court-Room, Roman Street, Slave Quarters, Bed-Chamber, Rocky Pass) and the property room (throne chair, scaffold, royal couches, trees, scepter, infant's cradle, spinning wheel, swords, rapiers, daggers, blunderbusses, paste jewels, casket, artificial flowers, goblets, champagne glasses, rubber asp, witches' cauldron, Yorick's skull); introduced her to the head scene-painter and the property-man and their dusty assistants; showed her the comforts of the star's dressing room and the dignified greenroom. There were no actors yet on the premises. Barton assured her she would like the company's Maurice, whom she guessed by the way he commended him ("a manly actor of the old school") would prove easy to work with and not very alert.

And when that was done—they were back in Barton's office—he offered her a week starting ten days from now, on September third; the California's general manager had insisted on booking a crowd-pleasing variety show for that week, but he would be delighted to cede the Georgia Minstrels, Hermann the Wizard, and Professor O. S. Fowler, the renowned phrenologist, to the Bush Theatre or to Maguire's. Then in October she could have three—four, if she liked—more weeks.

"There is one other thing. Your name, dear lady—of

course it's in the letters from your friends, but would you be so kind as to write it out for me?" He looked at the piece of paper. "M-A-R-Y-N-A Z-A- funny L-E-Z-O-W-S-K-A. Yes, I remember. And now, please, pronounce it for me."

She did.

"Would you say that again? The second name. I'm afraid it doesn't sound like what I'm looking at."

She explained that the Polish *l*, the barred *l*, was pronounced as a *w*, the *e* with a hook under it as "en," the *z* with the dot over it as "zh," and *w* as an *f* or *v*.

"I shall attempt it once. Just once. Zalen . . . no, Zawen . . . I have to lisp, right?" He laughed. "But let's be serious, dear lady. You realize, don't you, that no one in America will ever learn to pronounce your name correctly. Now, I'm sure you don't want to hear your name mispronounced all the time, and my worry is that only a few will make the effort to say it at all." He leaned back in his chair. "It's got to be shorter. Maybe you could drop the *z-o-w*. What do you say?"

"I shall be glad to improve my difficult foreign name," she said airily. "Isn't that what many people do when they come to America? I'm sure my late first husband, whose name I bear, Heinrich Załężowski—no, I think I'm not going to explain to you why he was Załężowski and I am Załężowska, that's *too* much for a Yankee mind—would have been very amused." And, amused by the prospect of marring Heinrich's last bit of sovereignty over her, she took back the paper, wrote on it, and handed it to him again.

"Z-A-L- We're forgetting about the Polish *l*, right?" He registered her nod. "Z-A-L-E-N-S-K-A. Zalenska. Not bad. Foreign, but not hard to say."

"Almost as easy as Ristori."

"You mock me, Madame Zalenska."

"Call me Madame Maryna."

"We'll have to do something about the first name too, I'm afraid."

"Ah, ça, non!" she cried. "That really is my name."

"But nobody can say it. Do you really want people saying Madame Mary-Naaah? Mary-Naaaaah. Mary-Naaaaaaah. No. You don't."

"Your suggestion, Mr. Barton?"

"Well, you can't be Mary. Too American. Marie, that's French. Say, how about changing just one letter? Look."

On the paper he had written: M-A-R-I-N-A.

"But that's how my name is spelled in Russian! No, Mr. Barton, a Polish actress could hardly have a Russian name." She was about to say, The Russians are our oppressors, and realized how puerile this would sound.

"Why not? Who in America would know the difference? And people can pronounce it. Mareena, they'll say. They'll think it's Italian. It sounds nice. What do you say? Marina Zalenska." He looked at her flirtatiously. "Madame Marina."

She frowned and turned away.

"Well then, that's settled. I shall have the contract drawn up this afternoon. And now—may I, to toast the occasion?" He was lifting a bottle of whiskey out of his desk drawer. "I must tell you," he said, "that anyone who works for me is fined five dollars if caught drinking in the theatre. Actors ten." He half-filled two glasses. "Except for Edwin Booth, of course. Exceptions are always made, and I say rightly so, for poor Booth. Neat or with water?"

Marina Zalenska. Marina Zalenska. Marina—what was the matter with Edwin Booth?—Zalenska. "I beg your pardon? Oh, no water." Marina, mother of Peter. Peter's last name would have to be changed too.

So all is settled, Henryk. The dates, the roles, my munificent salary, my mutilated name. No, the man is not a brother tippler. And when I took out a cigarette, he merely said, "Ah," and reached for his matches. He is the first American I have met who does not seem genuinely shocked to see a lady smoke. I think I shall get on with this Mr. Barton very well. He likes me, he is a

253

little afraid of me, and I like him, he is shrewd and he truly loves the theatre. I have dined with him and his charming wife, a simple home-cooked meal of creamed corn soup, deviled crabs, lamb chops in tomato sauce, stuffed potatoes, roast chickens, banana ice cream, jelly-roll, coffee, and I must not forget the stalks of uncooked celery set about the table in tall glasses to gnaw on *ad libitum* throughout the meal. You would have smiled at the heartiness of my appetite.

Applying to the mirror, the actor's only candid friend, Maryna acknowledged that she was thinner than when she left Poland, though she trusted that she would not look too thin, actually thin-looking, when all the costumes brought with her had been taken in; that her face had aged, especially around the eyes, though she knew that on a stage, with the normal wizardry of makeup and gaslight, she would appear no more than twenty-five. To be sure, she wrote to Henryk, the gush of animal spirits of a lighthearted girl is beyond me now, but my joy and enthusiasm are intact. I believe I can give a faultless imitation of the emotions that may elude me in real life. I was never a great instinctual actor, but I am tireless and strong.

Four days before she was to open, when the rehearsals began, Maryna moved to a pompous suite on the top floor of the Palace Hotel. It was Barton's idea, Barton's extravagance. As he explained it, "People will hear you're at the Palace, and that will make them take notice. Mr. Ralston put his all into the Palace. We're the second-best theatre in America. The Palace is the grandest hotel in the world." Maryna liked hotels: being in a hotel, any hotel, had meant, and would mean again, having a theatre to go to. And treating luxury as merely her due after the privations of the last months, while accepting inquisitive stares from across the immense Grand Court with its seven-story-high domed ceiling of amber-colored glass and breath to breath in the mirrored confines of the hydraulic elevator, was itself a kind of performance. Playbills around the city proclaimed the American debut of the great Polish actress Marina Zalenska, though Barton had not managed to prod a single journalist from one of the daily newspapers into requesting an interview. Members of the Polish community in San Francisco, abrim with anticipation of the imminent American triumph of their national treasure, sent trinkets and books and flowers, but the most thoughtful present of all was already waiting at the desk when Maryna checked into the Palace: a little velvet-lined box containing her black silver necklace and pendant earrings, the precious gift from Bogdan's grandmother, with a card: "From an anonymous"—this was crossed out, and "abject" written above—"admirer."

She wore them happily, her miraculously restored mourning jewelry, until Monday night, when she put on Adrienne's brilliant jewels.

Eager to coddle his astounding "discovery," Barton had offered four rehearsals of *Adrienne* with the full company, including a dress rehearsal on the day of the opening. Normally only new plays were rehearsed. For repertory, a few hours on the day of the performance with speeches rattled off and stage business reviewed was considered preparation enough. Maryna took note of the mild annoyance of her fellow actors at having to turn up four days in a row at ten o'clock; for her there could be nothing routine about these days. The first morning that Maryna was admitted to the California by the stage entrance seemed no less momentous an occasion than the evening long ago when, as Stefan's baby sister, she had passed through her first stage door. And hadn't the porter in the theatre in Kraków where Stefan was playing in *Don Carlos* been ill-tempered and slow to respond, like the one here with the baleful name of Chester Cant? But all theatres are alike, she thought gaily: the smells, the jokes, the envy. The porter at the Globe Theatre could well have been the model for the immortal grumbler in Macbeth's service who, tarrying to open the castle gate to some rackety late-night visitors, imagines himself the porter of hell.

"Your Shakespearean porter," she exclaimed to James Glenwood, her amiable Michonnet, who had also arrived for the rehearsal early, but only after some dispute with the surly porter—she could hear the din from the greenroom. *"I had thought to have let in some of all professions that go the primrose way to th' everlasting bonfire,"* Maryna recited companionably. "But let us hope our Mr. Cant does not." Seeing Glenwood's blank expression, she added, "*Macbeth*, Act Two."

Glenwood's face tightened. "I can see you don't know that we never say that name"—he coughed loudly—"either for the play or the character. We don't say it. Ever."

"How interesting! Is this some kind of American superstition?"

"*You* may call it a superstition," said Kate Egan, the company's over-age Princesse de Bouillon, who had just entered the greenroom with Thomas—Tom—Deane, its stolid Maurice.

"You mean, American actors when they perform the play can't utter the name Mac—"

"Oh, please don't say it again," said Deane. "Yes, of course the three witches have to say, *Upon the heath / There to meet with* . . . you know, and so do Banquo and Duncan and the others when their lines come. But anywhere except on stage—never!"

"In heaven's name, why?"

"Because the play is hexed," explained Deane. "Brings disaster. Always does. Why, some thirty years ago in New York, there were to be two productions of the Scottish play at the same time, one with Macready, who was thought the finest English Shakespearean after Kean, and the other with our great Edwin Forrest. Some people became upset about this, I believe there were many Irish among them, saying that for the Englishman to do the same play in another theatre was an insult to our American actor, and so gathered around that theatre on the night of Macready's opening and tore up paving stones and sent them crashing through the windows and were starting to batter down the doors. The militia opened fire, and dozens in the crowd were killed."

"Well, I shall be sure to bedeck myself with white-magic

charms when I come to play Lady—" Maryna looked about mischievously at her anxious colleagues. "The Scottish lady."

Ryszard hadn't dared ask when Bogdan would be arriving. Maryna had mentioned that she hoped he would soon resign himself to selling the farm back to the Fischers, since his losses would be covered several times over by her earnings from the first run of a week and the four weeks Barton had offered in October. For the moment, Ryszard's only rival was Miss Collingridge, who (for once!) was not waiting in the dressing room at the rehearsal's end, should Maryna want to do some more work on her lines.

"She's almost in love with you," he grumbled.

"She *is* in love with me, in her respectful way."

"Then my heart goes out to her. Who would have thought we had so much in common, your little diction teacher and I?"

"Ryszard, don't feel sorry for yourself. Miss Collingridge doesn't."

"Miss Collingridge is not disappointed. Miss Collingridge does not expect more intimacy from her idol than she already has."

"Oh," she cried. "Have I really disappointed you?"

Ryszard shook his head. "I'm a clod. I'm harassing you. It's unpardonable, what I just said. I shall go away." He grinned. "Until the day after tomorrow."

"And what would you think," she said, "if now I encourage you a little? If I admit that something has worked loose in my feelings and—" She flushed. "Maybe you *should* go away. I sit here alone, and worry that I might be getting a headache, and rub my forehead and temples with cologne, and then realize I am thinking not of Adrienne or Marguerite Gautier or Juliet but of you. And, thinking of you, I feel all sorts of physical sensations not unlike stage fright, as well as quickness of breath, restless limbs, and a few other stirrings that modesty prohibits my mentioning."

"Maryna!"

She raised her hand. "But the emperor, mind, has not said yes. For I ask myself, Is this love? Or is this the feminine yearning to yield to importunate male desire? I fear you have quite worn me down, Rich-ard"—she said his name in the American way, to annoy him. A little slap.

"Ma-ree-na," he said softly, and drew her hand to his heart.

Grateful as she had been that Bogdan had not yet joined her, and apprehensive as she was about his arrival for her opening, Maryna had not yet put it to herself that she would soon have to choose between the two men. But when she imagined them both standing about her dressing room while she was setting out her makeup and giving instructions to the seamstress, both solicitous, both anxious on her behalf, what did occur to her was, Whose face will I watch?

Then, on Saturday from Anaheim, a telegram:

ACCIDENT STOP FALL FROM HORSE STOP NO BROKEN BONES BUT BRUISES EVERYWHERE INCLUDING FACE HANDS STOP QUITE UNPRESENTABLE STOP ALAS SAN FRANCISCO UNTHINKABLE FOR NOW

Maryna said nothing to Ryszard about how disappointed she was; to herself she admitted that she was more angry than relieved. If Bogdan could not manage to be present at her opening, then he must feel— So be it, she thought. And wondered what she meant by that.

Sunday night Maryna dreamt that just before she went on stage Barton informed her that she was to do the role in Russian.

On Monday, Maryna was in her dressing room three hours before curtain, performing little rituals of order. Ryszard stood nearby, nervous as a husband in his new white kid gloves and patent-leather boots, hoping he had mustered the right shade of reassuring firmness to show his support and calm her nerves. (He remembered that look on Bogdan's expressive, ironic face.)

He had accompanied her from the hotel, seen her engaged with the dresser, pinned the many telegrams from Poland to a cork mat on the wall beside the mirror, leaving on top the ones she had singled out—from Henryk, her mother and Józefina, Barbara and Aleksander, and Tadeusz, Krystyna, and other young actors at the Imperial Theatre—then left to pace the corridor. At seven-thirty Ryszard came back, agreeably stocked with juicy lingo, to tell her that all illumination was ready (the gasman had lighted the "borders" with torch and long pole, and the "foots" in front of the curtain, and turned them "down to the blue"), the doors had been opened, and the audience—he could see their compatriots had turned out in force—was filing into the theatre.

Since Adrienne does not appear in Act One, there was plenty of time for Barton to report on the audience. True, the house was not full, but a goodly number of important theatregoers were there, as well as the reigning American Juliet, Rose Edwards, who was booked into the California for the following week to star in the ever popular British melodrama *East Lynne*.

"Wait until Rose sees *you*," Barton exclaimed. "She's a good actress, and she's no fool either. Maybe she'll tell me that she doesn't dare follow in your footsteps, and you can have her week."

"I doubt that any successful actress would make such an offer," said Maryna, smiling. "You are very clever, Mr. Barton, at keeping my spirits up."

But where is my fear, Maryna asked herself, after sending both men away to make her final inner preparation and mirror-check, and await the call-boy's summons for her entrance in the second act. Standing in the wings, she still registered none of the tumultuous symptoms of stage fright, the sweating palms, the racing heart, the knotted stomach. It seemed to her that she must be mad to have this certitude that everything would go well. And then she realized that she was more afraid than she had ever been in her life, but the fear was outside, like an impossible thickening of the air. She was strapped into her fear—a cold fear without physical resonance, except for a tightening of her skin—

and inside she felt calm and spacious. More than spacious enough for all these words she was carrying: English words, behind which were the words of the play in Polish, and behind them the French words of the original play, which she had studied when she first prepared the part in Warsaw . . . but everything had to be inside, protected against the fear. Her skin, all of it, from her scalp to her soles, was the barrier against the iron cladding of fear; her upper body—her mouth, her tongue and lips, her neck, her shoulders, her chest—was the vessel in which the moist words were stowed that would start streaming, in English, when she went on stage.

She would, as she reminded herself again just before she stepped into the light, be starting without the jolt of the ovation that in Poland had invariably greeted her entrance, bringing the play to a halt and preventing her for several minutes from uttering her first line. There would be—except from her compatriots—only brief polite applause. She had seen, even with the great Booth, that American audiences do not break into applause after the famous set speeches that many knew by heart. ("At the opera, yes," Barton had told her.) How did this new animal show enthusiasm, indifference, displeasure, the readiness to be tamed? She knew how to interpret Polish applause, as well as Polish coughs, whispers, shifting in the seats. But this audience seemed too quiet. How was she to interpret that? When she started the fable of the two pigeons (*Two pigeons were lovers both tender and true . . .*) all coughing stopped; when she finished, there was silence for a moment, and then a tempest of applause, cries, calls. Tom Deane tried five times to begin Maurice's lines before he succeeded in going on. He looked quite inconsolable. When the act was over Maryna left the stage in a trance, while the audience roared, clapped, and stamped its feet. In the interval Ryszard roamed the lobby with Barton and Miss Collingridge. "Splendid! Splendid!" he heard over and over, rising above the sprightly chatter, the mutual bows, smiles, handshakes, and waves. A man in a top hat greeted Barton with "Now she's worth thirty thousand dollars a year!"—the editor of the *Evening Post*, Ryszard learned from Barton afterward—and his wife, imposing in her trained evening skirt, said that while Madame Zalenska's English had a shade of foreignness, she must keep it as it is, for it was "sweetness incarnate." Miss Collingridge did not return Ryszard's treacherous smile.

Maryna floated back for the third act on a wave of energy that seemed to be coming from even further inside. She felt haloed, smooth, light-limbed, invulnerable. In the dark pavilion, scene of Adrienne's first encounter with her rival for Maurice's love, it was canonical staging for the Princesse de Bouillon to approach Adrienne with a candle to penetrate the disguise of the unknown woman who has chivalrously offered to rescue her from a compromising situation. Receptive, becalmed, Maryna watched the candle coming nearer and nearer, its flame pointed at the energy inside her, until gasps from the audience that fortunately covered Kate Egan's "Oh, hell!"—and "Sorry!"— made her aware that a corner of her veil had caught fire. Wondering whether Egan was apologizing for the profanity or for the mishap, Maryna flung the burning veil on the floor, in a single swift movement redraped her face with Adrienne's moiré silk shawl, and extended her hand to lead the wicked princess to safety. Some people thought it was all in the play; others applauded this daring bit of staging invented by the Polish actress.

She was recalled at the end of the third and the fourth acts for more applause.

The delivery of the words she had so long labored to say correctly was only a part of the flow of rhythmic events in her body. As for the inevitable rhyming of certain lines with some of her own feelings (what actor, whatever the role, does not feel this?), only once, and almost at the end, did Maryna allow herself to think about the words. When Adrienne says in her delirium, *Now in this play there are certain lines that I can say before everybody and no one will know that I am addressing them to him,* Maryna thought to herself, *If it is a success, then I have been addressing Adrienne's words of love to Ryszard.*

It is a clever thought, is it not?

One must love somebody.

It was as good a performance of Adrienne as she had ever given—and a triumph beyond anything she could have hoped for. Eleven curtain calls, eleven. And then hundreds thronging backstage to congratulate her, including all the Poles (except for their larcenous friend, though she was sure Halek had been in the audience), beaming and chattering and embracing one another. Bluff old Captain Znaniecki couldn't keep from chiding her for permitting her first name to be Russified, then burst into tears of joy and pride; Maryna cried too, and hugged him. What gave her most pleasure was the homage of an auburn-haired woman in brocade evening dress and shoes who was almost first to reach the greenroom and introduced herself as Rose Edwards. "I am at your feet, Madame," she said.

Two hours after the performance had ended, Maryna was finally able to leave the theatre.

Returning to the hotel with Ryszard, she stopped at the desk and sent a one-word telegram to Bogdan. VICTORY.

A half hour after they bid each other good night in the lobby, Ryszard, who had moved to the Palace two days before, came to Maryna's suite. She was waiting for him. She knew she was waiting for him because she had not undressed for bed, nor started preparing one of her more unsightly beauty secrets: the squares of brown paper soaked in cider vinegar that she wore against her temples while she slept, which kept the skin around her eyes smooth and free of wrinkles. She knew she was waiting for him because she turned down the jets in the sconces just so, until the room was bathed in shadow. She knew she was waiting for him because she stared for a long time at the enormous bed, mahogany, with a headboard that went halfway up to the fifteen-foot ceiling, wondered for the first time what she didn't like about it, and then removed first one, then two, then three of the six plump goose-down pillows and wedged them into the bottom of a wardrobe in the dressing room.

They kissed while she was closing the door; they were still kissing as she led him to the bedchamber, quick bruising kisses that were like words, like steps: she felt she was drawing him after her with her mouth. As they fell on the bed, still clothed, closed, the force of their bodies uniting pushed their heads apart. Maryna's mouth felt quite homeless. Meanwhile, tangled arms and legs were seeking the better position, the unlocking closeness. "I think I'm embarrassed," she murmured against his face. "You make me feel like a girl."

She rose to undress and Ryszard caught her by the wrist. "Don't take your clothes off yet. I know what you look like. I've lived with your body in my mind so long. Your breasts, your thighs, your love cave—I can tell you about them."

"But I'm not a girl," she said.

He released her arm and stood. Separately, solemnly, they removed their clothes. He folded the smooth length of her body in his arms.

"I can give you my heart, Ryszard. But I can't give you my life. I'm not Adrienne Lecouvreur"—she laughed. "Just another mature actress who relishes impersonating that impetuous girl."

He lay back on the bed and opened his arms to her. She lay on top of him. "You smell of soap," she whispered.

"Now you are making me feel shy," he said.

"It's been such a long journey for both of us to reach this bed."

"Maryna, Maryna."

"I shall know you don't love me anymore when you say my name only once."

"Maryna, Maryna, Maryna."

"When you wait for something too long, doesn't it become—? Oh . . ." She gasped.

"Who says we waited too long?" he said.

"No more questions!" she moaned, and drew him farther inside her, circling him with every part of her body.

After they had flooded each other with pleasure and fallen apart for a moment, lying side by side, Ryszard asked if she thought less of him because all this time he had been in love with her he had still gone with many women. "Be honest with me, Maryna."

She answered him with a vague, radiant smile.

Truth was, Ryszard had never fully believed that Maryna would one day be his. His love for Maryna, at its truest, had been draped by a stinging sense of the unlikelihood of its consummation. But he could not leap beyond desire. Like many writers, Ryszard did not really believe in the present, but only in the past and in the future. And he had hated wanting something he thought he could not have.

You get what you want, and that makes everything right.

She fell asleep after they made love a second time, her head on his chest and her leg thrown over his thighs: though he still wanted her, he had to let her be, for she must be exhausted; he tried to follow her into sleep, but was barred by unslaked desire, and joy. He spent the rest of the night drifting toward sleep, bearing Maryna's body, and at the edge of sleep coming awake again with the thought, But I am still awake. When dawn came, he did sleep, waking a few hours later to find her still flung across him, and wondered if he could move without her knowing; she must sleep on, as late as possible, to have all her strength for another *Adrienne* tonight.

But she was awake, and was covering him with kisses. "Oh, how alive I feel!" she cried. "You have given me back my body. What a second performance I shall give. And all our Polish friends, who must have been speculating about why Bogdan isn't here in San Francisco, will be sure it's because of you. My Maurice will surely notice, when I nestle against his chest to recite the fable of the two pigeons, that the girlish Adrienne is not as shy as she was last night. Mr. Barton will wonder, What has happened to that dignified lady from Poland? Success seems to have quite gone to her head. Her head!" She bent over and began to kiss his groin.

"The Polish lady is in love?" said Ryszard.

"The Polish lady is definitely—recklessly—indecently—imprudently—in love."

After two more performances of *Adrienne,* on Thursday night Maryna opened in *Camille* and, after a third *Camille* at the Saturday matinee, closed the week with another *Adrienne.* The houses were always full, the ovations more prolonged and rapturous, the cohort of opulently dressed admirers the jubilant Barton led backstage ever larger. She greeted them by name after only the first visit, the liquid energies of her performance quick-drying in the rush of these greenroom exchanges—she was winsome ("Yes, thank you, thank you . . . ah, you are too kind"), easily amused, inviolable. If they only knew the price I have paid—must go on paying—to do what I do! And now she had another secret: the usual after-the-show lightheadedness was thickened with sexual suspense. But the well-wishers had to be sent away, and their flowers given to her dresser and the property-men to make space for the next day's flowers, before, at last, she could return with Ryszard to the hotel.

Largest among the floral tributes massed together in her dressing room before the performance on Saturday evening was a giant basket plaited in the shape of a tower with tier upon tier of red, white, and blue flowers. From the belfry hung a square sheet of gold-bordered vellum.

"A poem," said Maryna. "Unsigned."

"Of course!" Ryszard exclaimed. "It was inevitable. You've captured the heart of another writer. Give me his poem and I'll tell you, with complete objectivity, whether my new rival has any talent or not."

"No"—Maryna laughed—"I shall read it to you. It can't be as difficult as a sonnet by Shakespeare, and, luckily for me, Miss Collingridge is not here to mend my pronunciation."

"The good fortune is mine."

"*Là, mon cher, tu exagères!* Jealous men may be exciting on the stage but in real life they soon become very boring."

"I *am* boring," said Ryszard. "Writers are boring."

"Ryszard, my sweet Ryszard," she cried—he groaned, happily—"you're going to stop thinking of yourself and just listen."

"When do I do anything else?"

"Sshhh . . ."

"But first I have to kiss you," he said.

They kissed, and did not feel like separating.

"You still want to oppress me with my rival's poem?"

"Yes!" She picked up the vellum again, held it before her, and declaimed, in what Polish critics had called her silver register:

Hither, unheralded by voice of fame,
Except as a fair foreigner you came.
Light was the welcome that we had prepared—
Even our sympathies you scarcely shared;
Not—

"Oh, Madame Mareena, dear Madame Mareena," Ryszard crowed, "sympathies. Not *sympaties*."

"Sympathies is what I did say, you dolt," Maryna exclaimed, and leaned over to kiss him before continuing:

Not as the artist whom your people knew—
As some fresh novice did we look on you.

"Aha, my rival is a mere drama critic!"

"Quiet!" she said. Curling her right hand, with her thumb and index finger Maryna tapped herself on the chest, twice, a venerable thespian gesture, mock-cleared her throat, and dropped into her celebrated velvet tone:

Mark the great change! Since that eventful night,
Only your wondrous art remains in sight.
Despite the fetters of a foreign tongue—

"Fetters," Ryszard hooted.

"Ryszard, I'm not going to let you stop me!"

Despite the fetters of a foreign tongue,
Jealousy round your matchless talent hung;
Enraptured we acknowledge your success—
Success the greater as expected less.

"But now he's going to kiss the hem of your robe, this little drama critic."

"And why not?"

Keep Polish memories in—

She stopped.

"What's the matter, Maryna? Darling!"

"I don't— I don't know if I can read the final couplet."

"What does the beast say about you? Tear it up!"

"No. Of course I can finish."

Keep Polish memories in your heart alone,
America now claims you for her own.

She put it down and turned away.

You get what you want, and then you're in despair.

"Maryna," said Ryszard. "Darling Maryna, please don't cry."

BY MID-MORNING on the day after the opening, seven journalists had set up restless, rivalrous encampments in the mammoth Parlor of the Palace Hotel; Maryna descended at noon. Ryszard had come down an hour earlier to say that Madame would soon be with them, and to send a telegram to the editor of the *Gazeta Polska* announcing his forthcoming full account of Maryna's American debut, which was certain to make all Polish hearts throb with pride. Learning a day later from his editor that a rival Warsaw newspaper was dispatching someone to San Francisco to cover the event, Ryszard rushed ahead with not one but two long articles, the first describing Maryna's performance in detail, the second its ecstatic reception by the first-night public and by the critics, who were, as he put it, "all, to a man, enraptured by the womanly charms and the incomparable genius of our Polish diva." No need to remind his readers who Maryna had been, only to recount what she had gloriously, and in truth, become.

Who—what—she had been, that was Maryna's subject in adroit conversation with the smitten local journalists waiting at the Palace that morning; and there were many more in the days that followed. Giving interviews entailed rewriting the past, starting with her age (she lopped off six years), her antecedents (the secondary-school Latin teacher became a professor at the Jagiellonian University), her beginnings as an actor (Heinrich became the director of an important private theatre in Warsaw where she made her debut at seventeen), her reasons for coming to America (to visit the Centennial Exposition) and then to California (to restore her health). By the end of the week Maryna had begun to believe some of the stories herself. After all, she'd had a plethora of reasons for emigrating. "I was ill." (*Was* I ill?) "I always dreamed of going on the stage in America." (*Did* I always mean to go back on the stage here?)

Then there were the unnecessary inventions. Maryna knew why she said she was thirty-one: she had already turned thirty-seven. Or why she said that only acute exhaustion brought on by years of overwork in Poland could have induced her to agree to a term of rustic seclusion ("Can you picture me, gentlemen, for ten months among chickens and cows?" she said, laughing): she didn't want anyone to think she'd been one of those simple-lifers. But why had she said that the farm was near Santa Barbara? No one would think less well of her if she said it was outside Anaheim. And why tell different stories to different interviewers? Usually her father was an eminent classics scholar still teaching at Kraków's noble, ancient university, who, when his daughter became, "what do you call it, stagestruck?" she said prettily, had vehemently opposed her hopes of an acting career ("but I was determined and left Kraków for Warsaw, where I made my debut in 1863"); but more than once he was a man of the mountains, a misfit only son, a dreamer, who committed to memory the verses of the great Polish poets during long solitary weeks in the high Tatras tending the family sheep, and having quit his village for Kraków hoping to gain admittance to the university, never succeeded in finding better than humble employment, never adjusted to city life, and did not live long enough to be proud, as she knew he would have been, of his actress daughter. Perhaps one tires of telling the same story again and again.

She could have said she was merely tailoring her reminiscences to make herself comprehensible: work of a foreigner. (And yes, she said, "Yes, I am especially pleased to have made my American debut in San Francisco.") Or acknowledged, with a smile, that fabulating was simply an actress's sport. Rachel, she had heard from one of the senior actors at the Imperial Theatre, told the most extraordinary untruths about herself to journalists when she came to perform in Warsaw twenty years ago. ("Like many exceedingly imaginative people," as this charming man had put it with great delicacy, "Rachel was given to what in other persons would be called lying.") But it's not easy to remember which of the stories you relate about your life are true when you relate all of them so often. And all stories respond to some inner truth.

Of course it is impossible, and imprudent, to explain oneself fully when one has become a foreigner. Some truths need to be emphasized to jibe with local ideas of seemliness (she knew Americans liked being told about early hardships and rebuffs by those crowned with wealth and success), while some truths, the ones that have their just weight only back home, are best not mentioned at all.

The morning after her debut three candidates for the role of Maryna's personal manager had also been waiting in the Palace lobby, eyeing each other sullenly, but Maryna signed on with the first with whom she conferred, Harry H. Warnock, who had come recommended by Barton. Ryszard was troubled, as he told Maryna later, by the speed with which she'd acquired this professional spouse. "Spouse?" Of course he didn't like him, Ryszard lumbered on, but that was not the point. Did she realize that from now on Warnock would always be with her (with us, he meant), was she sure he was the kind of man whose proximity she could tolerate for long, and so on, and perhaps Maryna hadn't understood how important a decision she had made, since personal managers did not exist in the Polish theatre. But Warnock was persuasive: he proposed a brief tour later that month in western Nevada (Virginia City and Reno) and northern California (Sacramento, San Jose), a debut in New York in December, and after that a four-month national tour. And Maryna was impatient and drunk with triumph. They agreed about repertory. Maryna would do mostly Shakespeare—she had played fourteen of Shakespeare's heroines in Poland and planned to redo them all—while continuing to offer *Adrienne Lecouvreur* and *Camille* and, in the more provincial communities that filled out any comprehensive tour, a few melodramas ("But not *East Lynne*!" she said; "What do you take me for, Madame? I know when I am dealing with an artist"). The money promised was stupendous. Indeed, they were on the way to agreeing about everything, until Warnock mentioned that he was glad some of her Polish friends had thought last night to tell him she was a countess. He'd find good use for that in making her a star!

"Ah, no, Mr. Warnock!"—Maryna wrinkled her nose with

distaste—"This would not be right at all." For such a profanation of the family name she would never be forgiven by Bogdan's brother. "That is my husband's title, not mine," she said. And, hoping to appeal to the democrat in this rotund man with the diamond scarfpin, "Artist—actress—is title enough for me."

"We're not talking about you, Madame Marina, we're talking about the public," said Warnock amiably.

"But it is I on the playbills! How can I be both Marina Zalenska and Countess Dembowska?"

"Easy," said Warnock.

"Unthinkable in Poland," she cried, and knew she had already lost the argument.

"Well, this is America," said Warnock, "and Americans love foreign titles."

"And— And it would be so vulgar for me to allow myself to be called a countess in my professional life."

"Vulgar? That's an awfully snobbish thing to say, Madame Marina. Americans don't feel chastened when they're told that something they enjoy is vulgar."

"But Americans like stars," she said, smiling severely.

"Yes," he said, "Americans like stars." He shook his head reproachfully. "And if they like you, you can make a lot of money."

"Mr. Warnock, I do not come from another planet. In Europe the public dotes on stars. People like to worship, we know that. Nevertheless, in Poland, as in France and the German-speaking lands, drama is first of all one of the fine arts, and our principal theatres, those maintained by the state, are devoted to an ideal of—"

While Maryna, sitting with Warnock in one of the reception rooms of the Palace, was calmly trying to make the manager of her future American career appreciate for just a moment the prestige and privileges that accrue from a career at Warsaw's Imperial Theatre—secure employment and steady promotion through the ranks, exemptions from conscription into the Czar's army, and the guarantee to all, upon retirement, of a handsome pension for life ("An actor is a civil servant," she said; "A what?" he exclaimed)—Rose Edwards, pacing back and forth in Barton's office, was in full cry. "As you know, Angus, I am not stupid, and I must tell you straight out that I cannot play after such a genius. And in dear old *East Lynne*!—I shall be trounced by the critics. Will you think badly of me if I cancel my week? You cannot, you are a friend. Announce that I am ill, Angus. And, as a friend, might you consider paying my hotel bill and the cost of my getting here and traveling on just as comfortably to the following week's engagement? Yes? No?"

"Dear, dear Rose!" Barton roared tenderly. "What I shall announce tomorrow in all the papers is that you have of your own free will withdrawn from your engagement here in favor of Madame Marina. The public will applaud your noble gesture, welcome you even more enthusiastically the next time you play at the California, and I'll give you not only the expenses you've asked for but five hundred dollars as well."

So Barton was able to report to Maryna that, as he had hoped, Rose Edwards was ceding her week.

In the second week Maryna repeated her Adrienne and Marguerite Gautier and, crossing at last truly into the English language, added Juliet. Tom Deane was delighted to do his Romeo, James Glenwood made an endearing Friar Laurence, and Kate Egan offered her crestfallen variation on Juliet's Nurse, which Maryna forgave, as she had forgiven Kate for igniting the veil—altogether inadvertently? of course not—on the first night. Last year's Juliet at the California Theatre had to feel glum about being shunted into the role of the Nurse, and obliged to be jolly and coarse with the subject of such headlines as "Debut at California Theatre Marks Epoch in Dramatic Art" and "World's Greatest Actress Makes American Debut in San Francisco."

Girding herself for the jealousy that invariably accompanies success, Maryna remembered her first year at the Imperial Theatre. Her coming had delivered a vivid insult to the old system, modeled on the Comédie-Française, in which the actors were recruited mostly from the Imperial's dramatic schools, and the few outsiders admitted to the company had to start at the lowest rank. There was no precedent for the invitation Maryna had received from the theatre's reform-minded new president, General Demichov, to come from Kraków to Warsaw for twelve guest-star performances; equally unheard of, and most galling to the other actors, was that the life contract Demichov then offered her included the right to choose her own roles. How well Maryna had understood the scowls and sulks of her new colleagues, before she compelled them to love her. *She* always felt green-eyed at the success of any putative rival. (An ignoble fantasy: Oh, if only Gabriela Ebert could see her now!) But American actors seemed astoundingly generous. (She would try to imitate these Americans and improve her character.) In America actors often spoke well of one another, seemed eager to admire.

It felt so natural to Maryna to be engulfed by admiration, as it did to have found the freedom to accept Ryszard's love. If there was a voice that said to her, Such an idyll cannot last, she could not hear it.

Ryszard heard it, conjured it up everywhere. He was leaden, reproachful: exactly what, a few days after they became lovers, he had promised Maryna he would not be. She had got *that* out of him by a chilling question. "Now that you have me"—they were lolling in bed late one morning—"what are you going to do with me?" But then, he thought, I would have said it anyway; I wanted her to think of me as light, light, light.

"What a question, my love! I'm going to look at you. As long as I can see you every day, I'll be happy."

"Just look at me? When could you not do that?"

"Now"—he drew her against his body—"I can look at you . . . closer."

But of course it wasn't as simple as this.

Ryszard thought he was a free spirit, unfettered by jealousy. How could he have known otherwise? Until now, the women he possessed he did not love and the woman he loved he did not possess. Now that he possessed her, or thought he did, he raged against all Maryna's admirers. And, of course, there were letters from Bogdan, and the occasional telegram, whose arrival Maryna made no attempt to hide, and that meant letters went from Maryna back to Bogdan. But Ryszard had no right to expect an account of this correspondence. At first he'd been grateful that Bogdan went unmentioned. It was as if the man had been magically banished from the universe. Now it felt as if Maryna were simply protecting Bogdan by never talking about him.

Everything spilled over in a tirade at the beginning of the second week, after her first Juliet.

"And that dullard, the Guatemalan consul who comes backstage every night, and he's not even Guatemalan, what's his name, Hangs—"

"Hanks," said Maryna. "Leslie C. Hanks."

"Hangs is better," said Ryszard. "You were flirting with him."

And perhaps she was. Every man seemed more attractive to her. Why couldn't Ryszard understand that *he* had made her more alive to the attentions of men; it was because she was with *him*—but no, he was simply jealous, more and more jealous. Bogdan had only been amused when other men flirted with her and she flirted back. He knew she meant nothing serious by it. He knew it was part of the normal giddiness and hypocrisy and insatiable craving to be loved to which every actress is prone. But then, she thought, Ryszard is a boy, Bogdan is a man.

And the next night, it was a stockbroker named John E. Daily, and the same scene all over again, with Ryszard storming about the parlor of Maryna's suite and on the verge of going back for the night to his own room on the second floor, when Maryna began laughing at him, just after Ryszard shouted, "I'm going to kill them both."

But there was no need for such desperate measures, as a scarcely chastened Ryszard was soon to report. Several days later, out for a stroll on Market Street, thinking (as he assured Maryna) of nothing but his mouth between her thighs, Ryszard saw the stockbroker stride out of a building (it was, Ryszard learned, the office of his brokerage firm), red-faced, glowering, yelling over his shoulder at a man hurrying after him through the door, then turn up the street—he was coming toward Ryszard—whereupon his pursuer, whom Ryszard now recognized, the Guatemalan consul, pulled out a pistol and fired at Daily's back. The stockbroker continued on a few steps, coughed, plucked at his collar, and fell dead at Ryszard's feet.

"Maybe I would have shot Dearly, if he kept on sending all those little *billets-doux*. Anyway, Hangs got there first."

"Ryszard, this isn't amusing."

"The nuisance is," he continued, "that now I can't stray too far from San Francisco. As a witness to the murder, I shall have to testify at the trial, which is unlikely to take place before November."

"And has Mr. Hanks confessed the motive for the crime?"

"No. He refuses to say. Doesn't matter, he'll hang for it. Unless he says that he'd just discovered that Dearly was his wife's lover and had gone out of his mind with the shock. Apparently, they don't hang you in San Francisco for killing your wife's lover, as long as you do it as soon as you find out about him. The police assume it was some bad speculation in Nevada mining stocks that Dearly had talked him into—"

"While you suspect they were brawling over me."

"Maryna, I didn't say that."

"But it occurred to you."

And so they were having their first quarrel, which ended handsomely that evening in bed. "I'm only jealous of everyone because I love you so much," explained Ryszard witlessly.

"I know," said Maryna. "But you still have to stop." She was about to say, Bogdan wasn't jealous of *you* back in Poland, but realized that she didn't know if this was true.

At the close of Maryna's second week of San Francisco triumph, and two days before she went out on a three-week tour

arranged by Warnock which would take her first to the phenomenally rich mining communities of western Nevada, Barton gave
a farewell party. When asked to propose a toast, she put out her
long arm, lifted her glass, and, looking into the blur of the candlelight, crooned, "To my new country!"

"Country," muttered Miss Collingridge. "Not *coun-n-try.*"

Ryszard would be at her side, and Warnock, who had already gone ahead to make everything ready, and Miss Collingridge, who had happily agreed to take on the duties of Maryna's
secretary but said that she hoped Madame would call her by her
first name from now on.

"Of course, Miss Collingridge, if you really insist," replied
Maryna with a smiling shrug.

"Collingridge," said Miss Collingridge. "As it is one word.
Not—"

"I shall be delighted, dear friend," said Maryna, "to address
you as Mildred."

It was three hundred miles to Virginia City, home of the
Comstock Lode, and the largest town between San Francisco and
St. Louis. "But it's not a normal town," Warnock had cautioned
before his departure, "and the trip's quite an experience too."
Hairpin turns on the iron road banded to the face of the snow-
capped granite wall, slim trestlework bridges strung over mile-
deep canyons—the Central Pacific's fabled crossing of "the Big
Hill," as he told her the Sierras were jocularly called, might seem
spectacular enough. But the best would come when they were almost there, after they had changed trains in Reno. The remaining distance to Virginia City, seventeen miles if you were a bird,
fifty-two miles if a passenger in one of the lemon-colored Pullman coaches of the Virginia and Truckee Railroad (another
wildly profitable venture of the late Mr. Ralston), would take
them along a track whose grade was steeper than steep, circling
and recircling the treeless mountain to reach the fabled town
near the peak. "But I know you have strong nerves, Madame Marina," he concluded.

"I do." She smiled. How Americans love their wonders. "Thanks to you, Mr. Warnock, I am prepared for everything."

He guaranteed Maryna that she would forget the drama of the journey to Virginia City when she discovered the big-city scale of the town's most famous theatre and the luxury of its six-story International Hotel, which rivaled the Palace in San Francisco in plush and ormolu, gilt and crystal, marquetry and cloisonné, crystal goblets from Vienna and richly brocaded bellpulls from Florence, all in gallant defiance of the occasional reminder that the town sat squarely on top of the mines. "You know," he said. "Doors that suddenly don't close, windows that you haven't tried to open which all of a sudden, well, shatter." Ryszard looked at him with unconcealed dislike. "Prepared for everything," Maryna repeated dreamily. "Subsidence," Miss Collingridge said crisply. "Exactly," Warnock said. "Now and then."

She opened her week of performances in the tilted town with *Camille*.

The manager in charge of the stage at Piper's Opera House told Maryna not to expect that his stock company could offer her a supporting cast as expert as the one at the California Theatre. "But they're good actors, mind you, and they've each got dozens of parts down line-perfect. The star can let us know at the last moment whether it's *Romeo and Juliet* or *The Octoroon* or *Richelieu* or *Our American Cousin* or *Camille*, whichever, and we're ready to play. And as I always tell my actors, the first rule is to give the star the center of the stage and keep out of his way. But if help is needed we can give that too. I remember the first time Booth came to do *Hamlet* here at Piper's. I guess he thought, this being a rough kind of town, maybe we weren't up to his standards. What seemed to worry him most was the fifth act, but I assured him that he'd have a practicable grave and whatever else he required, and we did a little better than that, we gave him something more lifelike, I'll wager, than he'd had in all his long career. I had a section sawed out of the stage floor, hired a couple of

miners from the Ophir to do valiant pick-work, and that night the gravediggers shoveled some interesting specimens of ore onto the stage before handing up Yorick's skull, and when Booth cried out, *This is I, Hamlet the Dane!* and leaped into Ophelia's grave to tussle with Laertes, he had a surprise, you should have seen the look on his face, when he found himself landing almost five feet down and on bedrock."

Of course the great thespian didn't say a word of thanks, and luckily he hadn't hurt himself, continued Piper's manager in charge of the stage. "Lord, he's a strange broody man. But geniuses are like that, I know." He told Maryna he had recommended to Booth that, after leaving Virginia City, he stop at a special spring situated a mile west of Carson City, much frequented by persons afflicted with rheumatism and melancholia. It's a "chicken-soup spring," so called because, with the addition of pepper and salt, the water acquires the taste of thin chicken soup and is actually quite nourishing.

"And I recommend it to you too, dear Madame."

"Thank you, Mr. Tyler, but I am neither rheumatic nor melancholiac. At least, not yet."

Cameel, Cameel, people called to her on the street. One was a tall man with a wide neat bandage under his chin, whom Ryszard decided must be recovering from a slit throat. Each of the three plays Maryna gave during the week called on her to counterfeit death—as Adrienne she died in an excruciating delirium; as Juliet, in a sensuous swoon, falling across the body of her Romeo; as Marguerite Gautier, in a convulsive protest against the injustice of death—but it was generally acknowledged that her greatest success in dying was in *Camille*, during one performance of which, reported the town's leading newspaper, *The Territorial Enterprise*, two members of the audience, in different parts of the thousand-seat theatre, were so transfixed with horror at seeing Marguerite spring from her couch and fall with a terrifying crash, dead, upon the floor, that both were struck with a rigidifying paralysis and remained unable to rise from their seats for a full hour after the performance had ended.

How else could the *Enterprise* convey to its readers the enchantment of Maryna's performances? Tall tales, hoaxes, and practical jokes were the paper's much admired, trademark method of responding to a landscape of improbabilities. Virginia City was itself a tall tale—the chance discovery by several ignorant prospectors, some twenty years before, of a lode of silver-rich quartz just below ground near the top of the mountain then called Sun Peak, which had been turned, by magnates from San Francisco who knew how to exploit it, into the most lucrative mining venture in the history of the world. Only recently some miners had cut into a block of almost pure silver fifty-four feet wide and thirty feet deep. Sober-sided reporting had little chance of being heard as long as were true stories like that.

Toward the end of the week Maryna let it be known that she would like to see the insides of this fabulous mountain, and promptly received an invitation signed by Jedediah Forster, the superintendent of the biggest of the bonanza mines, the Consolidated Virginia. Arriving with Ryszard at the mine office, she was provided with a cap, a pair of breeches, and a cloak, and, after donning her costume in an adjoining storeroom, returned to the office to be greeted by a very tall, handsome man in buckskins and silver buckles, Forster himself. He would be honored—he bowed—to be Madame Zalenska's guide, though he hoped she understood that the mine was ill-equipped to receive visitors, least of all so distinguished a lady visitor. Signaling one of the men in the office to follow with an oil lamp, he led Maryna and Ryszard outdoors to a brick shed housing an iron frame with a square plank floor, which he entered first. As the cage started its slow, clanking descent, the air thickened and the dampness acquired a sharp foul odor that pinched the nostrils and clogged the throat. They could hear water coursing down the shaft as they dropped lower and lower, and when the cage began to sway from side to side, Ryszard stretched out his arm to protect Maryna from contact with the rough wet wall. (What can *this* experience be good for, Maryna wondered, struggling not to give way to panic. One of those foolhardy adventures you get through by ignoring where you are and what you are feeling?) At last it stopped, discharging its passengers at the dim mouth of a low narrow tunnel. They began to walk, deeper and deeper still. The heat, unbearable, was being borne by miners stripped to the waist, wielding their pickaxes and shovels. Infernal work! "We are nineteen hundred feet under the ground," said their guide, who, after asking permission from Maryna, pulled off his buckskin jacket, exposing an immaculate silk shirt.

Ryszard determined not to remove his jacket, much as he would have liked to, even as he politely allowed himself to be taken off to look at the rising water in the next chamber and the new pumping machinery brought down to drain it. Con-Virginia's elegantly garbed superintendent, who remained with Maryna, did not suppose a lady would be interested in being shown how anything in the mine actually worked. He was very pleased, however, to be in her company.

"This is the second mine I have visited," Maryna remarked, for want of anything better to say. "Some years ago I was given a tour of the famous salt mine that lies south of Kraków, my native city in Poland."

"A salt mine. I'm afraid people around here wouldn't think that was much of a mine."

"Agreed, Colonel Forster"—all heads of mines, Maryna had been told, are addressed as Colonel—"salt is hardly as valuable as silver, but the mine itself is well worth visiting. You see, it has been in continuous operation since the thirteenth century."

"And they still haven't extracted all the salt? They must work very slowly in your country. But there can't be much incentive, considering what I guess the profit would be from salt."

"I can see, my dear Colonel, that I haven't explained properly what this great mine, this royal Polish mine, includes. It's not just a business, as everything is here in America. And you must not suppose our Polish miners are lacking in diligence. Their centuries of digging have hollowed out a vast underground world on five levels, with mile after mile of spacious galleries connecting more than a thousand halls or chambers, many of immense size. Some are supported by intricate lattices of timber, others by pillars of salt as thick as the great old trees of northern California, and several of these subterranean caverns, so long and wide as to appear boundless, are without any support in the middle. In two of the largest are grand lakes that can be crossed in a flatboat. But it is not only for these awesome Plutonic vistas that the mine has attracted so many distinguished tourists, starting with the great Polish astronomer Kopernik; even Goethe thought it worth a visit. Most interesting for the visitor is that, after the chambers have been bored and all the salt extracted, the miners carve life-size figures out of the salt to decorate the abandoned chambers."

"Statues," said Forster. "They take time off, while they're down in the mine, to make statues."

"Yes, statues of Polish kings and queens—there is a remarkable statue of one of my country's founding martyrs, Wanda, daughter of Krakus. And of course religious statues in the chapels on each level where the miners worship every morning, the grandest and most ancient being the one dedicated to Anthony of Padua, which has columns with ornamented capitals, arches, images of the Saviour, the Virgin, and the saint, altar and pulpit with all their decorations, and figures of two priests represented at prayers before the saint's shrine—all sculpted out of the dark rock salt. Here, once a month, a High Mass is celebrated."

"A church in a mine. Right."

Clearly, the Colonel did not believe her. He knew a tall story when he heard one.

Maryna enjoyed regaling Ryszard with the story of how she had flummoxed their imposing guide when they were back at the hotel.

"I know a story about another salt mine," said Ryszard,

"though, unfortunately, it's not I who made it up but Stendhal. At the salt mine of Hallein, near Salzburg, the miners have the pretty custom of throwing a wintry bough into one of the disused galleries and then retrieving it two or three months later when, thanks to the waters saturated with salt which have soaked the bough and then receded, it is thickly encrusted down to the tiniest twig with a shining deposit of little crystals, and these rare pieces of jewelry are presented to the lady tourists who visit the mine. Stendhal claims that falling in love is something like this process of crystallization. Dipping the idea of his beloved in his imagination, the lover endows her with all perfections, like the crystals on the leafless bough."

"As you've done with me."

"With other women, for a week or three, I admit." Ryszard laughed.

"Not with me."

"Dearest, peerless Maryna!"

"Why not me as well? Maybe I'm just a wintry bough. On a stage I scintillate and dazzle but—"

"Maryna!"

"I don't understand why you're telling me this story."

And Ryszard thought: I can't understand either. How could I be so stupid? What am I doing? And surely it was inane, no, cowardly, to reply, "Please, darling, let's not quarrel now." Now? "Ever!"

LEAVING THROUGH Piper's stage door near midnight after the final performance, Maryna and Ryszard and Miss Collingridge joined some two thousand people who, by bright moonlight and bonfires, were gazing upward as a woman clad in a short frock and tights stepped off the wrought-iron balustrade above the theatre's entrance into the air; followed with the crowd down Union Street as she too went down the steeply angled street, high above their heads; and applauded with the crowd as Miss Ella LaRue walked off the rope with a proud stamp of her foot onto the roof of a brick building on the corner of D and Union. "Cheering sight," said Ryszard to Maryna. "Immense across the hips, isn't she?" he added, hoping to annoy Miss Collingridge. Then, in search of further entertainment, they strolled back up to C Street and through a pair of double glass doors into the Polka Saloon.

As the mines were always working, so were the saloons. Miners arrived fresh from their shifts to wager their earnings at faro, monte, and poker (they distrusted fancy games and any sort of gambling machinery), and Maryna begged her companions to amuse themselves while she sat and watched the spectacle.

Ryszard went to stand at the bar and was soon being regaled by a reporter from the *Enterprise* with the news of the discovery in a sealed mountain cavern of a "silver man"—some poor Indian trapped in the cave long long ago, whose body over the centuries had been changed by the nature of the earth, steaming vapors, and the transfer of metallic substances into a mass of silver; more exactly, the body having been sent for assay to Carson City, into sulphuret of silver slightly mixed with copper and iron. Meanwhile, Miss Collingridge had become entranced by the saloon mascot, Black Billy, who, unlike the many goats living in old mine tunnels and foraging for scant herbage on the slopes of Mount Davidson, was one of a more privileged or daring band who had the run of the city: Billy lived and chewed tobacco on C Street.

Maryna remained undisturbed with her glass of champagne a full quarter of an hour before a bearded giant in a red-checked shirt rose from one of the nearby tables and lurched toward her, bottle in one hand and a red geranium in the other, bawling "O Jewelie-ette, Jewelie-ette, wherefore art thou Jewelie-ette!" She looked about the room for Ryszard's intervention, but a woman was right behind the intruder and already shooing him away with "Get along now, Nate. Don't bother the lady. She's worked hard too, and she has a right to sit here peaceable in my saloon and have a drink without bein' pestered by her admirers."

Her rescuer lingered next to the table. Fat, tightly corseted, beribboned, a little drunk, around forty-five or fifty, Maryna guessed. "I just want to tell you what an honor it is to have you in my saloon." She smiled, and Maryna saw that she had once been very pretty. "I just can't believe it's you, sittin' there. It's like a queen came in here. A queen! Here in the Polka!"

"Which we dance in Poland," said Maryna gaily.

"No kid?" said the woman. "And I thought it was a hundred percent American!" She paused. "You must want to be by yourself. I wouldn't blame you. You must be surrounded by people all the time."

"Do sit with me," said Maryna. "My friends will be back in a moment."

"May I?"—she sank into a chair—"May I? I won't talk too much, I promise." She gazed, awestruck, at Maryna. "I just have to tell you, you were so"—she sighed—"so wonderful last night. You know we get a lot of plays in Virginia and I always go when I can, I seen them all, almost, everyone comes here, even Booth, and I saw three of his Hamlets. And sometimes he'd stop by the Polka. Once he sat right at this table."

"I'm pleased to be sitting at Mr. Booth's table," said Maryna, smiling.

"Right there where you're sittin'. Very polite, no airs at all, but he seemed so sad. And he got drunk as a lord, though you'd never know it the next night. Well, he's grand, I don't say no, but I like actresses better, and you're the best. You can really feel somethin' when a woman suffers, at least that's what I think. Take the one you just did, the French lady who has to drive the nice young fellow who really loves her away and pretend she doesn't love him anymore, I can never say her name, it's not the same as the play."

"Marguerite Gautier."

"That's right. We've had a lot of Camilles, but you're the best. I never cried so much at a *Camille* in my life."

"It's a splendid role for an actress," said Maryna.

"And the way you do Juliet, that was wonderful, and the other one, I saw everything you did this week, the one about the French actress, what's her name, you know."

"Adrienne."

"That's it. You did it a whole lot better than that Italian who came here two years ago, I forget her name, and did it in Italian, but that didn't bother me, when someone is good you understand the feelin'."

"Adelaide Ristori."

"That's her. I like that play. But I like *Camille* the best."

"Ah, that interests me very much," said Maryna. "Could you tell me why you prefer *Camille*?"

"Because Juliet, she's just a sweet young thing, and she should of been happy, and it had nothin' to do with her, those families not gettin' along. And the French actress, I forgot her name again . . ."

"Adrienne."

"Right. She's good, too. And it isn't her fault that the man she loves has to be polite to that awful princess who goes ahead and poisons her. That's just bad luck, if you know what I mean. But Camille, she's more like real life. I mean, she hasn't been so good, she isn't innocent, how can she be, she's been with a lot of men, so she's kind of resigned, she doesn't believe in love, why should she, after all she's seen of men, and then she meets a man who's really different, and she wants to change her life. But she can't. They don't let her. She's got to be punished. She has to go back to bein' what she was." The woman started to cry.

"Here, Mrs. . . . Mrs. . . . I'm sorry, you didn't tell me your name," said Maryna, extending a handkerchief.

"Minnie," said the woman. "How'd you know I was married?"

"I didn't of course. I just assumed."

"Well, you're right. I am married." She dabbed at her eyes. "But you know how it is." She tilted her chair back unsteadily. "You don't marry the man you love."

"I'm sorry to hear that," said Maryna.

The woman signaled one of the waiters, who brought her a Sazerac. "I've gotten to like these fancy San Francisco drinks in my older years. When I was young, straight whiskey was good enough, bourbon, rye, corn, you name it. Somethin' else for you? My barman makes a real good Brandy Smash."

"Thank you, no. My friends will be back in a moment, and then I must leave."

"I hope I'm not gettin' out of my place. But you look like a woman I can confide in. You're an actress, you understand everything . . ."

"Hardly."

"Let me tell you why I said what I did, about marriage and all, it's a good story at the beginnin' though I don't think you could make much of a play out of it, not with the way it ended."

"I'm not looking for another role," said Maryna gently. "But I'm happy to hear your story. I like stories."

And Minnie began.

"It was twenty-five years ago, no, more . . . and I was livin' in California, in Cloudy Mountain, I don't know if you ever heard of it. There was this fellow who was after me, he was the sheriff, he was a big gambler too, but not a bad sort in his way, I could see that, and when he said he loved me, I knew he meant it, he wasn't just tryin' to get under my skirt. He'd keep sayin', Marry me, Girl, marry me, that's what he called me, Girl, and when I'd remind him that he had a wife back in New Orleans, he'd say that didn't matter, 'cause I was the wife he wanted to have. And maybe you won't believe it, lookin' at me now, but I wasn't bad-lookin', and I was pure in my heart, I was still a young thing, even though I had this saloon where all the miners came, the Polka, I call all my saloons the Polka, and most of 'em treated me real respectful, like I was their little sister, even though some didn't and there wasn't much I could do about it, I mean they were good customers. But I didn't like that part of the job, it got to makin' me feel sad, though I didn't let on, I was always singin' and laughin', and I was wonderin' if there was any way out of that life, but there wasn't. And then I thought, the sheriff's not a bad sort, at least he loves me, and I was sort of considerin' it, though I didn't let on.

"And then I met this other fellow I really did take a shine to, he was so romantic, he told me I had the face of an angel, me who was keepin' a saloon. But it was him that had the face of an angel, I never saw a man that looked like that. His face was all bony but smooth too, you wanted to touch his cheek, and he had a high forehead, and sometimes his hair fell into his eyes, big dark eyes with beautiful lashes, that got all crinkly when he smiled, it was a slow smile, real slow, that was like he was kissin' you with his smile. Just to look at him, it went right through me and made me weak in the knees. Trouble was, he was a bandit, that was his life, I suppose he just fell into it, and then he was known for a bandit, and wanted for murder, so he felt he had to go on. While he was bein' a bandit he was disguised as a Mexican, name of Ramerrez, 'cause everyone knows lots of Mexicans are bandits. But when he sneaked into Cloudy to court me he was got up as one of those high-toned shrimps from Sacramento and used his right name, Dick Johnson. And then he told me he was the one called Ramerrez everyone was after, but that since meetin' me he didn't want to be Ramerrez anymore, and he promised to reform, and I know he was sincere. And I talked to him too and told him all my secrets, and he listened, that was so nice, I never had that, someone you can talk to, someone you can turn your heart inside out to. I almost forgot who I was! And all this while, the sheriff was lookin' high and low for Ramerrez, and nobody knew Ramerrez was really Dick. But the sheriff, Jack, he never missed a trick when it came to me. He saw I was gettin' kinda interested in the fellow from Sacramento that he didn't know was Ramerrez. Interested! I was crazy for him! And what woman, if she's a real woman, doesn't love a bandit more than a sheriff, you know that, you're a woman, and you're an actress so you can play all women, angels and sinners . . .

"And guess who I hitched myself to? That's him over there by the strongbox with the six-shooter in his belt, we own this place together. The sheriff. But he gave that up, seein' as there was more money to be made in saloons, and ten years later, when they found the Comstock Lode, we came here, 'cause you didn't have to be real smart to see there'd be a lot of money to be made off thirsty silver miners comin' off their shifts. But why did I settle for him, that's what I ask myself, when I was so in love with Dick and had gotten up my courage and did go off with him, my head all full of dreams. We had to leave California, which I loved dearly, 'cause he was so wanted everywhere for murder, they would of hanged him if he got caught, and we came into Nevada, which wasn't a state then or even a territory, as long as nobody knew what lay under this mountain the whole place was just a county in Utah, and we wandered around awhile with no money, gettin' hungrier and hungrier. And then Dick went back to bein' Ramerrez, and I got scared, thinkin' of the life that was in front of me, always hidin' and runnin' and bein' afraid, and I left him and went crawlin' back to California, and Jack, he forgave me, and I saw he really did love me, 'cause he knew I'd never love him, not the way I loved Dick, and he still loved me, so that I had to think better of him, but that didn't mean I had to marry him. But I did. First we was sort of married there in Cloudy by the justice of the peace, a real one, even with that wife still alive in New Orleans, but I thought I should let him be serious, and finally she died, so I really am Mrs. Rance now, have been for a long time. And I ended up back in Nevada anyway, it's fifteen years already. And sometimes I lay awake all night next to Jack, up in the heights the goats run out on the flat tin roofs, like on our house, and their hoofs keep me awake, and I can't help thinkin' I should of stayed with Dick, even though he had to go back to bandit life. Maybe I just didn't think enough of myself. Or maybe I just wasn't brave. Dick always used to say, there was this poem he used to recite,

> *No star is ever lost we once have seen,*
> *We always may be what we might have been.*

I often say that to myself now." She took Maryna's hand and held it tightly. "But it ain't true."

"Maryna?" said Ryszard.

Assuring him with her glance that there was no "scene" from which she needed to be rescued, Maryna introduced them to each other.

"This your husband?" Minnie asked. "I seen him with you comin' out of the hotel."

"My bandit."

"Ah-ha!" said Minnie.

"What have you two women been talking about?" Ryszard said nervously. "Or is it not permitted for a mere man to be privy to your secret?"

"And are you goin' to make the same mistake?"

"Yes. I think so."

"Ladies, ladies," said Ryszard, feeling a surge of alarm. "Maryna, it's late. You must be tired. Let me take you back to the hotel."

"Sounds like a husband to me," said Minnie.

"That's why it may not be a mistake."

"Well, you'll know better than me. You're beautiful. You're a star. Everyone loves you. You can do anythin' you want."

"Can I? No, I can't."

Miss Collingridge, smelling of goat, was standing next to Ryszard. "Madame Marina, is there anything you need?"

"I guess she wants you to go back to the hotel, too," said Minnie.

THE QUESTION Ryszard had heard himself asking for days. The question. Finally, back in the hotel, after they had made love, he asked it.

"You're not going to let me stay with you, are you?"

He'd been hearing Maryna's answer, too. Still, it astonished him to hear it now.

"No."

"But you love me!" he cried.

"I do. And you have made me very happy. But, how can I say this, the *à deux* thing isn't, can never be that important to me. I understand that now. *Déformation professionelle*, if you will. I want to love and be loved, who does not, but I have to be calm . . . within myself. And with you I would worry, whether you were bored or restless or not writing enough. And I'd be right to worry. What have you got written in the last month—apart from writing about me?"

"That doesn't matter! I'm too happy to write!"

"But it does matter. Writing is your life, as theatre is mine. You don't want the life I lead. You don't know it now but you would find it out soon, in six months, at most a year. You're not made to be an actress's consort. Believe me, it won't last."

"Speak for yourself, you terrible creature!" He slammed his hand against the window frame.

"What do I hear, Ryszard? Could it be the sound of crystals dropping off the wintry bough?"

"Oh, Maryna!"

"You're asking me, and you have every right to ask me, if I really do love you. And I want to say—oh, dearest Ryszard, you know what I *want* to say. And that wanting is love, too, though not the kind you mean. But the truth is, I never know exactly what I feel when I'm not on a stage. No, that's not true. I feel intense interest, curiosity, pity, anxiety, desire to please—all that. But love, what you mean by love, what you want from me . . . I'm not sure. I know I don't feel love the way I represent it before an audience. Maybe I don't feel much of anything at all."

"Maryna, darling Maryna, you'll never convince me of that. I've held you in my arms, I've seen your face as no one has ever seen it—" He stopped. Have I, he wondered. He went on. "Maryna, I *know* you."

"Yes, now," she said. "I feel a great deal now, and it *is* for you, for no one else. But I can also feel it tilting away from you, and pouring back into the selves I create on the stage. You've given me so much, dear dear Ryszard."

"How miserable you're making me."

"Maybe," she mused, "it was because I thought I'd never be in love again that I didn't care about acting anymore, and thought I could give it up. But now I've known it again and—"

"And what?"

"I won't forget it again."

"You're going to live on a *memory* of our love? That's enough for you, Maryna?"

"Perhaps it is. Actors aren't so interested in real life. We just want to act."

"You think I'll be an impediment to your career? Too much of a distraction?"

"No, no, it's that I don't want to cheat you."

"I see. You're sending me away for my own good."

"I'm not saying that," she said.

"Actually, I think you're sending me away for your good. Only you haven't the courage to admit it. No, Maryna, your real reason for casting me away has nothing to do with your concern for my happiness."

"Oh Ryszard, Ryszard, there are many reasons."

"You're right. Let me see if I can guess them all. Fear of scandal—actress abandons husband and child for other man! Desire for security—actress leaves rich husband for impecunious writer! Unwillingness to lose class privileges—great actress exchanges aristocratic husband for lowborn—"

"Ah, I'm being treated to one of your virtuoso catalogues."

"Wait, I haven't finished, Maryna. Fear of flouting convention—actress leaves husband for man ten years her junior! Unwillingness to forfeit hard-won respectability, while bringing up bastard to whose father she claims to have been married. You thought I didn't know, I imagine, because dear Bogdan pretends not to know."

"I suppose I've no right now to ask you not to hurt me."

"Not to mention selfishness, hardheartedness, shallowness—" Ryszard stopped. Irrevocable words. Words that can't be unsaid. He began to cry.

It wasn't only because he was losing Maryna. It was the end of his youth: of his ability to love worshipfully, suffer unprotectedly. What would he dream of when he no longer dreamt of Maryna? This, thought Ryszard, is the most painful feeling I shall ever have. Was she suffering, too? And could she, too, be clambering over her feelings so as not to drown? This, he thought, is the saddest thing that will ever happen to me. He was in a dark place, where there were only wounds. And then a splinter of relief. Oh, the books he would write now, with only lesser obsessions to distract him! Never again—and the thought came to him on a wave of shame—will I be "too happy" to write.

Eight

MARYNA HAD NO CHOICE but to believe the story Bogdan related when he finally joined her at the Hotel Clarendon in New York in early January. It was not like Bogdan to fabulate. As he himself observed, he rarely felt the itch to tell any kind of story.

"And my fear—" The word was clipped before it could bloom. "And I worried that you were perishing of boredom and frustration back in Anaheim."

"Not at all," he said. "Something always flows in to fill the void."

"Poor Bogdan." Her smile was amorous, alert. They were side by side on the ottoman. She clasped the back of his head.

"Ah, you're not to feel sorry for me. You're supposed to believe me."

"Make me believe you," she said and drooped against his shoulder. "Will you think me credulous, or merely overfond, if I believe everything you say?"

"Overfond? I should like nothing better," he said, bringing her hand to his cheek. "Then I can be sure that even if you don't believe in my adventure, you won't disbelieve me either."

"Go on," she murmured.

"It was Ben Dreyfus, you remember him, don't you, who

293

told me that some years ago he'd heard talk of a bizarre cult in Sonora, each of whose members was charged with designing a feasible machine for sky travel. Not a hot-air balloon, at the mercy of the internal work of the wind, but a navigable air-ship that could be lifted off the ground by its own power and, once aloft, flown in any desired direction. A few of these bird-machines actually rose into the air, it was said, before they crashed. When he tried to find out more, he was told that the group had disbanded and its leader, a German named Christian von Roebling, had migrated south to Montoya Beach, near Carpinteria. Now it appeared that von Roebling might still be at it, since a friend of Dreyfus who came down from San Francisco in August by steamer swore to having seen a *something*, definitely not a balloon, high off the shore near Carpinteria cruising into a cloud. Since, as Dreyfus says, it can't be long before there are self-powered flying machines, he supposed it might be worth seeing how far these daredevils had got, thinking of a possible investment; and—he's been so decent, even lending me money to pay off those debts for machinery and supplies I'd not told you about—I offered to approach von Roebling on his behalf. So after I recovered from my accident I went up the coast—remember that week when we were entirely out of touch? You were in Virginia City, making miners weep and dropping down a shaft into the bowels of a treasure-hill. And I, I was chasing some quack Daedalus who could take me up in the air."

"What I did," Maryna exclaimed, "wasn't dangerous at all. Bogdan! Be careful!"

"Oh, Maryna, when am I not careful?" he said. "I took a room in the village inn, chatted with people in the saloons, none of whom knew anyone called von Roebling, and prowled the dunes, looking into the blue. After a few days, I was ready to give up, and went to buy some supplies for my return journey at the general store. The only other customer was a grizzled fellow wearing spectacles broad as a bandit's mask, who was purchasing . . . barrels of nails, I think. Hearing a blunt German accent, I introduced myself. He told me his name was Dellschau, something like that, but I suspected that I'd found von Roebling. Following him out of the store, I said in German that my scientific interests had brought me news of the work he was directing, and requested permission to watch the next time someone attempted to send his machine into the air. He was silent a long time; I was hoping he might prove to be one of those secretive people who actually crave as much as they fear another's intrusiveness. But then he let me know, in atrociously intermittent English, that my curiosity could have very unpleasant consequences"—"Bogdan!" cried Maryna—"because if there were any truth to the *phantastisch* story, this *Blödsinn* I'd heard about aeros and an Aero Club, his words, *I* hadn't used them, surely I would realize that seeing one of these machines up close, not to mention observing one in flight, would be *streng verboten* to all but bona-fide members of the club. His advice, and he repeated it, was to clear out of town *schnell*."

"But you didn't."

"Of course not."

"And did you ever see anything?"

"Not in the air. On the beach, late one night, I'd gone for a moonlit walk and there, some way ahead of me, was a dark thing that I mistook at first for a beached outrigger. It was canoe-shaped, though much bigger than a canoe, with four wings, two on either side, a sort of basket in the widest part where a pair of aeronauts would sit, and screw propellers attached to the bow and stern."

"I made some drawings of it, Mama."

"Peter, you weren't there!"

"Yes, but I know all about it and I—I'll show you!"

He ran into the other bedroom of the suite and returned with a large folder. Bogdan spread out the drawings at their feet.

"They're very prettily colored," said Maryna.

"Mama, this is science!"

"Yes, they're very accurate," said Bogdan. "The navigational part seemed clear—the propellers and, see, that's the rudder. But nothing I could make out gave any clue to how the contrivance is powered. No steam engine, which means engine, boiler, and a considerable weight of water and fuel, would be small enough, light enough. But if not steam, what? What can they have devised to lift something heavier than air off the ground?"

"A dragon comes," said Peter. "They have a pet dragon and it flips the machine into the air with its tail."

"Peter!"

"I'm not being childish, Mama. I'm being amusing."

"I wanted to get closer," Bogdan continued, "but then I saw four men with torches approaching. One of them was von Roebling. They were armed, so I decided to go back to town."

"Guns," said Peter. "They all had guns. Does everyone in New York have guns, too?"

"No, darling!" said Maryna. "We're not in the Wild West anymore. Now be good, and go to the other parlor and read."

"That was supposed to make you laugh," said Peter. "But since I'm not amusing you, I think I'll go down the hall and find Aniela or Miss Collingridge." He slammed the door.

Maryna frowned. "And then?"

"When I went out at dawn to the same spot, it was gone."

Maryna thought, Maybe he is making this up. Maybe Bogdan also thinks he has to entertain me.

"Of course, it must sound ridiculous that someone who had recently fallen off a horse would be hoping to be taken hundreds of feet up in the air in some fanciful contraption that couldn't possibly stay aloft very long."

Reminded of this accident in which she'd not really believed at the time, Maryna asked him, once again, just how badly he had been hurt in September.

"You want to know the exact nature of my injuries? Why? Do I seem scarred or disabled to you?" He stood. "I've told you. It's not worth retelling."

"I'm sorry," she said softly. And after a silence: "Did you tell von Roebling you'd sighted his machine?"

"Hardly. But I'll be back in California before long, and perhaps I'll attempt to talk to him again."

"And if these . . . these aeros really do fly, will you go into partnership with Dreyfus as an investor?"

"Surely not," said Bogdan. He sat beside her again and took her hand. "If there's one lesson I've learned from this past year's rural venture, it's that I shall never make a businessman. For the foreseeable future, my dear, the sole money-earner in this family is you."

Money was the reason they had not been reunited as soon as Maryna had decided to break with Ryszard. Money—and Ryszard's refusal to leave San Francisco, his excuse being that he was waiting to be called as a witness at the Hanks trial. Bogdan's affairs in Anaheim were still not settled, and it would have been foolish to liquidate everything in haste in order to come for Maryna's return engagement at the California Theatre in October as long as he and Peter still had a home in southern California: foolish and ruinously expensive. It might seem indecent to complain about having to scrimp and make sacrifices, as Maryna did every day to Warnock, when she was clearing a thousand dollars a week, far more, as dear old Captain Znaniecki had seen fit to remind her, than most workers in America earned in a year. But then most people did not have Maryna's expenses and responsibilities. At least she was able to send Bogdan some money to settle the debts he had accumulated in Anaheim; rescue the penniless family headed by Cyprian and Danuta, disillusioned with their life at Edenica and longing to return to Warsaw (she paid their passage); remit in full, as honor and indignation demanded, the outrageous fine of five thousand rubles exacted by the Imperial Theatre for breaking her contract (she had pleaded with the director—an erstwhile friend!—to extend her year's leave of absence by another year, but was refused). And before her loomed the outlay for the trip to New York, six weeks in a hotel until she would again be on salary when she opened in mid-December (Warnock would advance her the money for her hotel bill but could not be expected to pay for lodging Bogdan, Peter, and Aniela, and she would already have been paying for Miss Collingridge); and, most onerous of all the expenses she had to anticipate, the costumes. She had been able to make do in San Francisco. Costumes for Adrienne and Juliet were among those brought from Poland, while for *Camille* she had borrowed some money from Captain Znaniecki, hired a seamstress, and fitted herself out passably; but in New York she would be opening in *Camille,* and all five costumes had to be truly sumptuous. In New York, it didn't need to be explained to Maryna, a great deal was expected of a leading actress's costumes. Even more, Warnock observed, than in Paris.

But surely the advertising would not have been as vulgar in Paris. Warnock's work in that department—the playbills announcing the New York debut of "Countess Zalenska of the Russian Imperial Theatre, Warsaw"—had made her cringe. The *Countess* Zalenska, who in God's name is that? And, oh, must it say *Russian?* But Bogdan only laughed when he saw it. "*Que veux-tu, ma chère,* this is America. Why should they get anything about foreigners right at first? Warnock thinks there's a fortune to be made from you, but he's apprehensive all the same. Trust me, Maryna, he'll soon see that he needn't attach my irrelevant title to your charming new name."

She felt his calm, his benign calm, settle over her. He'd not changed too much: yes, country-brown when he arrived, a little heavier, and he'd taken to biting his nails; no, he was the same. Bogdan was kind, very kind, to feign lack of interest in Ryszard's whereabouts: Maryna volunteered the news that their friend, having the bad luck to see a man shoot down another in the street, had been detained in San Francisco to testify at the murderer's trial, after which he had returned to Poland. Heavy with unshareable thoughts, Maryna gratefully allowed herself to feel lightened, then steadied, by Bogdan's ingenious reserve. She'd been so nervous before he arrived. For a month her only untroubled relation had been to the wire-and-cloth dummy on which she elaborated the new costumes for *Camille*. With the seamstress Maryna had quarreled about both the magnificent ball dress for Act Four and the dying attire (a night robe of white India muslin) for Act Five. Everyone got on her nerves.

She had felt very agitated on opening night. The part she could identify as stage fright seemed appropriate, but it wasn't just stage fright and it didn't abate. Cynical and despairing in the first act, anxious and vulnerable and finally accepting Armand's love in the second—she knew she was simulating Marguerite Gautier's pathos and joy as well as she had ever done. It was the emotion that the story gave her no opportunity to deploy— anger—which was making her so nervous. At last, in the third act, she had a chance to vent it. A deliriously happy Marguerite is now living with her beloved Armand in the countryside just outside Paris; this morning he has gone into the city on a brief errand, and she is alone in a sunlit room looking onto the garden, dressed in a cashmere robe of peach-blossom pink, trimmed with a cascade of lace down the front and one narrow flounce around the bottom, lace ruffles on the elbow sleeves, a lace fraise at the neck, and one shell-shaped lace pocket on the left side ornamented with a pink rosette, which was to find particular favor with several of the reviewers. Her maid Nanine has just announced the arrival of a gentleman who wishes to speak to her. Marguerite, believing it to be her lawyer (unbeknownst to Armand, she has put up the entire contents of her grand house in Paris for sale), has asked for him to be shown in. Of course it is not the lawyer.

Mademoiselle Marguerite Gautier? A dignified older man has appeared at the door upstage right and continued past the live canary with which the stage manager, zealous for scenic realism, had seen fit to dress the set. *That is my name*, said Maryna. *To whom do I have the honor of speaking?* The canary started to chirp. *To Monsieur Duval.* Chirp. Chirp. You might have thought there were two birds in the cage. *Monsieur Duval?* Chirp, chirp, chirp. *Yes, madame, to Armand's father.* Maryna was supposed to say the next line in a troubled but calm tone—calm, she, with that bird's vile piping? *Armand is not here, monsieur.* Chirp, chirp, chirp, chirp. *I know. It is to you that I wish to speak. Be good enough to listen to what I have to say.* Listen? How could she listen to anything? *My son is ruining himself for you.* Chirp, chirr, squawk, cheep, trill, twitter, chirp. Having stood it as long as she could, Maryna walked to the rear of the set, took down the cage and hurled it out the open mullioned window, then turned and came gliding down the sloped stage floor to keep her appointment with heartbreak.

She did worry that she might have shocked some members of the audience—surely not everyone would think it part of the play!—but was reassured when, fifteen minutes later, as Marguerite finally realizes that her pure unselfish love for Armand is never going to be accepted by his father, Maryna heard the theatre fill with the sound of weeping spectators and saw the prompter toss the promptbook to the floor and flee for an orgy of nose-blowing to a corner of the wings. Unfortunately, one of the critics refused to let her forget the incident completely. The next day, the review in the *Sun* noted "a most original display of the fiery temperament characteristic of the greatest actresses, the defenestration of a raucous canary." Maryna was appalled to see it mentioned in print. Critics! They only want to mock and find fault! But she was even more furious with her relentlessly docile young secretary and diction coach, who had made a vehement incursion into her dressing room as soon as the performance ended. "The bird is not singing now, Madame Marina. That bird has a concussion, I'm sure!" Miss Collingridge *hated* what Maryna did to the bird.

Indeed, Maryna suspected, Miss Collingridge might well have been behind an admonitory visit by a pair of wide-eyed bumpkins from the American Society for the Prevention of Cruelty to Animals, who knocked at her dressing room an hour before the next evening's performance and requested that she produce for them an uninjured, chirping canary. Dispatching them brusquely, Maryna said that all birds and animals were in the care of her secretary, whom they could find by applying to her manager, down the hall, third door on the left. She hoped the canary would sing.

For a few days, Maryna was under the impression she had decided to send Miss Collingridge back to San Francisco. Was there no one she could count on for support and sympathy?

But then in the second week, just before Christmas, when she was performing *Adrienne Lecouvreur*, whose title Warnock convinced her should be definitively shortened to *Adrienne* ("*Adrienne Lecouvreur*, starring Countess Marina Zalenska? That's a bigger mouthful of foreignness than even New Yorkers can be asked to swallow." "Mr. Warnock, I can see you are bent on driving me mad. There is no such person as the Countess Zalenska. The Countess Dembowska, yes. My husband's name. But the actress whose fortunes you have so kindly undertaken to promote is plain, as you Americans say, plain Marina Zalenska." "OK," answered Warnock)—just as she was starting *Adrienne*, Maryna had news from Bogdan that he was on his way east, bringing her Peter and Aniela. And Bogdan had been so encouraging, and she needed encouragement because for the third week of her New York season she would be doing *Romeo and Juliet* and *As You Like It*. True, for *Camille* and *Adrienne* there had been nothing but panegyrics—the *Herald*: "She won all hearts"; the *Times*: "Popular Success, Artistic Triumph"; the *Tribune*: "She is a great actress"; the *Sun*: "Greatest actress since Rachel"; the *World*: "Not to be missed." No matter. She could always fail with Shakespeare.

"I see that not only have you performed as expected, but the critics have done the same," said Bogdan. "A pretty sheaf of accolades."

"Phrases for Warnock to splash all over the new playbill," said Maryna glumly.

"Forget Warnock."

"Alas, I can't forget him. He rules my life. But just tell me, was I as good as in Poland?"

"Better, I think. As you well know, my dear, you thrive on obstacles."

"And my English?"

"No, no"—he laughed—"for reassurance on that score, you must consult the indispensable Miss Collingridge."

"Armong, I loaf you," was Miss Collingridge's reply. Then, seeing Maryna's horrified look and Bogdan's smile, she added charitably, "But not always."

Bogdan brought support; Bogdan brought harmony. He gave his amused approval to this addition to Maryna's entourage, a new specimen of hearty asexual American womanhood. And Miss Collingridge liked Bogdan, was impressed by him, and, best of all, had instantly, effortlessly, made friends with Peter. Odd woman out in Maryna's newly reconstituted family was Aniela, her grainy pale face puckered with jealousy. This American woman who owned so many different hats, was she another ser- vant or Madame's friend? For ventures outside her Polish- speaking cocoon in Anaheim, Aniela had learned to count to twenty and say in her tuneful little voice, *That one, Half, More, Good, Thank you, It's too expensive, Good-bye.* In New York, she'd already acquired with Miss Collingridge's gentle tutoring such useful sentences as *Madame is busy, Madame is resting, Please put the flowers over there, I will give Madame your message.* And that was only a start. Aniela had to accept Miss Collingridge, what else could she do?

"Everything is back as it should be," Maryna said as they were falling asleep together in the big bed in the suite at the Clarendon Hotel. "I have you, if you can put up with me. I have Peter. I have the stage . . ."

"Is that really the right order?" he murmured.

"Oh, Bogdan," she cried, and kissed him fiercely on the mouth.

In contrast to the stage, where a woman's adultery never went unpunished, real life, as Maryna noted gratefully, did not have to be a melodrama. Life was a long hot soak in the tub, life was a glycerine massage and a pedicure. Life was never being idle, trying always to surpass oneself, having three new wigs made, throwing a canary out a stage window, making strangers cry. Life was a quiet talk with Bogdan about Peter.

"Wouldn't it be better to put him in boarding school before I go out on tour? That's no life for a child."

"I think we should keep him with us for the tour and at least through the summer. Miss Collingridge and I will give him his lessons. It's too soon for him to be separated from you again."

"He's furious with me."

She brought him some barber-pole candy. He threw it away. She bought him presents. He broke them. She read to him. He told her to stop.

Bogdan didn't answer.

"Yesterday he told me he loves Aniela more than he loves me."

"He'd have to be angry that you went away. And since he's a child he doesn't have to hide his feelings."

"But I can make it up to him. He'll forget. Do you think he'll forget? He can't stay angry."

"I think he won't stay angry," Bogdan said.

"I've promised that I'll never leave him again."

"Excellent promise," said Bogdan.

YOU COULD HAVE COME, Henryk. As far as I'm concerned, dear friend, you had no excuse anymore, once I was in New York, which is *much* closer to our old Europe. Bogdan would have liked you to be here, since he could not be. (He is with me now, I am glad to say.) But . . . *passons*. And so at last I have had my New York debut. Naturally—let me plume myself—it was a success. I have proved to myself once and for all that with a strong enough will one can surmount any obstacle. The theatre is always full (on gala nights the best tickets are sold at auction), the newspapers are enchanted with me, the women love me. And yet—will you be surprised by this?—I am consumed with anger. Or is it sadness? For I am truly alone in this triumph of mine; I can't deceive myself about that. Where were my friends? Where is the community of friends I believed in? Where is Poland? To be sure, all the Poles we met here last year were in the audience on opening night, but of real friends the only one present was Jakub, who, as you know, has been living in New York for six months now. And what has become of our splendid artist? He has found employment as an illustrator on a popular magazine, *Frank Leslie's Weekly*, and spends his days at a desk in the magazine office alongside the other illustrators. He says he hopes still to do some painting "on the side." What a pity. And Jakub has heard from a friend in Kraków that Wanda recently made another try at suicide. Why didn't *you* tell me about this? Awful, awful, awful! I know weak people will always succeed in harming themselves if that's what they really want to do. But even so—

Maryna had invoked the power of the will, as she often did with Henryk—there was a reproach in that, as well as a boast—but perhaps will was just another name for desire. She wanted this life, whatever it cost her: this loneliness, this euphoria. The quasi-amorous approval of innumerable, never to be known or barely known, others; her own painful, invigorating dissatisfactions. She would have been devastated had the reviews been anything other than paeans. If Maryna was to believe what she read about herself, hers was the opposite of declamatory acting. Her "simplicity," her "subtlety," her "delicate and refined art," her "utter naturalness" seemed very original to New York. But she did *not* believe what she read, especially when it consisted of nothing but praise, and for quite antithetical virtues. Certainly there was nothing natural about this naturalness, which was concocted for each role out of a thousand tiny judgments and decisions. Much, she knew, could be improved. Her voice still had its mighty throw, she allowed, but the yearlong absence from the stage had weakened the precision of her breath control. She felt the words sometimes lacked bite. She needed to vary still more the flow of certain passages. But when all this was corrected, as it would be by performing eight times a week (and on Sunday, Maryna came to the theatre for a few hours to work on the empty stage), would she not risk being too broad in her vocal effects?

Her fear was that these resurgent feelings of piratical masterfulness would provoke her to overacting. It is one thing to be uninterruptedly expressive, what acting is; another for the actor, out of vulgarity or defective self-awareness, to do too much. She said to Bogdan, "I would give ten years of my life to sit just once in the audience and see myself act, that I might learn what to avoid."

Authority on the stage is tantamount to the ability to project continuously, fluently, piercingly, a character's essence. In nature there are many off-duty moments, many unessential gestures; in the theatre characters reveal their essence all the time. (Anything else would be trivial, unfocused; oozing instead of signaling and shaping.) To act a role is to show what is emphatic in a person, what is sustained. Essential gestures are gestures that are repeated. If I am evil, I am evil all the time. Look at my leers, my scowls. I bare my teeth (if I am a man). Thinking of the suffering I'm about to wreak on my gullible victims, I quiver, visibly. Or, I am good (as women are good). Look, I am smiling, I am gazing tenderly, I bend forward to succor, or backward in pitiable recoil from the bestial advances of him-against-whom-I-am-powerless-to-defend-myself.

Everyone agreed that this was how to proceed. The audience can't be mistaken about whom to love, whom to pity, whom to despise. But must showing one's essence mean exaggerating the signs by which we recognize it? If one could have the courage to be not quite so pointed from the beginning, wouldn't that be finer, truer? More fascinating? Every night as she went on stage Maryna promised herself, I will hold something back. I will not be entirely legible. More variance, she bid herself, even at the risk of being confusing. More smolder.

And *my* essence? thought Maryna. What would I show if I were playing myself?

But an actor doesn't need to have an essence. Perhaps it would be a hindrance for an actor to have an essence. An actor needs only a mask.

Trying to analyze something ineffable which she brought to her roles, the critics fell back on words like "subtle" and "aristocratic." The presentation of the self that had charmed in San Francisco fell short in New York. Maryna had entranced many a reporter in California with her tales of rude beginnings, when touring in the Polish countryside meant playing in riding schools and barns as often as in theatres. Here in New York they were more interested in her ideas about the theatre, as long as these were uplifting. But what hope was there of correcting any of the impudent misunderstandings that dog the transfer of a great career to another country? Every actor (singer, instrumentalist, dancer) has been taught, has mentors, an artistic genealogy, a moral genealogy too; but Maryna Załężowska's, stocked with equally unpronounceable names, meant nothing here. Hers was an orphaned talent. And how to explain in America the distinctive sense of mission nourished by the Polish habits of devotion to impossible dreams. "We Poles are a very theatrical people," she declared with summary intention to the new batch of journalists who interrogated her.

In Poland she had represented the aspirations of a nation. Here she could only represent art, or culture, which many feared as something frivolous or snobbish or morally unhinging. Bogdan pointed out with a smile that Americans seemed to need perennial reassurance that art was not just art but served a higher moral or wholesomely civic purpose.

For her early interviews with the New York press, she had at the ready an English translation, made by Ryszard, of a cherished tribute published in the Warsaw theatrical journal *Antrakt*. "In every role she plays, Załężowska is fully responsive to the age in which she lives, as the music of Verdi sighs, weeps, suffers, loves, and cries out in the idiom of all humanity. As Verdi is the supreme composer of the age, Załężowska is its greatest actress." But Maryna suspected it would make no sense to anybody here that an eminent theatre critic in Poland had compared her, for the universality of her expressiveness—not for her role as bearer of her nation's aspirations—to Verdi. Americans might think what was meant was that her genius was unsubtle, merely operatic.

Instead, Maryna declared: "Gentlemen, you don't imagine me with a scrapbook, do you? I, who seldom read reviews and have never even thought of preserving what was written about me!"

She had won over the critics, including the redoubtable William Winter of the *Tribune*, the most powerful drama critic in the country. True, Winter could not resist mildly deploring Madame Zalenska's choice of opening vehicle. "Was it really necessary for this exquisite artist (and a countess, too, mind you!) to begin the conquest of our hearts by playing that dubious creature of frail lungs and even frailer virtue?" Of course Winter went on to forgive her. There had been not even a whisper of such censure in dear old San Francisco or blustery Virginia City, and Warnock had to explain to Maryna that the West was more broadminded (lax, some said), while eastern America ("Remember we're a whole continent and there are fifty million of us!"), especially the middle of the country, could get a "a bit" stirred up about the virtue of women depicted on the stage, meaning that Maryna should steel herself for "a fair amount" of sermonizing about the threat to public morals posed by Dumas's notorious and notoriously successful play.

Happily, not all the critics worried about whether their new idol had debased her art by playing a fallen woman. The influential Jeannette Gilder, of the *Herald*, who had become Maryna's special fan, was more interested in the courtesan's finery, an interest, observed Bogdan, one couldn't have inferred from Miss Gilder's own sartorial affectations, which included a high collar and cravat, a melon hat and man's coat. "The arms, which are bared by her gown, are encased in twelve-buttoned cream-colored kids below the elbow, and banded between that point and the shoulder with a velvet ribbon fastened with a jeweled pin," Miss Gilder noted in her description of Marguerite Gautier's stunning first-act entrance. And wasn't it amusing, continued Bogdan, that the clothes Maryna wore in *Camille* were of all her costumes the most copied by the censorious and the fashionable?

It was Bogdan who first pointed out to her (*she* would be the last person to see it, Maryna said) that ladies in New York were beginning to imitate her manners and gestures and hair styles (as in Act One of *Camille*, where her hair was dressed high on the head with puffs and bands), and Zalenska hats had made their appearance in the smartest shops, and Zalenska gloves, and Zalenska brooches, and "Polish Water," a new eau de cologne— the label showed an oval portrait of Maryna superimposed on a drawing-room scene with a young man at a piano who had Chopin's signature long hair and sensitive, consumptive face. Photographs of her in full *Camille* regalia were displayed in druggists' windows and for sale in cigar shops. The newspapers carried the daily news of Madame Zalenska's social engagements. Maryna still hadn't put back the weight she had lost, and if she were too wraithlike she would not look well in the much admired gown she wore in the first act of *Camille*, a composite evening crinoline of teal-blue silk with a green-black velvet train, cut to fit close to the body. But she was haunted by the photographs of the new reigning star in Paris, Sarah Bernhardt, she of the bird-like face and scrawny silhouette. Girding herself for future rivalry, Maryna vowed to remain underweight.

After the four weeks at the Fifth Avenue Theatre and a further week of work (taking in, letting out) on her stage wardrobe, which now filled two dozen trunks tended by a German seamstress, Maryna embarked on the conquest of America, appearing with stock companies all over the country except the Far West. In Philadelphia, the city's principal reviewer admired "the cross and tiara of diamonds worth forty thousand dollars" (as bruited by Warnock)—paste, of course—which she wore in Act Four of *Camille*. The mistake, Warnock's mistake, Maryna decided, had been to do only *Camille* for her week at the renowned Arch Street Theatre. Maryna was disappointed in Philadelphia. Baltimore and Washington, where she also offered *As You Like It* and *Romeo and Juliet*, were more appropriately beguiled. Then back up the coast by steamer to where, Warnock had told her, she would be playing—her Rosalind and Juliet only—to the most cultivated audience in the country, in one of its most venerable theatres. ("The Boston *Museum*, Mr. Warnock? Is that common in America, for a theatre to be called a museum?" "Just in Boston, dear lady.") Her new friend William Winter, a militant New Yorker, was more skeptical about the vaunted capital of high-minded America. Even Boston, he reassured Maryna teasingly, could not challenge her with audiences such as filled the theatres of London in David Garrick's day, who knew their Shakespeare so well that an actor who garbled the text, mispronounced a word, or even misplaced an emphasis risked being hissed or noisily corrected by the pit and gallery. But, yes, he conceded, Boston was full of discriminating Shakespeareans. Maryna looked forward to the challenge with confidence. Since, lulled by praise (her vigilance notwithstanding), she was spending less time monitoring her English, the shock was all the greater the day after she opened at the Boston Museum in what she thought had been her most fluent Rosalind yet, when she read in the *Evening Transcript* that its eminent drama critic found her accent enchanting, especially in the romantic passages of *As You Like It*, but an impediment when it came to the demands of Shakespeare's badinage.

"It's true, isn't it?" she wailed at Miss Collingridge, whom she had instantly summoned to her suite at the Langham Hotel for a coaching session. "How long have I been slipping?"

"In Philadelphia you said *ozer* for other, and in Washington you said *loaf* for love and *strent* for strength, and in Baltimore you said *bret* for breath and *trone* for throne and *lar-r-r-k* for lark.

It was the nightingale, and not the lark,
That pierced the fearful hollow of thine ear.

That was the worst."

"Dear Mildred, how do you put up with me?"

"Armong, I loaf you."

"Stop it, Mildred. I have taken the point."

If only Maryna's sole frustration were keeping her English fine-tuned enough to do justice to Shakespeare!

Toronto went better; Buffalo and Pittsburgh acknowledged themselves enchanted by this new, exotic ornament of the American stage; Cleveland and Columbus positively gleamed with approval. Since Maryna had made the mistake of telling Warnock that she never took more than two days to memorize a new role, it was just three days before they arrived in Cincinnati that he informed her that she was not only billed for *Adrienne* and *As You Like It* but, on the Saturday matinee, for *East Lynne*, too. Furious, Maryna reminded him that she'd said she would never stoop to *Beast Lynne*, as she called it—"I am an artist, Mr. Warnock," she thundered, "not a merchant of tears!"—but there she was, in the second month of touring, having succumbed to Warnock's pleas, Warnock's insistence, playing it in Cincinnati and Louisville and Savannah and Augusta and Memphis and St. Louis. Warnock had been right of course when he assured her, "It's money in the bank"—"It's what?"—"I mean, audiences love it." "Because they want to cry?" "Well, yes, people do like to cry in the theatre, almost as much as they like to laugh, and what's wrong with that, dear lady? But what they most like is watching great acting. And that's you!"

No exercise of histrionic prowess was more pleasing to audiences than that afforded by a plot requiring the main character to depart and then sneak back into the story, disguised for expediency or transformed by suffering, as somebody else, whose true identity, obvious enough to all who had paid to see the play, goes undetected by everyone on the stage. Such is the starring role in *East Lynne*—in effect, two roles. One is the weak-minded, gullible Lady Isabel, who deserts a loving husband and their children under the malign influence of a scheming rake. The other is the repentant sinner, prematurely aged by the agonies of contrition, who reenters her household as a bespectacled grey-haired governess, "Madame Vine," to care for her own children. Her cry, after the littlest of the three, a mere babe at the time she had left, dies in her arms—*Oh, Willie, my child, dead, dead, dead! And he never knew me, never called me mother!*—unleashed in audiences an explosion of grief. And the tears gushed again when she, dying, throws off her incognito and begs her husband's forgiveness—*Let what I am be erased from your memory, think of me (if you can) as the innocent trusting girl whom you made your wife*— is forgiven, and implores him not to punish their two remaining children for her own dereliction—*Be kind and loving to Lucy and little Archie*, she whispers hoarsely. *Do not let their mother's sin be visited on them!*

Never, never! cried the actor who played Archibald in this particular stock company—America had dozens of Archibalds, but there would be only one Isabel, the best, the most awesomely sad, as Maryna learned to play her. He bowed his head. She saw dandruff on his collar. She was spinning in a drum of unslakable grief. What am I doing, Maryna wondered as, little by little, she gave herself to the indestructible excitements and brazen pathos of *East Lynne*.

She was looking for a terrible tranquillity.

In Chicago, where she played at Hooley's Opera House for ten days, she was importuned with flowers and gifts and entreaties from the city's ever multiplying Polish settlement, the most numerous in America. On Sunday, following High Mass at St. Stanislaw's with Bogdan and an interminable luncheon given by Monsignor Klimowski, Maryna offered a program in the social hall adjoining the church (the proceeds to be distributed among needy parishioners) in which she recited poems of Mickiewicz, passages from Słowacki's *Mazepa*, and some of her famous moments from Shakespeare: Portia's mercy speech, Ophelia's mad scene, the Scottish lady's somnambulistic rave. It made her feel very carefree to be delivering Shakespeare wadded in Polish. Gruff shabby men and red-eyed women in kerchiefs came forward and kissed her hands.

So much journeying, to do the same thing in each new place, shrinks the world. A new town amounted to the size and appointments of her dressing room, the greater or lesser incompetence of the stock-company actors, the security of seeing Bogdan at his post (in the wings, as he preferred, or in a box, as Maryna often insisted, where she could see him better while on stage), and the warmth of his reassurance that all had gone well.

As a young actress in Heinrich's company, Maryna thought she had experienced the arduousness of touring to its fullest. But in America the need for respite was weakly acknowledged: Americans had invented the continuous tour, performance after performance, with only a day or two between one town and the next. Keeping to their compartment on the train, Maryna listened to the words of her roles in the clack of the wheels. Bogdan read. He would keep on reading when, after some desolate stop, they would be shunted to a siding to wait for an hour as more privileged trains hammered past them. Peter would gaze out the window, mumbling to himself, while Maryna stood and sat, sat and stood. She knew better than to interrupt him then, after having done it once.

"Twenty-eight what, my darling?"

"Mama, you're spoiling it!"

"For heaven's sake, Peter, spoiling what?"

"I was adding the numbers on the freight cars. There was a 1 and a 9 and an 8 and a 7 and a 3 and then you—"

"Sorry. Go back to your counting."

"Mama!"

"Now what have I done?"

"I have to wait for another train."

She often did not have a proper night's sleep, but her endurance was phenomenal. She could sleep whenever she wanted to and awaken refreshed after an hour.

Warnock waited for her to complain.

"I do not complain, as you see, Mr. Warnock," Maryna said in the middle of the night, sipping tea at the end of their car somewhere in icy Wisconsin. She was going from two evenings at the Grand Opera House in Milwaukee to three at the Academy of Music in Kansas City. They had halted in a freight yard, and the train had been lurching forward and backward, screeching and shuddering, for more than an hour. "These ghastly all-night train trips. The dingy hotels where you have lately been lodging me and my family. The terrible actors I am obliged to play with. This is Marina Zalenska's first American tour, and I have much to learn. I say only, please listen to me, for I shall not repeat myself, it will not be like *this* again."

Poland was circles—everything familiar, saturated, centrifugal. Here the country, ever more spacious and thinly marked, streamed and spiked in all directions. In constant movement from one unfamiliar place to the next, Maryna had never felt so concentrated, so sturdy, so impervious to her surroundings. Acting armored her with its urgencies, its satisfactions. Shakespeare's Juliet and Rosalind; Adrienne and Marguerite Gautier; even *East Lynne*'s wretched Lady Isabel—how comfortable she was in their company. Sometimes they entered her dreams, talking to one another. She wanted to console them. They succeeded in consoling her. It often seemed enough to have no thoughts but theirs.

Meanwhile, something was receding ever further from being spoken of. Something fitfully glimpsed was being covered over. She remembered when her hair fell out during the bout of typhoid fever three years ago, disclosing to her astonishment two dark pink stains on the back of her head, one below the crown and the other above the nape. Holding a hand mirror at the correct angle, she had stared with revulsion at the reflection of the birthmarks in the large dressing-room mirror behind her. But only her wig-maker and her dresser saw the back of her scalp, soon covered with a nap of obscuring first fuzz, and then the whole mass of hair grew back, and it was unlikely that she would ever be obliged to see her naked scalp again.

You see, you grasp, something upsetting, something unsightly looms into view . . . and then it is gone, and there is no point in chasing after it, no point in insisting on what is no longer there to be seen. How easily disturbing knowledge becomes useless knowledge.

Assume that, during their long separation last year, Maryna and Bogdan had both sought affection elsewhere, as needed: they were not going to force stories upon each other about what was known without being told. Love, married love, was full of generous silences. They were going to be generous with each other.

Maryna thought she knew what bound her so irrevocably to this man. He is just circumspect enough that I still feel free.

But wasn't it presumptuous to suppose that Bogdan would always be at her side, attending every performance? In Poland he was Count Dembowski, patriot, connoisseur. In America he was a man with a role instead of an occupation: to stand next to his wife in the burning center of her glory.

"I'm worried about you, dearest. The curse of my profession is that it requires me always to be thinking about myself. I am so grateful for your presence, your support, your love . . ."

"Are you worried about me?" Bogdan said. "I don't think so." Was he going to reproach her now? No. "You're asking me for reassurance."

"I suppose I am," said Maryna, chastened and relieved.

At the westernmost point of Maryna's tour—a week at the Boyd Opera House in Omaha—Bogdan left her and went back to southern California. His declared purpose was to look for a property to buy, a home to which they could retreat whenever Maryna was not touring. She supposed that Bogdan would be returning to Carpinteria to try to penetrate the mysterious Aero Club, and she was sure, knowing Bogdan, that once he had secured permission to witness a flight he would soon be asking to become an aeronaut himself.

"If something happened to you," said Maryna, "it would be unbearable to me. But you must do what you have to do."

Impossible for Bogdan to keep her reassured by letter while Maryna was constantly moving; and there would be telegrams, they agreed, only for an emergency. Her tour would end in June with a week in Brooklyn, at the Park Theatre, with *Camille*, *Adrienne*, and *Romeo and Juliet*. They had tickets on the S.S. *Europa* in early July. If all went well, Bogdan would have rejoined her in New York by then.

Of course, he wanted her to worry. That was his husbandly right. As it was Maryna's duty, to her art, to her sanity, not to worry too much.

Actually, she preferred that Bogdan not tell her all his plans; the least she could do was give him the right to have some secret adventure of his own. He wanted her credulity. Maybe they did fly. And surely they did crash.

NO, MAMA, I can't stay longer. The plan has always been that after a week I would go on to Zakopane. The doctor who took care of Stefan, and who's a great friend of mine, Dr. Tyszyń-ski, that's right, and whom I must visit while I'm here—no, he doesn't live in Kraków anymore. Yes, he lives year round now in Zakopane. Mama, I don't understand, do you *want* me to be uncomfortable? The hotel suits me perfectly. It's much better that way, and I've so much to do. My triumphal homecoming. Irony, Mama. This is a purely private visit, you know that. Everyone clawing at me. Why? My admirers will stop plaguing you and Józefina as soon as I leave, I guarantee it. Perhaps I shall write a

"Letter from America" for *Antrakt* while I'm here this week, what do you think, Bogdan? No, I'll never have the peace of mind I need in Kraków, I'll write it in Zakopane. In Warsaw? Why should I go to Warsaw, Mama? Out of the question. My Warsaw friends can take the train to Kraków if they want to see me. Because I'm mortally displeased with the administration of the Imperial Theatre. I did regard the director as a friend, yes. Until I learned he was only another vindictive bureaucrat. Bogdan, don't you agree? We've never considered it. I would make scenes. And I need to be calm. Much as I long to salute my former colleagues, and I especially regret not seeing Tadeusz on the Imperial's main stage, I am not going to Warsaw. Ask to be taken back? Mama, are you out of your mind? I certainly am still offended. But that's not why I'm staying in America. We always planned to return for July and August to visit relatives. To be visited by friends. Bogdan should leave directly for Poznań to call at several of the Dembowski estates, alas, he has inheritance matters to discuss with his brother. It's maddening that we came so near to seeing her again. We'd left New York, we were already on the high seas! Bogdan is heartbroken. She was an extraordinary woman, Józefina. Not modern at all, very irreverent. One doesn't find women like that in Poland anymore. Bogdan, my mother has a suitor, if I may put it so politely. Does everything in this country go on and on and *on*? She's close to eighty! Gliński, the baker on Floriańska Street, an oaf with a great domed head and flour-streaked mustache, I can count on finding him still there when I come by in the early morning to spend an hour with *le petit*. Am I? I don't mean to be. I suppose there's no harm in it. He lets Peter go with him to the bakery and putter about. Yes, Mama, he is called Peter now. No, really, it's an American name too, but I'm sure he'll let you call him Piotr. Mama, why the surprise that he's not forgotten Polish? He has to speak it with Aniela. My secretary? Did Aniela mention her or did Peter? She's American. Doesn't know a word of Polish. Of course she *could* learn, but why should she? It's America, Mama! Aniela glowed when I told her that she was coming with us and Miss Collingridge was returning to California for the two months. But being back in Poland doesn't seem to move her at all. Perhaps because she has no family. This awful ache in my heart. No, I'm talking to myself, Mama. I'm so glad to see you well, Mama. Believe me, Henryk, the greatest satisfaction I anticipate from this visit is seeing you. Bogdan, Bogdan dear, are you sure you don't want me to go with you to Wielkopolska? Ignacy wouldn't dare. Mama, stop trying to persuade me to go to Warsaw. Yes, there was a penalty. I already told you. Every theatre has a schedule of fines levied on actors for misconduct of every sort. Mama, of course I'd never been fined before! Ten thousand rubles, Mama. Yes, *ten*. That's how much it cost to purchase my freedom. Ah, now you understand. I've distributed all the presents I brought for my sisters and brothers and their families, Henryk, I've deposited Peter in the care of my mother and Józefina, he's being coddled by everyone. No, Peter, you can't come with me to Zakopane. But Aniela is staying with you. No, Mama isn't going for long. Mama will be back in a week or so. Mama, I don't want to eat the apple pancakes. I'm quite sated, thank you very much. Mama, I'm—I'm thirty-eight years old! Bogdan, guess what Aniela said this morning before I left Poselska Street. It's not as busy here as in America. She's certainly less busy! Alas, so am I. Henryk, you should have been at the train station when we arrived from Bremen. The crowds, the flowers, the songs. Just as when I left. I was very moved. I couldn't have known what I would feel coming home, Bogdan, could you? The whole of my American saga could seem now like a trip to the moon. But it doesn't, Bogdan, no. American adulation is depthless, while Polish adulation has depths that . . . you know what I mean. The interview, yes. Just one. Please sit here. Would you care for some coffee? I have only an hour. Yes, I am quite happy in America. To be sure, theatre is thought of very differently there. No, they have some excellent actors. I don't suppose you've ever heard of Edwin Booth? But it goes without saying that I intend to perform again in Poland! I shall always be before all else a Polish patriot and a

317

Polish actress. Still, as a modern artist, I want my art to be seen by many people. It feels altogether natural to act in English, and I'm planning for next year a season in London. With the miracles of modern transport, it is possible to take one's art everywhere. I shall never be daunted by great distances. In this respect, I have become quite American. Bogdan, must you leave now? Stay another few days. Bogdan, how small our beautiful old Kraków looks. Nothing has changed. Nothing! I know it's absurd, Henryk, but I dread coming to Zakopane. I'm afraid of finding it changed. You know how it is when you return somewhere after a long absence. Even a place you fled, you still want to find exactly as you left it. The same ugly pictures on the wall, the same sleepy dog under the table, the same pair of china dogs on the mantelpiece, the same leather-bound sets of unread classics in the bookcase, the same tuneless goldfinch singing in the window. He's coming to Kraków, Bogdan. He writes, he likes to make fun of me, that he cannot guarantee that Zakopane hasn't continued to change. Oh my dear. Those lines in your face, Henryk. I'm going to cry. No, it's not the lines, you know that. It's because you're here. And your hair has gone white. And what is that tremor in your hand? Let me embrace you again, my Henryk, my beloved friend. I should have come to Zakopane, forgive me. I could have averted my eyes when walking past the chalets being put up by moneyed people from Kraków. I might have said that I didn't recognize our Zakopane anymore, but you wouldn't believe me. You know how I exaggerate. You've not forgotten that your Maryna is an actress, have you? Let me kiss your cheeks again. It's true, I want nothing I've left to have changed, and why should it? I haven't been gone such a long time. Only two years. You *can't* call two years an eternity! Who's being histrionic now? Are you laughing at me, Henryk? Yes, to be sure, *I* want to be found changed, for the better, by those I left behind. Well? Yes, I *am* stronger. Yes. For the first time in my life, I understand what it is to stand alone. Though I'm never alone. You understand. No, I *haven't* left you for good, my dear, dear friend. It's only that, what is it to be the greatest

Polish actress? Remember when the peak of my ambition was to be better than Gabriela Ebert. Now, naturally, I want to be better than Sarah Bernhardt. But *am* I better than Bernhardt? I'll never find out if I remain in Poland. I need ordeals, challenges, mystery. I need to feel *not* at home. That's what makes me strong, I know that now. I need to fly out of myself, you can understand that, Henryk. And I don't mean just being on a stage, impersonating and transforming. For what is acting? Acting, of course I can say this only to you, Henryk, is *mis*representation. The theatre? Pretense and flummery. No, I'm not disillusioned. On the contrary. Bands of students serenading below my hotel window. Each day masses of fresh flowers banked beside the entrance. The other day I heard Peter telling my mother that what he liked about plays is that people don't really die, they're just pretending! Do rescue Peter from Mama and Józefina, and take him riding, Jarek. He mustn't stay all day in the apartment or the bakery. He needs exercise, he needs the outdoors. And after I left our phalanstery—no mockery, Henryk!—came difficult times, but I couldn't ask Bogdan to help me, he was having such problems with the farm. I sold what I could, pawned jewelry and lace, and sometimes I had no money even for a pound of tea and a little sugar and went to bed hungry. But poverty was the least of it. For after unexpected joy there was heartbreak, too. I am stronger for what I have sacrificed. Forgive me for saying no more than this. I feel that speaking about it, even to you, would be the greatest disloyalty of all to Bogdan. You know? He . . . he talked to you when he returned? No, of course he wouldn't. I was sure he would be the soul of discretion and dignity. Never mentioned me at all? Not once? That's because he's so angry with me. Then, Henryk, how *did* you know? But why am I asking? You know me better than anyone. I'm a monster. I've thrown love away. I'm a bad mother. I lie to everybody, including myself. No, I don't want absolution from you, Henryk. No, no, I suppose I do. Yes? I don't seem such a monster to you? I'm going to bury my head in your shoulder. And you will put your arm around me. How lovely this feels. My Henryk, my dearest friend, and how are *you*? All I do is talk about myself. Bogdan must go and contend with his fractious relatives. Bogdan must weep at the grave of his grandmother. She was ferocious. I admired her, and I feared her. For Bogdan she was *toute tendresse*. He'll come back and we'll have a little time in Paris before sailing from Cherbourg in late August, and all of September I'll be auditioning actors for the company I'm forming for my fall and winter tour, which starts with a six-week season in New York. Krystyna dear, let me look at you. Of course we can work together for a few days on your Ophelia. Nothing would give me more pleasure. Come to the hotel tomorrow afternoon. Good. Good. The graceless walk. I like it. You can even stumble when you offer the posy to Gertrude. Don't be afraid of being bold. You may try any effect, provided it is not sustained too long. Make the role your own, don't feel shadowed by how I portray her. When the great Rachel brought her Scottish lady (stop looking as if you don't know who I mean by the Scottish lady!) to London and was told that their great Mrs. Siddons had already exhausted every possible idea for playing the sleepwalking scene, Rachel replied, Surely not *every* idea. I intend to lick my hand. Your wildest fancy, Krystyna. Lurch, Krystyna! Brava. You have a large talent. But you are timid. An actor must deliver a pistol shot or two. Even Ophelia is not just a victim. Beware of limp lines, limp business, and limp exits. Don't say that, Henryk. I'll be back again soon. Why, to see how you are faring without me. Henryk, Henryk. May I not tease you? Must you be morose? Another tone, Henryk. Ah. You *will* ask me, you cannot stop yourself. Then you will have the answer: I suppose I don't miss anyone. I'm so busy. Sometimes I miss Bogdan, which may sound odd, since he's almost always with me. It doesn't sound odd to you? Indeed. The perfect husband? Remotecleverindulgent? Now you sound like Ryszard. That's something he might say. But *you* can't offend me, dearest Henryk. You know, I am not as self-absorbed as I appear. I worry that Bogdan doesn't have enough to do. He likes California best of all, and is negotiating for a property situated in a beautiful canyon in the Santa Ana Mountains, a place for us to be together when I'm not performing. Of course I'll always be performing. A successful actor in America does two hundred and fifty, as many as three hundred performances each year. Very helpful. She's less a secretary than she is a sort of governess, I suppose. Very strict and abject. Everyone needs a governess, even I need a governess, and Peter adores her. Józefina, have you ever thought of remarrying? I understand why you quit the stage, you are not vain or egotistical enough to be an actress, and it's more than commendable of you to stay on with Mama. But you must think of yourself, too. Don't frown, Józefina. Marriage may not always be the best solution for a woman, but you, my darling sister with the creases in your lovely brow, *you* need to devote yourself to someone. Better, to some ideal cause or service, as Henryk does. You should have been a teacher. Yes, he's a fascinating man. A noble soul. It's so admirable, his medical mission in Zakopane. And you could— Ah, you look even prettier when you blush, Józefina. Henryk, I have an idea for you. But I can't tell you yet. I shall make you think of it yourself. Yes, American tours are demanding, and they can last as long as thirty-two weeks. But a leading actor's life always has its ration of pleasures, mostly childhood pleasures: capering, daydreaming, making believe, throwing tantrums. Your smile, Henryk, does it mean you had supposed me altogether incapable of lucidity? And I'm expected, *expected* to be ardent, domineering, mercurial, avid for affection; and I'll have an indulgent elected family at the ready: the other actors, my tyrannical manager, Miss Collingridge, the wardrobe woman . . . and Bogdan will be with me part of the year, though I can't expect him just to travel around with me. In California he has adventures that are his alone. Has he formed some sort of attachment? He's not spoken of any, for which I'm grateful, but whatever it was, or is, he still wants to make his life with me. Peter, Mama is talking to Uncle Henryk. Yes, you and Aniela can go to the bakery. No, Mama, I shan't be here for dinner. Bogdan is returning tomorrow. In a few days we're going to

Poznań to stay for a week with Bogdan's sister. He's my guardian angel, Henryk. Yes, I know that's not what you asked me. I don't *know* if I do. But I want him. I need him. I feel well with him. He doesn't make me anxious. I am never bored with him. I *hope* that I love him. It would be so unfair if I didn't. I *do* love him. Ah. You are very severe with me, Henryk. But you are right of course. I told you, I'm a bad person. I don't love anybody. No, I don't feel crushed by other people's love. What an idea! But *you* shouldn't still care for me. You are too kind to me, Henryk. Much too kind. *Let* me weep. I spoil everything. I make no one happy. You are shaking your head. But I am inconsolable, Henryk. No, I am not acting. Shall I tell you what acting is, Tadeusz? Acting is *mis*representation. The art of the actor consists in exploiting an author's drama to show off his ability to allure and to counterfeit. An actor is like a forger. Bogdan, there's news. Tadeusz and Krystyna are going to marry. I don't mind when people behave predictably, do you? They were destined for each other. I trust the little fool isn't about to give up her career to be a wife. She's talented, more talented than Tadeusz. And I shall be the godmother of their first child. Oh Bogdan, it's so awful to be old. I *hate* becoming old. You say that because you're so kind, and you love me, but I know how I look. My beautiful Kraków. American cities are ugly beyond belief, Józefina. So ugly, so . . . disrespectful. But the land, the land, the mountains and deserts and prairies, and the wild rivers, are grander, more inspiring, and more disconcerting than in all our European fantasies of America. You cannot imagine how . . . heroic southern California is. I hope you will see it one day, Henryk. You breathe differently there. The ocean, the desert, in all their sublime neutrality, suggest quite another idea of how to live. You take deep breaths and you feel you can do anything you set your mind to. No, Mama, I'm not ill. I just need to be quiet for a day. Too many parties, and tears, and interviews. I'm told of imminent proposals for my return to the Polish stage which I won't be able to refuse, including the directorship of a theatre of my own. Bogdan, why don't I feel well here? Is it because I'm thinking of Stefan all the time? Now I remember why I wanted to leave Poland. It was because, because . . . no, I don't know why. Even now. All I know is that I feel so restless. A theatre of my own. A Polish theatre. What could I want more than that? I came back to preen and be admired, and make sure that I'm still loved and missed, and have everyone beg me to return, and it gives me no pleasure at all, none. Barbara, I can't remember your looking so contented, my dear. Do you think sometimes of our Arden? What an enchanting dream it was. And what stalwarts we were! I am very proud of us. Aleksander, we're buying land in Santiago Canyon. The Hunnecott ranch. You remember. We must all meet there a summer from now, after the house is finished. Bogdan wants to have livestock but we shall have proper help, you won't be asked to feed the horses or milk the goats, I promise! It will be wonderful. You two and Danuta and Cyprian and their girls and . . . Oh, don't remind me. I can't stop thinking about it. And there was no one to stop her! It's horrible. Horrible. Of course we would invite Julian. But I know he wouldn't come. And Jakub from New York. Ryszard? That goes without saying, doesn't it, Bogdan? Is he still in the same lodgings in Warsaw? Geneva? Since when? Why Geneva? No, we've not had news from him recently. And you'll come too, Henryk. Not to California, that's not for you. This year I'm going to have my own company and a much longer national tour. In America, a leading actor is "managed," like a business, and the manager comes along on the tour. And you'll travel with us as the company physician. There's always someone falling ill. Oh, it's such a lovely thought. Do consider it, Henryk. Perhaps I'll invite Józefina to come, too. My sister is a remarkable woman, don't you agree, Henryk? Nostalgia, Aleksander? For Poland? Spruce-lined Tatras trails, the chestnut alleys of Kraków, that sort of thing? Oh. For my old life. I think that's not what I feel. No, Henryk, nothing will make me nostalgic. I have set my heart against the past. America is good for that.

America, America! you retort—by the way, I prefer this tone. If you suspect that I find in my new country whatever I *want* to find there, you are right, Henryk. America is good for that as well. And you baked these kaiser rolls all by yourself, Peter darling? They're exquisite. Bogdan, I learned something very interesting the other day. According to Henryk, until not so long ago nostalgia was regarded as a serious, sometimes fatal, illness. Autumn was thought to be the most dangerous time, and soldiering a particularly vulnerable profession. Virtually anything, a love letter, a picture, a song, a spoonful of the tasty gruel of one's childhood, a few syllables in the accent of one's native region overheard on the street, could induce the onset of the disease. The case histories he's read have all appeared in French medical journals, but it seems unlikely that only the French were capable of dying of their attachment to the past. Poles, we agreed, must have been even more susceptible to this illness, just as Americans have turned out to excel at freeing themselves from the past. Yes, it's delicious, Mama. No, Mama, I don't want a pork cutlet or cauliflower topped with breadcrumbs and butter. (My God!) Mama, I'm *not* too thin. The most admired actress in Europe today, the queen of the French stage, weighs no more than . . . oh, never mind! Mama, have you any idea, any idea at *all*, who I am? The very question, Bogdan, I asked him. Presumably, the decline of this illness is one of the many benefits of the progress of civilization: of the steam engine, the telegraph, and regular mail. But you know Henryk—optimism being foreign to his nature, and also being unable ever to forgo the barbed observation—he says *he* thinks the decline of this sentiment in its lethal form merely portends the rise of a new illness, the inability to become attached to anything. Of course I think of Ryszard sometimes, Henryk. Doctor. Can you prescribe something to kill the pain? Or is it the numbness? I wasn't just being selfish. I panicked. He took my breath away. I felt too divided. Bogdan, Henryk said to me yesterday, you know how acerbic he can be, Poland loves you.

Poland needs you. But you don't need Poland anymore. What can I say to him? Henryk, there are two kinds of people. Those, like you, dear friend, who only feel well where everything is understandable, familiar. And those, the race to which I belong, who feel trapped, dull, irritable when they're at home. Which doesn't preclude my being fervently patriotic. What I most admire about Józefina, Henryk, is that she is largehearted. Oh Bogdan, how could Ignacy be so intransigent! It must be awful for you. We deserve a bit of holiday now. I'm glad we made the effort and accompanied Henryk back to Zakopane. Should a pair of seasoned southern Californians have flinched at a two-day wagon trip? Should we not rejoice in the progress that has come to the village, starting with Henryk's new, splendidly equipped dispensary? It's still our rough, pungent, deliciously isolated Zakopane, and we've feasted, what feasts, and walked, what walks, climbing farther than we meant to for a familiar panorama, and the highlanders have been so welcoming. I know you thought we were staying until Sunday. But we shall just make Henryk more unhappy. He'll miss us even more if we stay longer. Józefina's brow, her hair. Don't you think she's lovely, Henryk? You're blind, my friend. Where are we? We're in Zakopane. But I didn't want to come to Zakopane. We're in Kraków. But I don't want to stay in Kraków. Peter, embrace your grandmother and your aunts and your uncles and your cousins. Of course you can say good-bye to Mr. Gliński! Bogdan, Bogdan darling, I know you'll think me unpardonably capricious, but I don't want to stay as long as we planned. Let's leave for Paris now. I need clothes, yes, days and days of fittings. And every night we'll go to the theatre. *She* may be playing at the Comédie-Française. I know I'm going to hate her *and* fall in love with her. I already have a pang when I think of the sonorous vowels of Racine as she must launch them, and the majestic periods. Perhaps I wouldn't enjoy seeing her *Adrienne Lecouvreur* or her *Dame aux camélias*, but her *Hernani* and her *Phèdre*—more than anything in the world. As long as she doesn't know I'm in the audience. Mama, certainly I'll be back next summer. And you and Józefina shall come live with us in America, when Bogdan and I have our ranch. You, too old? Don't be ridiculous, Mama. Oh Poland. Don't be a lost love. Be my strength, be my pride, my shield that I carry out into the world. Oh Ryszard, your hands, your mouth, *ton sexe*. Bogdan, is everything still all right? For me, yes. I'm resigned *and* triumphant, Henryk. Who would have thought it would be like this?

THEY LEFT POLAND in late July; journeyed to Paris, where Maryna spent three weeks creating a dozen new wardrobes, sitting for her portrait, going to the theatre (she did see Sarah Bernhardt as Doña Sol in Victor Hugo's *Hernani*, and went backstage afterward to offer gracious homage to her magnificent rival), visiting the galleries and the Exposition Universelle; and sailed from Cherbourg on August 20th, arriving a week later, in time for the last month of New York's malodorous summer. They stayed again in the theatre district, off Union Square: the suite at the Clarendon Hotel filled with flowers, which quickly rotted in the lancing, muzzy heat. Maryna had found *her* hotel, where she would always stay when performing in New York; and she would accumulate, on this second national tour, other inflexible inclinations. Those who are professionally itinerant want to be greeted and fussed over reliably, familiarly, at the longer pauses on their circuits. Settling into the same room in the usual hotel, taking every supper at the same restaurant—the pleasure lies in having as little as possible to decide.

Maryna had been so happy to return to America, and then unable to repress a flare of disappointment (she felt let down by her imagination) as soon as they docked. But whether it was frustration at never being truly understood, or impatience with everyone for being so picturesquely, amusingly, earnestly, complacently American (had she imagined them otherwise?), disappointment, and frustration, and impatience were all quelled once she started auditioning actors for her company. To feel well, steady, it was enough to enter a theatre each morning and take command, the theatre where she would start playing in early October for six weeks. Emerging in the early afternoon, she felt weakened by the sunlight and the heat and the bumptious, adamant crowds. She had to remind herself that this was not America but only New York, so self-important and so sweaty, so narrow and so filled up. Home—the part of her new country Maryna could imagine claiming as home—was not New York, where the immigrant's America begins, but where America runs into the next ocean and ends. Bogdan needed California, the ending, the last beginning, and so did she.

For her second New York season at the Fifth Avenue Theatre, Maryna repeated, to even greater acclaim, her Adrienne and Marguerite Gautier and Juliet, and in the last two weeks forged a new triumph in the title role of *Frou-Frou*, another much loved French play about the wages of adultery. The story? Ah, the story! Vivacious, immature Gilberte de Sartorys, whose nickname is Frou-Frou, has introduced into her household her self-effacing unmarried sister, Louise, a paragon of female virtue, who inevitably comes to replace the spoiled child-wife in the affections of her little son and her husband, whereupon, imagining herself betrayed by her sister, Frou-Frou runs off with the caddish former suitor who had never stopped pursuing her, only to return several years later, penitent and mortally enfeebled, and be forgiven by her husband and permitted to embrace their child before she dies.

"I think it not quite as treacly as *East Lynne*," said Maryna. "Yes? No?"

"*East Lynne* is English, *Frou-Frou* is French," said Bogdan. "American audiences weep most liberally over the fate of disgraced women who are foreign."

"*And* rich. *And* titled," observed Miss Collingridge.

"Bogdan, tell me it's not as bad."

"How can I? Look at how they both end, with you laid out

and readying to expire in the nobly proportioned drawing room of the home you had foolishly, criminally abandoned. In *East Lynne* your last words are, and don't we all know them by heart, *Ah, is this death? 'Tis hard to part! Farewell, dear Archibald! my husband once, and loved now in death, as I never loved before! Farewell, until eternity! Think of me sometimes, keep one little corner in your heart for me — your poor — erring — lost Isabel!* Curtain."

"Mildewed, I expect," said Maryna. She was laughing.

"Ah, is this death?" said Peter.

"You're not to interrupt, you," said Maryna, pulling him into a hug.

"Think of me sometimes, keep one little corner in your heart for me," said Miss Collingridge.

"You too!" exclaimed Maryna.

"Whereas," continued Bogdan, "whereas in *Frou-Frou* you say instead — though you can use the same sofa, covered with another fabric — *Ah, at this time to die is very hard. Nay, do not grieve for me.* This to your woeful husband, sister, and father, all instructed to be sobbing into their handkerchiefs so the audience can better fix its attention on you. *What had I to expect but to die deserted by all, despairing and abandoned? In place of that, surrounded by those I love, I die peacefully — happy — no suffering — all calm, quiet —*"

"Spare me!" Maryna cried.

"And there is soft music and loud grief to escort you to your last words, *You all forgive — do you not? — Frou-Frou — poor Frou-Frou!* Curtain. Now, tell me, is this not the same play?"

"It is the same play."

"But why does Frou-Frou have to die?" said Peter. "She could jump up and say, I changed my mind."

"That would make a difference," said Maryna, kissing his hair.

"Then she could go out to California and go up in an airship and say, Try to catch me if you can."

"I like this end much better," Miss Collingridge said.

"So do I," said Maryna. "Yes, I am becoming quite American. I would much prefer to have a happy ending."

"IMPOSSIBLE," said Bogdan. The schedule was impossible. "You'll kill yourself."

On her first tour Maryna had been limited to playing in theatres that had resident companies, of which there were many fewer than a decade ago. With her own company, thirteen women and twelve men, she could perform wherever there was a theatre, and every town in America had a theatre, many of them called opera houses to make them sound more respectable, though no opera was ever performed there.

In New York State alone, Warnock had booked her for one or two performances in Poughkeepsie, Kingston, Hudson, Albany, Utica, Syracuse, Elmira, Troy, Ithaca, Rochester, and Buffalo.

After the week in Boston, this time at the Globe Theatre, came a string of nights in Lowell, Lawrence, Haverhill, Fall River, Holyoke, Brockton, Worcester, Northampton, and Springfield.

In Pennsylvania, between the week in Philadelphia and the four days in Pittsburgh, single performances in Bradford, Warren, Scranton, Erie, Wilkes-Barre, Easton, Oil City—"Oil City. An unusual name for a town in the eastern part of America, if I am not mistaken," murmured Bogdan.

In Ohio . . .

"Kalamazoo," said Peter. "It must be an Indian name."

"My stepson is reminding me," Bogdan continued, "that in Michigan *all* Madame's engagements are for a single night. Kalamazoo, Muskegon, Grand Rapids, Saginaw, Battle Creek, Ann Arbor, Bay City, Detroit. Eight cities in ten days."

"Chief Saginaw and his wife Detroit are camping by the Bay City under the Ann Arbor after the Battle Creek before they go on a raft down the Grand Rapids and return to Kalamazooooooo," said Peter.

"You left out Muskegon," said Miss Collingridge.

"But they won't forget to take their little son, named Muskegon."

"Perfect," said Miss Collingridge.

"Rushing around the country"—Bogdan refolded the map —"and for weeks at a time sleeping, if at all, in a different, uncomfortable hotel room every night? Do you want to kill your star, Mr. Warnock? These single evening engagements that follow mercilessly one after another will have to be dropped from the schedule."

"My dear sir, you must be joking. One-night stands bring in the biggest profit of the tour."

Maryna professed herself above the battle and ready for any exertion; Bogdan remained indignant; Warnock was frantic. He saw the whole tour collapsing unless . . .

Warnock's solution, Bogdan had to admit, was clever.

"Our own private railroad car? Is that common in America?" asked Maryna.

Not at all. Hers would be the very first company to travel the theatrical circuit by a means hitherto reserved for railroad magnates and slain presidents. Maryna liked being part of the wave of the future. Warnock liked the attention from the press which the car would command. In each town they visited, reporters were invited aboard to marvel at the double-height clerestory roof, watery legends on the frescoed ceiling (Moses in the bulrushes, Narcissus at his looking-glass pond, King Arthur on his funeral barge), carved black-walnut interiors, velvet window hangings, silver-plated gas lamps and hardware, Persian carpet and upright piano in Madame's saloon, zebra carpet and gilt-framed cheval glass and full-length portrait of the great actress on horseback in Western garb in her bedroom. Besides a large suite with its own dressing room and lavatory for Madame and her husband, there was a cozy office and adjoining bedroom for Madame's manager, bedrooms for Madame's son and Madame's secretary, and two tiers of comfortable sleeping berths for the actors and Madame's personal maid and the wardrobe mistress ("the sleeping arrangements of the ladies and gentlemen being separated at night by a screen in the middle of the car"), which folded back during the day to leave the floor clear for setting out the fauteuils and dining furniture; at the far end of the car were three washrooms, a galley kitchen, and clothes and bedding closets. Warnock let it be known that the interior redesign and outfitting of the seventy-foot-long former Wagner Sleeper had cost nine thousand dollars. On the exterior, painted a deep burgundy, oval panels on both sides announced in curly gold script: ZALENSKA AND COMPANY, HARRY H. WARNOCK, MANAGER. His middle name, he liked to mention, was Hannibal. The car's name, its new name, was *Poland*.

The acquisition of a private car and their own baggage wagon, with quarters for their skillful colored crew (cook, two waiters, and porter) and ingeniously sectioned storage space for the costumes and backdrops, made it possible for Warnock to add even more one-night stands.

No more packing and unpacking! They slept and ate on the train for weeks at a time, when every day or every other day there was a new town, a new theatre.

Upon arriving, Maryna and Warnock would go directly to the theatre, where Bogdan and the rest of the company would soon join them—Warnock to check on the box-office receipts and confer with scenery hands about any technical problems that could arise with their backdrops should the flies be too low or the wing space less than the requisite half of the proscenium opening, Maryna to take possession of the star's dressing room and post the itinerary next to the mirror so she would remember the name of the town, the theatre, the manager in charge of the stage. In the afternoon a brief rehearsal might need to be organized if tonight's play had not been done for a week or more, and time had to be set aside for polite exchanges with a delegation of local drama lovers, a poet with a flowing necktie, a stagestruck young lady and her mama, the editor of the town's newspaper, and the president of the local chapter of the Woman's Christian

Temperance Union. Then back to her dressing room to put on her makeup and don her costume, get on stage to do her performance, receive the local eminences in the greenroom, cull a few flowers from the many bouquets, and be at the railway station by midnight, where *Poland* and its baggage car would be hitched to the rear of whatever train was going to the town where they had their next engagement.

The economics of making an acting life entirely out of touring, without a home theatre where plays were rehearsed and maintained, meant that Maryna would never be able to deploy a large repertory in English. (At the Imperial Theatre she had played fifty-six roles!) Still, with six fully rehearsed plays, Zalenska and Company already offered more than did most of the leading actors in America crossing and recrossing the country. Indeed, some actors chose year after year to tour only their most popular role, becoming ever less ambitious for themselves and more contemptuous of their public. But an actor always, and rightly, mistrusts the public. (If audiences knew that the actors are judging *them*!) Giddy with fatigue and relief that the night's exertions are over, the actors peering into their dressing-room mirrors while slathering on cold cream to remove their makeup are also issuing verdicts on tonight's "house." Attentive? Stupid? Dead? Nothing to be done with stupidity, but Maryna had her ploys to dominate, correct, wake up a dead house—such as moving closer to the edge of the apron, looking out into the audience, turning up both volume and vibrato—or to silence a coughing one. Coughing tells you the audience wishes it were elsewhere. (In a recital, nobody coughs in the first ten minutes or during the encores.)

The theatres were not always full. The reasons could be bad weather, poor advertising, greedy theatre managers who had made the tickets too expensive, or organized outrage over plays judged to be offensively foreign or too associated with New York. "Let New York have its bedroom tragedies. Ohio will keep its mind on higher things," ended a letter to the newspaper in Lima urging a boycott of Zalenska and Company at the Faurot Theatre in *Camille*. It was signed: An American Mother. The reviewer in Terre Haute evoked Maryna's "womanly grace" in the role of Marguerite Gautier only to reproach her for "thereby making a career of sin seem tenderly appealing."

Maryna having flatly refused to program some additional, propitiatory performances of *East Lynne* in Ohio and Indiana, Warnock, hoping to distract the public, announced that Madame Zalenska had lost Marguerite Gautier's "cross and tiara of diamonds worth forty thousand dollars": although he had instantly cabled the finest jeweler in Paris, and the courier toting an even more costly diamond cross and tiara had already boarded the next steamship at Cherbourg, until the treasure reached Indiana he, Harry H. Warnock, could not answer for his star's mood. Maryna protested that he had made her look ridiculous. Not at all, explained Warnock, the American public expects a famous actress to be parted from her jewels at least once a year.

"Only her paste jewels? Or her real jewels as well?"

"Madame Marina"—he snorted with impatience—"a star is always careless with her valuables."

"Who has told you such nonsense, Mr. Warnock?"

"It was proven twenty years ago by Barnum—"

"But of course." Maryna sighed histrionically. "I have heard of this Barnum."

"—when he brought over Jenny Lind. The Swedish Nightingale, as P.T. dubbed her, and that was pure genius, lost all her jewels three times during her tour."

And Warnock was right. After he divulged the story about the jewels, the houses for *Camille* were always full.

Also to be endured: following seven curtain calls for a fast-paced *Camille* at the Academy of Music in Fort Wayne, the obese man, yellowing wig askew, pushing his way through the throng of present-bearing admirers in the greenroom (who had already pressed on her a bronze statuette of Hiawatha, the collected speeches of Ulysses S. Grant, and a music box, set on a nearby table and repeatedly wound up to unwind "Carnival in Venice")—*he* insisted on Maryna's accepting the gift of his own, dearest, fat, snuffling, champagne-colored English pug. "It ain't the jewels, Madame Zee, but I'll bet she keeps you happy for a while."

"I shall call her Ug," said Maryna, all smiles. She was tired, even peevish, that night.

"I beg your p?" said the fan.

Unexpectedly, Maryna, who was only fond of large dogs, and dogs without faulty breathing systems, had to promise Warnock she would not give Ug away. Another of Warnock's dicta: "All famous actresses have small dogs as pets"—and on this one he was unyielding. But Miss Collingridge, who would have charge of the beast, was allowed to rename her Indiana.

In Jacksonville, Maryna was presented with a pair of lime-green baby alligators.

"You don't have to keep these," said Warnock. Miss Collingridge had already found a larger cage for them, and was daintily emptying jars of insects and snails and some bleeding morsels of raw beef into their open jaws.

"Ah, but I will," said Maryna. "I've already bestowed Polish names on them. That one is Kasia. And her mate is Klemens. Miss Collingridge assures me that they are pleasant creatures, whose little white teeth are not yet sharp enough to do much harm."

"You are making fun of me, Madame Marina."

"How can you imagine such a thing? Have you not heard that Sarah Bernhardt has a pet lion cub, a cheetah, a parrot, and a monkey?"

"Sarah Bernhardt is a French actress, Madame Marina. You are an American actress."

"True, Mr. Warnock. Or should I say, True enough. Nevertheless, were I not condemned to live out my days in a railroad car, I would already have acquired a—"

"Right," said Warnock. "Keep the alligators."

When Warnock had her sit for a photograph with Kasia and Klemens, announcing to reporters that the alligators had been given to Madame Zalenska in New Orleans, Maryna, no amateur herself when it came to the enhancing falsehood, was curious to know why.

"Because New Orleans sounds better than Jacksonville."

"Better? In what sense better, Mr. Warnock?"

"More romantic. More foreign."

"And that is a good thing in America? Be patient with me. I am just trying to understand."

"Sometimes yes, sometimes no."

"But of course. Then do announce they were foisted on me in New Orleans by a ninety-four-year-old Creole soothsayer to ward off the evil spell she saw hanging over my head. And that, although I laughed at the old crone's prophecy, after a chunk of lead pipe dropped from the flies missing me by only an inch during the ovation for a *Romeo and Juliet* in Nashville, I have come to feel safer with these baleful creatures in my boudoir than without them."

"Now you're on board!" said Warnock. "I see, dear lady, you have understood . . . everything."

"Mr. Warnock, I have always understood. I have not agreed. That is all."

Before her *As You Like It* at the Schultz Opera House in Zanesville, Ohio, the audience was treated to a lecture by a Professor Steele Craven on "Shakespeare and the Comic Spirit." At Doheny's Opera House in Council Bluffs, Iowa, a program of variety acts (a ventriloquist, a unicyclist, dancing dogs) preceded her *Juliet* on the twenty-foot-wide apron stage. At Chatterton's Opera House in Springfield, Illinois, first came a minstrel show's twenty-minute *Eliza Escaping Across the Ice,* then *Frou-Frou.* In Owen's Academy of Music, in Charleston, South Carolina, *Adrienne* followed "A Medley of Short Pieces by Bellini, Meyerbeer, and Wagner." At Pillot's Opera House in Houston, the audience was prepared for *East Lynne* by a monologue entertainer, Thaddeus—"but I answer to Tadpole"—Murch. From the wings, Maryna heard him going on . . . and on: "Tadpole because I was very little when I was small. Murch because my daddy was Murch. Doodleball Murch. Now he was called Doodleball because—" Bogdan exploded. Either Warnock made sure that nothing, nothing was ever programmed before Zalenska and Company, or Madame would cancel the rest of the tour.

Another boon conferred by the snug duality of marriage: since Bogdan had taken up the indignation and dismay she was feeling, Maryna was free to lay claim to another, more indulgent response. Now it was her turn to say, "But what do you expect, dearest? This is America. They need to be sure they're being entertained. But the rude mechanicals enjoy what I offer them, too."

In Ming's Opera House in Helena, Montana, a Mrs. Aubertine Woodward De Kay played in Maryna's honor Chopin's Mazurka Op. 7, No. 1 and the A-flat major Polonaise before the curtain was allowed to go up on Zalenska and Company's *Camille*, and afterward offered a banquet for the whole company at the De Kay mansion. It was so naïve, so well-intended. My European fastidiousness is crumbling, Maryna thought. I am happy to please.

Her repertory now included three more of the Shakespeare roles she had done in Poland: Viola in *Twelfth Night* and Beatrice in *Much Ado About Nothing* (she loved these tales of mismatched or dueling couples where everything comes right in the end!), and Hermione in *The Winter's Tale*, in which Peter could play the tiny role of Hermione's ill-fated son, Mamillius. Though she knew Peter should be in boarding school, she could not bear to part with him yet. And she'd had to let Bogdan go.

"I envy you. I wouldn't know how to lead two lives," Maryna said, without looking at Bogdan's eyes. "I've paid too much just to lead this one."

"I won't go," he said.

"No, I want you to go. I'll hardly lack for employment while you're gone."

She felt heroic. It surprised her that some people thought her melancholiac. "You seemed a little sad when I came in," ventured the motherly reporter from the *Memphis Daily Avalanche.*

"What Polish face is without a touch of sadness?" Maryna replied. "But I am only a sad person when I am without my husband. We are together all the time, but lately he was obliged to go to California for a few months on business, and I miss him all the time."

THE DATE of the telegram was 23 February 1879:

VON ROEBLING AGREES TO OBSERVING FLIGHT STOP
AM NOT SEEKING PERMISSION TO GO UP

What was Bogdan doing? She hoped he would not alarm her, she'd not asked him to reassure her.

The next telegram came eight days later:

TIME ALOFT TEN MINUTES STOP INCOMPARABLE SPEC-
TACLE

Spectacle from the ground? Spectacle from the air? But how could she believe anything Bogdan said? She would have worried even more if there had not been six one-night stands in Missouri and five in Kentucky. Her repertory now stood at nine plays—five of them by Shakespeare—which she had played at thirty-four theatres in the last two months alone. She decided to add *Cymbe-line* as they reached Nebraska on the swing back across the Midwest. *Cymbeline*, she discovered, was one of the Bard's most popular plays in America. Audiences loved the stream of reconcil-iations at the end that washes over both the malign, would-be seducer of the virtuous Imogen and her choleric, easily duped husband.

Husbands are always right. A guilty wife must die. If really unfaithful, then really die. If suspected wrongfully of being unfaithful, then pretend to die—and wait, as long as it takes, for the foolishly enraged man to see reason and forgive her.

Of course it wasn't true anymore. These were modern times. A husband is not always right. But a woman is still expected to declare her poignant dependence on her husband.

Bogdan! Husband! Lie with me. Hold me. Warm me. I miss riding into sleep with you.

Another telegram, dated 17 March 1879:

MARYNA   MARYNA   MARYNA   STOP   EVERYTHING   IS
WHOLE STOP THERE IS WATER EVERYWHERE

Then silence. Had he gone mad? Would he disappear forever?

But of course I can live without him. As long as I keep on touring. These tours keep me in balance. Movement and excitement and the awareness of obligation drive away the bad thoughts, silence the foolish inclinations.

Husband! Friend! Do what you have to do. But don't torment me. I am not that strong. Yet.

"EACH CRAFT is constructed according to a different principle," Bogdan reported when he returned. "This one was called *Aero Heart. Aero Corazón.* Sometimes just *Corazón.*"

"Was? Then it crashed."

"Maryna, you haven't understood. It did go up. Almost straight up, the distinctive feature of this aero being that it has no wings. Straight up, without any outward skimming, to a hundred feet or so. There it hovered for ten astonishing, sublime minutes!"

"Tell me more," she said.

"Ah, Maryna. I feel very foolish. What am I doing to us? I'm possessed."

"No, you're not. You're telling me a story."

"I don't tell stories!"

"Yes, you do." She laughed softly.

"What do you want to know?"

"What it looks like."

"Like a giant bell, with the cabin completely enclosed and a huge, broad screw propeller sticking up from the roof that, when set in motion, is like a spinning top. I told you it has no wings, didn't I? Yes, of course I did. The lift-power is supplied by something the inventors call Air Squeezers, a tube through which compressed air is ejected below the craft. Squeezers and propeller send the craft straight up to a predetermined height, after which it stops, then flies horizontally—that part didn't work this time— in the direction in which it's pointed. Up to eighty miles an hour, Juan María and José claim."

"I thought the inventors were all Germans."

"Almost all."

"And they survived, unscathed, your Mexican friends, when the aero fell. You'd have told me if they were killed or . . ."

"Yes, *Corazón* is superbly prepared for catastrophe. A balloon three times its size, called a compensator, inflates rapidly to retard too sudden a descent, and elastic legs shoot out beneath the craft to break the fall on alighting."

"But you didn't go up with them?"

"Maryna, I told you I wouldn't."

"And so you didn't."

"I was on the verge of asking to be taken along. But I was afraid of being unable to master my fear. I knew, they knew, the landing would be subdued, disillusioning, not fatal. Still, there's no certainty. That's what an adventure is, isn't it? It's got flowers in its hair but it has no face"—"What, Bogdan?"—"Oh, and

339

Dreyfus *is* interested. And I think I can get von Roebling to meet with him. And then I'll have accomplished my mission. Maryna, Maryna, please don't shake your head like that!"

LEAVE AMERICA? Because—most American of reasons—it was "time to move on"? Warnock didn't understand. "But you've just begun in America. You can make a fortune here. Everyone loves you."

But how could a man like Warnock understand the lure of London for a true worshipper of Shakespeare? To be an actress in England, not just in English! In England she would bloom and surge beyond everything achieved on this second, even more successful American tour.

"No, you won't," said Warnock.

With the baffled, angry Warnock continuing to predict that her London venture would be a failure, Maryna put herself in the hands of Edward Dudley Brownlow, the English impresario. On May 1, 1879, she made her London debut with *Camille*, although not under that title, because *Camille*—as *La Dame aux camélias* was known, nonsensically, in English—lay under a ban from the Lord Chamberlain. Having always revered England as not only the land of Shakespeare but the birthplace of every civic freedom, Maryna was astonished to learn of the existence of a government censor in London. Just like Warsaw. No, not like Warsaw, if English censorship was so puny it could be thwarted by changing a play's title. And Maryna rather liked *Heartsease*, the new title, which seemed agreeably, meaninglessly conciliatory, and was disappointed to learn from Brownlow that heartsease was merely the name of another flower. She felt demoted, like the pure-hearted courtesan's signature flower. Surely this Lord Chamberlain could not oblige "the lady with the camellias" to die in the fifth act on a bed strewn with . . . pansies!

She'd chosen *Camille* over a play of Shakespeare for the same reason she started in America with *Adrienne Lecouvreur*:

her accent would matter less in a French play. The new mask through which she had learned to produce the sounds of English in America, with its jaw a little slack, had, with Miss Collingridge's help, to be tightened for London. Syllable breaks were reexamined and became crisper, consonants produced from the back of the mouth were moved forward, and the lips made thinner. "Snobs that they are, the English enjoy finding fault with our American accents," Miss Collingridge observed. "They particularly object to what they describe as the drawling intonation of American actors." "Drawl!" exclaimed Maryna. "Since when do I drawl?" Maryna could not admit to herself that she found the English intimidating. She had got used to the loose-mouthed American conversational attack—its garrulousness, its insistence on familiarity. In America, no one was interested in the tragic fate of her homeland, but she was made to feel welcome all the same. Here, both journalists with soiled collars and her titled dinner partners assumed she would want to bore them about Poland, while she was hoping to make English conversation. About the theatrical season in London. About Mr. Disraeli and Mr. Gladstone. About the weather.

Maryna had anticipated that the English were not to be conquered as swiftly as the Americans. She had not supposed that they weren't to be conquered at all, except conditionally. Her wager to herself was that if no more than half the reviews in the London newspapers mentioned her "enchanting" or "charming" accent, she would succeed in transferring her career, triumph and all, to England. All the reviews were flattering. Every critic mentioned the accent.

She was praised, but not embraced. Unlike Americans, the English didn't know what to do with questing foreigners. (Allowing them to become English was not an option.) And she, Marina Zalenska, was doubly a foreigner: a Pole from America.

At the end of May, when her run at the Court Theatre (*Heartsease, Romeo and Juliet, As You Like It*) had finished, she went with Bogdan and Miss Collingridge to see, possibly admire, the celebrated romantic pair of Ellen Terry and Henry Irving, at Irving's theatre, the Lyceum. Ready to incline her head to these new gods of the English stage, Maryna was almost disappointed, so she told Bogdan, to discover that she was as good as the Terry she studied closely that evening in the title role of Bulwer-Lytton's fusty, ever popular *The Lady of Lyons*; and as for the great Henry Irving, in the role of the lowborn hero, he seemed to her, with his dragging walk and weak guttural voice, altogether inferior in grace and distinction of speech to Edwin Booth.

At least Maryna had the satisfaction of knowing that, were she not barred from a career in England because she had committed herself body and soul to performing in English, she could have stood her own against Terry. But she couldn't compete with Sarah Bernhardt, who was about to arrive and would play at the Gaiety in French.

The day that Bernhardt and the Comédie-Française opened to worshipful acclaim in her *Phèdre*, Maryna went out on summer tour of the English provinces. There she offered her Rosalind and her Juliet, and also her Ophelia and Viola, which Brownlow was eager to present in another London season in the fall; but Maryna had no desire to stay on, campaigning for a more clinging approval. Perhaps, Maryna wondered gloomily, she had used up the allotted number of impossible feats her will could make possible. Even if that were so, there still remained the nearly impossible. The merely very difficult.

It had taken this sojourn in England to understand how much easier it was (*hadn't* it been easy?) to prevail in America: a whole country of people who believe in the will.

At a dinner party given in her honor by Lady Wolsington, Maryna had been seated next to the formidable American novelist and theatre critic Henry James, recently settled in London, and Mr. James had wondered if she might care to join him the following Tuesday for tea at the Café Royal, where he told her with circuitous bluntness that he hoped she'd not find him in the least predatory if . . . he hesitated, stroking his beautifully trimmed silky beard; he had already hesitated several times since they sat down at the marble-top table. "If what, dear Mr. James?" "If I confess to being what I can only describe as very interested, if not actually fascinated, both as a novelist and, I shall take the liberty of confiding in you one of my fonder hopes, a future playwright, fascinated, I say, in the actress as a contemporary *type*. I speak not of the actress as someone capable of an uncommon expressiveness, that expressiveness being to some extent conjoined with a flair for taking risks, necessary as such assets, expressiveness, audacity, are to her art, but the actress, the contemporary actress, as the most brilliant embodiment of feminine *success*." Mr. James spoke with decided emphases, sometimes at the beginning, usually at the close of his often meandering sentences.

"It doesn't feel as if I have been altogether a success in London," said Maryna. "At least not as much as I'd hoped, though I am most grateful for your friendly article."

"Ah, you must give the English a chance, dear Madame Zalenska. I'm afraid you may have been spoiled by our Yankee forthrightness. For all the want of *spread* in these compact isles there is much more *surface* here, one thing is said while another is meant, they are cautious, they can be suspicious, they are not keen on making a great effort, they would rather be thought a bit slow than too clever, they, how can I put it, *withhold*. But I predict they will come round."

He meant to be kind, no doubt. "England is not as vague and cushiony as America," he declared. *He* was a little vague and cushiony, in the nicest way—this fattish, wordy, manifestly brilliant man. It was futile, he pronounced encouragingly, to dwell on the differences between England and America, which he invited Maryna to look upon as "one big Anglo-Saxon total—" Had Mr. James recently revisited his birthplace, New York City? Had he ever set foot in California? Surely not. "—one big Anglo-Saxon total, destined to such an amount of melting together that an insistence on their difference is idle and pedantic," James was saying, "and that melting together will come the faster," he went on, "the more one takes it for granted and treats the life of the two countries as continuous or more or less *convertible*."

Convertible perhaps for an American, Maryna thought. Or this kind of American. For Mr. James—in accent, in hesitations, in stiffness, in ominous opaque courtesy—seemed quite English to her. Perhaps for a writer . . .

"Two chapters of the same book," James intoned, as if reading her mind.

"Or two acts of the same play."

"Just so," James said.

But no, not for actors. She could become an American, but never an English, actor.

She recognized the old American tune, which conflates willing strenuously and taking for granted. Henry James was very American after all. He'd contrived to have at his disposal a vast allotment of willing.

An English actor could always come to America: many had done so. Edwin Booth's father, Junius Brutus Booth, who as a young actor had played with and rivaled Edmund Kean on the London stage, deserted his wife and child for a flower seller on Bow Street and ran off with her to America, there to found a new family of ten children and make one of the great American acting careers. Unthinkable for an American actor to flee to England and have an equally illustrious career. Americans acclaimed by the London critics, as Charlotte Cushman had been a generation earlier with her Portia, Beatrice, Lady Macbeth, and her Romeo (played opposite her sister's Juliet), were not supposed to stay.

Maryna and Bogdan returned to America after a quick trip to Kraków in late August. A failure is a failure only if acknowledged. The English public had been most welcoming, the shoving, sweating, shouting crowd of journalists waiting for her at the White Star pier were told. Yes, she nodded, she *had* been tempted to remain in London. ("No, no! Please, gentlemen! I have not, I repeat, *not* said that I am abandoning the American stage.")

But she was wholly pleased—this part was true—to be back in America.

America: not just another country. While the unjust course of European history had ordained that a Pole could not be a citizen of Poland (but only of Russia or Austria or Prussia), the just course of world history had created America. Maryna would always be a Pole—no way to change that, nor would she want to. But she could, if she so chose, be an American too.

She immediately set to planning the next New York season and another national tour. Unable to forgive Warnock for, once again, being right, Maryna, in consultation with Bogdan, had engaged a zealous new personal manager with a "delicious" name, Ariel N. Peabody.

"Even more delicious than we thought," Maryna reported to Bogdan. "Recalling how pleased Mr. Warnock was with his middle name, I thought Mr. Peabody might like to be asked his. 'The N, you mean?' he cried." Maryna tilted her head as Peabody did; her mimicry of his voice was uncanny. " 'Ah, this may amuse you, Madame Marina. It stands for'—pause—'the name is'—flourish, bow—'Nothing.' "

"America never disappoints," observed Bogdan.

"*Nomen, omen*. Maybe he'll prove to be nothing like Mr. Warnock. No more humbug, I like this word, lost diamonds, lapdogs, alligators, tall tales—nothing of that."

"I shouldn't count on it," said Bogdan. "But a Marina Zalenska doesn't need A. Nothing Peabody to tell her what to do."

"HER SUCCESS has grown like an avalanche," announced the *Norfolk Public Ledger*. She continued to add Shakespeares: starting in 1880, *Measure for Measure*, and the following year *The Merchant of Venice* and, at last, "the Scottish play." As for being a star, American style: by the end of the third national tour Maryna thought she had got that role down pat.

345

It is to go about in your own sumptuously appointed apartment on wheels, a private railway car with etched-glass Gothic windows and velvet draperies and potted palms and a small library and a piano and a boudoir large enough for a mahogany dresser and four-poster bed, the other actors and your staff following in a second, private Pullman car; to have a pug named Indiana; to have a large watercolor painting of your pet pug adorning a panel of the parlor of your private car; to need the largest, most luxurious suite whenever you stop at hotels, the best hotels, and the most delicate food; to scribble notes on the finest linen paper with an embossed crest, the usual words of thanks to those who have attempted to entertain you or otherwise please you, kindly words to the bedazzled young women brave enough to request an interview ("You can't imagine how many girls write me every day to ask my advice on how to begin this profession, but how can I encourage them, so long as in America there are hardly any permanent theatres?"). It is to hobnob with other living legends: Longfellow is your special friend and Tennyson has received you in London and Oscar Wilde has greeted you with an armful of white lilies and announced he will write a play for you. It is to be unconventional, though hardly as unconventional as Oscar Wilde: your particular defiance of convention—you are a lady and you smoke—is the kind of thing people expected to learn about you. It is to be careless about possessions, to be unable to throw anything away, to be continually acquiring: you disembarked with sixty-five pieces of luggage when you came from the following summer's trip to Paris ("and a brief visit to her native Poland"), the New York papers recounted. It is to have many residences: "Soon she and her husband, Count Dembowski, will be going for a month to their ranch in southern California. The main house, recently completed, was designed by a friend of Madame Zalenska, the eminent architect and theatre-lover, Stanford White."

In Poland, you were allowed some practice of the arts of self-indulgence, but you were expected to be sincere and also to have high ideals—people respected you for that. In America, you were expected to exhibit the confusions of inner vehemence, to express opinions no one need take seriously, and have eccentric foibles and extravagant needs, which exhibited the force of your will, your appetitiveness, the spread of your self-regard—all excellent things.

Out for a drive (Boston, Philadelphia, Chicago) in your private brougham, you stop on impulse in front of a bookstore and come out with a dozen poets bound in choicest vellum, morocco, and tree-calf. Her tastes are all of the exclusive kind, the journalists reported. She spends money royally right and left, they said, with a princess-like freedom. At the same time, you were expected to be shrewd about money and a pitiless negotiator, but charitable too (you are pursued by heartrending letters from indigent Polish immigrants), and beyond reproach, that is, respectable, and a would-be homebody, and a devoted parent. A woman must always declare that her family matters more to her than her career.

Of course her real family was her company, whose ever-changing roster continued to advance in skill, thanks to Maryna's ferocious, supple mentoring.

"The curtain rises, you must seize the audience." Here she might seize the actor's wrist. "Fix the audience with a look, then ravish its soul with the voice. Making full use of your diaphragm, yes?" Here she would bellow. "Don't squeak or rant!"

She went over the tricks and pitfalls of the stage embrace. Dying, she explained, should be neither swift nor too drawn out. She gave instruction in techniques of coughing, fainting, and praying. To an actor who had the habit of agonizing in the wings with stage fright long before his entrance, she prescribed "a last-minute departure from the dressing room."

"Don't be afraid to turn upstage," she admonished. "The face may say too much, but the audience can read just what it needs, no more, from your back."

And: "Don't move your head when you talk. It makes the neck much less powerful."

And: "Don't let the voice go down. The voice should go out, but to another actor. Your voice is too much *at* the public."

At regular intervals packets of raw ginger arrived from San Francisco's Chinatown so Maryna could press on all members of her company the merits of frequent infusions of ginger tea: drinking it boiling hot, then eating the finely sliced raw ginger at the bottom of the cup, will solve almost all last-minute voice problems, she said. She pointed out that while fear and anxiety make men more thermic—"Thermic!" exclaimed Miss Collingridge appreciatively—so they need to be vigilant about perspiration stains that blossom on the upper part of their costumes, the same emotions make women feel chilled, so the women must be sure to bundle up before the performance and during intermissions.

"But, Madame," said Warren Bancroft (her Romeo and Benedick and Orlando and her Armand Duval and Maurice during the company's second season), "I always go cold as ice when I have stage fright."

"Nonsense," she said.

"Acting should never be easy," she said, spitting out *easy*. "That means you have forgotten yourself. You have forgotten where you are. You must never, never, never forget you are on a stage. Therefore you will always be afraid. You are afraid, but you are a conqueror. When you are on stage, whatever your role, you are a conqueror. You should feel very tall when you stand on a stage. Everything in you should straighten and contract around the fear. Even in grief, which is concave, you are still a line. And that line goes straight out to the last row of the highest balcony. Hold the line! Become a source of light. You are a candle. Keep your back straight, don't let your neck settle into your shoulders. Feel the flame rise from the top of your head."

Of Abner Dixey, dismissed after the first season (he had played Jaques in *As You Like It* and Malvolio in *Twelfth Night* and, even more woodenly, Captain Levison, the scheming rake in

East Lynne), she said, succinctly, "He didn't transform anything. An actor transforms."

"Most rules for behaving properly on a stage," she told them, "also apply to real life." ("Except," she said, smiling blithely, cryptically, "when they don't.") One such rule is: Never acknowledge a mishap. Once, in a *Measure for Measure* at the Taylor Opera House in Trenton, the actor playing Claudio, the brother, who has been condemned to death, in flinging himself at Isabella's feet to implore her to grant Angelo's base request (the price of sparing his life) knocked the prison bench over; sustaining the same frenzy of utterance that Claudio's wretchedness demanded, he deftly righted the bench. When the curtain fell on the last of numerous recalls that Maryna had generously shared with the young actor, a new recruit to the company, she said very softly to him: "Never try to repair an accident during a performance. It only prompts the audience to notice it."

To be sure, some accidents are harder to ignore, as when, in a *Macbeth* at McVicker's Theatre in Chicago ("Naturally, it was the Scottish play!"), having stupidly essayed her sleepwalking entrance with her eyes shut, Maryna stumbled and ruptured a tendon in her ankle. She continued the scene to the end without murmur, grimace, or alteration of her gait.

Your corrections are biting, maternal, just. Your example is luminous.

The members of your company repay you with adulation and fear and perfect, anxious devotion.

You show off, you amaze them. You are at the zenith. Your powers, so you feel now, are unlimited.

They were drawing full houses and enchanted audiences in Colorado. And after the final performance of a week at Denver's Tabor Grand Opera House—*Juliet* (as *Romeo and Juliet* was called in the company's schedule), *Adrienne, Camille, Winter's Tale*—Peabody organized a late supper with free liquor for the company in the empty saloon of their hotel. By the time Maryna

349

joined them, most of the men, and not only the men, were jovially drunk, and flirty Laura Fitch, who played the wicked Queen of England in *Cymbeline* and Audrey in *As You Like It* and Paulina in *The Winter's Tale,* was finishing her tabletop recitation of

> *When scarcely old enough to know*
> *The meaning of a tale of woe,*
> *'Twas then by mother we were told,*
> *That father in his grave was cold.*
> *For long we watched beside her bed,*
> *Then sobb'd to see her lie there dead;*
> *And now we wander hand in hand,*
> *Two orphan girls from Switzerland!*

"Ahem," said James Bridger, the new Mercutio in *Romeo and Juliet* and Touchstone in *As You Like It* and the faithful Gaston in *Camille,* who was in love with Laura. "Now where's my stage?" Leaping with Mercutio-like agility to the counter of the bar and slapping his hand to his chest, he bawled

> *I have ruined my health in the struggle for wealth!*
> *Said the banker in piteous tones—*

"Oh!" And jumped down.

At the sight of Maryna, everyone shrank into guilty, child-ish solemnity.

"Please! Let me not interrupt."

"We were only joking about, Madame, and reciting dog-gerel to each other," said Cornelia Scudder, the young actress to whom Maryna had given the roles of Celia in *As You Like It,* Perdita in *The Winter's Tale,* Hero in *Much Ado About Nothing,* and Louise, the virtuous sister in *Frou-Frou.*

"Then—I insist—you will continue." Maryna liked Cor-nelia. She looked from face to face. "No one wants to perform for me? No one wants to make me laugh?" She smiled at their discomfiture. "Very well." She nodded gravely. "Then I must perform for you. Something you'll find of special interest, I think, even though it's in Polish."

Maryna began in a whisper. Her dappled voice turned husky, then liquid. Her delivery was full of hesitations at first, revealing a mind heavy with feeling, amorous feeling, bitter feeling, unsure of what it wished to express. Then, gaining momentum, she passed to a high, mocking cadence. Rhapsodic, purling phrases were routed by harsh, slicing sounds, and a light, crazy laugh and then sobs and moans. Gazing out vacantly, she dropped into a hoarse tone, broken with grief, and finished with a pulsing vocal surge, telling of renewed hope and determination.

Clutched by Maryna's spell, the actors stared at her mutely. Miss Collingridge, sitting opposite Maryna, scribbled something on a piece of paper and passed it across the table. Maryna frowned. Finally, someone dared speak. "Tremendous," gasped Horace Petrie, their new Posthumus in *Cymbeline*, Angelo in *Measure for Measure*, and Banquo in *Macbeth*.

"Sshhh," said Mabel Hawley, typecast for maids (Juliet's Nurse and Nanine in *Camille* and Joyce in *East Lynne*) but, to cork her near-overflowing discontent, also awarded the role of *Adrienne*'s Princesse de Bouillon.

"Whatever it was, Madame, I was harpooned by it," said Harry Kellogg, the company's ringleted, portly Prince de Bouillon in *Adrienne*, Henri de Sartorys in *Frou-Frou*, Leontes in *The Winter's Tale*, and Duke Senior in *As You Like It*. He was from a whaling family in New Bedford, Massachusetts.

"Was it a poem, Madame?" said Mabel. "A monologue from an old Polish tragedy?"

Maryna smiled, and lit a cigarette.

"What was it, Madame? What was it?" exclaimed Charles Whiffen, her Iachimo in *Cymbeline* and Claudio in *Measure for Measure* and Orsino in *Twelfth Night* and Archibald Carlyle, the wronged husband in *East Lynne*.

"I merely—" she began, while idly unfolding Miss Colling-ridge's note. It read: "You recited the Polish alphabet. Twice." Maryna burst into laughter.

"Tell us! What was it, Madame?"

"You tell them, Mildred, what I was reciting."

"A prayer," declared the young woman defiantly. She was blushing.

"Exactly," said Maryna. "An actor's prayer. In my sad devout country, there is a prayer for everything."

Miss Collingridge smiled.

"Mildred, you've not been studying Polish behind my back, have you?" Maryna said the next morning on the train heading toward a night's *Frou-Frou* in Leadville. Dressed in a lacy tea gown, she was reclining on a chaise longue, waving her cigarette with a lazy gesture; Miss Collingridge shook her head. "Then, if I did not know you so well, I would say you were quite diaboli-cal."

"Madame Marina, that is the nicest thing you've ever said to me."

"And how was it, my alphabet?"

"In English, we say 'And how was my alphabet?' "

"Noted," Maryna said. "And the alphabet?"

"Grandiose," sighed Miss Collingridge.

Maryna could never understand why in America there was so much suspicion of the arts, even among educated people, and so much antipathy toward the theatre. A woman to whom Maryna was introduced in the lobby of the Plankinton Hotel in Milwaukee boasted that she had never set foot inside a theatre. "When I see a theatre entrance, I cross to the other side of the street." Yet there was no end of young women in every American city who thought (or whose mothers thought) they were born for the stage.

One or two might become actresses. None whom she saw—and Maryna wanted to be magnanimous—would ever be a star.

Authority, idiosyncrasy, velvetiness—these are what make a

star. And an unforgettable voice. You could do *everything* with the voice, once you knew which notes should be punched out, which left in shadow. Your breath control now gives you whatever you need: seamless phrasing, a bright range of colors, subtle timbral changes, the jolt of a cry or a crystalline whisper or an unexpected pause. Your voice rises, effortless, unhurried, and pure—enchanting the whole theatre into reverent silence. Who did not feel improved, then and there, by Isabella's noble plea?

> *But man, proud man,*
> *Dress'd in a little brief authority,*
> *Most ignorant of what he's most assur'd,*
> *His glassy essence, like an angry ape,*
> *Plays such fantastic tricks before high heaven*
> *As make the angels weep—*

You could make every member of the audience feel pensive, profound, if only for a moment. Or, with *Here's the smell of the blood ... still* and just a flutter of fingers at the end of a shapely arm clamped demurely to your side while looking down at the paralyzed guilty hand (no need to sniff it or lick it or hold it to the tip of your taper's flame) and groaning, sighing, resonating like a bell with *All the perfumes of Arabia will not sweeten this ... little hand. Oh, oh, oh!*—you could, you did, convulse every heart in the theatre.

SOMETIMES MARYNA rehearsed an actor in a new part from midnight to five in the morning, was up and at her first appointment at nine, and went on to have a full day and perform in the evening. She never looked tired. When asked, as she often was, about her beauty secrets, she at first replied, "A happy life ... my husband and child, my friends, my life in theatre, a reasonable amount of sleep, and good soap and water." In America it was common for a star to claim to be, under the wrappings of privilege, no different from everyone else, which everyone else, while only faintly imagining these privileges, knew was untrue. Maryna's women admirers were happier when she began "endorsing" something they could buy: Harriet Hubbard Ayer's Beauty Creams and Angel Star Hair Lotion.

She wished she could find a cream or lotion she liked, especially since she had reluctantly begun using the new grease-based makeup. Standardized like so much of modern life, the new makeup elements came ready-made in the form of round sticks, each numbered and labeled. It was quicker to apply than dry makeup, and safer, if one believed the rumor that certain chemicals used in preparing some of the powders, such as bismuth and red and white lead, were actually poisonous. (If only it were possible to use both dry and wet makeup—as the steamships plying the Atlantic, smoke streaming from their great funnels, also sported, in case of engine failure, a full complement of sails!) And Maryna had to resign herself to harsh, unflattering lighting, too. Odorless, safe (is safety *that* important?), brighter (oh, so much brighter)—what was thrilling on the street was a devastation in the theatre. Thick soft gaslight, with all the lovely specks and motes in it, conferred the necessary illusion on many a scene which electricity now revealed in all its naked trashiness. She'd heard that Henry Irving and Ellen Terry had refused to replace gas with electricity in the Lyceum—ever. But in America no one could refuse the often unlovely imperatives of progress. Gaslight was obsolete, and that was the end of it. The American partiality for the new decreed: whatever is, can be improved. Or ought to be replaced. Maryna soon forgot whether she had signed a letter, dated May 7, 1882, which appeared in many magazines under the heading "Madame Zalenska's Tribute to an American Invention," just for the fee she was paid, or whether for a time she had actually used this amusing new product.

My dear Sir: Last October while in Topeka, Kan., I purchased several boxes of your Felt Tablets (Ideal Tooth Polisher) for the teeth and have been using them ever since. I cheerfully add my testimony to others as to their value, and believe this invention will eventually almost entirely supersede the brush made of bristles. I am only afraid that at some time I may run out of Tablets in a place where none are procurable.

Yours sincerely,
Marina Zalenska

It became harder—does this always happen to great actors?—to remember the difference between what she said and what she thought. After she hailed her friend, Mr. Longfellow, as America's greatest poet—she had broken off her tour to recite "The Wreck of the Hesperus" and say a few words of tribute at his funeral—Bogdan ventured to rebuke her. "You can't *really* think Longfellow is as good a poet as Walt Whitman?" he exclaimed. "I . . . I don't know," Maryna said. "Do you think I'm becoming stupid, Bogdan? It's quite possible. Or just very conventional? I shouldn't like that at all."

Summoned at last to play opposite Edwin Booth, in a benefit performance of *Hamlet* at New York's Metropolitan Opera, Maryna sang Ophelia's songs to the music Moniuszko had composed for her when she played Ophelia in Warsaw many years before. "Ah, my father's ghost!" Booth shouted when Maryna knocked on his door an hour before curtain; she wanted to show him the precious original score. He was sitting in full costume in the dark, drinking; she could barely see his slender, important face. The dressing room smelled of urine. She'd heard it said so often that he was born pensive and sad, that his youth, given over to serving a tyrannical, antic father, had been comfortless, and that he had never recovered from the death of a beloved young wife after three years of marriage, followed, soon after, by the infamous deed of his younger brother, John Wilkes Booth. Maryna had her own reasons for being moody, but none of them could compare with his. She did not presume again on his solitude.

She felt serene. She hoped it wasn't just being old. Each

evening, after she finished her makeup and put on her costume, she would select one scene and work on freshening the reading of some lines: then she was lucid, focused, anxious. In her dressing room between the acts, a scarlet and magenta kimono (gift of the Japanese ambassador in Washington, an admirer) flung over her costume, woolen scarf around her throat to keep her vocal muscles warm, cigarette caught in a small gold clamp attached to a ring that she slipped on her forefinger, Maryna brooded over a lapboard accommodating cards hardly bigger than thumbnails . . . until the call-boy's summons wrenched her away from her game.

You don't cheat when you play solitaire. But neither do you accept every hand you deal yourself; you redeal and redeal until you see a hand (say, with two kings and at least one ace) that gives you a better chance to win. Sometimes she was thinking; or planning something; or remembering, for instance, about Ryszard. Often it was just the silky, insidious desire to play another game. There was news about Ryszard. He had married. Henryk had written her first, and then the others. Jealousy flashed, white-hot. (Yes, she had been vain enough to suppose he would never love anyone else.) Her insides felt scooped out with regret; then she iced with anger. (It didn't occur to her that he had married without love.) She dealt herself the cards. She lost. If you lose, you *have* to play again. You think, Just one more game. But even if you win, you still want to play again.

"I WISH TO SPEAK TO Madame Zalenska and her children," said the tall gaunt apparition in the doorway of Maryna's car.

An hour ago they had pulled into the train yard at Lexington, Kentucky, for two nights, and the wonder was how she had got past Melville, their clever porter, who was under orders to admit no one except members of the company. The young women who prowled about the stage door or haunted the pavement outside the hotel (if Maryna was in their city for a week's run), hoping for a glimpse of their idol, had even been known to venture into the railway station's darker precincts. But this, Maryna saw, was no aspirant to the stage.

"How may I help you?" said Maryna, rising.

"You are Madame Zalenska and"—her pale blue eyes scanned the long table where Bogdan, Miss Collingridge, Peabody, and a half dozen of the actors had just sat down to supper with Maryna—"these are your children?"

Thirty-five-year-old Maurice Barrymore (a gifted English actor and aspiring playwright who had been Maryna's Romeo, Orlando, Claudio, Maurice, and Armand Duval for several seasons now) and sixty-year-old Francis McGivern (her Friar Laurence, Angelo, Michonnet, and Armand's father) burst out laughing.

"Quiet, you youngsters, or you shall be spanked and sent to bed without your supper!" said Maryna. "As we all know that a great actress is ageless, I thank you for the compliment, Mrs.—"

"Mrs. Wenton."

"—but unfortunately I have only one child, and he is far away, in a boarding school near Boston."

"I am speaking of your company. These are your children too, the children of your soul, and their salvation depends entirely upon you."

"What would you guess the population of religious lunatics to be in America?" Bogdan murmured to Miss Collingridge.

"Why are you whispering, sir? You should listen to what I am saying to your mother."

"I am not an actor, madam, so perhaps my soul is exempt from immediate danger. And I defy anyone to construe my relation to this lady as filial."

Eben Stopford, their Charles the Wrestler in *As You Like It* and the Porter in *Macbeth*, banged the table with the flat of his huge hand.

"I see that I am being made fun of."

"Madame Marina, shall I escort the lady to the exit?"

357

"No, no, Eben. It's all right."

Mrs. Wenton smiled in triumph, then approached the table and looked intently into Maryna's face. "Permit me to have a talk with you. A private talk. I am sent to you on a holy mission by the one dearest to my heart."

"A private talk. Very well. But I shall invite the gentleman who has told you he is not an actor to join us."

In the sunken parlor at the end of the car, Bogdan picked a magazine from the reading table, sat on one of the sofas, crossed his legs, and frowned. Maryna seated the intruder opposite herself in the armchair by the bookcase. Melville, whom Maryna decided not to reproach for having failed in his sentry duty, appeared with the coffee. Sternly waving it away, their unwanted guest stared open-mouthed as Maryna inserted something into a short gold tube which she set between her lips, leaned forward when Bogdan rose, striking a match, so he could anoint its tip with a flame, and leaned back, resting her wrist on the lace antimacassar of the arm of the easy chair.

"You have never seen a lady with a cigarette?"

"No!"

"So now you have," said Maryna. "Do be so kind as to master your astonishment and tell me what you want from me, or let me return to my dinner."

"I may begin now? You will listen to me?"

"You may begin, Mrs. Fenton."

"Wenton. I don't know if I can, with that smoke coming out of your nostrils and mouth."

"You can," said Maryna. "Try."

"Last night my son appeared to me from the upper world. My little son, only three when he drowned in the pond near our house, and he had stars in his eyes. 'Mother,' he said, 'go to Madame Zalenska. Tell her that the floor of the stage is but a grating beneath which lie the flames of hell. Warn her, Mother, that if she continues to spread bad examples, there will be no pity for her. One day she will take a step, just one step, and that floor will break beneath her with a crash and she will fall into the fiery abyss, and the other actors with her.' " Mrs. Wenton gazed moist-eyed, imploringly, at Maryna.

"I am sorry to hear about your son. When did the dreadful accident happen?"

"Many years ago. But he is always with me. 'Mother,' he said last night, 'go in the name of the welfare of humanity, and beg Madame Zalenska to save herself and the many other souls she is dragging into corruption.' "

"Maryna, don't—"

"Corrupting? I corrupting anyone?"

"Yes!" And the intruder launched into a tirade against the plays Maryna was appearing in, singling out *Adrienne*, a story that glorifies the stage; *Camille*, the story of a courtesan; and *Frou-Frou*, the story of a frivolous woman who abandons her husband and little son. "All three"—she concluded—"the hellish conceptions of French authors."

"It does not appease you that these unhappy women, Adri-enne and Marguerite and poor Gilberte, all die at the end of the play? Even if they are as bad as you say, are they not sufficiently punished?"

"But before they are punished, you, Madame Zalenska, with your art, have made them seem very attractive."

"So I should be punished, too? Is that what you are saying?"

"Maryna, let me—"

"No, Bogdan, I want to hear Mrs. Wenton out. I want to un-derstand her."

"There is nothing to understand, Madame Zalenska. I come in the name of morality and religion."

"What religion, if I may ask?"

"I am an evangelist. I am of all religions."

"Really? In America there are so many kinds of churches and even—I'm told—families in which each member belongs to

359

a different church. And you believe in *all* of them, Mrs. Wenton? Extraordinary. I belong to just one, the Roman Catholic, and follow its precepts of charity and love."

"I thank heaven that I do not belong to Rome, but all of us, Roman or not, know the difference between good and evil. God has given you talent. Beautiful talent. Why not use it for good? Why do you present such immoral plays?"

"Surely you don't consider Shakespeare immoral."

"Another beautiful talent fatally misused! Not all of it, but yes, Shakespeare is rife with indecency! Lust, calling itself love, is the theme of *Romeo and Juliet,* and of *Midnight's Summer Dream,* which has all those couples sleeping together on the ground, and both *As You Like It* and *Twelfth Night* have a woman cavorting about the stage in *tights*! And there's witchcraft in the one that shows a wife enticing her husband to murder the king, after the witches prophesy to—"

"Please don't say it," said Maryna.

"Say what?"

"Mrs. Wenton, what plays would you like me to present? *The Passion Play,* perhaps."

"Is that another low French play? From its title I—"

"No, no, it is a religious play, performed in Austria. Its subject is the sufferings of Christ."

"Listen to me, Madame Zalenska. You have a great presence, a great voice. Something speaks through you. It is a woman's gift. Be a platform woman instead of a painted creature on a stage, pretending to be someone you are not. You could speak from your heart. You should be a preacher!"

"And what becomes of my art?"

"Art is a delusion! The greatest delusion in the world. Fame likewise."

"And money?"

"Money is not a delusion but a snare."

"A delicate distinction," said Maryna. "But then I cannot

imagine an American thinking money a delusion pure and simple."

"Why are you criticizing this great country, which has been so kind to you?"

"Ah," cried Maryna, stubbing out her cigarette and rising, "you are right. It *was* a criticism, glib and unoriginal even—who has not denounced the American romance with money?—but one I have the right, the very American right, to level against my adopted country. For as you may know, my husband and I have this year—it is seven years since we arrived—become American citizens. I am very grateful to this country. And, believe me, I do not think money a delusion, either."

"Maryna, it's time . . ." said Bogdan.

"Yes. Yes. May I ask you, Mrs. Wenton, if you go often to the theatre?"

"I am obliged to go"—she was looking up at Maryna with her head cocked—"to chart the progress of infamy."

"Then you will certainly want to see the play I am learning now and will present on Saturday in Louisville, at Macauley's. It has a scene where a young husband is terribly excited by his wife, who dances a fiery tarantella shaking her tambourine in front of him."

Mrs. Wenton rose hastily.

"Perhaps you would like me to dance it for you now."

"You persist in your hellish ways."

"I persist."

"My son will be very disappointed. 'Mother,' he will say, 'you failed to save Madame Zalenska.' I hope he will not be angry with me." She had turned to go, then turned back. "Remember, the gates of hell are open."

" 'Would that Mr. Lincoln had fallen elsewhere than at the very gates of hell!' " Maryna intoned. "I've been told that after he met his tragic end at Ford's Theatre, playhouses everywhere were closed for weeks, while Northern clergymen from their

361

Sunday pulpits unleashed the judgment of God against my devilish profession."

"Being Kentucky born and bred, I shed no tears over the passing of that atheist Mr. Lincoln. Still, a playhouse is a poor place to die in."

"I should not mind dying in a theatre," said Maryna. "Actually, I think I shall mind dying anywhere else."

"I shall pray for you, you poor misguided soul."

"Ah, Mrs. Wenton, what is one to do with people like you? You and your kind will ruin the chances of the theatre becoming anything other than shallow entertainment in this country. You will—you will ruin America!"

"In any case," said Bogdan, hurling his magazine to the floor, "you have ruined our supper. Maryna, come! Come!"

DECEMBER 3. The play with the tarantella. Writhing with lust. Incursion of a religious fanatic. Pathetic threats, tirades. Hellfire. Damnation. M. argumentative, fascinated.

December 4. Why, I suppose, M. is excited by this play. It's *Frou-Frou* turned upside down. The spoiled child-wife has only been pretending to be childish and silly, because that's the way her husband likes her to be. Turns out to be quite intelligent. Isn't deserting her family to pursue an illicit relationship. The problem: she's been made to realize that she's married to an unworthy husband. It's the husband who is at fault, who is not forgiven. No hint to the audience that her striking out on her own—to find out who she is!—may prove a disaster. The play condones her abandoning home, children. Three children, like *East Lynne*!

December 5. If desire is forbidden, it will swell and gush. The moon is smaller than the cloud covering it. This last sojourn in California. Reclining. Murmur of the stream. Fidgety smiles and downy, coppery, consenting . . . Things dreamed of became so well defined. I saddened. As if I had lost them. Smudged desire. Began to dream of M. Can't leave her. Ever. Ever. Ever. Ever.

December 6. East and west. Safety and recklessness. Home and danger. Love and lust. Bring Juan María east to join the company as a porter or a waiter? Is this what I want?

December 7. Probably a mistake to do the try-out in Louisville of our already notorious, new play from the Old World. Wife can't leave her husband and three children in Kentucky, I said to M. Kentucky will never permit. She'll have to stay, and make the best of things. M.'s look. At the least, we should change the title. Americans being very literal-minded, the audience may think it's a play for children. Next Saturday, the sidewalk outside Macauley's lined with perambulators. And Maurice thinks giving the wife a Scandinavian name will help public understanding of the play. Suggests Thora. Thora and her husband, Torwald? A bit too Scandinavian, no?

December 8. The problem is, of course, the end. Will American audiences accept the idea of a woman who leaves her husband and children not because she is wicked but because she is serious. Not likely. Wouldn't it be better, I say to M., if the play ended with the wife being reconciled with her husband? He does seem repentant. She can give him one more chance. And if she insists on leaving, walking out into a freezing winter night seems most improbable. It must be almost midnight. Where would she go at that hour? To a hotel, if there *is* a hotel in that little village? Isn't it all rather melodramatic? Couldn't she wait until morning?

December 9. I thought you liked happy endings, I say. I think this *is* a happy ending, M. says. You can't see why she wants to leave? All too well, I say. Everyone dreams of bursting the chains of marriage and starting over. Yes, M. says, but I don't now. And you, Bogdan? Do you want me to answer that? I reply. I thought we were discussing how to end this play. Husband, husband, M. says, we're always talking about ourselves when we talk of anything else. Yes, answer. Then why *can't* the ending be changed, I asked. I'm not leaving, I said.

363

December 11. M. agrees, reluctantly. Nora—no, Thora!—will think of leaving. But won't. Will forgive her husband. Should it go well here, we can restore the real ending when we bring it to New York.

December 12. *Thora* opened last night. M. magnificent. Maurice quite decent as the obtuse husband. Audience deplorable. Reviewers irate, even with the happy ending. Just as I feared. Offense to Christian morals and the American family. And oh, the tarantella.

HENRIK IBSEN'S *Thora,* with Marina Zalenska in the title role, had its only performance in Louisville, Kentucky.

While Maryna went on looking for another new play, Maurice Barrymore said he had decided to write one for her that could not fail, on the theme about which she'd often spoken so movingly in his presence: the martyrdom of Poland under the Russian oppressors. The title was *Nadjezda,* after one of the two roles he was creating for Maryna: a beautiful Polish woman whose husband has been imprisoned by the Russians for his part in the 1863 Uprising. Prince Zabouroff, the chief of police, convinces Nadjezda to yield to his lust in exchange for a promise to release her husband; instead, Zabouroff sends him to the firing squad, and returns the bullet-ridden corpse to Nadjezda, whereupon she consecrates their little daughter to revenge, swallows poison, falls on her husband's body, and dies. And Maryna would also play the beautiful daughter, Nadine, when grown, who avenges her parents' deaths. Zabouroff, ever dissolute, ever predatory, has invited Nadine to his office late one night; as he lunges at her, she manages to stab him with a knife seized from a nearby table set for their intimate supper. The play ends with Nadine swallowing poison and dying in the arms of her lover (the role Barrymore wrote for himself) when she discovers he is the son of the man she has killed.

Maryna couldn't refuse to do the play: it was Maurice's gift to her, and Maurice was a splendid actor. She was very very fond of Maurice. If only his fondness for her hadn't inspired this maudlin caricature of Polish patriotism, Polish suffering, Polish chivalry. For instance, when, before fleeing, Nadine sets two candles by Zabouroff's head and says a brief prayer . . . Maurice, really!

"Maudlin? Oh. What I meant is that she repents of her violence, you see. I should say the pious gesture is touching, Madame Marina. Don't you think?"

"I don't, Maurice. This is sentimentality, not piety. Nadine may be appalled by her own violence but she should not repent. The Czarist police chief deserves to die."

After a few performances in Baltimore, Maryna opened *Nadjezda* in February 1884 at the Star Theatre in New York and performed it more than fifty times in the spring and summer national tour.

When Maryna did not continue with *Nadjezda* the following year, its duplicitous author sent it to Sarah Bernhardt, declaring how honored he would be if she would read his play; the two leading roles, he barely had the courage to avow, had been written with her in mind.

And Bernhardt must have liked his play a little since obviously she had passed it on to Victorien Sardou, her regular dramatist and her lover: two years later she opened in Paris in a Sardou vehicle all too reminiscent of *Nadjezda*. To be sure, Sardou had made a few expert changes. A story stretching over twenty years had been compressed into an action taking place between late morning of one day and the following dawn. The failed Polish Uprising of 1863 had been turned into a failed Republican uprising in Rome at the end of the eighteenth century, the noble Polish wife into an impetuous Italian opera singer, and the husband awaiting execution into an ardent lover and a painter. Instead of a mother and a daughter, and two suicides, there was one heroine, the singer, who, after securing her lover's freedom (she thinks) and killing the vicious police chief, mounts to the roof of a castle on the Tiber for the fake execution she had been promised, discovers she has witnessed a real execution, and leaps to her death.

Maryna was unmoved by Maurice's distress. True, she had dropped *Nadjezda*. But he shouldn't have sent it to Bernhardt. He was justly punished.

Though Sardou had apparently retained those absurd candles set on either side of the police chief's corpse, it sounded to Maryna as if he'd much improved Maurice's play. Indeed, now that its protagonists were no longer Polish patriots, Maryna began to covet it. Peabody wrote Sardou with proposed terms for Maryna to acquire the rights to his play in America. Before she could consider seriously being so beastly to Maurice, Sardou cabled a polite refusal. Might he have suspected that Maurice planned to bring a lawsuit against him for plagiarism? More likely, a veto had come from Bernhardt, who would never allow the most successful of all the roles written for her to pass into Marina Zalenska's hands.

Unaware of Maryna's own projected treachery, and with his lawsuit foiled, the luckless author of *Nadjezda* suggested replagiarizing his own play and turning Sardou's *Tosca* into a Civil War story. Lydia—no, Annabelle, the beautiful wife of a spy for the Union cause who has been sentenced to death by a military court in Georgia, pleads with a Confederate general to spare her husband's life. Once her beau, the lecherous General Donnard offers a despicable bargain, which, moreover, he has no intention of keeping. In the conservatory of Donnard's Greek Revival mansion, George, the genial butler, has lit the gleaming silver candelabra on the table set for a late-night supper of oysters and champagne, while George's owner awaits the arrival of the lovely petitioner, who naïvely imagines—

Out of the question, Maurice! Out of the question. It was

Bogdan who vetoed that idea, and Maryna went back to her already secured triumphs.

"LISTEN, BOGDAN. 'The greatest actress on the American stage is a Pole. Indeed, Madame Zalenska has no living rival but Sarah Bernhardt, whom'—listen!—'whom to my mind she for the most part surpasses.' "

"Who wrote that? Not William Winter . . . ?"

"Hardly." She laughed, as she descended into Winter's raspy voice. " 'Americans must stand together in their stern determination to prevent an immoral use of the Theatre, made with the pretence of a serious purpose. I am speaking of the fashion of presenting nasty "problem plays." ' How he hated our little Ibsen venture, remember?"

"The ever worshipful Jeannette Gilder?"

"Not even! A critic in *Theatre* whom I've never met."

"So it's done, Maryna. You've won."

"What's left is for me to believe what I read."

Next year she would be doing a national tour with Edwin Booth: Ophelia to his Hamlet, Desdemona to his Othello, Portia to his Shylock, and in *Richelieu,* a Bulwer-Lytton drama in which Booth had enjoyed a success second only to his *Hamlet,* she would be playing Julie de Mortemar, the Cardinal's defenseless ward. Another woman victim!

"Poor Maryna," said Bogdan. "Such a strain life has placed on her credulity. Obsequious critics, who may not dare do other than praise her. Devious husband, who may not dare tell her the truth, but who has nevertheless tried to impart, if not tell . . . what seems too crude to tell."

"If you want to leave," Maryna said, "you should. I'm strong enough now."

"Pack a bag, pull off my wedding band and thrust it at you, open the door, slam the door, walk into the snowy night?"

"This isn't the only life you could lead."

"That could be said of many people," said Bogdan.

"But, Bogdan, right now I'm saying it of you."

"You think I'm a coward."

"No, I think you love me. Husbandly love. Friendship. But, as we both know, there are other kinds of love." She reached out one hand as she finished tying back her hair. He passed her the box of grease sticks. "I hope you believe that I always wish you would find what you need."

"I won't."

"Won't?"

"I'm too formed. Of a piece. Finished. My America is you. Still you. When I'm . . . there, I— You can't imagine how much I miss you."

"And you can't imagine, dearest Bogdan, because I haven't understood it myself, how much I love you. Would you like me to try to give up the stage again?"

"Maryna!"

"I would do it for you."

"Darling, Maryna, I forbid you even to consider making such a sacrifice for me."

"I don't know that it would be such a sacrifice." She was massaging a fine layer of cocoa butter into her forehead and cheeks. "As you say, I have—but I don't like this word—won. It only remains to go on, repeating myself, trying not to go coarse or stale. What kind of monster will I have become when I've made twenty national tours? Thirty? Forty?" She laughed girlishly. "When even I will be resigned to playing Juliet's Nurse? No, I could never resign myself to the Nurse! I'd rather play one of the witches in *Macbeth*."

"Maryna!"

"I adore shocking you, Bogdan," she said in her throatiest tones. "*Macbeth*. I'll say it again. *Macbeth*. Do you think we shall be struck by lightning?"

"You can always charm me, Maryna. You charm me quite

out of my mind. I did go up in the aero with Juan María and José. I've continued to fly with them."

"I thought so. How brave you are." She stood, and reached out to hold his face.

"How kind you are," he said. "I thought I would vanish into myself. Maybe I hoped it *would* hurtle and crash."

"But it didn't, dearest Bogdan." She tasted his mouth. He enfolded her in his arms. "And, you see, no bolt of lightning. Though it would have been lovely to die together just now. Crash. Fire. Ashes."

"Maryna!"

"And now, since you've succeeded in making me cry, you must vacate my little kingdom. How can I put on my makeup while I'm standing in a drizzle of reconciliations? Go, my love. Go!" Her smile was radiant. "And be sure"—her mouth parted and her eyes went ceilingward as memory bit—"be sure to set the lock so I don't have any unwelcome intruders."

Maryna sat down and looked into the mirror. Surely she was weeping because she was so happy—unless a happy life is impossible, and the highest a human being can attain is a heroic life. Happiness comes in many forms, to have lived for art is a privilege, a blessing, and women are talented at renouncing sexual felicity. She heard the closing creak of the dressing-room door. She listened for the click as it latched.

Nine

"YOU SEE, my dear Marina . . . I trust we may dispense with Madame Marina and Mr. Booth now that we're alone, and I am exhausted and sated with applause and quite as drunk as I need to be . . . I must tell you that I didn't approve when you came downstage and touched me tonight. Keep your eyes fixed on me throughout, ignoring the others in the courtroom, no objection to that. We both agree the speech is addressed to Shylock. *The quality of mercy is not strained, it droppeth as the gentle rain from heaven.* No, it doesn't, but that's not the point here, which is, my point, my point is . . . Portia is trying to convince Shylock, and thereby to move him. He's not easily moved. He has too many grievances. Portia may be moved herself by the wretched fellow. But Portia should never touch Shylock. Even if she only touches his shoulder. Touch his shoulder, touch any other part of him. No touching! Shylock is in pain. [*Stares into the glass he is holding.*] And being in pain is very . . . combustible. [*Looks up.*] I suppose you thought to show that Portia is very feminine under her red lawyer's robes, very feminine, and therefore knows, without needing to be told, that the ogre has senses, affections, passions, hurts. But that is a foolish sentimental gesture. [*Shakes his head.*] You are monstrously sentimental, woman, has anyone ever told you that? I myself prefer large, wrathful gestures. Which does not mean I shall not touch you before the evening is over, if I have a bit more to drink. Don't tell me that you're married, or that you're no longer young, or something of that kind. You are thirteen years younger than I am, unless you lie about your age, as does every attractive woman who can get away with it, but let's leave that, the touching and the rest, for later, as the whim strikes us. [*Stands by the fireplace.*] For now I shall only insist that you drink with me. No ladyish resistance? Excellent sign. Excellent. But nodding and smiling, your infallibly seductive smile, and touching the top of your lovely hair, aren't enough. I want to hear a robust 'Yes, Edwin. Yes . . . Edwin.' Brava! Well done. [*Finishes his glass.*] And a 'well done' to you, Ned! [*Sets the empty glass on the mantel.*] Ned is what I was called as a child. But you can't call me Ned. Not when you've just started to call me Edwin. Ned would be too intimate, don't you think? And we do best, you and I, on modest rations of intimacy. We're actors. [*Places his right foot on the fender.*] Do you ever wish you were a child again, Marina? Ah, *you* don't either. Something we have in common. Although I suspect we haven't *much* in common, you and I, besides being actors. Granted, that is a great deal. Is it not, Marina? Do I have your complete attention, Marina? I see your gaze wandering, in embarrassment, let's say, to the bust of Shakespeare on top of the bookcase. Stare away. You'll find a picture or a bust of Shakespeare in every room here. Shall I get it down for you? [*Walks to the bookcase.*] No? You see, you'd much rather stare at me. [*Pats Shakespeare on the head.*] Acting, Marina, is what you and I do. We played together before an audience this evening. Tolerably well, I might add. And, *sans* audience, we shall go on acting with each other, yes? But of course we shall be perfectly, perfectly sincere. [*Makes a stage bow.*] Whom shall I play? I think, let me see, I think I shall impersonate Edwin Booth. What an outstanding idea. He seems a much more interesting fellow than Shylock, and every bit as unhappy. Famously unhappy, brooding, wonderfully equipped to play tragic parts. However, don't think me too tyrannical, I'd prefer . . . tonight . . . that you not play Marina Zalenska.

[*Fetches a bottle of whiskey from a cabinet.*] Could you consider it? Just to humor me. Surely you have a few other selves in your repertory. I do think it very entertaining that for the last ten years everyone has agreed that the greatest actress in the English-speaking world is a Pole. A Pole with an accent. Yes, Marina. No one mentions your accent anymore, it is part of your magic, but eet ees ver-ree, verr-rree noticeable. Ah, for God's sake, don't pout, woman. I shall not deny that, accent and all, you phrase better than most who own the language. Another glass? Good. I'm curious to see when it will have an effect on you. [*Circles her.*] You are enchanting, Marina Zalenska. Either I'm being quite sincere or I just want to flatter you. Which do you think? Or neither. Perhaps I am a parrot. [*Squawks like a parrot.*] Don't be alarmed. My father sometimes did that. In the wings. Simpering and screeching and squawking. Just before he went on, and became instantly noble, eloquent, melodious. What was I saying? Oh, yes, *they* were saying. 'The most enchanting person I ever met.' Doesn't that ever trouble you, Marina? Do you never ask yourself, what in God's name must I have done to myself that people should find me so enchanting? [*Kisses her hand.*] You probably know that I had no success playing Romeo and soon dropped it from my repertory. As for Benedick . . . I was never a good Benedick! I could never be light enough. There is something earthbound in me. I shall never fly out of it. Ah, well. We must do what we do best. Don't you agree? I like playing villains best. Pity we're not doing *Richard III* on the tour. [*Twists his body, becomes misshapen.*] That was Father's first great role. And you've been Lady Anne—though not yet with me, alas—who cannot resist Dick Crookback when he plays the lover. [*Straightens up.*] Tell me, *are* you that much younger than I? Don't blush, woman! Do you think we're on a stage here? Well? Your secret shall be safe with me. I see you hesitating. I see you want to please me. I thought so. Well, you are still my junior by seven years. And quite good-looking. Capital for a woman. Am I being too sardonic? Are you in need of some balm? All actors need to be flattered. Who would know this better than Edwin Booth? Let's see, what can I say to please you that would also be true? Ah, yes. [*Points his finger at her.*] You walk well. I liked your walk tonight. You don't forget the play is set in Venice. Portia walks as if she is treading on marble. I shall remember that. That means, I shall steal it. From now on, Shylock too shall walk on marble. [*Walks across the room. Walk becomes mincing. Stops. Laughs.*] You see, I am still working on the role after all these years. My father would, when he had a run of Shylocks to do, go about muttering in Hebrew. Or something that sounded like Hebrew. Once while doing Shylock in Atlanta, he went into that city's finest restaurant and ordered ham and greens, and when the waiter brought it to his table, dashed the plate to the floor, shrieking 'Unclean! Faugh! Unclean! Faugh!' and stormed out. I of course, who am the very soul of rationality, don't for a minute think as Shylock when I am not on stage in the Jew's dark-brown gaberdine and tawny-yellow slouch hat, holding the knotted walking staff in my beringed right hand. [*Stretches out his hand to her.*] Nor do I think as Othello, except when I have made myself sooty as the Moor. Or even as Richard III, much as I relish the role. Ditto for Richelieu. Hamlet . . . perhaps. You could say I have a weakness for Hamlet. Not because everyone thinks I am Hamlet-like. I, Hamlet-like? As my father would say, faugh! Still, Hamlet reminds me of something in myself. Maybe it's that Hamlet is an actor. Yes, Marina, that's all he is. He is acting. He seems to be one thing, and underneath that seeming, what is there? Nothing. Nothing. Nothing. The inky-black suit he wears at court in the second scene. That tenacious, showy mourning for his father. Everyone's father dies, as Gertrude reminds him, and right she is, *Why seems it so particular with thee?* And Hamlet howls, he is howling, you know, *Seems, madam? Nay, it is. I know not 'seems.'* But he does know 'seems.' He knows nothing else. That's his problem. Hamlet would give anything, anything, not to be an actor, but he is condemned to it. Condemned to being an actor! He is waiting to break through seeming and performing, and just *be*, but there is nothing on the other side of seeming, Marina. Except death. Except Death. [*Looks around the room.*] I am looking for my Yorick-skull. Could I have misplaced it? Yorick! I mean, Philo! Where are you? What did I do with that skull? [*Pulls open the rolltop desk. Tosses papers on the floor.*] A prop, a prop. My kingdom for a prop! My last line would have gone so much more resoundingly if I could have brandished a skull. Except death. Except Death. Did you hear the capital D on the second 'death'? Of such wee details are great performances made. But I'm sure you did hear it, Marina. What better audience than you could a crushed tragedian have? [*Stretches out his hand to her.*] My little princess. My Polish queen. You have kindly consented to keep Ned company as he sinks into his cups. You know he is quite harmless, since he is so drunk, so your virtue is safe. Even if you are a respectable married woman, not so young, and so forth. But beware of old Ned. He's a sly one. [*Does a pirouette.*] He may only be pretending to be drunk. Perhaps he is really just deranged. And therefore just a leetle leetle dangerous. Like Hamlet, he's a sly one too. He pretends not to be acting. And he gives acting lessons to others. *Speak the speech, I pray you, as I pronounced it to you, trippingly on the tongue.* Don't you think his instructions to the actors are rather obvious? Very. *Suit the action to the word, the word to the action.* Why, he's as banal as Polonius! Where's the fire? Where's the recklessness? Perhaps I should play Hamlet on tiptoe, the whole play from start to finish, as my father once did Lear in Buffalo. Or in a whisper, as he once did Iago in Philadelphia. Of course my father was mad. Or drunk. Or both. One couldn't easily tell which. Like me, is that what you're thinking, Marina? It isn't? Oh. I thought you were going to be sincere with your old friend Ned. [*Sits beside her on the divan.*] But is Hamlet mad? Much ink spilled over that. I should say that Hamlet *must* be considered mad because only a mad person would think of disguising himself as a mad person, when there are so many other disguises to choose from. But perhaps not. Perhaps there aren't many disguises to choose from. Suppose being mad is the *only* one available, what do you think, Marina, in which case Hamlet's choice makes perfect sense. A most excellent, rational, charming . . . Prince of Denmark, I always say. A tad unhappy, to be sure. Very unhappy, indeed. But if to be unhappy were to be mad, why then we would all be mad. [*Takes off his shoes and rubs his feet.*] Am I boring you? I hope not, because now I'm coming to your role. [*Jumps up.*] But Ophelia *goes* mad, so it's not interesting. Raving about flowers. Hamlet wasn't nice to her. Poor girl. Hamlet stuck his blade into her father's gut. Well, his mother *was* getting on his nerves. *And* he thought there was a rat behind the curtain. [*Picks up the poker from the fireplace, brandishes it like a sword.*] And off she went into the water. Do you understand about madness, Marina? I don't think so. I'd lay odds that you are very expert at fending off your griefs. Not altogether of course. Am I right? A leetle leetle bit of suffering. Ah, you Europeans. You invented tragedy so you think you have a monopoly on it. And we Americans, we're all callow optimists. Right. I can feel an access of callow optimism coming on right now. How refreshing! Ahhhhhh . . . Another whiskey, Marina? You know, the only time I've seen you make Ophelia really seem mad was last week in Providence when, unusually for you, distracted, could it have been by me, gnashing my teeth alongside you in the wings, you made your entrance in Act Four empty-handed and, entirely unflustered, proceeded to distribute your posy to Gertrude and Claudius and Laertes. Invisible flowers. Father would have appreciated that. [*Pours himself a drink.*] Did I say my father squawked like a parrot? I remember a *Hamlet* in Natchez, when, during Ophelia's mad scene, a voice off stage began to crow like a rooster, and sure enough, it was Father, perched on top of a high ladder in the wings. [*Crows.*] Like that. So, dear Ophelia, do look about you when going mad. It can be contagious. My mother worried so about Father when he was on the road, and at fourteen sent me out with him to be his dresser and companion. Not to learn acting, anything but that! Johnny was to be the actor, the heir. Father said I ought to be a cabinetmaker, so it was a great sign when he invited me to eat Shakespeare with him one night in Waterbury. Bitter, I thought. Delicious, he said. Some pages from *Lear*. While Hamlet, we were talking about Hamlet, was a prince, who expected, rightly expected, to be the heir. [*Returns to the fireplace.*] Don't you think Hamlet's father is the mad one? It seems to me quite mad to turn yourself into a ghost and come back to haunt your son. But at least Hamlet didn't have a brother who could come back and haunt him. You know, after Johnny fired the shot he leaped from the presidential box onto the stage and shouted his line. *Sic semper*, you know. And broke his leg. [*Limps over to the desk.*] I am about to have another drink, Marina. Yes? One sign of an approaching paroxysm of my father's appetite for liquor was his use of a peculiar gesture, like this [*saws the air with his right hand beside his head*], and if I would try to stop him from drinking, which was part of my job, he would make that ominous gesture and shout, 'Go away, young man, go away! By God, sir, I'll put you aboard a man-o'-war, sir.' Sheer nonsense, as you see. Nothing could be done to stop him. Only undress him after and clean up his vomit. [*Lifts his glass.*] To you, old mole. He was a great actor. You must take my word for it, Marina. Truly great. He had astounded London as Richard III when he was twenty-one, and was hailed as the rival and successor to Kean. And he made his New York debut a few years later in the same role. My father as the hunchbacked villain was part of my life from early childhood on. He would enter the stage from the left amidst a tempest of boisterous hand-clapping. The first thing one saw was his lifted foot passing the wing, then the rest of him followed, head bent. He slowly walked down the stage to the footlights, musingly kicking his sword which he held by its sash away from his body. Forty years have passed and I can hear the clank of the sword and feel the eerie hush of three thousand people waiting for him to open his mouth. *Now is the winter of our discontent*— I suppose Father's style of acting was inflated and stagey. Certainly it would be considered so by today's standards. Nobody called *him* introspective and intellectual, as they do me. [*Laughs.*] He obeyed his terrors. He recognized the devil in himself. Father had sworn never to eat meat, 'dead flesh' he called it, and once when he broke his rule, did penance by filling his shoes with dried peas, then fitting them with lead soles and trudging all the way from Baltimore to Washington. He thought he was bad. He knew, some of the time he knew, he was mad. 'I can't read! I'm a charity boy! I can't read! Take me to the lunatic asylum!' he once shouted in the middle of a *Lear* at the Wieting in Syracuse. He was hustled off stage, to the sound of more than a few catcalls. But such outbursts on stage were rare. Oh. What do I see? I am still in my stocking feet! [*Puts his shoes back on.*] I gabble on about my father because it hurts so to talk about my brother. When I talk about Johnny I weep. [*Raises his hand imperiously.*] Not yet. Wait. 'To kill a king, that's a great deed,' Johnny would declaim. 'You'll see, soon the name of Booth will be known everywhere.' I thought it was Johnny posturing. How can an actor be taken seriously? It's all hocum, vanity, boasting. An actor is always trying to make himself interesting. First he has to make himself interesting to himself. Then to other people. Do you find yourself interesting, Marina? [*Looks about for his glass.*] Threats, augurs—and we hear only what we want to hear. Did Lincoln's wife heed him when the Great Emancipator told her the dream he'd had, in which he was drifting alone down a dark river? No, they went to the theatre. [*Laughs.*] Johnny was already much admired. Who knows if he would not have been more successful than I, even than Father, if he had not—if he had lived. He was wonderful in romantic roles. Romeo, the lot. Not for him the villains, Richard III and Iago and the Scottish lord, or the great self-deceivers, like Hamlet and Othello. He received hundreds of letters a week from lovesick women and girls, not to mention the missives from the women lucky enough to be granted his favors. [*Begins to cry.*] Johnny wanted to be loved. [*Takes out an embroidered handkerchief.*] If I weep now, will you think these are actor's tears? They are, you know. Hath not an actor eyes? If you prick him, doth he not bleed? I was playing at the Boston Theatre when it happened. It was thought, at first, to be a family conspiracy, and Junius, my older brother, was arrested, though soon let go. I wasn't arrested but my movements were watched by the police. All the Booths received death threats. [*Gazes at his hands.*] On politics Johnny and I quarreled like demons, since I was for the Union, and abolition. I had voted twice for Lincoln. Johnny thought he had killed a tyrant. He expected to be acclaimed as a hero. His death was excruciating. And the Booths will always be *his* family. What is an actor compared with a regicide—no, the assassin of a saint? Why wasn't I lynched? I was ready. When, many years later, someone actually did attempt to murder me— and then it wasn't a hater of the theatre but a theatre lover, a stagestruck lunatic he was called in the papers—I was no longer ready. Histriomania, I think this kind of insanity is called. You know the story. No? [*Sits again.*] It happened in Chicago, at McVicker's, during a *King Richard II.* One Mark Gray and his pistol were in the second balcony. I was on stage, in a dungeon in Pomfret Castle, well launched into the sad young king's last soliloquy.

> *I have been studying how I may compare*
> *This prison where I live unto the world;*
> *And, for because the world is populous,*
> *And here is not a creature but myself,*
> *I cannot do it.*

He fired at me twice. I survived only because I changed my usual business. On *I cannot do it* I always buried my head in my hands for a moment. That one time, on an impulse, I stood up. [*Stands.*] And then what happened after the poor fellow missed me? Oh, that was a fine performance. The great tragedian—that's myself, Marina, your humble servant—calmly advanced to the footlights and, pointing at the madman, asked that he be seized but not harmed, briefly left the stage to reassure his wife who, standing as usual in the wings, had gone quite hysterical, returned, and composedly finished his performance. [*Laughs.*] I was much admired for my *sang-froid*. Who could know that my heart was leaping around in my chest like a lion? And went on booming and banging about until another day and night had passed? I had been, well, I had *seemed*, so brave. But even that backfired. For it was said in several newspapers that I had arranged this attempt on my life to have more publicity for my week's run. An advertising stunt. Good God! But a society in which everything is for sale and every worthy occasion is *Barnumized* has to end by making cynics out of everybody. I suppose the only way the public would be convinced I hadn't hired a lunatic to fire on me would be to have been seriously wounded. Preferably slain. Then one could talk happily about the tragic curse of the Booth family, and all the rest. [*Pours himself another drink.*] Later I had one of the bullets, which had passed next to my head, pried out of the scenery where it had lodged and mounted on a gold cartridge cap inscribed 'To Edwin Booth, from Mark Gray,' which I wear as a charm on my watch chain. Would you like to see the sinister relic? [*Takes out the watch.*] Hell, it's late. Not that I'm tired. Your presence, Marina, has quite . . . revived me. You first saw me, when did you say, at the California, twelve, thirteen years ago? I was much better then. Much better. You like to admire, don't you? So do I. Let's drink to Henry Irving. No, you're wrong. He's a *very* good actor. His Hamlet may be even finer than mine. [*Lifts his glass.*] You won't drink to Irving? God, you are loyal, woman. I'm almost touched. I shall not say my Hamlet is without merit. Indeed, I have to my credit one pretty bit of stage business for the distraught Dane. When I was getting ready to do my Hamlet at the Winter Garden I bought a sword with a jeweled hilt and took it home and hung it at the foot of my bed. All night I kept getting up and lighting matches to see it, shifting its position, until it flashed on me that—*Angels and ministers of grace defend us!*—the sword was really a cross, and could be used, hilt raised high, to protect Hamlet against his father's ghost. Of course, too much originality and we will destroy Shakespeare. But

379

a leetle leetle originality, as you might say, dear Marina . . . I have been an original and really mad Prince of Denmark. The story is told that Mrs. David Garrick came to Kean and said, 'Davy used to do a wonderful thing in the closet scene in *Hamlet*, and you don't do it. He overturned a chair when he saw the ghost.' Kean tried it; when he saw the ghost he rose, put his heel under the leg of the chair, and knocked it over. But he could never get it right. He was thinking, Is this right? Fatal! [*Overturns a chair.*] You see, you can't repeat anything. I can overturn a chair until doomsday, and I'll never do it the way Garrick did. [*Kicks over another chair.*] Would you like to try? Maybe a woman could do the gesture now. Why shouldn't Ophelia, brokenhearted, overturn a chair? Hurry up, Marina, if you want to steal this idea from me. Everything is going faster now. That's modern life. I shall never get used to it. But then I don't have to. Neither do you. I remember a theatre manager in California, when I was very young, whose idea of conducting a rehearsal was to keep calling out to the company: 'Hurry up! This don't run smooth. More ginger! More ginger! Don't wait for cues!' I should like to see him rehearsing *Hamlet.* With *Hamlet* you have to go slowly. *O . . . what . . . a rogue . . . and peasant slave . . . am . . . I.* It was weakness that brought me back on the stage. After the . . . calamity, and given the justifiable hatred of anyone bearing the name of Booth, I had determined to abandon the stage forever. My retirement lasted less than six months. I had to make a living. Friends said I owed it to the Theatre to return. There was the imputation that I was a coward. And I did want to give people something else to think of when they heard the name Booth. I returned here, at the Winter Garden, as Hamlet. I kept everything of Johnny's until five years later. By then I'd opened my folly, my temple of theatrical art. Of course, we shall never have a national theatre, as in France, but we could have a theatre directed by a serious actor, in which artistic values would take precedence over the business point of view. Hah. You know how long Booth's Theatre lasted. Either I was an idiot at business or such an enterprise can't work in America, or both. Yes, both. [*Gathers some logs from the scuttle.*] And very late one night, with a stage carpenter I brought down to help me, I cast all Johnny's clothes, his books, his mementos, every last garment in his stage wardrobe (some of which were costumes inherited from Father) into a blazing furnace in the basement of Booth's. There were Johnny's diaries and packets and packets of letters, each in a different feminine hand, and nicely bound up in string. [*Pitches the logs into the fireplace.*] Women loved Johnny. The manner in which his head and throat rose from his shoulders was truly beautiful, and the ivory pallor of his skin, the blackness of his thick hair, the heavy lids of his glowing eyes, the fullness of his mouth . . . [*Stirs the fire with a poker.*] There is something Oriental about the Booths. Father boasted that we are part Jewish, his grandfather, John Booth, being a Jewish silversmith whose forebears, named Beth, had been driven out of Portugal. I should like that. It might even be true. [*Turns to face Maryna.*] Father was too short, as I am. He had bandy legs. That's his portrait over there. No, don't get up to look at it. [*Takes it off the wall, brings it to where Maryna is sitting.*] Father's lips formed a straight line, not the curve shown here. His beautiful aquiline nose was said to be his best feature, but when I was ten, still at home on the farm near Baltimore with my mother and brothers and sisters, there was a brawl with the manager of a stable in Charleston, where Father was performing. [*Rehangs the picture. Returns to the fireplace. Leans against the mantel.*] As you saw, Father's nose was broken at the bridge. William Winter places the deformity below it, toward the tip. But you know how accurate critics are. Crickets, my Edwina used to call them when she was little. 'Don't worry about the crickets, Papa.' They're no better than the audience. Flatter the audience, despise the audience. No. You must *hate* the audience. I suppose I should be grateful for the way I was welcomed back after . . . 1865. I'm not. They can lick your face. They blubber and dribble . . . I'll wager that *East Lynne* has caused more tears than the Civil War . . . and then they'll take your head off. [*Spits into the fireplace.*] Do they feel what they seem to be feeling? Then they really *are* idiots. All the more reason for the actor not to worry about being sincere. I hope to be inspired from time to time. But certainly not to 'feel' my part. What an idea! Anyway, one cannot endlessly repeat one's own heights of inspiration without being drawn to destructive gestures. Once, I managed to piss while standing in Ophelia's grave without anyone seeing except my thunderstruck Laertes. Once, when I lay dying in Horatio's arms, as he with his *Good night, sweet prince* pressed his cheek mournfully against mine, I whispered obscenities in his ear and watched him blanch. But that is what I do with men. With women I am very chivalrous and protective. [*Sits opposite Maryna and takes a cigar from the humidor on the small table beside his chair.*] Would you like to try one? Are you sure? How many have you smoked in your life? [*Lights the cigar.*] Not more than one, yes? But that's not the basis for an opinion. Everything takes getting used to, pleasures as much as griefs. [*Drops the cigar on the rug.*] No, no, don't worry. [*Jumps to his feet.*] I don't intend to set the house on fire. [*Throws the cigar into the fireplace.*] I'm feeling a little dizzy. Yes, I'll sit. [*Sits beside her.*] You're not afraid of old Ned? He's harmless, as you see. Dear old drunken Ned. [*Takes her hand.*] No danger that our late evening *tête-à-tête* might turn into a *corps-à-corps*. Ah, I've made you smile. Is it my foolish French? I am trying to impress you. You Europeans are born speaking French, isn't that so? But of course we have Shakespeare. Shakespeare makes us virtuous. His King Henry VIII says *'Tis a kind of good deed to say well.* Shakespeare could almost make me virtuous. How low I would be without him. I can always promote myself to some better plane with his words. But then I think, This seeing myself in Shakespeare has ruined Shakespeare. Shakespeare has been poisoned by me. I have killed Shakespeare. And then I think, No, you maniac, what are you saying? [*Slaps his forehead.*] It's not you, it's Shakespeare. Shakespeare is too good for us. What can the paradise of words mean to us now, to America? What use has a democracy for the beautiful and the noble in art? Nothing, nothing at all. What matters is that

I have been ponderously successful. I have made lots of money, and paid it out as fast as I could in various foolish ventures, like my theatre. I have been eye-deep in the quicksand of popular favor and I have dreamt my life away. There, Marina, you have a panorama of my mind. [*Stands.*] I'm better. No, I can stand. Marina, I have a grown daughter. You have a son at university. I trust he does not want to become an actor. Don't let the talent tree flourish. Cut it down, woman. Cut it down. [*Begins to sway.*] No, I'm all right. You don't think of returning to Poland, do you? One must never go back. Never. No, no . . . I just need to lean against something. [*Goes to the mantel.*] Here's a topic for us! Can a woman be a great actor? And Ned opines: Not as long as she wants to be a paragon of womanliness. There is something bland, appeasing, in you, Marina. Perhaps there is in all great actresses, with the possible exception of Bernhardt, don't wince, woman, except that her efforts not to be bland seem trivially theatrical. Pet lions, for God's sake! Sleeping in a satin-lined coffin. Not that I believe she does it. But she *says* she does it. No, a great actor is turbulent, rarely affable, profoundly . . . angry. Where is your vein of rage, Marina? [*Picks up the poker, holds it threateningly.*] There's nothing dangerous about you, Marina. You have not accepted your catastrophe. You have toyed with it, you have bargained with it. You have sold your soul so as to be able to think, from time to time, that you are happy. Yes, sold your soul, Marina. How perceptive you are, Edwin. [*Waves the poker.*] Of course that's not what you're thinking. You feel I am attacking you. And I am. That is the right of someone who has accepted *his* catastrophe. [*Replaces the poker.*] Ah, Marina, I should teach you how to curse. It might add character to those serene features. [*Begins to pace.*] Don't be so afraid of failing, Marina. It does the soul good. Lord, what a corrupting profession we exercise. We think we are upholding the beautiful and true, and we are merely propagating vanity and lies. Oh, you think I sound verr-rree American now. Well, I *am* an American. And so are you now, O abdicated Polish queen, and if you're not careful, the old New England verities will get you, too. You won't even notice your wits have gone astray, and you've become gloomy and censorious. However, you like California, a good sign in a European. So perhaps you're exempt. I doubt if I shall ever accept your invitation to visit you at your ranch. I have not the temperament for California anymore. I need to be cooped up, contained, *citied*. Tell me about that husband of yours out there. When he turned up during our week in Missouri, you were charming with each other. [*Picks up a small photograph from the top of the desk.*] Here's another picture. Edwina's mother. Mary. My first wife was an angel. You know what an angel is: a woman who thinks only of her husband. My second wife went insane. In the last years of her miserable life she was certain I had another wife hidden somewhere, with whom I was really happy. Would that I had! My father had two wives. The one he deserted in England and our mother. [*Sets the photograph down.*] Do you like happy endings, Marina? I crusade against 'em. Yes, I do. You probably like the way *King Lear* was mangled for a hundred years in England and America, with the Fool banished, a romance between Edgar and Cordelia, and Cordelia and Lear allowed to live. One of the few things I'm proud of is that I put a stop to that. I don't like happy endings. Not at all. But only because they don't exist. [*Sits. Takes Maryna's hand.*] The last act has to be an anticlimax, don't you think? As in life. Getting old is an anticlimax. Dying is, if one is lucky, an anticlimax. Who would fault a play for not ending on its highest note? *Hamlet* cannot end with Hamlet's dying words, can it, Marina? Fortinbras must come on and detach the audience from Hamlet's pitiable fate. We may then mourn for him, if we like. Or not. [*Stands again.*] It's late, does this feel like an anticlimax? It is nearly midnight. *What do I fear? Myself? There's none else by,* as King Dick says when the ghosts come after him at Bosworth Field. I don't feel like letting you go, Marina. *We have heard the chimes at midnight, Master Shallow!* . . . but an American has never heard them. You must have heard chimes at midnight, Marina, back in Poland. We don't have chimes at midnight in America. I would like to go through one day, one day, when I do not think of a line of Shakespeare! Time for one last, anticlimactic drink. [*Pours out more whiskey.*] It's not true that Shakespeare's lines are always tumbling about in my head. Days go by in which I think of nothing when I'm not speaking, reciting. I drink. I sleep. I pace. I look moody. Give me your hand, Marina. No, I have a better idea. Close your eyes, Marina. Don't be afraid. And presto change-o! abracadabra! and other mountebank cries and gibberings. Open your eyes. Here's the skull! [*Flourishes it.*] My Yorick-skull. This is no ordinary wretch's skull, Marina, dug up from a potter's field and sold to a theatre. This is the skull of a criminal. I even know his name. Philo Perkins. Hanged for stealing a horse. No mercy for him dropping like the gentle rain and so forth. Now when the poor fellow mounted the scaffold and was asked for his last request, what was it? Why, that afterward, his head being likely to be almost wrenched away from his neck, would they please sever it, and peel it nice and clean, and send the skull as a gift, with his compliments, its use would be obvious, to the great tragedian Junius Brutus Booth. Yes, the horse thief was an ardent theatregoer. A particular admirer of Father, whom he went to see perform whenever he could. And so his executioners gallantly fulfilled his request, and this grey woody *thing* was Father's Yorick-skull for many years, and then passed to me. And people say Americans don't really care about serious theatre! Well, well, well . . . [*Places the skull in the center of the rug. Stands back to gaze at it.*] Am I suffering? I hear people whispering behind my back. Poor Edwin Booth. Poor Edwin Booth. And I don't want to disappoint them. So I do suffer. It's my role. A lifetime of looking moody, tormented, harrowed by grief. I'd be the worst of monsters if I were not suffering. But I wouldn't mind being the worst of monsters. Mary's death. Johnny's . . . death. Maybe I did not suffer at all. I only became very thin, like a page in a book. If you can say 'I am suffering,' you are not really suffering, Marina. You are an actor. [*Places a lamp on the rug beside the skull.*] Sometimes I think I am simply becoming my father. That all those processes which are making me more and more like my father are gathering strength, gathering speed, rushing to the edge, like a waterfall, and then they will throw me over into the murk and dark water, and I shall drown in his madness. Except that I shall die first. I'll make sure of that. Even if the Everlasting *has* fixed His canon 'gainst self-slaughter . . . I'm acting, Marina. You must have noticed. Naughty Ned. Hardly means a word he says. I shall not kill myself. I'm too afraid. Father was alone when he died, completely alone. I was already nineteen. He had left me in San Francisco. In New Orleans he boarded a Mississippi riverboat bound for Cincinnati; on the fifth day out, he fell over, like this. [*Collapses on the floor.*] No, don't help me up. I have lost the level run of time and events, and am living in a mist. I am told I am better than I ever was. That can't be true. Eh, Philo? [*Stands with difficulty.*] But we were quite good tonight, I think. And you consented to come back to the club with me. I can invite a respectable woman back to my quarters because I live in an actors' club. But it is my house, as you know, and you are in my private apartment. May I touch your face? I will touch your face, whether you like it or not. I see you do like it. You're damned attractive, Marina. [*Hiccups.*] I told you that I am no Romeo. [*More hiccups.*] There is just so much suffering you can endure, and then it is time for the comedy of desire. Or not. *Was ever woman in this humour woo'd? Was ever woman in this humour won?* Sometimes I wish I had given as much time to learning the names of the constellations as I have to committing to memory the Bard's great roles. When you are falling into the dark, Marina, it becomes hard to imagine that, after you are gone, the light will still exist. Yes, once we understand, really understand, that we are going to die, astronomy is the only consolation. Look at the celestial theatre, Marina. [*Throws open the window.*] Let's be cold. It's snowing. You shall want to be back at the Clarendon soon. Look at the stars, Marina. And the trees, and the lights going up the avenue. Are you cold? Do you need someone to warm you? Come into the bedroom, Marina. I shall show you a secret. I keep a framed picture of Johnny beside my bed. You can come into the bed with me. Perhaps I am not too drunk to make love to you. [*Maryna stands.*] Yes, lean on me. No, damn it, I shall lean on you. Wait, wait. How do I know so much about you, you may wonder. Why, I've *acted* with you, woman. I've seen how you pretend. Nothing more revealing than that. You are as naked to me as if you were my bride. And I am your husband in art. Your elderly husband. Your decrepit, demented husband. Your squat, thin-lipped, lank-haired, mad—"

"That's enough, Edwin," she said. "Dear Edwin."

"Ah, a woman's mercy. Quite undeserved. Most gratefully accepted. A woman's generous, well-meant, incomprehending call to surcease."

"Stop, Edwin."

"I shall. Actually, there's a bit of business that I'd like to go over now, if you wouldn't mind. It's after you enter, and Portia says to me . . . I mean, it's that moment when Shylock says, to you, to Portia . . . I mean, Marina, I think we can improve the moment. Maybe, I'm not sure, you *can* touch me. I'm not entirely averse to a new piece of business here. I am not so pledged to tradition. And I have an absolute loathing of empty repetition. But I hate improvisation. An actor can't just *make it up*. Shall we promise each other, here and now, always to tell first when we're going to do something new? We have a long tour ahead of us."

DELUXE
ESSENTIAL
HANDBOOK

The need-to-know stats and facts on over 700 Pokémon

SCHOLASTIC INC.

Welcome to the World of Pokémon!

Kanto . . . Johto . . . Hoenn. . . Sinnoh . . . Unova . . . Kalos . . .

There are six Pokémon regions bursting with fascinating Pokémon. And this book is bursting with information about them!

The key to success in raising, battling, and evolving your Pokémon is staying informed. Information about each Pokémon's type, species, height, and weight can make all the difference in Gym battles, in the wild, and anywhere else you might meet Pokémon.

In this book, you'll get all the stats and facts you need about over 700 Pokémon. You'll find out how each Pokémon evolves, which moves it uses, and learn which Pokémon can evolve into Mega-Evolved Pokémon during battle.

So get ready, Trainers: With this *Deluxe Essential Handbook*, you'll be ready to master almost any Pokémon challenge!

3

HOW TO USE THIS BOOK

Here are the basics you'll discover about each Pokémon:

NAME

HOW TO SAY IT

When it comes to Pokémon pronunciation, it's easy to get tongue-tied! There are many Pokémon with unusual names, so we'll help you sound them out. Soon you'll be saying Pokémon names so perfectly, you'll sound like a professor!

HEIGHT AND WEIGHT

How does each Pokémon measure up? Find out by checking its height and weight stats. And remember, good things come in all shapes and sizes. It's up to every Trainer to work with his/her Pokémon and play up its size.

POSSIBLE MOVES

Every Pokémon has its own unique combination of Moves. Before you hit the battlefield, we'll tell you all about each Pokémon's awesome attacks. And don't forget, with a good Trainer, they can always learn more!

DESCRIPTION

Knowledge is power! Pokémon Trainers have to know their stuff. Find out everything you need to know about your Pokémon here.

EVOLUTION

If your Pokémon has an evolved form or pre-evolved form, we'll show you its place in the chain and how it evolves.

MEGA EVOLUTION

Certain key Pokémon have an all-new skill—during battle, they can Mega Evolve. Mega-Evolved Pokémon can tap into strength far greater than anything they've ever experienced. Mega Pokémon can change height, weight, and even type. You'll get the new stats in this book.

TYPE

Each Pokémon has a type, and some even have two! (Pokémon with two types are called dual-type Pokémon.) Every type of Pokémon comes with its advantages and disadvantages. We'll break them all down for you here.

REGION

There are different regions in the Pokémon world, like Kanto, Johto, Hoenn, Sinnoh, Unova, and Kalos. Each region has Pokémon particular to it.

Curious about what Pokémon types you'll spot on your Pokémon journey? Find out about all eighteen types on the next page . . .

GUIDE TO POKÉMON TYPES

A Pokémon's type can tell you a lot about it—from where to find it in the wild to the Moves it'll be able to use on the battlefield. Type is the key to unlocking a Pokémon's power.

A clever Trainer should always consider type when picking a Pokémon for a match, because type shows a Pokémon's strengths and weaknesses. For example, a Fire-type may melt an Ice-type, but against a Water-type, it might find it's the one in hot water. And while a Water-type usually has the upper hand in battle with a Fire-type, a Water-type move would act like a sprinkler on a Grass-type Pokémon. But when that same Grass-type is battling a Fire-type, it just might get scorched.

Keep in mind that Moves can be mightier based on the location of the battle. Rock-type Pokémon rock at mountainside battles, Electric-types get charged up near power plants, and Ground-types like to get down and dirty right in the dirt. And if a Pokémon has two types—that is, if it's a dual type—well, then it's double trouble!

Here are the eighteen different Pokémon types:

FIRE

GRASS

WATER

NORMAL

ELECTRIC

BUG

GHOST

FLYING

FIGHTING

PSYCHIC

STEEL

ROCK

GROUND

ICE

POISON

DARK

DRAGON

FAIRY

Ready to discover more about each Pokémon?
Then let's begin!

ABOMASNOW
Frost Tree Pokémon

TYPE: GRASS-ICE

Snow-covered mountains are Abomasnow's preferred habitat. It creates blizzards to hide itself and keep others away.

How to say it: ah-BOM-ah-snow

Height: 7' 03"
Weight: 298.7 lbs.

Possible Moves: Ice Punch, Powder Snow, Leer, Razor Leaf, Icy Wind, Grass Whistle, Swagger, Mist, Ice Shard, Ingrain, Wood Hammer, Blizzard, Sheer Cold

MEGA ABOMASNOW
Frost Tree Pokémon

TYPE: GRASS-ICE

Height: 8' 10"
Weight: 407.9 lbs.

Snover   Abomasnow   Mega Abomasnow

ABRA
Psi Pokémon

TYPE: PSYCHIC

Even while Abra is sleeping, which is most of the time, it can escape a foe by teleporting away. If it doesn't get enough sleep, its powers fade.

How to say it: AH-bra

Height: 2' 11"
Weight: 43.0 lbs.

Possible Move: Teleport

Abra   Kadabra   Alakazam   Mega Alakazam

ABSOL

Disaster Pokémon

REGIONS
**HOENN,
KALOS
(COASTAL)**

TYPE: DARK

Absol doesn't often appear to people, but when it does, they should pay attention. It leaves its mountain home to warn others of an approaching disaster.

How to say it: AB-sol

Height: 3' 11"
Weight: 103.6 lbs.

Possible Moves: Perish Song, Me First, Razor Wind, Detect, Taunt, Scratch, Feint, Leer, Quick Attack, Pursuit, Bite, Double Team, Slash, Swords Dance, Future Sight, Night Slash, Detect, Psycho Cut, Sucker Punch

MEGA ABSOL

Disaster Pokémon

TYPE: DARK

Height: 3' 11"
Weight: 108.0 lbs.

Absol ➡ Mega Absol

ACCELGOR
Shell Out Pokémon

TYPE: BUG

After coming out of its shell, Accelgor is light and quick, moving with the speed of a ninja. It wraps its body up to keep from drying out.

How to say it: ak-SELL-gohr

Height: 2' 07"
Weight: 55.8 lbs.

Possible Moves: Final Gambit, Power Swap, Leech Life, Acid Spray, Double Team, Quick Attack, Struggle Bug, Mega Drain, Swift, Me First, Agility, Giga Drain, U-turn, Bug Buzz, Recover

Shelmet   Accelgor

Shield Forme

AEGISLASH
Royal Sword Pokémon

TYPE: STEEL-GHOST

Aegislash has long been seen as a symbol of royalty. In olden days, these Pokémon often accompanied the king.

How to say it: EE-jih-SLASH

Height: 5' 07"   **Weight:** 116.8 lbs.

Possible Moves: Fury Cutter, Pursuit, Autotomize, Shadow Sneak, Slash, Iron Defense, Night Slash, Power Trick, Iron Head, Head Smash, Swords Dance, Aerial Ace, King's Shield, Sacred Sword

Blade Forme

Honedge   Doublade   Aegislash   11

AERODACTYL
Fossil Pokémon

TYPE: ROCK-FLYING

This Pokémon was restored from a piece of fossilized amber. It's said that Aerodactyl ruled the skies in its ancient world.

How to say it: AIR-row-DACK-tull

Height: 5' 11"
Weight: 130.1 lbs.

Possible Moves: Iron Head, Ice Fang, Fire Fang, Thunder Fang, Wing Attack, Supersonic, Bite, Scary Face, Roar, Agility, Ancient Power, Crunch, Take Down, Sky Drop, Hyper Beam, Rock Slide, Giga Impact

MEGA AERODACTYL
Fossil Pokémon

TYPE: ROCK-FLYING

Height: 6' 11"
Weight: 174.2 lbs.

Aerodactyl   Mega Aerodactyl

TYPE: STEEL-ROCK

Aggron is extremely protective of the mountain it claims as its territory. After a natural disaster, it will work tirelessly to restore its mountain, rebuilding the topsoil and planting trees.

How to say it: AGG-ron

Height: 6' 11"
Weight: 793.7 lbs.

Possible Moves: Tackle, Harden, Mud-Slap, Headbutt, Metal Claw, Iron Defense, Roar, Take Down, Iron Head, Protect, Metal Sound, Iron Tail, Autotomize, Heavy Slam, Double-Edge, Metal Burst

REGIONS HOENN, KALOS (MOUNTAIN)

AGGRON
Iron Armor Pokémon

MEGA AGGRON
Iron Armor Pokémon

TYPE: STEEL

Height: 7' 03"
Weight: 870.8 lbs.

Aron ⟹ Lairon ⟹ Aggron ⟹ Mega Aggron

13

TYPE: NORMAL

Aipom uses the appendage at the end of its tail just like a hand. Its actual hands have lost their dexterity because it relies so much on its tail.

How to say it: AY-pom

Height: 2' 07"   **Weight:** 25.4 lbs.

Possible Moves: Scratch, Tail Whip, Sand Attack, Astonish, Baton Pass, Tickle, Fury Swipes, Swift, Screech, Agility, Double Hit, Fling, Nasty Plot, Last Resort

Aipom   Ambipom

TYPE: PSYCHIC

Because its brain never stops growing, Alakazam must use telekinesis to hold up its heavy head. On the plus side, its memory and intellect are amazing.

How to say it: AH-la-kuh-ZAM

Height: 4' 11"
Weight: 105.8 lbs.

Possible Moves: Teleport, Kinesis, Confusion, Disable, Miracle Eye, Ally Switch, Psybeam, Reflect, Telekinesis, Recover, Psycho Cut, Calm Mind, Psychic, Future Sight, Trick

REGIONS
KALOS (CENTRAL), KANTO

ALAKAZAM
Psi Pokémon

MEGA ALAKAZAM
Psi Pokémon

TYPE: PSYCHIC

Height: 3' 11"
Weight: 105.8 lbs.

Abra ⇨ Kadabra ⇨ Alakazam ⇨ Mega Alakazam

TYPE: WATER

When Alomomola finds injured Pokémon in the open sea where it lives, it gently wraps its healing fins around them and guides them to shore.

How to say it: uh-LOH-muh-MOH-luh

Height: 3' 11"   **Weight:** 69.7 lbs.

Possible Moves: Hydro Pump, Wide Guard, Healing Wish, Pound, Water Sport, Aqua Ring, Aqua Jet, Double Slap, Heal Pulse, Protect, Water Pulse, Wake-Up Slap, Soak, Wish, Brine, Safeguard, Helping Hand

Does not evolve

ALTARIA
Humming Pokémon

TYPE:
DRAGON-FLYING

When Altaria sings through the sky in its beautiful soprano voice, anyone listening falls into a happy daydream. Its soft, cottony wings are perfect for catching updrafts.

How to say it: ahl-TAR-ee-uh

Height: 3' 07"
Weight: 45.4 lbs.

Possible Moves: Sky Attack, Pluck, Peck, Growl, Astonish, Sing, Fury Attack, Safeguard, Mist, Round, Natural Gift, Take Down, Refresh, Dragon Dance, Dragon Breath, Cotton Guard, Dragon Pulse, Perish Song, Moonblast

MEGA ALTARIA
Humming Pokémon

TYPE: DRAGON-FAIRY

Height: 4' 11"
Weight: 45.4 lbs.

Swablu   Altaria   Mega Altaria

AMAURA
Tundra Pokémon

REGION
**KALOS
(COASTAL)**

TYPE: ROCK-ICE

In the ancient world, Amaura's cold habitat kept predators at bay. It was restored from a frozen fragment.

How to say it: ah-MORE-uh

Height: 4' 03"   **Weight:** 55.6 lbs.

Possible Moves: Growl, Powder Snow, Thunder Wave, Rock Throw, Icy Wind, Take Down, Mist, Aurora Beam, Ancient Power, Round, Avalanche, Hail, Nature Power, Encore, Light Screen, Ice Beam, Hyper Beam, Blizzard

Amaura   Aurorus

TYPE: NORMAL

REGION SINNOH

AMBIPOM
Long Tail Pokémon

Because Ambipom's two tails are so dexterous, it rarely uses its arms after evolving. Groups of Ambipom will sometimes link tails as a sign of friendship.

How to say it: AM-bih-pom

Height: 3' 11"
Weight: 44.8 lbs.

Possible Moves: Scratch, Tail Whip, Sand Attack, Astonish, Baton Pass, Tickle, Fury Swipes, Swift, Screech, Agility, Double Hit, Fling, Nasty Plot, Last Resort

Aipom   Ambipom

TYPE: GRASS-POISON

REGIONS KALOS (MOUNTAIN), UNOVA

AMOONGUSS
Mushroom Pokémon

In a swaying dance, Amoonguss waves its arm caps, which look like Poké Balls, in an attempt to lure the unwary. It doesn't often work.

How to say it: uh-MOON-gus

Height: 2' 00"
Weight: 23.1 lbs.

Possible Moves: Absorb, Growth, Astonish, Bide, Mega Drain, Ingrain, Feint Attack, Sweet Scent, Giga Drain, Toxic, Synthesis, Clear Smog, Solar Beam, Rage Powder, Spore

Foongus   Amoonguss

19

AMPHAROS

Light Pokémon

TYPE: ELECTRIC

Ampharos shines so brightly that its light can be seen over long distances. Long ago, people used this light to send signals from far away.

How to say it: AMF-fah-rahs

Height: 4' 07"　　**Weight:** 135.6 lbs.

Possible Moves: Zap Cannon, Magnetic Flux, Ion Deluge, Dragon Pulse, Fire Punch, Tackle, Growl, Thunder Wave, Thunder Shock, Cotton Spore, Charge, Take Down, Electro Ball, Confuse Ray, Thunder Punch, Power Gem, Discharge, Cotton Guard, Signal Beam, Light Screen, Thunder

MEGA AMPHAROS

Light Pokémon

TYPE: ELECTRIC-DRAGON

Height: 4' 07"
Weight: 135.6 lbs.

Mareep　　Flaaffy　　Ampharos　Mega Ampharos

TYPE: ROCK-BUG

The eight wings along Anorith's body wave in sequence to propel it through the warm seas where it lives. It was restored from a fossil.

How to say it: AN-no-rith

Height: 2' 04"
Weight: 27.6 lbs.

Possible Moves: Scratch, Harden, Mud Sport, Water Gun, Metal Claw, Protect, Ancient Power, Fury Cutter, Slash, Rock Blast, Crush Claw, X-Scissor

ANORITH
Old Shrimp Pokémon

Anorith ⇨ **Armaldo**

TYPE: POISON

A powerful constrictor, Arbok can crush a steel barrel in its mighty coils. Getting out of its grip is no small feat.

How to say it: ARE-bock

Height: 11' 06"
Weight: 143.3 lbs.

Possible Moves: Ice Fang, Thunder Fang, Fire Fang, Wrap, Leer, Poison Sting, Bite, Glare, Screech, Acid, Crunch, Stockpile, Swallow, Spit Up, Acid Spray, Mud Bomb, Gastro Acid, Belch, Haze, Coil, Gunk Shot

REGIONS
KALOS
(MOUNTAIN),
KANTO

ARBOK
Cobra Pokémon

Ekans ⇨ **Arbok**

ARCANINE
Legendary Pokémon

TYPE: FIRE

Arcanine's internal flame is the fuel for its amazing speed and endurance. If it runs for a whole day, it can cover more than 6,000 miles.

How to say it: ARE-ka-nine

Height: 6' 03"   **Weight:** 341.7 lbs.

Possible Moves: Thunder Fang, Bite, Roar, Fire Fang, Odor Sleuth, Extreme Speed

Growlithe   Arcanine

ARCEUS
Alpha Pokémon

REGION
SINNOH

TYPE: NORMAL

In the mythology of the Sinnoh region, Arceus emerged from its Egg into complete nothingness, and then shaped the world and everything in it.

How to say it: AR-key-us

Height: 10' 06"   **Weight:** 705.5 lbs.

Possible Moves: Seismic Toss, Cosmic Power, Natural Gift, Punishment, Gravity, Earth Power, Hyper Voice, Extreme Speed, Refresh, Future Sight, Recover, Hyper Beam, Perish Song, Judgment

MYTHICAL POKÉMON

Does not evolve

22

ARCHEN
First Bird Pokémon

TYPE: ROCK-FLYING

It is believed that modern-day flying Pokémon descended from the ancient Archen, even though its wings aren't strong enough for flight. It was restored from a fossil.

How to say it: AR-ken

Height: 1' 08"   **Weight:** 20.9 lbs.

Possible Moves: Quick Attack, Leer, Wing Attack, Rock Throw, Double Team, Scary Face, Pluck, Ancient Power, Agility, Quick Guard, Acrobatics, Dragon Breath, Crunch, Endeavor, U-turn, Rock Slide, Dragon Claw, Thrash

Archen   Archeops

ARCHEOPS
First Bird Pokémon

TYPE: ROCK-FLYING

After evolving, Archeops can fly, though they aren't very good at it. They need a running start to get airborne and can generally get around more reliably by running.

How to say it: AR-kee-ops

Height: 4' 07"   **Weight:** 70.5 lbs.

Possible Moves: Quick Attack, Leer, Wing Attack, Rock Throw, Double Team, Scary Face, Pluck, Ancient Power, Agility, Quick Guard, Acrobatics, Dragon Breath, Crunch, Endeavor, U-turn, Rock Slide, Dragon Claw, Thrash

Archen   Archeops

ARIADOS
Long Leg Pokémon

**REGIONS
JOHTO,
KALOS
(MOUNTAIN)**

TYPE: BUG-POISON

The web Ariados spins is made of thin silk, strong enough to bind and hold an enemy. The tiny hooks on its feet make it an excellent climber.

How to say it: AIR-ree-uh-dose

Height: 3' 07"   **Weight:** 73.9 lbs.

Possible Moves: Venom Drench, Fell Stinger, Bug Bite, Poison Sting, String Shot, Scary Face, Constrict, Leech Life, Night Shade, Shadow Sneak, Fury Swipes, Sucker Punch, Spider Web, Agility, Pin Missile, Psychic, Poison Jab, Cross Poison, Sticky Web

Spinarak   **Ariados**

ARMALDO
Plate Pokémon

**REGION
HOENN**

TYPE: ROCK-BUG

With its huge claws and armored body, Armaldo is well equipped for battle. It has adapted to walk on its hind legs so it can live on land.

How to say it: ar-MAL-do

Height: 4' 11"   **Weight:** 150.4 lbs.

Possible Moves: Scratch, Harden, Mud Sport, Water Gun, Metal Claw, Protect, Ancient Power, Fury Cutter, Slash, Rock Blast, Crush Claw, X-Scissor

Anorith   **Armaldo**

 REGION KALOS (CENTRAL)

AROMATISSE
Fragrance Pokémon

TYPE: FAIRY

Aromatisse uses its powerful scent as a weapon in battle. It can overpower an opponent with a strategic stench.

How to say it: uh-ROME-uh-teece

Height: 2' 07"
Weight: 34.2 lbs.

Possible Moves: Aromatic Mist, Heal Pulse, Sweet Scent, Fairy Wind, Sweet Kiss, Odor Sleuth, Echoed Voice, Calm Mind, Draining Kiss, Aromatherapy, Attract, Moonblast, Charm, Flail, Misty Terrain, Skill Swap, Psychic, Disarming Voice, Reflect, Psych Up

Spritzee   **Aromatisse**

TYPE: STEEL-ROCK

Aron chews up metal objects, from iron ore to steel bridges, and uses the metal to build up its body. It can destroy a heavy truck with a full-speed charge.

How to say it: AIR-ron

Height: 1' 04"   **Weight:** 132.3 lbs.

Possible Moves: Tackle, Harden, Mud-Slap, Headbutt, Metal Claw, Iron Defense, Roar, Take Down, Iron Head, Protect, Metal Sound, Iron Tail, Autotomize, Heavy Slam, Double-Edge, Metal Burst

 REGIONS HOENN, KALOS (MOUNTAIN)

ARON
Iron Armor Pokémon

Aron   **Lairon**   **Aggron**   **Mega Aggron**   25

ARTICUNO
Freeze Pokémon

REGIONS
KALOS (COASTAL), KANTO

LEGENDARY POKÉMON

TYPE: ICE-FLYING

When Articuno flaps its wings, the air turns chilly. This Legendary Pokémon often brings snowfall in its wake.

How to say it: ART-tick-COO-no

Height: 5' 07"   **Weight:** 122.1 lbs.

Possible Moves: Roost, Hurricane, Freeze-Dry, Tailwind, Sheer Cold, Gust, Powder Snow, Mist, Ice Shard, Mind Reader, Ancient Power, Agility, Ice Beam, Reflect, Hail, Blizzard

Does not evolve

TYPE: NORMAL

With the sensitive feelers on their ears, Audino can listen to people's heartbeats to pick up on their current state. Egg hatching can be predicted as well.

How to say it: AW-dih-noh

Height: 3' 07"
Weight: 68.3 lbs.

Possible Moves: Last Resort, Play Nice, Pound, Growl, Helping Hand, Refresh, Double Slap, Attract, Secret Power, Entrainment, Take Down, Heal Pulse, After You, Simple Beam, Double-Edge

REGIONS
KALOS (CENTRAL), UNOVA

AUDINO
Hearing Pokémon

MEGA AUDINO
Light Pokémon

TYPE: NORMAL-FAIRY

Height: 4' 11"
Weight: 70.5 lbs.

Audino   **Mega Audino**

AURORUS
Tundra Pokémon

TYPE: ROCK-ICE

With the icy crystals that line its sides, Aurorus can freeze the surrounding air and trap its foes in ice.

How to say it: ah-ROAR-us

Height: 8' 10"
Weight: 496.0 lbs.

Possible Moves: Freeze-Dry, Growl, Powder Snow, Thunder Wave, Rock Throw, Icy Wind, Take Down, Mist, Aurora Beam, Ancient Power, Round, Avalanche, Hail, Nature Power, Encore, Light Screen, Ice Beam, Hyper Beam, Blizzard

Amaura   Aurorus

AVALUGG
Iceberg Pokémon

TYPE: ICE

Avalugg's broad, flat back is a common resting place for groups of Bergmite. Its big, bulky body can crush obstacles in its path.

How to say it: AV-uh-lug

Height: 6' 07"
Weight: 1,113.3 lbs.

Possible Moves: Iron Defense, Crunch, Skull Bash, Tackle, Bite, Harden, Powder Snow, Icy Wind, Take Down, Sharpen, Curse, Ice Fang, Ice Ball, Rapid Spin, Avalanche, Blizzard, Recover, Double-Edge

Bergmite   Avalugg

AXEW
Tusk Pokémon

TYPE: DRAGON

If one of Axew's tusks breaks off, it quickly regrows, even stronger and sharper than before. It uses its tusks to crush berries and mark territory.

How to say it: AKS-yoo

Height: 2' 00"
Weight: 39.7 lbs.

Possible Moves: Scratch, Leer, Assurance, Dragon Rage, Dual Chop, Scary Face, Slash, False Swipe, Dragon Claw, Dragon Dance, Taunt, Dragon Pulse, Swords Dance, Guillotine, Outrage, Giga Impact

Axew   Fraxure   Haxorus

AZELF
Willpower Pokémon

TYPE: PSYCHIC

According to legend, Azelf brought a lasting balance to the world. It is known as "the Being of Willpower."

How to say it: AZ-elf

Height: 1' 00"   **Weight:** 0.7 lbs.

Possible Moves: Rest, Confusion, Imprison, Detect, Swift, Uproar, Future Sight, Nasty Plot, Extrasensory, Last Resort, Natural Gift, Explosion

LEGENDARY POKÉMON

Does not evolve

AZUMARILL

Aqua Rabbit Pokémon

TYPE: WATER-FAIRY

When Azumarill spots a Pokémon struggling in the water, it creates a balloon of air so the other Pokémon can breathe. It has excellent hearing.

How to say it: ah-ZU-mare-rill

Height: 2' 07"
Weight: 62.8 lbs.

Possible Moves: Tackle, Water Gun, Tail Whip, Water Sport, Bubble, Defense Curl, Rollout, Bubble Beam, Helping Hand, Aqua Tail, Double-Edge, Aqua Ring, Rain Dance, Superpower, Hydro Pump, Play Rough

Azurill 　　 Marill 　　 Azumarill

AZURILL

Polka Dot Pokémon

REGIONS
HOENN,
KALOS
(CENTRAL)

TYPE: NORMAL-FAIRY

Azurill can fling itself more than ten yards by spinning the large ball at the end of its tail and then throwing it. It can also use the tail to bounce around.

How to say it: uh-ZOO-rill

Height: 0' 08"
Weight: 4.4 lbs.

Possible Moves: Splash, Water Gun, Tail Whip, Water Sport, Bubble, Charm, Bubble Beam, Helping Hand, Slam, Bounce

Azurill 　　 Marill 　　 Azumarill

BAGON
Rock Head Pokémon

TYPE: DRAGON

Chasing its dream of flight, Bagon practices by jumping from high places. To protect it during these leaps, its head has become hard enough to smash boulders.

How to say it: BAY-gon

Height: 2' 00"   **Weight:** 92.8 lbs.

Possible Moves: Rage, Bite, Leer, Headbutt, Focus Energy, Ember, Dragon Breath, Zen Headbutt, Scary Face, Crunch, Dragon Claw, Double-Edge

Bagon   **Shelgon**   **Salamence**   **Mega Salamence**

REGION
HOENN

BALTOY
Clay Doll Pokémon

TYPE: GROUND-PSYCHIC

Baltoy can spin on its single foot to keep itself upright when moving or sleeping. Apparently, these Pokémon lived among people in ancient times.

How to say it: BAL-toy

Height: 1' 08"   **Weight:** 47.4 lbs.

Possible Moves: Confusion, Harden, Rapid Spin, Mud-Slap, Psybeam, Rock Tomb, Self-Destruct, Ancient Power, Power Trick, Sandstorm, Cosmic Power, Extrasensory, Guard Split, Power Split, Earth Power, Heal Block, Explosion

Baltoy   **Claydol**

BANETTE
Marionette Pokémon

REGIONS
HOENN,
KALOS
(MOUNTAIN)

TYPE: GHOST

Banette keeps its mouth zipped tightly shut so its energy doesn't escape. It sticks itself with pins to curse others.

How to say it: bane-NETT

Height: 3' 07"
Weight: 27.6 lbs.

Possible Moves: Knock Off, Screech, Night Shade, Curse, Spite, Will-O-Wisp, Shadow Sneak, Feint Attack, Hex, Shadow Ball, Sucker Punch, Embargo, Snatch, Grudge, Trick

MEGA BANETTE
Marionette Pokémon

TYPE: GHOST

Height: 3' 11"
Weight: 28.7 lbs.

Shuppet   **Banette**   **Mega Banette**

32

TYPE: ROCK-WATER

When seven Binacle come together to fight as one, a Barbaracle is formed. The head gives the orders, but the limbs don't always listen.

How to say it: bar-BARE-uh-kull

Height: 4' 03"   **Weight:** 211.6 lbs.

Possible Moves: Stone Edge, Skull Bash, Shell Smash, Scratch, Sand Attack, Water Gun, Withdraw, Fury Swipes, Slash, Mud-Slap, Clamp, Rock Polish, Ancient Power, Hone Claws, Fury Cutter, Night Slash, Razor Shell, Cross Chop

Binacle   **Barbaracle**

BARBOACH

Whiskers Pokémon

TYPE: WATER-GROUND

Barboach buries itself in the mud, leaving its whiskers exposed to sense when something is moving nearby. The slimy coating on its body makes it very hard to grab.

How to say it: bar-BOACH

Height: 1' 04"
Weight: 4.2 lbs.

Possible Moves: Mud-Slap, Mud Sport, Water Sport, Water Gun, Mud Bomb, Amnesia, Water Pulse, Magnitude, Rest, Snore, Aqua Tail, Earthquake, Future Sight, Fissure

Barboach   **Whiscash**

BASCULIN

Hostile Pokémon

Red Stripe

Blue Stripe

TYPE: WATER

An ongoing feud exists between Basculin with blue stripes and Basculin with red stripes. Because they're constantly fighting, they are rarely found in the same place.

How to say it: BASS-kyoo-lin

Height: 3' 03"
Weight: 39.7 lbs.

Possible Moves: Thrash, Flail, Tail Whip, Tackle, Water Gun, Uproar, Headbutt, Bite, Aqua Jet, Chip Away, Take Down, Crunch, Aqua Tail, Soak, Double-Edge, Scary Face, Final Gambit

Does not evolve

BASTIODON
Shield Pokémon

TYPE: ROCK-STEEL

When several Bastiodon stand shoulder to shoulder, no attack can penetrate the shield wall formed by their rocky faces. Despite their imposing appearance, they are quite gentle.

How to say it: BAS-tee-oh-donn

Height: 4' 03"   **Weight:** 329.6 lbs.

Possible Moves: Tackle, Protect, Taunt, Metal Sound, Take Down, Iron Defense, Swagger, Ancient Power, Block, Endure, Metal Burst, Iron Head, Heavy Slam

Shieldon   Bastiodon

BAYLEEF
Leaf Pokémon

TYPE: GRASS

The tree shoots that form a wreath around Bayleef's neck give off an invigorating fragrance. A tube-shaped leaf protects each shoot.

How to say it: BAY-leaf

Height: 3' 11"   **Weight:** 34.8 lbs.

Possible Moves: Tackle, Growl, Razor Leaf, Poison Powder, Synthesis, Reflect, Magical Leaf, Natural Gift, Sweet Scent, Light Screen, Body Slam, Safeguard, Aromatherapy, Solar Beam

Chikorita   Bayleef   Meganium

BEARTIC
Freezing Pokémon

TYPE: ICE

Beartic live in the far north, where the seas are very cold. Their fangs and claws are made of ice formed by their own freezing breath.

How to say it: BAIR-tick

Height: 8' 06"
Weight: 573.2 lbs.

Possible Moves: Sheer Cold, Thrash, Superpower, Aqua Jet, Growl, Powder Snow, Bide, Icy Wind, Play Nice, Fury Swipes, Brine, Endure, Swagger, Slash, Flail, Icicle Crash, Rest, Blizzard, Hail

Cubchoo   Beartic

BEAUTIFLY
Butterfly Pokémon

REGION
HOENN

TYPE: BUG-FLYING

To attract a Beautifly, plant flowers near your windows. This Pokémon uncoils its long mouth to gather pollen from flowers.

How to say it: BUE-tee-fly

Height: 3' 03"
Weight: 62.6 lbs.

Possible Moves: Absorb, Gust, Stun Spore, Morning Sun, Mega Drain, Whirlwind, Attract, Silver Wind, Giga Drain, Bug Buzz, Quiver Dance

Wurmple   Silcoon   Beautifly

BEEDRILL
Poison Bee Pokémon

TYPE: BUG-POISON

Stay far away from a Beedrill nest. These territorial Pokémon will swarm any intruder in a furious attack.

How to say it: BEE-dril

Height: 3' 03"   **Weight:** 65.0 lbs.

Possible Moves: Fury Attack, Focus Energy, Twineedle, Rage, Pursuit, Toxic Spikes, Pin Missile, Agility, Assurance, Poison Jab, Endeavor, Fell Stinger

MEGA BEEDRILL
Poison Bee Pokémon

TYPE: BUG-POISON

Height: 4' 07"
Weight: 89.4 lbs.

Weedle   Kakuna   Beedrill   Mega Beedrill

BEHEEYEM

Cerebral Pokémon

REGION
UNOVA

TYPE: PSYCHIC

Beheeyem flashes its fingers in three different colors to communicate, but the patterns aren't yet understood. With its psychic power, it can take control of an opponent's mind.

How to say it: BEE-hee-ehm

Height: 3' 03"
Weight: 76.1 lbs.

Possible Moves: Confusion, Growl, Heal Block, Miracle Eye, Psybeam, Headbutt, Hidden Power, Imprison, Simple Beam, Zen Headbutt, Psych Up, Psychic, Calm Mind, Recover, Guard Split, Power Split, Synchronoise, Wonder Room

Elgyem ➡ Beheeyem

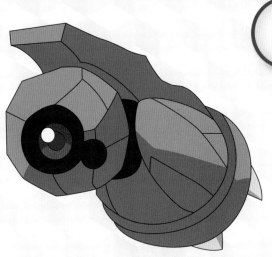

BELDUM
Iron Ball Pokémon

TYPE: STEEL-PSYCHIC

The magnetic force that runs through Beldum's body keeps it hovering in midair. It can send magnetic pulses to communicate with others.

How to say it: BELL-dum

Height: 2' 00" **Weight:** 209.9 lbs.

Possible Move: Take Down

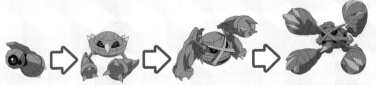

Beldum → Metang → Metagross → Mega Metagross

BELLOSSOM
Flower Pokémon

TYPE: GRASS

In strong sunlight, this Pokémon's leaves spin in a joyful dance. Bellossom that evolve from a particularly stinky Gloom will grow the most beautiful flowers.

How to say it: bell-LAHS-um

Height: 1' 04" **Weight:** 12.8 lbs.

Possible Moves: Leaf Storm, Leaf Blade, Mega Drain, Sweet Scent, Stun Spore, Sunny Day, Magical Leaf, Petal Blizzard

Oddish → Gloom → Vileplume

Gloom → Bellossom

BELLSPROUT

Flower Pokémon

REGIONS
KALOS (MOUNTAIN), KANTO

TYPE: GRASS-POISON

Bellsprout's long, thin body can bend in any direction, so it's good at dodging attacks. The liquid it spits is highly corrosive.

How to say it: BELL-sprout

Height: 2' 04"
Weight: 8.8 lbs.

Possible Moves: Vine Whip, Growth, Wrap, Sleep Powder, Poison Powder, Stun Spore, Acid, Knock Off, Sweet Scent, Gastro Acid, Razor Leaf, Slam, Wring Out

Bellsprout   Weepinbell   Victreebel

BERGMITE

Ice Chunk Pokémon

REGION
KALOS (MOUNTAIN)

TYPE: ICE

When cracks form in Bergmite's icy body, it uses freezing air to patch itself up with new ice. It lives high in the mountains.

How to say it: BERG-mite

Height: 3' 03"
Weight: 219.4 lbs.

Possible Moves: Tackle, Bite, Harden, Powder Snow, Icy Wind, Take Down, Sharpen, Curse, Ice Fang, Ice Ball, Rapid Spin, Avalanche, Blizzard, Recover, Double-Edge

Bergmite   Avalugg

TYPE: NORMAL-WATER

BIBAREL
Beaver Pokémon

With their large, sharp teeth, Bibarel busily cut up trees to build nests. Sometimes these nests block small streams and divert the flow of the water.

How to say it: bee-BER-rel

Height: 3' 03"
Weight: 69.4 lbs.

Possible Moves: Rototiller, Tackle, Growl, Defense Curl, Rollout, Water Gun, Headbutt, Hyper Fang, Yawn, Amnesia, Take Down, Super Fang, Superpower, Curse

Bidoof   Bibarel

TYPE: NORMAL

BIDOOF
Plump Mouse Pokémon

Bidoof live beside the water, where they gnaw on rock or wood to keep their front teeth worn down. They have a steady nature and are not easily upset.

How to say it: BEE-doof

Height: 1' 08"
Weight: 44.1 lbs.

Possible Moves: Tackle, Growl, Defense Curl, Rollout, Headbutt, Hyper Fang, Yawn, Amnesia, Take Down, Super Fang, Superpower, Curse

Bidoof   Bibarel

BINACLE

Two-Handed Pokémon

REGION
KALOS
(COASTAL)

TYPE: ROCK-WATER

Binacle live in pairs, two on the same rock. They comb the beach for seaweed to eat.

How to say it: BY-nuh-kull

Height: 1' 08"
Weight: 68.3 lbs.

Possible Moves: Shell Smash, Scratch, Sand Attack, Water Gun, Withdraw, Fury Swipes, Slash, Mud-Slap, Clamp, Rock Polish, Ancient Power, Hone Claws, Fury Cutter, Night Slash, Razor Shell, Cross Chop

Binacle   **Barbaracle**

BISHARP

Sword Blade Pokémon

REGIONS
KALOS
(MOUNTAIN),
UNOVA

TYPE: DARK-STEEL

When Pawniard hunt in a pack, Bisharp leads them and gives the orders. It's often the one that deals the final blow.

How to say it: BIH-sharp

Height: 5' 03"
Weight: 154.3 lbs.

Possible Moves: Guillotine, Iron Head, Metal Burst, Scratch, Leer, Fury Cutter, Torment, Feint Attack, Scary Face, Metal Claw, Slash, Assurance, Metal Sound, Embargo, Iron Defense, Night Slash, Swords Dance

Pawniard   **Bisharp**

BLASTOISE
Shellfish Pokémon

TYPE: WATER

From the spouts on its shell, Blastoise can fire water bullets with amazing accuracy. It can hit a target more than one hundred sixty feet away!

How to say it: BLAS-toyce

Height: 5' 03"
Weight: 188.5 lbs.

Possible Moves: Flash Cannon, Tackle, Tail Whip, Water Gun, Withdraw, Bubble, Bite, Rapid Spin, Protect, Water Pulse, Aqua Tail, Skull Bash, Iron Defense, Rain Dance, Hydro Pump

MEGA BLASTOISE
Shellfish Pokémon

TYPE: WATER

Height: 5' 03"
Weight: 222.9 lbs.

Squirtle ⇨ Wartortle ⇨ Blastoise ⇨ Mega Blastoise

BLAZIKEN

Blaze Pokémon

REGION
HOENN

TYPE: FIRE-FIGHTING

With continued strengthening of its legs, Blaziken can leap over a thirty-story building. The flames that flare from its wrists burn hotter against a worthy foe.

How to say it: BLAZE-uh-ken

Height: 6' 03"
Weight: 114.6 lbs.

Possible Moves: Fire Punch, High Jump Kick, Scratch, Growl, Focus Energy, Ember, Double Kick, Peck, Sand Attack, Bulk Up, Quick Attack, Blaze Kick, Slash, Brave Bird, Sky Uppercut, Flare Blitz

MEGA BLAZIKEN

Blaze Pokémon

TYPE: FIRE-FIGHTING

Height: 6' 03"
Weight: 114.6 lbs.

Torchic Combusken Blaziken Mega Blaziken

BLISSEY
Happiness Pokémon

TYPE: NORMAL

Blissey is extremely sensitive to people's emotions. If it senses sorrow, it leaps into action, rushing to the sad person's side with the gift of a special egg.

How to say it: BLISS-sey

Height: 4' 11"   **Weight:** 103.2 lbs.

Possible Moves: Defense Curl, Pound, Growl, Tail Whip, Refresh, Double Slap, Softboiled, Bestow, Minimize, Take Down, Sing, Fling, Heal Pulse, Egg Bomb, Light Screen, Healing Wish, Double-Edge

Happiny   Chansey   Blissey

BLITZLE

Electrified Pokémon

REGION
UNOVA

TYPE: ELECTRIC

Blitzle's mane attracts lightning and stores the electricity. It can discharge this electricity in controlled flashes to communicate with others.

How to say it: BLIT-zul

Height: 2' 07"   **Weight:** 65.7 lbs.

Possible Moves: Quick Attack, Tail Whip, Charge, Shock Wave, Thunder Wave, Flame Charge, Pursuit, Spark, Stomp, Discharge, Agility, Wild Charge, Thrash

Blitzle   Zebstrika

BOLDORE

Ore Pokémon

REGIONS
**KALOS
(COASTAL),
UNOVA**

TYPE: ROCK

The energy within Boldore's body overflows, leaks out, and forms into orange crystals. Though its head always points in the same direction, it can quickly move sideways and backward.

How to say it: BOHL-dohr

Height: 2' 11"   **Weight:** 224.9 lbs.

Possible Moves: Tackle, Harden, Sand Attack, Headbutt, Rock Blast, Mud-Slap, Iron Defense, Smack Down, Power Gem, Rock Slide, Stealth Rock, Sandstorm, Stone Edge, Explosion

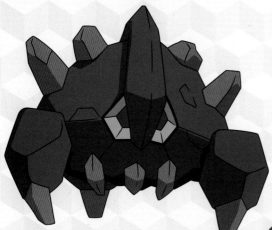

Roggenrola   Boldore   Gigalith

TYPE: ROCK

Bonsly prefers to live in dry places. When its body stores excess moisture, it releases water from its eyes, making it look like it's crying.

How to say it: BON-slye

Height: 1' 08"
Weight: 33.1 lbs.

Possible Moves: Fake Tears, Copycat, Flail, Low Kick, Rock Throw, Mimic, Feint Attack, Rock Tomb, Block, Rock Slide, Counter, Sucker Punch, Double-Edge

REGIONS
KALOS (MOUNTAIN), SINNOH

BONSLY
Bonsai Pokémon

Bonsly   Sudowoodo

TYPE: NORMAL

Though Bouffalant can knock a train off the rails with the force of its headbutt, it doesn't worry about hurting itself, because its fluffy fur absorbs the impact.

How to say it: BOO-fuh-lahnt

Height: 5' 03"
Weight: 208.6 lbs.

Possible Moves: Pursuit, Leer, Rage, Fury Attack, Horn Attack, Scary Face, Revenge, Head Charge, Focus Energy, Megahorn, Reversal, Thrash, Swords Dance, Giga Impact

REGION
UNOVA

BOUFFALANT
Bash Buffalo Pokémon

Does not evolve

BRAIXEN

Fox Pokémon

TYPE: FIRE

When Braixen pulls the twig out of its tail, the friction from its fur sets the wood on fire. It can use this flaming twig as a tool or a weapon.

How to say it: BRAKE-sen

Height: 3' 03"
Weight: 32.0 lbs.

Possible Moves: Scratch, Tail Whip, Ember, Howl, Flame Charge, Psybeam, Fire Spin, Lucky Chant, Light Screen, Psyshock, Flamethrower, Will-O-Wisp, Psychic, Sunny Day, Magic Room, Fire Blast

Fennekin   Braixen   Delphox

BRAVIARY

Valiant Pokémon

TYPE: NORMAL-FLYING

To protect its friends, Braviary will keep battling even when it's hurt. Its wings and talons are so strong that it can carry a car through the air.

How to say it: BRAY-vee-air-ee

Height: 4' 11"
Weight: 90.4 lbs.

Possible Moves: Peck, Leer, Fury Attack, Wing Attach, Hone Claws, Scary Face, Aerial Ace, Slash, Defog, Tailwind, Air Slash, Crush Claw, Sky Drop, Superpower, Whirlwind, Brave Bird, Thrash

Rufflet   Braviary

TYPE: GRASS-FIGHTING

REGION
HOENN

BRELOOM
Mushroom Pokémon

If a seed falls from Breloom's tail, you really shouldn't eat it. The seeds are toxic and taste terrible. Its arms stretch to throw impressive punches.

How to say it: BRELL-loom

Height: 3' 11"   **Weight:** 86.4 lbs.

Possible Moves: Absorb, Tackle, Stun Spore, Leech Seed, Mega Drain, Headbutt, Mach Punch, Counter, Force Palm, Sky Uppercut, Mind Reader, Seed Bomb, Dynamic Punch

Shroomish   Breloom

TYPE: STEEL-PSYCHIC

REGION
SINNOH

BRONZONG
Bronze Bell Pokémon

In ancient times, people thought Bronzong was responsible for making the rain fall, so they often asked it for help to make their crops flourish.

How to say it: brawn-ZONG

Height: 4' 03"   **Weight:** 412.3 lbs.

Possible Moves: Sunny Day, Rain Dance, Tackle, Confusion, Hypnosis, Imprison, Confuse Ray, Extrasensory, Iron Defense, Safeguard, Block, Gyro Ball, Future Sight, Feint Attack, Payback, Heal Block, Heavy Slam

Bronzor   Bronzong

BRONZOR

Bronze Pokémon

TYPE: STEEL-PSYCHIC

In ancient times, people thought a mystical power was contained within Bronzor's back pattern. Artifacts matching its shape have been discovered in tombs from that era.

How to say it: BRAWN-zorr

Height: 1' 08"
Weight: 133.4 lbs.

Possible Moves: Tackle, Confusion, Hypnosis, Imprison, Confuse Ray, Extrasensory, Iron Defense, Safeguard, Gyro Ball, Future Sight, Feint Attack, Payback, Heal Block, Heavy Slam

Bronzor　　Bronzong

BUDEW

Bud Pokémon

REGIONS
KALOS
(CENTRAL),
SINNOH

TYPE: GRASS-POISON

When the weather turns cold, Budew's bud is tightly closed. In the springtime, it opens up again and gives off its pollen.

How to say it: buh-DOO

Height: 0' 08"
Weight: 2.6 lbs.

Possible Moves: Absorb, Growth, Water Sport, Stun Spore, Mega Drain, Worry Seed

Budew　　Roselia　　Roserade

BUIZEL
Sea Weasel Pokémon

TYPE: WATER

Buizel rapidly spins its two tails to propel itself through the water. The flotation sac around its neck keeps its head up without effort, and it can deflate the sac to dive.

How to say it: BWEE-zul

Height: 2' 04"
Weight: 65.0 lbs.

Possible Moves: Sonic Boom, Growl, Water Sport, Quick Attack, Water Gun, Pursuit, Swift, Aqua Jet, Double Hit, Whirlpool, Razor Wind, Aqua Tail, Agility, Hydro Pump

Buizel ⇨ **Floatzel**

REGIONS
KALOS
(CENTRAL),
KANTO

BULBASAUR
Seed Pokémon

TYPE: GRASS-POISON

Bulbasaur likes to take a nap in the sunshine. While it sleeps, the seed on its back catches the rays and uses the energy to grow.

How to say it: BUL-ba-sore

Height: 2' 04"   **Weight:** 15.2 lbs.

Possible Moves: Tackle, Growl, Leech Seed, Vine Whip, Poison Powder, Sleep Powder, Take Down, Razor Leaf, Sweet Scent, Growth, Double-Edge, Worry Seed, Synthesis, Seed Bomb

Bulbasaur ⇨ **Ivysaur** ⇨ **Venusaur** ⇨ **Mega Venusaur**

BUNEARY

Rabbit Pokémon

TYPE: NORMAL

Buneary keeps its ears rolled up except when attacking or scouting for danger. It can extend its ears with enough force to pulverize a boulder.

How to say it: buh-NEER-ree

Height: 1' 04"
Weight: 12.1 lbs.

Possible Moves: Splash, Pound, Defense Curl, Foresight, Endure, Frustration, Quick Attack, Jump Kick, Baton Pass, Agility, Dizzy Punch, After You, Charm, Entrainment, Bounce, Healing Wish

Buneary   Lopunny   Mega Lopunny

BUNNELBY

Digging Pokémon

TYPE: NORMAL

Bunnelby can use its ears like shovels to dig holes in the ground. Eventually, its ears become strong enough to cut through thick tree roots while it digs.

How to say it: BUN-ell-bee

Height: 1' 04"   **Weight:** 11.0 lbs.

Possible Moves: Tackle, Agility, Leer, Quick Attack, Double Slap, Mud-Slap, Take Down, Mud Shot, Double Kick, Odor Sleuth, Flail, Dig, Bounce, Super Fang, Facade, Earthquake

Bunnelby   Diggersby

BURMY (GRASS CLOAK)

Bagworm Pokémon

TYPE: BUG

Burmy creates a cloak for itself out of whatever materials it can find. The cloak protects it from chilly temperatures and shields it in battle.

How to say it: BURR-mee

Height: 0' 08" **Weight:** 7.5 lbs.

Possible Moves: Protect, Tackle, Bug Bite, Hidden Power

Burmy

Wormadam Female Form

Mothim Male Form

BURMY (SANDY CLOAK)

Bagworm Pokémon

TYPE: BUG

Did you know that each Burmy covers up with the objects around it? This Burmy uses rocks and sand for protection.

How to say it: BURR-mee

Height: 0' 08" **Weight:** 7.5 lbs.

Possible Moves: Protect, Tackle, Bug Bite, Hidden Power

Burmy

Wormadam Female Form

Mothim Male Form

BURMY (TRASH CLOAK)
Bagworm Pokémon

TYPE: BUG

If you're looking for Burmy with a Trash Cloak, try poking around inside a few buildings. You might get lucky!

How to say it: BURR-mee

Height: 0' 08"   **Weight:** 7.5 lbs.

Possible Moves: Protect, Tackle, Bug Bite, Hidden Power

Burmy → Wormadam Female Form

Mothim Male Form

BUTTERFREE
Butterfly Pokémon

TYPE: BUG-FLYING

Butterfree is excellent at seeking out flowers with the most delicious nectar. It sometimes flies more than six miles to locate its favorite food.

How to say it: BUT-er-free

Height: 3' 07"
Weight: 70.5 lbs.

Possible Moves: Confusion, Poison Powder, Stun Spore, Sleep Powder, Gust, Supersonic, Whirlwind, Psybeam, Silver Wind, Tailwind, Rage Powder, Safeguard, Captivate, Bug Buzz, Quiver Dance

Caterpie ⇒ Metapod ⇒ Butterfree

54

TYPE: GRASS

CACNEA
Cactus Pokémon

Cacnea produce the most beautiful and fragrant flowers when they live in particularly harsh and dry environments. They can shoot their thorns to attack.

How to say it: CACK-nee-uh

Height: 1' 04"   **Weight:** 113.1 lbs.

Possible Moves: Poison Sting, Leer, Absorb, Growth, Leech Seed, Sand Attack, Pin Missile, Ingrain, Feint Attack, Spikes, Sucker Punch, Payback, Needle Arm, Cotton Spore, Sandstorm, Destiny Bond

Cacnea   Cacturne

CACTURNE
Scarecrow Pokémon

TYPE: GRASS-DARK

Cacturne stand very still during the day so as not to waste energy or moisture in the heat of the desert sun. After dark, they hunt in packs, often attacking travelers who weren't prepared for the environment.

How to say it: CACK-turn

Height: 4' 03"   **Weight:** 170.6 lbs.

Possible Moves: Revenge, Poison Sting, Leer, Absorb, Growth, Leech Seed, Sand Attack, Pin Missile, Ingrain, Feint Attack, Spikes, Sucker Punch, Payback, Needle Arm, Cotton Spore, Sandstorm, Destiny Bond

Cacnea   Cacturne

CAMERUPT

Eruption Pokémon

REGION
HOENN

TYPE: FIRE-GROUND

When Camerupt gets angry, the volcanic humps on its back tend to erupt. The magma that sprays out is superheated and very dangerous.

How to say it: CAM-err-rupt

Height: 6' 03"
Weight: 485.0 lbs.

Possible Moves: Growl, Tackle, Ember, Magnitude, Focus Energy, Flame Burst, Take Down, Amnesia, Lava Plume, Rock Slide, Earth Power, Earthquake, Fissure

MEGA CAMERUPT

Eruption Pokémon

TYPE: FIRE-GROUND

Height: 8' 02"
Weight: 706.6 lbs.

Numel　　　Camerupt　　　Mega Camerupt

CARBINK
Jewel Pokémon

TYPE: ROCK-FAIRY

While excavating caves, miners and archeologists sometimes stumble upon Carbink sleeping deep underground. The stone on top of its head can fire beams of energy.

How to say it: CAR-bink

Height: 1' 0"
Weight: 12.6 lbs.

Possible Moves: Tackle, Harden, Rock Throw, Sharpen, Smack Down, Reflect, Stealth Rock, Guard Split, Ancient Power, Flail, Skill Swap, Power Gem, Stone Edge, Moonblast, Light Screen, Safeguard

Does not evolve

CARNIVINE
Bug Catcher Pokémon

TYPE: GRASS

Carnivine wraps itself around trees in swampy areas. It gives off a sweet aroma that lures others close, then attacks.

How to say it: CAR-neh-vine

Height: 4' 07"
Weight: 59.5 lbs.

Possible Moves: Bind, Growth, Bite, Vine Whip, Sweet Scent, Ingrain, Feint Attack, Leaf Tornado, Stockpile, Spit Up, Swallow, Crunch, Wring Out, Power Whip

Does not evolve

CARRACOSTA

Prototurtle Pokémon

TYPE: WATER-ROCK

With its powerful jaws and massive front flippers, Carracosta is a formidable fighter. It can break through the hull of a tanker ship with a single slap.

How to say it: kar-ruh-KOSS-tuh

Height: 3' 11"
Weight: 178.6 lbs.

Possible Moves: Bide, Withdraw, Water Gun, Rollout, Bite, Protect, Aqua Jet, Ancient Power, Crunch, Wide Guard, Brine, Smack Down, Curse, Shell Smash, Aqua Tail, Rock Slide, Rain Dance, Hydro Pump

Tirtouga   Carracosta

CARVANHA

Savage Pokémon

REGIONS
HOENN,
KALOS
(CENTRAL)

TYPE: WATER-DARK

Carvanha descend in a swarm to attack anything that enters their territory. When they work together, their strong jaws and sharp teeth can rip a hole in a boat's hull.

How to say it: car-VAH-na

Height: 2' 07"   **Weight:** 45.9 lbs.

Possible Moves: Leer, Bite, Rage, Focus Energy, Scary Face, Ice Fang, Screech, Swagger, Assurance, Crunch, Aqua Jet, Agility, Take Down

Carvanha   Sharpedo   Mega Sharpedo

TYPE: BUG

When Cascoon is ready to evolve, it wraps itself up in silk, which hardens around its body. If something attacks its cocoon, it takes the hit without moving so as not to use up energy . . . but it also remembers the attacker.

How to say it: CAS-koon

Height: 2' 04"
Weight: 25.4 lbs.

Possible Move: Harden

REGION
HOENN

CASCOON
Cocoon Pokémon

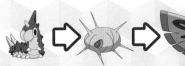

Wurmple   **Cascoon**   **Dustox**

Regular Form

REGION
HOENN

CASTFORM
Weather Pokémon

TYPE: NORMAL

Changes in the weather alter Castform's appearance and its mood. It draws on the power of nature to transform and protect itself from the elements.

How to say it: CAST-form

Height: 1' 00"   **Weight:** 1.8 lbs.

Possible Moves: Tackle, Water Gun, Ember, Powder Snow, Headbutt, Rain Dance, Sunny Day, Hail, Weather Ball, Hydro Pump, Fire Blast, Blizzard

Snowy Form

Rainy Form

Sunny Form   **Does not evolve**

CATERPIE
Worm Pokémon

REGIONS
KALOS (CENTRAL), KANTO

TYPE: BUG

A ravenous Caterpie can quickly gobble up leaves that are bigger than itself. Its antenna can produce a terrible smell.

How to say it: CAT-ur-pee

Height: 1' 00"
Weight: 6.4 lbs.

Possible Moves: Tackle, String Shot, Bug Bite

Caterpie   Metapod   Butterfree

CELEBI
Time Travel Pokémon

REGION
JOHTO

MYTHICAL POKÉMON

TYPE: PSYCHIC-GRASS

Celebi traveled back in time to come to this world. According to myth, its presence is a sign of a bright future.

How to say it: SEL-ih-bee

Height: 2' 00"   **Weight:** 11.0 lbs.

Possible Moves: Leech Seed, Confusion, Recover, Heal Bell, Safeguard, Magical Leaf, Ancient Power, Baton Pass, Natural Gift, Heal Block, Future Sight, Healing Wish, Leaf Storm, Perish Song

Does not evolve

CHANDELURE
Luring Pokémon

TYPE: GHOST-FIRE

Chandelure's spooky flames can burn the spirit right out of someone. If that happens, the spirit becomes trapped in this world, endlessly wandering.

How to say it: shan-duh-LOOR

Height: 3' 03"
Weight: 75.6 lbs.

Possible Moves: Pain Split, Smog, Confuse Ray, Flame Burst, Hex

Litwick   **Lampent**   **Chandelure**

CHANSEY
Egg Pokémon

TYPE: NORMAL

The eggs Chansey produces every day are full of nutrition and flavor. Even people suffering a loss of appetite eat them up with delight.

How to say it: CHAN-see

Height: 3' 07"
Weight: 76.3 lbs.

Possible Moves: Defense Curl, Pound, Growl, Tail Whip, Refresh, Double Slap, Softboiled, Bestow, Minimize, Take Down, Sing, Fling, Heal Pulse, Egg Bomb, Light Screen, Healing Wish, Double-Edge

Happiny   **Chansey**   **Blissey**

CHARIZARD
Flame Pokémon

REGIONS
KALOS (CENTRAL), KANTO

TYPE: FIRE-FLYING

Charizard seeks out stronger foes and only breathes fire during battles with worthy opponents. The fiery breath is so hot that it can turn any material to slag.

How to say it: CHAR-iz-ard

Height: 5' 07"   **Weight:** 199.5 lbs.

Possible Moves: Flare Blitz, Heat Wave, Dragon Claw, Shadow Claw, Air Slash, Scratch, Growl, Ember, Smokescreen, Dragon Rage, Scary Face, Fire Fang, Flame Burst, Wing Attack, Slash, Flamethrower, Fire Spin, Inferno

MEGA CHARIZARD X
Flame Pokémon

TYPE: FIRE-DRAGON
Height: 5' 07"   **Weight:** 243.6 lbs.

MEGA CHARIZARD Y
Flame Pokémon

TYPE: FIRE-FLYING
Height: 5' 07"   **Weight:** 221.6 lbs.

Charmander ⇨ Charmeleon ⇨ Charizard ⇨

Mega Charizard X

Mega Charizard Y

TYPE: FIRE

The flame on Charmander's tail tip indicates how the Pokémon is feeling. It flares up in a fury when Charmander is angry!

How to say it: CHAR-man-der

Height: 2' 00"
Weight: 18.7 lbs.

Possible Moves: Scratch, Growl, Ember, Smokescreen, Dragon Rage, Scary Face, Fire Fang, Flame Burst, Slash, Flamethrower, Fire Spin, Inferno

REGIONS
KALOS (CENTRAL), KANTO

CHARMANDER
Lizard Pokémon

Mega Charizard X

Mega Charizard Y

Charmander Charmeleon Charizard

TYPE: FIRE

When Charmeleon takes on a powerful opponent in battle, its tail flame glows white-hot. Its claws are very sharp.

How to say it: char-MEE-lee-un

Height: 3' 07"
Weight: 41.9 lbs.

Possible Moves: Scratch, Growl, Ember, Smokescreen, Dragon Rage, Scary Face, Fire Fang, Flame Burst, Slash, Flamethrower, Fire Spin, Inferno

REGIONS
KALOS (CENTRAL), KANTO

CHARMELEON
Flame Pokémon

Mega Charizard X

Charmander Charmeleon Charizard

Mega Charizard Y

CHATOT
Music Note Pokémon

REGIONS
KALOS (COASTAL), SINNOH

TYPE: NORMAL-FLYING

Chatot can mimic other Pokémon's cries and even human speech. A group of them will often pick up the same phrase and keep repeating it among themselves.

How to say it: CHAT-tot

Height: 1' 08"
Weight: 4.2 lbs.

Possible Moves: Hyper Voice, Chatter, Confide, Taunt, Peck, Growl, Mirror Move, Sing, Fury Attack, Round, Mimic, Echoed Voice, Roost, Uproar, Synchronoise, Feather Dance

Does not evolve

CHERRIM
Blossom Pokémon

REGION
SINNOH

TYPE: GRASS

Cherrim keeps its petals folded around itself except in bright sunshine. When the weather is nice, its bloom opens wide to absorb as much sunlight as it can.

How to say it: chuh-RIM

Height: 1' 08"   **Weight:** 20.5 lbs.

Possible Moves: Morning Sun, Tackle, Growth, Leech Seed, Helping Hand, Magical Leaf, Sunny Day, Petal Dance, Worry Seed, Take Down, Solar Beam, Lucky Chant

Cherubi   Cherrim

TYPE: GRASS

CHERUBI
Cherry Pokémon

Cherubi stores nutrients in the small red ball attached to its head. When it's ready to evolve, it uses up all the nutrients at once, making the small ball wither.

How to say it: chuh-ROO-bee

Height: 1' 04"
Weight: 7.3 lbs.

Possible Moves: Morning Sun, Tackle, Growth, Leech Seed, Helping Hand, Magical Leaf, Sunny Day, Worry Seed, Take Down, Solar Beam, Lucky Chant

Cherubi   Cherrim

CHESNAUGHT
Spiny Armor Pokémon

TYPE: GRASS-FIGHTING

When its friends are in trouble, Chesnaught uses its own body as a shield. Its shell is tough enough to protect it from a powerful explosion.

How to say it: CHESS-nawt

Height: 5' 03"   **Weight:** 198.4 lbs.

Possible Moves: Feint, Hammer Arm, Belly Drum, Tackle, Growl, Vine Whip, Rollout, Bite, Leech Seed, Pin Missile, Needle Arm, Take Down, Seed Bomb, Spiky Shield, Mud Shot, Bulk Up, Body Slam, Pain Split, Wood Hammer, Giga Impact

Chespin   Quilladin   Chesnaught

CHESPIN

Spiny Nut Pokémon

REGION
KALOS
(CENTRAL)

TYPE: GRASS

When Chespin flexes its soft quills, they become tough spikes with sharp, piercing points. It relies on its nutlike shell for protection in battle.

How to say it: CHESS-pin

Height: 1' 04"
Weight: 19.8 lbs.

Possible Moves: Tackle, Growl, Vine Whip, Rollout, Bite, Leech Seed, Pin Missile, Take Down, Seed Bomb, Mud Shot, Bulk Up, Body Slam, Pain Split, Wood Hammer

Chespin   Quilladin   Chesnaught

CHIKORITA

Leaf Pokémon

REGION
JOHTO

TYPE: GRASS

Chikorita brandishes its leaf in battle to fend off a foe. When it does this, the leaf gives off a lovely aroma that calms everyone down.

How to say it: CHICK-oh-REE-ta

Height: 2' 11"   **Weight:** 14.1 lbs.

Possible Moves: Tackle, Growl, Razor Leaf, Poison Powder, Synthesis, Reflect, Magical Leaf, Natural Gift, Sweet Scent, Light Screen, Body Slam, Safeguard, Aromatherapy, Solar Beam

Chikorita   Bayleef   Meganium

66

TYPE: FIRE

Chimchar's rear is always on fire, even when it stands in the rain. If it's not feeling well, the flame flickers weakly.

How to say it: CHIM-char

Height: 1' 08"
Weight: 13.7 lbs.

Possible Moves: Scratch, Leer, Ember, Taunt, Fury Swipes, Flame Wheel, Nasty Plot, Torment, Facade, Fire Spin, Acrobatics, Slack Off, Flamethrower

CHIMCHAR
Chimp Pokémon

Chimchar   Monferno   Infernape

CHIMECHO
Wind Chime Pokémon

TYPE: PSYCHIC

The sucker on the top of Chimecho's head can attach to a tree branch or building. Its hollow body amplifies its chiming cries.

How to say it: chime-ECK-ko

Height: 2' 00"
Weight: 2.2 lbs.

Possible Moves: Healing Wish, Synchronoise, Wrap, Growl, Astonish, Confusion, Uproar, Take Down, Yawn, Psywave, Double-Edge, Heal Bell, Safeguard, Extrasensory, Heal Pulse

Chingling   Chimecho

CHINCHOU

Angler Pokémon

TYPE: WATER-ELECTRIC

With its two antennae, Chinchou can release an electric charge for use as a weapon, or flash lights to communicate. It sometimes gets a tingly feeling if it generates too much electricity.

How to say it: CHIN-chow

Height: 1' 08"   **Weight:** 26.5 lbs.

Possible Moves: Water Gun, Supersonic, Thunder Wave, Flail, Bubble, Confuse Ray, Spark, Take Down, Electro Ball, Bubble Beam, Signal Beam, Discharge, Aqua Ring, Hydro Pump, Ion Deluge, Charge

Chinchou   Lanturn

CHINGLING

Bell Pokémon

TYPE: PSYCHIC

When Chingling hops about, a small orb bounces around inside its mouth, producing a noise like the sound of bells. It uses high-pitched sounds to attack its opponents' hearing.

How to say it: CHING-ling

Height: 0' 08"
Weight: 1.3 lbs.

Possible Moves: Wrap, Growl, Astonish, Confusion, Uproar, Last Resort, Entrainment

Chingling   Chimecho

TYPE: NORMAL

A special oil coats Cinccino's soft white fur. This oil repels dust and dirt, deflects enemy attacks, and keeps static electricity at bay.

How to say it: chin-CHEE-noh

Height: 1' 08"
Weight: 16.5 lbs.

Possible Moves: Bullet Seed, Rock Blast, Helping Hand, Tickle, Sing, Tail Slap

REGION
UNOVA

CINCCINO
Scarf Pokémon

Minccino ⇨ Cinccino

TYPE: WATER

Even as Clamperl's soft body grows inside its hard shell, the shell stays the same size until it evolves. In addition to protecting itself, it uses the shell to catch food or to grab onto an opponent in battle.

How to say it: CLAM-perl

Height: 1' 04"   **Weight:** 115.7 lbs.

Possible Moves: Clamp, Water Gun, Whirlpool, Iron Defense, Shell Smash

REGIONS
HOENN, KALOS (COASTAL)

CLAMPERL
Bivalve Pokémon

Clamperl

Huntail

Gorebyss

69

CLAUNCHER
Water Gun Pokémon

REGION
**KALOS
(COASTAL)**

TYPE: WATER

Clauncher shoots water from its claws with a force that can pulverize rock. Its range is great enough to knock flying Pokémon out of the air.

How to say it: CLAWN-chur

Height: 1' 08"
Weight: 18.3 lbs.

Possible Moves: Splash, Water Gun, Water Sport, Vice Grip, Bubble, Flail, Bubble Beam, Swords Dance, Crabhammer, Water Pulse, Smack Down, Aqua Jet, Muddy Water

Clauncher   Clawitzer

CLAWITZER
Howitzer Pokémon

REGION
**KALOS
(COASTAL)**

TYPE: WATER

Clawitzer's giant claw can expel massive jets of water at high speed. It fires the water forward to attack, or backward to propel itself through the sea.

How to say it: CLOW-wit-zur

Height: 4' 03"   **Weight:** 77.8 lbs.

Possible Moves: Heal Pulse, Dark Pulse, Dragon Pulse, Aura Sphere, Splash, Water Gun, Water Sport, Vice Grip, Bubble, Flail, Bubble Beam, Swords Dance, Crabhammer, Water Pulse, Smack Down, Aqua Jet, Muddy Water

Clauncher   Clawitzer

CLAYDOL

Clay Doll Pokémon

TYPE: GROUND-PSYCHIC

Claydol is thought to have originated from an ancient clay statue. It levitates to move and can shoot energy beams from its hands.

How to say it: CLAY-doll

Height: 4' 11"   **Weight:** 238.1 lbs.

Possible Moves: Teleport, Confusion, Harden, Rapid Spin, Mud-Slap, Psybeam, Rock Tomb, Self-Destruct, Ancient Power, Power Trick, Sandstorm, Hyper Beam, Extrasensory, Cosmic Power, Guard Split, Power Split, Earth Power, Heal Block, Explosion

Baltoy   Claydol

CLEFABLE

Fairy Pokémon

TYPE: FAIRY

Clefable moves with such lightness that it can skip across the water—perfect for a moonlight stroll on the surface of a lake.

How to say it: cluh-FAY-bull

Height: 4' 03"
Weight: 88.2 lbs.

Possible Moves: Sing, Double Slap, Minimize, Metronome

Cleffa   Clefairy   Clefable

71

CLEFAIRY

Fairy Pokémon

TYPE: FAIRY

Groups of Clefairy gather to play under the full moon. When the sun rises, they retreat to their mountain home and snuggle together to sleep.

How to say it: cluh-FAIR-ee

Height: 2' 00"   **Weight:** 16.5 lbs.

Possible Moves: Pound, Growl, Encore, Sing, Double Slap, Defense Curl, Follow Me, Minimize, Wake-Up Slap, Bestow, Cosmic Power, Lucky Chant, Metronome, Gravity, Moonlight, Stored Power, Light Screen, Healing Wish, After You

Cleffa   Clefairy   Clefable

CLEFFA

Star Shape Pokémon

REGION **JOHTO**

TYPE: FAIRY

During a meteor shower, groups of Cleffa gather to dance in a circle. Their dance lasts until dawn and makes them very thirsty, so they sip dewdrops to rehydrate.

How to say it: CLEFF-uh

Height: 1' 00"   **Weight:** 6.6 lbs.

Possible Moves: Pound, Charm, Encore, Sing, Sweet Kiss, Copycat, Magical Leaf

Cleffa   Clefairy   Clefable

CLOYSTER
Bivalve Pokémon

TYPE: WATER-ICE

By sucking in water and then shooting it out, Cloyster can propel itself through the sea. It also uses this method to fire its shell spikes in battle.

How to say it: CLOY-stur

Height: 4' 11"
Weight: 292.1 lbs.

Possible Moves: Hydro Pump, Shell Smash, Toxic Spikes, Withdraw, Supersonic, Protect, Aurora Beam, Spike Cannon, Spikes, Icicle Crash

Shellder ⇨ Cloyster

LEGENDARY POKÉMON

REGION
UNOVA

COBALION
Iron Will Pokémon

TYPE: STEEL-FIGHTING

Like its body, Cobalion's heart is tough as steel. Legends say that in the past, it protected Pokémon from harmful people.

How to say it: koh-BAY-lee-un

Height: 6' 11"   **Weight:** 551.2 lbs.

Possible Moves: Quick Attack, Leer, Double Kick, Metal Claw, Take Down, Helping Hand, Retaliate, Iron Head, Sacred Sword, Swords Dance, Quick Guard, Work Up, Metal Burst, Close Combat

Does not evolve

COFAGRIGUS

Coffin Pokémon

TYPE: GHOST

Cofagrigus resembles a coffin covered in solid gold. Stories say that when would-be thieves approach, it opens its lid and traps them inside.

How to say it: kof-uh-GREE-guss

Height: 5' 07"
Weight: 168.7 lbs.

Possible Moves: Astonish, Protect, Disable, Haze, Night Shade, Hex, Will-O-Wisp, Ominous Wind, Curse, Power Split, Guard Split, Scary Face, Shadow Ball, Grudge, Mean Look, Destiny Bond

Yamask   Cofagrigus

COMBEE

Tiny Bee Pokémon

TYPE: BUG-FLYING

Combee are always in search of honey, which they bring to their Vespiquen leader. They cluster together to sleep in a formation that resembles a hive.

How to say it: COMB-bee

Height: 1' 00"   **Weight:** 12.1 lbs.

Possible Moves: Sweet Scent, Gust, Bug Bite, Bug Buzz

Combee   Vespiquen

TYPE: FIRE-FIGHTING

Combusken runs through meadows and up mountains to strengthen its legs. It can deliver kicks at high speed and with crushing power.

How to say it: com-BUS-ken

Height: 2' 11"
Weight: 43.0 lbs.

Possible Moves: Scratch, Growl, Focus Energy, Ember, Double Kick, Peck, Sand Attack, Bulk Up, Quick Attack, Slash, Mirror Move, Sky Uppercut, Flare Blitz

REGION
HOENN

COMBUSKEN
Young Fowl Pokémon

Torchic Combusken Blaziken Mega Blaziken

REGIONS
KALOS (MOUNTAIN), UNOVA

CONKELDURR
Muscular Pokémon

TYPE: FIGHTING

Conkeldurr spin their concrete pillars to attack. It's said that long ago, people first learned about concrete from these Pokémon.

How to say it: kon-KELL-dur

Height: 4' 07"   **Weight:** 191.8 lbs.

Possible Moves: Pound, Leer, Focus Energy, Bide, Low Kick, Rock Throw, Wake-Up Slap, Chip Away, Bulk Up, Rock Slide, Dynamic Punch, Scary Face, Hammer Arm, Stone Edge, Focus Punch, Superpower

Timburr Gurdurr Conkeldurr

75

CORPHISH
Ruffian Pokémon

REGIONS
HOENN,
KALOS
(COASTAL)

TYPE: WATER

Corphish aren't picky about what they eat or where they live. Because of this, their numbers have increased substantially.

How to say it: COR-fish

Height: 2' 00"
Weight: 25.4 lbs.

Possible Moves: Bubble, Harden, Vice Grip, Leer, Bubble Beam, Protect, Knock Off, Taunt, Night Slash, Crabhammer, Swords Dance, Crunch, Guillotine

Corphish   Crawdaunt

CORSOLA
Coral Pokémon

REGIONS
JOHTO,
KALOS
(COASTAL)

TYPE: WATER-ROCK

Corsola prefer warm water and migrate south when it gets cold. When the sun hits their branches just right, they sparkle in many colors.

How to say it: COR-soh-la

Height: 2' 00"
Weight: 11.0 lbs.

Possible Moves: Tackle, Harden, Bubble, Recover, Refresh, Bubble Beam, Ancient Power, Lucky Chant, Spike Cannon, Iron Defense, Rock Blast, Endure, Aqua Ring, Power Gem, Mirror Coat, Earth Power, Flail

Does not evolve

TYPE: GRASS-FAIRY

COTTONEE
Cotton Puff Pokémon

When threatened, it releases cotton from its body to act as a decoy while it escapes. When several Cottonee stick together, they resemble a cloud drifting through the sky.

How to say it: KAHT-ton-ee

Height: 1' 00"
Weight: 1.3 lbs.

Possible Moves: Absorb, Growth, Leech Seed, Stun Spore, Mega Drain, Cotton Spore, Razor Leaf, Poison Powder, Giga Drain, Charm, Helping Hand, Energy Ball, Cotton Guard, Sunny Day, Endeavor, Solar Beam

Cottonee   Whimsicott

TYPE: ROCK-GRASS

CRADILY
Barnacle Pokémon

After evolving, Cradily leaves its rock and wanders freely to find food along the bottom of the sea. It can also anchor its body to withstand rough seas.

How to say it: cray-DILLY

Height: 4' 11"
Weight: 133.2 lbs.

Possible Moves: Astonish, Constrict, Acid, Ingrain, Confuse Ray, Amnesia, Ancient Power, Gastro Acid, Energy Ball, Stockpile, Spit Up, Swallow, Wring Out

Lileep   Cradily

CRANIDOS

Head Butt Pokémon

REGION
SINNOH

TYPE: ROCK

Cranidos lived in the ancient jungle and cleared its path by headbutting trees to make them fall down. It was restored from a fossil.

How to say it: CRANE-ee-dose

Height: 2' 11"
Weight: 69.4 lbs.

Possible Moves: Headbutt, Leer, Focus Energy, Pursuit, Take Down, Scary Face, Assurance, Chip Away, Ancient Power, Zen Headbutt, Screech, Head Smash

Cranidos   Rampardos

CRAWDAUNT

Rogue Pokémon

REGIONS
**HOENN,
KALOS
(CENTRAL)**

TYPE: WATER-DARK

Crawdaunt doesn't tolerate company, and if another Pokémon enters its territory, it's in for a battle. The only time Crawdaunt isn't itching for a fight is just after it sheds its shell, when its soft body is vulnerable.

How to say it: CRAW-daunt

Height: 3' 07"   **Weight:** 72.3 lbs.

Possible Moves: Guillotine, Bubble, Harden, Vice Grip, Leer, Bubble Beam, Protect, Knock Off, Swift, Taunt, Night Slash, Crabhammer, Swords Dance, Crunch

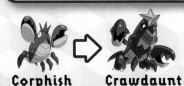

Corphish   Crawdaunt

TYPE: PSYCHIC

The glimmering particles that trail from Cresselia's wings resemble a veil. This Legendary Pokémon, which brings happy dreams, is said to be a symbol of the crescent moon.

How to say it: cres-SEL-ee-uh

Height: 4' 11"
Weight: 188.7 lbs.

Possible Moves: Confusion, Double Team, Safeguard, Mist, Aurora Beam, Future Sight, Slash, Moonlight, Psycho Cut, Psycho Shift, Psychic

REGION
SINNOH

CRESSELIA
Lunar Pokémon

LEGENDARY POKÉMON

Does not evolve

CROAGUNK
Toxic Mouth Pokémon

REGIONS
KALOS
(CENTRAL),
SINNOH

TYPE: POISON-FIGHTING

Croagunk produces its distinctive croaking sound by inflating the poison sacs in its cheeks. The sound often startles an opponent so it can get in a poisonous jab.

How to say it: CROW-gunk

Height: 2' 04"   **Weight:** 50.7 lbs.

Possible Moves: Astonish, Mud-Slap, Poison Sting, Taunt, Pursuit, Feint Attack, Revenge, Swagger, Mud Bomb, Sucker Punch, Venoshock, Nasty Plot, Poison Jab, Sludge Bomb, Belch, Flatter

Croagunk   Toxicroak

CROBAT
Bat Pokémon

REGIONS
JOHTO,
KALOS
(CENTRAL)

TYPE: POISON-FLYING

Crobat's four wings cut through the air with barely a sound. If it's been flying a long way, it starts alternating wings, flapping with one pair and letting the other pair rest.

How to say it: CROW-bat

Height: 5' 11"   **Weight:** 165.3 lbs.

Possible Moves: Cross Poison, Screech, Leech Life, Supersonic, Astonish, Bite, Wing Attack, Confuse Ray, Swift, Air Cutter, Acrobatics, Mean Look, Poison Fang, Haze, Air Slash

Zubat   Golbat   Crobat

CROCONAW
Big Jaw Pokémon

TYPE: WATER

Each of Croconaw's fangs ends in a barb that resembles a fishhook. When it grips a foe in its fearsome jaws, escape is nearly impossible.

How to say it: CROCK-oh-naw

Height: 3' 07"   **Weight:** 55.1 lbs.

Possible Moves: Scratch, Leer, Water Gun, Rage, Bite, Scary Face, Ice Fang, Flail, Crunch, Chip Away, Slash, Screech, Thrash, Aqua Tail, Superpower, Hydro Pump

Totodile   Croconaw   Feraligatr

TYPE: BUG-ROCK

CRUSTLE
Stone Home Pokémon

Because Crustle carries a heavy slab of rock everywhere it goes, its legs are extremely strong. Battles between them are determined by whose rock breaks first.

How to say it: KRUS-tul

Height: 4' 07"   **Weight:** 440.9 lbs.

Possible Moves: Shell Smash, Rock Blast, Withdraw, Sand Attack, Feint Attack, Smack Down, Rock Polish, Bug Bite, Stealth Rock, Rock Slide, Slash, X-Scissor, Flail, Rock Wrecker

Dwebble   Crustle

81

CRYOGONAL
Crystallizing Pokémon

REGIONS
KALOS (MOUNTAIN), UNOVA

TYPE: ICE

Cryogonal's crystalline structure is made of ice formed in snow clouds. With its long chains of ice crystals, it unleashes a freezing attack.

How to say it: kry-AH-guh-nul

Height: 3' 07"
Weight: 326.3 lbs.

Possible Moves: Bind, Ice Shard, Sharpen, Rapid Spin, Icy Wind, Mist, Haze, Aurora Beam, Acid Armor, Ice Beam, Light Screen, Reflect, Slash, Confuse Ray, Recover, Solar Beam, Night Slash, Sheer Cold

Does not evolve

CUBCHOO
Chill Pokémon

REGIONS
KALOS (MOUNTAIN), UNOVA

TYPE: ICE

Even a healthy Cubchoo always has a runny nose. Its sniffles power its freezing attacks.

How to say it: cub-CHOO

Height: 1' 08"
Weight: 18.7 lbs.

Possible Moves: Growl, Powder Snow, Bide, Icy Wind, Play Nice, Fury Swipes, Brine, Endure, Charm, Slash, Flail, Rest, Blizzard, Hail, Thrash, Sheer Cold

Cubchoo   Beartic

CUBONE
Lonely Pokémon

TYPE: GROUND

When Cubone looks at the full moon, it often sees an image of its lost mother. Its tears leave stains on the skull it wears.

How to say it: CUE-bone

Height: 1' 04"
Weight: 14.3 lbs.

Possible Moves: Growl, Tail Whip, Bone Club, Headbutt, Leer, Focus Energy, Bonemerang, Rage, False Swipe, Thrash, Fling, Bone Rush, Endeavor, Double-Edge, Retaliate

Cubone   Marowak

CYNDAQUIL
Fire Mouse Pokémon

TYPE: FIRE

The protective flames on Cyndaquil's back are an indicator of its mood. A sputtering fire means it's tired, while anger makes the flames burn high and hot.

How to say it: SIN-da-kwill

Height: 1' 08"   **Weight:** 17.4 lbs.

Possible Moves: Tackle, Leer, Smokescreen, Ember, Quick Attack, Flame Wheel, Defense Curl, Flame Charge, Swift, Lava Plume, Flamethrower, Inferno, Rollout, Double-Edge

Cyndaquil   Quilava   Typhlosion

DARKRAI
Pitch-Black Pokémon

MYTHICAL POKÉMON

TYPE: DARK

Darkrai defends its territory by sending intruders into a deep sleep, where they are tormented by terrible nightmares.

How to say it: DARK-rye

Height: 4' 11" **Weight:** 111.3 lbs.

Possible Moves: Ominous Wind, Disable, Quick Attack, Hypnosis, Feint Attack, Nightmare, Double Team, Haze, Nasty Plot, Dream Eater, Dark Pulse

Does not evolve

REGION
UNOVA

DARMANITAN
Blazing Pokémon

TYPE: FIRE

Fueled by its internal fire, Darmanitan can throw a punch hard enough to destroy a dump truck. To recover from a serious battle, it turns to stone so it can meditate undisturbed.

How to say it: dar-MAN-ih-tan

Height: 4' 03"
Weight: 204.8 lbs.

Possible Moves: Tackle, Rollout, Incinerate, Rage, Fire Fang, Headbutt, Swagger, Facade, Fire Punch, Work Up, Thrash, Belly Drum, Flare Blitz, Hammer Arm, Taunt, Superpower, Overheat

Darumaka   Darmanitan

REGION
UNOVA

DARUMAKA
Zen Charm Pokémon

TYPE: FIRE

Darumaka tucks its hands and feet into its body to sleep, but its internal fire still burns at searing temperatures. Long ago, people used its intense body heat to warm themselves.

How to say it: dah-roo-MAH-kuh

Height: 2' 00"   **Weight:** 82.7 lbs.

Possible Moves: Tackle, Rollout, Incinerate, Rage, Fire Fang, Headbutt, Uproar, Facade, Fire Punch, Work Up, Thrash, Belly Drum, Flare Blitz, Taunt, Superpower, Overheat

Darumaka   Darmanitan

DEDENNE

Antenna Pokémon

TYPE: ELECTRIC-FAIRY

Dedenne uses its whiskers like antennae to communicate over long distances using electrical waves. It can soak up electricity through its tail.

How to say it: deh-DEN-nay

Height: 0' 08"
Weight: 4.9 lbs.

Possible Moves: Tackle, Tail Whip, Thunder Shock, Charge, Charm, Parabolic Charge, Nuzzle, Thunder Wave, Volt Switch, Rest, Snore, Charge Beam, Entrainment, Play Rough, Thunder, Discharge

Does not evolve

DEERLING

Season Pokémon

TYPE: NORMAL-GRASS

Deerling's fur changes with the seasons. Shifts in temperature and humidity affect the color and even the scent of its fur.

How to say it: DEER-ling

Height: 2' 00"   **Weight:** 43.0 lbs.

Possible Moves: Tackle, Camouflage, Growl, Sand Attack, Double Kick, Leech Seed, Feint Attack, Take Down, Jump Kick, Aromatherapy, Energy Ball, Charm, Nature Power, Double-Edge, Solar Beam

**Autumn
Form**

**Summer
Form**

**Winter
Form**

**Spring
Form**

Deerling   Sawsbuck

DEINO
Irate Pokémon

TYPE: DARK-DRAGON

Deino can't see, so they explore their surroundings by biting and crashing into things. Because of this, they are often covered in cuts and scratches.

How to say it: DY-noh

Height: 2' 07"
Weight: 38.1 lbs.

Possible Moves: Tackle, Dragon Rage, Focus Energy, Bite, Headbutt, Dragon Breath, Roar, Crunch, Slam, Dragon Pulse, Work Up, Dragon Rush, Body Slam, Scary Face, Hyper Voice, Outrage

Deino   Zweilous   Hydreigon

TYPE: NORMAL

Delcatty lives according to its own whims, eating and sleeping as the mood strikes it. If awakened by another Pokémon, it moves elsewhere to continue its nap.

How to say it: dell-CAT-tee

Height: 3' 07"
Weight: 71.9 lbs.

Possible Moves: Fake Out, Attract, Sing, Double Slap

DELCATTY
Prim Pokémon

Skitty   Delcatty

DELIBIRD
Delivery Pokémon

REGIONS
JOHTO, KALOS (MOUNTAIN)

TYPE: ICE-FLYING

With Delibird's help, a famous climber was able to summit the tallest mountain in the world! This Pokémon always stores extra food in its rolled-up tail and shares it with travelers.

How to say it: DELL-ee-bird

Height: 2' 11"
Weight: 35.3 lbs.

Possible Move: Present

Does not evolve

DELPHOX
Fox Pokémon

REGION
KALOS (CENTRAL)

TYPE: FIRE-PSYCHIC

The mystical Delphox uses a flaming branch as a focus for its psychic visions. When it gazes into the fire, it can see the future.

How to say it: DELL-fox

Height: 4' 11"   **Weight:** 86.0 lbs.

Possible Moves: Future Sight, Role Play, Switcheroo, Shadow Ball, Scratch, Tail Whip, Ember, Howl, Flame Charge, Psybeam, Fire Spin, Lucky Chant, Light Screen, Psyshock, Mystical Fire, Flamethrower, Will-O-Wisp, Psychic, Sunny Day, Magic Room, Fire Blast

Fennekin ⇨ Braixen ⇨ Delphox

TYPE: PSYCHIC

From the crystal on its chest, Deoxys can shoot out laser beams. This highly intelligent Pokémon came into being when a virus mutated during a fall from space.

How to say it: dee-OCKS-iss

Height: 5' 07"   **Weight:** 134.0 lbs.

Possible Moves: Leer, Wrap, Night Shade, Teleport, Knock Off, Pursuit, Psychic, Snatch, Psycho Shift, Zen Headbutt, Cosmic Power, Recover, Hyper Beam

Does not evolve

DEWGONG

Sea Lion Pokémon

REGION
KANTO

TYPE: WATER-ICE

Long ago, a sailor saw Dewgong taking a nap on the ice and thought it was a mermaid. It sleeps best in the bitter cold.

How to say it: DOO-gong

Height: 5' 07"
Weight: 264.6 lbs.

Possible Moves: Headbutt, Growl, Signal Beam, Icy Wind, Encore, Ice Shard, Rest, Aqua Ring, Aurora Beam, Aqua Jet, Brine, Sheer Cold, Take Down, Dive, Aqua Tail, Ice Beam, Safeguard, Hail

Seel **Dewgong**

DEWOTT

Discipline Pokémon

REGION
UNOVA

TYPE: WATER

Dewott must undergo disciplined training to master the flowing techniques it uses when wielding its two scalchops in battle.

How to say it: DOO-wot

Height: 2' 07"   **Weight:** 54.0 lbs.

Possible Moves: Tackle, Tail Whip, Water Gun, Water Sport, Focus Energy, Razor Shell, Fury Cutter, Water Pulse, Revenge, Aqua Jet, Encore, Aqua Tail, Retaliate, Swords Dance, Hydro Pump

Oshawott **Dewott** **Samurott**

DIALGA
Temporal Pokémon

TYPE: STEEL-DRAGON

It is said Dialga can control time with its mighty roar. In ancient times, it was revered as a legend.

How to say it: dee-AL-guh

Height: 17' 09"
Weight: 1,505.8 lbs.

Possible Moves: Dragon Breath, Scary Face, Metal Claw, Ancient Power, Slash, Power Gem, Metal Burst, Dragon Claw, Earth Power, Aura Sphere, Iron Tail, Flash Cannon

LEGENDARY POKÉMON

Does not evolve

DIANCIE
Jewel Pokémon

MYTHICAL POKÉMON

TYPE: ROCK-FAIRY

According to myth, when Carbink suddenly transforms into Diancie, its dazzling appearance is the most beautiful sight in existence. It has the power to compress carbon from the atmosphere, forming diamonds between its hands.

How to say it: die-AHN-see

Height: 2' 04"
Weight: 19.4 lbs.

Possible Moves: Tackle, Harden, Rock Throw, Sharpen, Smack Down, Reflect, Stealth Rock, Guard Split, Ancient Power, Flail, Skill Swap, Trick Room, Stone Edge, Moonblast, Diamond Storm, Light Screen, Safeguard

MEGA DIANCIE
Jewel Pokémon

TYPE: ROCK-FAIRY

Height: 3' 07"
Weight: 61.3 lbs.

Does not evolve

TYPE: NORMAL-GROUND

Diggersby can use their ears like excavators to move heavy boulders. Construction workers like having them around.

How to say it: DIH-gurz-bee

Height: 3' 03"   **Weight:** 93.5 lbs.

Possible Moves: Hammer Arm, Rototiller, Bulldoze, Swords Dance, Tackle, Agility, Leer, Quick Attack, Mud-Slap, Take Down, Mud Shot, Double Kick, Odor Sleuth, Flail, Dig, Bounce, Super Fang, Facade, Earthquake

DIGGERSBY
Digging Pokémon

Bunnelby   **Diggersby**

TYPE: GROUND

Farmers love having Diglett around. As these Pokémon burrow through the ground, they leave the soil in perfect condition for planting.

How to say it: DIG-let

Height: 0' 08"
Weight: 1.8 lbs.

Possible Moves: Scratch, Sand Attack, Growl, Astonish, Mud-Slap, Magnitude, Bulldoze, Sucker Punch, Mud Bomb, Earth Power, Dig, Slash, Earthquake, Fissure

DIGLETT
Mole Pokémon

Diglett   **Dugtrio**

DITTO
Transform Pokémon

TYPE: NORMAL

Ditto can alter the structure of its cells to change its shape. This works best if it has an example to copy—if it tries to copy another shape from memory, it sometimes gets things wrong.

How to say it: DIT-toe

Height: 1' 00"
Weight: 8.8 lbs.

Possible Move: Transform

Does not evolve

DODRIO
Triple Bird Pokémon

REGIONS
KALOS (CENTRAL), KANTO

TYPE: NORMAL-FLYING

Dodrio has three heads, three hearts, and three sets of lungs. It can keep watch in all directions and run a long way without getting tired.

How to say it: doe-DREE-oh

Height: 5' 11"
Weight: 187.8 lbs.

Possible Moves: Pluck, Peck, Growl, Quick Attack, Rage, Fury Attack, Pursuit, Uproar, Acupressure, Tri Attack, Agility, Drill Peck, Endeavor, Thrash

Doduo   Dodrio

DODUO
Twin Bird Pokémon

TYPE: NORMAL-FLYING

While one of Doduo's heads sleeps, the other stays alert to watch for danger. Its brains are identical.

How to say it: doe-DOO-oh

Height: 4' 07" **Weight:** 86.4 lbs.

Possible Moves: Peck, Growl, Quick Attack, Rage, Fury Attack, Pursuit, Uproar, Acupressure, Double Hit, Agility, Drill Peck, Endeavor, Thrash

Doduo   Dodrio

TYPE: NORMAL

Donphan curls up in a ball to attack with a high-speed rolling tackle. Such an attack can knock down a house!

How to say it: DON-fan

Height: 3' 07"
Weight: 264.6 lbs.

Possible Moves: Fire Fang, Thunder Fang, Horn Attack, Growl, Defense Curl, Bulldoze, Rapid Spin, Knock Off, Rollout, Magnitude, Slam, Fury Attack, Assurance, Scary Face, Earthquake, Giga Impact

DONPHAN
Armor Pokémon

Phanpy   Donphan

DOUBLADE
Sword Pokémon

TYPE: STEEL-GHOST

The two swords that make up Doublade's body fight together in intricate slashing patterns that bewilder even accomplished swordsmen.

How to say it: DUH-blade

Height: 2' 07"
Weight: 9.9 lbs.

Possible Moves: Tackle, Swords Dance, Fury Cutter, Metal Sound, Pursuit, Autotomize, Shadow Sneak, Aerial Ace, Retaliate, Slash, Iron Defense, Night Slash, Power Trick, Iron Head, Sacred Sword

Honedge ⇨ Doublade ⇨ Aegislash

DRAGALGE
Mock Kelp Pokémon

TYPE: POISON-DRAGON

Toxic and territorial, Dragalge defend their homes from anything that enters. Even large ships aren't safe from their poison.

How to say it: druh-GAL-jee

Height: 5' 11"
Weight: 179.7 lbs.

Possible Moves: Dragon Tail, Twister, Tackle, Smokescreen, Water Gun, Feint Attack, Tail Whip, Bubble, Acid, Camouflage, Poison Tail, Water Pulse, Double Team, Toxic, Aqua Tail, Sludge Bomb, Hydro Pump, Dragon Pulse

Skrelp ⇨ Dragalge

DRAGONAIR
Dragon Pokémon

TYPE: DRAGON

Dragonair's internal energy can be discharged from special crystals on its body. Apparently, when this happens, it can change the local weather.

How to say it: DRAG-gon-AIR

Height: 13' 01"   **Weight:** 36.4 lbs.

Possible Moves: Wrap, Leer, Thunder Wave, Twister, Dragon Rage, Slam, Agility, Dragon Tail, Aqua Tail, Dragon Rush, Safeguard, Dragon Dance, Outrage, Hyper Beam

Dratini   Dragonair   Dragonite

DRAGONITE
Dragon Pokémon

TYPE: DRAGON-FLYING

Dragonite can fly around the whole world in less than a day. It lives far out at sea and comes to the aid of wrecked ships.

How to say it: DRAG-gon-ite

Height: 7' 03"
Weight: 463.0 lbs.

Possible Moves: Hurricane, Fire Punch, Thunder Punch, Roost, Wrap, Leer, Thunder Wave, Twister, Dragon Rage, Slam, Agility, Dragon Tail, Aqua Tail, Dragon Rush, Safeguard, Wing Attack, Dragon Dance, Outrage, Hyper Beam

Dratini → Dragonair → Dragonite

DRAPION
Ogre Scorpion Pokémon

TYPE: POISON-DARK

Drapion's strong arms could tear a car into scrap metal. The claws on its arms and tail are extremely toxic.

How to say it: DRAP-ee-on

Height: 4' 03"
Weight: 135.6 lbs.

Possible Moves: Thunder Fang, Ice Fang, Fire Fang, Bite, Poison Sting, Leer, Knock Off, Pin Missile, Acupressure, Pursuit, Bug Bite, Poison Fang, Venoshock, Hone Claws, Toxic Spikes, Night Slash, Scary Face, Crunch, Fell Stinger, Cross Poison

Skorupi → Drapion

DRATINI
Dragon Pokémon

TYPE: DRAGON

As Dratini grows, it is constantly in molt, shedding its skin to accommodate the life energy that builds up within it.

How to say it: dra-TEE-nee

Height: 5' 11"
Weight: 7.3 lbs.

Possible Moves: Wrap, Leer, Thunder Wave, Twister, Dragon Rage, Slam, Agility, Dragon Tail, Aqua Tail, Dragon Rush, Safeguard, Dragon Dance, Outrage, Hyper Beam

Dratini   Dragonair   Dragonite

DRIFBLIM
Blimp Pokémon

TYPE: GHOST-FLYING

During the day, Drifblim tend to be sleepy. They take flight at dusk, but since they can't control their direction, they'll drift away wherever the wind blows them.

How to say it: DRIFF-blim

Height: 3' 11"   **Weight:** 33.1 lbs.

Possible Moves: Phantom Force, Constrict, Minimize, Astonish, Gust, Focus Energy, Payback, Ominous Wind, Stockpile, Hex, Swallow, Spit Up, Shadow Ball, Amnesia, Baton Pass, Explosion

Drifloon   Drifblim

99

DRIFLOON
Balloon Pokémon

TYPE: GHOST-FLYING

Known as "the Signpost for Wandering Spirits," Drifloon itself was formed by spirits. It prefers humid weather and is happiest when it's floating through damp air.

How to say it: DRIFF-loon

Height: 1' 04"
Weight: 2.6 lbs.

Possible Moves: Constrict, Minimize, Astonish, Gust, Focus Energy, Payback, Ominous Wind, Stockpile, Hex, Swallow, Spit Up, Shadow Ball, Amnesia, Baton Pass, Explosion

Drifloon   Drifblim

DRILBUR
Mole Pokémon

TYPE: GROUND

Drilbur bores through the ground by bringing its claws together to form a sharp point and rotating its entire body. In this way, it can travel underground as fast as thirty MPH.

How to say it: DRIL-bur

Height: 1' 00"   **Weight:** 18.7 lbs.

Possible Moves: Scratch, Mud Sport, Rapid Spin, Mud-Slap, Fury Swipes, Metal Claw, Dig, Hone Claws, Slash, Rock Slide, Earthquake, Swords Dance, Sandstorm, Drill Run, Fissure

Drilbur   Excadrill

TYPE: PSYCHIC

Ever wake up with an itchy nose? It might be because a Drowzee was lurking nearby, trying to draw out your dreams.

How to say it: DROW-zee

Height: 3' 03"
Weight: 71.4 lbs.

Possible Moves: Pound, Hypnosis, Disable, Confusion, Headbutt, Poison Gas, Meditate, Psybeam, Psych Up, Synchronoise, Zen Headbutt, Swagger, Psychic, Nasty Plot, Psyshock, Future Sight

DROWZEE
Hypnosis Pokémon

Drowzee   **Hypno**

TYPE: DRAGON

Druddigon can't move if it gets too cold, so it soaks up the sun with its wings. It can navigate tight caves at a brisk pace.

How to say it: DRUD-dih-gahn

Height: 5' 03"
Weight: 306.4 lbs.

Possible Moves: Leer, Scratch, Hone Claws, Bite, Scary Face, Dragon Rage, Slash, Crunch, Dragon Claw, Chip Away, Revenge, Night Slash, Dragon Tail, Rock Climb, Superpower, Outrage

DRUDDIGON
Cave Pokémon

Does not evolve

DUCKLETT
Water Bird Pokémon

REGIONS
KALOS (CENTRAL), UNOVA

TYPE: WATER-FLYING

Skilled swimmers, Ducklett dive underwater in search of delicious peat moss. When enemies approach, they kick up water with their wings to cover their retreat.

How to say it: DUK-lit

Height: 1' 08"
Weight: 12.1 lbs.

Possible Moves: Water Gun, Water Sport, Defog, Wing Attack, Water Pulse, Aerial Ace, Bubble Beam, Feather Dance, Aqua Ring, Air Slash, Roost, Rain Dance, Tailwind, Brave Bird, Hurricane

Ducklett   Swanna

DUGTRIO
Mole Pokémon

REGIONS
KALOS (MOUNTAIN), KANTO

TYPE: GROUND

When it comes to digging, Dugtrio knows that three heads are better than one. The triplets think alike and work together.

How to say it: dug-TREE-oh

Height: 2' 04"   **Weight:** 73.4 lbs.

Possible Moves: Rototiller, Night Slash, Tri Attack, Scratch, Sand Attack, Growl, Astonish, Mud-Slap, Magnitude, Bulldoze, Sucker Punch, Sand Tomb, Mud Bomb, Earth Power, Dig, Slash, Earthquake, Fissure

Diglett   Dugtrio

TYPE: NORMAL

Dunsparce uses its tail like a drill to dig a burrow, scooting backward into the tunnel. Its underground nest is like a maze.

How to say it: DUN-sparce

Height: 4' 11"
Weight: 30.9 lbs.

Possible Moves: Rage, Defense Curl, Rollout, Spite, Pursuit, Screech, Yawn, Ancient Power, Take Down, Roost, Glare, Dig, Double-Edge, Coil, Endure, Drill Run, Endeavor, Flail

REGIONS
JOHTO, KALOS (CENTRAL)

DUNSPARCE
Land Snake Pokémon

Does not evolve

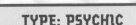

TYPE: PSYCHIC

Duosion's brain is divided into two, so sometimes it tries to do two different things at the same time. When the brains are thinking together, Duosion's psychic power is at its strongest.

How to say it: doo-OH-zhun

Height: 2' 00"   **Weight:** 17.6 lbs.

Possible Moves: Psywave, Reflect, Rollout, Snatch, Hidden Power, Light Screen, Charm, Recover, Psyshock, Endeavor, Future Sight, Pain Split, Psychic, Skill Swap, Heal Block, Wonder Room

REGIONS
KALOS (COASTAL), UNOVA

DUOSION
Mitosis Pokémon

Solosis   **Duosion**   **Reuniclus**

DURANT
Iron Ant Pokémon

TYPE: BUG-STEEL

The heavily armored Durant work together to keep attackers away from their colony. Durant and Heatmor are natural enemies.

How to say it: dur-ANT

Height: 1' 00"
Weight: 72.8 lbs.

Possible Moves:
Guillotine, Iron Defense, Metal Sound, Vice Grip, Sand Attack, Fury Cutter, Bite, Agility, Metal Claw, Bug Bite, Crunch, Iron Head, Dig, Entrainment, X-Scissor

Does not evolve

DUSCLOPS
Beckon Pokémon

REGION HOENN

TYPE: GHOST

There is no escape for anything absorbed into the hollow body of Dusclops. When it waves its hands and focuses its single eye, it can entrance a foe to do its will.

How to say it: DUS-klops

Height: 5' 03"   **Weight:** 67.5 lbs.

Possible Moves: Fire Punch, Ice Punch, Thunder Punch, Gravity, Bind, Leer, Night Shade, Disable, Foresight, Astonish, Confuse Ray, Shadow Sneak, Pursuit, Curse, Will-O-Wisp, Shadow Punch, Hex, Mean Look, Payback, Future Sight

Duskull   Dusclops   Dusknoir

TYPE: GHOST

Dusknoir senses signals from the spirit world with the antenna on its head. The signals tell it to guide lost spirits . . . and sometimes people.

How to say it: DUSK-nwar

Height: 7' 03"   **Weight:** 235.0 lbs.

Possible Moves: Fire Punch, Ice Punch, Thunder Punch, Gravity, Bind, Leer, Night Shade, Disable, Foresight, Astonish, Confuse Ray, Shadow Sneak, Pursuit, Curse, Will-O-Wisp, Shadow Punch, Hex, Mean Look, Payback, Future Sight

DUSKNOIR
Gripper Pokémon

Duskull   Dusclops   Dusknoir

DUSKULL
Requiem Pokémon

TYPE: GHOST

Parents sometimes threaten misbehaving children with a visit from Duskull. It can pass through walls in pursuit of its target, but gives up the chase at sunrise.

How to say it: DUS-kull

Height: 2' 07"   **Weight:** 33.1 lbs.

Possible Moves: Leer, Night Shade, Disable, Foresight, Astonish, Confuse Ray, Shadow Sneak, Pursuit, Curse, Will-O-Wisp, Hex, Mean Look, Payback, Future Sight

Duskull   Dusclops   Dusknoir

DUSTOX

Poison Moth Pokémon

REGION
HOENN

TYPE: BUG-POISON

City lights attract Dustox in swarms. This is unfortunate, because their wings scatter poisonous dust, and their feeding habits quickly strip trees bare.

How to say it: DUS-tocks

Height: 3' 11"
Weight: 69.7 lbs.

Possible Moves: Confusion, Gust, Protect, Moonlight, Psybeam, Whirlwind, Light Screen, Silver Wind, Toxic, Bug Buzz, Quiver Dance

Wurmple   Cascoon   Dustox

DWEBBLE

Rock Inn Pokémon

REGIONS
KALOS (COASTAL), UNOVA

TYPE: BUG-ROCK

Using a special liquid from its mouth, Dwebble hollows out a rock to use as its shell. It becomes very anxious without a proper rock.

How to say it: DWEHB-bul

Height: 1' 00"
Weight: 32.0 lbs.

Possible Moves: Fury Cutter, Rock Blast, Withdraw, Sand Attack, Feint Attack, Smack Down, Rock Polish, Bug Bite, Stealth Rock, Rock Slide, Slash, X-Scissor, Shell Smash, Flail, Rock Wrecker

Dwebble   Crustle

EELEKTRIK
Elefish Pokémon

TYPE: ELECTRIC

Eelektrik wraps its long body around its opponent and gives off a paralyzing electric shock from the round markings on its sides. Its appetite is quite large.

How to say it: ee-LEK-trik

Height: 3' 11"
Weight: 48.5 lbs.

Possible Moves: Headbutt, Thunder Wave, Spark, Charge Beam, Bind, Acid, Discharge, Crunch, Thunderbolt, Acid Spray, Coil, Wild Charge, Gastro Acid, Zap Cannon, Thrash

Tynamo   Eelektrik   Eelektross

EELEKTROSS
Elefish Pokémon

TYPE: ELECTRIC

With their gaping sucker mouths, electrically charged fangs, and long arms that allow them to crawl up on land, Eelektross are dangerous opponents.

How to say it: ee-LEK-trahs

Height: 6' 11"
Weight: 177.5 lbs.

Possible Moves: Crush Claw, Headbutt, Acid, Discharge, Crunch

Tynamo   Eelektrik   Eelektross

EEVEE
Evolution Pokémon

TYPE: NORMAL

The amazingly adaptive Eevee can evolve into many different Pokémon, depending on its environment. This allows it to withstand harsh conditions.

How to say it: EE-vee

Height: 1' 00"
Weight: 14.3 lbs.

Possible Moves: Helping Hand, Growl, Tackle, Tail Whip, Sand Attack, Baby-Doll Eyes, Swift, Quick Attack, Bite, Refresh, Covet, Take Down, Charm, Baton Pass, Double-Edge, Last Resort, Trump Card

Jolteon

Flareon

Glaceon

Vaporeon

Eevee

Espeon

Umbreon

Leafeon

Sylveon

TYPE: POISON

When Ekans rests, it coils its long body up into a spiral. In this position, it can quickly raise its head to challenge a foe.

How to say it: ECK-kins

Height: 6' 07"
Weight: 15.2 lbs.

Possible Moves: Wrap, Leer, Poison Sting, Bite, Glare, Screech, Acid, Stockpile, Swallow, Spit Up, Acid Spray, Mud Bomb, Gastro Acid, Belch, Haze, Coil, Gunk Shot

EKANS
Snake Pokémon

Ekans   **Arbok**

ELECTABUZZ
Electric Pokémon

TYPE: ELECTRIC

During thunderstorms, Electabuzz climb to high places, hoping to be struck by lightning. Because they can absorb the bolts safely, they sometimes act as lightning rods.

How to say it: ee-LECK-tuh-buzz

Height: 3' 07"   **Weight:** 66.1 lbs.

Possible Moves: Quick Attack, Leer, Thunder Shock, Low Kick, Swift, Shock Wave, Light Screen, Electro Ball, Thunder Punch, Discharge, Thunderbolt, Screech, Thunder

Elekid   **Electabuzz**   **Electivire**

ELECTIVIRE

Thunderbolt Pokémon

REGION
SINNOH

TYPE: ELECTRIC

Electricity crackles between Electivire's horns and the tips of its tails. When it forms a circuit with its tails, its opponent receives a powerful shock.

How to say it: e-LECT-uh-vire

Height: 5' 11"
Weight: 305.6 lbs.

Possible Moves: Fire Punch, Quick Attack, Leer, Thunder Shock, Low Kick, Swift, Shock Wave, Light Screen, Electro Ball, Thunder Punch, Discharge, Thunderbolt, Screech, Thunder, Giga Impact

Elekid   Electabuzz   Electivire

ELECTRIKE

Lightning Pokémon

REGIONS
**HOENN,
KALOS
(COASTAL)**

TYPE: ELECTRIC

Electrike's long fur stores up static electricity when it runs at blinding speed. It can use this electricity to charge up its leg muscles and run even faster.

How to say it: eh-LEK-trike

Height: 2' 00"
Weight: 33.5 lbs.

Possible Moves: Tackle, Thunder Wave, Leer, Howl, Quick Attack, Spark, Odor Sleuth, Bite, Thunder Fang, Roar, Discharge, Charge, Wild Charge, Thunder

Electrike   Manectric   Mega Manectric

TYPE: ELECTRIC

Electrode feeds by absorbing electricity, often from power plants or lightning storms. If it eats too much at once, it explodes.

How to say it: ee-LECK-trode

Height: 3' 11"
Weight: 146.8 lbs.

Possible Moves: Magnetic Flux, Charge, Tackle, Sonic Boom, Spark, Eerie Impulse, Rollout, Screech, Charge Beam, Light Screen, Electro Ball, Self-Destruct, Swift, Magnet Rise, Gyro Ball, Explosion, Mirror Coat

REGIONS
KALOS
(MOUNTAIN),
KANTO

ELECTRODE
Ball Pokémon

Voltorb **Electrode**

REGION
JOHTO

ELEKID
Electric Pokémon

TYPE: ELECTRIC

Elekid tries to avoid touching metal, because doing so discharges the electricity it stores inside its body. If that happens, it spins its arms to charge up again.

How to say it: el-EH-kid

Height: 2' 00"   **Weight:** 51.8 lbs.

Possible Moves: Quick Attack, Leer, Thunder Shock, Low Kick, Swift, Shock Wave, Light Screen, Electro Ball, Thunder Punch, Discharge, Thunderbolt, Screech, Thunder

Elekid **Electabuzz** **Electivire**

ELGYEM

Cerebral Pokémon

TYPE: PSYCHIC

It's said Elgyem were first discovered in the desert after a UFO crashed there fifty years ago. Their psychic power can compress an opponent's brain and cause terrible headaches.

How to say it: ELL-jee-ehm

Height: 1' 08"
Weight: 19.8 lbs.

Possible Moves: Confusion, Growl, Heal Block, Miracle Eye, Psybeam, Headbutt, Hidden Power, Imprison, Simple Beam, Zen Headbutt, Psych Up, Psychic, Calm Mind, Recover, Guard Split, Power Split, Synchronoise, Wonder Room

Elgyem   Beheeyem

EMBOAR

Mega Fire Pig Pokémon

TYPE: FIRE-FIGHTING

With the fiery beard that covers its chin, Emboar can set its fists ablaze and throw flaming punches. Its battle moves are speedy and powerful.

How to say it: EHM-bohr

Height: 5' 03"   **Weight:** 330.7 lbs.

Possible Moves: Hammer Arm, Tackle, Tail Whip, Ember, Odor Sleuth, Defense Curl, Flame Charge, Arm Thrust, Smog, Rollout, Take Down, Heat Crash, Assurance, Flamethrower, Head Smash, Roar, Flare Blitz

Tepig   Pignite   Emboar

TYPE: ELECTRIC-FLYING

When Emolga stretches out its limbs, the membrane connecting them spreads like a cape and allows it to glide through the air. It makes its abode high in the trees.

How to say it: ee-MAHL-guh

Height: 1' 04"
Weight: 11.0 lbs.

Possible Moves: Thunder Shock, Quick Attack, Tail Whip, Charge, Spark, Nuzzle, Pursuit, Double Team, Shock Wave, Electro Ball, Acrobatics, Light Screen, Encore, Volt Switch, Agility, Discharge

REGIONS
KALOS (COASTAL), UNOVA

EMOLGA
Sky Squirrel Pokémon

Does not evolve

TYPE: WATER-STEEL

With the sharp edges of its wings, Empoleon can slash through drifting ice as it swims faster than a speedboat. The length of its trident-like horns indicates its power.

How to say it: em-PO-lee-on

Height: 5' 07"   **Weight:** 186.3 lbs.

Possible Moves: Tackle, Growl, Bubble, Swords Dance, Peck, Metal Claw, Bubble Beam, Swagger, Fury Attack, Brine, Aqua Jet, Whirlpool, Mist, Drill Peck, Hydro Pump

REGION
SINNOH

EMPOLEON
Emperor Pokémon

Piplup   Prinplup   Empoleon

ENTEI
Volcano Pokémon

REGION
JOHTO

LEGENDARY POKÉMON

TYPE: FIRE

People say that Entei came into being when a volcano erupted. This Legendary Pokémon carries the heat of magma in its fiery heart.

How to say it: EN-tay

Height: 6' 11"   **Weight:** 436.5 lbs.

Possible Moves: Bite, Leer, Ember, Roar, Fire Spin, Stomp, Flamethrower, Swagger, Fire Fang, Lava Plume, Extrasensory, Fire Blast, Calm Mind, Eruption

Does not evolve

TYPE: BUG-STEEL

ESCAVALIER
Cavalry Pokémon

The stolen Shelmet shell protects Escavalier's body like armor. It uses its double lances to attack.

How to say it: ess-KAH-vuh-LEER

Height: 3' 03"
Weight: 72.8 lbs.

Possible Moves: Double-Edge, Fell Stinger, Peck, Leer, Quick Guard, Twineedle, Fury Attack, Headbutt, False Swipe, Bug Buzz, Slash, Iron Head, Iron Defense, X-Scissor, Reversal, Swords Dance, Giga Impact

Karrablast → **Escavalier**

TYPE: PSYCHIC

ESPEON
Sun Pokémon

When Espeon finds its Trainer worthy, its loyalty knows no bounds. It apparently learned to predict danger so it could keep its Trainer safe.

How to say it: ESS-pee-on

Height: 2' 11"
Weight: 58.4 lbs.

Possible Moves: Helping Hand, Tackle, Tail Whip, Sand Attack, Confusion, Quick Attack, Swift, Psybeam, Future Sight, Psych Up, Morning Sun, Psychic, Last Resort, Power Swap

Eevee → **Espeon**

ESPURR
Restraint Pokémon

REGION
KALOS (CENTRAL)

TYPE: PSYCHIC

Espurr emits powerful psychic energy from organs in its ears. It has to fold its ears down to keep the power contained.

How to say it: ESS-purr

Height: 1' 00"   **Weight:** 7.7 lbs.

Possible Moves: Scratch, Leer, Covet, Confusion, Light Screen, Psybeam, Fake Out, Disarming Voice, Psyshock

Espurr   **Meowstic**

EXCADRILL
Subterrene Pokémon

REGION
UNOVA

TYPE: GROUND-STEEL

Excadrill live several hundred feet underground, where they use their strong steel claws to dig out nests and tunnels. Sometimes that causes big trouble for subway systems.

How to say it: EKS-kuh-dril

Height: 2' 04"   **Weight:** 89.1 lbs.

Possible Moves: Scratch, Mud Sport, Rapid Spin, Mud-Slap, Fury Swipes, Metal Claw, Dig, Hone Claws, Slash, Rock Slide, Horn Drill, Earthquake, Swords Dance, Sandstorm, Drill Run, Fissure

Drilbur   **Excadrill**

TYPE: GRASS-PSYCHIC

The six eggs that make up Exeggcute's body spin around a common center. When the eggs begin to crack, this Pokémon is ready to evolve.

How to say it: ECKS-egg-cute

Height: 1' 04"   **Weight:** 5.5 lbs.

Possible Moves: Barrage, Uproar, Hypnosis, Reflect, Leech Seed, Bullet Seed, Stun Spore, Poison Powder, Sleep Powder, Confusion, Worry Seed, Natural Gift, Solar Beam, Extrasensory, Bestow

REGIONS
KALOS (COASTAL), KANTO

EXEGGCUTE
Egg Pokémon

Exeggcute   Exeggutor

TYPE: GRASS-PSYCHIC

A tropical Pokémon, Exeggutor has three heads that keep growing when they get enough sun. Exeggcute are thought to form from the fallen heads of Exeggutor.

How to say it: ecks-EGG-u-tore

Height: 6' 07"
Weight: 264.6 lbs.

Possible Moves: Seed Bomb, Barrage, Hypnosis, Confusion, Stomp, Psyshock, Egg Bomb, Wood Hammer, Leaf Storm

REGIONS
KALOS (COASTAL), KANTO

EXEGGUTOR
Coconut Pokémon

Exeggcute   Exeggutor

EXPLOUD
Loud Noise Pokémon

REGIONS
**HOENN,
KALOS
(CENTRAL)**

TYPE: NORMAL

When Exploud takes a deep breath through the tubes that cover its body, watch out! It's about to unleash a thunderous bellow that will shake the ground around it.

How to say it: ecks-PLOWD

Height: 4' 11"   **Weight:** 185.2 lbs.

Possible Moves: Boomburst, Ice Fang, Fire Fang, Thunder Fang, Pound, Uproar, Astonish, Howl, Bite, Supersonic, Stomp, Screech, Crunch, Roar, Synchronoise, Rest, Sleep Talk, Hyper Voice, Hyper Beam

Whismur   Loudred   Exploud

TYPE: NORMAL-FLYING

Farfetch'd always carries its trusty plant stalk. Sometimes, two of them will fight over a superior stalk.

How to say it: FAR-fetched

Height: 2' 07"
Weight: 33.1 lbs.

Possible Moves: Brave Bird, Poison Jab, Peck, Sand Attack, Leer, Fury Cutter, Fury Attack, Aerial Ace, Knock Off, Slash, Air Cutter, Swords Dance, Agility, Night Slash, Acrobatics, Feint, False Swipe, Air Slash

REGIONS KALOS (CENTRAL), KANTO

FARFETCH'D
Wild Duck Pokémon

Does not evolve

TYPE: NORMAL-FLYING

Fearow's long, thin beak is the perfect tool for digging up food from the dirt or catching it in the water.

How to say it: FEER-oh

Height: 3' 11"
Weight: 83.8 lbs.

Possible Moves: Drill Run, Pluck, Peck, Growl, Leer, Fury Attack, Pursuit, Aerial Ace, Mirror Move, Agility, Assurance, Roost, Drill Peck

REGIONS KALOS (MOUNTAIN), KANTO

FEAROW
Beak Pokémon

Spearow   Fearow

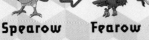

FEEBAS

Fish Pokémon

TYPE: WATER

Feebas isn't much to look at, but its hardy nature and persistent survival instinct let it live in any aquatic environment.

How to say it: FEE-bass

Height: 2' 00"
Weight: 16.3 lbs.

Possible Moves: Splash, Tackle, Flail

Feebas ⇨ Milotic

FENNEKIN

Fox Pokémon

TYPE: FIRE

Searing heat radiates from Fennekin's large ears to keep opponents at a distance. It often snacks on twigs to gain energy.

How to say it: FEN-ik-in

Height: 1' 04"   **Weight:** 20.7 lbs.

Possible Moves: Scratch, Tail Whip, Ember, Howl, Flame Charge, Psybeam, Fire Spin, Lucky Chant, Light Screen, Psyshock, Flamethrower, Will-O-Wisp, Psychic, Sunny Day, Magic Room, Fire Blast

Fennekin ⇨ Braixen ⇨ Delphox

TYPE: WATER

Feraligatr uses its gaping maw as an intimidation tactic. Its powerful legs propel it into a high-speed charge.

How to say it: fer-AL-ee-gay-tur

Height: 7' 07"
Weight: 195.8 lbs.

Possible Moves: Scratch, Leer, Water Gun, Rage, Bite, Scary Face, Ice Fang, Flail, Agility, Crunch, Chip Away, Slash, Screech, Thrash, Aqua Tail, Superpower, Hydro Pump

**REGION
JOHTO**

FERALIGATR
Big Jaw Pokémon

Totodile   Croconaw   Feraligatr

**REGIONS
KALOS
(COASTAL),
UNOVA**

FERROSEED
Thorn Seed Pokémon

TYPE: GRASS-STEEL

Ferroseed use their spikes to cling to cave ceilings and absorb iron. They can also shoot those spikes to cover their escape when enemies approach.

How to say it: fer-AH-seed

Height: 2' 00"
Weight: 41.4 lbs.

Possible Moves: Tackle, Harden, Rollout, Curse, Metal Claw, Pin Missile, Gyro Ball, Iron Defense, Mirror Shot, Ingrain, Self-Destruct, Iron Head, Payback, Flash Cannon, Explosion

Ferroseed   Ferrothorn

121

FERROTHORN
Thorn Pod Pokémon

TYPE: GRASS-STEEL

Ferrothorn swings its spiked feelers to attack. It likes to hang from the ceiling of a cave and shower spikes on anyone passing below.

How to say it: fer-AH-thorn

Height: 3' 03"   **Weight:** 242.5 lbs.

Possible Moves: Rock Climb, Tackle, Harden, Rollout, Curse, Metal Claw, Pin Missile, Gyro Ball, Iron Defense, Mirror Shot, Ingrain, Self-Destruct, Power Whip, Iron Head, Payback, Flash Cannon, Explosion

Ferroseed   Ferrothorn

FINNEON
Wing Fish Pokémon

REGION
SINNOH

TYPE: WATER

If Finneon soaks up enough sunlight during the day, the patterns on its body give off light when night falls on the sea where it lives.

How to say it: FINN-ee-onn

Height: 1' 04"
Weight: 15.4 lbs.

Possible Moves: Pound, Water Gun, Attract, Rain Dance, Gust, Water Pulse, Captivate, Safeguard, Aqua Ring, Whirlpool, U-turn, Bounce, Silver Wind, Soak

Finneon   Lumineon

FLAAFFY
Wool Pokémon

TYPE: ELECTRIC

Parts of Flaaffy's body are covered in wool that generates static electricity and builds up a charge. Its skin is resistant to electricity, so it doesn't shock itself by accident.

How to say it: FLAH-fee

Height: 2' 07"
Weight: 29.3 lbs.

Possible Moves: Tackle, Growl, Thunder Wave, Thunder Shock, Cotton Spore, Charge, Take Down, Electro Ball, Confuse Ray, Power Gem, Discharge, Cotton Guard, Signal Beam, Light Screen, Thunder

Mareep　**Flaaffy**　**Ampharos**　**Mega Ampharos**

FLABÉBÉ
Single Bloom Pokémon

TYPE: FAIRY

Each Flabébé has a special connection with the flower it holds. They take care of their flowers and use them as an energy source.

How to say it: flah-BAY-BAY

Height: 0' 04"　　**Weight:** 0.2 lbs.

Possible Moves: Tackle, Vine Whip, Fairy Wind, Lucky Chant, Razor Leaf, Wish, Magical Leaf, Grassy Terrain, Petal Blizzard, Aromatherapy, Misty Terrain, Moonblast, Petal Dance, Solar Beam

Flabébé　**Floette**　**Florges**

FLAREON

Flame Pokémon

REGIONS
KALOS (COASTAL), KANTO

TYPE: FIRE

Flareon's body can become very hot, so it fluffs out its soft fur to release excess heat into its surroundings. Even so, it can reach more than 1,600 degrees Fahrenheit.

How to say it: FLAIR-ee-on

Height: 2' 11"
Weight: 55.1 lbs.

Possible Moves: Helping Hand, Tackle, Tail Whip, Sand Attack, Ember, Quick Attack, Bite, Fire Fang, Fire Spin, Scary Face, Smog, Lava Plume, Last Resort, Flare Blitz

Eevee ⇨ Flareon

FLETCHINDER

Ember Pokémon

REGION
KALOS (CENTRAL)

TYPE: FIRE-FLYING

As the flame sac on Fletchinder's belly slowly heats up, it flies faster and faster. It produces embers from its beak.

How to say it: FLETCH-in-der

Height: 2' 04"
Weight: 35.3 lbs.

Possible Moves: Tackle, Growl, Quick Attack, Peck, Agility, Flail, Ember, Roost, Razor Wind, Natural Gift, Flame Charge, Acrobatics, Me First, Tailwind, Steel Wing

Fletchling ⇨ Fletchinder ⇨ Talonflame

FLETCHLING
Tiny Robin Pokémon

TYPE: NORMAL-FLYING

Flocks of Fletchling sing to one another in beautiful voices to communicate. If an intruder threatens their territory, they will defend it fiercely.

How to say it: FLETCH-ling

Height: 1' 00"
Weight: 3.7 lbs.

Possible Moves: Tackle, Growl, Quick Attack, Peck, Agility, Flail, Roost, Razor Wind, Natural Gift, Flame Charge, Acrobatics, Me First, Tailwind, Steel Wing

Fletchling Fletchinder Talonflame

TYPE: WATER

The flotation sac that surrounds its entire body makes Floatzel very good at rescuing people in the water. It can float them to safety like an inflatable raft.

How to say it: FLOAT-zul

Height: 3' 07"   **Weight:** 73.9 lbs.

Possible Moves: Ice Fang, Crunch, Sonic Boom, Growl, Water Sport, Quick Attack, Water Gun, Pursuit, Swift, Aqua Jet, Double Hit, Whirlpool, Razor Wind, Aqua Tail, Agility, Hydro Pump

FLOATZEL
Sea Weasel Pokémon

Buizel Floatzel

FLOETTE
Single Bloom Pokémon

REGION
**KALOS
(CENTRAL)**

TYPE: FAIRY

Floette keeps watch over flower beds and will rescue a flower if it starts to droop. It dances to celebrate the spring bloom.

How to say it: floh-ET

Height: 0' 08"
Weight: 2.0 lbs.

Possible Moves: Tackle, Vine Whip, Fairy Wind, Lucky Chant, Razor Leaf, Wish, Magical Leaf, Grassy Terrain, Petal Blizzard, Aromatherapy, Misty Terrain, Moonblast, Petal Dance, Solar Beam

Flabébé   Floette   Florges

FLORGES
Garden Pokémon

REGION
**KALOS
(CENTRAL)**

TYPE: FAIRY

Long ago, Florges were a welcome sight on castle grounds, where they would create elaborate flower gardens.

How to say it: FLORE-jess

Height: 3' 07"
Weight: 22.0 lbs.

Possible Moves: Disarming Voice, Lucky Chant, Wish, Magical Leaf, Flower Shield, Grass Knot, Grassy Terrain, Petal Blizzard, Misty Terrain, Moonblast, Petal Dance, Aromatherapy

Flabébé   Floette   Florges

FLYGON
Mystic Pokémon

TYPE: GROUND-DRAGON

When Flygon flaps its wings, it stirs up the sand to create a concealing sandstorm. The vibration of the wings also produces musical tones, making it sound like the Pokémon is singing through the sandstorm.

How to say it: FLY-gon

Height: 6' 07"   **Weight:** 180.8 lbs.

Possible Moves: Sonic Boom, Sand Attack, Feint Attack, Sand Tomb, Mud-Slap, Bide, Bulldoze, Rock Slide, Supersonic, Screech, Dragon Breath, Earth Power, Sandstorm, Dragon Tail, Hyper Beam, Dragon Claw

Trapinch   Vibrava   Flygon

TYPE: GRASS-POISON

Foongus uses its deceptive Poké Ball pattern to lure people or Pokémon close. Then it attacks with poison spores.

How to say it: FOON-gus

Height: 0' 08"
Weight: 2.2 lbs.

Possible Moves: Absorb, Growth, Astonish, Bide, Mega Drain, Ingrain, Feint Attack, Sweet Scent, Giga Drain, Toxic, Synthesis, Clear Smog, Solar Beam, Rage Powder, Spore

FOONGUS
Mushroom Pokémon

Foongus   Amoonguss

FORRETRESS
Bagworm Pokémon

TYPE: BUG-STEEL

Forretress is protected by a shell of solid steel. It opens the shell to catch food, but slams it shut again so quickly that no one can see inside.

How to say it: FOR-it-TRESS

Height: 3' 11"
Weight: 277.3 lbs.

Possible Moves: Toxic Spikes, Tackle, Protect, Self-Destruct, Bug Bite, Take Down, Rapid Spin, Bide, Natural Gift, Spikes, Mirror Shot, Autotomize, Payback, Explosion, Iron Defense, Gyro Ball, Double-Edge, Magnet Rise, Zap Cannon, Heavy Slam

Pineco   Forretress

FRAXURE
Axe Jaw Pokémon

TYPE: DRAGON

Fraxure clash in intense battles over territory. After a battle is over, they always remember to sharpen their tusks on smooth stones so they'll be ready for the next battle.

How to say it: FRAK-shur

Height: 3' 03"   **Weight:** 79.4 lbs.

Possible Moves: Scratch, Leer, Assurance, Dragon Rage, Dual Chop, Scary Face, Slash, False Swipe, Dragon Claw, Dragon Dance, Taunt, Dragon Pulse, Swords Dance, Guillotine, Outrage, Giga Impact

Axew   Fraxure   Haxorus

TYPE: WATER-GHOST

When battling underwater, Frillish uses poison to stun its opponent, then wraps the foe in its veil-like arms and drags it down into the depths.

How to say it: FRIL-lish

Height: 3' 11"
Weight: 72.8 lbs.

Possible Moves: Bubble, Water Sport, Absorb, Night Shade, Bubble Beam, Recover, Water Pulse, Ominous Wind, Brine, Rain Dance, Hex, Hydro Pump, Wring Out, Water Spout

Male Form

Female Form

Frillish   Jellicent

TYPE: WATER

The foamy bubbles that cover Froakie's body protect its sensitive skin from damage. It's always alert to any changes in its environment.

How to say it: FRO-kee

Height: 1' 00"
Weight: 15.4 lbs.

Possible Moves: Pound, Growl, Bubble, Quick Attack, Lick, Water Pulse, Smokescreen, Round, Fling, Smack Down, Substitute, Bounce, Double Team, Hydro Pump

REGION
KALOS (CENTRAL)

FROAKIE
Bubble Frog Pokémon

Froakie   Frogadier   Greninja

FROGADIER
Bubble Frog Pokémon

TYPE: WATER

Swift and sure, Frogadier coats pebbles in a bubbly foam and then flings them with pinpoint accuracy. It has spectacular jumping and climbing skills.

How to say it: FROG-uh-deer

Height: 2' 00"
Weight: 24.0 lbs.

Possible Moves: Pound, Growl, Bubble, Quick Attack, Lick, Water Pulse, Smokescreen, Round, Fling, Smack Down, Substitute, Bounce, Double Team, Hydro Pump

Froakie   Frogadier   Greninja

FROSLASS
Snow land Pokémon

TYPE: ICE-GHOST

With its icy breath, Froslass can freeze its opponents solid. Some believe the first Froslass was created when a woman became lost in the snowy mountains.

How to say it: FROS-lass

Height: 4' 03"
Weight: 58.6 lbs.

Possible Moves: Powder Snow, Leer, Double Team, Astonish, Icy Wind, Confuse Ray, Ominous Wind, Wake-Up Slap, Captivate, Ice Shard, Hail, Blizzard, Destiny Bond

Snorunt   Froslass

TYPE: NORMAL

An experienced groomer can trim Furfrou's fluffy coat into many different styles. Being groomed in this way makes the Pokémon both fancier and faster.

How to say it: FUR-froo

Height: 3' 11"
Weight: 61.7 lbs.

Possible Moves: Tackle, Growl, Sand Attack, Baby-Doll Eyes, Headbutt, Tail Whip, Bite, Odor Sleuth, Retaliate, Take Down, Charm, Sucker Punch, Cotton Guard

REGION
**KALOS
(CENTRAL)**

FURFROU
Poodle Pokémon

Does not evolve

TYPE: NORMAL

With its long, thin body and impressive speed, Furret has an evasive edge in battle. It can often wriggle right out of an opponent's grasp.

How to say it: FUR-ret

Height: 5' 11"
Weight: 71.6 lbs.

Possible Moves: Scratch, Foresight, Defense Curl, Quick Attack, Fury Swipes, Helping Hand, Follow Me, Slam, Rest, Sucker Punch, Amnesia, Baton Pass, Me First, Hyper Voice

REGIONS
**JOHTO,
KALOS
(CENTRAL)**

FURRET
Long Body Pokémon

Sentret ⇨ Furret

GABITE
Cave Pokémon

TYPE: DRAGON-GROUND

While digging to expand its nest, Gabite sometimes finds sparkly gems that then become part of its hoard.

How to say it: gab-BITE

Height: 4' 07"　　**Weight:** 123.5 lbs.

Possible Moves: Tackle, Sand Attack, Dragon Rage, Sandstorm, Take Down, Sand Tomb, Dual Chop, Slash, Dragon Claw, Dig, Dragon Rush

Gible　　Gabite　　Garchomp　　Mega Garchomp

GALLADE
Blade Pokémon

TYPE: PSYCHIC-FIGHTING

A master of the blade, Gallade battles using the swordlike appendages that extend from its elbows.

How to say it: GAL-laid

Height: 5' 03"
Weight: 114.6 lbs.

Possible Moves: Stored Power, Close Combat, Leaf Blade, Night Slash, Leer, Confusion, Double Team, Teleport, Fury Cutter, Slash, Heal Pulse, Swords Dance, Psycho Cut, Helping Hand, Feint, False Swipe, Protect

MEGA GALLADE
Blade Pokémon

TYPE: PSYCHIC-FIGHTING

Height: 5' 03"
Weight: 124.3 lbs.

Ralts → Kirlia → Gallade → Mega Gallade

133

GALVANTULA
Elespider Pokémon

TYPE: BUG-ELECTRIC

Galvantula's webs crackle with electricity, which shocks anything that blunders into them. It can also spin an electric barrier in battle.

How to say it: gal-VAN-choo-luh

Height: 2' 07"
Weight: 31.5 lbs.

Possible Moves: String Shot, Leech Life, Spider Web, Thunder Wave, Screech, Fury Cutter, Electroweb, Bug Bite, Gastro Acid, Slash, Electro Ball, Signal Beam, Agility, Sucker Punch, Discharge, Bug Buzz

Joltik   **Galvantula**

GARBODOR
Trash Heap Pokémon

TYPE: POISON

Garbodor wraps its long left arm around an opponent to bring it within range of its poisonous breath. It creates new kinds of poison by eating garbage.

How to say it: gar-BOH-dur

Height: 6' 03"   **Weight:** 236.6 lbs.

Possible Moves: Pound, Poison Gas, Recycle, Toxic Spikes, Acid Spray, Double Slap, Sludge, Stockpile, Swallow, Body Slam, Sludge Bomb, Clear Smog, Toxic, Amnesia, Belch, Gunk Shot, Explosion

Trubbish   **Garbodor**

GARCHOMP
Mach Pokémon

TYPE: DRAGON-GROUND

Garchomp can fly faster than the speed of sound. When it assumes a streamlined position for flight, it looks like a fighter jet.

How to say it: gar-CHOMP

Height: 6' 03"
Weight: 209.4 lbs.

Possible Moves: Fire Fang, Tackle, Sand Attack, Dragon Rage, Sandstorm, Take Down, Sand Tomb, Dual Chop, Slash, Dragon Claw, Dig, Crunch, Dragon Rush

MEGA GARCHOMP
Mach Pokémon

TYPE: DRAGON-GROUND

Height: 6' 03"
Weight: 209.4 lbs.

Gible   Gabite   Garchomp   Mega Garchomp

GARDEVOIR

Embrace Pokémon

TYPE: PSYCHIC-FAIRY

Fiercely protective of its Trainer, Gardevoir can see into the future to detect a threat to that Trainer. It responds by unleashing the full strength of its psychic powers.

How to say it: GAR-dee-VWAR

Height: 5' 03"
Weight: 106.7 lbs.

Possible Moves: Moonblast, Stored Power, Misty Terrain, Healing Wish, Growl, Confusion, Double Team, Teleport, Wish, Magical Leaf, Heal Pulse, Calm Mind, Psychic, Imprison, Future Sight, Captivate, Hypnosis, Dream Eater

MEGA GARDEVOIR

Embrace Pokémon

TYPE: PSYCHIC-FAIRY

Height: 5' 03"
Weight: 106.7 lbs.

Ralts　　Kirlia　　Gardevoir　　Mega Gardevoir

GASTLY
Gas Pokémon

TYPE: GHOST-POISON

Gastly's body is made of gas clouds that can be disrupted by strong winds. Groups of them sometimes huddle close to a house for protection.

How to say it: GAST-lee

Height: 4' 03"
Weight: 0.2 lbs.

Possible Moves: Hypnosis, Lick, Spite, Mean Look, Curse, Night Shade, Confuse Ray, Sucker Punch, Payback, Shadow Ball, Dream Eater, Dark Pulse, Destiny Bond, Hex, Nightmare

Gastly → Haunter → Gengar → Mega Gengar

GASTRODON EAST SEA
Sea Slug Pokémon

REGION
SINNOH

TYPE: WATER-GROUND

It's said that Gastrodon were once covered by protective shells, but over the ages, those shells have vanished. When threatened, they release purple fluid to cover their escape.

How to say it: GAS-tro-donn

Height: 2' 11"   **Weight:** 65.9 lbs.

Possible Moves: Mud-Slap, Mud Sport, Harden, Water Pulse, Mud Bomb, Hidden Power, Rain Dance, Body Slam, Muddy Water, Recover

Shellos
(East Sea)   Gastrodon
(East Sea)

137

GASTRODON WEST SEA

Sea Slug Pokémon

TYPE:
WATER-GROUND

Gastrodon lives in shallow waters. It can grow back any body part that is ripped off.

How to say it: GAS-tro-donn

Height: 2' 11"
Weight: 65.9 lbs.

Possible Moves: Mud-Slap, Mud Sport, Harden, Water Pulse, Mud Bomb, Hidden Power, Rain Dance, Body Slam, Muddy Water, Recover

Shellos
(West Sea)

Gastrodon
(West Sea)

GENESECT

Paleozoic Pokémon

TYPE: BUG-STEEL

The powerful cannon on Genesect's back is the result of Team Plasma's meddling. This Mythical Pokémon is 300 million years old.

How to say it: JEN-uh-sekt

Height: 4' 11"
Weight: 181.9 lbs.

Possible Moves: Fell Stinger, Techno Blast, Quick Attack, Magnet Rise, Metal Claw, Screech, Fury Cutter, Lock-On, Flame Charge, Magnet Bomb, Slash, Metal Sound, Signal Beam, Tri Attack, X-Scissor, Bug Buzz, Simple Beam, Zap Cannon, Hyper Beam, Self-Destruct

MYTHICAL POKÉMON

Does not evolve

GENGAR
Shadow Pokémon

TYPE:
GHOST-POISON

If your shadow suddenly runs away, it might be a Gengar stalking you through the darkness.

How to say it: GHEN-gar

Height: 4' 11"
Weight: 89.3 lbs.

Possible Moves:
Hypnosis, Lick, Spite, Mean Look, Curse, Night Shade, Confuse Ray, Sucker Punch, Shadow Punch, Payback, Shadow Ball, Dream Eater, Dark Pulse, Destiny Bond, Hex, Nightmare

MEGA GENGAR
Shadow Pokémon

TYPE: GHOST-POISON

Height: 4' 07"
Weight: 89.3 lbs.

Gastly   Haunter   Gengar   Mega Gengar

GEODUDE
Rock Pokémon

REGIONS
KALOS (MOUNTAIN), KANTO

TYPE: ROCK-GROUND

As a Geodude grows older, its rough edges are smoothed away. When it sleeps, it digs into the ground, where it resembles a rock.

How to say it: JEE-oh-dude

Height: 1' 04"
Weight: 44.1 lbs.

Possible Moves: Tackle, Defense Curl, Mud Sport, Rock Polish, Rollout, Magnitude, Rock Throw, Rock Blast, Smack Down, Self-Destruct, Bulldoze, Stealth Rock, Earthquake, Explosion, Double-Edge, Stone Edge

Geodude   Graveler   Golem

GIBLE
Land Shark Pokémon

REGIONS
KALOS (MOUNTAIN), SINNOH

TYPE: DRAGON-GROUND

Gible dig holes in the walls of warm caves to make their nests. Don't get too close, or they might pounce!

How to say it: GIB-bull

Height: 2' 04"   **Weight:** 45.2 lbs.

Possible Moves: Tackle, Sand Attack, Dragon Rage, Sandstorm, Take Down, Sand Tomb, Slash, Dragon Claw, Dig, Dragon Rush

Gible   Gabite   Garchomp   Mega Garchomp

GIGALITH
Compressed Pokémon

TYPE: ROCK

After Gigalith soaks up the sun's rays, it uses its energy core to process that energy into a weapon. A blast of its compressed energy can destroy a mountain.

How to say it: GIH-gah-lith

Height: 5' 07"
Weight: 573.2 lbs.

Possible Moves: Tackle, Harden, Sand Attack, Headbutt, Rock Blast, Mud-Slap, Iron Defense, Smack Down, Power Gem, Rock Slide, Stealth Rock, Sandstorm, Stone Edge, Explosion

Roggenrola   Boldore   Gigalith

TYPE: NORMAL-PSYCHIC

The brain that controls Girafarig's secondary head is too small to think and just reacts to its surroundings. It tends to attack anyone who approaches from behind.

How to say it: jir-RAF-uh-rig

Height: 4' 11"
Weight: 91.5 lbs.

Possible Moves: Power Swap, Guard Swap, Astonish, Tackle, Growl, Confusion, Odor Sleuth, Stomp, Agility, Psybeam, Baton Pass, Assurance, Double Hit, Psychic, Zen Headbutt, Crunch

GIRAFARIG
Long Neck Pokémon

Does not evolve

Origin Forme

Altered Forme

TYPE: GHOST-DRAGON

As punishment, the Legendary Pokémon Giratina was banished to another dimension, where everything is distorted and reversed.

How to say it: gear-uh-TEE-na

Height: 22' 08"   **Weight:** 1,433.0 lbs.

Possible Moves: Dragon Breath, Scary Face, Ominous Wind, Ancient Power, Slash, Shadow Sneak, Destiny Bond, Dragon Claw, Earth Power, Aura Sphere, Shadow Claw, Shadow Force, Hex

Does not evolve

GLACEON
Fresh Snow Pokémon

TYPE: ICE

The icy Glaceon has amazing control over its body temperature. It can freeze its own fur and then fire the frozen hairs like needles at an opponent.

How to say it: GLACE-ee-on

Height: 2' 07" **Weight:** 57.1 lbs.

Possible Moves: Helping Hand, Tackle, Tail Whip, Sand Attack, Icy Wind, Quick Attack, Bite, Ice Fang, Ice Shard, Barrier, Mirror Coat, Hail, Last Resort, Blizzard

Eevee   Glaceon

GLALIE

Face Pokémon

TYPE: ICE

Glalie's rocky body is surrounded by a sturdy shell of ice, which it creates by freezing water vapor in the air around it. It can also create amazing ice sculptures with this power.

How to say it: GLAY-lee

Height: 4' 11"
Weight: 565.5 lbs.

Possible Moves: Powder Snow, Leer, Double Team, Bite, Icy Wind, Headbutt, Protect, Ice Fang, Crunch, Ice Beam, Hail, Blizzard, Sheer Cold

MEGA GLALIE

Face Pokémon

TYPE: ICE

Height: 6' 11"
Weight: 772.1 lbs.

Snorunt   Glalie   Mega Glalie

144

TYPE: NORMAL

When it's feeling happy and friendly, Glameow purrs winningly and performs a lovely dance with its spiraling tail. When it's in a bad mood, however, the claws come out.

How to say it: GLAM-meow

Height: 1' 08"
Weight: 8.6 lbs.

Possible Moves: Fake Out, Scratch, Growl, Hypnosis, Feint Attack, Fury Swipes, Charm, Assist, Captivate, Slash, Sucker Punch, Attract, Hone Claws

REGION
SINNOH

GLAMEOW
Catty Pokémon

Glameow Purugly

TYPE: GROUND-FLYING

Gliding silently through the air, Gligar can strike from above to grab on to an opponent's face with all four of its claws. The barb on its tail is poisonous.

How to say it: GLY-gar

Height: 3' 07"   **Weight:** 142.9 lbs.

Possible Moves: Poison Sting, Sand Attack, Harden, Knock Off, Quick Attack, Fury Cutter, Feint Attack, Acrobatics, Slash, U-turn, Screech, X-Scissor, Sky Uppercut, Swords Dance, Guillotine

REGIONS
JOHTO,
KALOS
(MOUNTAIN)

GLIGAR
Fly Scorpion Pokémon

Gligar Gliscor

GLISCOR

Fang Scorpion Pokémon

TYPE: GROUND-FLYING

Gliscor hangs upside down from trees, watching for its chance to attack. At the right moment, it silently swoops, with its long tail ready to seize its opponent.

How to say it: GLY-score

Height: 6' 07"
Weight: 93.7 lbs.

Possible Moves: Guillotine, Thunder Fang, Ice Fang, Fire Fang, Poison Jab, Sand Attack, Harden, Knock Off, Quick Attack, Fury Cutter, Feint Attack, Acrobatics, Night Slash, U-turn, Screech, X-Scissor, Sky Uppercut, Swords Dance

Gligar ⇨ Gliscor

GLOOM

Weed Pokémon

TYPE: GRASS-POISON

Gloom doesn't always smell terrible—when it feels safe and relaxed, its aroma fades. However, its nectar usually carries an awful stench.

How to say it: GLOOM

Height: 2' 07"   **Weight:** 19.0 lbs.

Possible Moves: Absorb, Sweet Scent, Acid, Poison Powder, Stun Spore, Sleep Powder, Mega Drain, Lucky Chant, Natural Gift, Moonlight, Giga Drain, Petal Blizzard, Petal Dance, Grassy Terrain

Oddish ⇨ Gloom ⇨ Vileplume / Bellossom

TYPE: GRASS

This perceptive Pokémon can read its riders' feelings by paying attention to their grip on its horns. Gogoat also use their horns in battles for leadership.

How to say it: GO-goat

Height: 5' 07"
Weight: 200.6 lbs.

Possible Moves: Aerial Ace, Tackle, Growth, Vine Whip, Tail Whip, Leech Seed, Razor Leaf, Worry Seed, Synthesis, Take Down, Bulldoze, Seed Bomb, Bulk Up, Double-Edge, Horn Leech, Leaf Blade, Milk Drink, Earthquake

REGION
KALOS
(CENTRAL)

GOGOAT
Mount Pokémon

Skiddo   Gogoat

REGIONS
KALOS
(CENTRAL),
KANTO

GOLBAT
Bat Pokémon

TYPE: POISON-FLYING

With its four sharp fangs, Golbat feeds on living beings. Darkness gives it an advantage in battle, and it prefers to attack on pitch-black nights.

How to say it: GOL-bat

Height: 5' 03"   **Weight:** 121.3 lbs.

Possible Moves: Screech, Leech Life, Supersonic, Astonish, Bite, Wing Attack, Confuse Ray, Swift, Air Cutter, Acrobatics, Mean Look, Poison Fang, Haze, Air Slash

Zubat   Golbat   Crobat

147

GOLDEEN
Goldfish Pokémon

REGIONS
KALOS (CENTRAL), KANTO

TYPE: WATER

Goldeen's long, elegant fins wave gracefully in the water. It's hard to keep this lovely Pokémon in an aquarium, because its horn can break through thick glass.

How to say it: GOL-deen

Height: 2' 00"
Weight: 33.1 lbs.

Possible Moves: Peck, Tail Whip, Water Sport, Supersonic, Horn Attack, Water Pulse, Flail, Aqua Ring, Fury Attack, Waterfall, Horn Drill, Agility, Soak, Megahorn

Goldeen   Seaking

GOLDUCK
Duck Pokémon

REGIONS
KALOS (CENTRAL), KANTO

TYPE: WATER

The webbing on its legs makes Golduck an excellent swimmer. Even when facing strong currents and towering waves, it can cut through the water to rescue shipwreck victims.

How to say it: GOL-duck

Height: 5' 07"   **Weight:** 168.9 lbs.

Possible Moves: Aqua Jet, Water Sport, Scratch, Tail Whip, Water Gun, Disable, Confusion, Water Pulse, Fury Swipes, Screech, Zen Headbutt, Aqua Tail, Soak, Psych Up, Amnesia, Hydro Pump, Wonder Room

Psyduck   Golduck

TYPE: ROCK-GROUND

People who live on mountainsides sometimes dig grooves to keep Golem from rolling right into their houses.

How to say it: GO-lum

Height: 4' 07"
Weight: 661.4 lbs.

Possible Moves: Heavy Slam, Tackle, Defense Curl, Mud Sport, Rock Polish, Steamroller, Magnitude, Rock Throw, Rock Blast, Smack Down, Self-Destruct, Bulldoze, Stealth Rock, Earthquake, Explosion, Double-Edge, Stone Edge

REGIONS
KALOS (MOUNTAIN), KANTO

GOLEM
Megaton Pokémon

Geodude   Graveler   Golem

TYPE: GROUND-GHOST

Sculpted from clay and animated by a mysterious internal energy, Golett are the product of ancient science.

How to say it: GO-let

Height: 3' 03"
Weight: 202.8 lbs.

Possible Moves: Pound, Astonish, Defense Curl, Mud-Slap, Rollout, Shadow Punch, Iron Defense, Mega Punch, Magnitude, Dynamic Punch, Night Shade, Curse, Earthquake, Hammer Arm, Focus Punch

REGIONS
KALOS (COASTAL), UNOVA

GOLETT
Automaton Pokémon

Golett   Golurk

149

GOLURK
Automaton Pokémon

TYPE: GROUND-GHOST

The seal on Golurk's chest keeps its energy contained and stops it from going wild. Long ago, these Pokémon were created as protectors.

How to say it: GO-lurk

Height: 9' 02"
Weight: 727.5 lbs.

Possible Moves: Phantom Force, Focus Punch, Pound, Astonish, Defense Curl, Mud-Slap, Rollout, Shadow Punch, Iron Defense, Mega Punch, Magnitude, Dynamic Punch, Night Shade, Curse, Heavy Slam, Earthquake, Hammer Arm

Golett   **Golurk**

GOODRA
Dragon Pokémon

TYPE: DRAGON

The affectionate Goodra just loves to give its Trainer a big hug! Unfortunately, its hugs leave the recipient covered in goo.

How to say it: GOO-druh

Height: 6' 07"   **Weight:** 331.8 lbs.

Possible Moves: Outrage, Feint, Tackle, Bubble, Absorb, Protect, Bide, Dragon Breath, Rain Dance, Flail, Body Slam, Muddy Water, Dragon Pulse, Aqua Tail, Power Whip

Goomy   **Sliggoo**   **Goodra**

TYPE: DRAGON

The slippery membrane that covers Goomy's body deflects the fists and feet of its attackers. To keep itself from drying out, it stays away from the sun.

How to say it: GOO-mee

Height: 1' 00"
Weight: 6.2 lbs.

Possible Moves: Tackle, Bubble, Absorb, Protect, Bide, Dragon Breath, Rain Dance, Flail, Body Slam, Muddy Water, Dragon Pulse

REGION KALOS (MOUNTAIN)

GOOMY
Soft Tissue Pokémon

Goomy   Sliggoo   Goodra

TYPE: WATER

Gorebyss is tougher than it looks. Its long, slender body is built to withstand the crushing pressure at the bottom of the ocean. Regular attacks just won't do much.

How to say it: GORE-a-biss

Height: 5' 11"
Weight: 49.8 lbs.

Possible Moves: Whirlpool, Confusion, Agility, Water Pulse, Amnesia, Aqua Ring, Captivate, Baton Pass, Dive, Psychic, Aqua Tail, Hydro Pump

REGIONS HOENN, KALOS (COASTAL)

GOREBYSS
South Sea Pokémon

Clamperl   Gorebyss

GOTHITA
Fixation Pokémon

REGIONS
KALOS (MOUNTAIN), UNOVA

TYPE: PSYCHIC

Gothita's wide eyes are always fixed on something. It seems when they stare like that, they're seeing what others cannot.

How to say it: GAH-THEE-tah

Height: 1' 04"
Weight: 12.8 lbs.

Possible Moves: Pound, Confusion, Tickle, Play Nice, Fake Tears, Double Slap, Psybeam, Embargo, Feint Attack, Psyshock, Flatter, Future Sight, Heal Block, Psychic, Telekinesis, Charm, Magic Room

Gothita   Gothorita   Gothitelle

GOTHITELLE
Astral Body Pokémon

REGIONS
KALOS (MOUNTAIN), UNOVA

TYPE: PSYCHIC

Gothitelle observes the stars to predict the future. It sometimes distorts the air around itself to reveal faraway constellations.

How to say it: GAH-thih-tell

Height: 4' 11"
Weight: 97.0 lbs.

Possible Moves: Pound, Confusion, Tickle, Play Nice, Fake Tears, Double Slap, Psybeam, Embargo, Feint Attack, Psyshock, Flatter, Future Sight, Heal Block, Psychic, Telekinesis, Charm, Magic Room

Gothita   Gothorita   Gothitelle

152

TYPE: PSYCHIC

Gothorita draw their power from starlight. On starry nights, they can make stones float and control people's movements with their enhanced psychic power.

How to say it: GAH-thoh-REE-tah

Height: 2' 04"   **Weight:** 39.7 lbs.

Possible Moves: Pound, Confusion, Tickle, Play Nice, Fake Tears, Double Slap, Psybeam, Embargo, Feint Attack, Psyshock, Flatter, Future Sight, Heal Block, Psychic, Telekinesis, Charm, Magic Room

REGIONS
KALOS (MOUNTAIN), UNOVA

GOTHORITA
Manipulate Pokémon

Gothita Gothorita Gothitelle

TYPE: GHOST-GRASS

During the new moon, the eerie song of the Gourgeist echoes through town, bringing woe to anyone who hears it.

How to say it: GORE-guyst

Height: 2' 11"   **Weight:** 27.6 lbs.

Possible Moves: Explosion, Phantom Force, Trick, Astonish, Confuse Ray, Scary Face, Trick-or-Treat, Worry Seed, Razor Leaf, Leech Seed, Bullet Seed, Shadow Sneak, Shadow Ball, Pain Split, Seed Bomb

REGION
KALOS (MOUNTAIN)

GOURGEIST
Pumpkin Pokémon

Pumpkaboo Gourgeist

GRANBULL

Fairy Pokémon

TYPE: FAIRY

The weight of the huge fangs in Granbull's lower jaw throw the Pokémon off balance, so it has to walk with its head tilted back. It generally doesn't bite unless startled.

How to say it: GRAN-bull

Height: 4' 07"
Weight: 107.4 lbs.

Possible Moves: Outrage, Ice Fang, Fire Fang, Thunder Fang, Tackle, Scary Face, Tail Whip, Charm, Bite, Lick, Headbutt, Roar, Rage, Play Rough, Payback, Crunch

Snubbull   Granbull

GRAVELER

Rock Pokémon

TYPE: ROCK-GROUND

Graveler loves to eat rocks, and moss-covered rocks are a favorite snack. It will munch its way up the side of a mountain if it's hungry.

How to say it: GRAV-el-ler

Height: 3' 03"
Weight: 231.5 lbs.

Possible Moves: Tackle, Defense Curl, Mud Sport, Rock Polish, Rollout, Magnitude, Rock Throw, Rock Blast, Smack Down, Self-Destruct, Bulldoze, Stealth Rock, Earthquake, Explosion, Double-Edge, Stone Edge

Geodude   Graveler   Golem

GRENINJA
Ninja Pokémon

TYPE: WATER-DARK

Greninja can compress water into sharp-edged throwing stars. With the grace of a ninja, it slips in and out of sight to attack from the shadows.

How to say it: greh-NIN-jah

Height: 4' 11"   **Weight:** 88.2 lbs.

Possible Moves: Night Slash, Role Play, Mat Block, Pound, Growl, Bubble, Quick Attack, Lick, Water Pulse, Smokescreen, Shadow Sneak, Spikes, Feint Attack, Water Shuriken, Substitute, Extrasensory, Double Team, Haze, Hydro Pump

Froakie   Frogadier   Greninja

GRIMER
Sludge Pokémon

TYPE: POISON

Because its body is like sludge, Grimer can squeeze itself into small openings like sewer pipes. The fluid it gives off is full of germs.

How to say it: GRIME-er

Height: 2' 11"
Weight: 66.1 lbs.

Possible Moves: Poison Gas, Pound, Harden, Mud-Slap, Disable, Minimize, Sludge, Mud Bomb, Fling, Screech, Sludge Bomb, Acid Armor, Sludge Wave, Gunk Shot, Memento

Grimer   Muk

GROTLE
Grove Pokémon

REGION
SINNOH

TYPE: GRASS

Grotle leaves the shade of its forest home to soak up sunlight with its shell. It's good at finding clear water, and smaller Pokémon often ride on its back when they're thirsty.

How to say it: GRAHT-ull

Height: 3' 07"   **Weight:** 213.8 lbs.

Possible Moves: Tackle, Withdraw, Absorb, Razor Leaf, Curse, Bite, Mega Drain, Leech Seed, Synthesis, Crunch, Giga Drain, Leaf Storm

Turtwig   Grotle   Torterra

REGION
HOENN

GROUDON
Continent Pokémon

TYPE: GROUND

Legends say that Groudon is the land personified. When it channels the full power of nature, it can expand the landmass with eruptions of magma. This Pokémon often clashes with Kyogre.

How to say it: GRAU-don

Height: 11' 06"
Weight: 2,094.4 lbs.

Possible Moves: Mud Shot, Scary Face, Lava Plume, Hammer Arm, Rest, Earthquake, Ancient Power, Eruption, Bulk Up, Earth Power, Fissure, Solar Beam, Fire Blast

PRIMAL GROUDON
Continent Pokémon

TYPE: GROUND-FIRE

Height: 16' 05"
Weight: 2,204.0 lbs.

Groudon   Primal Groudon

GROVYLE
Wood Gecko Pokémon

REGION
HOENN

TYPE: GRASS

Grovyle can travel so swiftly from branch to branch that it looks like it's flying through the forest. The leaves on its body are excellent camouflage.

How to say it: GROW-vile

Height: 2' 11"   **Weight:** 47.6 lbs.

Possible Moves: Pound, Leer, Absorb, Quick Attack, Fury Cutter, Pursuit, Screech, Leaf Blade, Agility, Slam, Detect, False Swipe, Leaf Storm

Treecko   **Grovyle**   **Sceptile**   **Mega Sceptile**

GROWLITHE
Puppy Pokémon

REGION
KANTO

TYPE: FIRE

Growlithe has an excellent nose and a good memory for scents. It can even sniff out people's emotions.

How to say it: GROWL-ith

Height: 2' 04"   **Weight:** 41.9 lbs.

Possible Moves: Bite, Roar, Ember, Leer, Odor Sleuth, Helping Hand, Flame Wheel, Reversal, Fire Fang, Flame Burst, Take Down, Flamethrower, Agility, Crunch, Retaliate, Heat Wave, Flare Blitz

Growlithe   **Arcanine**

GRUMPIG
Manipulate Pokémon

TYPE: PSYCHIC

Grumpig breaks into a strange dance when it's using its black pearls to focus its psychic power. Many collectors consider the pearls to be priceless artwork.

How to say it: GRUM-pig

Height: 2' 11"
Weight: 157.6 lbs.

Possible Moves: Splash, Psywave, Odor Sleuth, Psybeam, Psych Up, Confuse Ray, Magic Coat, Zen Headbutt, Rest, Snore, Power Gem, Psyshock, Payback, Psychic, Bounce

Spoink ⇨ Grumpig

GULPIN
Stomach Pokémon

TYPE: POISON

Gulpin's stomach takes up most of its body, so there's not much room for its other organs. Its powerful digestive enzymes make short work of anything it swallows.

How to say it: GULL-pin

Height: 1' 04"
Weight: 22.7 lbs.

Possible Moves: Pound, Yawn, Poison Gas, Sludge, Amnesia, Encore, Toxic, Acid Spray, Stockpile, Spit Up, Swallow, Belch, Sludge Bomb, Gastro Acid, Wring Out, Gunk Shot

Gulpin ⇨ Swalot

GURDURR
Muscular Pokémon

REGIONS
KALOS (MOUNTAIN), UNOVA

TYPE: FIGHTING

With its strong muscles, Gurdurr can wield its steel beam with ease in battle. It's so sturdy that a whole team of wrestlers couldn't knock it down.

How to say it: GUR-dur

Height: 3' 11"   **Weight:** 88.2 lbs.

Possible Moves: Pound, Leer, Focus Energy, Bide, Low Kick, Rock Throw, Wake-Up Slap, Chip Away, Bulk Up, Rock Slide, Dynamic Punch, Scary Face, Hammer Arm, Stone Edge, Focus Punch, Superpower

Timburr   Gurdurr   Conkeldurr

GYARADOS
Atrocious Pokémon

TYPE:
WATER-FLYING

After evolving, Gyarados experiences a shift in the cellular structure of its brain. This may explain why it is so violent, sometimes going on month-long rampages.

How to say it: GARE-uh-dos

Height: 21' 04"
Weight: 518.1 lbs.

Possible Moves: Thrash, Bite, Dragon Rage, Leer, Twister, Ice Fang, Aqua Tail, Rain Dance, Hydro Pump, Dragon Dance, Hyper Beam

MEGA GYARADOS
Atrocious Pokémon

TYPE: WATER-DARK

Height: 21' 04"
Weight: 672.4 lbs.

Magikarp   Gyarados   Mega Gyarados

161

HAPPINY
Playhouse Pokémon

REGION
SINNOH

TYPE: NORMAL

In the pouch on its belly, Happiny carefully stores a round, white stone that resembles an egg. It sometimes offers this stone to those it likes.

How to say it: hap-PEE-nee

Height: 2' 00"
Weight: 53.8 lbs.

Possible Moves: Pound, Charm, Copycat, Refresh, Sweet Kiss

Happiny **Chansey** **Blissey**

HARIYAMA
Arm Thrust Pokémon

REGIONS
HOENN, KALOS (COASTAL)

TYPE: FIGHTING

Don't let Hariyama's bulk fool you—it's made of pure muscle. A single strike from its open palm can snap a thick tree in half.

How to say it: HAR-ee-YAH-mah

Height: 7' 07"   **Weight:** 559.5 lbs.

Possible Moves: Brine, Tackle, Focus Energy, Sand Attack, Arm Thrust, Vital Throw, Fake Out, Whirlwind, Knock Off, Smelling Salts, Belly Drum, Force Palm, Seismic Toss, Wake-Up Slap, Endure, Close Combat, Reversal, Heavy Slam

Makuhita **Hariyama**

TYPE: GHOST-POISON

Don't ever let a Haunter lick you! Its ghostly tongue can steal your life energy.

How to say it: HAUNT-ur

Height: 5' 03"   **Weight:** 0.2 lbs.

Possible Moves: Hypnosis, Lick, Spite, Mean Look, Curse, Night Shade, Confuse Ray, Sucker Punch, Shadow Punch, Payback, Shadow Ball, Dream Eater, Dark Pulse, Destiny Bond, Hex, Nightmare

REGIONS
**KALOS
(MOUNTAIN),
KANTO**

HAUNTER
Gas Pokémon

Gastly ⇒ Haunter ⇒ Gengar ⇒ Mega Gengar

TYPE: FIGHTING-FLYING

Hawlucha prefers to fight by diving at its foes from above. This aerial advantage makes up for its small size.

How to say it: haw-LOO-cha

Height: 2' 07"   **Weight:** 47.4 lbs.

Possible Moves: Detect, Tackle, Hone Claws, Karate Chop, Wing Attack, Roost, Aerial Ace, Encore, Fling, Flying Press, Bounce, Endeavor, Feather Dance, High Jump Kick, Sky Attack, Sky Drop, Swords Dance

REGION
**KALOS
(COASTAL)**

HAWLUCHA
Wrestling Pokémon

Does not evolve

HAXORUS
Axe Jaw Pokémon

REGIONS
KALOS
(CENTRAL),
UNOVA

TYPE: DRAGON

Haxorus can cut through steel with its mighty tusks, which stay sharp no matter what. Its body is heavily armored.

How to say it: HAK-soar-us

Height: 5' 11"
Weight: 232.6 lbs.

Possible Moves: Outrage, Scratch, Leer, Assurance, Dragon Rage, Dual Chop, Scary Face, Slash, False Swipe, Dragon Claw, Dragon Dance, Taunt, Dragon Pulse, Swords Dance, Guillotine, Giga Impact

Axew ⇨ Fraxure ⇨ Haxorus

HEATMOR
Anteater Pokémon

REGIONS
KALOS
(MOUNTAIN),
UNOVA

TYPE: FIRE

Heatmor can control the flame from its mouth like a tongue, and the fire is so hot that it can melt through steel. Heatmor and Durant are natural enemies.

How to say it: HEET-mohr

Height: 4' 07"
Weight: 127.9 lbs.

Possible Moves: Inferno, Hone Claws, Tackle, Incinerate, Lick, Odor Sleuth, Bind, Fire Spin, Fury Swipes, Snatch, Flame Burst, Bug Bite, Slash, Amnesia, Flamethrower, Stockpile, Spit Up, Swallow

Does not evolve

HEATRAN
Lava Dome Pokémon

TYPE: FIRE-STEEL

Heatran makes its home in caves carved out by volcanic eruptions. This Legendary Pokémon's feet can dig into rock, allowing it to walk on walls and ceilings.

How to say it: HEE-tran

Height: 5' 07"   **Weight:** 948.0 lbs.

Possible Moves: Ancient Power, Leer, Fire Fang, Metal Sound, Crunch, Scary Face, Lava Plume, Fire Spin, Iron Head, Earth Power, Heat Wave, Stone Edge, Magma Storm

Does not evolve

HELIOLISK
Generator Pokémon

TYPE: ELECTRIC-NORMAL

Heliolisk generates electricity by spreading its frill out wide to soak up the sun. It uses this energy to boost its speed.

How to say it: HEE-lee-oh-lisk

Height: 3' 03"
Weight: 46.3 lbs.

Possible Moves: Eerie Impulse, Electrify, Razor Wind, Quick Attack, Thunder, Charge, Parabolic Charge

Helioptile → Heliolisk

HELIOPTILE
Generator Pokémon

TYPE: ELECTRIC-NORMAL

The frills on Helioptile's head soak up sunlight and create electricity. In this way, they can generate enough energy to keep them going without food.

How to say it: hee-lee-AHP-tile

Height: 1' 08"   **Weight:** 13.2 lbs.

Possible Moves: Pound, Tail Whip, Thunder Shock, Charge, Mud-Slap, Quick Attack, Razor Wind, Parabolic Charge, Thunder Wave, Bulldoze, Volt Switch, Electrify, Thunderbolt

Helioptile → Heliolisk

HERACROSS
Single Horn Pokémon

TYPE: BUG-FIGHTING

Though its feet end in sharp claws, Heracross doesn't use them as a weapon. Instead, it digs them into the ground to brace itself while it uses its giant horn to scoop up an enemy.

How to say it: HAIR-uh-cross

Height: 4' 11"
Weight: 119.0 lbs.

Possible Moves: Arm Thrust, Bullet Seed, Night Slash, Tackle, Leer, Horn Attack, Endure, Fury Attack, Aerial Ace, Chip Away, Counter, Brick Break, Take Down, Pin Missile, Close Combat, Feint, Reversal, Megahorn

MEGA HERACROSS
Single Horn Pokémon

TYPE: BUG-FIGHTING

Height: 5' 07"
Weight: 137.8 lbs.

Heracross   Mega Heracross

HERDIER
Loyal Dog Pokémon

TYPE: NORMAL

Herdier is known for its unwavering loyalty, even helping its Trainer take care of other Pokémon. The black fur on its back protects it like a cape.

How to say it: HERD-ee-er

Height: 2' 11"
Weight: 32.4 lbs.

Possible Moves: Leer, Tackle, Odor Sleuth, Bite, Helping Hand, Take Down, Work Up, Crunch, Roar, Retaliate, Reversal, Last Resort, Giga Impact

Lillipup → **Herdier** → **Stoutland**

HIPPOPOTAS
Hippo Pokémon

REGIONS
**KALOS
(COASTAL),
SINNOH**

TYPE: GROUND

Hippopotas lives in a dry environment. Its body gives off sand instead of sweat, and this sandy shield keeps it protected from water and germs.

How to say it: HIP-poh-puh-TOSS

Height: 2' 07"
Weight: 109.1 lbs.

Possible Moves: Tackle, Sand Attack, Bite, Yawn, Take Down, Dig, Sand Tomb, Crunch, Earthquake, Double-Edge, Fissure

Hippopotas → **Hippowdon**

TYPE: GROUND

HIPPOWDON
Heavyweight Pokémon

REGIONS
KALOS (COASTAL), SINNOH

Hippowdon stores sand inside its body and expels it through the ports on its sides to create a twisting sandstorm in battle.

How to say it: hip-POW-don

Height: 6' 07"
Weight: 661.4 lbs.

Possible Moves: Ice Fang, Fire Fang, Thunder Fang, Tackle, Sand Attack, Bite, Yawn, Take Down, Dig, Sand Tomb, Crunch, Earthquake, Double-Edge, Fissure

Hippopotas   **Hippowdon**

TYPE: FIGHTING

HITMONCHAN
Punching Pokémon

REGION
KANTO

Hitmonchan has the fighting spirit of a world-class boxer. It's extremely driven and never gives up.

How to say it: HIT-mon-chan

Height: 4' 07"
Weight: 110.7 lbs.

Possible Moves: Revenge, Comet Punch, Agility, Pursuit, Mach Punch, Bullet Punch, Feint, Vacuum Wave, Quick Guard, Thunder Punch, Ice Punch, Fire Punch, Sky Uppercut, Mega Punch, Detect, Focus Punch, Counter, Close Combat

Tyrogue

Hitmonlee

Hitmontop

Hitmonchan

HITMONLEE

Kicking Pokémon

REGION
KANTO

TYPE: FIGHTING

Hitmonlee can extend its legs like springs to deliver kicks with tremendous force. It's always careful to stretch and loosen up after battle.

How to say it: HIT-mon-lee

Height: 4' 11"
Weight: 109.8 lbs.

Possible Moves: Revenge, Double Kick, Meditate, Rolling Kick, Jump Kick, Brick Break, Focus Energy, Feint, High Jump Kick, Mind Reader, Foresight, Wide Guard, Blaze Kick, Endure, Mega Kick, Close Combat, Reversal

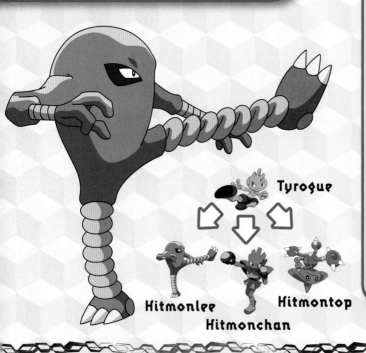

Tyrogue

Hitmonlee
Hitmonchan
Hitmontop

HITMONTOP

Handstand Pokémon

REGION
JOHTO

TYPE: FIGHTING

Hitmontop's spinning kicks balance offense and defense. Walking is a less efficient mode of travel for it than spinning.

How to say it: HIT-mon-TOP

Height: 4' 07"   **Weight:** 105.8 lbs.

Possible Moves: Revenge, Rolling Kick, Focus Energy, Pursuit, Quick Attack, Triple Kick, Rapid Spin, Counter, Feint, Agility, Gyro Ball, Wide Guard, Quick Guard, Detect, Close Combat, Endeavor

Tyrogue

Hitmonlee
Hitmonchan
Hitmontop

LEGENDARY POKÉMON

HO-OH
Rainbow Pokémon

TYPE: FIRE-FLYING

When Ho-Oh's feathers catch the light at different angles, they glow in a rainbow of colors. Legend says these feathers bring joy to whoever holds one.

How to say it: HOE-OH

Height: 12' 06"
Weight: 438.7 lbs.

Possible Moves: Whirlwind, Weather Ball, Gust, Brave Bird, Extrasensory, Sunny Day, Fire Blast, Sacred Fire, Punishment, Ancient Power, Safeguard, Recover, Future Sight, Natural Gift, Calm Mind, Sky Attack

Does not evolve

TYPE: DARK-FLYING

When Honchkrow cries out in its deep voice, several Murkrow will appear to answer the call. Honchkrow is most active after dark.

How to say it: HONCH-krow

Height: 2' 11"
Weight: 60.2 lbs.

Possible Moves: Night Slash, Sucker Punch, Astonish, Pursuit, Haze, Wing Attack, Swagger, Nasty Plot, Foul Play, Quash, Dark Pulse

HONCHKROW
Big Boss Pokémon

Murkrow Honchkrow

HONEDGE
Sword Pokémon

REGION
KALOS (CENTRAL)

TYPE: STEEL-GHOST

Beware when approaching a Honedge! Those foolish enough to wield it like a sword will quickly find themselves wrapped in its blue cloth and drained of energy.

How to say it: HONE-ej

Height: 2' 07"
Weight: 4.4 lbs.

Possible Moves: Tackle, Swords Dance, Fury Cutter, Metal Sound, Pursuit, Autotomize, Shadow Sneak, Aerial Ace, Retaliate, Slash, Iron Defense, Night Slash, Power Trick, Iron Head, Sacred Sword

Honedge   Doublade   Aegislash

HOOPA
The Mischief Pokémon

REGION
KALOS

MYTHICAL POKÉMON

TYPE: PSYCHIC-GHOST

According to myth, Hoopa can summon whatever it wants with the enormous power of its six rings. When that power is confined, it is much smaller and less destructive.

How to say it: HOOP-ah

Height: 1' 08"   **Weight:** 19.8 lbs.

Possible Moves: Trick, Destiny Bond, Ally Switch, Confusion, Astonish, Magic Coat, Light Screen, Psybeam, Skill Swap, Power Split, Guard Split, Phantom Force, Zen Headbutt, Wonder Room, Trick Room, Shadow Ball, Nasty Plot, Psychic, Hyperspace Hole

Hoopa
Confined

Hoopa
Unbound

Does not evolve

HOOTHOOT
Owl Pokémon

TYPE: NORMAL-FLYING

Hoothoot has a special sense organ that allows it to track the rotation of the planet. It always starts to hoot at the same time of day, and this timing is so exact you could set your watch by it.

How to say it: HOOT-HOOT

Height: 2' 04"   **Weight:** 46.7 lbs.

Possible Moves: Tackle, Growl, Foresight, Hypnosis, Peck, Uproar, Reflect, Confusion, Echoed Voice, Take Down, Air Slash, Zen Headbutt, Synchronoise, Extrasensory, Psycho Shift, Roost, Dream Eater

Hoothoot   Noctowl

HOPPIP
Cottonweed Pokémon

TYPE: GRASS-FLYING

Since Hoppip floats on the wind, it must cluster together with others to withstand strong gusts. Otherwise, it might be blown away!

How to say it: HOP-pip

Height: 1' 04"
Weight: 1.1 lbs.

Possible Moves: Splash, Synthesis, Tail Whip, Tackle, Fairy Wind, Poison Powder, Stun Spore, Sleep Powder, Bullet Seed, Leech Seed, Mega Drain, Acrobatics, Rage Powder, Cotton Spore, U-turn, Worry Seed, Giga Drain, Bounce, Memento

Hoppip   Skiploom   Jumpluff

HORSEA
Dragon Pokémon

TYPE: WATER

Horsea wraps its tail around solid objects on the seafloor to avoid being swept away in a strong current. When threatened, it spits a cloud of ink to cover its escape.

How to say it: HOR-see

Height: 1' 04"   **Weight:** 17.6 lbs.

Possible Moves: Water Gun, Smokescreen, Leer, Bubble, Focus Energy, Bubble Beam, Agility, Twister, Brine, Hydro Pump, Dragon Dance, Dragon Pulse

Horsea   Seadra   Kingdra

TYPE: DARK-FIRE

Houndoom choose who will lead their pack by engaging in fierce battles. You can often identify a pack leader by its sharply angled horns.

How to say it: HOWN-doom

Height: 4' 07"
Weight: 77.2 lbs.

Possible Moves: Inferno, Nasty Plot, Thunder Fang, Leer, Ember, Howl, Smog, Roar, Bite, Odor Sleuth, Beat Up, Fire Fang, Feint Attack, Embargo, Foul Play, Flamethrower, Crunch

HOUNDOOM
Dark Pokémon

MEGA HOUNDOOM
Dark Pokémon

TYPE: DARK-FIRE

Height: 6' 03"
Weight: 109.1 lbs.

Houndour ⇨ Houndoom ⇨ Mega Houndoom

HOUNDOUR
Dark Pokémon

TYPE: DARK-FIRE

Houndour are known for their teamwork. They hunt in packs and use different kinds of cries to coordinate their group attacks.

How to say it: HOWN-dowr

Height: 2' 00"
Weight: 23.8 lbs.

Possible Moves: Leer, Ember, Howl, Smog, Roar, Bite, Odor Sleuth, Beat Up, Fire Fang, Feint Attack, Embargo, Foul Play, Flamethrower, Crunch, Nasty Plot, Inferno

Houndour   Houndoom   Mega Houndoom

HUNTAIL
Deep Sea Pokémon

TYPE: WATER

Huntail lives in the darkest depths of the sea, so people didn't know about it for a long time. Its tail, which resembles a small creature, sometimes tricks others into attacking.

How to say it: HUN-tail

Height: 5' 07"
Weight: 59.5 lbs.

Possible Moves: Whirlpool, Bite, Screech, Water Pulse, Scary Face, Ice Fang, Brine, Baton Pass, Dive, Crunch, Aqua Tail, Hydro Pump

Clamperl   Huntail

HYDREIGON
Brutal Pokémon

TYPE: DARK-DRAGON

The smaller heads on Hydreigon's arms don't have brains, but they can still eat. Any movement within its line of sight will be greeted with a frightening attack.

How to say it: hy-DRY-gahn

Height: 5' 11"   **Weight:** 352.7 lbs.

Possible Moves: Outrage, Hyper Voice, Tri Attack, Dragon Rage, Focus Energy, Bite, Headbutt, Dragon Breath, Roar, Crunch, Slam, Dragon Pulse, Work Up, Dragon Rush, Body Slam, Scary Face

Deino   Zweilous   Hydreigon

HYPNO
Hypnosis Pokémon

TYPE: PSYCHIC

As Hypno's pendulum swings and shines, anyone watching falls into a hypnotic trance. To enhance the effect, it always keeps the pendulum polished.

How to say it: HIP-no

Height: 5' 03"   **Weight:** 166.7 lbs.

Possible Moves: Nightmare, Switcheroo, Pound, Hypnosis, Disable, Confusion, Headbutt, Poison Gas, Meditate, Psybeam, Psych Up, Synchronoise, Zen Headbutt, Swagger, Psychic, Nasty Plot, Psyshock, Future Sight

Drowzee   Hypno

IGGLYBUFF
Balloon Pokémon

TYPE: NORMAL-FAIRY

Before it evolves, Igglybuff's vocal cords are under-developed, and singing hurts its throat. Its soft, squishy body gives off a sweet, calming aroma.

How to say it: IG-lee-buff

Height: 1' 00"
Weight: 2.2 lbs.

Possible Moves: Sing, Charm, Defense Curl, Pound, Sweet Kiss, Copycat

Igglybuff   Jigglypuff   Wigglytuff

ILLUMISE
Firefly Pokémon

TYPE: BUG

Illumise gives off a sweet scent that attracts Volbeat by the dozen. Then, it directs the swarm in drawing patterns of light across the night sky.

How to say it: EE-loom-MEE-zay

Height: 2' 00"
Weight: 39.0 lbs.

Possible Moves: Tackle, Play Nice, Sweet Scent, Charm, Moonlight, Quick Attack, Wish, Encore, Flatter, Helping Hand, Zen Headbutt, Bug Buzz, Covet

Does not evolve

INFERNAPE
Flame Pokémon

TYPE: FIRE-FIGHTING

Swift and agile, Infernape puts all four of its limbs to use in its distinctive fighting style. The fire on its head mirrors the fire in its spirit.

How to say it: in-FER-nape

Height: 3' 11"   **Weight:** 121.3 lbs.

Possible Moves: Scratch, Leer, Ember, Taunt, Mach Punch, Fury Swipes, Flame Wheel, Feint, Punishment, Close Combat, Fire Spin, Acrobatics, Calm Mind, Flare Blitz

Chimchar   Monferno   Infernape

INKAY
Revolving Pokémon

TYPE: DARK-PSYCHIC

The spots on Inkay's body emit a flashing light. This light confuses its opponents, giving it a chance to escape.

How to say it: in-kay

Height: 1' 04"
Weight: 7.7 lbs.

Possible Moves: Tackle, Peck, Constrict, Reflect, Foul Play, Swagger, Psywave, Topsy-Turvy, Hypnosis, Psybeam, Switcheroo, Payback, Light Screen, Pluck, Psycho Cut, Slash, Night Slash, Superpower

Inkay   Malamar

IVYSAUR
Seed Pokémon

REGIONS
KALOS (CENTRAL), KANTO

TYPE: GRASS-POISON

Carrying the weight of the bud on its back makes Ivysaur's legs stronger. When the bud is close to blooming, the Pokémon spends more time sleeping in the sun.

How to say it: EYE-vee-sore

Height: 3' 03"   **Weight:** 28.7 lbs.

Possible Moves: Tackle, Growl, Leech Seed, Vine Whip, Poison Powder, Sleep Powder, Take Down, Razor Leaf, Sweet Scent, Growth, Double-Edge, Worry Seed, Synthesis, Solar Beam

Bulbasaur   Ivysaur   Venusaur   Mega Venusaur

TYPE: WATER-GHOST

Though most of its body is made of seawater, Jellicent should not be underestimated. Stories tell of a whole fleet of shipwrecks on the floor of its ocean home.

How to say it: JEL-ih-sent

Height: 7' 03"
Weight: 297.6 lbs.

Possible Moves: Bubble, Water Sport, Absorb, Night Shade, Bubble Beam, Recover, Water Pulse, Ominous Wind, Brine, Rain Dance, Hex, Hydro Pump, Wring Out, Water Spout

JELLICENT
Floating Pokémon

Male Form

Female Form

Frillish   Jellicent

TYPE: NORMAL-FAIRY

Jigglypuff's primary weapon is its song, which lulls opponents to sleep. Because it never stops to breathe while singing, long battles can put it in danger.

How to say it: JIG-lee-puff

Height: 1' 08"   **Weight:** 12.1 lbs.

Possible Moves: Sing, Defense Curl, Pound, Play Nice, Disable, Round, Rollout, Double Slap, Rest, Body Slam, Gyro Ball, Wake-Up Slap, Mimic, Hyper Voice, Disarming Voice, Double-Edge

JIGGLYPUFF
Balloon Pokémon

Igglybuff   Jigglypuff   Wigglytuff

MYTHICAL POKÉMON

TYPE: STEEL-PSYCHIC

According to myth, if you write your wish on one of the notes attached to Jirachi's head and then sing to it in a pure voice, the Pokémon will awaken from its thousand-year slumber and grant your wish.

How to say it: jer-AH-chi

Height: 1' 00"   **Weight:** 2.4 lbs.

Possible Moves: Wish, Confusion, Rest, Swift, Helping Hand, Psychic, Refresh, Rest, Zen Headbutt, Double-Edge, Gravity, Healing Wish, Future Sight, Cosmic Power, Last Resort, Doom Desire

Does not evolve

JOLTEON
Lightning Pokémon

TYPE: ELECTRIC

Jolteon's fur carries a static charge, and its body generates electricity. It can channel this electricity during battle to call down a thunderbolt!

How to say it: JOL-tee-on

Height: 2' 07" **Weight:** 54.0 lbs.

Possible Moves: Helping Hand, Tackle, Tail Whip, Sand Attack, Thunder Shock, Quick Attack, Double Kick, Thunder Fang, Pin Missile, Agility, Thunder Wave, Discharge, Last Resort, Thunder

Eevee   Jolteon

TYPE: BUG-ELECTRIC

Joltik can't produce their own electricity, so they attach to larger Pokémon and suck up the static electricity given off. They store this energy in a special pouch.

How to say it: JOHL-tik

Height: 0' 04" **Weight:** 1.3 lbs.

Possible Moves: String Shot, Leech Life, Spider Web, Thunder Wave, Screech, Fury Cutter, Electroweb, Bug Bite, Gastro Acid, Slash, Electro Ball, Signal Beam, Agility, Sucker Punch, Discharge, Bug Buzz

REGION
UNOVA

JOLTIK
Attaching Pokémon

Joltik   Galvantula

JUMPLUFF
Cottonweed Pokémon

TYPE: GRASS-FLYING

If Jumpluff hits a patch of cold air while it's drifting on the wind, it will return to the ground to await a warm breeze. The winds carry its fluffy body across the sea and around the world.

How to say it: JUM-pluff

Height: 2' 07"
Weight: 6.6 lbs.

Possible Moves: Splash, Synthesis, Tail Whip, Tackle, Fairy Wind, Poison Powder, Stun Spore, Sleep Powder, Bullet Seed, Leech Seed, Mega Drain, Acrobatics, Rage Powder, Cotton Spore, U-turn, Worry Seed, Giga Drain, Bounce, Memento

Hoppip Skiploom Jumpluff

JYNX
Human Shape Pokémon

TYPE: ICE-PSYCHIC

Jynx has a hypnotic, rhythmic walk that makes it look like it's dancing. People who watch it move often find themselves dancing along.

How to say it: JINX

Height: 4' 07"   **Weight:** 89.5 lbs.

Possible Moves: Draining Kiss, Perish Song, Pound, Lick, Lovely Kiss, Powder Snow, Double Slap, Ice Punch, Heart Stamp, Mean Look, Fake Tears, Wake-Up Slap, Avalanche, Body Slam, Wring Out, Blizzard

Smoochum Jynx

KABUTO
Shellfish Pokémon

TYPE: ROCK-WATER

Kabuto has remained unchanged for three hundred million years. It was restored from a fossil, but every once in a while, a living specimen is discovered in the wild.

How to say it: kuh-BOO-toe

Height: 1' 08"
Weight: 25.4 lbs.

Possible Moves: Scratch, Harden, Absorb, Leer, Mud Shot, Sand Attack, Endure, Aqua Jet, Mega Drain, Metal Sound, Ancient Power, Wring Out

Kabuto   Kabutops

TYPE: ROCK-WATER

Long ago, Kabutops swam through ancient seas in search of food. Its legs and gills are just beginning to adapt to a life on land.

How to say it: KA-boo-tops

Height: 4' 03"
Weight: 89.3 lbs.

Possible Moves: Feint, Scratch, Harden, Absorb, Leer, Mud Shot, Sand Attack, Endure, Aqua Jet, Mega Drain, Slash, Metal Sound, Ancient Power, Wring Out, Night Slash

KABUTOPS
Shellfish Pokémon

Kabuto   Kabutops

KADABRA
Psi Pokémon

REGIONS
KALOS (CENTRAL), KANTO

TYPE: PSYCHIC

The silver spoon Kadabra carries intensifies its brain waves. Only those with strong minds should attempt to train this Pokémon.

How to say it: kuh-DAH-bra

Height: 4' 03"   **Weight:** 124.6 lbs.

Possible Moves: Teleport, Kinesis, Confusion, Disable, Miracle Eye, Ally Switch, Psybeam, Reflect, Telekinesis, Recover, Psycho Cut, Role Play, Psychic, Future Sight, Trick

Abra   Kadabra   Alakazam   Mega Alakazam

KAKUNA
Cocoon Pokémon

REGIONS
KALOS (CENTRAL), KANTO

TYPE: BUG-POISON

Kakuna appears motionless from the outside, but inside its shell, it's busily preparing to evolve. Sometimes the shell heats up from this activity.

How to say it: kah-KOO-na

Height: 2' 00"
Weight: 22.0 lbs.

Possible Move: Harden

Weedle   Kakuna   Beedrill   Mega Beedrill

KANGASKHAN
Parent Pokémon

TYPE: NORMAL

A little Kangaskhan playing on its own should be left alone. The Parent Pokémon always keeps careful watch and will attack any aggressor.

How to say it: KANG-gas-con

Height: 7' 03"
Weight: 176.4 lbs.

Possible Moves: Comet Punch, Leer, Fake Out, Tail Whip, Bite, Double Hit, Rage, Mega Punch, Chip Away, Dizzy Punch, Crunch, Endure, Outrage, Sucker Punch, Reversal

MEGA KANGASKHAN
Parent Pokémon

TYPE: NORMAL

Height: 7' 03"
Weight: 220.5 lbs.

Kangaskhan   Mega Kangaskhan

KARRABLAST

Clamping Pokémon

TYPE: BUG

Karrablast often attack Shelmet, trying to steal their shells. When electrical energy envelops them at the same time, they both evolve.

How to say it: KAIR-ruh-blast

Height: 1' 08"
Weight: 13.0 lbs.

Possible Moves: Peck, Leer, Endure, Fury Cutter, Fury Attack, Headbutt, False Swipe, Bug Buzz, Slash, Take Down, Scary Face, X-Scissor, Flail, Swords Dance, Double-Edge

Karrablast   **Escavalier**

KECLEON

Color Swap Pokémon

TYPE: NORMAL

Kecleon is a master of camouflage and can change the color of its skin to hide in any environment. However, its zigzag pattern is always the same.

How to say it: KEH-clee-on

Height: 3' 03"   **Weight:** 48.5 lbs.

Possible Moves: Synchronoise, Ancient Power, Thief, Tail Whip, Astonish, Lick, Scratch, Bind, Feint Attack, Fury Swipes, Feint, Psybeam, Shadow Sneak, Slash, Screech, Substitute, Sucker Punch, Shadow Claw

Does not evolve

Ordinary Forme

Resolute Forme

TYPE: WATER-FIGHTING

Keldeo travels the world visiting beaches and riverbanks, where it can race across the water. When this Mythical Pokémon is filled with resolve, it gains a blinding speed.

How to say it: KELL-dee-oh

Height: 4' 07"   **Weight:** 106.9 lbs.

Possible Moves: Aqua Jet, Leer, Double Kick, Bubble Beam, Take Down, Helping Hand, Retaliate, Aqua Tail, Sacred Sword, Swords Dance, Quick Guard, Work Up, Hydro Pump, Close Combat

Does not evolve

KINGDRA
Dragon Pokémon

**REGIONS
JOHTO,
KALOS
(COASTAL)**

TYPE: WATER-DRAGON

Kingdra makes its home so deep in the ocean that nothing else lives there. Some people think its yawn influences the currents.

How to say it: KING-dra

Height: 5' 11"
Weight: 335.1 lbs.

Possible Moves: Dragon Pulse, Yawn, Water Gun, Smokescreen, Leer, Bubble, Focus Energy, Bubble Beam, Agility, Twister, Brine, Hydro Pump, Dragon Dance

Horsea　　Seadra　　Kingdra

KINGLER
Pincer Pokémon

**REGION
KANTO**

TYPE: WATER

When one Kingler waves to another with its giant claw, it's sending a message. They can't hold long conversations this way, though, because waving those heavy claws is tiring.

How to say it: KING-ler

Height: 4' 03"　　**Weight:** 132.3 lbs.

Possible Moves: Wide Guard, Mud Sport, Bubble, Vice Grip, Leer, Harden, Bubble Beam, Mud Shot, Metal Claw, Stomp, Protect, Guillotine, Slam, Brine, Crabhammer, Flail

Krabby　　Kingler

TYPE: PSYCHIC-FAIRY

A Kirlia whose Trainer has a positive attitude develops a shining beauty. When this Pokémon uses its psychic powers, strange mirages surround it.

How to say it: KERL-lee-ah

Height: 2' 07"   **Weight:** 44.5 lbs.

Possible Moves: Growl, Confusion, Double Team, Teleport, Lucky Chant, Magical Leaf, Heal Pulse, Calm Mind, Psychic, Imprison, Future Sight, Charm, Hypnosis, Dream Eater, Stored Power

REGIONS
HOENN,
KALOS
(CENTRAL)

KIRLIA
Emotion Pokémon

Ralts   Kirlia

Gardevoir   Mega Gardevoir

Gallade   Mega Gallade

191

KLANG
Gear Pokémon

TYPE: STEEL

Klang's body is made up of one mini-gear and one bigger gear, which change their rotation to communicate with other Klang. It can shoot the mini-gear at an opponent in battle.

How to say it: KLANG

Height: 2' 00"
Weight: 112.4 lbs.

Possible Moves: Vice Grip, Charge, Thunder Shock, Gear Grind, Bind, Charge Beam, Autotomize, Mirror Shot, Screech, Discharge, Metal Sound, Shift Gear, Lock-On, Zap Cannon, Hyper Beam

Klink   Klang   Klinklang

KLEFKI
Key Ring Pokémon

REGION
**KALOS
(MOUNTAIN)**

TYPE: STEEL-FAIRY

To keep valuables locked up tight, give the key to a Klefki. This Pokémon loves to collect keys, and it will guard its collection with all its might.

How to say it: KLEF-key

Height: 0' 08"   **Weight:** 6.6 lbs.

Possible Moves: Fairy Lock, Tackle, Fairy Wind, Astonish, Metal Sound, Spikes, Draining Kiss, Crafty Shield, Foul Play, Torment, Mirror Shot, Imprison, Recycle, Play Rough, Magic Room, Heal Block

Does not evolve

TYPE: STEEL

REGION UNOVA

KLINK
Gear Pokémon

The two mini-gears that make up Klink's body are meant for each other. If they get separated, they won't mesh with any other mini-gear until they find each other again.

How to say it: KLEENK

Height: 1' 00"
Weight: 46.3 lbs.

Possible Moves: Vice Grip, Charge, Thunder Shock, Gear Grind, Bind, Charge Beam, Autotomize, Mirror Shot, Screech, Discharge, Metal Sound, Shift Gear, Lock-On, Zap Cannon, Hyper Beam

Klink   Klang   Klinklang

TYPE: STEEL

REGION UNOVA

KLINKLANG
Gear Pokémon

Klinklang stores energy in its red core and charges itself up by spinning that gear rapidly. It can shoot the energy from the spikes on its outer ring.

How to say it: KLEENK-klang

Height: 2' 00"
Weight: 178.6 lbs.

Possible Moves: Vice Grip, Charge, Thunder Shock, Gear Grind, Bind, Charge Beam, Autotomize, Mirror Shot, Screech, Discharge, Metal Sound, Shift Gear, Lock-On, Zap Cannon, Hyper Beam

Klink   Klang   Klinklang

KOFFING

Poison Gas Pokémon

TYPE: POISON

The gases that fill Koffing's body are extremely toxic. When it's under attack, it releases this poisonous gas from jets on its surface.

How to say it: CAWF-ing

Height: 2' 00"
Weight: 2.2 lbs.

Possible Moves: Poison Gas, Tackle, Smog, Smokescreen, Assurance, Clear Smog, Self-Destruct, Sludge, Haze, Gyro Ball, Explosion, Sludge Bomb, Destiny Bond, Memento

Koffing   Weezing

KRABBY

River Crab Pokémon

TYPE: WATER

Krabby dig holes in sandy beaches to make their homes. When the food supply is limited, they sometimes fight over territory.

How to say it: CRA-bee

Height: 1' 04"
Weight: 614.3 lbs.

Possible Moves: Mud Sport, Bubble, Vice Grip, Leer, Harden, Bubble Beam, Mud Shot, Metal Claw, Stomp, Protect, Guillotine, Slam, Brine, Crabhammer, Flail

Krabby   Kingler

KRICKETOT
Cricket Pokémon

TYPE: BUG

The sound of Kricketot's antennae knocking together resembles the sound of a xylophone. They use these sounds to communicate.

How to say it: KRICK-eh-tot

Height: 1' 00"   **Weight:** 4.9 lbs.

Possible Moves: Growl, Bide, Struggle Bug, Bug Bite

Kricketot   Kricketune

KRICKETUNE
Cricket Pokémon

TYPE: BUG

Kricketune composes many different melodies that reflect its emotional state. Researchers are trying to determine whether the patterns of its music have a deeper meaning.

How to say it: KRICK-eh-toon

Height: 3' 03"   **Weight:** 56.2 lbs.

Possible Moves: Growl, Bide, Fury Cutter, Leech Life, Sing, Focus Energy, Slash, X-Scissor, Screech, Taunt, Night Slash, Bug Buzz, Perish Song

Kricketot   Kricketune

195

KROKOROK

Desert Croc Pokémon

REGIONS
KALOS (COASTAL), UNOVA

TYPE: GROUND-DARK

The membranes that cover Krokorok's eyes not only protect them during sandstorms, but also act like heat sensors, enabling it to navigate in total darkness.

How to say it: KRAHK-oh-rahk

Height: 3' 03"   **Weight:** 73.6 lbs.

Possible Moves: Leer, Rage, Bite, Sand Attack, Torment, Sand Tomb, Assurance, Mud-Slap, Embargo, Swagger, Crunch, Dig, Scary Face, Foul Play, Sandstorm, Earthquake, Thrash

Sandile   Krokorok   Krookodile

KROOKODILE

Intimidation Pokémon

REGIONS
KALOS (COASTAL), UNOVA

TYPE: GROUND-DARK

Krookodile's formidable jaws are capable of crunching up cars. Triggered into violence by nearby movement, Krookodile will clamp onto its prey with all the might of those jaws.

How to say it: KROOK-oh-dyle

Height: 4' 11"   **Weight:** 212.3 lbs.

Possible Moves: Outrage, Leer, Rage, Bite, Sand Attack, Torment, Sand Tomb, Assurance, Mud-Slap, Embargo, Swagger, Crunch, Dig, Scary Face, Foul Play, Sandstorm, Earthquake

Sandile   Krokorok   Krookodile

REGION HOENN

KYOGRE
Sea Basin Pokémon

TYPE: WATER

Legends say that Kyogre is the sea personified. When it channels the full power of nature, it can raise sea levels with mighty storms. This Pokémon often clashes with Groudon.

How to say it: kai-OH-gurr

Height: 14' 09"
Weight: 776.0 lbs.

Possible Moves: Water Pulse, Scary Face, Body Slam, Muddy Water, Aqua Ring, Ice Beam, Ancient Power, Water Spout, Calm Mind, Aqua Tail, Sheer Cold, Double-Edge, Hydro Pump

PRIMAL KYOGRE
Sea Basin Pokémon

TYPE: WATER

Height: 32' 02"
Weight: 948.0 lbs.

Kyogre → Primal Kyogre

LEGENDARY POKÉMON

Black Kyurem

White Kyurem

TYPE: DRAGON-ICE

When the freezing energy inside Kyurem leaked out, its entire body froze. Legends say it will become whole with the help of a hero who will bring truth or ideals.

How to say it: KYOO-rem

Height: 9' 10"   **Weight:** 716.5 lbs.

Possible Moves: Icy Wind, Dragon Rage, Imprison, Ancient Power, Ice Beam, Dragon Breath, Slash, Scary Face, Glaciate, Dragon Pulse, Imprison, Endeavor, Blizzard, Outrage, Hyper Voice

Does not evolve

TYPE: STEEL-ROCK

Lairon lives near tasty, mineral-rich springs, where it tempers its body with iron from the water and rocks. It sometimes comes into conflict with miners going after the same iron ore it uses as a food source.

How to say it: LAIR-ron

Height: 2' 11"
Weight: 264.6 lbs.

Possible Moves: Tackle, Harden, Mud-Slap, Headbutt, Metal Claw, Iron Defense, Roar, Take Down, Iron Head, Protect, Metal Sound, Iron Tail, Autotomize, Heavy Slam, Double-Edge, Metal Burst

LAIRON
Iron Armor Pokémon

Aron → Lairon → Aggron → Mega Aggron

LAMPENT
Lamp Pokémon

TYPE: GHOST-FIRE

Lampent tends to lurk grimly around hospitals, waiting for someone to take a bad turn so it can absorb the departing spirit. The stolen spirits keep its fire burning.

How to say it: LAM-pent

Height: 2' 00"   **Weight:** 28.7 lbs.

Possible Moves: Ember, Astonish, Minimize, Smog, Fire Spin, Confuse Ray, Night Shade, Will-O-Wisp, Flame Burst, Imprison, Hex, Memento, Inferno, Curse, Shadow Ball, Pain Split, Overheat

Litwick → Lampent → Chandelure

199

LEGENDARY POKÉMON

TYPE: GROUND-FLYING

Because its arrival helps crops grow, Landorus is welcomed as "the Guardian of the Fields." This Legendary Pokémon uses the energy of wind and lightning to enrich the soil.

How to say it: LAN-duh-rus

Height: 4' 11" **Weight:** 149.9 lbs.

Possible Moves: Block, Mud Shot, Rock Tomb, Imprison, Punishment, Bulldoze, Rock Throw, Extrasensory, Swords Dance, Earth Power, Rock Slide, Earthquake, Sandstorm, Fissure, Stone Edge, Hammer Arm, Outrage

Does not evolve

LANTURN
Light Pokémon

TYPE: WATER-ELECTRIC

Lanturn's antenna produces a light bright enough to be seen from the surface when it's swimming deep in the ocean. Its nickname is "the Deep-sea Star."

How to say it: LAN-turn

Height: 3' 11" **Weight:** 49.6 lbs.

Possible Moves: Eerie Impulse, Water Gun, Supersonic, Thunder Wave, Flail, Bubble, Confuse Ray, Spark, Take Down, Stockpile, Swallow, Spit Up, Electro Ball, Bubble Beam, Signal Beam, Discharge, Aqua Ring, Hydro Pump, Ion Deluge, Charge

Chinchou   Lanturn

TYPE: WATER-ICE

When a Lapras sings a sad song at twilight, it's said to be looking for other Lapras. Because of human activity, these Pokémon are growing more rare.

How to say it: LAP-rus

Height: 8' 02" **Weight:** 485.0 lbs.

Possible Moves: Sing, Growl, Water Gun, Mist, Confuse Ray, Ice Shard, Water Pulse, Body Slam, Rain Dance, Perish Song, Ice Beam, Brine, Safeguard, Hydro Pump, Sheer Cold

LAPRAS
Transport Pokémon

Does not evolve

LARVESTA

Torch Pokémon

TYPE: BUG-FIRE

From its five horns, Larvesta sends out flames to keep attackers at bay. When it's ready to evolve, it spins a fiery cocoon.

How to say it: lar-VESS-tuh

Height: 3' 07"
Weight: 63.5 lbs.

Possible Moves: Ember, String Shot, Leech Life, Take Down, Flame Charge, Bug Bite, Double-Edge, Flame Wheel, Bug Buzz, Amnesia, Thrash, Flare Blitz

Larvesta   Volcarona

LARVITAR

Rock Skin Pokémon

REGIONS
**JOHTO,
KALOS
(MOUNTAIN)**

TYPE: ROCK-GROUND

Larvitar hatches from an egg buried deep underground. It has to eat its way to the surface by devouring the soil above it.

How to say it: LAR-vuh-tar

Height: 2' 00" **Weight:** 158.7 lbs.

Possible Moves: Bite, Leer, Sandstorm, Screech, Chip Away, Rock Slide, Scary Face, Thrash, Dark Pulse, Payback, Crunch, Earthquake, Stone Edge, Hyper Beam

Larvitar   Pupitar   Tyranitar   Mega Tyranitar

REGION
HOENN

LATIAS
Eon Pokémon

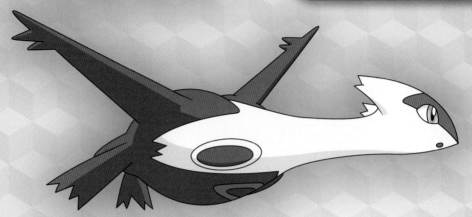

TYPE: DRAGON-PSYCHIC

Sensitive and intelligent, Latias can pick up on people's emotions and understand what they're saying. The down that covers its body can refract light to change its appearance.

How to say it: LAT-ee-ahs

Height: 4' 07"   **Weight:** 88.2 lbs.

Possible Moves: Psywave, Wish, Helping Hand, Safeguard, Dragon Breath, Water Sport, Refresh, Mist Ball, Zen Headbutt, Recover, Psycho Shift, Charm, Psychic, Heal Pulse, Reflect Type, Guard Split, Dragon Pulse, Healing Wish

MEGA LATIAS
Eon Pokémon

TYPE: DRAGON-PSYCHIC

Height: 5' 11"
Weight: 114.6 lbs.

Latias   Mega Latias

LATIOS
Eon Pokémon

REGION
HOENN

LEGENDARY POKÉMON

TYPE: DRAGON-PSYCHIC

Latios can project images into someone else's mind to share information. When it folds its forelegs back against its body, it could beat a jet plane in a race through the sky.

How to say it: LAT-ee-ose

Height: 6' 07"   **Weight:** 132.3 lbs.

Possible Moves: Psywave, Heal Block, Helping Hand, Safeguard, Dragon Breath, Protect, Refresh, Luster Purge, Zen Headbutt, Recover, Psycho Shift, Dragon Dance, Psychic, Heal Pulse, Telekinesis, Power Split, Dragon Pulse, Memento

MEGA LATIOS
Eon Pokémon

TYPE: DRAGON-PSYCHIC

Height: 7' 07"
Weight: 154.3 lbs.

Latios   Mega Latios

LEAFEON
Verdant Pokémon

TYPE: GRASS

When Leafeon soaks up the sun for use in photosynthesis, it gives off clean, fresh air. It often takes naps in a sunny area to gather energy.

How to say it: LEAF-ee-on

Height: 3' 03"
Weight: 56.2 lbs.

Possible Moves: Tail Whip, Tackle, Helping Hand, Sand Attack, Razor Leaf, Quick Attack, Grass Whistle, Magical Leaf, Giga Drain, Swords Dance, Synthesis, Sunny Day, Last Resort, Leaf Blade

Eevee   Leafeon

REGION
UNOVA

LEAVANNY
Nurturing Pokémon

TYPE: BUG-GRASS

Leavanny loves to make warm clothes for smaller Pokémon, cutting up leaves with its arms and sewing them together with sticky silk from its mouth.

How to say it: lee-VAN-nee

Height: 3' 11"   **Weight:** 45.2 lbs.

Possible Moves: False Swipe, Tackle, String Shot, Bug Bite, Razor Leaf, Struggle Bug, Slash, Helping Hand, Leaf Blade, X-Scissor, Entrainment, Swords Dance, Leaf Storm

Sewaddle Swadloon Leavanny

LEDIAN
Five Star Pokémon

TYPE: BUG-FLYING

Ledian channels starlight for use as an energy source. Where the sky is clear and the stars shine bright, these Pokémon gather in large numbers.

How to say it: LEH-dee-an

Height: 4' 07"
Weight: 78.5 lbs.

Possible Moves: Tackle, Supersonic, Comet Punch, Light Screen, Reflect, Safeguard, Mach Punch, Baton Pass, Silver Wind, Agility, Swift, Double-Edge, Bug Buzz

Ledyba   Ledian

LEDYBA
Five Star Pokémon

TYPE: BUG-FLYING

Ledyba gives off a fragrant fluid that it uses to communicate with others. It changes the scent to indicate its emotions.

How to say it: LEH-dee-bah

Height: 3' 03"   **Weight:** 23.8 lbs.

Possible Moves: Tackle, Supersonic, Comet Punch, Light Screen, Reflect, Safeguard, Mach Punch, Baton Pass, Silver Wind, Agility, Swift, Double-Edge, Bug Buzz

Ledyba   Ledian

LICKILICKY
Licking Pokémon

TYPE: NORMAL

Lickilicky can make its long tongue even longer, stretching it out to wrap around food or foe. Its drool causes a lasting numbness.

How to say it: LICK-ee-LICK-ee

Height: 5' 07"
Weight: 308.6 lbs.

Possible Moves: Wring Out, Power Whip, Lick, Supersonic, Defense Curl, Knock Off, Wrap, Stomp, Disable, Slam, Rollout, Chip Away, Me First, Refresh, Screech, Gyro Ball

Lickitung   Lickilicky

TYPE: NORMAL

Lickitung learns about new things by licking them to discover their taste and texture. Sour tastes are not its favorite.

How to say it: LICK-it-tung

Height: 3' 11"
Weight: 144.4 lbs.

Possible Moves: Lick, Supersonic, Defense Curl, Knock Off, Wrap, Stomp, Disable, Slam, Rollout, Chip Away, Me First, Refresh, Screech, Power Whip, Wring Out

LICKITUNG
Licking Pokémon

Lickitung   Lickilicky

LIEPARD
Cruel Pokémon

REGIONS
KALOS (MOUNTAIN), UNOVA

TYPE: DARK

Elegant and swift, Liepard can move through the night without a sound. It uses this stealth to execute sneak attacks.

How to say it: LY-purd

Height: 3' 07"
Weight: 82.7 lbs.

Possible Moves: Scratch, Growl, Assist, Sand Attack, Fury Swipes, Pursuit, Torment, Fake Out, Hone Claws, Assurance, Slash, Taunt, Night Slash, Snatch, Nasty Plot, Sucker Punch, Play Rough

Purrloin   Liepard

LILEEP
Sea Lily Pokémon

REGION
HOENN

TYPE: ROCK-GRASS

Lileep clings to a rock at the bottom of the sea and uses its tentacles to catch food. It was restored from a fossil.

How to say it: lil-LEEP

Height: 3' 03"   **Weight:** 52.5 lbs.

Possible Moves: Astonish, Constrict, Acid, Ingrain, Confuse Ray, Amnesia, Gastro Acid, Ancient Power, Energy Ball, Stockpile, Spit Up, Swallow, Wring Out

Lileep   Cradily

TYPE: GRASS

Unless Lilligant gets just the right kind of care, it will wither and refuse to bloom. The blossom is so beautiful and fragrant that many Trainers decide they're up for the challenge.

How to say it: LIL-lih-gunt

Height: 3' 07"
Weight: 35.9 lbs.

Possible Moves: Growth, Leech Seed, Mega Drain, Synthesis, Teeter Dance, Quiver Dance, Petal Dance

LILLIGANT
Flowering Pokémon

Petilil **Lilligant**

TYPE: NORMAL

Lillipup doesn't let its courage override its intelligence when it comes to battling stronger opponents. With the sensitive hair around its face, it can pick up on slight movements nearby.

How to say it: LIL-ee-pup

Height: 1' 04"
Weight: 9.0 lbs.

Possible Moves: Leer, Tackle, Odor Sleuth, Bite, Helping Hand, Take Down, Work Up, Crunch, Roar, Retaliate, Reversal, Last Resort, Giga Impact

LILLIPUP
Puppy Pokémon

Lillipup **Herdier** **Stoutland**

LINOONE
Rushing Pokémon

REGIONS
**HOENN,
KALOS
(CENTRAL)**

TYPE: NORMAL

Because Linoone can only run in straight lines, curving roads pose quite a navigation problem. It charges ahead at top speed when hunting.

How to say it: line-NOON

Height: 1' 08"
Weight: 71.6 lbs.

Possible Moves:
Play Rough, Rototiller, Switcheroo, Tackle, Growl, Tail Whip, Headbutt, Sand Attack, Odor Sleuth, Mud Sport, Fury Swipes, Covet, Bestow, Slash, Rest, Belly Drum, Fling

Zigzagoon ⇨ Linoone

LITLEO
Lion Cub Pokémon

REGION
**KALOS
(CENTRAL)**

TYPE: FIRE-NORMAL

When Litleo is ready to get stronger, it leaves its pride to live alone. During a battle, its mane radiates intense heat.

How to say it: LIT-lee-oh

Height: 2' 00"
Weight: 29.8 lbs.

Possible Moves: Tackle, Leer, Ember, Work Up, Headbutt, Noble Roar, Take Down, Fire Fang, Endeavor, Echoed Voice, Flamethrower, Crunch, Hyper Voice, Incinerate, Overheat

Litleo ⇨ Pyroar

TYPE: GHOST-FIRE

Litwick pretends to guide people and Pokémon with its light, but following it is a bad idea. The ghostly flame absorbs life energy for use as fuel.

How to say it: LIT-wik

Height: 1' 00"   **Weight:** 6.8 lbs.

Possible Moves: Ember, Astonish, Minimize, Smog, Fire Spin, Confuse Ray, Night Shade, Will-O-Wisp, Flame Burst, Imprison, Hex, Memento, Inferno, Curse, Shadow Ball, Pain Split, Overheat

LITWICK
Candle Pokémon

Litwick   Lampent   Chandelure

TYPE: WATER-GRASS

When the mischievous Lombre spots someone fishing, it swims up to tug on the line. The film that covers its body is unpleasantly slimy to the touch.

How to say it: LOM-brey

Height: 3' 11"   **Weight:** 71.6 lbs.

Possible Moves: Astonish, Growl, Absorb, Nature Power, Fake Out, Fury Swipes, Water Sport, Bubble Beam, Zen Headbutt, Uproar, Hydro Pump

LOMBRE
Jolly Pokémon

Lotad   Lombre   Ludicolo

LOPUNNY

Rabbit Pokémon

TYPE: NORMAL

Because its ears are quite fragile, Lopunny reacts to any rough touch with a kick. If it detects a threat, it leaps away.

How to say it: LAH-puh-nee

Height: 3' 11"
Weight: 73.4 lbs.

Possible Moves: Mirror Coat, Magic Coat, Splash, Pound, Defense Curl, Foresight, Endure, Return, Quick Attack, Jump Kick, Baton Pass, Agility, Dizzy Punch, After You, Charm, Entrainment, Bounce, Healing Wish

MEGA LOPUNNY

Caring Pokémon

TYPE: NORMAL

Height: 4' 03"
Weight: 62.4 lbs.

Buneary　Lopunny　Mega Lopunny

TYPE: WATER-GRASS

The leaf on Lotad's head is too big and heavy for it to carry on land, so it floats on the surface of the water.

How to say it: LOW-tad

Height: 1' 08"
Weight: 5.7 lbs.

Possible Moves: Astonish, Growl, Absorb, Nature Power, Mist, Natural Gift, Mega Drain, Bubble Beam, Zen Headbutt, Rain Dance, Energy Ball

REGIONS
HOENN, KALOS (MOUNTAIN)

LOTAD
Water Weed Pokémon

Lotad   **Lombre**   **Ludicolo**

TYPE: NORMAL

Loudred shouts at such volume that it temporarily deafens itself. The sound waves it produces can knock down a wooden house.

How to say it: LOUD-red

Height: 3' 03"   **Weight:** 89.3 lbs.

Possible Moves: Pound, Uproar, Astonish, Howl, Bite, Supersonic, Stomp, Screech, Roar, Synchronoise, Rest, Sleep Talk, Hyper Voice

REGIONS
HOENN, KALOS (CENTRAL)

LOUDRED
Big Voice Pokémon

Whismur   **Loudred**   **Exploud**

213

LUCARIO

Aura Pokémon

TYPE: FIGHTING-STEEL

Sensing the auras that all beings emanate allows Lucario to read minds and predict movements. Lucario is also very sensitive to others' emotions.

How to say it: loo-CAR-ee-oh

Height: 3' 11"
Weight: 119.0 lbs.

Possible Moves: Extreme Speed, Dragon Pulse, Close Combat, Aura Sphere, Foresight, Quick Attack, Detect, Metal Claw, Counter, Feint, Power-Up Punch, Swords Dance, Metal Sound, Bone Rush, Quick Guard, Me First, Calm Mind, Heal Pulse

MEGA LUCARIO

Aura Pokémon

TYPE: FIGHTING-STEEL

Height: 4' 03"
Weight: 126.8 lbs.

Riolu   Lucario   Mega Lucario

REGIONS
HOENN,
KALOS
(MOUNTAIN)

LUDICOLO
Carefree Pokémon

TYPE: WATER-GRASS

Ludicolo just can't help leaping into a joyful dance when it hears a festive tune. Children who sing while hiking often attract its attention.

How to say it: LOO-dee-KO-low

Height: 4' 11"   **Weight:** 121.3 lbs.

Possible Moves: Astonish, Growl, Mega Drain, Nature Power

Lotad   Lombre   Ludicolo

TYPE: PSYCHIC-FLYING

Lugia can knock down a house with one flutter of its enormously powerful wings. For the safety of others, this Legendary Pokémon lives at the bottom of the sea.

How to say it: LOO-gee-uh

Height: 17' 01"   **Weight:** 476.2 lbs.

Possible Moves: Whirlwind, Weather Ball, Gust, Dragon Rush, Extrasensory, Rain Dance, Hydro Pump, Aeroblast, Punishment, Ancient Power, Safeguard, Recover, Future Sight, Natural Gift, Calm Mind, Sky Attack

Does not evolve

TYPE: WATER

Lumineon lives at the bottom of the deep blue sea. The patterns on its tail give off light, and it can use its front fins to crawl along the sand unnoticed.

How to say it: loo-MIN-ee-onn

Height: 3' 11"
Weight: 52.9 lbs.

Possible Moves: Pound, Water Gun, Attract, Rain Dance, Gust, Water Pulse, Captivate, Safeguard, Aqua Ring, Whirlpool, U-turn, Bounce, Silver Wind, Soak

**REGION
SINNOH**

LUMINEON
Neon Pokémon

Finneon   Lumineon

TYPE: ROCK-PSYCHIC

People think Lunatone came from space because it was first discovered near a meteorite. It floats to get around instead of walking, and its red eyes can freeze a foe with fear.

How to say it: LOO-nuh-tone

Height: 3' 03"
Weight: 370.4 lbs.

Possible Moves: Magic Room, Rock Throw, Tackle, Harden, Confusion, Hypnosis, Rock Polish, Psywave, Embargo, Rock Slide, Cosmic Power, Psychic, Heal Block, Stone Edge, Future Sight, Explosion, Moonblast

**REGIONS
HOENN,
KALOS
(COASTAL)**

LUNATONE
Meteorite Pokémon

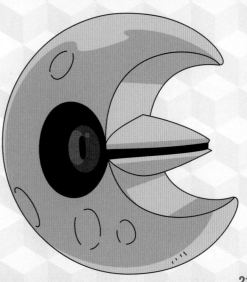

Does not evolve

LUVDISC
Rendezvous Pokémon

REGIONS
**HOENN,
KALOS
(COASTAL)**

TYPE: WATER

Because of its pink, heart-shaped body and its habit of swimming around affectionate couples in shallow tropical seas, Luvdisc is considered a symbol of romance.

How to say it: LOVE-disk

Height: 2' 00"
Weight: 19.2 lbs.

Possible Moves: Tackle, Charm, Water Gun, Agility, Take Down, Lucky Chant, Water Pulse, Attract, Flail, Sweet Kiss, Hydro Pump, Aqua Ring, Captivate, Safeguard

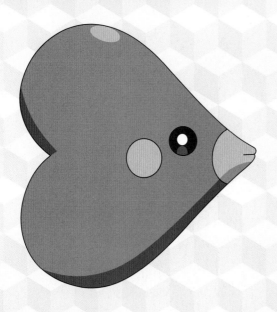

Does not evolve

LUXIO
Spark Pokémon

REGION
SINNOH

TYPE: ELECTRIC

A powerful electric current arcs between Luxio's claws, making it a dangerous opponent in battle. They form small groups and live together.

How to say it: LUCKS-ee-oh

Height: 2' 11"
Weight: 67.2 lbs.

Possible Moves: Tackle, Leer, Charge, Spark, Bite, Roar, Swagger, Thunder Fang, Crunch, Scary Face, Discharge

Shinx　　Luxio　　Luxray

LUXRAY
Gleam Eyes Pokémon

TYPE: ELECTRIC

Luxray's gleaming golden eyes can see right through solid objects. This is very useful when it's keeping watch for approaching threats or looking for food.

How to say it: LUCKS-ray

Height: 4' 07"   **Weight:** 92.6 lbs.

Possible Moves: Tackle, Leer, Charge, Spark, Bite, Roar, Swagger, Thunder Fang, Crunch, Scary Face, Discharge, Wild Charge

Shinx Luxio Luxray

MACHAMP
Superpower Pokémon

TYPE: FIGHTING

Though it is a master of martial arts, Machamp sometimes gets its four arms tangled up when trying to do more intricate tasks.

How to say it: muh-CHAMP

Height: 5' 03"
Weight: 286.6 lbs.

Possible Moves: Wide Guard, Low Kick, Leer, Focus Energy, Karate Chop, Low Sweep, Foresight, Seismic Toss, Revenge, Vital Throw, Submission, Wake-Up Slap, Cross Chop, Scary Face, Dynamic Punch

Machop   Machoke   Machamp

MACHOKE
Superpower Pokémon

TYPE: FIGHTING

Machoke never stop training. Even when they have jobs helping people with heavy labor, they spend their free time building up their muscles.

How to say it: muh-CHOKE

Height: 4' 11"
Weight: 155.4 lbs.

Possible Moves: Low Kick, Leer, Focus Energy, Karate Chop, Low Sweep, Foresight, Seismic Toss, Revenge, Vital Throw, Submission, Wake-Up Slap, Cross Chop, Scary Face, Dynamic Punch

Machop   Machoke   Machamp

MACHOP
Superpower Pokémon

TYPE: FIGHTING

Machop lifts a Graveler like a weight to make its muscles stronger. No matter how much it exercises, it never gets sore.

How to say it: muh-CHOP

Height: 2' 07"
Weight: 43.0 lbs.

Possible Moves: Low Kick, Leer, Focus Energy, Karate Chop, Low Sweep, Foresight, Seismic Toss, Revenge, Vital Throw, Submission, Wake-Up Slap, Cross Chop, Scary Face, Dynamic Punch

Machop   Machoke   Machamp

MAGBY
Live Coal Pokémon

TYPE: FIRE

A Magby that's breathing yellow flames is a healthy Magby. If the flames are smoking and sputtering, it probably needs to get some rest.

How to say it: MAG-bee

Height: 2' 04"
Weight: 47.2 lbs.

Possible Moves: Smog, Leer, Ember, Smokescreen, Feint Attack, Fire Spin, Confuse Ray, Flame Burst, Fire Punch, Lava Plume, Flamethrower, Sunny Day, Fire Blast

Magby   Magmar   Magmortar

MAGCARGO

Lava Pokémon

TYPE: FIRE-ROCK

Magcargo's body is so hot that it vaporizes any nearby water. When the weather turns rainy, Magcargo is surrounded by a thick cloud of steam.

How to say it: mag-CAR-go

Height: 2' 07"
Weight: 121.3 lbs.

Possible Moves: Earth Power, Yawn, Smog, Ember, Rock Throw, Harden, Recover, Flame Burst, Ancient Power, Amnesia, Lava Plume, Shell Smash, Rock Slide, Body Slam, Flamethrower

Slugma　Magcargo

MAGIKARP

Fish Pokémon

TYPE: WATER

Though Magikarp is an exceptionally weak Pokémon when it comes to battle skills, it has an extremely strong constitution. It can live in the most polluted of water.

How to say it: MADGE-eh-karp

Height: 2' 11"
Weight: 22.0 lbs.

Possible Moves: Splash, Tackle, Flail

Magikarp　Gyarados　Mega Gyarados

MAGMAR
Spitfire Pokémon

TYPE: FIRE

When Magmar releases bursts of flame during a battle, any nearby plant life is in danger of catching fire.

How to say it: MAG-mar

Height: 4' 03"
Weight: 98.1 lbs.

Possible Moves: Smog, Leer, Ember, Smokescreen, Feint Attack, Fire Spin, Confuse Ray, Flame Burst, Fire Punch, Lava Plume, Flamethrower, Sunny Day, Fire Blast

Magby → Magmar → Magmortar

TYPE: FIRE

Magmortar makes its home inside a volcano's crater. Its breath is searingly hot, as are the fireballs it blasts out of its arms.

How to say it: mag-MOR-tur

Height: 5' 03"
Weight: 149.9 lbs.

Possible Moves: Thunder Punch, Smog, Leer, Ember, Smokescreen, Feint Attack, Fire Spin, Confuse Ray, Flame Burst, Fire Punch, Lava Plume, Flamethrower, Sunny Day, Fire Blast, Hyper Beam

MAGMORTAR
Blast Pokémon

Magby → Magmar → Magmortar

MAGNEMITE
Magnet Pokémon

REGIONS KALOS (MOUNTAIN), KANTO

TYPE: ELECTRIC-STEEL

A sudden power failure can sometimes be traced to many Magnemite draining energy from the power lines that feed a building.

How to say it: MAG-nuh-mite

Height: 1' 00"
Weight: 13.2 lbs.

Possible Moves: Tackle, Supersonic, Thunder Shock, Sonic Boom, Thunder Wave, Magnet Bomb, Spark, Mirror Shot, Metal Sound, Electro Ball, Flash Cannon, Screech, Discharge, Lock-On, Magnet Rise, Gyro Ball, Zap Cannon

Magnemite   Magneton   Magnezone

MAGNETON
Magnet Pokémon

REGIONS KALOS (MOUNTAIN), KANTO

TYPE: ELECTRIC-STEEL

The magnetic field that surrounds Magneton can wreak havoc on electronics and other machines. Having this Pokémon around can be very bad for business.

How to say it: MAG-nuh-ton

Height: 3' 03"   **Weight:** 132.3 lbs.

Possible Moves: Zap Cannon, Tri Attack, Tackle, Supersonic, Thunder Shock, Sonic Boom, Electric Terrain, Thunder Wave, Magnet Bomb, Spark, Mirror Shot, Metal Sound, Electro Ball, Flash Cannon, Screech, Discharge, Lock-On, Magnet Rise, Gyro Ball

Magnemite   Magneton   Magnezone

TYPE: ELECTRIC-STEEL

MAGNEZONE
Magnet Area Pokémon

Magnezone give off a strong magnetic field that they can't always control. Sometimes they attract one another by accident and stick so tightly that they have trouble separating.

How to say it: MAG-nuh-zone

Height: 3' 11"
Weight: 396.8 lbs.

Possible Moves: Zap Cannon, Magnetic Flux, Mirror Coat, Barrier, Tackle, Supersonic, Sonic Boom, Thunder Shock, Electric Terrain, Thunder Wave, Magnet Bomb, Spark, Mirror Shot, Metal Sound, Electro Ball, Flash Cannon, Screech, Discharge, Lock-On, Magnet Rise, Gyro Ball

Magnemite ⇨ Magneton ⇨ Magnezone

TYPE: FIGHTING

MAKUHITA
Guts Pokémon

If the tireless Makuhita gets knocked down in battle, it always gets up again. Every time it does so, it builds up energy for Evolution.

How to say it: MAK-oo-HEE-ta

Height: 3' 03"
Weight: 190.5 lbs.

Possible Moves: Tackle, Focus Energy, Sand Attack, Arm Thrust, Vital Throw, Fake Out, Whirlwind, Knock Off, Smelling Salts, Belly Drum, Force Palm, Seismic Toss, Wake-Up Slap, Endure, Close Combat, Reversal, Heavy Slam

Makuhita   Hariyama

MALAMAR

Overturning Pokémon

REGION
KALOS (COASTAL)

TYPE: DARK-PSYCHIC

With hypnotic compulsion, Malamar can control the actions of others, forcing them to do its will. The movement of its tentacles can put anyone watching into a trance.

How to say it: MAL-uh-MAR

Height: 4' 11"
Weight: 103.6 lbs.

Possible Moves: Superpower, Reversal, Tackle, Peck, Constrict, Reflect, Foul Play, Swagger, Psywave, Topsy-Turvy, Hypnosis, Psybeam, Switcheroo, Payback, Light Screen, Pluck, Psycho Cut, Slash, Night Slash

Inkay **Malamar**

MAMOSWINE

Twin Tusk Pokémon

REGIONS
KALOS (MOUNTAIN), SINNOH

TYPE: ICE-GROUND

Mamoswine have been around since the last ice age, but the warmer climate reduced their population. Their huge twin tusks are formed of ice.

How to say it: MAM-oh-swine

Height: 8' 02"
Weight: 641.5 lbs.

Possible Moves: Scary Face, Ancient Power, Peck, Odor Sleuth, Mud Sport, Powder Snow, Mud-Slap, Endure, Mud Bomb, Hail, Ice Fang, Take Down, Double Hit, Mist, Thrash, Earthquake, Blizzard

Swinub   Piloswine   Mamoswine

TYPE: WATER

From its earliest days, Manaphy has possessed the power to form close bonds with any Pokémon, no matter what kind.

How to say it: man-UH-fee

Height: 1' 00"   **Weight:** 3.1 lbs.

Possible Moves: Tail Glow, Bubble, Water Sport, Charm, Supersonic, Bubble Beam, Acid Armor, Whirlpool, Water Pulse, Aqua Ring, Dive, Rain Dance, Heart Swap

Does not evolve

TYPE: DARK-FLYING

Mandibuzz flies in slow circles, high in the sky, to keep an eye out for a weak opponent. Then it swoops down in an aerial attack.

How to say it: MAN-dih-buz

Height: 3' 11"   **Weight:** 87.1 lbs.

Possible Moves: Gust, Leer, Fury Attack, Pluck, Nasty Plot, Flatter, Feint Attack, Punishment, Defog, Tailwind, Air Slash, Dark Pulse, Embargo, Bone Rush, Whirlwind, Brave Bird, Mirror Move

Vullaby   Mandibuzz

TYPE: ELECTRIC

When Manectric enters battle, thunderclouds follow. Its mane gives off a strong electric charge.

How to say it: mane-EK-trick

Height: 4' 11"
Weight: 88.6 lbs.

Possible Moves: Electric Terrain, Fire Fang, Tackle, Thunder Wave, Leer, Howl, Quick Attack, Spark, Odor Sleuth, Bite, Thunder Fang, Roar, Discharge, Charge, Wild Charge, Thunder

REGIONS
**HOENN,
KALOS
(COASTAL)**

MANECTRIC
Discharge Pokémon

MEGA MANECTRIC
Discharge Pokémon

TYPE: ELECTRIC

Height: 5' 11"
Weight: 97.0 lbs.

Electrike   Manectric   Mega Manectric

MANKEY

Pig Monkey Pokémon

REGION
KANTO

TYPE: FIGHTING

Mankey flies into a rage at the slightest provocation. These fits of temper are usually preceded by violent tremors, but there's rarely enough time to get away.

How to say it: MANK-ee

Height: 1' 08" **Weight:** 61.7 lbs.

Possible Moves: Covet, Scratch, Low Kick, Leer, Focus Energy, Fury Swipes, Karate Chop, Seismic Toss, Screech, Assurance, Swagger, Cross Chop, Thrash, Punishment, Close Combat, Final Gambit

Mankey ⇨ Primeape

MANTINE

Kite Pokémon

REGIONS
**JOHTO,
KALOS
(COASTAL)**

TYPE:
WATER-FLYING

When the weather is nice, Mantine often leap gracefully out of the waves into the bright sunlight. Sometimes Remoraid go along for the ride.

How to say it: MAN-tine

Height: 6' 11"
Weight: 485.0 lbs.

Possible Moves: Psybeam, Bullet Seed, Signal Beam, Tackle, Bubble, Supersonic, Bubble Beam, Confuse Ray, Wing Attack, Headbutt, Water Pulse, Wide Guard, Take Down, Agility, Air Slash, Aqua Ring, Bounce, Hydro Pump

Mantyke ⇨ Mantine

MANTYKE
Kite Pokémon

TYPE: WATER-FLYING

Mantyke that live in different regions have different patterns on their backs. They're often found in the company of Remoraid.

How to say it: MAN-tike

Height: 3' 03"
Weight: 143.3 lbs.

Possible Moves: Tackle, Bubble, Supersonic, Bubble Beam, Confuse Ray, Wing Attack, Headbutt, Water Pulse, Wide Guard, Take Down, Agility, Air Slash, Aqua Ring, Bounce, Hydro Pump

Mantyke   ⟹   **Mantine**

REGION
UNOVA

MARACTUS
Cactus Pokémon

TYPE: GRASS

Maractus live in dry places, where they dance with rhythmic movements of their prickly limbs to keep others away. This motion gives off a sound like the shaking of maracas.

How to say it: mah-RAK-tus

Height: 3' 03"   **Weight:** 61.7 lbs.

Possible Moves: Peck, Absorb, Sweet Scent, Growth, Pin Missile, Mega Drain, Synthesis, Cotton Spore, Needle Arm, Giga Drain, Acupressure, Ingrain, Petal Dance, Sucker Punch, Sunny Day, Solar Beam, Cotton Guard, After You

Does not evolve

MAREEP

Wool Pokémon

TYPE: ELECTRIC

When Mareep's woolly coat builds up static electricity, the end of its tail glows brightly. The static charge grows as Mareep moves and its wool rubs together.

How to say it: mah-REEP

Height: 2' 00"   **Weight:** 17.2 lbs.

Possible Moves: Tackle, Growl, Thunder Wave, Thunder Shock, Cotton Spore, Charge, Take Down, Electro Ball, Confuse Ray, Power Gem, Discharge, Cotton Guard, Signal Beam, Light Screen, Thunder

Mareep   Flaaffy   Ampharos   Mega Ampharos

MARILL

Aqua Mouse Pokémon

TYPE: WATER-FAIRY

When Marill dives underwater in search of plants to eat, its buoyant tail bobs on the surface. The tail is flexible enough to wrap around a tree as an anchor.

How to say it: MARE-rull

Height: 1' 04"   **Weight:** 18.7 lbs.

Possible Moves: Tackle, Water Gun, Tail Whip, Water Sport, Bubble, Defense Curl, Rollout, Bubble Beam, Helping Hand, Aqua Tail, Double-Edge, Aqua Ring, Rain Dance, Superpower, Hydro Pump, Play Rough

Azurill   Marill   Azumarill

TYPE: GROUND

After overcoming its grief and evolving, Marowak has become extremely tough. Its spirit, tempered by adversity, can withstand just about anything.

How to say it: MAR-oh-wack

Height: 3' 03"
Weight: 99.2 lbs.

Possible Moves: Growl, Tail Whip, Bone Club, Headbutt, Leer, Focus Energy, Bonemerang, Rage, False Swipe, Thrash, Fling, Bone Rush, Endeavor, Double-Edge, Retaliate

REGIONS KALOS (COASTAL), KANTO

MAROWAK
Bone Keeper Pokémon

Cubone   Marowak

TYPE: WATER-GROUND

When the tide goes out, Marshtomp loves to play in the mud. Its well-developed hind legs offer stability, so it can travel over mud faster than it can swim.

How to say it: MARSH-stomp

Height: 2' 04"
Weight: 61.7 lbs.

Possible Moves: Tackle, Growl, Mud-Slap, Water Gun, Bide, Mud Shot, Foresight, Mud Bomb, Take Down, Muddy Water, Protect, Earthquake, Endeavor

REGION HOENN

MARSHTOMP
Mud Fish Pokémon

Mudkip   Marshtomp   Swampert   Mega Swampert

MASQUERAIN

Eyeball Pokémon

TYPE: BUG-FLYING

The eye patterns on Masquerain's large antennae usually have an angry expression, which sometimes scares would-be opponents. If the eyes look sad, it's a sign that heavy rain is coming.

How to say it: mas-ker-RAIN

Height: 2' 07"   **Weight:** 7.9 lbs.

Possible Moves: Quiver Dance, Bug Buzz, Whirlwind, Ominous Wind, Bubble, Quick Attack, Sweet Scent, Water Sport, Gust, Scary Face, Stun Spore, Silver Wind, Air Slash

Surskit   Masquerain

MAWILE
Deceiver Pokémon

TYPE: STEEL-FAIRY

An enemy fooled by Mawile's sweet face will quickly find itself in the crushing grip of the massive steel jaws on the back of this Pokémon's head.

How to say it: MAW-while

Height: 2' 00"
Weight: 25.4 lbs.

Possible Moves: Play Rough, Iron Head, Taunt, Growl, Fairy Wind, Astonish, Fake Tears, Bite, Sweet Scent, Vice Grip, Feint Attack, Baton Pass, Crunch, Iron Defense, Sucker Punch, Stockpile, Swallow, Spit Up

MEGA MAWILE
Deceiver Pokémon

TYPE: STEEL-FAIRY

Height: 3' 03"
Weight: 51.8 lbs.

Mawile   Mega Mawile

MEDICHAM
Meditate Pokémon

TYPE: FIGHTING-PSYCHIC

Medicham has developed a sixth sense and psychic powers through long meditation training. It can disappear into its mountain home if danger approaches.

How to say it: MED-uh-cham

Height: 4' 03"
Weight: 69.4 lbs.

Possible Moves: Zen Headbutt, Fire Punch, Thunder Punch, Ice Punch, Bide, Meditate, Confusion, Detect, Hidden Power, Mind Reader, Feint, Calm Mind, Force Palm, High Jump Kick, Psych Up, Acupressure, Power Trick, Reversal, Recover

MEGA MEDICHAM
Meditate Pokémon

TYPE: FIGHTING-PSYCHIC

Height: 4' 03"
Weight: 69.4 lbs.

Meditite → Medicham → Mega Medicham

TYPE: FIGHTING-PSYCHIC

MEDITITE
Meditate Pokémon

REGIONS
HOENN,
KALOS
(CENTRAL)

Through intense meditation and extreme hunger, Meditite works hard to train its mental powers.

How to say it: MED-uh-tite

Height: 2' 00"   **Weight:** 24.7 lbs.

Possible Moves: Zen Headbutt, Fire Punch, Thunder Punch, Ice Punch, Bide, Meditate, Confusion, Detect, Hidden Power, Mind Reader, Feint, Calm Mind, Force Palm, High Jump Kick, Psych Up, Acupressure, Power Trick, Reversal, Recover

Meditite   Medicham   Mega Medicham

TYPE: GRASS

REGION
JOHTO

MEGANIUM
Herb Pokémon

Meganium's flower wafts a soothing aroma. During a battle, the fragrance grows stronger as this Pokémon attempts to calm its enemies.

How to say it: meg-GAY-nee-um

Height: 5' 11"
Weight: 221.6 lbs.

Possible Moves: Tackle, Growl, Razor Leaf, Poison Powder, Synthesis, Reflect, Magical Leaf, Natural Gift, Petal Dance, Sweet Scent, Light Screen, Body Slam, Safeguard, Aromatherapy, Solar Beam

Chikorita   Bayleef   Meganium

237

MELOETTA

Melody Pokémon

MYTHICAL POKÉMON

Aria Forme

Pirouette Forme

TYPE: NORMAL-PSYCHIC

When Meloetta sings, its voice can control the emotions of people or Pokémon. The beautiful melodies of this Mythical Pokémon can bring aching sadness or radiant joy.

How to say it: mell-oh-ET-uh

Height: 2' 00"   **Weight:** 14.3 lbs.

Possible Moves: Round, Quick Attack, Confusion, Sing, Teeter Dance, Acrobatics, Psybeam, Echoed Voice, U-turn, Wake-Up Slap, Psychic, Hyper Voice, Role Play, Close Combat, Perish Song

Does not evolve

MEOWSTIC
Constraint Pokémon

Male Form

Female Form

TYPE: PSYCHIC

When Meowstic unfolds its ears, the psychic blast created by the eyeball patterns inside can pulverize heavy machinery. It keeps its ears tightly folded unless it's in danger.

How to say it: MYOW-stik

Height: 2' 00"   **Weight:** 18.7 lbs.

Possible Moves (male): Quick Guard, Mean Look, Helping Hand, Scratch, Leer, Covet, Confusion, Light Screen, Psybeam, Fake Out, Disarming Voice, Psyshock, Charm, Miracle Eye, Reflect, Psychic, Role Play, Imprison, Sucker Punch, Misty Terrain

Possible Moves (female): Stored Power, Me First, Magical Leaf, Scratch, Leer, Covet, Confusion, Light Screen, Psybeam, Fake Out, Disarming Voice, Psyshock, Charge Beam, Extrasensory, Psychic, Role Play, Signal Beam, Sucker Punch, Future Sight

Meowstic
(Male Form)

Espurr

Meowstic
(Female Form)

MEOWTH

Scratch Cat Pokémon

REGION
KANTO

TYPE: NORMAL

When Meowth retracts its sharp claws, it can move without making a sound or leaving a footprint. It's drawn to shiny things like coins.

How to say it: me-OUTH

Height: 1' 04"
Weight: 9.3 lbs.

Possible Moves: Scratch, Growl, Bite, Fake Out, Fury Swipes, Screech, Feint Attack, Taunt, Pay Day, Slash, Nasty Plot, Assurance, Captivate, Night Slash, Feint

Meowth Persian

MESPRIT

Emotion Pokémon

REGION
SINNOH

LEGENDARY POKÉMON

TYPE: PSYCHIC

According to legend, Mesprit brought the first taste of joy and sorrow to people's hearts. It is known as "the Being of Emotion."

How to say it: MES-prit

Height: 1' 00"   **Weight:** 0.7 lbs.

Possible Moves: Rest, Confusion, Imprison, Protect, Swift, Lucky Chant, Future Sight, Charm, Extrasensory, Copycat, Natural Gift, Healing Wish

240   Does not evolve

METAGROSS

Iron Leg Pokémon

TYPE: STEEL-PSYCHIC

Metagross is formed when two Metang combine, linking their four brains together. It is intimidating both physically and mentally—it can easily pin a foe underneath its massive steel body and perform complicated calculations in the blink of an eye.

How to say it: MET-uh-gross

Height: 5' 03"
Weight: 1,212.5 lbs.

Possible Moves: Magnet Rise, Take Down, Metal Claw, Confusion, Scary Face, Pursuit, Bullet Punch, Psychic, Iron Defense, Agility, Hammer Arm, Meteor Mash, Zen Headbutt, Hyper Beam

MEGA METAGROSS

Iron Leg Pokémon

TYPE: STEEL-PSYCHIC

Height: 8' 02"
Weight: 2,078.7 lbs.

Beldum   Metang   Metagross   Mega Metagross

METANG
Iron Claw Pokémon

REGION
HOENN

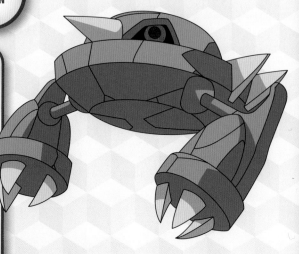

TYPE: STEEL-PSYCHIC

Metang is formed when two Beldum combine, linking their brains and bodies. The power of its linked brains makes it capable of psychokinesis.

How to say it: met-TANG

Height: 3' 11"   **Weight:** 446.4 lbs.

Possible Moves: Magnet Rise, Take Down, Metal Claw, Confusion, Scary Face, Pursuit, Bullet Punch, Psychic, Iron Defense, Agility, Meteor Mash, Zen Headbutt, Hyper Beam

Beldum   Metang   Metagross   Mega Metagross

METAPOD
Cocoon Pokémon

REGIONS
KALOS (CENTRAL), KANTO

TYPE: BUG

Inside its iron-hard shell, Metapod patiently prepares to evolve. It doesn't move much, so it relies on its shell for protection.

How to say it: MET-uh-pod

Height: 2' 04"
Weight: 21.8 lbs.

Possible Move: Harden

Caterpie   Metapod   Butterfree

MYTHICAL POKÉMON

MEW
New Species Pokémon

TYPE: PSYCHIC

It is said that within Mew's cells rests the entirety of the Pokémon genetic code. This Mythical Pokémon can turn invisible to keep others from noticing it.

How to say it: MUE

Height: 1' 04"   **Weight:** 8.8 lbs.

Possible Moves: Pound, Reflect Type, Transform, Mega Punch, Metronome, Psychic, Barrier, Ancient Power, Amnesia, Me First, Baton Pass, Nasty Plot, Aura Sphere

Does not evolve

MEWTWO
Genetic Pokémon

LEGENDARY POKÉMON

TYPE: PSYCHIC

Scientists created Mewtwo by manipulating its genes. If only they could have given it a sense of compassion . . .

How to say it: MUE-TOO

Height: 6' 07"   **Weight:** 269.0 lbs.

Possible Moves: Confusion, Disable, Barrier, Swift, Future Sight, Psych Up, Miracle Eye, Mist, Psycho Cut, Amnesia, Power Swap, Guard Swap, Psychic, Me First, Recover, Safeguard, Aura Sphere, Psystrike

MEGA MEWTWO X
Genetic Pokémon

TYPE: PSYCHIC-FIGHTING

Height: 7' 07"
Weight: 280.0 lbs.

MEGA MEWTWO Y
Genetic Pokémon

TYPE: PSYCHIC

Height: 4' 11"
Weight: 72.8 lbs.

Mega
Mewtwo X

Mewtwo

Mega
Mewtwo Y

MIENFOO
Martial Arts Pokémon

TYPE: FIGHTING

In battle, Mienfoo never stops moving, flowing through one attack after another with grace and speed. Its claws are very sharp.

How to say it: MEEN-FOO

Height: 2' 11"
Weight: 44.1 lbs.

Possible Moves: Pound, Meditate, Detect, Fake Out, Double Slap, Swift, Calm Mind, Force Palm, Drain Punch, Jump Kick, U-turn, Quick Guard, Bounce, High Jump Kick, Reversal, Aura Sphere

Mienfoo　　Mienshao

MIENSHAO
Martial Arts Pokémon

TYPE: FIGHTING

With the long, whiplike fur on its arms, Mienshao can unleash a flurry of attacks so fast they're almost invisible. Its battle combos are unstoppable.

How to say it: MEEN-SHOW

Height: 4' 07"　　**Weight:** 78.3 lbs.

Possible Moves: Aura Sphere, Reversal, Pound, Meditate, Detect, Fake Out, Double Slap, Swift, Calm Mind, Force Palm, Drain Punch, Jump Kick, U-turn, Wide Guard, Bounce, High Jump Kick

Mienfoo　　Mienshao

MIGHTYENA

Bite Pokémon

REGIONS
**HOENN,
KALOS
(MOUNTAIN)**

TYPE: DARK

Mightyena sounds a deep growl before attacking. In the wild, these Pokémon live together in packs.

How to say it: MY-tee-EH-nah

Height: 3' 03"
Weight: 81.6 lbs.

Possible Moves: Crunch, Tackle, Howl, Sand Attack, Bite, Howl, Odor Sleuth, Roar, Swagger, Assurance, Scary Face, Taunt, Embargo, Take Down, Thief, Sucker Punch

Poochyena   Mightyena

MILOTIC

Tender Pokémon

REGION
HOENN

TYPE: WATER

The astoundingly beautiful Milotic live on lake bottoms and radiate calming energy. When they give off a bright pink glow, people stop fighting.

How to say it: my-LOW-tic

Height: 20' 04"
Weight: 357.1 lbs.

Possible Moves: Water Gun, Wrap, Water Sport, Refresh, Water Pulse, Twister, Recover, Captivate, Aqua Tail, Rain Dance, Hydro Pump, Attract, Safeguard, Aqua Ring

Feebas   Milotic

REGIONS
JOHTO,
KALOS
(COASTAL)

MILTANK
Milk Cow Pokémon

TYPE: NORMAL

Miltank produces more than five gallons of milk every day! The milk has a sweet flavor that people of all ages enjoy.

How to say it: MILL-tank

Height: 3' 11"
Weight: 166.4 lbs.

Possible Moves: Tackle, Growl, Defense Curl, Stomp, Milk Drink, Bide, Rollout, Body Slam, Zen Headbutt, Captivate, Gyro Ball, Heal Bell, Wake-Up Slap

Does not evolve

REGIONS
KALOS
(COASTAL),
SINNOH

MIME JR.
Mime Pokémon

TYPE: PSYCHIC-FAIRY

To enthrall and confuse an attacker, Mime Jr. copies its movements. While the opponent is bewildered, it makes its escape.

How to say it: mime JOO-nyur

Height: 2' 00"   **Weight:** 28.7 lbs.

Possible Moves: Tickle, Barrier, Confusion, Copycat, Meditate, Double Slap, Mimic, Encore, Light Screen, Reflect, Psybeam, Substitute, Recycle, Trick, Psychic, Role Play, Baton Pass, Safeguard

Mime Jr. → Mr. Mime

247

MINCCINO

Chinchilla Pokémon

REGION
UNOVA

TYPE: NORMAL

The very tidy Minccino uses its tail as a broom to rid its habitat of any wayward dust or dirt. They even groom one another with their tails.

How to say it: min-CHEE-noh

Height: 1' 04"
Weight: 12.8 lbs.

Possible Moves: Pound, Growl, Helping Hand, Tickle, Double Slap, Encore, Swift, Sing, Tail Slap, Charm, Wake-Up Slap, Echoed Voice, Slam, Captivate, Hyper Voice, Last Resort, After You

Minccino　　**Cinccino**

MINUN

Cheering Pokémon

REGIONS
**HOENN,
KALOS
(CENTRAL)**

TYPE: ELECTRIC

Minun shoots out sparks when cheering on its teammates. If the battle isn't going well, the spark showers get more intense.

How to say it: MIE-nun

Height: 1' 04"　　**Weight:** 9.3 lbs.

Possible Moves: Nasty Plot, Nuzzle, Entrainment, Play Nice, Growl, Thunder Wave, Quick Attack, Helping Hand, Spark, Encore, Charm, Copycat, Electro Ball, Swift, Fake Tears, Charge, Thunder, Baton Pass, Agility, Trump Card

Does not evolve

MISDREAVUS
Screech Pokémon

TYPE: GHOST

Misdreavus likes to scare people by making a dreadful wailing sound. The red spheres around its neck seem to soak up the fear so the Pokémon can use it for food.

How to say it: mis-DREE-vuss

Height: 2' 04"
Weight: 2.2 lbs.

Possible Moves: Growl, Psywave, Spite, Astonish, Confuse Ray, Mean Look, Hex, Psybeam, Pain Split, Payback, Shadow Ball, Perish Song, Grudge, Power Gem

Misdreavus → Mismagius

MISMAGIUS
Magical Pokémon

TYPE: GHOST

Mismagius shows up unexpectedly, muttering in its chanting voice. Its chants often bring torment to those who listen.

How to say it: mis-MAG-ee-us

Height: 2' 11"   **Weight:** 9.7 lbs.

Possible Moves: Lucky Chant, Magical Leaf, Growl, Psywave, Spite, Astonish

Misdreavus → Mismagius

MOLTRES
Flame Pokémon

REGIONS
KALOS (COASTAL), KANTO

LEGENDARY POKÉMON

TYPE: FIRE-FLYING

When Moltres gets hurt, some say it dives into an active volcano and heals itself by bathing in lava. This Legendary Pokémon can give off flames and control fire.

How to say it: MOL-trays

Height: 6' 07"   **Weight:** 132.3 lbs.

Possible Moves: Roost, Hurricane, Sky Attack, Heat Wave, Wing Attack, Ember, Fire Spin, Agility, Endure, Ancient Power, Flamethrower, Safeguard, Air Slash, Sunny Day, Solar Beam

Does not evolve

MONFERNO
Playful Pokémon

REGION
SINNOH

TYPE: FIRE-FIGHTING

An excellent climber, Monferno can strike from above. It can flare up its tail flame to keep enemies at bay.

How to say it: mon-FERN-oh

Height: 2' 11"   **Weight:** 48.5 lbs.

Possible Moves: Scratch, Leer, Ember, Taunt, Mach Punch, Fury Swipes, Flame Wheel, Feint, Torment, Close Combat, Fire Spin, Acrobatics, Slack Off, Flare Blitz

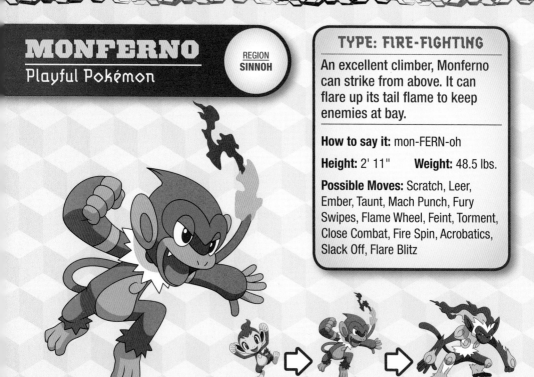

Chimchar   Monferno   Infernape

TYPE: BUG-FLYING

Mothim loves the taste of Combee's honey. Sometimes it will raid a hive at night to steal the sweet substance.

How to say it: MOTH-im

Height: 2' 11"   **Weight:** 51.4 lbs.

Possible Moves: Tackle, Protect, Bug Bite, Hidden Power, Confusion, Gust, Poison Powder, Psybeam, Camouflage, Silver Wind, Air Slash, Psychic, Bug Buzz, Quiver Dance

Burmy
(Male Form)

Mothim

MR. MIME
Barrier Pokémon

REGIONS
KALOS (COASTAL), KANTO

TYPE: PSYCHIC-FAIRY

Sometimes, Mr. Mime's gestures convince an onlooker that the invisible thing it's miming actually exists. Then that thing becomes real.

How to say it: MIS-ter MIME

Height: 4' 03"   **Weight:** 120.1 lbs.

Possible Moves: Misty Terrain, Magical Leaf, Quick Guard, Wide Guard, Power Swap, Guard Swap, Barrier, Confusion, Copycat, Meditate, Double Slap, Mimic, Psywave, Encore, Light Screen, Reflect, Psybeam, Substitute, Recycle, Trick, Psychic, Role Play, Baton Pass, Safeguard

Mime Jr.   Mr. Mime

MUDKIP
Mud Fish Pokémon

REGION
HOENN

TYPE: WATER

Because its fin is so sensitive to the motion of air and water, Mudkip knows what's going on nearby without opening its eyes. The flared gills on its cheeks allow it to breathe underwater.

How to say it: MUD-kip

Height: 1' 04"
Weight: 16.8 lbs.

Possible Moves: Tackle, Growl, Mud-Slap, Water Gun, Bide, Foresight, Mud Sport, Take Down, Whirlpool, Protect, Hydro Pump, Endeavor

Mudkip   Marshtomp   Swampert   Mega Swampert

MUK
Sludge Pokémon

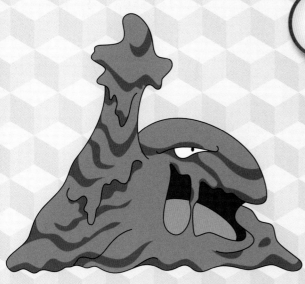

TYPE: POISON

Muk really stinks. The fluid it oozes gives off a terrible smell and pollutes clean water. Cities with a trash problem may also find they have a Muk problem.

How to say it: MUCK

Height: 3' 11"
Weight: 66.1 lbs.

Possible Moves: Poison Gas, Pound, Harden, Mud-Slap, Disable, Minimize, Sludge, Mud Bomb, Fling, Screech, Sludge Bomb, Acid Armor, Sludge Wave, Gunk Shot, Memento

Grimer → Muk

TYPE: NORMAL

Munchlax's long fur is a perfect place to hide snacks. With this permanent food stash, it never goes hungry.

How to say it: MUNCH-lax

Height: 2' 00"
Weight: 231.5 lbs.

Possible Moves: Last Resort, Snatch, Lick, Metronome, Odor Sleuth, Tackle, Defense Curl, Amnesia, Chip Away, Screech, Body Slam, Stockpile, Swallow, Rollout, Fling, Belly Drum, Natural Gift

MUNCHLAX
Big Eater Pokémon

Munchlax → Snorlax

TYPE: PSYCHIC

When people and Pokémon sleep, Munna appears to eat their dreams and nightmares. After eating a happy dream, it gives off pink mist.

How to say it: MOON-nuh

Height: 2' 00"   **Weight:** 51.4 lbs.

Possible Moves: Psywave, Defense Curl, Lucky Chant, Yawn, Psybeam, Imprison, Moonlight, Hypnosis, Zen Headbutt, Synchronoise, Nightmare, Future Sight, Calm Mind, Psychic, Dream Eater, Telekinesis, Stored Power

Munna   Musharna

MURKROW
Darkness Pokémon

TYPE: DARK-FLYING

People used to think Murkrow brought bad luck, so they were afraid of it and kept their distance. It's drawn to sparkly things and sometimes tries to steal them.

How to say it: MUR-crow

Height: 1' 08"
Weight: 4.6 lbs.

Possible Moves: Peck, Astonish, Pursuit, Haze, Wing Attack, Night Shade, Assurance, Taunt, Feint Attack, Mean Look, Foul Play, Tailwind, Sucker Punch, Torment, Quash

Murkrow ➡ Honchkrow

TYPE: PSYCHIC

The dream mist that rises from Musharna's forehead is influenced by the dreams it eats. It can take on many different colors.

How to say it: moo-SHAHR-nuh

Height: 3' 07"
Weight: 133.4 lbs.

Possible Moves: Defense Curl, Lucky Chant, Psybeam, Hypnosis

MUSHARNA
Drowsing Pokémon

Munna ➡ Musharna

NATU
Tiny Bird Pokémon

REGION
JOHTO

TYPE: PSYCHIC-FLYING

With its underdeveloped wings, Natu can't fly, but it's a great jumper, able to leap onto a tree branch higher than a grown man's head. It tends to engage in staring contests with those who meet its eyes.

How to say it: NAH-too

Height: 0' 08" **Weight:** 4.4 lbs.

Possible Moves: Peck, Leer, Night Shade, Teleport, Lucky Chant, Miracle Eye, Me First, Confuse Ray, Wish, Psycho Shift, Future Sight, Stored Power, Ominous Wind, Power Swap, Guard Swap, Psychic

Natu   Xatu

NIDOKING
Drill Pokémon

REGIONS
KALOS
(COASTAL),
KANTO

TYPE: POISON-GROUND

When Nidoking swings its massive tail, it can knock down a radio tower. Nothing can stand in the way of its furious rampage.

How to say it: NEE-doe-king

Height: 4' 07"
Weight: 136.7 lbs.

Possible Moves: Megahorn, Peck, Focus Energy, Double Kick, Poison Sting, Chip Away, Thrash, Earth Power

Nidoran ♂   Nidorino   Nidoking

TYPE: POISON-GROUND

When defending its nest, Nidoqueen hurls its hard-scaled body at an intruder. The impact is often enough to send the enemy flying through the air.

How to say it: NEE-doe-kween

Height: 4' 03"
Weight: 132.3 lbs.

Possible Moves: Superpower, Scratch, Tail Whip, Double Kick, Poison Sting, Chip Away, Body Slam, Earth Power

REGIONS
KANTO
KALOS
(COASTAL),

NIDOQUEEN
Drill Pokémon

Nidoran ♀   Nidorina   Nidoqueen

TYPE: POISON

Though Nidoran ♀ is small, it's quite dangerous. The barbs in its fur and the horn on its head are both extremely poisonous.

How to say it: NEE-doe-ran

Height: 1' 04"
Weight: 15.4 lbs.

Possible Moves: Growl, Scratch, Tail Whip, Double Kick, Poison Sting, Fury Swipes, Bite, Helping Hand, Toxic Spikes, Flatter, Crunch, Captivate, Poison Fang

REGIONS
KALOS
(COASTAL),
KANTO

NIDORAN ♀
Poison Pin Pokémon

Nidoran ♀   Nidorina   Nidoqueen

NIDORAN ♂

Poison Pin Pokémon

TYPE: POISON

Nidoran ♂ has excellent hearing and, thanks to specialized muscles, it can move and rotate its ears to pick up the slightest sound.

How to say it: NEE-doe-ran

Height: 1' 04"   **Weight:** 15.4 lbs.

Possible Moves: Leer, Peck, Focus Energy, Double Kick, Poison Sting, Fury Attack, Horn Attack, Helping Hand, Toxic Spikes, Flatter, Poison Jab, Captivate, Horn Drill

Nidoran ♂   Nidorino   Nidoking

NIDORINA

Poison Pin Pokémon

TYPE: POISON

Nidorina are very social and become nervous on their own. When among friends, their poisonous barbs retract so they don't hurt anyone.

How to say it: NEE-doe-REE-na

Height: 2' 07"
Weight: 44.1 lbs.

Possible Moves: Growl, Scratch, Tail Whip, Double Kick, Poison Sting, Fury Swipes, Bite, Helping Hand, Toxic Spikes, Flatter, Crunch, Captivate, Poison Fang

Nidoran ♀   Nidorina   Nidoqueen

REGIONS
**KALOS
(COASTAL),
KANTO**

NIDORINO
Poison Pin Pokémon

TYPE: POISON

The horn on Nidorino's forehead is made of an extremely hard substance. When challenged, its body bristles with poisonous barbs.

How to say it: NEE-doe-REE-no

Height: 2' 11"
Weight: 43.0 lbs.

Possible Moves: Leer, Peck, Focus Energy, Double Kick, Poison Sting, Fury Attack, Horn Attack, Helping Hand, Toxic Spikes, Flatter, Poison Jab, Captivate, Horn Drill

Nidoran ♂   Nidorino   Nidoking

REGIONS
**HOENN,
KALOS
(CENTRAL)**

NINCADA
Trainee Pokémon

TYPE: BUG-GROUND

Nincada prefers to stay out of the sun, living underground and feeding on tree roots. When Evolution approaches, it stops moving altogether.

How to say it: nin-KAH-da

Height: 1' 08"   **Weight:** 12.1 lbs.

Possible Moves: Scratch, Harden, Leech Life, Sand Attack, Fury Swipes, Mind Reader, False Swipe, Mud-Slap, Metal Claw, Dig

Ninjask

Nincada   Shedinja

NINETALES

Fox Pokémon

REGION
KANTO

TYPE: FIRE

Ninetales can control an opponent's mind with the light from its red eyes. Stories say this Pokémon was formed when nine wizards merged into a single being.

How to say it: NINE-tails

Height: 3' 07"
Weight: 43.9 lbs.

Possible Moves: Nasty Plot, Ember, Quick Attack, Confuse Ray, Safeguard

Vulpix   Ninetales

NINJASK

Ninja Pokémon

REGIONS
**HOENN,
KALOS
(CENTRAL)**

TYPE: BUG-FLYING

Ninjask moves so fast that it's hard to see, although its cry is quite audible. Proper training is a must to keep its defiant nature in check.

How to say it: NIN-jask

Height: 2' 07"   **Weight:** 26.5 lbs.

Possible Moves: Bug Bite, Scratch, Harden, Leech Life, Sand Attack, Fury Swipes, Mind Reader, Double Team, Fury Cutter, Screech, Swords Dance, Slash, Agility, Baton Pass, X-Scissor

Ninjask

Nincada   Shedinja

NOCTOWL
Owl Pokémon

TYPE: NORMAL-FLYING

With its excellent night vision and its silent wings, Noctowl is an expert when it comes to hunting in the darkness.

How to say it: NAHK-towl

Height: 5' 03"   **Weight:** 89.9 lbs.

Possible Moves: Dream Eater, Sky Attack, Tackle, Growl, Foresight, Hypnosis, Peck, Uproar, Reflect, Confusion, Echoed Voice, Take Down, Air Slash, Zen Headbutt, Synchronoise, Extrasensory, Psycho Shift, Roost

Hoothoot   Noctowl

TYPE: FLYING-DRAGON

Noibat live in lightless caves and communicate with ultrasonic waves emitted from their ears. These waves can make a strong man dizzy.

How to say it: NOY-bat

Height: 1' 08"
Weight: 17.6 lbs.

Possible Moves: Screech, Supersonic, Tackle, Leech Life, Gust, Bite, Wing Attack, Agility, Air Cutter, Roost, Razor Wind, Tailwind, Whirlwind, Super Fang, Air Slash, Hurricane

NOIBAT
Sound Wave Pokémon

Noibat   Noivern

NOIVERN

Sound Wave Pokémon

REGION
KALOS
(MOUNTAIN)

TYPE: FLYING-DRAGON

Noivern are masters when it comes to battling in the dark. The ultrasonic waves they release from their ears are powerful enough to crush a boulder.

How to say it: NOY-vurn

Height: 4' 11"
Weight: 187.4 lbs.

Possible Moves: Moonlight, Boomburst, Dragon Pulse, Hurricane, Screech, Supersonic, Tackle, Leech Life, Gust, Bite, Wing Attack, Agility, Air Cutter, Roost, Razor Wind, Tailwind, Whirlwind, Super Fang, Air Slash

Noibat Noivern

NOSEPASS

Compass Pokémon

REGIONS
HOENN,
KALOS
(COASTAL)

TYPE: ROCK

It's impossible for two Nosepass to stand face-to-face because their magnetic noses repel each other. They move at a glacial pace.

How to say it: NOSE-pass

Height: 3' 03"   **Weight:** 213.8 lbs.

Possible Moves: Tackle, Harden, Block, Rock Throw, Thunder Wave, Rock Blast, Rest, Spark, Rock Slide, Power Gem, Sandstorm, Discharge, Earth Power, Stone Edge, Lock-On, Zap Cannon

Nosepass   Probopass

NUMEL
Numb Pokémon

TYPE: FIRE-GROUND

The rather dull Numel sometimes doesn't notice when it's being attacked. Its body is full of magma, so Numel takes care to stay dry. Rain can make the magma cool and harden.

How to say it: NUM-mull

Height: 2' 04"
Weight: 52.9 lbs.

Possible Moves: Growl, Tackle, Ember, Magnitude, Focus Energy, Flame Burst, Take Down, Amnesia, Lava Plume, Earth Power, Earthquake, Flamethrower, Double-Edge

Numel   **Camerupt**   **Mega Camerupt**

TYPE: GRASS-DARK

Nuzleaf can play the leaf on its head like a flute, and the music makes listeners nervous. It lives in dense forests and doesn't like visitors.

How to say it: NUZ-leaf

Height: 3' 03"
Weight: 61.7 lbs.

Possible Moves: Razor Leaf, Pound, Harden, Growth, Nature Power, Fake Out, Torment, Feint Attack, Razor Wind, Swagger, Extrasensory

NUZLEAF
Wily Pokémon

Seedot   **Nuzleaf**   **Shiftry**

OCTILLERY

Jet Pokémon

TYPE: WATER

In battle, Octillery wraps its opponent up in its tentacles to keep it from moving. If that doesn't work, it sprays a cloud of ink to cover its escape.

How to say it: ock-TILL-er-ree

Height: 2' 11"
Weight: 62.8 lbs.

Possible Moves: Gunk Shot, Rock Blast, Water Gun, Constrict, Psybeam, Aurora Beam, Bubble Beam, Focus Energy, Octazooka, Wring Out, Signal Beam, Ice Beam, Bullet Seed, Hydro Pump, Hyper Beam, Soak

Remoraid → Octillery

ODDISH

Weed Pokémon

TYPE: GRASS-POISON

Oddish seeks out fertile ground where it can absorb nutrients from the soil. When it finds the perfect spot, it buries itself, and its feet apparently become like tree roots.

How to say it: ODD-ish

Height: 1' 08"   **Weight:** 11.9 lbs.

Possible Moves: Absorb, Sweet Scent, Acid, Poison Powder, Stun Spore, Sleep Powder, Mega Drain, Lucky Chant, Natural Gift, Moonlight, Giga Drain, Petal Dance, Grassy Terrain

Oddish → Gloom → Vileplume

Bellossom

OMANYTE
Spiral Pokémon

TYPE: ROCK-WATER

Omanyte's sturdy shell protects it from enemy attacks. This ancient Pokémon was restored from a fossil.

How to say it: AH-man-ite

Height: 1' 04"   **Weight:** 16.5 lbs.

Possible Moves: Constrict, Withdraw, Bite, Water Gun, Rollout, Leer, Mud Shot, Brine, Protect, Ancient Power, Tickle, Rock Blast, Shell Smash, Hydro Pump

Omanyte   Omastar

TYPE: ROCK-WATER

Some suspect that Omastar went extinct because it could no longer carry its heavy shell with ease. It seeks out food with its tentacles.

How to say it: AHM-uh-star

Height: 3' 03"   **Weight:** 77.2 lbs.

Possible Moves: Constrict, Withdraw, Bite, Water Gun, Rollout, Leer, Mud Shot, Brine, Protect, Ancient Power, Spike Cannon, Tickle, Rock Blast, Shell Smash, Hydro Pump

OMASTAR
Spiral Pokémon

Omanyte   Omastar

ONIX
Rock Snake Pokémon

REGIONS
KALOS
(COASTAL),
KANTO

TYPE: ROCK-GROUND

Thanks to its internal magnet, Onix never loses its way while boring through the ground. Its body grows smoother with age as the rough edges wear away.

How to say it: ON-icks

Height: 28' 10"   **Weight:** 463.0 lbs.

Possible Moves: Mud Sport, Tackle, Harden, Bind, Curse, Rock Throw, Rock Tomb, Rage, Stealth Rock, Rock Polish, Gyro Ball, Smack Down, Dragon Breath, Slam, Screech, Rock Slide, Sand Tomb, Iron Tail, Dig, Stone Edge, Double-Edge, Sandstorm

Onix   Steelix   Mega Steelix

OSHAWOTT
Sea Otter Pokémon

REGION
UNOVA

TYPE: WATER

Oshawott can detach the scalchop on its belly and use it as a weapon in battle or as a tool for cutting up food and other things.

How to say it: AH-shuh-wot

Height: 1' 08"   **Weight:** 13.0 lbs.

Possible Moves: Tackle, Tail Whip, Water Gun, Water Sport, Focus Energy, Razor Shell, Fury Cutter, Water Pulse, Revenge, Aqua Jet, Encore, Aqua Tail, Retaliate, Swords Dance, Hydro Pump

Oshawott   Dewott   Samurott

PACHIRISU
EleSquirrel Pokémon

TYPE: ELECTRIC

When Pachirisu affectionately rub their cheeks together, they're sharing electric energy with one another. The balls of fur they shed crackle with static.

How to say it: patch-ee-REE-sue

Height: 1' 04"   **Weight:** 8.6 lbs.

Possible Moves: Growl, Bide, Quick Attack, Charm, Spark, Endure, Nuzzle, Swift, Electro Ball, Sweet Kiss, Thunder Wave, Super Fang, Discharge, Last Resort, Hyper Fang

Does not evolve

PALKIA

Spatial Pokémon

LEGENDARY POKÉMON

TYPE: WATER-DRAGON

It is said Palkia can cause rents and distortions in space. In ancient times, it was revered as a legend.

How to say it: PAL-kee-uh

Height: 13' 09"   **Weight:** 740.8 lbs.

Possible Moves: Dragon Breath, Scary Face, Water Pulse, Ancient Power, Slash, Power Gem, Aqua Tail, Dragon Claw, Earth Power, Aura Sphere, Aqua Tail, Spacial Rend, Hydro Pump

Does not evolve

TYPE: WATER-GROUND

With the vibrations of its head bumps, Palpitoad can make ripples in the water or cause seismic activity. Its long tongue is coated in a sticky substance.

How to say it: PAL-pih-tohd

Height: 2' 07"   **Weight:** 37.5 lbs.

Possible Moves: Bubble, Growl, Supersonic, Round, Bubble Beam, Mud Shot, Aqua Ring, Uproar, Muddy Water, Rain Dance, Flail, Echoed Voice, Hydro Pump, Hyper Voice

Tympole   Palpitoad   Seismitoad

PANCHAM

Playful Pokémon

TYPE: FIGHTING

Pancham tries to be intimidating, but it's just too cute. When someone pats it on the head, it drops the tough-guy act and grins.

How to say it: PAN-chum

Height: 2' 00"   **Weight:** 17.6 lbs.

Possible Moves: Tackle, Leer, Arm Thrust, Work Up, Karate Chop, Comet Punch, Slash, Circle Throw, Vital Throw, Body Slam, Crunch, Entrainment, Parting Shot, Sky Uppercut

Pancham   Pangoro

PANGORO

Daunting Pokémon

TYPE: FIGHTING-DARK

The leafy sprig Pangoro holds in its mouth helps the Pokémon track its opponents' movements. Taking hits in battle doesn't seem to bother it at all.

How to say it: PAN-go-roh

Height: 6' 11"   **Weight:** 299.8 lbs.

Possible Moves: Entrainment, Hammer Arm, Tackle, Leer, Arm Thrust, Work Up, Karate Chop, Comet Punch, Slash, Circle Throw, Vital Throw, Body Slam, Crunch, Parting Shot, Sky Uppercut, Taunt, Low Sweep

Pancham   Pangoro

PANPOUR
Spray Pokémon

REGIONS KALOS (CENTRAL), UNOVA

TYPE: WATER

Panpour's head tuft is full of nutrient-rich water. It uses its tail to water plants, which then grow big and healthy.

How to say it: PAN-por

Height: 2' 00"
Weight: 29.8 lbs.

Possible Moves: Scratch, Play Nice, Leer, Lick, Water Gun, Fury Swipes, Water Sport, Bite, Scald, Taunt, Fling, Acrobatics, Brine, Recycle, Natural Gift, Crunch

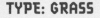

Panpour Simipour

TYPE: GRASS

Chewing the leaf from Pansage's head is a known method of stress relief. It willingly shares its leaf—along with any berries it's collected—with those who need it.

How to say it: PAN-sayj

Height: 2' 00"   **Weight:** 23.1 lbs.

Possible Moves: Scratch, Play Nice, Leer, Lick, Vine Whip, Fury Swipes, Leech Seed, Bite, Seed Bomb, Torment, Fling, Acrobatics, Grass Knot, Recycle, Natural Gift, Crunch

REGIONS KALOS (CENTRAL), UNOVA

PANSAGE
Grass Monkey Pokémon

Pansage Simisage

271

PANSEAR
High Temp Pokémon

REGIONS
KALOS (CENTRAL), UNOVA

TYPE: FIRE

Clever and helpful, Pansear prefers to cook its berries rather than eating them raw. Its natural habitat is volcanic caves, so it's no surprise that its fiery tuft burns at six hundred degrees Fahrenheit.

How to say it: PAN-seer

Height: 2' 00"
Weight: 24.3 lbs.

Possible Moves: Scratch, Play Nice, Leer, Lick, Incinerate, Fury Swipes, Yawn, Bite, Flame Burst, Amnesia, Fling, Acrobatics, Fire Blast, Recycle, Natural Gift, Crunch

Pansear   Simisear

PARAS
Mushroom Pokémon

REGION
KANTO

TYPE: BUG-GRASS

Mushrooms called tochukaso grow on Paras's back. Some people use them in medicines.

How to say it: PAR-iss

Height: 1' 00"
Weight: 11.9 lbs.

Possible Moves: Scratch, Stun Spore, Poison Powder, Leech Life, Fury Cutter, Spore, Slash, Growth, Giga Drain, Aromatherapy, Rage Powder, X-Scissor

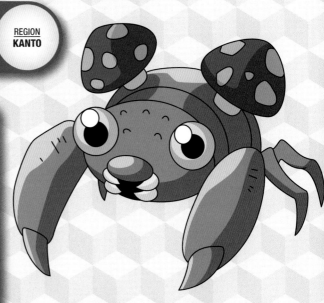

Paras   Parasect

TYPE: BUG-GRASS

Parasect feed on the roots of trees. If a group of them infests the same tree, they can be very destructive.

How to say it: PAR-i-sect

Height: 3' 03"
Weight: 65.0 lbs.

Possible Moves: Cross Poison, Scratch, Stun Spore, Poison Powder, Leech Life, Fury Cutter, Spore, Slash, Growth, Giga Drain, Aromatherapy, Rage Powder, X-Scissor

PARASECT
Mushroom Pokémon

Paras ➡ **Parasect**

PATRAT
Scout Pokémon

TYPE: NORMAL

Wary and cautious, Patrat are very serious about their job as lookouts. They store food in their cheeks so they don't have to leave their posts.

How to say it: pat-RAT

Height: 1' 08"
Weight: 25.6 lbs.

Possible Moves: Tackle, Leer, Bite, Bide, Detect, Sand Attack, Crunch, Hypnosis, Super Fang, After You, Work Up, Hyper Fang, Mean Look, Baton Pass, Slam

Patrat ➡ **Watchog**

PAWNIARD
Sharp Blade Pokémon

REGIONS
KALOS (MOUNTAIN), UNOVA

TYPE: DARK-STEEL

Pawniard's body is covered in blades, which it keeps sharp by polishing them after battle. Even when hurt, it's a relentless hunter.

How to say it: PAWN-yard

Height: 1' 08"
Weight: 22.5 lbs.

Possible Moves: Scratch, Leer, Fury Cutter, Torment, Feint Attack, Scary Face, Metal Claw, Slash, Assurance, Metal Sound, Embargo, Iron Defense, Night Slash, Iron Head, Swords Dance, Guillotine

Pawniard　　Bisharp

PELIPPER
Water Bird Pokémon

REGIONS
HOENN, KALOS (COASTAL)

TYPE: WATER-FLYING

Flying low over the waves, Pelipper catches food by dipping its huge bill into the water. Its bill is big enough that it can even carry small Pokémon from place to place.

How to say it: PEL-ip-purr

Height: 3' 11"　　**Weight:** 61.7 lbs.

Possible Moves: Hydro Pump, Tailwind, Soak, Growl, Water Gun, Water Sport, Wing Attack, Supersonic, Mist, Water Pulse, Payback, Protect, Roost, Brine, Stockpile, Swallow, Spit Up, Fling, Hurricane

Wingull　　Pelipper

TYPE: NORMAL

Persian uses its distinctive whiskers as sensors to find out about its surroundings. Grabbing the whiskers makes it meek and docile.

How to say it: PURR-shin

Height: 3' 03"
Weight: 70.5 lbs.

Possible Moves: Switcheroo, Scratch, Growl, Bite, Fake Out, Fury Swipes, Screech, Feint Attack, Taunt, Power Gem, Slash, Nasty Plot, Assurance, Captivate, Night Slash, Feint

REGION
KANTO

PERSIAN
Classy Cat Pokémon

Meowth ⇨ Persian

TYPE: GRASS

When many Petilil settle in an area, gardeners and farmers pay attention, because these Pokémon seek out rich soil that's good for growing plants. Their leaves have healing properties.

How to say it: PEH-tih-lil

Height: 1' 08"   **Weight:** 14.6 lbs.

Possible Moves: Absorb, Growth, Leech Seed, Sleep Powder, Mega Drain, Synthesis, Magical Leaf, Stun Spore, Giga Drain, Aromatherapy, Helping Hand, Energy Ball, Entrainment, Sunny Day, After You, Leaf Storm

REGION
UNOVA

PETILIL
Bulb Pokémon

Petilil ⇨ Lilligant

PHANPY

Long Nose Pokémon

TYPE: GROUND

Phanpy sucks up water with its long trunk to spray itself for a bath or to playfully squirt others. It makes its nest by digging into a riverbank.

How to say it: FAN-pee

Height: 1' 08"
Weight: 73.9 lbs.

Possible Moves: Odor Sleuth, Tackle, Growl, Defense Curl, Flail, Take Down, Rollout, Natural Gift, Slam, Endure, Charm, Last Resort, Double-Edge

Phanpy   Donphan

PHANTUMP

Stump Pokémon

TYPE: GHOST-GRASS

It is said that when the spirits of wandering children inhabit old tree stumps, these Pokémon are created. Phantump dwell in lonely forests, far away from people.

How to say it: FAN-tump

Height: 1' 04"   **Weight:** 15.4 lbs.

Possible Moves: Tackle, Confuse Ray, Astonish, Growth, Ingrain, Feint Attack, Leech Seed, Curse, Will-O-Wisp, Forest's Curse, Destiny Bond, Phantom Force, Wood Hammer, Horn Leech

Phantump   Trevenant

TYPE: WATER

Phione gather in large groups as they drift with the current through warm seas. After floating for a time, they always return home, no matter how far they have traveled.

How to say it: fee-OWN-ay

Height: 1' 04"   **Weight:** 6.8 lbs.

Possible Moves: Bubble, Water Sport, Charm, Supersonic, Bubble Beam, Acid Armor, Whirlpool, Water Pulse, Aqua Ring, Dive, Rain Dance

Does not evolve

PICHU
Tiny Mouse Pokémon

REGIONS
JOHTO,
KALOS
(CENTRAL)

TYPE: ELECTRIC

Sometimes, when two Pichu play together, the static electricity that crackles off their bodies produces an unexpected shower of sparks. This often startles them into crying.

How to say it: PEE-choo

Height: 1' 00"   **Weight:** 4.4 lbs.

Possible Moves: Thunder Shock, Charm, Tail Whip, Sweet Kiss, Thunder Wave, Nasty Plot

Pichu   Pikachu   Raichu

PIDGEOT
Bird Pokémon

TYPE: NORMAL-FLYING

Many Trainers are drawn to Pidgeot because of its lovely feathers. The beautiful colors of its crest are particularly striking.

How to say it: PIDG-ee-ott

Height: 4' 11"
Weight: 87.1 lbs.

Possible Moves: Hurricane, Tackle, Sand Attack, Gust, Quick Attack, Whirlwind, Twister, Feather Dance, Agility, Wing Attack, Roost, Tailwind, Mirror Move, Air Slash

MEGA PIDGEOT
Bird Pokémon

TYPE: NORMAL-FLYING

Height: 7' 03"
Weight: 111.3 lbs.

Pidgey ⇨ Pidgeotto ⇨ Pidgeot ⇨ Mega Pidgeot

PIDGEOTTO

Bird Pokémon

TYPE: NORMAL-FLYING

Very territorial, Pidgeotto keeps up a steady patrol of the large area it claims as its own. Any intruder will be driven off with merciless attacks from its sharp claws.

How to say it: PIDG-ee-OH-toe

Height: 3' 07"   **Weight:** 66.1 lbs.

Possible Moves: Tackle, Sand Attack, Gust, Quick Attack, Whirlwind, Twister, Feather Dance, Agility, Wing Attack, Roost, Tailwind, Mirror Move, Air Slash, Hurricane

Pidgey   Pidgeotto   Pidgeot   Mega Pidgeot

PIDGEY

Tiny Bird Pokémon

TYPE: NORMAL-FLYING

Thanks to Pidgey's excellent sense of direction, it can always find its way home, no matter how far it has traveled.

How to say it: PIDG-ee

Height: 1' 00"   **Weight:** 4.0 lbs.

Possible Moves: Tackle, Sand Attack, Gust, Quick Attack, Whirlwind, Twister, Feather Dance, Agility, Wing Attack, Roost, Tailwind, Mirror Move, Air Slash, Hurricane

Pidgey   Pidgeotto   Pidgeot   Mega Pidgeot

PIDOVE
Tiny Pigeon Pokémon

TYPE: NORMAL-FLYING

Even wild Pidove are used to having people around. They live in cities and often flock to places where people spend time like plazas and parks.

How to say it: pih-DUV

Height: 1' 00"   **Weight:** 4.6 lbs.

Possible Moves: Gust, Growl, Leer, Quick Attack, Air Cutter, Roost, Detect, Taunt, Air Slash, Razor Wind, Feather Dance, Swagger, Facade, Tailwind, Sky Attack

Pidove   Tranquill   Unfezant

PIGNITE
Fire Pig Pokémon

TYPE: FIRE-FIGHTING

"Food is fuel"—for Pignite, that common phrase is a bit more literal. When it eats, its internal fire is stoked, which increases its power and speed.

How to say it: pig-NYTE

Height: 3' 03"   **Weight:** 122.4 lbs.

Possible Moves: Tackle, Tail Whip, Ember, Odor Sleuth, Defense Curl, Flame Charge, Arm Thrust, Smog, Rollout, Take Down, Heat Crash, Assurance, Flamethrower, Head Smash, Roar, Flare Blitz

Tepig   Pignite   Emboar

PIKACHU
Mouse Pokémon

REGIONS
KALOS (CENTRAL), KANTO

Pichu ⟹ Pikachu ⟹ Raichu

TYPE: ELECTRIC

The red pouches on Pikachu's cheeks store up electricity while it sleeps. It often delivers a zap when encountering something unfamiliar.

How to say it: PEE-ka-choo

Height: 1' 04"   **Weight:** 13.2 lbs.

Possible Moves: Tail Whip, Thunder Shock, Growl, Play Nice, Quick Attack, Thunder Wave, Electro Ball, Double Team, Nuzzle, Slam, Thunderbolt, Feint, Agility, Discharge, Light Screen, Thunder

REGION
HOENN

Pikachu Libre
Special Move:
Flying Press

Pikachu Belle
Special Move:
Icicle Crash

Pikachu PhD
Special Move:
Electric Terrain

Pikachu Pop Star
Special Move:
Draining Kiss

Pikachu Rock Star
Special Move:
Meteor Mash

Does not evolve

TYPE: ICE-GROUND

REGIONS
JOHTO,
KALOS
(MOUNTAIN)

PILOSWINE
Swine Pokémon

Piloswine's long, thick hair helps protect it from the intense cold of its surroundings. Its tusks can dig through the ice to find buried food.

How to say it: PILE-oh-swine

Height: 3' 07"
Weight: 123.0 lbs.

Possible Moves: Ancient Power, Peck, Odor Sleuth, Mud Sport, Powder Snow, Mud-Slap, Endure, Mud Bomb, Icy Wind, Ice Fang, Take Down, Fury Attack, Mist, Thrash, Earthquake, Blizzard, Amnesia

Swinub   Piloswine   Mamoswine

TYPE: BUG

REGION
JOHTO

PINECO
Bagworm Pokémon

Don't disturb Pineco while it's eating! Most of the time it patiently hangs onto a branch, but if it's dislodged during a meal, it will fall to the ground and explode.

How to say it: PINE-co

Height: 2' 00"   **Weight:** 15.9 lbs.

Possible Moves: Tackle, Protect, Self-Destruct, Bug Bite, Take Down, Rapid Spin, Bide, Natural Gift, Spikes, Payback, Explosion, Iron Defense, Gyro Ball, Double-Edge

Pineco   Forretress

PINSIR
Stag Beetle Pokémon

REGIONS
KALOS (COASTAL), KANTO

TYPE: BUG

When its strong pincer gets a grip, Pinsir can lift an enemy much bigger than itself. The thorns that line its horns dig into its opponent, making it hard to get away.

How to say it: PIN-sir

Height: 4' 11"
Weight: 121.3 lbs.

Possible Moves: Vice Grip, Focus Energy, Bind, Seismic Toss, Harden, Revenge, Brick Break, Vital Throw, Submission, X-Scissor, Storm Throw, Thrash, Swords Dance, Superpower, Guillotine

MEGA PINSIR
Stag Beetle Pokémon

TYPE: BUG-FLYING

Height: 5' 07"
Weight: 130.1 lbs.

Pinsir   Mega Pinsir

TYPE: WATER

Proud and stubborn, Piplup can be a challenge to train. It's quite independent, preferring to take care of itself and find its own food.

How to say it: PIP-plup

Height: 1' 04"
Weight: 11.5 lbs.

Possible Moves: Pound, Growl, Bubble, Water Sport, Peck, Bubble Beam, Bide, Fury Attack, Brine, Whirlpool, Mist, Drill Peck, Hydro Pump

REGION
SINNOH

PIPLUP
Penguin Pokémon

Piplup   **Prinplup**   **Empoleon**

TYPE: ELECTRIC

Plusle can short out the electricity in its body to create a crackling shower of sparks! It always cheers on its friends in battle.

How to say it: PLUS-ull

Height: 1' 04"
Weight: 9.3 lbs.

Possible Moves: Nasty Plot, Nuzzle, Entrainment, Play Nice, Growl, Thunder Wave, Quick Attack, Helping Hand, Spark, Encore, Copycat, Electro Ball, Swift, Fake Tears, Charge, Thunder, Baton Pass, Agility, Last Resort

REGIONS
HOENN,
KALOS
(CENTRAL)

PLUSLE
Cheering Pokémon

Does not evolve

POLITOED

Frog Pokémon

REGIONS
JOHTO, KALOS (MOUNTAIN)

TYPE: WATER

Politoed has a single long, curly hair on the top of its head, which marks it as a ruler. Apparently, a longer hair with more curl is more respected by others.

How to say it: PAUL-lee-TOED

Height: 3' 07"
Weight: 74.7 lbs.

Possible Moves: Bubble Beam, Hypnosis, Double Slap, Perish Song, Swagger, Bounce, Hyper Voice

Poliwag   Poliwhirl   Politoed

POLIWAG

Tadpole Pokémon

REGIONS
KALOS (MOUNTAIN), KANTO

TYPE: WATER

Poliwag's skin is so thin that you can see right through it to the Pokémon's spiral-shaped insides. Fortunately, it's also very resilient and flexible.

How to say it: PAUL-lee-wag

Height: 2' 00"   **Weight:** 27.3 lbs.

Possible Moves: Water Sport, Water Gun, Hypnosis, Bubble, Double Slap, Rain Dance, Body Slam, Bubble Beam, Mud Shot, Belly Drum, Wake-Up Slap, Hydro Pump, Mud Bomb

Poliwrath

Poliwag   Poliwhirl   Politoed

POLIWHIRL
Tadpole Pokémon

TYPE: WATER

Poliwhirl is covered with a slick, slippery, slimy fluid that allows it to wriggle out of sticky situations.

How to say it: PAUL-lee-wirl

Height: 3' 03"
Weight: 44.1 lbs.

Possible Moves: Water Sport, Water Gun, Hypnosis, Bubble, Double Slap, Rain Dance, Body Slam, Bubble Beam, Mud Shot, Belly Drum, Wake-Up Slap, Hydro Pump, Mud Bomb

Poliwag Poliwhirl → Poliwrath

→ Politoed

TYPE: WATER-FIGHTING

Burly and muscular, Poliwrath can exercise for hours without getting tired. It swims effortlessly through the ocean.

How to say it: PAUL-lee-rath

Height: 4' 03"
Weight: 119.0 lbs.

Possible Moves: Circle Throw, Bubble Beam, Hypnosis, Double Slap, Submission, Dynamic Punch, Mind Reader

POLIWRATH
Tadpole Pokémon

Poliwag Poliwhirl Poliwrath

PONYTA

Fire Horse Pokémon

**REGION
KANTO**

TYPE: FIRE

At the beginning of its life, Ponyta's legs are too weak to hold it up. It quickly learns to run by chasing after its elders.

How to say it: PO-nee-tuh

Height: 3' 03"
Weight: 66.1 lbs.

Possible Moves: Growl, Tackle, Tail Whip, Ember, Flame Wheel, Stomp, Flame Charge, Fire Spin, Take Down, Inferno, Agility, Fire Blast, Bounce, Flare Blitz

Ponyta   Rapidash

POOCHYENA

Bite Pokémon

**REGIONS
HOENN,
KALOS
(MOUNTAIN)**

TYPE: DARK

Poochyena tries to look bigger than it is by bristling up its tail. It tends to react to unexpected movement by biting, and it easily chases prey to exhaustion.

How to say it: POO-chee-EH-nah

Height: 1' 08"   **Weight:** 30.0 lbs.

Possible Moves: Tackle, Howl, Sand Attack, Bite, Odor Sleuth, Roar, Swagger, Assurance, Scary Face, Taunt, Embargo, Take Down, Sucker Punch, Crunch

Poochyena   Mightyena

PORYGON
Virtual Pokémon

TYPE: NORMAL

Porygon was created from programming code, and it can return to that form to navigate cyberspace. It can't be copied like regular data.

How to say it: POR-ee-gon

Height: 2' 07"
Weight: 80.5 lbs.

Possible Moves: Conversion 2, Tackle, Conversion, Sharpen, Psybeam, Agility, Recover, Magnet Rise, Signal Beam, Recycle, Discharge, Lock-On, Tri Attack, Magic Coat, Zap Cannon

Porygon Porygon2 Porygon-Z

PORYGON2
Virtual Pokémon

TYPE: NORMAL

Porygon2 is the product of human ingenuity. Programmed with artificial intelligence, it is capable of learning new things.

How to say it: POR-ee-gon TOO

Height: 2' 00"   **Weight:** 71.6 lbs.

Possible Moves: Conversion 2, Tackle, Conversion, Defense Curl, Psybeam, Agility, Recover, Magnet Rise, Signal Beam, Recycle, Discharge, Lock-On, Tri Attack, Magic Coat, Zap Cannon, Hyper Beam

Porygon Porygon2 Porygon-Z

289

PORYGON-Z

Virtual Pokémon

TYPE: NORMAL

Changes in its programming were intended to allow Porygon-Z to travel to other dimensions, but something went awry during the upgrade, and it began behaving erratically.

How to say it: POR-ee-gon ZEE

Height: 2' 11"   **Weight:** 75.0 lbs.

Possible Moves: Trick Room, Conversion 2, Tackle, Conversion, Nasty Plot, Psybeam, Agility, Recover, Magnet Rise, Signal Beam, Embargo, Discharge, Lock-On, Tri Attack, Magic Coat, Zap Cannon, Hyper Beam

Porygon   Porygon2   Porygon-Z

PRIMEAPE

Pig Monkey Pokémon

TYPE: FIGHTING

Fury increases Primeape's blood flow and powers up its muscles. Its intelligence drops sharply during a rage.

How to say it: PRIME-ape

Height: 3' 03"   **Weight:** 70.5 lbs.

Possible Moves: Fling, Scratch, Low Kick, Leer, Focus Energy, Fury Swipes, Karate Chop, Seismic Toss, Screech, Assurance, Rage, Swagger, Cross Chop, Thrash, Punishment, Close Combat, Final Gambit

Mankey   Primeape

TYPE: WATER

Because Prinplup have a strong sense of self-importance, they tend to live alone. They can topple trees by striking with their wings.

How to say it: PRIN-plup

Height: 2' 07"
Weight: 50.7 lbs.

Possible Moves: Tackle, Growl, Bubble, Water Sport, Peck, Metal Claw, Bubble Beam, Bide, Fury Attack, Brine, Whirlpool, Mist, Drill Peck, Hydro Pump

REGION
SINNOH

PRINPLUP
Penguin Pokémon

Piplup   Prinplup   Empoleon

TYPE: ROCK-STEEL

Probopass uses the strong magnetic field it generates to control the three smaller Mini-Noses attached to the sides of its body.

How to say it: PRO-bow-pass

Height: 4' 07"   **Weight:** 749.6 lbs.

Possible Moves: Magnet Rise, Gravity, Tackle, Iron Defense, Block, Magnet Bomb, Thunder Wave, Rock Blast, Rest, Spark, Rock Slide, Power Gem, Sandstorm, Discharge, Earth Power, Stone Edge, Lock-On, Zap Cannon

REGIONS
KALOS
(COASTAL),
SINNOH

PROBOPASS
Compass Pokémon

Nosepass   Probopass

PSYDUCK

Duck Pokémon

REGIONS
KALOS
(CENTRAL),
KANTO

TYPE: WATER

Though Psyduck can use mysterious psychic powers, it can never remember doing so. Apparently, this power creates strange brain waves that resemble deep slumber.

How to say it: SY-duck

Height: 2' 07" **Weight:** 43.2 lbs.

Possible Moves: Water Sport, Scratch, Tail Whip, Water Gun, Disable, Confusion, Water Pulse, Fury Swipes, Screech, Zen Headbutt, Aqua Tail, Soak, Psych Up, Amnesia, Hydro Pump, Wonder Room

Psyduck   Golduck

PUMPKABOO

Pumpkin Pokémon

REGION
KALOS
(MOUNTAIN)

TYPE: GHOST-GRASS

The nocturnal Pumpkaboo tends to get restless as darkness falls. Stories say it serves as a guide for wandering spirits, leading them through the night to find their true home.

How to say it: PUMP-kuh-boo

Height: 1' 04" **Weight:** 11.0 lbs.

Possible Moves: Trick, Astonish, Confuse Ray, Scary Face, Trick-or-Treat, Worry Seed, Razor Leaf, Leech Seed, Bullet Seed, Shadow Sneak, Shadow Ball, Pain Split, Seed Bomb

Pumpkaboo   Gourgeist

TYPE: ROCK-GROUND

Pupitar moves by propulsion, expelling compressed gases to launch itself forward. Its hard surface protects it when it hits solid objects.

How to say it: PUE-puh-tar

Height: 3' 11"
Weight: 335.1 lbs.

Possible Moves: Bite, Leer, Sandstorm, Screech, Chip Away, Rock Slide, Scary Face, Thrash, Dark Pulse, Payback, Crunch, Earthquake, Stone Edge, Hyper Beam

PUPITAR
Hard Shell Pokémon

Larvitar Pupitar Tyranitar Mega Tyranitar

PURRLOIN
Devious Pokémon

TYPE: DARK

Purrloin acts cute and innocent to trick people into trusting it. Then it steals their stuff.

How to say it: PUR-loyn

Height: 1' 04"
Weight: 22.3 lbs.

Possible Moves: Scratch, Growl, Assist, Sand Attack, Fury Swipes, Pursuit, Torment, Fake Out, Hone Claws, Assurance, Slash, Captivate, Night Slash, Snatch, Nasty Plot, Sucker Punch, Play Rough

Purrloin Liepard

PURUGLY

Tiger Cat Pokémon

REGION
SINNOH

TYPE: NORMAL

Purugly wraps its two tails around its waist to make itself look bigger. It's been known to kick other Pokémon out of their comfortable nests and take over.

How to say it: purr-UG-lee

Height: 3' 03"
Weight: 96.6 lbs.

Possible Moves: Fake Out, Scratch, Growl, Hypnosis, Feint Attack, Fury Swipes, Charm, Assist, Captivate, Slash, Swagger, Body Slam, Attract, Hone Claws

Glameow   Purugly

PYROAR

Royal Pokémon

REGION
KALOS
(CENTRAL)

TYPE: FIRE-NORMAL

Pyroar live together in prides, led by the male whose fiery mane is the biggest. The females of the pride guard the young.

How to say it: PIE-roar

Height: 4' 11"   **Weight:** 179.7 lbs.

Possible Moves: Hyper Beam, Tackle, Leer, Ember, Work Up, Headbutt, Noble Roar, Take Down, Fire Fang, Endeavor, Echoed Voice, Flamethrower, Crunch, Hyper Voice, Incinerate, Overheat

Male Form

Female Form

Litleo   Pyroar

294

TYPE: WATER-GROUND

Quagsire doesn't exactly hunt for food—it hangs out in the water with its mouth open and waits for something to drift in. Fortunately, this lack of movement means it doesn't need to eat much.

How to say it: KWAG-sire

Height: 4' 07"   **Weight:** 165.3 lbs.

Possible Moves: Water Gun, Tail Whip, Mud Sport, Mud Shot, Slam, Mud Bomb, Amnesia, Yawn, Earthquake, Rain Dance, Mist, Haze, Muddy Water

QUAGSIRE
Water Fish Pokémon

Wooper   **Quagsire**

QUILAVA
Volcano Pokémon

TYPE: FIRE

To keep opponents from getting too close, Quilava heats up the air around it by flaring the flames on its body. It's extremely nimble and good at dodging.

How to say it: kwil-LA-va

Height: 2' 11"   **Weight:** 41.9 lbs.

Possible Moves: Tackle, Leer, Smokescreen, Ember, Quick Attack, Flame Wheel, Defense Curl, Swift, Flame Charge, Lava Plume, Flamethrower, Inferno, Rollout, Double-Edge, Eruption

Cyndaquil   Quilava   Typhlosion

QUILLADIN

Spiny Armor Pokémon

REGION
**KALOS
(CENTRAL)**

TYPE: GRASS

Quilladin often train for battle by charging forcefully into one another. Despite their spiky appearance, they have a gentle nature and don't like confrontation.

How to say it: QUILL-uh-din

Height: 2' 04"
Weight: 63.9 lbs.

Possible Moves: Tackle, Growl, Vine Whip, Rollout, Bite, Leech Seed, Pin Missile, Needle Arm, Take Down, Seed Bomb, Mud Shot, Bulk Up, Body Slam, Pain Split, Wood Hammer

Chespin   Quilladin   Chesnaught

QWILFISH

Balloon Pokémon

REGIONS
**JOHTO,
KALOS
(COASTAL)**

TYPE: WATER-POISON

Qwilfish puffs up its body by sucking in water, and then uses that water pressure to send the poisonous spikes that cover it shooting outward at an opponent.

How to say it: KWILL-fish

Height: 1' 08"   **Weight:** 8.6 lbs.

Possible Moves: Fell Stinger, Hydro Pump, Destiny Bond, Water Gun, Spikes, Tackle, Poison Sting, Harden, Minimize, Bubble, Rollout, Toxic Spikes, Stockpile, Spit Up, Revenge, Brine, Pin Missile, Take Down, Aqua Tail, Poison Jab

Does not evolve

REGIONS
**KALOS
(CENTRAL),
KANTO**

RAICHU
Mouse Pokémon

TYPE: ELECTRIC

When overcharged with electricity, Raichu sinks its tail into the ground to get rid of the excess. The charge makes it glow faintly in the dark.

How to say it: RYE-choo

Height: 2' 07"   **Weight:** 66.1 lbs.

Possible Moves: Thunder Shock, Tail Whip, Quick Attack, Thunderbolt

Pichu   Pikachu   Raichu

RAIKOU
Thunder Pokémon

LEGENDARY POKÉMON

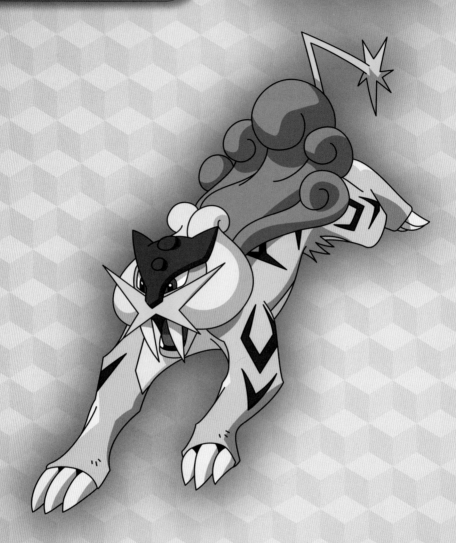

TYPE: ELECTRIC

When Raikou roars, the air and land shudder. This Legendary Pokémon moves with lightning speed.

How to say it: RYE-coo

Height: 6' 03"   **Weight:** 392.4 lbs.

Possible Moves: Bite, Leer, Thunder Shock, Roar, Quick Attack, Spark, Reflect, Crunch, Thunder Fang, Discharge, Extrasensory, Rain Dance, Calm Mind, Thunder

Does not evolve

RALTS
Feeling Pokémon

TYPE: PSYCHIC-FAIRY

With its horns, Ralts can sense people's emotions. Its own mood tends to reflect what it senses, and it's drawn to people with a positive attitude.

How to say it: RALTS

Height: 1' 04"
Weight: 14.6 lbs.

Possible Moves: Growl, Confusion, Double Team, Teleport, Lucky Chant, Magical Leaf, Heal Pulse, Calm Mind, Psychic, Imprison, Future Sight, Charm, Hypnosis, Dream Eater, Stored Power

Ralts Kirlia

Gardevoir Mega Gardevoir

Gallade Mega Gallade

RAMPARDOS

Head Butt Pokémon

REGION
SINNOH

TYPE: ROCK

Rampardos can smash through anything with its skull, which is iron-hard and incredibly thick. Unfortunately, this means its brain has no room to grow.

How to say it: ram-PAR-dose

Height: 5' 03"
Weight: 226.0 lbs.

Possible Moves: Headbutt, Leer, Focus Energy, Pursuit, Take Down, Scary Face, Assurance, Chip Away, Endeavor, Ancient Power, Zen Headbutt, Screech, Head Smash

Cranidos ⟹ Rampardos

RAPIDASH

Fire Horse Pokémon

REGION
KANTO

TYPE: FIRE

Most of the time, Rapidash travels at a casual canter across the flat lands where it lives. When it breaks into a gallop, its mane blazes brightly.

How to say it: RAP-i-dash

Height: 3' 11"
Weight: 69.7 lbs.

Possible Moves: Poison Jab, Megahorn, Growl, Quick Attack, Tail Whip, Ember, Flame Wheel, Stomp, Flame Charge, Fire Spin, Take Down, Inferno, Agility, Fury Attack, Fire Blast, Bounce, Flare Blitz

Ponyta ⟹ Rapidash

RATICATE
Mouse Pokémon

TYPE: NORMAL

Because Raticate's fangs never stop growing, it has to gnaw on hard objects to whittle them down. Logs and rocks often serve this purpose, but sometimes it chews on houses!

How to say it: RAT-i-kate

Height: 2' 04"
Weight: 40.8 lbs.

Possible Moves: Swords Dance, Tackle, Tail Whip, Quick Attack, Focus Energy, Bite, Pursuit, Hyper Fang, Sucker Punch, Scary Face, Crunch, Assurance, Super Fang, Double-Edge, Endeavor

Rattata **Raticate**

RATTATA
Mouse Pokémon

TYPE: NORMAL

Rattata is always on the alert, keeping an ear out for the slightest sound even in its sleep. It's happy to nest just about anywhere.

How to say it: ruh-TA-tah

Height: 1' 00"
Weight: 7.7 lbs.

Possible Moves: Tackle, Tail Whip, Quick Attack, Focus Energy, Bite, Pursuit, Hyper Fang, Sucker Punch, Crunch, Assurance, Super Fang, Double-Edge, Endeavor

Rattata **Raticate**

RAYQUAZA
Sky High Pokémon

LEGENDARY POKÉMON

TYPE: DRAGON-FLYING

Legends say the ancient Pokémon Rayquaza flies through the upper atmosphere and feeds on meteoroids. It's known for stopping the endless battles between Kyogre and Groudon.

How to say it: ray-KWAZ-uh

Height: 23' 00"
Weight: 455.2 lbs.

Possible Moves: Twister, Scary Face, Crunch, Hyper Voice, Rest, Air Slash, Ancient Power, Outrage, Dragon Dance, Fly, Extreme Speed, Hyper Beam, Dragon Pulse

MEGA RAYQUAZA
Sky High Pokémon

TYPE: DRAGON-FLYING

Height: 35' 05"
Weight: 864.2 lbs.

Rayquaza   Mega Rayquaza

TYPE: ICE

Created during an ice age, Regice's body is frozen solid, and even lava can't melt it. It can lower the temperature of the air around it by several hundred degrees.

How to say it: REDGE-ice

Height: 5' 11"   **Weight:** 385.8 lbs.

Possible Moves: Explosion, Stomp, Icy Wind, Curse, Superpower, Ancient Power, Amnesia, Charge Beam, Lock-On, Zap Cannon, Ice Beam, Hammer Arm, Hyper Beam

Does not evolve

TYPE: NORMAL

According to legend, Regigigas built smaller models of itself out of rock, ice, and magma. It's so enormous that it could tow an entire continent behind it.

How to say it: REDGE-ee-gee-gus

Height: 12' 02"   **Weight:** 925.9 lbs.

Possible Moves: Fire Punch, Ice Punch, Thunder Punch, Dizzy Punch, Knock Off, Confuse Ray, Foresight, Revenge, Wide Guard, Zen Headbutt, Payback, Crush Grip, Heavy Slam, Giga Impact

Does not evolve

REGIROCK
Rock Peak Pokémon

TYPE: ROCK

Regirock's body is made entirely of rocks, and these rocks were recently discovered to be from all around the world. It repairs itself after battle by seeking out new rocks.

How to say it: REDGE-ee-rock

Height: 5' 07" **Weight:** 507.1 lbs.

Possible Moves: Explosion, Stomp, Rock Throw, Curse, Superpower, Ancient Power, Iron Defense, Charge Beam, Lock-On, Zap Cannon, Stone Edge, Hammer Arm, Hyper Beam

Does not evolve

REGISTEEL

Iron Pokémon

REGION
HOENN

LEGENDARY
POKÉMON

TYPE: STEEL

Registeel isn't actually made of steel—it's a strange substance harder than any known metal. Ancient people sealed it away in a prison.

How to say it: REDGE-ee-steel

Height: 6' 03"   **Weight:** 451.9 lbs.

Possible Moves: Explosion, Stomp, Metal Claw, Curse, Superpower, Ancient Power, Iron Defense, Amnesia, Charge Beam, Lock-On, Zap Cannon, Iron Head, Flash Cannon, Hammer Arm, Hyper Beam

Does not evolve

RELICANTH
Longevity Pokémon

REGIONS
HOENN,
KALOS
(COASTAL)

TYPE: WATER-ROCK

Relicanth today look much the same as they did one hundred million years ago. These ancient Pokémon are covered in rocky scales to protect them in the ocean depths.

How to say it: REL-uh-canth

Height: 3' 03"
Weight: 51.6 lbs.

Possible Moves: Head Smash, Hydro Pump, Ancient Power, Mud Sport, Tackle, Harden, Water Gun, Rock Tomb, Yawn, Take Down, Double-Edge, Dive, Rest

Does not evolve

REMORAID
Jet Pokémon

REGIONS
JOHTO,
KALOS
(COASTAL)

TYPE: WATER

Remoraid can knock flying targets out of the air with precise jets of high-velocity water. It swims downstream when it's time to evolve.

How to say it: REM-oh-raid

Height: 2' 00"
Weight: 26.5 lbs.

Possible Moves: Water Gun, Lock-On, Psybeam, Aurora Beam, Bubble Beam, Focus Energy, Water Pulse, Signal Beam, Ice Beam, Bullet Seed, Hydro Pump, Hyper Beam, Soak

Remoraid **Octillery**

RESHIRAM
Vast White Pokémon

LEGENDARY POKÉMON

TYPE: DRAGON-FIRE

Legends say Reshiram is drawn to those who value the truth. The flare of its fiery tail can disrupt the atmosphere and cause strange weather patterns.

How to say it: RESH-i-ram

Height: 10' 06"   **Weight:** 6,727.5 lbs.

Possible Moves: Fire Fang, Dragon Rage, Imprison, Ancient Power, Flamethrower, Dragon Breath, Slash, Extrasensory, Fusion Flare, Dragon Pulse, Imprison, Crunch, Fire Blast, Outrage, Hyper Voice, Blue Flare

Does not evolve

TYPE: PSYCHIC

Reuniclus shake hands with one another to create a network between their brains. Working together boosts their psychic power, and they can crush huge rocks with their minds.

How to say it: ree-yoo-NIH-klus

Height: 3' 03"
Weight: 44.3 lbs.

Possible Moves: Psywave, Reflect, Rollout, Snatch, Hidden Power, Light Screen, Charm, Recover, Psyshock, Endeavor, Future Sight, Pain Split, Psychic, Dizzy Punch, Skill Swap, Heal Block, Wonder Room

REGIONS
KALOS (COASTAL), UNOVA

REUNICLUS
Multiplying Pokémon

Solosis   Duosion   Reuniclus

REGIONS
KALOS (COASTAL), KANTO

RHYDON
Drill Pokémon

TYPE: GROUND-ROCK

Rhydon's horn, which it uses as a drill, is hard enough to crush diamonds. Its hide is like armor, and it can run right through molten lava without feeling a thing.

How to say it: RYE-don

Height: 6' 03"   **Weight:** 264.6 lbs.

Possible Moves: Megahorn, Horn Drill, Horn Attack, Tail Whip, Stomp, Fury Attack, Scary Face, Rock Blast, Bulldoze, Chip Away, Take Down, Hammer Arm, Drill Run, Stone Edge, Earthquake

Rhyhorn   Rhydon   Rhyperior

RHYHORN

Spikes Pokémon

TYPE: GROUND-ROCK

A charging Rhyhorn is so single-minded that it doesn't think about anything else until it demolishes its target.

How to say it: RYE-horn

Height: 3' 03"
Weight: 253.5 lbs.

Possible Moves: Horn Attack, Tail Whip, Stomp, Fury Attack, Scary Face, Rock Blast, Bulldoze, Chip Away, Take Down, Drill Run, Stone Edge, Earthquake, Horn Drill, Megahorn

Rhyhorn   Rhydon   Rhyperior

RHYPERIOR

Drill Pokémon

TYPE: GROUND-ROCK

Rhyperior uses the holes in its hands to bombard its opponents with rocks. Sometimes it even hurls a Geodude! Rhyperior's rocky hide is thick enough to protect it from molten lava.

How to say it: rye-PEER-ee-or

Height: 7' 10"
Weight: 623.5 lbs.

Possible Moves: Rock Wrecker, Megahorn, Horn Drill, Poison Jab, Horn Attack, Tail Whip, Stomp, Fury Attack, Scary Face, Rock Blast, Chip Away, Take Down, Hammer Arm, Drill Run, Stone Edge, Earthquake

Rhyhorn   Rhydon   Rhyperior

RIOLU
Emanation Pokémon

TYPE: FIGHTING

The aura surrounding Riolu's body indicates its emotional state. It alters the shape of this aura to communicate.

How to say it: ree-OH-loo

Height: 2' 04"
Weight: 44.5 lbs.

Possible Moves: Foresight, Quick Attack, Endure, Counter, Feint, Force Palm, Copycat, Screech, Reversal, Nasty Plot, Final Gambit

Riolu   Lucario   Mega Lucario

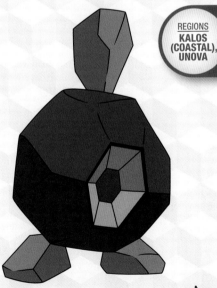

ROGGENROLA
Mantle Pokémon

TYPE: ROCK

Each Roggenrola has an energy core at its center. The intense pressure in their underground home has compressed their bodies into a steely toughness.

How to say it: rah-gen-ROH-lah

Height: 1' 04"   **Weight:** 39.7 lbs.

Possible Moves: Tackle, Harden, Sand Attack, Headbutt, Rock Blast, Mud-Slap, Iron Defense, Smack Down, Rock Slide, Stealth Rock, Sandstorm, Stone Edge, Explosion

Roggenrola   Boldore   Gigalith

ROSELIA

Thorn Pokémon

TYPE: GRASS-POISON

Thieves sometimes try to swipe the lovely blossoms Roselia grows. It responds with a shower of sharp, poisonous thorns.

How to say it: roh-ZEH-lee-uh

Height: 1' 00"   **Weight:** 4.4 lbs.

Possible Moves: Absorb, Growth, Poison Sting, Stun Spore, Mega Drain, Leech Seed, Magical Leaf, Grass Whistle, Giga Drain, Toxic Spikes, Sweet Scent, Ingrain, Petal Dance, Toxic, Aromatherapy, Synthesis, Petal Blizzard

Budew   Roselia   Roserade

ROSERADE

Bouquet Pokémon

REGIONS
KALOS
(CENTRAL),
SINNOH

TYPE: GRASS-POISON

With its beautiful blooms, enticing aroma, and graceful movements, Roserade is quite enchanting—but watch out! Its arms conceal thorny whips, and the thorns carry poison.

How to say it: ROSE-raid

Height: 2' 11"
Weight: 32.0 lbs.

Possible Moves: Venom Drench, Grassy Terrain, Weather Ball, Poison Sting, Mega Drain, Magical Leaf, Sweet Scent

Budew   Roselia   Roserade

ROTOM
Plasma Pokémon

REGIONS
KALOS (MOUNTAIN), SINNOH

TYPE: ELECTRIC-GHOST

Scientists are conducting ongoing research on Rotom, which shows potential as a power source. Sometimes it sneaks into electrical appliances and causes trouble.

How to say it: ROW-tom

Height: 1' 00"
Weight: 0.7 lbs.

Possible Moves: Discharge, Charge, Trick, Astonish, Thunder Wave, Thunder Shock, Confuse Ray, Uproar, Double Team, Shock Wave, Ominous Wind, Substitute, Electro Ball, Hex

Does not evolve

RUFFLET
Eaglet Pokémon

REGION
UNOVA

TYPE: NORMAL-FLYING

Rufflet is absolutely fearless when challenging opponents. It will pick a fight with just about anyone, becoming stronger in the process.

How to say it: RUF-lit

Height: 21' 08"   **Weight:** 23.1 lbs.

Possible Moves: Peck, Leer, Fury Attack, Wing Attack, Hone Claws, Scary Face, Aerial Ace, Slash, Defog, Tailwind, Air Slash, Crush Claw, Sky Drop, Whirlwind, Brave Bird, Thrash

Rufflet   Braviary

SABLEYE
Darkness Pokémon

TYPE: DARK-GHOST

Sableye lives deep in a cave, where it uses its sharp claws to dig up rocks for food. Minerals from these rocks then become part of its gemstone eyes and the crystals on its body.

How to say it: SAY-bull-eye

Height: 1' 08" **Weight:** 24.3 lbs.

Possible Moves: Mean Look, Zen Headbutt, Leer, Scratch, Foresight, Night Shade, Astonish, Fury Swipes, Fake Out, Detect, Shadow Sneak, Knock Off, Feint Attack, Punishment, Shadow Claw, Power Gem, Confuse Ray, Foul Play, Shadow Ball

MEGA SABLEYE
Darkness Pokémon

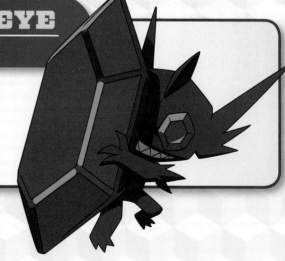

TYPE: DARK-GHOST

Height: 1' 08"
Weight: 24.3 lbs.

Sableye   Mega Sableye

TYPE: DRAGON-FLYING

When it evolves, Salamence finally grows the wings it's always dreamed of. It trails fire across the sky in a soaring celebration.

How to say it: SAL-uh-mence

Height: 4' 11"
Weight: 226.2 lbs.

Possible Moves: Double-Edge, Fire Fang, Thunder Fang, Rage, Bite, Leer, Headbutt, Focus Energy, Ember, Protect, Dragon Breath, Zen Headbutt, Scary Face, Fly, Crunch, Dragon Claw, Dragon Tail

REGIONS
**HOENN,
KALOS
(COASTAL)**

SALAMENCE
Dragon Pokémon

MEGA SALAMENCE
Dragon Pokémon

TYPE: DRAGON-FLYING

Height: 5' 11"
Weight: 248.2 lbs.

Bagon   Shelgon   Salamence   Mega Salamence

SAMUROTT
Formidable Pokémon

REGION
UNOVA

TYPE: WATER

From the armor on its front legs, Samurott can draw its swordlike seamitars in a heartbeat. Its glare can make everyone behave.

How to say it: SAM-uh-rot

Height: 4' 11"　　**Weight:** 208.6 lbs.

Possible Moves: Megahorn, Tackle, Tail Whip, Water Gun, Water Sport, Focus Energy, Razor Shell, Fury Cutter, Water Pulse, Revenge, Aqua Jet, Slash, Encore, Aqua Tail, Retaliate, Swords Dance, Hydro Pump

Oshawott **Dewott** **Samurott**

SANDILE
Desert Croc

REGIONS
**KALOS
(COASTAL),
UNOVA**

TYPE: GROUND-DARK

Sandile travels just below the surface of the desert sand, with only its nose and eyes sticking out. The warmth of the sand keeps it from getting too cold.

How to say it: SAN-dyle

Height: 2' 04"
Weight: 33.5 lbs.

Possible Moves: Leer, Rage, Bite, Sand Attack, Torment, Sand Tomb, Assurance, Mud-Slap, Embargo, Swagger, Crunch, Dig, Scary Face, Foul Play, Sandstorm, Earthquake, Thrash

Sandile **Krokorok** **Krookodile**

TYPE: GROUND

When Sandshrew rolls up into a ball, its tough hide helps keep it safe. It lives in the desert and sleeps in a burrow under the sand.

How to say it: SAND-shroo

Height: 2' 00"
Weight: 26.5 lbs.

Possible Moves: Scratch, Defense Curl, Sand Attack, Poison Sting, Rollout, Rapid Spin, Swift, Fury Cutter, Magnitude, Fury Swipes, Sand Tomb, Slash, Dig, Gyro Ball, Swords Dance, Sandstorm, Earthquake

REGIONS
KALOS (MOUNTAIN), KANTO

SANDSHREW
Mouse Pokémon

Sandshrew **Sandslash**

TYPE: GROUND

Sections of hardened hide form the spikes that cover Sandslash's body. The spikes protect it in battle and can also be used as a weapon.

How to say it: SAND-slash

Height: 3' 03"   **Weight:** 65.0 lbs.

Possible Moves: Scratch, Defense Curl, Sand Attack, Poison Sting, Rollout, Rapid Spin, Swift, Fury Cutter, Magnitude, Fury Swipes, Crush Claw, Sand Tomb, Slash, Dig, Gyro Ball, Swords Dance, Sandstorm, Earthquake

REGIONS
KALOS (MOUNTAIN), KANTO

SANDSLASH
Mouse Pokémon

Sandshrew **Sandslash**

317

SAWK
Karate Pokémon

TYPE: FIGHTING

Sawk go deep into the mountains to train their fighting skills relentlessly. If they are disturbed during this training, they become very angry.

How to say it: SAWK

Height: 4' 07"
Weight: 112.4 lbs.

Possible Moves: Rock Smash, Leer, Bide, Focus Energy, Double Kick, Low Sweep, Counter, Karate Chop, Brick Break, Bulk Up, Retaliate, Endure, Quick Guard, Close Combat, Reversal

Does not evolve

SAWSBUCK
Season Pokémon

REGION
UNOVA

TYPE: NORMAL-GRASS

As the seasons change, their horns display different kinds of plant growth. Because of their seasonal migration, some people regard Sawsbuck's appearance as a sign of spring.

How to say it: SAWZ-buk

Height: 6' 03"
Weight: 203.9 lbs.

Possible Moves: Megahorn, Tackle, Camouflage, Growl, Sand Attack, Double Kick, Leech Seed, Feint Attack, Take Down, Jump Kick, Aromatherapy, Energy Ball, Charm, Horn Leech, Nature Power, Double-Edge, Solar Beam

Winter Form

Spring Form

Summer Form

Autumn Form

Deerling ⟹ Sawsbuck

SCATTERBUG
Scatterdust Pokémon

TYPE: BUG

When threatened, Scatterbug protects itself with a cloud of black powder that can paralyze its attacker. This powder also serves as protection from the elements.

How to say it: SCAT-ter-BUG

Height: 1' 00"   **Weight:** 5.5 lbs.

Possible Moves: Tackle, String Shot, Stun Spore, Bug Bite

Scatterbug   Spewpa   Vivillon

SCEPTILE
Forest Pokémon

TYPE: GRASS

Razor-edged leaves and nutritious seeds sprout from Sceptile's back. It wields the leaves in battle, and cares for trees by planting its seeds nearby to enrich the soil.

How to say it: SEP-tile

Height: 5' 07"
Weight: 115.1 lbs.

Possible Moves: Night Slash, Pound, Leer, Absorb, Quick Attack, X-Scissor, Pursuit, Screech, Leaf Blade, Agility, Slam, Detect, False Swipe, Leaf Storm

MEGA SCEPTILE
Forest Pokémon

TYPE: GRASS
Height: 6' 03"
Weight: 121.7 lbs.

Treecko Grovyle Sceptile Mega Sceptile

320

SCIZOR
Pincer Pokémon

TYPE: BUG-STEEL

Scizor's exoskeleton is as hard as steel, easily shrugging off most ordinary attacks. It controls its internal temperature by flapping its wings.

How to say it: SI-zor

Height: 5' 11"   **Weight:** 260.1 lbs.

Possible Moves: Feint, Bullet Punch, Quick Attack, Leer, Focus Energy, Pursuit, False Swipe, Agility, Metal Claw, Fury Cutter, Slash, Razor Wind, Iron Defense, X-Scissor, Night Slash, Double Hit, Iron Head, Swords Dance

MEGA SCIZOR
Pincer Pokémon

TYPE: BUG-STEEL

Height: 6' 07"
Weight: 275.6 lbs.

Scyther   Scizor   Mega Scizor

SCOLIPEDE
Megapede Pokémon

TYPE: BUG-POISON

The claws near Scolipede's head can be used to grab, immobilize, and poison its opponent. Scolipede moves quickly when chasing down enemies.

How to say it: SKOH-lih-peed

Height: 8' 02"
Weight: 442.0 lbs.

Possible Moves: Megahorn, Defense Curl, Rollout, Poison Sting, Screech, Pursuit, Protect, Poison Tail, Bug Bite, Venoshock, Baton Pass, Agility, Steamroller, Toxic, Venom Drench, Rock Climb, Double-Edge

Venipede ⇨ **Whirlipede** ⇨ **Scolipede**

SCRAFTY
Hoodlum Pokémon

TYPE: DARK-FIGHTING

A group of Scrafty is led by the one with the biggest crest. Their powerful kicks can shatter concrete.

How to say it: SKRAF-tee

Height: 3' 07"
Weight: 66.1 lbs.

Possible Moves: Leer, Low Kick, Sand Attack, Feint Attack, Headbutt, Swagger, Brick Break, Payback, Chip Away, High Jump Kick, Scary Face, Crunch, Facade, Rock Climb, Focus Punch, Head Smash

Scraggy ⇨ **Scrafty**

SCRAGGY
Shedding Pokémon

TYPE: DARK-FIGHTING

Scraggy can pull its loose, rubbery skin up around its neck to protect itself from attacks. With its tough skull, it delivers headbutts without warning.

How to say it: SKRAG-ee

Height: 2' 00"   **Weight:** 26.0 lbs.

Possible Moves: Leer, Low Kick, Sand Attack, Feint Attack, Headbutt, Swagger, Brick Break, Payback, Chip Away, High Jump Kick, Scary Face, Crunch, Facade, Rock Climb, Focus Punch, Head Smash

Scraggy   Scrafty

SCYTHER
Mantis Pokémon

TYPE: BUG-FLYING

With its impressive speed and razor-sharp scythes, Scyther is a formidable opponent. It can slash through a log with one blow.

How to say it: SY-thur

Height: 4' 11"   **Weight:** 123.5 lbs.

Possible Moves: Vacuum Wave, Quick Attack, Leer, Focus Energy, Pursuit, False Swipe, Agility, Wing Attack, Fury Cutter, Slash, Razor Wind, Double Team, X-Scissor, Night Slash, Double Hit, Air Slash, Swords Dance, Feint

Scyther   Scizor   Mega Scizor

SEADRA
Dragon Pokémon

TYPE: WATER

When Seadra spins around in the water, it can cause a whirlpool with enough force to capsize a small boat. It sleeps among coral branches.

How to say it: SEE-dra

Height: 3' 11"
Weight: 55.1 lbs.

Possible Moves: Water Gun, Smokescreen, Leer, Bubble, Focus Energy, Bubble Beam, Agility, Twister, Brine, Hydro Pump, Dragon Dance, Dragon Pulse

Horsea Seadra Kingdra

SEAKING
Goldfish Pokémon

TYPE: WATER

Male Seaking become brilliantly colored during the autumn, when they perform their courtship dance. The pair take turns keeping watch over their nests.

How to say it: SEE-king

Height: 4' 03"
Weight: 86.0 lbs.

Possible Moves: Megahorn, Poison Jab, Peck, Tail Whip, Water Sport, Supersonic, Horn Attack, Water Pulse, Flail, Aqua Ring, Fury Attack, Waterfall, Horn Drill, Agility, Soak

Goldeen Seaking

SEALEO
Ball Roll Pokémon

TYPE: ICE-WATER

Sealeo learns about new things by exploring them with its nose, examining the fragrance and texture. It particularly enjoys spinning round objects on its nose.

How to say it: SEEL-ee-oh

Height: 3' 07"
Weight: 193.1 lbs.

Possible Moves: Powder Snow, Growl, Water Gun, Encore, Ice Ball, Body Slam, Aurora Beam, Hail, Swagger, Rest, Snore, Blizzard, Sheer Cold

Spheal ➡ Sealeo ➡ Walrein

SEEDOT
Acorn Pokémon

TYPE: GRASS

Because Seedot hangs from branches by the top of its head, it looks just like an acorn when it isn't moving. For a glossy finish, it drinks plenty of water and polishes itself with leaves.

How to say it: SEE-dot

Height: 1' 08"
Weight: 8.8 lbs.

Possible Moves: Bide, Harden, Growth, Nature Power, Synthesis, Sunny Day, Explosion

Seedot ➡ Nuzleaf ➡ Shiftry

325

SEEL

Sea Lion Pokémon

TYPE: WATER

In frozen seas, Seel swims under the ice in search of food. It uses the point on its head to break through the ice when it comes up for air.

How to say it: SEEL

Height: 3' 07"
Weight: 198.4 lbs.

Possible Moves: Headbutt, Growl, Water Sport, Icy Wind, Encore, Ice Shard, Rest, Aqua Ring, Aurora Beam, Aqua Jet, Brine, Take Down, Dive, Aqua Tail, Ice Beam, Safeguard, Hail

Seel ⇨ Dewgong

SEISMITOAD

Vibration Pokémon

TYPE: WATER-GROUND

When Seismitoad vibrates the bumps on its hands, its punches get a serious power boost—enough to pulverize a boulder with a single hit.

How to say it: SYZ-mih-tohd

Height: 4' 11"
Weight: 136.7 lbs.

Possible Moves: Bubble, Growl, Supersonic, Round, Bubble Beam, Mud Shot, Aqua Ring, Uproar, Muddy Water, Rain Dance, Acid, Flail, Drain Punch, Echoed Voice, Hydro Pump, Hyper Voice

Tympole ⇨ Palpitoad ⇨ Seismitoad

TYPE: NORMAL

Sentret always sleep in groups of two or more so one of them can keep watch and alert its friends if danger threatens. When alone, they're too nervous to sleep.

How to say it: SEN-tret

Height: 2' 07"   **Weight:** 13.2 lbs.

Possible Moves: Scratch, Foresight, Defense Curl, Quick Attack, Fury Swipes, Helping Hand, Follow Me, Slam, Rest, Sucker Punch, Amnesia, Baton Pass, Me First, Hyper Voice

REGIONS
JOHTO,
KALOS
(CENTRAL)

SENTRET
Scout Pokémon

Sentret ➡️ **Furret**

REGION
UNOVA

SERPERIOR
Regal Pokémon

TYPE: GRASS

A single glare from Serperior can stop most opponents in their tracks. The energy it absorbs from the sun gets a boost inside its body.

How to say it: sur-PEER-ee-ur

Height: 10' 10"
Weight: 138.9 lbs.

Possible Moves: Tackle, Leer, Vine Whip, Wrap, Growth, Leaf Tornado, Leech Seed, Mega Drain, Slam, Leaf Blade, Coil, Giga Drain, Wring Out, Gastro Acid, Leaf Storm

Snivy ➡️ **Servine** ➡️ **Serperior**

327

SERVINE

Grass Snake Pokémon

REGION
UNOVA

TYPE: GRASS

Dirt on its leaves blocks its photosynthesis, so Servine is fussy about staying clean. It confounds its enemies with quick movements before it strikes with its whiplike vines.

How to say it: SUR-vine

Height: 2' 07"
Weight: 35.3 lbs.

Possible Moves: Tackle, Leer, Vine Whip, Wrap, Growth, Leaf Tornado, Leech Seed, Mega Drain, Slam, Leaf Blade, Coil, Giga Drain, Wring Out, Gastro Acid, Leaf Storm

Snivy   Servine   Serperior

SEVIPER

Fang Snake Pokémon

REGIONS
**HOENN,
KALOS
(COASTAL)**

TYPE: POISON

The sharp blade on Seviper's tail also gives off a powerful poison. These Pokémon constantly feud with Zangoose.

How to say it: seh-VIE-per

Height: 8' 10"
Weight: 115.7 lbs.

Possible Moves: Wrap, Swagger, Bite, Lick, Poison Tail, Screech, Venoshock, Glare, Poison Fang, Venom Drench, Night Slash, Gastro Acid, Haze, Poison Jab, Crunch, Belch, Coil, Wring Out

Does not evolve

SEWADDLE
Sewing Pokémon

TYPE: BUG-GRASS

Sewaddle makes clothing for itself by sewing leaves together with the sticky thread it produces from its mouth. Fashion designers often use it as a mascot.

How to say it: seh-WAH-dul

Height: 1' 00"   **Weight:** 5.5 lbs.

Possible Moves: Tackle, String Shot, Bug Bite, Razor Leaf, Struggle Bug, Endure, Bug Buzz, Flail

Sewaddle   Swadloon   Leavanny

329

SHARPEDO

Brutal Pokémon

TYPE: WATER-DARK

Though Sharpedo isn't great at swimming long distances, it can shoot forward at seventy-five MPH by propelling seawater through its body. If a tooth falls out, it grows back immediately.

How to say it: shar-PEE-do

Height: 5' 11"
Weight: 195.8 lbs.

Possible Moves: Night Slash, Feint, Leer, Bite, Rage, Focus Energy, Scary Face, Ice Fang, Screech, Swagger, Assurance, Crunch, Slash, Aqua Jet, Taunt, Agility, Skull Bash

MEGA SHARPEDO

Brutal Pokémon

TYPE: WATER-DARK

Height: 8' 02"
Weight: 287.3 lbs.

Carvanha   Sharpedo   Mega Sharpedo

SHAYMIN (LAND FORME)
Gratitude Pokémon

TYPE: GRASS

When the Gracidea flower blooms, Shaymin gains the power of flight. Wherever it goes, it clears the air of toxins and brings feelings of gratitude.

How to say it: SHAY-min

Height: 0' 08"   **Weight:** 4.6 lbs.

Possible Moves: Growth, Magical Leaf, Leech Seed, Synthesis, Sweet Scent, Natural Gift, Worry Seed, Aromatherapy, Energy Ball, Sweet Kiss, Healing Wish, Seed Flare

MYTHICAL POKÉMON

Does not evolve

SHAYMIN (SKY FORME)
Gratitude Pokémon

TYPE: GRASS-FLYING

Shaymin has the power to clean the environment in this forme, too. Once it has transformed, Shaymin Sky Forme flies off to find a new home.

How to say it: SHAY-min

Height: 1' 04"   **Weight:** 11.5 lbs.

Possible Moves: Growth, Magical Leaf, Leech Seed, Quick Attack, Sweet Scent, Natural Gift, Worry Seed, Air Slash, Energy Ball, Sweet Kiss, Leaf Storm, Seed Flare

MYTHICAL POKÉMON

Does not evolve

SHEDINJA

Shed Pokémon

TYPE: BUG-GHOST

Shedinja is a strange Pokémon. It doesn't move, it doesn't breathe, and no one really knows where it came from. Its body seems to be nothing more than a hollow shell.

How to say it: sheh-DIN-ja

Height: 2' 07" **Weight:** 2.6 lbs.

Possible Moves: Scratch, Harden, Leech Life, Sand Attack, Fury Swipes, Mind Reader, Spite, Confuse Ray, Shadow Sneak, Grudge, Phantom Force, Heal Block, Shadow Ball

Ninjask

Nincada   Shedinja

SHELGON

Endurance Pokémon

TYPE: DRAGON

A shell of thick armor protects Shelgon while it prepares to evolve. It's hard enough to repel enemy attacks, and so heavy that it makes the Pokémon move slowly.

How to say it: SHELL-gon

Height: 3' 07" **Weight:** 243.6 lbs.

Possible Moves: Rage, Bite, Leer, Headbutt, Focus Energy, Ember, Protect, Dragon Breath, Zen Headbutt, Scary Face, Crunch, Dragon Claw, Double-Edge

Bagon   Shelgon   Salamence   Mega Salamence

TYPE: WATER

When Shellder's shell is closed, its large tongue tends to hang out. It uses its tongue as a shovel to dig a nest in the sand.

How to say it: SHELL-der

Height: 1' 00"
Weight: 8.8 lbs.

Possible Moves: Tackle, Withdraw, Supersonic, Icicle Spear, Protect, Leer, Clamp, Ice Shard, Razor Shell, Aurora Beam, Whirlpool, Brine, Iron Defense, Ice Beam, Shell Smash, Hydro Pump

REGIONS
KALOS
(COASTAL),
KANTO

SHELLDER
Bivalve Pokémon

Shellder   Cloyster

REGION
SINNOH

SHELLOS (EAST SEA)
Sea Slug Pokémon

TYPE: WATER

Shellos come in different colors and shapes, depending on where they live. Their squishy bodies give off a strange purple fluid when pressure is applied.

How to say it: SHELL-oss

Height: 1' 00"
Weight: 13.9 lbs.

Possible Moves: Mud-Slap, Mud Sport, Harden, Water Pulse, Mud Bomb, Hidden Power, Rain Dance, Body Slam, Muddy Water, Recover

Shellos   Gastrodon
(East Sea)   (East Sea)

333

SHELLOS (WEST SEA)
Sea Slug Pokémon

TYPE: WATER

Like Gastrodon, Shellos will look quite different depending upon where it lives.

How to say it: SHELL-oss

Height: 1' 00"
Weight: 13.9 lbs.

Possible Moves: Mud-Slap, Mud Sport, Harden, Water Pulse, Mud Bomb, Hidden Power, Rain Dance, Body Slam, Muddy Water, Recover

Shellos (West Sea)   Gastrodon (West Sea)

SHELMET
Snail Pokémon

REGIONS
KALOS (MOUNTAIN), UNOVA

TYPE: BUG

Shelmet evolves when exposed to electricity, but only if Karrablast is nearby. It's unclear why this is the case.

How to say it: SHELL-mett

Height: 1' 04"
Weight: 17.0 lbs.

Possible Moves: Leech Life, Acid, Bide, Curse, Struggle Bug, Mega Drain, Yawn, Protect, Acid Armor, Giga Drain, Body Slam, Bug Buzz, Recover, Guard Swap, Final Gambit

Shelmet   Accelgor

TYPE: ROCK-STEEL

Though Shieldon's face is well protected by its polished armor, it's vulnerable if a foe strikes from behind. It was restored from a fossil.

How to say it: SHEEL-donn

Height: 1' 08"
Weight: 125.7 lbs.

Possible Moves: Tackle, Protect, Taunt, Metal Sound, Take Down, Iron Defense, Swagger, Ancient Power, Endure, Metal Burst, Iron Head, Heavy Slam

SHIELDON
Shield Pokémon

Shieldon   Bastiodon

SHIFTRY
Wicked Pokémon

TYPE: GRASS-DARK

Shiftry makes its home in the tops of ancient trees. Its leafy fans can stir up powerful gusts of wind.

How to say it: SHIFF-tree

Height: 4' 03"
Weight: 131.4 lbs.

Possible Moves: Feint Attack, Whirlwind, Nasty Plot, Razor Leaf, Leaf Tornado, Leaf Storm

Seedot   Nuzleaf   Shiftry

SHINX
Flash Pokémon

REGION
SINNOH

TYPE: ELECTRIC

When Shinx senses danger, its fur gives off a bright flash. This brilliant light blinds its attacker so Shinx can make a hasty escape.

How to say it: SHINKS

Height: 1' 08"
Weight: 20.9 lbs.

Possible Moves: Tackle, Leer, Charge, Spark, Bite, Roar, Swagger, Thunder Fang, Crunch, Scary Face, Discharge, Wild Charge

Shinx   Luxio   Luxray

SHROOMISH
Mushroom Pokémon

REGION
HOENN

TYPE: GRASS

Shroomish live deep in the forest and make their home in moist soil, using rotted plant material as food. The spores it shakes from its cap are poisonous.

How to say it: SHROOM-ish

Height: 1' 04"   **Weight:** 9.9 lbs.

Possible Moves: Absorb, Tackle, Stun Spore, Leech Seed, Mega Drain, Headbutt, Poison Powder, Worry Seed, Growth, Giga Drain, Seed Bomb, Spore

Shroomish   Breloom

TYPE: BUG-ROCK

Shuckle stores berries in its shell so it always has a food supply. This comes in handy when it hides away under the rocks.

How to say it: SHUCK-kull

Height: 2' 00"
Weight: 45.2 lbs.

Possible Moves: Sticky Web, Withdraw, Constrict, Bide, Rollout, Encore, Wrap, Struggle Bug, Safeguard, Rest, Rock Throw, Gastro Acid, Power Trick, Shell Smash, Rock Slide, Bug Bite, Power Split, Guard Split, Stone Edge

REGIONS JOHTO, KALOS (MOUNTAIN)

SHUCKLE
Mold Pokémon

Does not evolve

TYPE: GHOST

If someone is consumed by thoughts of revenge, it's likely a Shuppet is lurking nearby, drawing energy from those dark feelings.

How to say it: SHUP-pett

Height: 2' 00"
Weight: 5.1 lbs.

Possible Moves: Knock Off, Screech, Night Shade, Spite, Will-O-Wisp, Shadow Sneak, Curse, Feint Attack, Hex, Shadow Ball, Sucker Punch, Embargo, Snatch, Grudge, Trick

REGIONS HOENN, KALOS (MOUNTAIN)

SHUPPET
Puppet Pokémon

Shuppet   ⇨   **Banette**   ⇨   **Mega Banette**

SIGILYPH
Avianoid Pokémon

TYPE: PSYCHIC-FLYING

Sigilyph were appointed to keep watch over an ancient city. Their patrol route never varies.

How to say it: SIH-jih-liff

Height: 4' 07"
Weight: 30.9 lbs.

Possible Moves: Gust, Miracle Eye, Hypnosis, Psywave, Tailwind, Whirlwind, Psybeam, Air Cutter, Light Screen, Reflect, Synchronoise, Mirror Move, Gravity, Air Slash, Psychic, Cosmic Power, Sky Attack

Does not evolve

SILCOON
Cocoon Pokémon

REGION
HOENN

TYPE: BUG

While waiting to evolve, Silcoon wraps its body in silk and attaches itself to a branch. It leaves a tiny hole so it can see. The cocoon protects the Pokémon and collects rainwater so it can drink.

How to say it: sill-COON

Height: 2' 00"
Weight: 22.0 lbs.

Possible Move: Harden

Wurmple   Silcoon   Beautifly

SIMIPOUR
Geyser Pokémon

TYPE: WATER

Simipour can shoot water out of its tail with such force that it can punch right through a concrete wall. When its stores run low, it dips its tail into clean water to suck up a refill.

How to say it: SIH-mee-por

Height: 3' 03"
Weight: 63.9 lbs.

Possible Moves: Leer, Lick, Fury Swipes, Scald

Panpour   Simipour

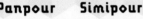

SIMISAGE
Thorn Monkey Pokémon

TYPE: GRASS

Simisage's tail is covered in thorns, and it uses the tail like a whip to lash out at opponents. It always seems to be in a bad mood.

How to say it: SIH-mee-sayj

Height: 3' 07"
Weight: 67.2 lbs.

Possible Moves: Leer, Lick, Fury Swipes, Seed Bomb

Pansage   Simisage

SIMISEAR
Ember Pokémon

TYPE: FIRE

Simisear's head and tail give off embers in the heat of battle . . . or any time it's excited. It has quite a sweet tooth.

How to say it: SIH-mee-seer

Height: 3' 03"
Weight: 61.7 lbs.

Possible Moves: Leer, Lick, Fury Swipes, Flame Burst

Pansear   Simisear

SKARMORY
Armor Bird Pokémon

TYPE: STEEL-FLYING

The steel that makes up Skarmory's wings gets dinged up and dented during battles. Every year, the sharp edges renew themselves.

How to say it: SKAR-more-ree

Height: 5' 07"
Weight: 111.3 lbs.

Possible Moves: Leer, Peck, Sand Attack, Swift, Agility, Fury Attack, Feint, Air Cutter, Spikes, Metal Sound, Steel Wing, Autotomize, Air Slash, Slash, Night Slash

Does not evolve

TYPE: GRASS

REGION KALOS (CENTRAL)

SKIDDO
Mount Pokémon

Calm and gentle, Skiddo have been living side by side with people for many generations. They can create energy via photosynthesis.

How to say it: skid-OO

Height: 2' 11"
Weight: 68.3 lbs.

Possible Moves: Tackle, Growth, Vine Whip, Tail Whip, Leech Seed, Razor Leaf, Worry Seed, Synthesis, Take Down, Bulldoze, Seed Bomb, Bulk Up, Double-Edge, Horn Leech, Leaf Blade, Milk Drink

Skiddo   Gogoat

TYPE: GRASS-FLYING

REGIONS JOHTO, KALOS (CENTRAL)

SKIPLOOM
Cottonweed Pokémon

In mild temperatures, the flower on Skiploom's head begins to bloom. The petals start to open at just above sixty-four degrees Fahrenheit, and warmer temperatures coax them into full blossom.

How to say it: SKIP-loom

Height: 2' 00"
Weight: 2.2 lbs.

Possible Moves: Splash, Synthesis, Tail Whip, Tackle, Fairy Wind, Poison Powder, Stun Spore, Sleep Powder, Bullet Seed, Leech Seed, Mega Drain, Acrobatics, Rage Powder, Cotton Spore, U-turn, Worry Seed, Giga Drain, Bounce, Memento

Hoppip   Skiploom   Jumpluff

341

SKITTY

Kitten Pokémon

TYPE: NORMAL

Anything that moves, including its own tail, draws Skitty's attention and starts a playful game of chase. Wild Skitty live in trees.

How to say it: SKIT-tee

Height: 2' 00"
Weight: 24.3 lbs.

Possible Moves: Fake Out, Growl, Tail Whip, Tackle, Foresight, Attract, Sing, Double Slap, Copycat, Assist, Charm, Feint Attack, Wake-Up Slap, Covet, Heal Bell, Double-Edge, Captivate, Play Rough

Skitty   Delcatty

SKORUPI

Scorpion Pokémon

REGIONS
KALOS
(MOUNTAIN),
SINNOH

TYPE: POISON-BUG

After burying itself in the sand, Skorupi lurks in hiding. If an intruder gets too close, it latches on with the poisonous claws on its tail.

How to say it: skor-ROOP-ee

Height: 2' 07"   **Weight:** 26.5 lbs.

Possible Moves: Bite, Poison Sting, Leer, Knock Off, Pin Missile, Acupressure, Pursuit, Bug Bite, Poison Fang, Venoshock, Hone Claws, Toxic Spikes, Night Slash, Scary Face, Crunch, Fell Stinger, Cross Poison

Skorupi   Drapion

TYPE: POISON-WATER

Skrelp disguises itself as rotten kelp to hide from enemies. It defends itself by spraying a poisonous liquid.

How to say it: Skrelp

Height: 1' 08"
Weight: 16.1 lbs.

Possible Moves: Tackle, Smokescreen, Water Gun, Feint Attack, Tail Whip, Bubble, Acid, Camouflage, Poison Tail, Water Pulse, Double Team, Toxic, Aqua Tail, Sludge Bomb, Hydro Pump, Dragon Pulse

Skrelp → Dragalge

SKUNTANK
Skunk Pokémon

REGIONS
KALOS
(COASTAL),
SINNOH

TYPE: POISON-DARK

From the end of its tail, Skuntank can shoot a noxious fluid more than 160 feet. This fluid smells awful, and the stench only gets worse if it's not cleaned up immediately.

How to say it: SKUN-tank

Height: 3' 03"   **Weight:** 83.8 lbs.

Possible Moves: Scratch, Focus Energy, Poison Gas, Screech, Fury Swipes, Smokescreen, Feint, Slash, Toxic, Acid Spray, Flamethrower, Night Slash, Memento, Belch, Explosion

Stunky → Skuntank

343

SLAKING

Lazy Pokémon

TYPE: NORMAL

Slaking lies in one place and pulls up grass to eat. Circular bare spots in a meadow might be a sign that a Slaking lives nearby. After eating everything within reach, it moves to another spot, but it's not happy about that.

How to say it: SLAH-king

Height: 6' 07" **Weight:** 287.7 lbs.

Possible Moves: Scratch, Yawn, Encore, Slack Off, Feint Attack, Amnesia, Covet, Swagger, Chip Away, Counter, Flail, Fling, Punishment, Hammer Arm

Slakoth   **Vigoroth**   **Slaking**

SLAKOTH

Slacker Pokémon

REGION
HOENN

TYPE: NORMAL

It's rare to see a Slakoth move. It's awake for only a few hours per day, its heart beats extremely slowly, and it doesn't require much food.

How to say it: SLAH-koth

Height: 2' 07" **Weight:** 52.9 lbs.

Possible Moves: Scratch, Yawn, Encore, Slack Off, Feint Attack, Amnesia, Covet, Chip Away, Counter, Flail

Slakoth   **Vigoroth**   **Slaking**

SLIGGOO
Soft Tissue Pokémon

TYPE: DRAGON

The four horns on Sliggoo's head are sense organs that allow the Pokémon to find its way by sound and smell.

How to say it: SLIH-goo

Height: 2' 07"   **Weight:** 38.6 lbs.

Possible Moves: Tackle, Bubble, Absorb, Protect, Bide, Dragon Breath, Rain Dance, Flail, Body Slam, Muddy Water, Dragon Pulse

Goomy   Sliggoo   Goodra

SLOWBRO
Hermit Crab Pokémon

TYPE: WATER-PSYCHIC

Because of the Shellder chomping on its tail, Slowbro can no longer spend its days fishing. It can swim to catch food, but it's not happy about that.

How to say it: SLOW-bro

Height: 5' 03"
Weight: 173.1 lbs.

Possible Moves: Heal Pulse, Curse, Yawn, Tackle, Growl, Water Gun, Confusion, Disable, Headbutt, Water Pulse, Zen Headbutt, Slack Off, Withdraw, Amnesia, Psychic, Rain Dance, Psych Up

MEGA SLOWBRO
Hermit Crab Pokémon

TYPE: WATER-PSYCHIC

Height: 6' 07"
Weight: 264.6 lbs.

Slowpoke

Slowbro

Slowking

Mega
Slowbro

REGIONS JOHTO, KALOS (COASTAL)

SLOWKING
Royal Pokémon

TYPE: WATER-PSYCHIC

If the Shellder on its head were to let go, Slowking would forget all its knowledge. It spends time in research every day, trying to solve the world's greatest mysteries.

How to say it: SLOW-king

Height: 6' 07"   **Weight:** 175.3 lbs.

Possible Moves: Heal Pulse, Power Gem, Hidden Power, Curse, Yawn, Tackle, Growl, Water Gun, Confusion, Disable, Headbutt, Water Pulse, Zen Headbutt, Nasty Plot, Swagger, Psychic, Trump Card, Psych Up

Slowpoke   Slowking

REGIONS KALOS (COASTAL), KANTO

SLOWPOKE
Dopey Pokémon

Slowbro   Mega Slowbro

Slowpoke

Slowking

TYPE: WATER-PSYCHIC

Slowpoke spends much of its time along the riverbank, where it uses its tail for fishing. Often, its mind wanders and it spends the whole day lazing about.

How to say it: SLOW-poke

Height: 3' 11"   **Weight:** 79.4 lbs.

Possible Moves: Curse, Yawn, Tackle, Growl, Water Gun, Confusion, Disable, Headbutt, Water Pulse, Zen Headbutt, Slack Off, Amnesia, Psychic, Rain Dance, Psych Up, Heal Pulse

SLUGMA

Lava Pokémon

TYPE: FIRE

The magma that circulates within Slugma's body serves as its blood, supplying its organs with oxygen and nutrients. It has to stay warm, or the magma will harden.

How to say it: SLUG-ma

Height: 2' 04"
Weight: 77.2 lbs.

Possible Moves: Yawn, Smog, Ember, Rock Throw, Harden, Recover, Flame Burst, Ancient Power, Amnesia, Lava Plume, Rock Slide, Body Slam, Flamethrower, Earth Power

Slugma   Magcargo

SLURPUFF

Meringue Pokémon

TYPE: FAIRY

Pastry chefs love having a Slurpuff in the kitchen. With its incredibly sensitive nose, it can tell exactly when a dessert is baked to perfection.

How to say it: SLUR-puff

Height: 2' 07"   **Weight:** 11.0 lbs.

Possible Moves: Sweet Scent, Tackle, Fairy Wind, Play Nice, Fake Tears, Round, Cotton Spore, Endeavor, Aromatherapy, Draining Kiss, Energy Ball, Cotton Guard, Wish, Play Rough, Light Screen, Safeguard

Swirlix   Slurpuff

TYPE: NORMAL

Smeargle's tail tip produces a fluid that it uses like paint to draw thousands of different territorial markings.

How to say it: SMEAR-gull

Height: 3' 11"
Weight: 127.9 lbs.

Possible Move: Sketch

REGIONS
JOHTO,
KALOS
(CENTRAL)

SMEARGLE
Painter Pokémon

Does not evolve

TYPE: ICE-PSYCHIC

Very active but a little clumsy, Smoochum falls down a lot when it runs. After falling, it seeks out a reflective surface so it can make sure its face isn't smudged.

How to say it: SMOO-chum

Height: 1' 04"   **Weight:** 13.2 lbs.

Possible Moves: Pound, Lick, Sweet Kiss, Powder Snow, Confusion, Sing, Heart Stamp, Mean Look, Fake Tears, Lucky Chant, Avalanche, Psychic, Copycat, Perish Song, Blizzard

REGIONS
JOHTO,
KALOS
(MOUNTAIN)

SMOOCHUM
Kiss Pokémon

Smoochum   Jynx

349

SNEASEL
Sharp Claw Pokémon

TYPE: DARK-ICE

When Sneasel climbs trees, its hooklike claws sink into the bark to give it a good grip. It sometimes raids unprotected nests for food.

How to say it: SNEE-zul

Height: 2' 11"
Weight: 61.7 lbs.

Possible Moves: Scratch, Leer, Taunt, Quick Attack, Feint Attack, Icy Wind, Fury Swipes, Agility, Metal Claw, Hone Claws, Beat Up, Screech, Slash, Snatch, Punishment, Ice Shard

Sneasel   Weavile

SNIVY
Grass Snake Pokémon

REGION
UNOVA

TYPE: GRASS

Soaking up sunlight with its tail increases Snivy's speed. Though it has hands, it generally uses the vines that extend from its neck instead.

How to say it: SNY-vee

Height: 2' 00"   **Weight:** 17.9 lbs.

Possible Moves: Tackle, Leer, Vine Whip, Wrap, Growth, Leaf Tornado, Leech Seed, Mega Drain, Slam, Leaf Blade, Coil, Giga Drain, Wring Out, Gastro Acid, Leaf Storm

Snivy   Servine   Serperior

TYPE: NORMAL

Snorlax spends most of its time eating and sleeping. Small children sometimes play by bouncing on this gentle Pokémon's vast belly.

How to say it: SNOR-lacks

Height: 6' 11"
Weight: 1,014.1 lbs.

Possible Moves: Tackle, Defense Curl, Amnesia, Lick, Chip Away, Yawn, Body Slam, Rest, Snore, Sleep Talk, Rollout, Block, Belly Drum, Crunch, Heavy Slam, Giga Impact

Munchlax   Snorlax

TYPE: ICE

They say that when a Snorunt visits your home, it brings good fortune that will last. It eats snow and spends the warmer seasons hidden deep in caves.

How to say it: SNOW-runt

Height: 2' 04"   **Weight:** 37.0 lbs.

Possible Moves: Powder Snow, Leer, Double Team, Bite, Icy Wind, Headbutt, Protect, Ice Fang, Crunch, Ice Shard, Hail, Blizzard

Froslass

Snorunt   Glalie   Mega Glalie

SNOVER
Frost Tree Pokémon

TYPE: GRASS-ICE

Snover live high in the mountains most of the year, but in the winter, they migrate to lower elevations.

How to say it: SNOW-vur

Height: 3' 03"
Weight: 111.3 lbs.

Possible Moves: Powder Snow, Leer, Razor Leaf, Icy Wind, Grass Whistle, Swagger, Mist, Ice Shard, Ingrain, Wood Hammer, Blizzard, Sheer Cold

Snover   Abomasnow   Mega Abomasnow

SNUBBULL
Fairy Pokémon

TYPE: FAIRY

Snubbull can drive off smaller Pokémon by making scary faces at them. After they run away, it seems to regret its behavior.

How to say it: SNUB-bull

Height: 2' 00"
Weight: 17.2 lbs.

Possible Moves: Ice Fang, Fire Fang, Thunder Fang, Tackle, Scary Face, Tail Whip, Charm, Bite, Lick, Headbutt, Roar, Rage, Play Rough, Payback, Crunch

Snubbull   Granbull

TYPE: PSYCHIC

The special liquid that surrounds Solosis protects it from any harsh conditions. They communicate with telepathy.

How to say it: soh-LOH-sis

Height: 1' 00"
Weight: 2.2 lbs.

Possible Moves: Psywave, Reflect, Rollout, Snatch, Hidden Power, Light Screen, Charm, Recover, Psyshock, Endeavor, Future Sight, Pain Split, Psychic, Skill Swap, Heal Block, Wonder Room

SOLOSIS
Cell Pokémon

REGIONS KALOS (COASTAL), UNOVA

Solosis   Duosion   Reuniclus

REGIONS HOENN, KALOS (COASTAL)

SOLROCK
Meteorite Pokémon

TYPE: ROCK-PSYCHIC

When Solrock spins, it gives off heat and light. It uses sunlight for energy and can apparently pick up on others' emotions.

How to say it: SOLE-rock

Height: 3' 11"   **Weight:** 339.5 lbs.

Possible Moves: Wonder Room, Rock Throw, Tackle, Harden, Confusion, Fire Spin, Rock Polish, Psywave, Embargo, Rock Slide, Cosmic Power, Psychic, Heal Block, Stone Edge, Solar Beam, Explosion

Does not evolve

SPEAROW
Tiny Bird Pokémon

TYPE: NORMAL-FLYING

When many Spearow sound their loud, high-pitched cry all at once, it usually means danger is nearby.

How to say it: SPEAR-oh

Height: 1' 00"
Weight: 4.4 lbs.

Possible Moves: Peck, Growl, Leer, Fury Attack, Pursuit, Aerial Ace, Mirror Move, Agility, Assurance, Roost, Drill Peck

Spearow   Fearow

SPEWPA
Scatterdust Pokémon

REGION
KALOS
(CENTRAL)

TYPE: BUG

Like Scatterbug, Spewpa releases a protective cloud of powder when attacked. It can also bristle up its thick fur in an attempt to scare off any aggressors.

How to say it: SPEW-puh

Height: 1' 00"
Weight: 18.5 lbs.

Possible Moves: Harden, Protect

Scatterbug   Spewpa   Vivillon

SPHEAL
Clap Pokémon

TYPE: ICE-WATER

Spheal can roll across the ice faster than it can walk. When it's happy, it bursts into applause by clapping its fins together, so a group of joyful Spheal is rather noisy.

How to say it: SFEEL

Height: 2' 07"
Weight: 87.1 lbs.

Possible Moves: Defense Curl, Powder Snow, Growl, Water Gun, Encore, Ice Ball, Body Slam, Aurora Beam, Hail, Rest, Snore, Blizzard, Sheer Cold

Spheal   Sealeo   Walrein

SPINARAK
String Spit Pokémon

TYPE: BUG-POISON

Spinarak uses its web like another sensory organ. It can read the vibration of the strands to tell what's happening nearby.

How to say it: SPIN-uh-rack

Height: 1' 08"   **Weight:** 18.7 lbs.

Possible Moves: Poison Sting, String Shot, Scary Face, Constrict, Leech Life, Night Shade, Shadow Sneak, Fury Swipes, Sucker Punch, Spider Web, Agility, Pin Missile, Psychic, Poison Jab, Cross Poison, Sticky Web

Spinarak   Ariados

SPINDA
Spot Panda Pokémon

REGIONS
HOENN, KALOS (MOUNTAIN)

TYPE: NORMAL

It's said that no two Spinda have the same pattern of spots. They stumble and totter when they walk, making their opponents dizzy.

How to say it: SPIN-dah

Height: 3' 07"
Weight: 11.0 lbs.

Possible Moves: Tackle, Uproar, Copycat, Feint Attack, Psybeam, Hypnosis, Dizzy Punch, Sucker Punch, Teeter Dance, Psych Up, Double-Edge, Flail, Thrash

Does not evolve

SPIRITOMB
Forbidden Pokémon

REGION
SINNOH

TYPE: GHOST-DARK

Long ago, Spiritomb was bound to an odd keystone as punishment for bad behavior. Its body is formed of more than a hundred spirits.

How to say it: SPIRI-toom

Height: 3' 03"
Weight: 238.1 lbs.

Possible Moves: Curse, Pursuit, Confuse Ray, Spite, Shadow Sneak, Feint Attack, Hypnosis, Dream Eater, Ominous Wind, Sucker Punch, Nasty Plot, Memento, Dark Pulse

Does not evolve

SPOINK
Bounce Pokémon

TYPE: PSYCHIC

The constant bouncing motion of Spoink's springy tail regulates its heartbeat. It's always looking for a bigger pearl for its head, because the jewel focuses its psychic powers.

How to say it: SPOINK

Height: 2' 04"   **Weight:** 67.5 lbs.

Possible Moves: Splash, Psywave, Odor Sleuth, Psybeam, Psych Up, Confuse Ray, Magic Coat, Zen Headbutt, Rest, Snore, Power Gem, Psyshock, Payback, Psychic, Bounce

Spoink   Grumpig

SPRITZEE
Perfume Pokémon

TYPE: FAIRY

Long ago, this Pokémon was popular among the nobility for its lovely scent. Instead of spraying perfume, ladies would keep a Spritzee close at hand.

How to say it: SPRIT-zee

Height: 0' 08"   **Weight:** 1.1 lbs.

Possible Moves: Sweet Scent, Fairy Wind, Sweet Kiss, Odor Sleuth, Echoed Voice, Calm Mind, Draining Kiss, Aromatherapy, Attract, Moonblast, Charm, Flail, Misty Terrain, Skill Swap, Psychic, Disarming Voice

Spritzee   Aromatisse

357

SQUIRTLE
Tiny Turtle Pokémon

TYPE: WATER

With its aerodynamic shape and grooved surface, Squirtle's shell helps it cut through the water very quickly. It also offers protection in battle.

How to say it: SKWIR-tul

Height: 1' 08"   **Weight:** 19.8 lbs.

Possible Moves: Tackle, Tail Whip, Water Gun, Withdraw, Bubble, Bite, Rapid Spin, Protect, Water Pulse, Aqua Tail, Skull Bash, Iron Defense, Rain Dance, Hydro Pump

Squirtle   Wartortle   Blastoise   Mega Blastoise

STANTLER
Big Horn Pokémon

TYPE: NORMAL

The intricately curved antlers that grow from Stantler's head have been regarded as priceless works of art by collectors.

How to say it: STAN-tler

Height: 4' 07"
Weight: 157.0 lbs.

Possible Moves: Tackle, Leer, Astonish, Hypnosis, Stomp, Sand Attack, Take Down, Confuse Ray, Calm Mind, Role Play, Zen Headbutt, Jump Kick, Imprison, Captivate, Me First

Does not evolve

TYPE: NORMAL-FLYING

After evolving, Staraptor go off on their own, leaving their flocks behind. With their strong wings, they can fly with ease even when carrying a burden.

How to say it: star-RAP-tor

Height: 3' 11"
Weight: 54.9 lbs.

Possible Moves: Tackle, Growl, Quick Attack, Wing Attack, Double Team, Endeavor, Whirlwind, Aerial Ace, Take Down, Close Combat, Agility, Brave Bird, Final Gambit

REGIONS
KALOS (COASTAL), SINNOH

STARAPTOR
Predator Pokémon

Starly　　**Staravia**　　**Staraptor**

REGIONS
KALOS (COASTAL), SINNOH

STARAVIA
Starling Pokémon

TYPE: NORMAL-FLYING

Staravia travel in large flocks that can be very territorial. Battles sometimes break out between two competing flocks.

How to say it: star-AY-vee-ah

Height: 2' 00"
Weight: 34.2 lbs.

Possible Moves: Tackle, Growl, Quick Attack, Wing Attack, Double Team, Endeavor, Whirlwind, Aerial Ace, Take Down, Agility, Brave Bird, Final Gambit

Starly　　**Staravia**　　**Staraptor**

359

STARLY
Starling Pokémon

TYPE: NORMAL-FLYING

Huge flocks of Starly gather in fields and mountains. In such large numbers, their wings flap with impressive power . . . and their noisy singing is quite a nuisance!

How to say it: STAR-lee

Height: 1' 00"
Weight: 4.4 lbs.

Possible Moves: Tackle, Growl, Quick Attack, Wing Attack, Double Team, Endeavor, Whirlwind, Aerial Ace, Take Down, Agility, Brave Bird, Final Gambit

Starly → Staravia → Staraptor

STARMIE
Mysterious Pokémon

REGIONS
KALOS (COASTAL), KANTO

TYPE: WATER-PSYCHIC

Because of the glowing rainbow of colors produced by Starmie's core, this Pokémon is known as "the Gem of the Sea." It spins its body like a propeller to swim.

How to say it: STAR-mee

Height: 3' 07"
Weight: 176.4 lbs.

Possible Moves: Hydro Pump, Water Gun, Rapid Spin, Recover, Swift, Confuse Ray

Staryu → Starmie

STARYU
Star Shape Pokémon

TYPE: WATER

Staryu's red core glows brightly in the dark. When it flashes this light, it is said to be communing with the stars.

How to say it: STAR-you

Height: 2' 07"   **Weight:** 76.1 lbs.

Possible Moves: Tackle, Harden, Water Gun, Rapid Spin, Recover, Camouflage, Swift, Bubble Beam, Minimize, Gyro Ball, Light Screen, Brine, Reflect Type, Power Gem, Cosmic Power, Hydro Pump

Staryu   Starmie

STEELIX

Iron Snake Pokémon

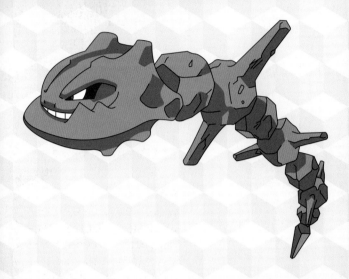

TYPE: STEEL-GROUND

Steelix lives deep underground and can tunnel straight down more than half a mile below the surface.

How to say it: STEE-licks

Height: 30' 02"
Weight: 881.8 lbs.

Possible Moves: Thunder Fang, Ice Fang, Fire Fang, Mud Sport, Tackle, Harden, Bind, Curse, Rock Throw, Rock Tomb, Rage, Stealth Rock, Autotomize, Gyro Ball, Smack Down, Dragon Breath, Slam, Screech, Rock Slide, Crunch, Iron Tail, Dig, Stone Edge, Double-Edge, Sandstorm

MEGA STEELIX

Iron Snake Pokémon

TYPE: STEEL-GROUND

Height: 34' 05"
Weight: 1,631.4 lbs.

Onix   Steelix   Mega Steelix

STOUTLAND
Big-Hearted Pokémon

TYPE: NORMAL

Stoutland excels at cold-weather rescues. Wrapped up in its warm, shaggy fur, someone could even spend the night on a snowy mountain and be okay.

How to say it: STOWT-lund

Height: 3' 11"
Weight: 134.5 lbs.

Possible Moves: Ice Fang, Fire Fang, Thunder Fang, Leer, Tackle, Odor Sleuth, Bite, Helping Hand, Take Down, Work Up, Crunch, Roar, Retaliate, Reversal, Last Resort, Giga Impact

Lillipup ⇨ **Herdier** ⇨ **Stoutland**

TYPE: GROUND-ELECTRIC

Stunfisk buries its flat body in mud, so it's hard to see and often gets stepped on. When that happens, its thick skin keeps it from being hurt, and Stunfisk zaps the offender with a cheery smile.

How to say it: STUN-fisk

Height: 2' 04"
Weight: 24.3 lbs.

Possible Moves: Fissure, Flail, Tackle, Water Gun, Mud-Slap, Mud Sport, Bide, Thunder Shock, Mud Shot, Camouflage, Mud Bomb, Discharge, Endure, Bounce, Muddy Water, Thunderbolt, Revenge

REGIONS
KALOS
(MOUNTAIN),
UNOVA

STUNFISK
Trap Pokémon

Does not evolve

STUNKY

Skunk Pokémon

REGIONS
KALOS (COASTAL), SINNOH

TYPE: POISON-DARK

The terrible-smelling fluid that Stunky sprays from its rear can keep others far away from it for a whole day.

How to say it: STUNK-ee

Height: 1' 04"
Weight: 42.3 lbs.

Possible Moves: Scratch, Focus Energy, Poison Gas, Screech, Fury Swipes, Smokescreen, Feint, Slash, Toxic, Acid Spray, Night Slash, Memento, Belch, Explosion

Stunky → Skuntank

SUDOWOODO

Imitation Pokémon

REGIONS
JOHTO, KALOS (MOUNTAIN)

TYPE: ROCK

For most of the year, Sudowoodo can easily disguise itself as a tree for protection. However, in the winter, its green hands give it away.

How to say it: SOO-doe-WOO-doe

Height: 3' 11"   **Weight:** 83.8 lbs.

Possible Moves: Wood Hammer, Copycat, Flail, Low Kick, Rock Throw, Mimic, Slam, Feint Attack, Rock Tomb, Block, Rock Slide, Counter, Sucker Punch, Double-Edge, Stone Edge, Hammer Arm

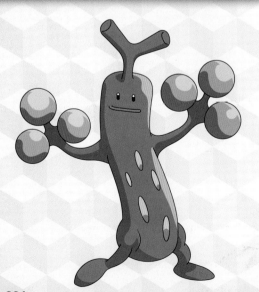

Bonsly → Sudowoodo

364

TYPE: WATER

Suicune can clear pollution from lakes and rivers. This Legendary Pokémon's heart is as pure as clear water.

How to say it: SWEE-koon

Height: 6' 07"   **Weight:** 412.3 lbs.

Possible Moves: Bite, Leer, Bubble Beam, Rain Dance, Gust, Aurora Beam, Mist, Mirror Coat, Ice Fang, Tailwind, Extrasensory, Hydro Pump, Calm Mind, Blizzard

Does not evolve

SUNFLORA

Sun Pokémon

REGION
JOHTO

TYPE: GRASS

Sunflora soaks up the sun's rays and transforms that energy into nutrients. It's very active during the warmth of the day, but when sunset arrives, it stops moving.

How to say it: sun-FLOR-a

Height: 2' 07"
Weight: 18.7 lbs.

Possible Moves: Absorb, Pound, Growth, Mega Drain, Ingrain, Grass Whistle, Leech Seed, Bullet Seed, Worry Seed, Razor Leaf, Petal Dance, Sunny Day, Solar Beam, Leaf Storm

Sunkern   Sunflora

SUNKERN

Seed Pokémon

REGION
JOHTO

TYPE: GRASS

Sunkern doesn't consume food but lives entirely on dewdrops. It avoids movement as much as possible so it doesn't use up its stored energy.

How to say it: SUN-kurn

Height: 1' 00"
Weight: 4.0 lbs.

Possible Moves: Absorb, Growth, Mega Drain, Ingrain, Grass Whistle, Leech Seed, Endeavor, Worry Seed, Razor Leaf, Synthesis, Sunny Day, Giga Drain, Seed Bomb

Sunkern   Sunflora

TYPE: BUG-WATER

The point on Surskit's head produces a sweet syrup that attracts some Pokémon. The points on its feet give off an oil that lets it skate across the surface of the water.

How to say it: SUR-skit

Height: 1' 08"
Weight: 3.7 lbs.

Possible Moves: Bubble, Quick Attack, Sweet Scent, Water Sport, Bubble Beam, Agility, Mist, Haze, Baton Pass, Sticky Web

REGIONS
HOENN,
KALOS
(CENTRAL)

SURSKIT
Pond Skater Pokémon

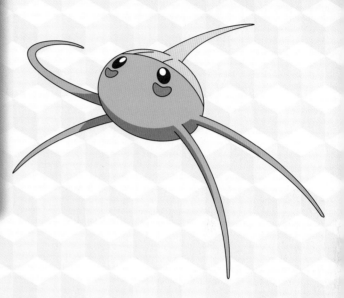

Surskit   **Masquerain**

TYPE: NORMAL-FLYING

Swablu uses its cottony wings to polish everything around it. It also likes to land on people's heads, so a woman walking down the sidewalk could suddenly discover she's wearing a fluffy Swablu hat.

How to say it: swah-BLUE

Height: 1' 04"   **Weight:** 2.6 lbs.

Possible Moves: Peck, Growl, Astonish, Sing, Fury Attack, Safeguard, Mist, Round, Natural Gift, Take Down, Refresh, Mirror Move, Cotton Guard, Dragon Pulse, Perish Song, Moonblast

REGIONS
HOENN,
KALOS
(MOUNTAIN)

SWABLU
Cotton Bird Pokémon

Swablu   **Altaria**   **Mega Altaria**

367

SWADLOON

Leaf-Wrapped Pokémon

TYPE: BUG-GRASS

When many Swadloon live in a forest, the plants grow strong and healthy. These Pokémon eat fallen leaves and give off nutrients that enrich the soil.

How to say it: swahd-LOON

Height: 1' 08"
Weight: 16.1 lbs.

Possible Moves: Grass Whistle, Tackle, String Shot, Bug Bite, Razor Leaf, Protect

Sewaddle   Swadloon   Leavanny

SWALOT

Poison Bag Pokémon

TYPE: POISON

Swalot's mouth can open wide enough to swallow a car tire easily. It defends itself by secreting a poisonous fluid.

How to say it: SWAH-lot

Height: 5' 07"   **Weight:** 176.4 lbs.

Possible Moves: Gunk Shot, Wring Out, Pound, Yawn, Poison Gas, Sludge, Amnesia, Encore, Body Slam, Toxic, Acid Spray, Stockpile, Spit Up, Swallow, Belch, Sludge Bomb, Gastro Acid

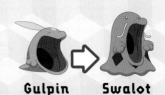

Gulpin   Swalot

TYPE: WATER-GROUND

Swampert can tell when a storm is coming by shifts in the winds and waves. It's strong enough to drag and lift heavy boulders, so it builds a fort to take shelter.

How to say it: SWAM-pert

Height: 4' 11"
Weight: 180.6 lbs.

Possible Moves: Tackle, Growl, Mud-Slap, Water Gun, Bide, Mud Shot, Foresight, Mud Bomb, Take Down, Muddy Water, Protect, Earthquake, Endeavor, Hammer Arm

SWAMPERT
Mud Fish Pokémon

MEGA SWAMPERT
Mud Fish Pokémon

TYPE: WATER-GROUND

Height: 6' 03"
Weight: 224.9 lbs.

Mudkip   Marshtomp   Swampert   Mega Swampert

SWANNA
White Bird Pokémon

REGIONS
KALOS (CENTRAL), UNOVA

TYPE: WATER-FLYING

In the evening, a flock of Swanna performs an elegant dance around its leader. Their exceptional stamina and wing strength allow them to fly thousands of miles at a time.

How to say it: SWAH-nuh

Height: 4' 03"
Weight: 53.4 lbs.

Possible Moves: Water Gun, Water Sport, Defog, Wing Attack, Water Pulse, Aerial Ace, Bubble Beam, Feather Dance, Aqua Ring, Air Slash, Roost, Rain Dance, Tailwind, Brave Bird, Hurricane

Ducklett → Swanna

SWELLOW
Swallow Pokémon

REGIONS
HOENN, KALOS (COASTAL)

TYPE: NORMAL-FLYING

Soaring gracefully through the sky, Swellow will go into a steep dive if it spots food on the ground. It's very vain about keeping its wings properly groomed.

How to say it: SWELL-low

Height: 2' 04"
Weight: 43.7 lbs.

Possible Moves: Air Slash, Pluck, Peck, Growl, Focus Energy, Quick Attack, Wing Attack, Double Team, Endeavor, Aerial Ace, Agility

Taillow → Swellow

SWINUB
Pig Pokémon

TYPE: ICE-GROUND

Swinub keeps its nose to the ground in search of food. Its favorite thing to eat is a certain kind of mushroom found under dead grass. Sometimes, it finds a hot spring while it's sniffing about.

How to say it: SWY-nub

Height: 1' 04"   **Weight:** 14.3 lbs.

Possible Moves: Tackle, Odor Sleuth, Mud Sport, Powder Snow, Mud-Slap, Endure, Mud Bomb, Icy Wind, Ice Shard, Take Down, Mist, Earthquake, Flail, Blizzard, Amnesia

Swinub   Piloswine   Mamoswine

TYPE: FAIRY

Swirlix loves to snack on sweets. Its sugary eating habits have made its white fur sweet and sticky, just like cotton candy.

How to say it: SWUR-licks

Height: 1' 04"
Weight: 7.7 lbs.

Possible Moves: Sweet Scent, Tackle, Fairy Wind, Play Nice, Fake Tears, Round, Cotton Spore, Endeavor, Aromatherapy, Draining Kiss, Energy Ball, Cotton Guard, Wish, Play Rough, Light Screen, Safeguard

SWIRLIX
Cotton Candy Pokémon

Swirlix   Slurpuff

SWOOBAT

Courting Pokémon

TYPE: PSYCHIC-FLYING

When a male Swoobat is trying to impress a female, it gives off ultrasonic waves that put everyone in a good mood. Under other circumstances, Swoobat's waves can pulverize concrete.

How to say it: SWOO-bat

Height: 2' 11"
Weight: 23.1 lbs.

Possible Moves: Confusion, Odor Sleuth, Gust, Assurance, Heart Stamp, Imprison, Air Cutter, Attract, Amnesia, Calm Mind, Air Slash, Future Sight, Psychic, Endeavor

Woobat   Swoobat

SYLVEON

Intertwining Pokémon

REGION **KALOS (COASTAL)**

TYPE: FAIRY

To keep others from fighting, Sylveon projects a calming aura from its feelers, which look like flowing ribbons. It wraps those ribbons around its Trainer's arm when they walk together.

How to say it: SIL-vee-on

Height: 3' 03"   **Weight:** 51.8 lbs.

Possible Moves: Disarming Voice, Tail Whip, Tackle, Helping Hand, Sand Attack, Fairy Wind, Quick Attack, Swift, Draining Kiss, Skill Swap, Misty Terrain, Light Screen, Moonblast, Last Resort, Psych Up

Eevee   Sylveon

TYPE: NORMAL-FLYING

Although Taillow is fierce and courageous in battle, even against stronger foes, hunger or loneliness sometimes makes it cry.

How to say it: TAY-low

Height: 1' 00"
Weight: 5.1 lbs.

Possible Moves: Peck, Growl, Focus Energy, Quick Attack, Wing Attack, Double Team, Endeavor, Aerial Ace, Agility, Air Slash

REGIONS HOENN, KALOS (COASTAL)

TAILLOW
Tiny Swallow Pokémon

Taillow → **Swellow**

REGION KALOS (CENTRAL)

TALONFLAME
Scorching Pokémon

TYPE: FIRE-FLYING

Talonflame can swoop at incredible speeds when attacking. During intense battles, its wings give off showers of embers as it flies.

How to say it: TAL-un-flame

Height: 3' 11"   **Weight:** 54.0 lbs.

Possible Moves: Brave Bird, Flare Blitz, Tackle, Growl, Quick Attack, Peck, Agility, Flail, Ember, Roost, Razor Wind, Natural Gift, Flame Charge, Acrobatics, Me First, Tailwind, Steel Wing

Fletchling   Fletchinder   Talonflame

TANGELA

Vine Pokémon

REGION
KANTO

TYPE: GRASS

If grabbed by an attacker, Tangela can break away and leave the foe with a handful of vines. The vines grow back within a day.

How to say it: TANG-guh-luh

Height: 3' 03"
Weight: 77.2 lbs.

Possible Moves: Ingrain, Constrict, Sleep Powder, Absorb, Growth, Poison Powder, Vine Whip, Bind, Mega Drain, Stun Spore, Knock Off, Ancient Power, Natural Gift, Slam, Tickle, Wring Out, Power Whip

Tangela   Tangrowth

TANGROWTH

Vine Pokémon

REGION
SINNOH

TYPE: GRASS

During warmer times of the year, Tangrowth's vines grow so rapidly that they cover its eyes. It can control its vines like arms.

How to say it: TANG-growth

Height: 6' 07"
Weight: 283.5 lbs.

Possible Moves: Ingrain, Constrict, Sleep Powder, Absorb, Growth, Poison Powder, Vine Whip, Bind, Mega Drain, Stun Spore, Ancient Power, Knock Off, Natural Gift, Slam, Tickle, Wring Out, Power Whip, Block

Tangela   Tangrowth

TAUROS
Wild Bull Pokémon

TYPE: NORMAL

Tauros just isn't happy unless it's battling. If nobody's up for the challenge, it blows off steam by charging at trees and knocking them over.

How to say it: TORE-ros

Height: 4' 07"
Weight: 194.9 lbs.

Possible Moves: Tackle, Tail Whip, Rage, Horn Attack, Scary Face, Pursuit, Rest, Payback, Work Up, Zen Headbutt, Take Down, Swagger, Thrash, Giga Impact

Does not evolve

TYPE: NORMAL

Teddiursa changes the flavor of its honey-soaked paws by incorporating different kinds of berries and pollen.

How to say it: TED-dy-UR-sa

Height: 2' 00"
Weight: 19.4 lbs.

Possible Moves: Fling, Covet, Scratch, Baby-Doll Eyes, Lick, Fake Tears, Fury Swipes, Feint Attack, Sweet Scent, Play Nice, Slash, Charm, Rest, Snore, Thrash

TEDDIURSA
Little Bear Pokémon

Teddiursa　Ursaring

TENTACOOL

Jellyfish Pokémon

REGIONS **KALOS (COASTAL), KANTO**

TYPE: WATER-POISON

If a Tentacool spends too much time out of water, its body will dry out. In the sea, it can focus and redirect sunlight into energy beams.

How to say it: TEN-ta-cool

Height: 2' 11"
Weight: 100.3 lbs.

Possible Moves: Poison Sting, Supersonic, Constrict, Acid, Toxic Spikes, Bubble Beam, Wrap, Acid Spray, Barrier, Water Pulse, Poison Jab, Screech, Hex, Hydro Pump, Sludge Wave, Wring Out

Tentacool   Tentacruel

TENTACRUEL

Jellyfish Pokémon

REGIONS **KALOS (COASTAL), KANTO**

TYPE: WATER-POISON

When the red orbs on Tentacruel's head glow, it's about to unleash a sonic blast that stirs up the sea. Its poisonous tentacles can extend to catch food.

How to say it: TEN-ta-crool

Height: 5' 03"   **Weight:** 121.3 lbs.

Possible Moves: Reflect Type, Wring Out, Poison Sting, Supersonic, Constrict, Acid, Toxic Spikes, Bubble Beam, Wrap, Acid Spray, Barrier, Water Pulse, Poison Jab, Screech, Hex, Hydro Pump, Sludge Wave

Tentacool   Tentacruel

TEPIG
Fire Pig Pokémon

TYPE: FIRE

Tepig uses the fireballs from its nose in battle—and in cooking! It likes to roast berries rather than eating them raw, though sometimes they get a little overdone.

How to say it: TEH-pig

Height: 1' 08"   **Weight:** 21.8 lbs.

Possible Moves: Tackle, Tail Whip, Ember, Odor Sleuth, Defense Curl, Flame Charge, Smog, Rollout, Take Down, Heat Crash, Assurance, Flamethrower, Head Smash, Roar, Flare Blitz

Tepig   Pignite   Emboar

TERRAKION
Cavern Pokémon

REGION
UNOVA

LEGENDARY
POKÉMON

TYPE: ROCK-FIGHTING

Legends tell of a time when Terrakion attacked a mighty castle to protect its Pokémon friends. They say it knocked down a giant wall with the force of its charge.

How to say it: tur-RAK-ee-un

Height: 6' 03"   **Weight:** 573.2 lbs.

Possible Moves: Quick Attack, Leer, Double Kick, Smack Down, Take Down, Helping Hand, Retaliate, Rock Slide, Sacred Sword, Swords Dance, Quick Guard, Work Up, Stone Edge, Close Combat

Does not evolve

REGIONS KALOS (COASTAL), UNOVA

THROH
Judo Pokémon

TYPE: FIGHTING

Throh make belts for themselves out of vines, and pull those belts tight to power up their muscles. They can't resist the challenge of throwing a bigger opponent.

How to say it: THROH

Height: 4' 03"   **Weight:** 122.4 lbs.

Possible Moves: Bind, Leer, Bide, Focus Energy, Seismic Toss, Vital Throw, Revenge, Storm Throw, Body Slam, Bulk Up, Circle Throw, Endure, Wide Guard, Superpower, Reversal

Does not evolve

379

TYPE: ELECTRIC-FLYING

Thundurus can discharge powerful electric bolts from the spikes on its tail. This Legendary Pokémon causes terrible lightning storms, which often result in forest fires.

How to say it: THUN-duh-rus

Height: 4' 11"   **Weight:** 134.5 lbs.

Possible Moves: Uproar, Astonish, Thunder Shock, Swagger, Bite, Revenge, Shock Wave, Heal Block, Agility, Discharge, Crunch, Charge, Nasty Plot, Thunder, Dark Pulse, Hammer Arm, Thrash

Does not evolve

TIMBURR
Muscular Pokémon

TYPE: FIGHTING

Timburr always carries a wooden beam, which it trades for bigger ones as it grows. These Pokémon can be a big help to construction workers.

How to say it: TIM-bur

Height: 2' 00"
Weight: 27.6 lbs.

Possible Moves: Pound, Leer, Focus Energy, Bide, Low Kick, Rock Throw, Wake-Up Slap, Chip Away, Bulk Up, Rock Slide, Dynamic Punch, Scary Face, Hammer Arm, Stone Edge, Focus Punch, Superpower

Timburr → **Gurdurr** → **Conkeldurr**

TIRTOUGA
Prototurtle Pokémon

TYPE: WATER-ROCK

Tirtouga is an excellent swimmer and diver, reaching depths of half a mile. It can also leave its ocean home to search for food on land. It was restored from a fossil.

How to say it: teer-TOO-guh

Height: 2' 04"
Weight: 36.4 lbs.

Possible Moves: Bide, Withdraw, Water Gun, Rollout, Bite, Protect, Aqua Jet, Ancient Power, Crunch, Wide Guard, Brine, Smack Down, Curse, Shell Smash, Aqua Tail, Rock Slide, Rain Dance, Hydro Pump

Tirtouga → **Carracosta**

381

TOGEKISS

Jubilee Pokémon

TYPE: FAIRY-FLYING

Togekiss flies around the world to seek out places of peace, bringing gifts and blessings to those who practice respect and harmony toward one another.

How to say it: TOE-geh-kiss

Height: 4' 11"
Weight: 83.8 lbs.

Possible Moves: Sky Attack, Extreme Speed, Aura Sphere, Air Slash

Togepi → Togetic → Togekiss

TOGEPI

Spike Ball Pokémon

REGION
JOHTO

TYPE: FAIRY

Togepi soaks up good vibes from other beings for use as energy. Its shell is filled with happy feelings and warm fuzzies.

How to say it: TOE-geh-pee

Height: 1' 00"   **Weight:** 3.3 lbs.

Possible Moves: Growl, Charm, Metronome, Sweet Kiss, Yawn, Encore, Follow Me, Bestow, Wish, Ancient Power, Safeguard, Baton Pass, Double-Edge, Last Resort, After You

Togepi → Togetic → Togekiss

TOGETIC
Happiness Pokémon

TYPE: FAIRY-FLYING

Widely regarded as a bringer of good luck, Togetic seeks out people with pure hearts and showers happiness upon them.

How to say it: TOE-geh-tick

Height: 2' 00"   **Weight:** 7.1 lbs.

Possible Moves: Magical Leaf, Growl, Charm, Metronome, Sweet Kiss, Yawn, Encore, Follow Me, Bestow, Wish, Ancient Power, Safeguard, Baton Pass, Double-Edge, Last Resort, After You

Togepi   Togetic   Togekiss

TYPE: FIRE

Torchic's internal fire and soft feathers make it a perfect cuddle buddy. In battle, it can breathe flames and shoot fireballs!

How to say it: TOR-chick

Height: 1' 04"   **Weight:** 5.5 lbs.

Possible Moves: Scratch, Growl, Focus Energy, Ember, Peck, Sand Attack, Fire Spin, Quick Attack, Slash, Mirror Move, Flamethrower

TORCHIC
Chick Pokémon

Torchic   Combusken   Blaziken   Mega Blaziken

TORKOAL

Coal Pokémon

TYPE: FIRE

Torkoal gets its energy by burning coal, which it digs up from mountains and uses to fill the hollow parts of its shell. The coal burns faster if it's fueling up for battle.

How to say it: TOR-coal

Height: 1' 08"   **Weight:** 177.2 lbs.

Possible Moves: Inferno, Heat Wave, Protect, Flail, Shell Smash, Ember, Smog, Withdraw, Curse, Fire Spin, Smokescreen, Flame Wheel, Rapid Spin, Flamethrower, Body Slam, Protect, Lava Plume, Iron Defense, Amnesia

Does not evolve

TORNADUS

Cyclone Pokémon

REGION
UNOVA

LEGENDARY POKÉMON

TYPE: FLYING

Wrapped in its cloud, Tornadus flies at two hundred MPH. This Legendary Pokémon causes fierce windstorms with gales that can knock down houses.

How to say it: tohr-NAY-dus

Height: 4' 11"
Weight: 138.9 lbs.

Possible Moves: Uproar, Astonish, Gust, Swagger, Bite, Revenge, Air Cutter, Extrasensory, Agility, Air Slash, Crunch, Tailwind, Rain Dance, Hurricane, Dark Pulse, Hammer Arm, Thrash

Does not evolve

TORTERRA
Continent Pokémon

TYPE: GRASS-GROUND

There's enough room on Torterra's enormous back for several small Pokémon to make their nests. According to ancient folklore, a particularly large one lived under the ground.

How to say it: tor-TERR-uh

Height: 7' 03" **Weight:** 683.4 lbs.

Possible Moves: Wood Hammer, Tackle, Withdraw, Absorb, Razor Leaf, Curse, Bite, Mega Drain, Earthquake, Leech Seed, Synthesis, Crunch, Giga Drain, Leaf Storm

Turtwig **Grotle** **Torterra**

TYPE: WATER

Be careful around a playful Totodile! It tends to nibble on friends as a sign of affection, but its jaws are strong enough to cause serious harm.

How to say it: TOE-toe-dyle

Height: 2' 00"
Weight: 20.9 lbs.

Possible Moves: Scratch, Leer, Water Gun, Rage, Bite, Scary Face, Ice Fang, Flail, Crunch, Chip Away, Slash, Screech, Thrash, Aqua Tail, Superpower, Hydro Pump

TOTODILE
Big Jaw Pokémon

Totodile **Croconaw** **Feraligatr**

TOXICROAK
Toxic Mouth Pokémon

REGIONS
KALOS (CENTRAL), SINNOH

TYPE: POISON-FIGHTING

Toxicroak's dangerous poison is stored in its throat sac and delivered through the claws on its knuckles.

How to say it: TOX-uh-croak

Height: 4' 03"   **Weight:** 97.9 lbs.

Possible Moves: Astonish, Mud-Slap, Poison Sting, Taunt, Pursuit, Feint Attack, Revenge, Swagger, Mud Bomb, Sucker Punch, Venoshock, Nasty Plot, Poison Jab, Sludge Bomb, Belch, Flatter

Croagunk → Toxicroak

TRANQUILL
Wild Pigeon Pokémon

REGION
UNOVA

TYPE: NORMAL-FLYING

Tranquill can always find its way back home, whether to its nest deep in the forest or to its Trainer's side. It's said that when these Pokémon nest together, peace surrounds the area.

How to say it: TRAN-kwil

Height: 2' 00"   **Weight:** 33.1 lbs.

Possible Moves: Gust, Growl, Leer, Quick Attack, Air Cutter, Roost, Detect, Taunt, Air Slash, Razor Wind, Feather Dance, Swagger, Facade, Tailwind, Sky Attack

Pidove → Tranquill → Unfezant

TRAPINCH
Ant Pit Pokémon

TYPE: GROUND

Trapinch lives in the desert, where it can go without water for several days. It digs a bowl-shaped pit in the sand and hides at the bottom, waiting for something to fall in.

How to say it: TRAP-inch

Height: 2' 04"
Weight: 33.1 lbs.

Possible Moves: Fissure, Superpower, Feint, Bite, Sand Attack, Feint Attack, Sand Tomb, Mud-Slap, Bide, Bulldoze, Rock Slide, Dig, Crunch, Earth Power, Sandstorm, Hyper Beam, Earthquake

Trapinch   Vibrava   Flygon

TREECKO
Wood Gecko Pokémon

TYPE: GRASS

The tiny hooks on Treecko's feet allow it to climb straight up walls. With its calm attitude, it coolly stands up to bigger opponents.

How to say it: TREE-ko

Height: 1' 08"   **Weight:** 11.0 lbs.

Possible Moves: Pound, Leer, Absorb, Quick Attack, Pursuit, Screech, Mega Drain, Agility, Slam, Detect, Giga Drain, Energy Ball

Treecko   Grovyle   Sceptile   Mega Sceptile

TREVENANT

Elder Tree Pokémon

TYPE: GHOST-GRASS

Using its roots, Trevenant can control the trees around it to protect its forest home. Smaller Pokémon sometimes live in its hollow body.

How to say it: TREV-uh-nunt

Height: 4' 11"
Weight: 156.5 lbs.

Possible Moves: Horn Leech, Tackle, Confuse Ray, Astonish, Growth, Ingrain, Feint Attack, Leech Seed, Curse, Will-O-Wisp, Forest's Curse, Destiny Bond, Phantom Force, Wood Hammer, Shadow Claw

Phantump ⇨ Trevenant

TROPIUS

Fruit Pokémon

TYPE: GRASS-FLYING

Tropius eats so much fruit that it started to grow its own fruit around its neck. The fruit is a popular snack for youngsters.

How to say it: TROH-pee-us

Height: 6' 07"
Weight: 220.5 lbs.

Possible Moves: Leer, Gust, Growth, Razor Leaf, Stomp, Sweet Scent, Whirlwind, Magical Leaf, Body Slam, Synthesis, Leaf Tornado, Air Slash, Bestow, Solar Beam, Natural Gift, Leaf Storm

Does not evolve

TYPE: POISON

Trubbish live in grungy, germy, grimy places and release a gas that induces sleep in anyone who breathes it. They were created when household garbage reacted with chemical waste.

How to say it: TRUB-bish

Height: 2' 00"   **Weight:** 68.3 lbs.

Possible Moves: Pound, Poison Gas, Recycle, Toxic Spikes, Acid Spray, Double Slap, Sludge, Stockpile, Swallow, Take Down, Sludge Bomb, Clear Smog, Toxic, Amnesia, Belch, Gunk Shot, Explosion

REGIONS
KALOS (MOUNTAIN), UNOVA

TRUBBISH
Trash Bag Pokémon

Trubbish ⇨ **Garbodor**

REGION
SINNOH

TURTWIG
Tiny Leaf Pokémon

TYPE: GRASS

Turtwig's shell is made of soil, and its whole body can produce energy via photosynthesis. If it goes too long without water, its leaf wilts.

How to say it: TUR-twig

Height: 1' 04"
Weight: 22.5 lbs.

Possible Moves: Tackle, Withdraw, Absorb, Razor Leaf, Curse, Bite, Mega Drain, Leech Seed, Synthesis, Crunch, Giga Drain, Leaf Storm

Turtwig ⇨ **Grotle** ⇨ **Torterra**

389

TYMPOLE
Tadpole Pokémon

TYPE: WATER

Tympole creates sound waves with the vibrations of its cheeks. People can't hear these sounds, so it can communicate with others undetected.

How to say it: TIM-pohl

Height: 1' 08"
Weight: 9.9 lbs.

Possible Moves: Bubble, Growl, Supersonic, Round, Bubble Beam, Mud Shot, Aqua Ring, Uproar, Muddy Water, Rain Dance, Flail, Echoed Voice, Hydro Pump, Hyper Voice

Tympole   Palpitoad   Seismitoad

TYNAMO
Elefish Pokémon

TYPE: ELECTRIC

A single Tynamo can't generate much power, but when several of them join forces, they can unleash an electric shock with the force of a lightning strike.

How to say it: TY-nuh-moh

Height: 0' 08"
Weight: 0.7 lbs.

Possible Moves: Tackle, Thunder Wave, Spark, Charge Beam

Tynamo   Eelektrik   Eelektross

TYPHLOSION
Volcano Pokémon

TYPE: FIRE

The heat shimmer given off by Typhlosion's flames serves to conceal the Pokémon's movements. It can unleash a fiery explosion to scorch everything around it.

How to say it: tie-FLOW-zhun

Height: 5' 07"   **Weight:** 175.3 lbs.

Possible Moves: Gyro Ball, Tackle, Leer, Smokescreen, Ember, Quick Attack, Flame Wheel, Defense Curl, Swift, Flame Charge, Lava Plume, Flamethrower, Inferno, Rollout, Double-Edge, Eruption

Cyndaquil   Quilava   Typhlosion

TYRANITAR

Armor Pokémon

TYPE: ROCK-DARK

Tyranitar lives in the mountains, where it often goes wandering in search of battle opponents. It has been known to topple a mountain when building a nest.

How to say it: tie-RAN-uh-tar

Height: 6' 07"
Weight: 445.3 lbs.

Possible Moves: Thunder Fang, Ice Fang, Fire Fang, Bite, Leer, Sandstorm, Screech, Chip Away, Rock Slide, Scary Face, Thrash, Dark Pulse, Payback, Crunch, Earthquake, Stone Edge, Hyper Beam, Giga Impact

MEGA TYRANITAR

Armor Pokémon

TYPE: ROCK-DARK

Height: 8' 02"
Weight: 562.2 lbs.

Larvitar   Pupitar   Tyranitar   Mega Tyranitar

TYPE: ROCK-DRAGON

Tyrantrum's enormous and powerful jaws made it the boss of its ancient world. Nothing could challenge its rule.

How to say it: tie-RAN-trum

Height: 8' 02"
Weight: 595.2 lbs.

Possible Moves: Head Smash, Tail Whip, Tackle, Roar, Stomp, Bide, Stealth Rock, Bite, Charm, Ancient Power, Dragon Tail, Crunch, Dragon Claw, Thrash, Earthquake, Horn Drill, Head Smash, Rock Slide, Giga Impact

REGION **KALOS (COASTAL)**

TYRANTRUM
Despot Pokémon

Tyrunt   **Tyrantrum**

TYPE: FIGHTING

Training and working out every day is a must for keeping Tyrogue's stress levels under control. Its Trainer must take a disciplined approach.

How to say it: tie-ROAG

Height: 2' 04"   **Weight:** 46.3 lbs.

Possible Moves: Tackle, Helping Hand, Fake Out, Foresight

REGION **JOHTO**

TYROGUE
Scuffle Pokémon

Tyrogue

Hitmonlee   **Hitmontop**

Hitmonchan

TYRUNT
Royal Heir Pokémon

KALOS (COASTAL)

TYPE: ROCK-DRAGON

Tyrunt often responds to frustration by pitching a fit. This ancient Pokémon lived millions of years ago.

How to say it: TIE-runt

Height: 2' 07"   **Weight:** 57.3 lbs.

Possible Moves: Tail Whip, Tackle, Roar, Stomp, Bide, Stealth Rock, Bite, Charm, Ancient Power, Dragon Tail, Crunch, Dragon Claw, Thrash, Earthquake, Horn Drill

Tyrunt   Tyrantrum

TYPE: DARK

When Umbreon springs into battle, the ring pattern in its fur begins to glow. The influence of moonlight caused it to evolve.

How to say it: UM-bree-on

Height: 3' 03"
Weight: 59.5 lbs.

Possible Moves: Helping Hand, Tackle, Tail Whip, Sand Attack, Pursuit, Quick Attack, Confuse Ray, Feint Attack, Assurance, Screech, Moonlight, Mean Look, Last Resort, Guard Swap

REGIONS
JOHTO, KALOS (COASTAL)

UMBREON
Moonlight Pokémon

Eevee   Umbreon

TYPE: NORMAL-FLYING

Unfezant has a prickly personality and rarely bonds with anyone other than its Trainer. The males have impressive head plumage, and the females are better at flying.

How to say it: un-FEZ-ent

Height: 3' 11"   **Weight:** 63.9 lbs.

Possible Moves: Gust, Growl, Leer, Quick Attack, Air Cutter, Roost, Detect, Taunt, Air Slash, Razor Wind, Feather Dance, Swagger, Facade, Tailwind, Sky Attack

REGION
UNOVA

UNFEZANT
Proud Pokémon

Male Form

Female Form

Pidove   Tranquill   Unfezant

UNOWN
Symbol Pokémon

REGION
JOHTO

TYPE: PSYCHIC

Unown can be found in many different shapes that resemble ancient writing. It's not known which came first.

How to say it: un-KNOWN

Height: 1' 08"
Weight: 11.0 lbs.

Possible Move: Hidden Power

Does not evolve

URSARING
Hibernator Pokémon

REGIONS
**JOHTO,
KALOS
(MOUNTAIN)**

TYPE: NORMAL

Ursaring makes daily rounds through the forest where it lives, climbing high into the trees and splashing through the streams to find food.

How to say it: UR-sa-ring

Height: 5' 11"   **Weight:** 277.3 lbs.

Possible Moves: Hammer Arm, Covet, Scratch, Leer, Lick, Fake Tears, Fury Swipes, Feint Attack, Sweet Scent, Play Nice, Slash, Scary Face, Rest, Snore, Thrash

Teddiursa   Ursaring

TYPE: PSYCHIC

According to legend, Uxie brought the gift of intelligence to humankind. It is known as "the Being of Knowledge."

How to say it: YUKE-see

Height: 1' 00"   **Weight:** 0.7 lbs.

Possible Moves: Rest, Confusion, Imprison, Endure, Swift, Yawn, Future Sight, Amnesia, Extrasensory, Flail, Natural Gift, Memento

Does not evolve

VANILLISH
Icy Snow Pokémon

TYPE: ICE

Vanillish live in snow-covered mountains and battle using particles of ice they create by chilling the air around them.

How to say it: vuh-NIHL-lish

Height: 3' 07"
Weight: 90.4 lbs.

Possible Moves: Icicle Spear, Harden, Astonish, Uproar, Icy Wind, Mist, Avalanche, Taunt, Mirror Shot, Acid Armor, Ice Beam, Hail, Mirror Coat, Blizzard, Sheer Cold

Vanillite   Vanillish   Vanilluxe

VANILLITE
Fresh Snow Pokémon

TYPE: ICE

When the sun rose and cast its light on icicles, Vanillite were created. With their icy breath, they can surround themselves with snow showers.

How to say it: vuh-NIHL-lyte

Height: 1' 04"
Weight: 12.6 lbs.

Possible Moves: Icicle Spear, Harden, Astonish, Uproar, Icy Wind, Mist, Avalanche, Taunt, Mirror Shot, Acid Armor, Ice Beam, Hail, Mirror Coat, Blizzard, Sheer Cold

Vanillite   Vanillish   Vanilluxe

VANILLUXE
Snowstorm Pokémon

TYPE: ICE

From the water it gulps down, Vanilluxe creates snowy stormclouds inside its body. When it becomes angry, it uses those clouds to form a raging blizzard.

How to say it: vuh-NIHL-lux

Height: 4' 03"   **Weight:** 126.8 lbs.

Possible Moves: Sheer Cold, Freeze-Dry, Weather Ball, Icicle Spear, Harden, Astonish, Uproar, Icy Wind, Mist, Avalanche, Taunt, Mirror Shot, Acid Armor, Ice Beam, Hail, Mirror Coat, Blizzard

Vanillite   Vanillish   Vanilluxe

TYPE: WATER

With its gills and fins, Vaporeon has adapted to an aquatic life. It can control its watery habitat with ease.

How to say it: vay-POUR-ree-on

Height: 3' 03"   **Weight:** 63.9 lbs.

Possible Moves: Helping Hand, Tackle, Tail Whip, Sand Attack, Water Gun, Quick Attack, Water Pulse, Aurora Beam, Aqua Ring, Acid Armor, Haze, Muddy Water, Last Resort, Hydro Pump

VAPOREON
Bubble Jet Pokémon

Eevee   Vaporeon

VENIPEDE

Centipede Pokémon

REGIONS
KALOS
(CENTRAL),
UNOVA

TYPE: BUG-POISON

Venipede uses the feelers at both ends of its body to explore its surroundings. It's extremely aggressive, and its bite is poisonous.

How to say it: VEHN-ih-peed

Height: 1' 04"
Weight: 11.7 lbs.

Possible Moves: Defense Curl, Rollout, Poison Sting, Screech, Pursuit, Protect, Poison Tail, Bug Bite, Venoshock, Agility, Steamroller, Toxic, Rock Climb, Double-Edge

Venipede   Whirlipede   Scolipede

VENOMOTH

Poison Moth Pokémon

REGION
KANTO

TYPE: BUG-POISON

When they become active after dark, Venomoth are often drawn to streetlamps. It isn't the light that attracts them, but the promise of food.

How to say it: VENN-oh-moth

Height: 4' 11"
Weight: 27.6 lbs.

Possible Moves: Silver Wind, Tackle, Disable, Foresight, Supersonic, Confusion, Poison Powder, Leech Life, Stun Spore, Psybeam, Sleep Powder, Gust, Signal Beam, Zen Headbutt, Poison Fang, Psychic, Bug Buzz, Quiver Dance

Venonat   Venomoth

REGION
KANTO

VENONAT
Insect Pokémon

TYPE: BUG-POISON

Venonat's large, sensitive eyes pick up even the tiniest movement. The stiff hair that covers its body protects it from harm.

How to say it: VENN-oh-nat

Height: 3' 03"　　**Weight:** 66.1 lbs.

Possible Moves: Tackle, Disable, Foresight, Supersonic, Confusion, Poison Powder, Leech Life, Stun Spore, Psybeam, Sleep Powder, Signal Beam, Zen Headbutt, Poison Fang, Psychic

Venonat　　Venomoth

VENUSAUR

Seed Pokémon

TYPE: GRASS-POISON

When Venusaur is well nourished and spends enough time in the sun, the flower on its back is brightly colored. The blossom gives off a soothing scent.

How to say it: VEE-nuh-sore

Height: 6' 07"
Weight: 220.5 lbs.

Possible Moves: Tackle, Growl, Vine Whip, Leech Seed, Poison Powder, Sleep Powder, Take Down, Razor Leaf, Sweet Scent, Growth, Double-Edge, Petal Dance, Worry Seed, Synthesis, Petal Blizzard, Solar Beam

MEGA VENUSAUR

Seed Pokémon

TYPE: GRASS-POISON

Height: 7' 10"
Weight: 342.8 lbs.

Bulbasaur ➡ **Ivysaur** ➡ **Venusaur** ➡ **Mega Venusaur**

TYPE: BUG-FLYING

Vespiquen controls the colony that lives in its honeycomb body by releasing pheromones. It feeds the colony with honey provided by Combee.

How to say it: VES-pih-kwen

Height: 3' 11"   **Weight:** 84.9 lbs.

Possible Moves: Fell Stinger, Destiny Bond, Sweet Scent, Gust, Poison Sting, Confuse Ray, Fury Cutter, Pursuit, Fury Swipes, Defend Order, Slash, Power Gem, Heal Order, Toxic, Air Slash, Captivate, Attack Order, Swagger

VESPIQUEN
Beehive Pokémon

REGIONS KALOS (CENTRAL), SINNOH

Combee   Vespiquen

TYPE: GROUND-DRAGON

Vibrava's wings aren't strong enough to fly very far, but it can vibrate them to produce ultrasonic waves that can give anyone listening a bad headache.

How to say it: VY-BRAH-va

Height: 3' 07"   **Weight:** 33.7 lbs.

Possible Moves: Sonic Boom, Sand Attack, Feint Attack, Sand Tomb, Mud-Slap, Bide, Bulldoze, Rock Slide, Supersonic, Screech, Dragon Breath, Earth Power, Sandstorm, Hyper Beam

VIBRAVA
Vibration Pokémon

REGIONS HOENN, KALOS (MOUNTAIN)

Trapinch   Vibrava   Flygon

403

MYTHICAL POKÉMON

TYPE: PSYCHIC-FIRE

According to myth, Victini can bring victory in any kind of competition. Because it creates unlimited energy, it can share the overflow with others.

How to say it: vik-TEE-nee

Height: 1' 04"   **Weight:** 8.8 lbs.

Possible Moves: Searing Shot, Focus Energy, Confusion, Incinerate, Quick Attack, Endure, Headbutt, Flame Charge, Reversal, Flame Burst, Zen Headbutt, Inferno, Double-Edge, Flare Blitz, Final Gambit, Stored Power, Overheat

Does not evolve

VICTREEBEL
Flycatcher Pokémon

REGIONS
KALOS (MOUNTAIN), KANTO

TYPE: GRASS-POISON

Victreebel uses its long vine like a fishing lure, swishing and flicking it to draw prey closer to its gaping mouth.

How to say it: VICK-tree-bell

Height: 5' 07"
Weight: 34.2 lbs.

Possible Moves: Stockpile, Swallow, Spit Up, Vine Whip, Sleep Powder, Sweet Scent, Razor Leaf, Leaf Tornado, Leaf Storm, Leaf Blade

Bellsprout **Weepinbell** **Victreebel**

VIGOROTH
Wild Monkey Pokémon

REGION
HOENN

TYPE: NORMAL

Vigoroth just can't sit still! If it spends too much time inactive, it gets stressed out and goes on a rampage. It doesn't sleep very well.

How to say it: VIG-er-roth

Height: 4' 07"   **Weight:** 102.5 lbs.

Possible Moves: Scratch, Focus Energy, Encore, Uproar, Fury Swipes, Endure, Slash, Counter, Chip Away, Focus Punch, Reversal

Slakoth **Vigoroth** **Slaking**

405

VILEPLUME

Flower Pokémon

REGIONS
KALOS (CENTRAL), KANTO

TYPE: GRASS-POISON

Many people are terribly allergic to the poisonous pollen Vileplume gives off. The petals of its flower are truly enormous.

How to say it: VILE-ploom

Height: 3' 11"
Weight: 41.0 lbs.

Possible Moves: Mega Drain, Aromatherapy, Stun Spore, Poison Powder, Petal Blizzard, Petal Dance, Solar Beam

Vileplume

Oddish   Gloom

Bellossom

VIRIZION

Grassland Pokémon

REGION
UNOVA

LEGENDARY POKÉMON

TYPE: GRASS-FIGHTING

According to legend, Virizion can move so swiftly that its opponents are left bewildered. Its horns are lovely and graceful—and as sharp as blades.

How to say it: vih-RY-zee-un

Height: 6' 07"   **Weight:** 440.9 lbs.

Possible Moves: Quick Attack, Leer, Double Kick, Magical Leaf, Take Down, Helping Hand, Retaliate, Giga Drain, Sacred Sword, Swords Dance, Quick Guard, Work Up, Leaf Blade, Close Combat

Does not evolve

TYPE: BUG-FLYING

The colorful patterns on Vivillon's wings are determined by the Pokémon's habitat. Vivillon from different parts of the world have different wing patterns.

How to say it: VIH-vee-yon

Height: 3' 11"   **Weight:** 37.5 lbs.

Possible Moves: Powder, Sleep Powder, Poison Powder, Stun Spore, Gust, Light Screen, Struggle Bug, Psybeam, Supersonic, Draining Kiss, Aromatherapy, Bug Buzz, Safeguard, Quiver Dance, Hurricane

REGION
KALOS (CENTRAL)

VIVILLON
Scale Pokémon

Scatterbug   **Spewpa**   **Vivillon**

TYPE: BUG

When night falls, Volbeat flashes the light on its tail in different patterns to send messages to others. It follows the sweet scent of Illumise.

How to say it: VOLL-beat

Height: 2' 04"
Weight: 39.0 lbs.

Possible Moves: Flash, Tackle, Double Team, Confuse Ray, Moonlight, Quick Attack, Tail Glow, Signal Beam, Protect, Helping Hand, Zen Headbutt, Bug Buzz, Double-Edge

REGIONS
HOENN, KALOS (CENTRAL)

VOLBEAT
Firefly Pokémon

Does not evolve

VOLCARONA

Sun Pokémon

TYPE: BUG-FIRE

The scales that cover Volcarona's six wings are like embers, and it scatters them to engulf the battlefield in flames. Its fire shines as bright as the sun.

How to say it: vol-kah-ROH-nuh

Height: 5' 03"
Weight: 101.4 lbs.

Possible Moves: Ember, String Shot, Leech Life, Gust, Fire Spin, Whirlwind, Silver Wind, Quiver Dance, Heat Wave, Bug Buzz, Rage Powder, Hurricane, Fiery Dance

Larvesta   Volcarona

VOLTORB

Ball Pokémon

REGIONS
KALOS (MOUNTAIN), KANTO

TYPE: ELECTRIC

Voltorb looks a lot like a Poké Ball, and it was first spotted at a Poké Ball factory. What's the connection? Nobody knows.

How to say it: VOLT-orb

Height: 1' 08"   **Weight:** 22.9 lbs.

Possible Moves: Charge, Tackle, Sonic Boom, Eerie Impulse, Spark, Rollout, Screech, Charge Beam, Light Screen, Electro Ball, Self-Destruct, Swift, Magnet Rise, Gyro Ball, Explosion, Mirror Coat

Voltorb   Electrode

TYPE: DARK-FLYING

Vullaby's wings aren't yet big enough to carry it through the air. The bones it wears around its lower half are gathered by Mandibuzz.

How to say it: VUL-luh-bye

Height: 1' 08"   **Weight:** 19.8 lbs.

Possible Moves: Gust, Leer, Fury Attack, Pluck, Nasty Plot, Flatter, Feint Attack, Punishment, Defog, Tailwind, Air Slash, Dark Pulse, Embargo, Whirlwind, Brave Bird, Mirror Move

REGION
UNOVA

VULLABY
Diapered Pokémon

Vullaby   **Mandibuzz**

TYPE: FIRE

Vulpix starts its life with a single tail that splits into six as it grows. The fire inside its body is constantly burning.

How to say it: VULL-picks

Height: 2' 00"
Weight: 21.8 lbs.

Possible Moves: Ember, Tail Whip, Roar, Quick Attack, Fire Spin, Confuse Ray, Imprison, Flame Burst, Safeguard, Will-O-Wisp, Payback, Flamethrower, Captivate, Inferno, Grudge, Extrasensory, Fire Blast

REGION
KANTO

VULPIX
Fox Pokémon

Vulpix   **Ninetales**

409

WAILMER
Ball Whale Pokémon

REGIONS
HOENN, KALOS (COASTAL)

TYPE: WATER

Wailmer is so round because it stores seawater inside its body. It can use this water to inflate itself for higher bounces, or shoot the water from its nostrils.

How to say it: WAIL-murr

Height: 6' 07"
Weight: 286.6 lbs.

Possible Moves: Splash, Growl, Water Gun, Rollout, Whirlpool, Astonish, Water Pulse, Mist, Rest, Brine, Water Spout, Amnesia, Dive, Bounce, Hydro Pump, Heavy Slam

Wailmer   Wailord

WAILORD
Float Whale Pokémon

REGIONS
HOENN, KALOS (COASTAL)

TYPE: WATER

The enormous Wailord makes its home in the open sea, where it swims with its mouth open to gather food. Sometimes it leaps out of the water, crashing back down with a massive splash.

How to say it: WAI-lord

Height: 47' 07"   **Weight:** 877.4 lbs.

Possible Moves: Splash, Growl, Water Gun, Rollout, Whirlpool, Astonish, Water Pulse, Mist, Rest, Brine, Water Spout, Amnesia, Dive, Bounce, Hydro Pump, Heavy Slam

Wailmer   Wailord

WALREIN
Ice Break Pokémon

TYPE: ICE-WATER

Walrein's giant tusks are capable of smashing through icebergs. Its thick blubber keeps it warm in frigid seas and is great for fending off hits in battle.

How to say it: WAL-rain

Height: 4' 07"
Weight: 332.0 lbs.

Possible Moves: Crunch, Powder Snow, Growl, Water Gun, Encore, Ice Ball, Body Slam, Aurora Beam, Hail, Swagger, Rest, Snore, Ice Fang, Blizzard, Sheer Cold

Spheal ⟹ Sealeo ⟹ Walrein

TYPE: WATER

The fur on Wartortle's tail darkens with age. Its shell bears the scratches of many battles.

How to say it: WOR-TORE-tul

Height: 3' 03"
Weight: 49.6 lbs.

Possible Moves: Tackle, Tail Whip, Water Gun, Withdraw, Bubble, Bite, Rapid Spin, Protect, Water Pulse, Aqua Tail, Skull Bash, Iron Defense, Rain Dance, Hydro Pump

WARTORTLE
Turtle Pokémon

Squirtle ⟹ Wartortle ⟹ Blastoise ⟹ Mega Blastoise

WATCHOG

Lookout Pokémon

TYPE: NORMAL

Watchog can make its stripes and eyes glow in the dark. Its tail stands straight up to alert others when it spots an intruder.

How to say it: WAH-chawg

Height: 3' 07"   **Weight:** 59.5 lbs.

Possible Moves: Rototiller, Tackle, Leer, Bite, Low Kick, Bide, Detect, Sand Attack, Crunch, Hypnosis, Confuse Ray, Super Fang, After You, Psych Up, Hyper Fang, Mean Look, Baton Pass, Slam

Patrat ⇨ Watchog

WEAVILE

Sharp Claw Pokémon

TYPE: DARK-ICE

In the snowy places where they live, Weavile communicate with others in the area by leaving carvings in tree trunks. They work together to hunt for food.

How to say it: WEE-vile

Height: 3' 07"   **Weight:** 75.0 lbs.

Possible Moves: Embargo, Revenge, Assurance, Scratch, Leer, Taunt, Quick Attack, Feint Attack, Icy Wind, Fury Swipes, Nasty Plot, Metal Claw, Hone Claws, Fling, Screech, Night Slash, Snatch, Punishment, Dark Pulse

Sneasel ⇨ Weavile

WEEDLE
Hairy Bug Pokémon

TYPE: BUG-POISON

Weedle's sense of smell is excellent. With its large red nose, it can sniff out the leaves it likes best.

How to say it: WEE-dull

Height: 1' 00"   **Weight:** 7.1 lbs.

Possible Moves: Poison Sting, String Shot, Bug Bite

Weedle   Kakuna   Beedrill   Mega Beedrill

WEEPINBELL
Flycatcher Pokémon

TYPE: GRASS-POISON

The hooked stem behind its head lets Weepinbell hang from a tree branch to sleep. Sometimes it falls to the ground during the night.

How to say it: WEE-pin-bell

Height: 3' 03"   **Weight:** 14.1 lbs.

Possible Moves: Vine Whip, Growth, Wrap, Sleep Powder, Poison Powder, Stun Spore, Acid, Knock Off, Sweet Scent, Gastro Acid, Razor Leaf, Slam, Wring Out

Bellsprout   Weepinbell   Victreebel

WEEZING

Poison Gas Pokémon

REGION
KANTO

TYPE: POISON

Rotting food gives off a noxious gas that attracts Weezing. Its twin bodies take turns inflating and deflating to keep its poisonous gases churning.

How to say it: WEEZE-ing

Height: 3' 11"
Weight: 20.9 lbs.

Possible Moves: Poison Gas, Tackle, Smog, Smokescreen, Assurance, Clear Smog, Self-Destruct, Sludge, Haze, Double Hit, Explosion, Sludge Bomb, Destiny Bond, Memento

Koffing   Weezing

WHIMSICOTT

Windveiled Pokémon

REGION
UNOVA

TYPE: GRASS-FAIRY

Where the winds whirl, Whimsicott appear, slipping into homes through the tiniest cracks and playing tricks on people. The white fluff they leave behind sometimes gives them away.

How to say it: WHIM-zih-kot

Height: 2' 04"
Weight: 14.6 lbs.

Possible Moves: Growth, Leech Seed, Mega Drain, Cotton Spore, Gust, Tailwind, Hurricane

Cottonee   Whimsicott

WHIRLIPEDE

Curlipede Pokémon

TYPE: BUG-POISON

Covered in a sturdy shell, Whirlipede doesn't move much unless it's attacked. Then it leaps into action, spinning at high velocity and smashing into the attacker.

How to say it: WHIR-lih-peed

Height: 3' 11"   **Weight:** 129.0 lbs.

Possible Moves: Defense Curl, Rollout, Poison Sting, Screech, Pursuit, Protect, Poison Tail, Iron Defense, Bug Bite, Venoshock, Agility, Steamroller, Toxic, Venom Drench, Rock Climb, Double-Edge

Venipede   Whirlipede   Scolipede

TYPE: WATER-GROUND

If you get too close to a pond where a Whiscash lives, it might thrash so violently to protect its territory that it sets off an earthquake. It can also sense when a regular earthquake is coming.

How to say it: WISS-cash

Height: 2' 11"   **Weight:** 52.0 lbs.

Possible Moves: Zen Headbutt, Tickle, Mud-Slap, Mud Sport, Water Sport, Water Gun, Mud Bomb, Amnesia, Water Pulse, Magnitude, Rest, Snore, Aqua Tail, Earthquake, Future Sight, Fissure

WHISCASH

Whiskers Pokémon

Barboach   Whiscash

415

WHISMUR

Whisper Pokémon

REGIONS
HOENN, KALOS (CENTRAL)

TYPE: NORMAL

When Whismur isn't in trouble, the noises it makes are very quiet. As soon as danger approaches, it sounds an earsplitting wail.

How to say it: WHIS-mur

Height: 2' 00"
Weight: 35.9 lbs.

Possible Moves: Pound, Uproar, Astonish, Howl, Supersonic, Stomp, Screech, Roar, Synchronoise, Rest, Sleep Talk, Hyper Voice

Whismur　　Loudred　　Exploud

WIGGLYTUFF

Balloon Pokémon

REGIONS
KALOS (MOUNTAIN), KANTO

TYPE: NORMAL-FAIRY

A protective coating of tears covers Wigglytuff's enormous eyes, keeping the dust away. It can suck in air to inflate its flexible body until it resembles a balloon.

How to say it: WIG-lee-tuff

Height: 3' 03"
Weight: 26.5 lbs.

Possible Moves: Double-Edge, Play Rough, Sing, Disable, Defense Curl, Double Slap

Igglybuff　　Jigglypuff　　Wigglytuff

REGIONS
**HOENN,
KALOS
(COASTAL)**

WINGULL
Seagull Pokémon

TYPE:
WATER-FLYING

With its long wings, Wingull can catch updrafts from the sea and glide across the sky as if on skates. It hides food and other treasures in various places.

How to say it: WING-gull

Height: 2' 00"
Weight: 20.9 lbs.

Possible Moves: Growl, Water Gun, Supersonic, Wing Attack, Mist, Water Pulse, Quick Attack, Roost, Pursuit, Air Cutter, Agility, Aerial Ace, Air Slash, Hurricane

Wingull ➡ **Pelipper**

TYPE: PSYCHIC

Relying on its powers of endurance, Wobbuffet prefers not to attack—unless a foe goes after its tail. Then, it unleashes a powerful counterstrike.

How to say it: WAH-buf-fett

Height: 4' 03"
Weight: 62.8 lbs.

Possible Moves: Counter, Mirror Coat, Safeguard, Destiny Bond

REGIONS
**JOHTO,
KALOS
(COASTAL)**

WOBBUFFET
Patient Pokémon

Wynaut ➡ **Wobbuffet**

WOOBAT
Bat Pokémon

TYPE: PSYCHIC-FLYING

When Woobat attaches itself to something, it leaves a heart-shaped mark with its nose. The nose is also the source of its echolocation signals.

How to say it: WOO-bat

Height: 1' 04"
Weight: 4.6 lbs.

Possible Moves: Confusion, Odor Sleuth, Gust, Assurance, Heart Stamp, Imprison, Air Cutter, Attract, Amnesia, Calm Mind, Air Slash, Future Sight, Psychic, Endeavor

Woobat Swoobat

WOOPER
Water Fish Pokémon

TYPE: WATER-GROUND

Though Wooper usually live in the water, they sometimes come ashore to look for food. To protect their bodies, they cover themselves with a sticky substance that is poisonous to the touch.

How to say it: WOOP-pur

Height: 1' 04"   **Weight:** 18.7 lbs.

Possible Moves: Water Gun, Tail Whip, Mud Sport, Mud Shot, Slam, Mud Bomb, Amnesia, Yawn, Earthquake, Rain Dance, Mist, Haze, Muddy Water

Wooper Quagsire

WORMADAM (PLANT CLOAK)

Bagworm Pokémon

TYPE: BUG-GRASS

The cloak it wore as Burmy becomes a permanent part of Wormadam's body. Its appearance is determined by its surroundings at the time of Evolution.

How to say it: WUR-muh-dam

Height: 1' 08"   **Weight:** 14.3 lbs.

Possible Moves: Tackle, Protect, Bug Bite, Hidden Power, Confusion, Razor Leaf, Growth, Psybeam, Captivate, Flail, Attract, Psychic, Leaf Storm

**Burmy
(Female Form)   Wormadam**

WORMADAM (SANDY CLOAK)

Bagworm Pokémon

TYPE: BUG-GROUND

If you want a Bug- and Ground-type Wormadam, make sure your Burmy has a Sandy Cloak! Once Burmy evolves, there's no going back.

How to say it: WUR-muh-dam

Height: 1' 08"   **Weight:** 14.3 lbs.

Possible Moves: Tackle, Protect, Bug Bite, Hidden Power, Confusion, Rock Blast, Harden, Psybeam, Captivate, Flail, Attract, Psychic, Fissure

**Burmy
(Female Form)   Wormadam**

419

WORMADAM (TRASH CLOAK)

Bagworm Pokémon

TYPE: BUG-STEEL

Looking for a Wormadam with awesome Steel-type moves? You'll need to evolve a Burmy with a Trash Cloak.

How to say it: WUR-muh-dam

Height: 1' 08"   **Weight:** 14.3 lbs.

Possible Moves: Tackle, Protect, Bug Bite, Hidden Power, Confusion, Mirror Shot, Metal Sound, Psybeam, Captivate, Flail, Attract, Psychic, Iron Head

Burmy (Female Form)   **Wormadam**

WURMPLE

Worm Pokémon

REGION **HOENN**

TYPE: BUG

With the spikes on its tail, Wurmple strips away tree bark to get at the delicious sap underneath. The spikes also come in handy when fending off an attacker.

How to say it: WERM-pull

Height: 1' 00"   **Weight:** 7.9 lbs.

Possible Moves: Tackle, String Shot, Poison Sting, Bug Bite

Silcoon   **Beautifly**

Wurmple

Cascoon   **Dustox**

WYNAUT
Bright Pokémon

TYPE: PSYCHIC

If a Wynaut is smacking its tail against the ground that means it's angry, regardless of the big smile on its face.

How to say it: WHY-not

Height: 2' 00"   **Weight:** 30.9 lbs.

Possible Moves: Splash, Charm, Encore, Counter, Mirror Coat, Safeguard, Destiny Bond

Wynaut   Wobbuffet

TYPE: PSYCHIC-FLYING

Some people believe Xatu can see the future, and they respect its mystical powers. When it stands still for hours on end, they say it's petrified by terrible visions.

How to say it: ZAH-too

Height: 4' 11"   **Weight:** 33.1 lbs.

Possible Moves: Peck, Leer, Night Shade, Teleport, Lucky Chant, Miracle Eye, Me First, Confuse Ray, Tailwind, Wish, Psycho Shift, Future Sight, Stored Power, Ominous Wind, Power Swap, Guard Swap, Psychic

Natu   Xatu

LEGENDARY POKÉMON

REGION
**KALOS
(MOUNTAIN)**

XERNEAS
Life Pokémon

TYPE: FAIRY

Xerneas's horns shine in all the colors of the rainbow. It is said that this Legendary Pokémon can share the gift of endless life.

How to say it: ZURR-nee-us

Height: 9' 10"   **Weight:** 474.0 lbs.

Possible Moves: Heal Pulse, Aromatherapy, Ingrain, Take Down, Light Screen, Aurora Beam, Gravity, Geomancy, Moonblast, Megahorn, Night Slash, Horn Leech, Psych Up, Misty Terrain, Nature Power, Close Combat, Giga Impact, Outrage

Does not evolve

YAMASK

Spirit Pokémon

TYPE: GHOST

The mask that Yamask carries is said to represent its face from a former life. Sometimes, remembering that former life makes it very sad.

How to say it: YAH-mask

Height: 1' 08"
Weight: 3.3 lbs.

Possible Moves: Astonish, Protect, Disable, Haze, Night Shade, Hex, Will-O-Wisp, Ominous Wind, Curse, Power Split, Guard Split, Shadow Ball, Grudge, Mean Look, Destiny Bond

Yamask   Cofagrigus

YANMA

Clear Wing Pokémon

TYPE: BUG-FLYING

With its compound eyes, Yanma can see in every direction without moving its head. It can make quick stops and turns during flight.

How to say it: YAN-ma

Height: 3' 11"
Weight: 83.8 lbs.

Possible Moves: Tackle, Foresight, Quick Attack, Double Team, Sonic Boom, Detect, Supersonic, Uproar, Pursuit, Ancient Power, Hypnosis, Wing Attack, Screech, U-turn, Air Slash, Bug Buzz

Yanma   Yanmega

YANMEGA
Ogre Darner Pokémon

TYPE: BUG-FLYING

With four wings on its back and two more on its tail to keep it balanced, Yanmega is capable of extremely high-speed flight. It can carry a full-grown person through the air.

How to say it: yan-MEG-ah

Height: 6' 03"   **Weight:** 113.5 lbs.

Possible Moves: Bug Buzz, Air Slash, Night Slash, Bug Bite, Tackle, Foresight, Quick Attack, Double Team, Sonic Boom, Detect, Supersonic, Uproar, Pursuit, Ancient Power, Feint, Slash, Screech, U-turn

Yanma   Yanmega

YVELTAL
Destruction Pokémon

REGION
**KALOS
(MOUNTAIN)**

LEGENDARY
POKÉMON

TYPE: DARK-FLYING

When Yveltal spreads its dark wings, its feathers give off a red glow. It is said that this Legendary Pokémon can absorb the life energy of others.

How to say it: ee-VELL-tall

Height: 19' 00"   **Weight:** 447.5 lbs.

Possible Moves: Hurricane, Razor Wind, Taunt, Roost, Double Team, Air Slash, Snarl, Oblivion Wing, Disable, Dark Pulse, Foul Play, Phantom Force, Psychic, Dragon Rush, Focus Blast, Sucker Punch, Hyper Beam, Sky Attack

Does not evolve

TYPE: NORMAL

Zangoose slashes at opponents with its sharp claws extended. These Pokémon constantly feud with Seviper.

How to say it: ZANG-goose

Height: 4' 03"
Weight: 88.8 lbs.

Possible Moves: Scratch, Leer, Quick Attack, Fury Cutter, Pursuit, Slash, Embargo, Crush Claw, Revenge, False Swipe, Detect, X-Scissor, Taunt, Swords Dance, Close Combat

Does not evolve

REGIONS
HOENN, KALOS (COASTAL)

ZANGOOSE
Cat Ferret Pokémon

TYPE: ELECTRIC-FLYING

When Zapdos is hit by a bolt of lightning, its power increases. This Legendary Pokémon can bend electricity to its will.

How to say it: ZAP-dose

Height: 5' 03"
Weight: 116.0 lbs.

Possible Moves: Roost, Zap Cannon, Drill Peck, Peck, Thunder Shock, Thunder Wave, Detect, Pluck, Ancient Power, Charge, Agility, Discharge, Rain Dance, Light Screen, Thunder

Does not evolve

REGIONS
KALOS (COASTAL), KANTO

ZAPDOS
Electric Pokémon

LEGENDARY POKÉMON

ZEBSTRIKA
Thunderbolt Pokémon

REGION
UNOVA

TYPE: ELECTRIC

A herd of Zebstrika running at top speed gives off a noise like thunder.
If they get angry, their manes shoot off lightning.

How to say it: zehb-STRY-kuh

Height: 5' 03"   **Weight:** 175.3 lbs.

Possible Moves: Quick Attack, Tail Whip, Charge, Thunder Wave, Shock Wave,
Flame Charge, Pursuit, Spark, Stomp, Discharge, Agility, Wild Charge, Thrash

Blitzle   Zebstrika

ZEKROM
Deep Black Pokémon

TYPE: DRAGON-ELECTRIC

Legends say Zekrom helps those who pursue their ideals. It surrounds itself with thunderclouds to travel unseen, and its tail can generate electricity.

How to say it: ZECK-rahm

Height: 9' 06"   **Weight:** 760.6 lbs.

Possible Moves: Thunder Fang, Dragon Rage, Imprison, Ancient Power, Thunderbolt, Dragon Breath, Slash, Zen Headbutt, Fusion Bolt, Dragon Claw, Imprison, Crunch, Thunder, Outrage, Hyper Voice, Bolt Strike

Does not evolve

ZIGZAGOON

TinyRaccoon Pokémon

REGIONS
**HOENN,
KALOS
(CENTRAL)**

TYPE: NORMAL

Zigzagoon's curiosity drives it to wander constantly and restlessly. It rubs the sturdy bristles on its back against trees to mark its territory.

How to say it: ZIG-zag-GOON

Height: 1' 04"
Weight: 38.6 lbs.

Possible Moves: Growl, Tackle, Tail Whip, Headbutt, Baby-Doll Eyes, Sand Attack, Odor Sleuth, Mud Sport, Pin Missile, Covet, Bestow, Flail, Rest, Belly Drum, Fling

Zigzagoon   Linoone

ZOROARK

Illusion Fox Pokémon

REGIONS
**KALOS
(MOUNTAIN),
UNOVA**

TYPE: DARK

Masters of deception, Zoroark are able to create entire landscapes out of illusions. In this way, they can scare or trick people away from their territory and protect their pack.

How to say it: ZORE-oh-ark

Height: 5' 03"   **Weight:** 178.8 lbs.

Possible Moves: Night Daze, Imprison, U-turn, Scratch, Leer, Pursuit, Hone Claws, Fury Swipes, Feint Attack, Scary Face, Taunt, Foul Play, Night Slash, Torment, Agility, Embargo, Punishment, Nasty Plot

Zorua   Zoroark

ZORUA

Tricky Fox Pokémon

TYPE: DARK

Zorua can use the power of illusion to make itself look like a person or a different Pokémon. It sometimes uses the resulting confusion to flee from a battle.

How to say it: ZORE-oo-ah

Height: 2' 04"
Weight: 27.6 lbs.

Possible Moves: Scratch, Leer, Pursuit, Fake Tears, Fury Swipes, Feint Attack, Scary Face, Taunt, Foul Play, Torment, Agility, Embargo, Punishment, Nasty Plot, Imprison, Night Daze

Zorua   Zoroark

ZUBAT

Bat Pokémon

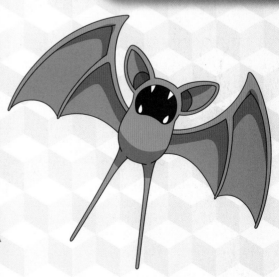

TYPE: POISON-FLYING

Sunlight isn't good for Zubat, so it stays hidden during the day. It prefers dark places like caves and old houses.

How to say it: ZOO-bat

Height: 2' 07"
Weight: 16.5 lbs.

Possible Moves: Leech Life, Supersonic, Astonish, Bite, Wing Attack, Confuse Ray, Swift, Air Cutter, Acrobatics, Mean Look, Poison Fang, Haze, Air Slash

Zubat   Golbat   Crobat

ZWEILOUS

Hostile Pokémon

TYPE: DARK-DRAGON

Zweilous has a ravenous appetite and exhausts the local food supply before moving on. Rather than working together, its two heads compete for food.

How to say it: ZVY-lus

Height: 4' 07"   **Weight:** 110.2 lbs.

Possible Moves: Double Hit, Dragon Rage, Focus Energy, Bite, Headbutt, Dragon Breath, Roar, Crunch, Slam, Dragon Pulse, Work Up, Dragon Rush, Body Slam, Scary Face, Hyper Voice, Outrage

Deino   Zweilous   Hydreigon

ZYGARDE

Order Pokémon

LEGENDARY POKÉMON

TYPE: DRAGON-GROUND

Zygarde dwells deep within a cave in the Kalos region. It is said that this Legendary Pokémon is a guardian of the ecosystem.

How to say it: ZY-gard

Height: 16' 05"   **Weight:** 672.4 lbs.

Possible Moves: Glare, Bulldoze, Dragon Breath, Bite, Safeguard, Dig, Bind, Land's Wrath, Sandstorm, Haze, Crunch, Earthquake, Camouflage, Dragon Pulse, Dragon Dance, Coil, Extreme Speed, Outrage

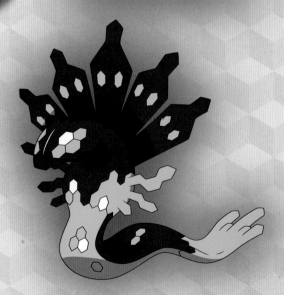

Does not evolve